I0823473

# THE AMERICAN SHORT STORY
# THE NINETEENTH CENTURY

## VOLUME I

# THE AMERICAN SHORT STORY

## THE NINETEENTH CENTURY

---

### VOLUME 1

*Charles Brockden Brown to Mark Twain*

---

John Stauffer, *editor*

THE LIBRARY OF AMERICA

THE AMERICAN SHORT STORY
THE NINETEENTH CENTURY, VOLUME 1


Published in the United States by Library of America,
14 East 60th Street, New York, NY 10022.
Visit our website at www.loa.org.



This paper exceeds the requirements of
ANSI/NISO Z39.48–1992 (Permanence of Paper).

Distributed to the trade in the United States
by Penguin Random House Inc.
and in Canada by Penguin Random House Canada Ltd.

The authorized representative in the EU for product safety and compliance is
eucomply OÜ, Pärnu mnt 139b-14, 11317 Tallinn, Estonia.
hello@eucompliancepartner.com

Library of Congress Control Number: 2025937866
ISBN 978–1–59853–820–5

First Printing
The Library of America—394

Manufactured in the United States of America

# *Contents*

# *Preface*

This two-volume anthology, gathering 103 stories by fifty-one authors, tracks the development of the American short story in the nineteenth century and showcases its vitality, its inventiveness, and its rich diversity. The nineteenth century was marked by tremendous change and innovation in American writing, and the short story was at the center of that creative and intellectual ferment, fueled by the evolution of new printing technologies, the rapid growth of periodical literature, and rising literacy rates.

The contents of this anthology—reprinted from nineteenth-century periodicals and gift books, modern critical editions, and, in one instance, an author typescript—have not been chosen to meet the requirements of a narrow, formal definition of the short story. Indeed, that would not be possible since the modern short story as a distinct form was still evolving in the nineteenth century. Prior to the 1880s the term "short story" referred primarily to children's stories. What we now call "short stories" were, through most of the nineteenth century, known as "tales," "sketches," "legends," "fables," or "anecdotes," depending on the piece.

Joyce Carol Oates once observed that formal definitions of the short story abound, but none are "democratic enough to accommodate an art that includes so much variety and an art that so readily lends itself to experimentation and idiosyncratic voices. Perhaps length alone should be the sole criterion?" As a practical matter at least, we excluded from consideration any stories lengthier than forty pages in the Library of America series format. The shortest, as a matter of interest, are two and a half pages.

The earliest stories in this anthology were published in 1805 and 1807 (Charles Brockden Brown's "Somnambulism" and Washington Irving's "The Little Man in Black"). There is nothing before Charles Brockden Brown and Washington Irving—from 1800 to 1804—that we felt deserved inclusion, though other early stories by Brown were considered. What stories by writers working in 1900 and beyond should be included? Frank Norris, Stephen Crane, and Paul Laurence Dunbar are among the last-born writers in this anthology: they were all dead by 1906, and belong to the nineteenth century.

Other writers presented slightly more difficult challenges. Mark Twain, William Dean Howells, Francis Hopkinson Smith, Harriett Prescott Spofford, George Washington Cable, Joel Chandler Harris, Mary E. Wilkins Freeman, Thomas Nelson Page, Alice Brown, Charles Chesnutt, Pauline Hopkins, Charlotte Perkins Gilman, Hamlin Garland, Sadakichi Hartmann, and Alice Dunbar-Nelson all lived a decade or longer into the twentieth century. More than a few of these writers had abandoned fiction writing early in the new century or found that tastes had changed, leaving them without readers. Their best work is associated with the prior century, and these writers are represented by stories published or written in the nineteenth century, or in a few instances, by stories written in the first few years of the twentieth.

Two master practitioners of the form, we realized, could not be contained within the nineteenth century—Edith Wharton and Henry James. Both belong as much to the twentieth century as to the nineteenth. Wharton was only just getting started as a professional writer in the 1890s, but she was then already an extremely accomplished story writer. It seemed impossible not to include some of her earlier stories in this anthology; readers will find two of her best early stories represented here. Henry James, the most influential writer of the second half of the nineteenth century, lived until 1916. Some of his late stories—"The Jolly Corner" (1908) comes immediately to mind—are acknowledged masterpieces, but readers will not find them here. As with Wharton, James is represented in this anthology by stories that appeared before 1900. In fairness to the editors of a future Library of America edition dedicated to the twentieth-century American short story, we leave for their consideration stories by James and Wharton published after 1900, as we do the interesting work of Native American short story writers who were starting out at the beginning of the twentieth century.

# THE AMERICAN SHORT STORY
# THE NINETEENTH CENTURY

## VOLUME I

# CHARLES BROCKDEN BROWN

(1771–1810)

## *Somnambulism*

### *A fragment*

[The following fragment will require no other preface or commentary than an extract from the Vienna Gazette of June 14, 1784. "At Great Glogau, in Silesia, the attention of physicians, and of the people, has been excited by the case of a young man, whose behaviour indicates perfect health in all respects but one. He has a habit of rising in his sleep, and performing a great many actions with as much order and exactness as when awake. This habit for a long time showed itself in freaks and achievements merely innocent, or, at least, only troublesome and inconvenient, till about six weeks ago. At that period a shocking event took place about three leagues from the town, and in the neighbourhood where the youth's family resides. A young lady, travelling with her father by night, was shot dead upon the road, by some person unknown. The officers of justice took a good deal of pains to trace the author of the crime, and at length, by carefully comparing circumstances, a suspicion was fixed upon this youth. After an accurate scrutiny, by the tribunal of the circle, he has been declared author of the murder: but what renders the case truly extraordinary is, that there are good reasons for believing that the deed was perpetrated by the youth while asleep, and was entirely unknown to himself. The young woman was the object of his affection, and the journey in which she had engaged had given him the utmost anxiety for her safety."]

OUR GUESTS were preparing to retire for the night, when somebody knocked loudly at the gate. The person was immediately admitted, and presented a letter to Mr. Davis. This letter was from a friend, in which he informed our guest of certain concerns of great importance, on which the letter-writer was extremely anxious to have a personal conference with his friend; but knowing that he intended to set out from —— four days previous to his writing, he was hindered from setting out by the apprehension of missing him upon the way. Meanwhile, he had deemed it best to send a special messsage to quicken his motions, should he be able to find him.

The importance of this interview was such, that Mr. Davis declared his intention of setting out immediately. No solicitations could induce him to delay a moment. His daughter, convinced of the urgency of his motives, readily consented to brave the perils and discomforts of a nocturnal journey.

This event had not been anticipated by me. The shock that it produced in me was, to my own apprehension, a subject of surprise. I could not help perceiving that it was greater than the occasion would justify. The pleasures of this intercourse were, in a moment, to be ravished from me. I was to part from my new friend, and when we should again meet it was impossible to foresee. It was then that I recollected her expressions, that assured me that her choice was fixed upon another. If I saw her again, it would probably be as a wife. The claims of friendship, as well as those of love, would then be swallowed up by a superior and hateful obligation.

But, though betrothed, she was not wedded. That was yet to come; but why should it be considered as inevitable? Our dispositions and views must change with circumstances. Who was he that Constantia Davis had chosen? Was he born to outstrip all competitors in ardour and fidelity? We cannot fail of chusing that which appears to us most worthy of choice. He had hitherto been unrivalled; but was not this day destined to introduce to her one, to whose merits every competitor must yield? He that would resign this prize, without an arduous struggle, would, indeed, be of all wretches the most pusillanimous and feeble.

Why, said I, do I cavil at her present choice? I will maintain that it does honour to her discernment. She would not be that accomplished being which she seems, if she had acted otherwise. It would be sacrilege to question the rectitude of her conduct. The object of her choice was worthy. The engagement of her heart in his favour was unavoidable, because her experience had not hitherto produced one deserving to be placed in competition with him. As soon as his superior is found, his claims will be annihilated. Has not this propitious accident supplied the defects of her former observation? But soft! is she not betrothed? If she be, what have I to dread? The engagement is accompanied with certain conditions. Whether they be openly expressed or not, they necessarily limit it. Her vows are binding on condition that the present situation continues, and that another does not arise, previously to marriage, by whom claims those of the present lover will be justly superseded.

But how shall I contend with this unknown admirer? She is going whither it will not be possible for me to follow her. An interview of a few hours is not sufficient to accomplish the important purpose that I meditate; but even this is now at an end. I shall speedily be forgotten by her. I have done nothing that entitles me to a place in her remembrance. While my rival will be left at liberty to prosecute his suit, I shall be abandoned to solitude, and have no other employment than to ruminate on the bliss that has eluded my grasp. If scope were allowed to my exertions, I might hope that they would ultimately be crowned with success; but, as it is, I am manacled and powerless. The good would easily be reached, if my hands were at freedom: now that they are fettered, the attainment is impossible.

But is it true that such is my forlorn condition? What is it that irrecoverably binds me to this spot? There are seasons of respite from my present occupations, in which I commonly indulge myself in journeys. This lady's habitation is not at an immeasurable distance from mine. It may be easily comprised within the sphere of my excursions. Shall I want a motive or excuse for paying her a visit? Her father has claimed to be better acquainted with my uncle. The lady has intimated, that the sight of me, at any future period, will give her pleasure. This will furnish ample apology for visiting their house. But why should I delay my visit? Why not immediately attend them on their way? If not on their whole journey, at least for a part of it? A journey in darkness is not unaccompanied with peril. Whatever be the caution or knowledge of their guide, they cannot be supposed to surpass mine, who have trodden this part of the way so often, that my chamber floor is scarcely more familiar to me. Besides, there is danger, from which, I am persuaded, my attendance would be a sufficient, an indispensable safeguard.

I am unable to explain why I conceived this journey to be attended with uncommon danger. My mind was, at first, occupied with the remoter consequences of this untimely departure, but my thoughts gradually returned to the contemplation of its immediate effects. There were twenty miles to a ferry, by which the travellers designed to cross the river, and at which they expected to arrive at sun-rise the next morning. I have said that the intermediate way was plain and direct. Their guide professed to be thoroughly acquainted with it.—From what quarter, then, could danger be expected to arise? It was easy to enumerate and magnify possibilities; that a tree, or ridge, or stone unobserved might overturn the carriage; that their horse might fail, or be urged, by some accident, to flight, were far from being impossible. Still they were such as justified caution. My vigilance would, at least, contribute to their security. But I could not for a moment divest myself of the belief, that my aid was indispensable. As I pondered on this image my emotions arose to terror.

All men are, at times, influenced by inexplicable sentiments. Ideas haunt them in spite of all their efforts to discard them. Prepossessions are entertained, for which their reason is unable to discover any adequate cause. The strength of a belief, when it is destitute of any rational foundation, seems, of itself, to furnish a new ground for credulity. We first admit a powerful persuasion, and then, from reflecting on the insufficiency of the ground on which it is built, instead of being prompted to dismiss it, we become more forcibly attached to it.

I had received little of the education of design. I owed the formation of my character chiefly to accident. I shall not pretend to determine in what degree I was credulous or superstitious. A belief, for which I could not rationally account, I was sufficiently prone to consider as the work of some invisible agent; as an intimation from the great source of existence and knowledge. My imagination was vivid. My passions, when I allowed them sway, were incontroulable. My conduct, as my feelings, was characterised by precipitation and headlong energy.

On this occasion I was eloquent in my remonstrances. I could not suppress my opinion, that unseen danger lurked in their way. When called upon to state the reasons of my apprehensions, I could only enumerate possibilities of which they were already apprised, but which they regarded in their true light. I made bold enquiries into the importance of the motives that should induce them to expose themselves to the least hazard. They could not urge their horse beyond his real strength. They would be compelled to suspend their journey for some time the next day. A few hours were all that they could hope to save by their utmost expedition. Were a few hours of such infinite moment?

In these representations I was sensible that I had over-leaped the bounds of rigid decorum. It was not my place to weigh his motives and inducements. My age and situation, in this family, rendered silence and submission my peculiar province. I had hitherto confined myself within bounds of scrupulous propriety, but now I had suddenly lost sight of all regards but those which related to the safety of the travellers.

Mr. Davis regarded my vehemence with suspicion. He eyed me with more attention than I had hitherto received from him. The impression which this unexpected interference made upon him, I was, at the time, too much absorbed in other considerations to notice. It was afterwards plain that he suspected my zeal to originate in a passion for his daughter, which it was by no means proper for him to encourage. If this idea occurred to him, his humanity would not suffer it to generate indignation or resentment in his bosom. On the contrary, he treated my arguments with mildness, and assured me that I had overrated the inconveniences and perils of the journey. Some regard was to be paid to his daughter's ease and health. He did not believe them to be materially endangered. They should make suitable provision of cloaks and caps against the inclemency of the air. Had not the occasion been extremely urgent, and of that urgency he alone could be the proper judge, he should certainly not consent to endure even these trivial inconveniences. "But you seem," continued he, "chiefly anxious for my daughter's sake. There is, without doubt, a large portion of gallantry in your fears. It is natural and venial in a young man to take infinite pains for the service of the ladies; but, my dear, what say you? I will refer this important question to your decision. Shall we go, or wait till the morning?"

"Go, by all means," replied she. "I confess the fears that have been expressed appear to be groundless. I am bound to our young friend for the concern he takes in our welfare, but certainly his imagination misleads him. I am not so much a girl as to be scared merely because it is dark."

I might have foreseen this decision; but what could I say? My fears and my repugnance were strong as ever.

The evil that was menaced was terrible. By remaining where they were till the next day they would escape it. Was no other method sufficient for their preservation? My attendance would effectually obviate the danger.

This scheme possessed irresistible attractions. I was thankful to the danger for suggesting it. In the fervour of my conceptions, I was willing to run to the world's end to show my devotion to the lady. I could sustain, with alacrity, the fatigue of many nights of travelling and watchfulness. I should unspeakably prefer them to warmth and ease, if I could thereby extort from this lady a single phrase of gratitude or approbation.

I proposed to them to bear them company, at least till the morning light. They would not listen to it. Half my purpose was indeed answered by the glistening eyes and affectionate looks of Miss Davis, but the remainder I was pertinaciously bent on likewise accomplishing. If Mr. Davis had not suspected my motives, he would probably have been less indisposed to compliance. As it was, however, his objections were insuperable. They earnestly insisted on my relinquishing my design. My uncle, also, not seeing any thing that justified extraordinary precautions, added his injunctions. I was conscious of my inability to show any sufficient grounds for my fears. As long as their representations rung in my ears, I allowed myself to be ashamed of my weakness, and conjured up a temporary persuasion that my attendance was, indeed, superfluous, and that I should show most wisdom in suffering them to depart alone.

But this persuasion was transient. They had no sooner placed themselves in their carriage, and exchanged the parting adieus, but my apprehensions returned upon me as forcibly as ever. No doubt part of my despondency flowed from the idea of separation, which, however auspicious it might prove to the lady, portended unspeakable discomforts to me. But this was not all. I was breathless with fear of some unknown and terrible disaster that awaited them. A hundred times I resolved to disregard their remonstrances, and hover near them till the morning. This might be done without exciting their displeasure. It was easy to keep aloof and be unseen by them. I should doubtless have pursued this method if my fears had assumed any definite and consistent form; if, in reality, I had been able distinctly to tell what it was that I feared. My guardianship would be of no use against the obvious sources of danger in the ruggedness and obscurity of the way. For that end I must have tendered them my services, which I knew would be refused, and, if pertinaciously obtruded on them, might justly excite displeasure. I was not insensible, too, of the obedience that was due to my uncle. My absence would be remarked. Some anger and much disquietude would have been the consequences with respect to him. And after all, what was this groundless and ridiculous persuasion that governed me? Had I profited nothing by experience of the effects of similar follies? Was I never to attend to the lessons of sobriety and truth? How ignominious to be thus the slave of a fortuitous and inexplicable impulse! To be the victim of terrors more chimerical than those which haunt the dreams of idiots and children! *They* can describe clearly, and attribute a real existence to the object of their terrors. Not so can I.

Influenced by these considerations, I shut the gate at which I had been standing, and turned towards the house. After a few steps I paused, turned, and listened to the distant sounds of the carriage. My courage was again on the point of yielding, and new efforts were requisite before I could resume my first resolutions.

I spent a drooping and melancholy evening. My imagination continually hovered over our departed guests. I recalled every circumstance of the road. I reflected by what means they were to pass that bridge, or extricate themselves from this slough. I imagined the possibility of their guide's forgetting the position of a certain oak that grew in the road. It was an ancient tree, whose boughs extended, on all sides, to an extraordinary distance. They seemed disposed by nature in that way in which they would produce the most ample circumference of shade. I could not recollect any other obstruction from which much was to be feared. This indeed was several miles distant, and its appearance was too remarkable not to have excited attention.

The family retired to sleep. My mind had been too powerfully excited to permit me to imitate their example. The incidents of the last two days passed over my fancy like a vision. The revolution was almost incredible which my mind had undergone, in consequence of these incidents. It was so abrupt and entire that my soul seemed to have passed into a new form. I pondered on every incident till the surrounding scenes disappeared, and I forgot my real situation. I mused upon the image of Miss Davis till my whole soul was dissolved in tenderness, and my eyes overflowed with tears. There insensibly arose a sort of persuasion that destiny had irreversably decreed that I should never see her more.

While engaged in this melancholy occupation, of which I cannot say how long it lasted, sleep overtook me as I sat. Scarcely a minute had elapsed during this period without conceiving the design, more or less strenuously, of sallying forth, with a view to overtake and guard the travellers; but this design was embarrassed with invincible objections, and was alternately formed and laid aside. At length, as I have said, I sunk into profound slumber, if that slumber can be termed profound, in which my fancy was incessantly employed in calling up the forms, into new combinations, which had constituted my waking reveries.—The images were fleeting and transient, but the events of the morrow recalled them to my remembrance with sufficient distinctness. The terrors which I had so deeply and unaccountably imbibed could not fail of retaining some portion of their influence, in spite of sleep.

In my dreams, the design which I could not bring myself to execute while awake I embraced without hesitation. I was summoned, methought, to defend this lady from the attacks of an assassin. My ideas were full of confusion and inaccuracy. All that I can recollect is, that my efforts had been unsuccessful to avert the stroke of the murderer. This, however, was not accomplished without drawing on his head a bloody retribution. I imagined myself engaged, for a long time, in pursuit of the guilty, and, at last, to have detected him in an artful disguise. I did not employ the usual preliminaries which honour prescribes, but, stimulated by rage, attacked him with a pistol, and terminated his career by a mortal wound.

I should not have described these phantoms had there not been a remarkable coincidence between them and the real events of that night. In the morning, my uncle, whose custom it was to rise first in the family, found me quietly reposing in the chair in which I had fallen asleep. His summons roused and startled me. This posture was so unusual that I did not readily recover my recollection, and perceive in what circumstances I was placed.

I shook off the dreams of the night. Sleep had refreshed and invigorated my frame, as well as tranquillized my thoughts. I still mused on yesterday's adventures, but my reveries were more cheerful and benign. My fears and bodements were dispersed with the dark, and I went into the fields, not merely to perform the duties of the day, but to ruminate on plans for the future.

My golden visions, however, were soon converted into visions of despair. A messenger arrived before noon, intreating my presence, and that of my uncle, at the house of Dr. Inglefield, a gentleman who resided at the distance of three miles from our house. The messenger explained the intention of this request. It appeared that the terrors of the preceding evening had some mysterious connection with truth. By some deplorable accident, Miss Davis had been shot on the road, and was still lingering in dreadful agonies at the house of this physician. I was in a field near the road when the messenger approached the house. On observing me, he called me. His tale was meagre and imperfect, but the substance of it it was easy to gather. I stood for a moment motionless and aghast. As soon as I recovered my thoughts I set off full speed, and made not a moment's pause till I reached the house of Inglefield.

The circumstances of this mournful event, as I was able to collect them at different times, from the witnesses, were these. After they had parted from us, they proceeded on their way for some time without molestation. The clouds disappearing, the star-light enabled them with less difficulty to discern their path. They met not a human being till they came within less than three miles of the oak which I have before described. Here Miss Davis looked forward with some curiosity and said to her father, "Do you not see some one in the road before us? I saw him this moment move across from the fence on the right hand and stand still in the middle of the road."

"I see nothing, I must confess," said the father: "but that is no subject of wonder; your young eyes will of course see farther than my old ones."

"I see him clearly at this moment," rejoined the lady. "If he remain a short time where he is, or seems to be, we shall be able to ascertain his properties. Our horse's head will determine whether his substance be impassive or not."

The carriage slowly advancing, and the form remaining in the same spot, Mr. Davis at length perceived it, but was not allowed a clearer examination, for the person, having, as it seemed, ascertained the nature of the cavalcade, shot across the road, and disappeared. The behaviour of this unknown person furnished the travellers with a topic of abundant speculation.

Few possessed a firmer mind than Miss Davis; but whether she was assailed, on this occasion, with a mysterious foreboding of her destiny; whether the eloquence of my fears had not, in spite of resolution, infected her; or whether she imagined evils that my incautious temper might draw upon me, and which might originate in our late interview, certain it was that her spirits were visibly depressed. This accident made no sensible alteration in her. She was still disconsolate and incommunicative. All the efforts of her father were insufficient to inspire her with cheerfulness. He repeatedly questioned her as to the cause of this unwonted despondency. Her answer was, that her spirits were indeed depressed, but she believed that the circumstance was casual. She knew of nothing that could justify despondency. But such is humanity. Cheerfulness and dejection will take their turns in the best regulated bosoms, and come and go when they will, and not at the command of reason. This observation was succeeded by a pause. At length Mr. Davis said, "A thought has just occurred to me. The person whom we just now saw is young Althorpe."

Miss Davis was startled: "Why, my dear father, should you think so? It is too dark to judge, at this distance, by resemblance of figure. Ardent and rash as he appears to be, I should scarcely suspect him on this occasion. With all the fiery qualities of youth, unchastised by experience, untamed by adversity, he is capable no doubt of extravagant adventures, but what could induce him to act in this manner?"

"You know the fears that he expressed concerning the issue of this night's journey. We know not what foundation he might have had for these fears. He told us of no danger that ought to deter us, but it is hard to conceive that he should have been thus vehement without cause. We know not what motives might have induced him to conceal from us the sources of his terror. And since he could not obtain our consent to his attending us, he has taken these means, perhaps, of effecting his purpose. The darkness might easily conceal him from our observation. He might have passed us without our noticing him, or he might have made a circuit in the woods we have just passed, and come out before us."

"That I own," replied the daughter, "is not improbable. If it be true, I shall be sorry for his own sake, but if there be any danger from which his attendance can secure us, I shall be well pleased for all our sakes. He will reflect with some satisfaction, perhaps, that he has done or intended us a service. It would be cruel to deny him a satisfaction so innocent."

"Pray, my dear, what think you of this young man? Does his ardour to serve us flow from a right source?"

"It flows, I have no doubt, from a double source. He has a kind heart, and delights to oblige others: but this is not all. He is likewise in love, and imagines that he cannot do too much for the object of his passion."

"Indeed!" exclaimed Mr. Davis, in some surprise. "You speak very positively. That is no more than it suspected; but how came you to know it with so much certainty?"

"The information came to me in the directest manner. He told me so himself."

"So ho! why, the impertinent young rogue!"

"Nay, my dear father, his behavior did not merit that epithet. He is rash and inconsiderate. That is the utmost amount of his guilt. A short absence will show him the true state of his feelings. It was unavoidable, in one of his character, to fall in love with the first woman whose appearance was in any degree specious. But attachments like these will be extinguished as easily as they are formed. I do not fear for him on this account."

"Have you reason to fear for him on any account?"

"Yes. The period of youth will soon pass away. Overweening and fickle, he will go on committing one mistake after another, incapable of repairing his errors, or of profiting by the daily lessons of experience. His genius will be merely an implement of mischief. His greater capacity will be evinced merely by the greater portion of unhappiness that, by means of it, will accrue to others or rebound upon himself."

"I see, my dear, that your spirits are low. Nothing else, surely, could suggest such melancholy presages. For my part, I question not, but he will one day be a fine fellow and a happy one. I like him exceedingly. I shall take pains to be acquainted with his future adventures, and do him all the good that I can."

"That intention," said his daughter, "is worthy of the goodness of your heart. He is no less an object of regard to me than to you. I trust I shall want neither the power nor inclination to contribute to his welfare. At present, however, his welfare will be best promoted by forgetting me. Hereafter, I shall solicit a renewal of intercourse."

"Speak lower," said the father. "If I mistake not, there is the same person again." He pointed to the field that skirted the road on the left hand. The young lady's better eyes enabled her to detect his mistake. It was the trunk of a cherry-tree that he had observed.

They proceeded in silence. Contrary to custom, the lady was buried in musing. Her father, whose temper and inclinations were moulded by those of his child, insensibly subsided into the same state.

The re-appearance of the same figure that had already excited their attention diverted them anew from their contemplations. "As I live," exclaimed Mr. Davis, "that thing, whatever it be, haunts us. I do not like it. This is strange conduct for young Althorpe to adopt. Instead of being our protector, the danger, against which he so pathetically warned us, may be, in some inscrutable way, connected with this personage. It is best to be upon our guard."

"Nay, my father," said the lady, "be not disturbed. What danger can be dreaded by two persons from one? This thing, I dare say, means us no harm. What is at present inexplicable might be obvious enough if we were better acquainted with this neighbourhood. It is not worth a thought. You see it is now gone." Mr. Davis looked again, but it was no longer discernible.

They were now approaching a wood. Mr. Davis called to the guide to stop. His daughter enquired the reason of this command. She found it arose from his uncertainty as to the propriety of proceeding.

"I know not how it is," said he, "but I begin to be affected with the fears of young Althorpe. I am half resolved not to enter this wood.—That light yonder informs that a house is near. It may not be unadvisable to stop. I cannot think of delaying our journey till morning; but, by stopping a few minutes, we may possibly collect some useful information. Perhaps it will be expedient and practicable to procure the attendance of another person. I am not well pleased with myself for declining our young friend's offer."

To this proposal Miss Davis objected the inconveniences that calling at a farmer's house, at this time of night, when all were retired to rest, would probably occasion. "Besides," continued she, "the light which you saw is gone: a sufficient proof that it was nothing but a meteor."

At this moment they heard a noise, at a small distance behind them, as of shutting a gate. They called. Speedily an answer was returned in a tone of mildness. The person approached the chaise, and enquired who they were, whence they came, whither they were going, and, lastly, what they wanted.

Mr. Davis explained to this inquisitive person, in a few words, the nature of their situation, mentioned the appearance on the road, and questioned him, in his turn, as to what inconveniences were to be feared from prosecuting his journey. Satisfactory answers were returned to these enquiries.

"As to what you seed in the road," continued he, "I reckon it was nothing but a sheep or a cow. I am not more scary than some folks, but I never goes out a' nights without I sees some *sich* thing as that, that I takes for a man or woman, and am scared a little oftentimes, but not much. I'm sure after to find that it's not nothing but a cow, or hog, or tree, or something. If it wasn't some sich thing you seed, I reckon it was *Nick Handyside.*"

"Nick Handyside! who was he?"

"It was a fellow that went about the country a' nights. A shocking fool to be sure, that loved to plague and frighten people. Yes. Yes. It couldn't be nobody, he reckoned, but Nick. Nick was a droll thing. He wondered they'd never heard of Nick. He reckoned they were strangers in these here parts."

"Very true, my friend. But who is Nick? Is he a reptile to be shunned, or trampled on?"

"Why I don't know how as that. Nick is an odd soul to be sure; but he don't do nobody no harm, as ever I heard, except by scaring them. He is easily skeart though, for that matter, himself. He loves to frighten folks, but he's shocking apt to be frightened himself. I reckon you took Nick for a ghost. That's a shocking good story, I declare. Yet it's happened hundreds and hundreds of times, I guess, and more."

When this circumstance was mentioned, my uncle, as well as myself, was astonished at our own negligence. While enumerating, on the preceding evening, the obstacles and inconveniences which the travellers were likely to encounter, we entirely and unaccountably overlooked one circumstance, from which inquietude might reasonably have been expected. Near the spot where they now were, lived a Mr. Handyside, whose only son was an idiot. He also merited the name of monster, if a projecting breast, a mis-shapen head, features horrid and distorted, and a voice that resembled nothing that was ever before heard, could entitle him to that appellation. This being, besides the natural deformity of his frame, wore looks and practised gesticulations that were, in an inconceivable degree, uncouth and hideous. He was mischievous, but his freaks were subjects of little apprehension to those who were accustomed to them, though they were frequently occasions of alarm to strangers. He particularly delighted in imposing on the ignorance of strangers and the timidity of women. He was a perpetual rover. Entirely bereft of reason, his sole employment consisted in sleeping, and eating, and roaming. He would frequently escape at night, and a thousand anecdotes could have been detailed respecting the tricks which Nick Handyside had played upon way-farers.

Other considerations, however, had, in this instance, so much engrossed our minds, that Nick Handyside had never been once thought of or mentioned. This was the more remarkable, as there had very lately happened an adventure, in which this person had acted a principal part. He had wandered from home, and got bewildered in a desolate tract, known by the name of Norwood. It was a region, rude, sterile, and lonely, bestrewn with rocks, and embarrassed with bushes.

He had remained for some days in this wilderness. Unable to extricate himself, and, at length, tormented with hunger, he manifested his distress by the most doleful shrieks. These were uttered with most vehemence, and heard at greatest distance, by night. At first, those who heard them were panic-struck; but, at length, they furnished a clue by which those who were in search of him were guided to the spot. Notwithstanding the recentness and singularity of this adventure, and the probability that our guests would suffer molestation from this cause, so strangely forgetful had we been, that no caution on this head had been given. This caution, indeed, as the event testified, would have been superfluous, and yet I cannot enough wonder that in hunting for some reason, by which I might justify my fears to them or to myself, I had totally overlooked this mischief-loving idiot.

After listening to an ample description of Nick, being warned to proceed with particular caution in a part of the road that was near at hand, and being assured that they had nothing to dread from human interference, they resumed their journey with new confidence.

Their attention was frequently excited by rustling leaves or stumbling footsteps, and the figure which they doubted not to belong to Nick Handyside, occasionally hovered in their sight. This appearance no longer inspired them with apprehension. They had been assured that a stern voice was sufficient to repulse him, when most importunate. This antic being treated all others as children. He took pleasure in the effects which the sight of his own deformity produced, and betokened his satisfaction by a laugh, which might have served as a model to the poet who has depicted the ghastly risibilities of Death. On this occasion, however, the monster behaved with unusual moderation. He never came near enough for his peculiarities to be distinguished by star-light. There was nothing fantastic in his motions, nor any thing surprising, but the celerity of his transitions. They were unaccompanied by those howls, which reminded you at one time of a troop of hungry wolves, and had, at another, something in them inexpressibly wild and melancholy. This monster possessed a certain species of dexterity. His talents, differently applied, would have excited rational admiration. He was fleet as a deer. He was patient, to an incredible degree, of watchfulness, and cold, and hunger. He had improved the flexibility of his voice, till his cries, always loud and rueful, were capable of being diversified without end. Instances had been known, in which the stoutest heart was appalled by them; and some, particularly in the case of women, in which they had been productive of consequences truly deplorable.

When the travellers had arrived at that part of the wood where, as they had been informed, it was needful to be particularly cautious, Mr. Davis, for their greater security, proposed to his daughter to alight. The exercise of walking, he thought, after so much time spent in a close carriage, would be salutary and pleasant. The young lady readily embraced the proposal. They forthwith alighted, and walked at a small distance before the chaise, which was now conducted by the servant. From this moment the spectre, which, till now, had been occasionally visible, entirely disappeared. This incident naturally led the conversation to this topic. So singular a specimen of the forms which human nature is found to assume could not fail of suggesting a variety of remarks.

They pictured to themselves many combinations of circumstances in which Handyside might be the agent, and in which the most momentous effects might flow from his agency, without its being possible for others to conjecture the true nature of the agent. The propensities of this being might contribute to realize, on an American road, many of those imaginary tokens and perils which abound in the wildest romance. He would be an admirable machine, in a plan whose purpose was to generate or foster, in a given subject, the frenzy of quixotism.—No theatre was better adapted than Norwood to such an exhibition. This part of the country had long been deserted by beasts of prey. Bears might still, perhaps, be found during a very rigorous season, but wolves which, when the country was a desert, were extremely numerous, had now, in consequence of increasing population, withdrawn to more savage haunts. Yet the voice of Handyside, varied with the force and skill of which he was known to be capable, would fill these shades with outcries as ferocious as those which are to be heard in Siamese or Abyssinian forests. The tale of his recent elopement had been told by the man with whom they had just parted, in a rustic but picturesque style.

"But why," said the lady, "did not our kind host inform us of this circumstance? He must surely have been well acquainted with the existence and habits of this Handyside. He must have perceived to how many groundless alarms our ignorance, in this respect, was likely to expose us. It is strange that he did not afford us the slightest intimation of it."

Mr. Davis was no less surprised at this omission. He was at a loss to conceive how this should be forgotten in the midst of those minute directions, in which every cause had been laboriously recollected from which he might incur danger or suffer obstruction.

This person, being no longer an object of terror, began to be regarded with a very lively curiosity. They even wished for his appearance and near approach, that they might carry away with them more definite conceptions of his figure. The lady declared she should be highly pleased by hearing his outcries, and consoled herself with the belief, that he would not allow them to pass the limits which he had prescribed to his wanderings, without greeting them with a strain or two. This wish had scarcely been uttered, when it was completely gratified.

The lady involuntarily started, and caught hold of her father's arm. Mr. Davis himself was disconcerted. A scream, dismally loud, and piercingly shrill, was uttered by one at less than twenty paces from them.

The monster had shown some skill in the choice of a spot suitable to his design. Neighbouring precipices, and a thick umbrage of oaks, on either side, contributed to prolong and to heighten his terrible notes. They were rendered more awful by the profound stillness that preceded and followed them. They were able speedily to quiet the trepidations which this hideous outcry, in spite of preparation and foresight, had produced, but they had not foreseen one of its unhappy consequences.

In a moment Mr. Davis was alarmed by the rapid sound of footsteps behind him. His presence of mind, on this occasion, probably saved himself and his daughter from instant destruction. He leaped out of the path, and, by a sudden exertion, at the same moment, threw the lady to some distance from the tract. The horse that drew the chaise rushed by them with the celerity of lightning. Affrighted at the sounds which had been uttered at a still less distance from the horse than from Mr. Davis, possibly with a malicious design to produce this very effect, he jerked the bridle from the hands that held it, and rushed forward with headlong speed. The man, before he could provide for his own safety, was beaten to the earth. He was considerably bruised by the fall, but presently recovered his feet, and went in pursuit of the horse.

This accident happened at about a hundred yards from the *oak*, against which so many cautions had been given. It was not possible, at any time, without considerable caution, to avoid it. It was not to be wondered at, therefore, that, in a few seconds, the carriage was shocked against the trunk, overturned, and dashed into a thousand fragments. The noise of the crash sufficiently informed them of this event. Had the horse been inclined to stop, a repetition, for the space of some minutes, of the same savage and terrible shrieks would have added tenfold to his consternation and to the speed of his flight. After this dismal strain had ended, Mr. Davis raised his daughter from the ground. She had suffered no material injury. As soon as they recovered from the confusion into which this accident had thrown them, they began to consult upon the measures proper to be taken upon this emergency. They were left alone. The servant had gone in pursuit of the flying horse. Whether he would be able to retake him was extremely dubious. Meanwhile they were surrounded by darkness. What was the distance of the next house could not be known. At that hour of the night they could not hope to be directed, by the far-seen taper, to any hospitable roof. The only alternative, therefore, was to remain where they were, uncertain of the fate of their companion, or to go forward with the utmost expedition.

They could not hesitate to embrace the latter. In a few minutes they arrived at the oak. The chaise appeared to have been dashed against a knotty projecture of the trunk, which was large enough for a person to be conveniently seated on it. Here they again paused.—Miss Davis desired to remain here a few minutes to recruit her exhausted strength. She proposed to her father to leave her here, and go forward in quest of the horse and the servant. He might return as speedily as he thought proper. She did not fear to be alone. The voice was still. Having accomplished his malicious purposes, the spectre had probably taken his final leave of them. At all events, if the report of the rustic was true, she had no personal injury to fear from him.

Through some deplorable infatuation, as he afterwards deemed it, Mr. Davis complied with her intreaties, and went in search of the missing. He had engaged in a most unpromising undertaking. The man and horse were by this time at a considerable distance. The former would, no doubt, shortly return. Whether his pursuit succeeded or miscarried, he would surely see the propriety of hastening his return with what tidings he could obtain, and to ascertain his master's situation. Add to this, the impropriety of leaving a woman, single and unarmed, to the machinations of this demoniac. He had scarcely parted with her when these reflections occurred to him. His resolution was changed. He turned back with the intention of immediately seeking her. At the same moment, he saw the flash and heard the discharge of a pistol. The light proceeded from the foot of the oak. His imagination was filled with horrible forebodings. He ran with all his speed to the spot. He called aloud upon the name of his daughter, but, alas! she was unable to answer him. He found her stretched at the foot of the tree, senseless, and weltering in her blood. He lifted her in his arms, and seated her against the trunk. He found himself stained with blood, flowing from a wound, which either the darkness of the night, or the confusion of his thoughts, hindered him from tracing. Overwhelmed with a catastrophe so dreadful and unexpected, he was divested of all presence of mind. The author of his calamity had vanished. No human being was at hand to succour him in his uttermost distress. He beat his head against the ground, tore away his venerable locks, and rent the air with his cries.

Fortunately there was a dwelling at no great distance from this scene. The discharge of a pistol produces a sound too loud not to be heard far and wide, in this lonely region. This house belonged to a physician. He was a man noted for his humanity and sympathy. He was roused, as well as most of his family, by a sound so uncommon. He rose instantly, and calling up his people proceeded with lights to the road. The lamentations of Mr. Davis directed them to the place. To the physician the scene was inexplicable. Who was the author of this distress; by whom the pistol was discharged; whether through some untoward chance or with design, he was as yet uninformed, nor could he gain any information from the incoherent despair of Mr. Davis.

Every measure that humanity and professional skill could suggest were employed on this occasion. The dying lady was removed to the house. The ball had lodged in her brain, and to extract it was impossible. Why should I dwell on the remaining incidents of this tale? She languished till the next morning, and then expired.

1805

# WILLIAM AUSTIN

(1778–1841)

---

## *Peter Rugg, the Missing Man*

### SOME ACCOUNT OF PETER RUGG, THE MISSING MAN, LATE OF BOSTON, NEW-ENGLAND. IN A LETTER TO MR. HERMAN KRAUFF

SIR,—Agreeably to my promise, I now relate to you all the particulars of the lost man and child, which I have been able to collect. It is entirely owing to the humane interest you seemed to take in the report, that I have pursued the inquiry to the following result.

You may remember that business called me to Boston in the summer of 1820. I sailed in the packet to Providence, and when I arrived there, I learnt that every seat in the Stage was engaged. I was thus obliged either to wait a few hours, or accept a seat with the driver, who civilly offered me that accommodation. Accordingly, I took my seat by his side, and soon found him intelligent and communicative. When we had travelled about ten miles, the horses suddenly threw their ears on their necks, as flat as a hare's. Said the driver, "have you a surtout with you?" "No," said I, "why do you ask?" "You will want one soon," said he. "Do you observe the ears of all the horses?" "Yes," and was just about to ask the reason. "They see the storm breeder, and we shall see him soon." At this moment there was not a cloud visible in the firmament. Soon after, a small speck appeared in the road. "There," said my companion, "comes the storm breeder; he always leaves a Scotch mist behind him. By many a wet jacket do I remember him. I suppose the poor fellow suffers much himself, much more than is known to the world." Presently, a man with a child beside him, with a large black horse, and a weather-beaten chair, once built for a chaise body, passed in great haste, apparently at the rate of twelve miles an hour. He seemed to grasp the reins of his horse with firmness, and appeared to anticipate his speed. He seemed dejected, and looked anxiously at the passengers, particularly at the stage driver and myself. In a moment after he passed us, the horses' ears were up, and bent themselves forward so that they nearly met. "Who is that man," said I, "he seems in great trouble." "Nobody knows who he is, but his person and the child are familiar to me. I have met them more than a hundred times, and have been so often asked the way to Boston, by that man, even when he was travelling directly from that town, that of late, I have refused any communication with him; and that is the reason he gave me such a fixed look." "But does he never stop any where?" "I have never known him to stop any where, longer than to inquire the way to Boston; and let him be where he may, he will tell you he cannot stay a moment, for he must reach Boston that night."

We were now ascending a high hill in Walpole; and as we had a fair view of the heavens, I was rather disposed to jeer the driver for thinking of his surtout, as not a cloud as big as a marble, could be discerned. "Do you look," said he, "in the direction whence the man came, that is the place to look: the storm never meets him, it follows him." We presently approached another hill, and when at the height, the driver pointed out in an eastern direction a little black speck, about as big as a hat. "There," said he, "is the seed storm; we may possibly reach Polley's before it reaches us, but the wanderer and his child will go to Providence through rain, thunder and lightning." And now the horses, as though taught by instinct, hastened with increased speed. The little black cloud came on rolling over the turnpike, and doubled and trebled itself in all directions. The appearance of this cloud attracted the notice of all the passengers; for after it had spread itself to a great bulk, it suddenly became more limited in circumference, grew more compact, dark and consolidated. And now the successive flashes of chain lightning caused the whole cloud to appear like a sort of irregular net work, and displayed a thousand fantastic images. The driver bespoke my attention to a remarkable configuration in the cloud: He said every flash of lightning near its centre discovered to him distinctly the form of a man sitting in an open carriage drawn by a black horse. But in truth, I saw no such thing. The man's fancy was doubtless at fault. It is a very common thing for the imagination to paint for the senses, both in the visible and invisible world.

In the mean time the distant thunder gave notice of a shower at hand; and just as we reached Polley's tavern the rain poured down in torrents. It was soon over, the cloud passing in the direction of the turnpike toward Providence. In a few moments after, a respectable looking man in a chaise stopped at the door. The man and child in the chair having excited some little sympathy among the passengers, the gentleman was asked if he had observed them? He said, he had met them, that the man seemed bewildered, and inquired the way to Boston: that he was driving at great speed, as though he expected to outstrip the tempest; that the moment he had passed him, a thunder clap broke distinctly over the man's head, and seemed to envelope both man and child, horse and carriage. "I stopped," said the gentleman, "supposing the lightning had struck him, but the horse only seemed to loam up and increase his speed, and as well as I could judge he travelled just as fast as the thunder cloud." While this man was speaking, a pedlar with a cart of tin merchandize came up, all dripping; and on being questioned, he said he had met that man and carriage, within a fortnight in four different states; that at each time he had inquired the way to Boston, and that a thunder shower like the present had each time, deluged him, his waggon and his wares, setting his tinpots, &c. afloat, so that he had determined to get marine insurance done for the future. But that which excited his surprise most, was the strange conduct of his horse, for that long before he could distinguish the man in the chair, his own horse stood still in the road, and flung back his ears. "In short," said the pedlar, "I wish never to see that man and horse again; they do not look to me as though they belonged to this world."

This is all that I could learn at that time; and the occurrence soon after, would have become with me, "like one of those things which had never happened," had I not, as I stood recently on the door-step of Bennett's hotel in Hartford, heard a man say, "there goes Peter Rugg and his child! he looks wet and weary, and farther from Boston than ever." I was satisfied it was the same man that I had seen more than three years before; for whoever has once seen Peter Rugg can never after be deceived as to his identity. "Peter Rugg!" said I? "and who is Peter Rugg?" "That," said the stranger, "is more than any one can tell exactly. He is a famous traveller, held in light esteem by all innholders, for he never stops to eat, drink, or sleep. I wonder why the government do not employ him to carry the mail." "Aye," said a bystander, "that is a thought bright only on one side; how long would it take in that case to send a letter to Boston, for Peter has already to my knowledge been more than twenty years travelling to that place." "But," said I, "does the man never stop any where, does he never converse with any one? I saw the same man more than three years since, near Providence, and I heard a strange story about him. Pray, Sir, give me some account of this man." "Sir," said the stranger, "those who know the most respecting that man, say the least. I have heard it asserted that heaven sometimes sets a mark on a man, either for a judgment or a trial. Under which Peter Rugg now labours, I cannot say; therefore I am rather inclined to pity, than to judge." "You speak like a humane man," said I, "and pray if you have known him so long, I pray you will give me some account of him. Has his appearance much altered in that time?" "Why, yes. He looks as though he never ate, drank or slept; and his child looks older than himself, and he looks like time broke off from eternity, and anxious to gain a resting place." "And how does his horse look?" said I. "As for his horse, he looks fatter, and gayer, and shews more animation and courage, than he did twenty years ago. The last time Rugg spoke to me, he enquired how far it was to Boston. I told him just one hundred miles. 'Why,' said he, 'how can you deceive me so? It is cruel to mislead a traveller. I have lost my way; pray direct me the nearest way to Boston.' I repeated it was one hundred miles. 'How can you say so,' said he, 'I was told last evening it was but fifty, and I have travelled all night.' 'But,' said I, 'you are now travelling from Boston. You must turn back.' 'Alas,' said he, 'it is all turn back! Boston shifts with the wind, and plays all around the compass. One man tells me it is to the East, another to the West; and the guide posts, too, they all point the wrong way.' 'But will you not stop and rest,' said I. 'You seem wet and weary.' 'Yes,' said he, 'it has been foul weather since I left home.' 'Stop, then, and refresh yourself.' 'I must not stop, I must reach home to-night, if possible: though I think you must be mistaken in the distance to Boston.' He then gave the reins to his horse, which he restrained with difficulty, and disappeared in a moment. A few days afterwards, I met the man a little this side Claremont, winding around the hills in Unity, at the rate, I believe, of twelve miles an hour."

"Is Peter Rugg his real name, or has he accidentally gained that name?" "I know not, but presume he will not deny his name; you can ask him, for see, he has turned his horse, and is passing this way." In a moment, a dark coloured, high spirited horse approached, and would have passed without stopping, but I had resolved to speak to Peter Rugg, or whoever the man might be. Accordingly, I stepped into the street, and as the horse approached, I made a feint of stopping him. The man immediately reined in his horse. "Sir," said I, "may I be so bold as to inquire if you are not Mr. Rugg? for I think I have seen you before." "My name is Peter Rugg," said he, "I have unfortunately lost my way; I am wet and weary, and will take it kindly of you to direct me to Boston." "You live in Boston, do you, and in what street?" "In Middle-street." "When did you leave Boston?" "I cannot tell precisely; it seems a considerable time." "But how did you and your child become so wet? It has not rained here to-day." "It has just rained a heavy shower up the river. But I shall not reach Boston to-night, if I tarry. Would you advise me to take the old road, or the turnpike?" "Why, the old road is one hundred and seventeen miles, and the turnpike is ninety-seven." "How can you say so? you impose on me; it is wrong to trifle with a traveller; you know it is but forty miles from Newburyport to Boston." "But this is not Newburyport; this is Hartford." "Do not deceive me, sir. Is not this town Newburyport, and the river that I have been following, the Merrimac?" "No, Sir, this is Hartford, and the river, the Connecticut." He wrung his hands and looked incredulous. "Have the rivers, too, changed their courses, as the cities have changed places? But see, the clouds are gathering in the south, and we shall have a rainy night. Ah, that fatal oath!" He would tarry no longer, his impatient horse leaped off, his hind flanks rising like wings, he seemed to devour all before him, and to scorn all behind.

I had now, as I thought, discovered a clue to the history of Peter Rugg, and I determined, the next time my business called me to Boston, to make a further inquiry. Soon after, I was enabled to collect the following particulars from Mrs. Croft, an aged lady in Middle-street, who has resided in Boston, during the last twenty years. Her narration is this—The last summer, a person, just at twilight, stopped at the door of the late Mrs. Rugg. Mrs. Croft, on coming to the door, perceived a stranger, with a child by his side, in an old weather-beaten carriage, with a black horse. The stranger asked for Mrs. Rugg, and was informed that Mrs. Rugg had died in a good old age, more than twenty years before that time. The stranger replied, "how can you deceive me so? do ask Mrs. Rugg to step to the door." "Sir, I assure you Mrs. Rugg has not lived here these nineteen years; no one lives here but myself, and my name is Betsey Croft." The stranger paused, and looked up and down the street, and said, "though the painting is rather faded, this looks like my house." "Yes," said the child, "that is the stone before the door, that I used to sit on to eat my bread and milk." "But," said the stranger, "it seems to be on the wrong side of the street. Indeed, every thing here seems to be misplaced. The streets are all changed, the people are all changed, the town seems changed, and what is strangest of all, Catherine Rugg has deserted her husband and child. Pray," continued the stranger, "has John Foy come home from sea? he went a long voyage, he is my kinsman. If I could see him, he could give me some account of Mrs. Rugg." "Sir," said Mrs. Croft, "I never heard of John Foy. Where did he live?" "Just above here, in Orange Tree Lane." "There is no such place in this neighborhood." "What do you tell me! Are the streets gone? Orange Tree Lane is at the head of Hanover-street, near Pemberton's hill." "There is no such lane now." "Madam! you cannot be serious. But you doubtless know my brother, William Rugg. He lives in Royal Exchange Lane, near King-street." "I know of no such lane; and I am sure there is no such street as King-street, in this town." "No such street as King-street! Why, woman! you mock me. You may as well tell me there is no King George. However, madam, you see I am wet and weary, I must find a resting place. I will go to Hart's tavern near the market." "Which market, sir? for you seem perplexed; we have several markets." "You know there is but one market, near the town dock." "O, the old market, but no such man as Hart has kept there these twenty years." Here the stranger seemed disconcerted, and uttered to himself quite audibly, "Strange mistake, how much this looks like the town of Boston! It certainly has a great resemblance to it; but I perceive my mistake now. Some other Mrs. Rugg, some other Middle-street." Then said he, "madam, can you direct me to Boston?" "Why, this is Boston, the city of Boston, I know of no other Boston." "City of Boston it may be; but it is not the Boston where I live. I recollect now, I came over a bridge instead of a ferry. Pray, what bridge is that, I just came over." "It is Charles River Bridge." "I perceive my mistake, there is a ferry between Boston and Charlestown, there is no bridge. Ah, I perceive my mistake, if I was in Boston my horse would carry me directly to my own door. But my horse shews by his impatience, that he is in a strange place. Absurd, that I should have mistaken this place for the old town of Boston! it is a much finer city than the town of Boston. It has been built long since Boston. I fancy Boston must lie at a distance from this city, as the good woman seems ignorant of it." At these words, his horse began to chafe, and strike the pavement with his fore feet; the stranger seemed a little bewildered, and said, "no home to-night," and giving the reins to his horse, passed up the street, and Mrs. Croft saw no more of him.

It was evident that the generation to which Peter Rugg belonged had passed away.

This was all the account of Peter Rugg, I could obtain from Mrs. Croft; but she directed me to an elderly man, Mr. James Felt, who lived near her, and who had kept a record of the principal occurrences for the last fifty years. At my request, she sent for him; and after I had related to him the object of my inquiry, Mr. Felt told me he had known Rugg in his youth; that his disappearance had caused some surprise; but as it sometimes happens that men run away; sometimes to be rid of others, and sometimes to be rid of themselves; and as Rugg took his child with him, and his own horse and chair; and as it did not appear that any creditors made a stir, the occurrence soon mingled itself in the stream of oblivion; and Rugg and his child, horse and chair, were soon forgotten. "It is true," said Mr. Felt, "sundry stories grew out of Rugg's affair, whether true or false I cannot tell; but stranger things have happened in my day, without even a newspaper notice." "Sir," said I, "Peter Rugg is now living. I have lately seen Peter Rugg and his child, horse and chair; therefore, I pray you to relate to me all you know or ever heard of him." "Why, my friend," said James Felt, "that Peter Rugg is now a living man I will not deny; but that you have seen Peter Rugg and his child, is impossible, if you mean a small child, for Jenny Rugg, if living, must be at least—let me see—Boston massacre, 1770—Jenny Rugg was about ten years old. Why, sir, Jenny Rugg, if living, must be more than sixty years of age. That Peter Rugg is living, is highly probable, as he was only ten years older than myself; and I was only eighty last March; and I am as likely to live twenty years longer, as any man." Here I perceived that Mr. Felt was in his dotage, and I despaired from gaining any intelligence from him, on which I could depend.

I took my leave of Mrs. Croft, and proceeded to my lodgings at the Marlborough Hotel.

If Peter Rugg, thought I, has been travelling since the Boston massacre, there is no reason, why he should not travel to the end of time. If the present generation know little of him, the next will know less, and Peter and his child will have no hold on this world.

In the course of the evening, I related my adventure in Middle-street. "Hah!" said one of the company, smiling, "do you really think you have seen Peter Rugg? I have heard my grandfather speak of him, as though he seriously believed his own story." "Sir," said I, "pray let us compare your grandfather's story of Mr. Rugg, with my own." "Peter Rugg, sir, if my grandfather was worthy of credit, once lived in Middle-street, in this city. He was a man in comfortable circumstances, had a wife and one daughter, and was generally esteemed for his sober life and manners. But unhappily his temper, at times was altogether ungovernable, and then, his language was terrible. In these fits of passion, if a door stood in his way, he would never do less than kick a pannel through. He would sometimes throw his heels over his head, and come down on his feet, uttering oaths in a circle; and thus in a rage, he was the first who performed a summersett, and did what others have since learnt to do for merriment and money. Once, Rugg was seen to bite a ten-penny nail in halves. In those days, every body, both men and boys, wore wigs; and Peter, at these moments of violent passion, would become so profane that his wig would rise up from his head. Some said, it was on account of his terrible language. Others accounted for it in a more philosophical way, and said it was caused by the expansion of his scalp; as violent passion, we know, will swell the veins and expand the head. While these fits were on him, Rugg had no respect for heaven or earth. Except this infirmity, all agreed that Rugg was a good sort of a man; for when his fits were over, nobody was so ready to commend a placid temper as Peter.

"It was late in autumn, one morning, that Rugg, in his own chair, with a fine large bay horse, took his daughter, and proceeded to Concord. On his return, a violent storm overtook him. At dark, he stopped in Menotomy (now West-Cambridge), at the door of a Mr. Cutter, a friend of his, who urged him to tarry the night. On Rugg's declining to stop, Mr. Cutter urged him vehemently. 'Why, Mr. Rugg,' said Cutter, 'the storm is overwhelming you; the night is exceeding dark; your little daughter will perish; you are in an open chair, and the tempest is increasing.' 'Let the storm increase,' said Rugg, with a fearful oath, 'I will see home to-night, in spite of the last tempest! or may I never see home!' At these words, he gave his whip to his high spirited horse, and disappeared in a moment. But Peter Rugg did not reach home that night, nor the next; nor, when he became a missing man, could he ever be traced beyond Mr. Cutter's in Menotomy. For a long time after, on every dark and stormy night, the wife of Peter Rugg would fancy she heard the crack of a whip, and the fleet tread of a horse, and the rattling of a carriage, passing her door. The neighbours, too, heard the same noises, and some said they knew it was Rugg's horse; the tread on the pavement was perfectly familiar to them. This occurred so repeatedly, that at length the neighbours watched with lanterns, and saw the real Peter Rugg, with his own horse and chair, and child sitting beside him, pass directly before his own door, his head turning toward his house, and himself making every effort to stop his horse, but in vain. The next day, the friends of Mrs. Rugg exerted themselves to find her husband and child. They inquired at every public house and stable in town; but it did not appear that Rugg made any stay in Boston. No one, after Rugg had passed his own door, could give any account of him; though it was asserted by some that the clatter of Rugg's horse and carriage over the pavements shook the houses on both sides of the streets. And this is credible, if indeed Rugg's horse and carriage did pass on that night. For at this day, in many of the streets, a loaded truck or team in passing will shake the houses like an earthquake. However, Rugg's neighbours never afterwards watched again; some of them treated it all as a delusion, and thought no more of it. Others, of a different opinion, shook their heads, and said nothing. Thus Rugg, and his child, horse and chair, were soon forgotten; and probably many in the neighborhood never heard a word on the subject.

"There was indeed a rumour, that Rugg afterwards was seen in Connecticut, between Suffield and Hartford, passing through the country, like a streak of chalk. This gave occasion to Rugg's friends to make further inquiry. But the more they inquired, the more they were baffled. If they heard of Rugg, one day in Connecticut,—the next, they heard of him winding around the hills in New-Hampshire; and soon after, a man in a chair, with a small child, exactly answering the description of Peter Rugg, would be seen in Rhode-Island, inquiring the way to Boston.

"But that which chiefly gave a colour of mystery to the story of Peter Rugg, was the affair at Charlestown bridge. The toll-gatherer asserted that sometimes, on the darkest, and most stormy nights, when no object could be discerned, about the time Rugg was missing, a horse and wheel carriage, with a noise equal to a troop, would at midnight, in utter contempt of the rates of toll, pass over the bridge. This occurred so frequently, that the toll-gatherer resolved to attempt a discovery. Soon after, at the usual time, apparently the same horse and carriage approached the bridge from Charlestown square. The toll-gatherer, prepared, took his stand as near the middle of the bridge as he dared, with a large three-legged stool in his hand. As the appearance passed, he threw the stool at the horse, but heard nothing, except the noise of the stool skipping across the bridge. The toll-gatherer, on the next day, asserted that the stool went directly through the body of the horse; and he persisted in that belief ever after. Whether Rugg, or whoever the person was, ever passed the bridge again, the toll-gatherer would never tell—and when questioned seemed anxious to wave the subject. And thus, Peter Rugg and his child, horse and carriage, remain a mystery to this day."

This, sir, is all that I could learn of Peter Rugg in Boston. When I see him again, you shall hear further from your friend and humble servant,

JONATHAN DUNWELL.

New-York, Aug. 28, 1824.

## SOME FURTHER ACCOUNT OF PETER RUGG, THE MISSING MAN, LATE OF BOSTON, NEW-ENGLAND.

To the Editor of the Galaxy,

Sir,—Perhaps you may recollect that in the summer of 1824, I communicated a few particulars respecting a man called Peter Rugg. I intimated to you that if I ever heard any thing more of the man, I would inform you. A short time after, I noticed in the Galaxy, a very inconsiderate complaint of yours, "that nothing more was heard of Peter Rugg;" as if it was in my power to follow Mr. Rugg and relate his adventures. I have now the pleasure to inform you that I have not only, since that time, seen Mr. Rugg, but have sitten by the side of him, and conversed with him in his own chair.

In the autumn of 1825, I attended the races at Richmond in Virginia; as two new horses of great promise were run, the race ground was never better attended, nor was expectation ever more deeply excited. The partisans of Dart and Lightning, the two race horses, were equally anxious, and equally dubious of the result. To an indifferent spectator it was impossible to perceive any difference. They were equally beautiful to behold, alike in colour and height, and as they stood side by side, they measured from heel to fore feet within half an inch of each other. The eyes of each were full, prominent and resolute, and when at times they regarded each other, they assumed a lofty demeanour, seemed to shorten their necks, project their eyes and rest their bodies equally on their four hoofs. They certainly discovered signs of intelligence, and displayed a courtesy to each other, unusual even with statesmen. It was now nearly twelve o'clock, the hour of expectation, doubt and anxiety. The riders mounted their horses; and so trim, light and airy, they sat on the animals, they seemed a part of them. The spectators, many deep, in a solid column, had taken their places; and as many thousand breathing statues were there, as spectators. All eyes were turned to Dart and Lightning, and their two fairy riders. There was nothing to disturb this calm, except a busy woodpecker on a neighboring tree. The signal was given, and Dart and Lightning answered the signal with ready intelligence. At first they proceed on a slow trot, then they quicken to a canter, and then a gallop. Presently they sweep the plain; both horses lay themselves, flat on the ground, their riders bending forward, and resting their chins between their horses' ears. Had not the ground been perfectly level, had there been any undulation, the least rise and fall, the spectator, every moment, for a moment, would have lost sight of both horses and riders. While these horses, side by side, thus appeared, flying without wings, flat as a hare, and neither gained on the other, all eyes were diverted to a new spectacle. Directly in the rear of Dart and Lightning, a majestic black horse of unusual size, drawing an old weather-beaten chair, strode over the plain; and although he appeared to make no effort, for he maintained a steady trot, before Dart and Lightning approached the goal, the black horse and chair had overtaken the racers, who, on perceiving this new competitor pass them, threw back their ears, and suddenly stopped in their course. Thus neither Dart nor Lightning carried away the purse. The spectators now, were exceedingly curious to learn whence came the black horse and chair. With many it was the opinion that nobody was in the vehicle. Indeed, this began to be the prevalent opinion, for those at a short distance, so fleet was the black horse, could not easily discern, who, if any body, was in the carriage. But both the riders, whom the black horse passed very nearly, agreed in this particular, that a sad looking man with a little girl, was in the chair. When they stated this, I was satisfied it was Peter Rugg. But what caused no little surprise, John Spring, one of the riders, he who rode Lightning, asserted that no earthly horse, without breaking his trot, could in a carriage outstrip his race horse: and he persisted with some passion that it was not a horse, he was sure it was not a horse, but a large black ox. "What a great black ox can do," said John, "I cannot pretend to say; but no race horse, not even Flying Childers, could out-trot Lightning in a fair race." This opinion of John Spring excited no little merriment, for it was clearly obvious to every one, that it was a powerful black horse that interrupted the race: but John Spring, jealous of Lightning's reputation as a horse, would rather have it thought that any other beast, even an ox, had been the victor. However, the horse-laugh at John Spring's expence was soon suppressed; for as soon as Dart and Lightning began to breathe more freely, it was observed that both of them walked deliberately to the tract of the race ground, and putting their heads to the earth, they suddenly raised them again, and began to snort. They repeated this, till John Spring said, "these horses have discovered something strange; they suspect foul play; let me go and talk with Lightning." And he went up to Lightning and took hold of his main, and Lightning put his nose toward the ground and smelt of the earth without touching it, and then reared his head very high, and snorted so loudly that the sound echoed from the next hill. Dart did the same. John Spring stooped down to examine the spot where Lightning smelt. In a moment he raised himself up, and the countenance of the man was changed; his strength failed him, and he sidled against Lightning. At length John Spring recovered from his stupor, and exclaimed, "it was an ox! I told you it was an ox, no real horse ever yet beat Lightning." And now, on a close inspection of the black horse's tracks in the path, it was evident to every one, that the fore feet of the black horse were cloven. Notwithstanding these appearances, to me it was evident that the strange horse, was in reality a horse. Yet when the people left the race ground, I presume one half of all those present, would have testified that a large black ox had distanced two of the fleetest coursers that had ever trod the Virginia turf. So uncertain are all things called historical facts.

While I was proceeding to my lodgings, pondering on the events of the day, a stranger rode up to me, and accosted me thus, "I think your name is Dunwell, sir?" "Yes, sir," I replied. "Did I not see you, a year or two since in Boston, at the Marlborough Hotel?" "Very likely, sir, for I was there." "And you heard a story about one Peter Rugg?" "I recollect it all," said I. "The account you heard in Boston must be true, for here he was to-day. The man has found his way to Virginia, and for aught that appears has been to Cape Horn. I have seen him before to-day, but never saw him travel with such fearful velocity.

Pray, sir, where does Peter Rugg spend his winters? for I have seen him only in summer, and always in foul weather, except at this time." I replied, "no one knows where Peter Rugg spends his winters, where or when he eats, drinks, sleeps or lodges. He seems to have an indistinct idea of day and night, time and space, storm and sunshine. His only object is Boston. It appears to me that Rugg's horse has some controul of the chair: and that Rugg himself is, in some sort, under the controul of his horse." I then inquired of the stranger where he first saw the man and horse. "Why, sir," said the stranger, "in the summer of 1824, I travelled to the North for my health, and soon after I saw you at the Marlborough Hotel, I returned homeward to Virginia, and if my memory is correct, I saw this man and horse in every State between here and Massachusetts. Sometimes he would meet me, but oftener overtake me. He never spoke but once, and that once was in Delaware. On his approach he checked his horse with some difficulty. A more beautiful horse I never saw; his hide was as fair, and rotund and glossy as the skin of a Congo beauty. When Rugg's horse approached mine, he reined in his neck, bent his ears forward until they met, and looked my horse full in the face. My horse immediately withered into half a horse: his hide curled up like a piece of burnt leather; spell bound, he was fixed to the earth as though a nail had been drove through each hoof. 'Sir,' said Rugg, 'perhaps you are travelling to Boston, and if so, I should be happy to accompany you, for I have lost my way, and I must reach home to-night. See how sleepy this little girl looks; poor thing, she is a picture of patience.' 'Sir,' said I, 'it is impossible for you to reach home to-night, for you are in Concord in the County of Sussex, in the State of Delaware.' 'What do you mean,' said he, 'by State of Delaware? If I was in Concord, that is only twenty miles from Boston, and my horse Lightfoot could carry me to Charlestown Ferry in less than two hours. You mistake, sir; you are a stranger here; this town is nothing like Concord. I am well acquainted with Concord. I went to Concord when I left Boston.' 'But,' said I, 'you are in Concord in the State of Delaware.' 'What do you mean by State?' said Rugg. 'Why, one of the United States.' 'States,' said he, in a low voice, 'the man is a wag, and would persuade me I am in Holland.' Then, raising his voice, he said, 'you seem, sir, to be a gentleman, and I entreat you to mislead me not; tell me quickly, for pity's sake, the right road to Boston, for you see my horse will swallow his bitts; for he has eaten nothing since I left Concord.' 'Sir,' said I, 'this town is Concord, Concord in Delaware, not Concord in Massachusetts; and you are now five hundred miles from Boston.' Rugg looked at me for a moment, more in sorrow than resentment, and then repeated, 'five hundred miles! unhappy man, who would have thought he had been deranged, but nothing is so deceitful as appearances, in this world. Five hundred miles! this beats Connecticut River.' What he meant by Connecticut River, I know not; his horse broke away, and Rugg disappeared in a moment."

I explained to the stranger the meaning of Rugg's expression, "Connecticut River," and the incident respecting him that occurred at Hartford, as I stood on the door stone of Mr. Bennett's excellent hotel. We both agreed that the man we had seen that day was the true Peter Rugg.

Soon after, I saw Rugg again, at the toll gate on the Turnpike, between Alexandria and Middleburgh. While I was paying the toll, I observed to the toll gatherer, that the drought was more severe in his vicinity, than further South. "Yes," said he, "the drought is excessive; but if I had not heard yesterday by a traveller, that the man with the black horse was seen in Kentucky a day or two since, I should be sure of a shower in a few minutes." I looked all around the horizon, and could not discern a cloud that could hold a pint of water. "Look, sir," said the toll gatherer, "you perceive to the Eastward, just rising that hill, a small black cloud not bigger than a black-berry, and while I am speaking it is doubling and trebling itself, and rolling up the turnpike steadily, as if its sole design was to deluge some object." "True," said I, "I do perceive it; but what connexion is there between a thunder cloud and a man and horse?" "More than you imagine, or I can tell you; but stop a moment, sir, I may need your assistance. I know that cloud, I have seen it several times before; and can testify to its identity. You will soon see a man and black horse under it." While he was yet speaking, true enough, we began to hear the distant thunder, and soon the chain lightning performed all the figures of a country dance. About a mile distant, we saw the man and black horse under the cloud; but before he arrived at the toll gate, the thunder cloud had spent itself, and not even a sprinkle fell near us. As the man, whom I instantly knew to be Rugg, attempted to pass, the toll gatherer swung the gate across the road, seized Rugg's horse by the reins and demanded two dollars. Feeling some little regard for Rugg, I interfered, and began to question the toll gatherer, and requested him not to be wroth with the man. The toll gatherer replied he had just cause, for the man had run his toll ten times, and moreover that the horse had discharged a cannon ball at him, to the great danger of his life; that the man had always before, approached so rapidly that he was too quick for the rusty hinges of the toll gate; but that now he would have full satisfaction. Rugg looked wishfully at me, and said, "I entreat you, sir, to delay me not, I have found at length the direct road to Boston, and shall not reach home before night if you detain me: you see I am dripping wet, and ought to change my clothes." The toll gatherer then demanded why he had run his toll, so many times? "Toll! why," said Rugg, "do you demand toll? there is no toll to pay on the King's highway." "King's highway! do you not perceive this is a turnpike?" "Turnpike! there are no turnpikes in Massachusetts." "That may be, but we have several in Virginia." "Virginia! do you pretend I am in Virginia?" Rugg then, appealing to me, asked how far it was to Boston? Said I, "Mr. Rugg, I perceive you are bewildered, and am sorry to see you so far from home; you are, indeed, in Virginia." "You know me then, sir, it seems; and you say I am in Virginia. Give me leave to tell you, sir, you are the most impudent man alive; for I was never forty miles from Boston, and I never saw a Virginian in my life. This beats Delaware!" "Your toll, sir, your toll!" "I will not pay you a penny," said Rugg, "you are both of you highway robbers; there are no turnpikes in this country. Take toll on the King's highway! Robbers take toll on the King's highway." Then in a low tone he said, "here is evidently a conspiracy against me; alas, I shall never see Boston! The highways refuse me a passage, the rivers change their courses, and there is no faith in the compass." But Rugg's horse had no idea of stopping more than one minute, for in the midst of this altercation, the horse, whose nose was resting on the upper bar of the turnpike gate, seized it between his teeth, lifted it gently off its staples, and trotted off with it. The toll gatherer, confounded, strained his eyes after his gate. "Let him go," said I, "the horse will soon drop your gate, and you will get it again."

I then questioned the toll gatherer respecting his knowledge of this man; and he related the following particulars. "The first time," said he, "that man ever passed this toll gate was in the year 1806, at the moment of the great eclipse. I thought the horse was frightened at the sudden darkness and concluded he had run away with the man. But within a few days after, the same man and horse repassed with equal speed, without the least respect to the toll gate, or to me, except by a vacant stare. Some few years afterward, during the late war, I saw the same man approaching again, and I resolved to check his career. Accordingly, I stepped into the middle of the road, and stretched wide both of my arms, and cried, 'stop, sir, on your peril!' At this, the man said, 'now Lightfoot, confound the robber!' At the same time, he gave the whip liberally to the flank of his horse, who bounded off with such force, that it appeared to me, two such horses, give them a place to stand, would check the diurnal motion of the earth. An ammunition wagon which had just passed on to Baltimore, had dropped an eighteen pounder in the road; this unlucky ball lay in the way of the horse's heels, and the beast, with the sagacity of a demon, clinched it with one of his heels and hurled it behind him. I feel dizzy in relating the fact, but so nearly did the ball pass my head that the wind thereof blew off my hat, and the ball bedded itself in that gate post, as you may see, if you will cast your eye to the post. I have permitted it to remain there in memory of the occurrence, as the people of Boston, I am told, preserve the eighteen pounder, which is now to be seen half bedded in Brattle-street church."

I then took leave of the toll gatherer, and promised him, if I saw, or heard of his gate, I would send him notice.

A strong inclination had possessed me to arrest Rugg, and search his pockets, thinking great discoveries might be made in the examination; but what I saw and heard that day convinced me that no human force could detain Peter Rugg against his consent. I therefore determined if I ever saw Rugg again to treat him in the gentlest manner.

In pursuing my way to New-York, I entered on the Turnpike in Trenton; and when I arrived at New-Brunswick, I perceived the road was newly McAdamised. The small stones had just been laid thereon. As I passed this piece of road, I observed at regular distances of about eight feet, the stones entirely displaced from spots as large as the circumference of a half-bushel measure. This singular appearance induced me to inquire the cause of it at the turnpike gate. "Sir," said the toll gatherer, "I wonder not at the question, but I am unable to give you a satisfactory answer. Indeed, sir, I believe I am bewitched, and that the turnpike is under a spell of enchantment; for what appeared to me last night cannot be a real transaction; otherwise a turnpike gate is a useless thing." "I do not believe in witchcraft or enchantment," said I, "and if you will relate circumstantially what happened, last night, I will endeavour to account for it by natural means." "You may recollect, the night was uncommonly dark. Well, sir, just after I had closed the gate for the night, down the turnpike, as far as my eye could reach, I beheld, what at first appeared to me, two armies engaged. The report of the musketry, and the flashes of their firelocks were incessant and continuous. As this strange spectacle approached me with the fury of a tornado, the noise increased, and the appearance rolled on in one compact body over the surface of the ground. The most splendid fireworks rose out of the earth, and encircled this moving spectacle. The divers tints of the rainbow, the most brilliant dies that the sun lays on the lap of spring, added to the whole family of gems, could not display a more beautiful, radiant and dazzling spectacle than accompanied the black horse. You would have thought all the stars of heaven had met in merriment on the turnpike. In the midst of this luminous configuration sat a man, distinctly to be seen, in a miserable looking chair drawn by a black horse. The turnpike gate, ought, by the laws of nature, and the laws of the state, to have made a wreck of the whole, and have dissolved the enchantment; but no, the horse, without an effort, passed over the gate, and drew the man and chair horizontally after him without touching the bar. This was what I call enchantment—what think you, sir?" "My friend," said I, "you have grossly magnified a natural occurrence. The man was Peter Rugg on his way to Boston. It is true, his horse travelled with unequalled speed, but as he reared high his fore feet, he could not help displacing the thousand small stones on which he trod, which flying in all directions struck each other, and resounded and scintillated. The top bar of your gate is not more than two feet from the ground, and Rugg's horse at every vault could easily lift the carriage over that gate." This satisfied Mr. McDoubt; and I was pleased at that occurrence, for otherwise Mr. McDoubt, who is a worthy man, late from the Highlands, might have added to his calender of superstitions. Having thus disenchanted the McAdamised road, and the turnpike gate, and also Mr. McDoubt, I pursued my journey homeward to New-York.

Little did I expect to see or hear any thing further of Mr. Rugg, for he was now more than twelve hours in advance of me. I could hear nothing of him on my way to Elizabethtown. I therefore concluded that during the past night he had turned off from the turnpike, and pursued a Westerly direction. But just before I arrived at Powles's Hook, I observed a considerable collection of passengers in the ferry boat, all standing motionless, and steadily looking at the same object. One of the ferrymen, Mr. Hardy, who well knew me, observing my approach, delayed a minute, in order to afford me a passage, and coming up, said, "Mr. Dunwell, we have got a curiosity on board, that would puzzle Dr. Mitchill." "Some strange fish, I suppose, has found its way into the Hudson." "No," said he, "it is a man, who looks as if he had lain hid in the ark, and had just now ventured out. He has a little girl with him, the counterpart of himself; and the finest horse you ever saw, harnessed to the queerest looking carriage that ever was made." "Ah, Mr. Hardy," said I, "you have, indeed, hooked a prize; no one before you could ever detain Peter Rugg long enough to examine him." "Do you know the man," said Mr. Hardy. "No, nobody knows him, but every body has seen him. Detain him as long as possible, delay the boat under any pretence; cut the gear of the horse; do any thing to detain him." As I entered the ferry boat, I was struck at the spectacle before me; there, indeed, sat Peter Rugg and Jenny Rugg in the chair, and there stood the black horse, all as quiet as lambs, surrounded by more than fifty men and women, who seemed to have lost all their senses but one. Not a motion, not a breath, not a nestle. They were all eye. Rugg appeared to them to be a man not of this world; and they appeared to Rugg a strange generation of men. Rugg spoke not, and they spoke not; nor was I disposed to disturb the calm; satisfied, to reconnoitre Rugg in a state of rest. Presently, Rugg observed in a low voice, addressed to nobody, "A new contrivance, horses instead of oars, Boston folks are full of notions." It was plain that Rugg was of Dutch extract—he had on three pairs of small clothes, called in former days of simplicity, breeches, not much the worse for wear; but time had proved the fabric, and shrunk each of them more than the other, so that they discovered at the knees, their different qualities and colours. His several waistcoats, the flaps of all which rested on his knees, gave him an appearance rather corpulent. His capacious drab coat would supply the stuff for half a dozen modern ones. The sleeves were like meal bags—in the cuffs of which you might nurse a child to sleep. His hat, probably once black, now of a tan colour, was neither round, nor cocked, but much in shape like the one President Monroe wore on his late tour. This dress gave the rotund face of Rugg an antiquated dignity. The man, though deeply sun-burnt, did not appear to be more than thirty years of age. He had lost his sad and anxious look, was quite composed, and seemed happy. The chair in which Rugg sat, was very capacious, evidently made for service, and calculated to last for ages. The timber would supply material for three modern carriages. This chair, like a Nantucket coach, would answer for every thing that ever went on wheels. The horse, too, was an object of curiosity—his majestic height, his natural main and tail gave him a commanding appearance—and his large open nostrils indicated inexhaustible wind. It was apparent that the hoofs of his fore feet had been split, probably on some newly McAdamised road, and were now growing together again; so that John Spring was not altogether in the wrong.

How long this dumb scene would otherwise have continued, I cannot tell. Rugg discovered no sign of impatience. But Rugg's horse, having been quiet more than five minutes, had no idea of standing idle; he began to whinny, and in a moment after, with his right fore foot, he started a plank. Said Rugg, "my horse is impatient, he sees the North End. You must be quick, or he will be ungovernable." At these words, the horse raised his left fore foot; and when he laid it down, every inch of the ferry boat trembled. Two men immediately seized Rugg's horse by the nostrils. The horse nodded, and both of them were in the Hudson. While we were fishing up the men, the horse was perfectly quiet. "Fret not the horse," said Rugg, "and he will do no harm. He is only anxious like myself to arrive at yonder beautiful shore. He sees the North Church, and smells his own stable." "Sir," said I to Rugg, practising a little deception, "pray tell me, for I am a stranger here, what river is this, and what city is that opposite? for you seem to be an inhabitant of it." "This river, sir, is called Mystic River, and this is Winnisimet ferry, we have retained the Indian names, and that town is Boston. You must, indeed, be a stranger in these parts, not to know that yonder is Boston, the capital of the New-England provinces." "Pray, sir, how long have you been absent from Boston?" "Why, that I cannot exactly tell. I lately went with this little girl of mine, to Concord to see my friends; and I am ashamed to tell you in returning lost the way, and have been travelling ever since. No one would direct me right. It is cruel to mislead a traveller. My horse, Lightfoot, has boxed the compass, and it seems to me he has boxed it back again. But, sir, you perceive my horse is uneasy; Lightfoot, as yet, has given only a hint and a nod. I cannot be answerable for his heels." At these words, Lightfoot reared his long tail, and snapped it as you would a whip lash. The Hudson reverberated with the sound. Instantly the six horses began to move the boat. The Hudson was a sea of glass, smooth as oil, not a ripple. The horses, from a smart trot, soon pressed into a gallop; water now ran over the gunnel; the ferry boat was soon buried in an ocean of foam and the noise of the spray was like the roaring of many waters. When we arrived at New-York, you might see the beautiful white wake of the ferry boat across the Hudson.

Though Rugg refused to pay toll at turnpikes, when Mr. Hardy reached his hand for the ferriage, Rugg readily put his hand into one of his many pockets, and took out a piece of silver, and handed it to Hardy. "What is this," said Mr. Hardy. "It is thirty shillings," said Rugg. "It might have once been thirty shillings, old tenor," said Mr. Hardy, "but it is not at present." "The money is good English coin," said Rugg, "my grandfather brought a bag of them from England, and he had them hot from the mint." Hearing this, I approached near to Rugg, and asked permission to see the coin. It was a half crown, coined by the English Parliament, dated in the year 1649. On one side, "The Commonwealth of England," and St. George's cross encircled with a wreath of laurel. On the other, "God with us," and a harp and St. George's cross united. I winked to Mr. Hardy, and pronounced it good, current money; and said loudly, I would not permit the gentleman to be imposed on, for I would exchange the money myself. On this, Rugg spoke, "please to give me your name, sir." "My name is Dunwell, sir," I replied. "Mr. Dunwell," said Rugg, "you are the only honest man I have seen since I left Boston. As you are a stranger here, my house is your home, dame Rugg will be happy to see her husband's friend. Step into my chair, sir, there is room enough; move a little, Jenny, for the gentleman, and we will be in Middle-street in a minute." Accordingly, I took a seat by Peter Rugg. "Were you never in Boston before?" said Rugg. "No," said I. "Well, you will now see the queen of New-England, a town second only to Philadelphia, in all North America." "You forget New-York," said I. "Poh, New-York is nothing; though I never was there, I am told you might put all New-York in our Mill Pond. No, Sir, New-York, I assure you, is but a sorry affair, no more to be compared to Boston than a wigwam to a palace."

As Rugg's horse turned into Pearl street, I looked Rugg as fully in the face as good manners would allow, and said, "Sir, if this is Boston, I acknowledge New-York is not worthy to be one of its suburbs." Before we had proceeded far in Pearl street, Rugg's countenance changed, he began to twitter under his ears, his eyes trembled in their sockets; he was evidently bewildered. "What is the matter, Mr. Rugg? you seem disturbed." "This surpasses all human comprehension; if you know, sir, where we are, I beseech you to tell me." "If this place," I replied, "is not Boston, it must be New-York." "No, sir, it is not Boston; nor can it be New-York. How could I be in New-York, which is nearly two hundred miles from Boston!" By this time we had passed into Broadway, and then Rugg, in truth, discovered a chaotic mind. "There is no such place as this in North America, this is all the effect of enchantment; this is a grand delusion, nothing real; here is seemingly a great city, magnificent houses, shops and goods, men and women innumerable, and as busy as in real life, all sprung up in one night from the wilderness. Or what is more probable, some tremendous convulsion of nature has thrown London or Amsterdam on the shores of New-England. Or, possibly, I may be dreaming, though the night seems rather long, but before now I have sailed in one night to Amsterdam, bought goods of Vandogger, and returned to Boston before morning." At this moment a hue and cry was heard, "stop the madmen, they will endanger the lives of thousands!" In vain hundreds attempted to stop Rugg's horse; Lightfoot interfered with nothing, his course was straight as a shooting star. But on my part fearful that before night I should find myself behind the Alleghanies, I addressed Mr. Rugg in a tone of entreaty, and requested him to restrain the horse and permit me to alight. "My friend," said he, "we shall be in Boston before dark, and dame Rugg will be most exceeding glad to see us." "Mr. Rugg," said I, "you must excuse me; pray look to the West, see that thunder cloud swelling with rage, as if in pursuit of us." "Ah," said Rugg, "it is in vain to attempt to escape, I know that cloud, it is collecting new wrath to spend on my head." Then, checking his horse, he permitted me to descend, saying, "farewell, Mr. Dunwell, I shall be happy to see you in Boston, I live in Middle-street."

If ever I see Peter Rugg again, Mr. Editor, you may possibly hear more from

Your obedient servant,
JONATHAN DUNWELL.
New-York, Aug. 26, 1826.

## ARRIVAL OF MR. PETER RUGG IN BOSTON.

It is uncertain in what direction Mr. Rugg pursued his course, after he disappeared in Broadway: but one thing is sufficiently known to every body, that in the course of two months, after he was seen in New-York, he found his way most opportunely to Boston.

It seems the estate of Peter Rugg had recently escheated to the Commonwealth of Massachusetts for want of heirs; and the legislature had ordered the Solicitor General to advertise, and sell it, at public auction. Happening to be in Boston at the time, and observing this advertisement, which described a considerable extent of land, I felt a kindly curiosity to see the spot where Rugg once lived. Taking the advertisement in my hand, I wandered a little way down Middle-street, and without asking a question of any one, when I came to a certain spot, I said to myself, "This is Rugg's estate, I will proceed no further, this must be the spot; it is a counterpart of Peter Rugg." The premises, indeed, looked as if they had accomplished a sad prophesy. Fronting on Middle-street, they extended in the rear to Ann-street, and embraced about half an acre of land. It was not uncommon in former times to have half an acre for a house lot; for an acre of land then, in many parts of Boston, was not more valuable than a foot, in some places at present. The old mansion house had become powder-post, and been blown away. One other building, uninhabited, stood ominous, courting dilapidation. The street had been so much raised, that the bed chamber had descended to the kitchen and was level with the street. The house seemed conscious of its fate, and as though tired of standing there, the front was fast retreating from the rear, and waiting the next south wind to project itself into the street. If the most wary animals had sought a place of refuge, here they would have rendevoused. Here, under the ridge pole, the crow would have perched in security, and in the recesses below, you might have caught the fox and the weasel asleep. "The hand of destiny," said I, "has pressed heavy on this spot; still heavier on the former owners. Strange that so large a lot of land as this should want an heir! Yet Peter Rugg, at this day, might pass by his own door stone, and ask, 'who once lived there?'"

The auctioneer, appointed by the Solicitor, to sell this estate, was a man of eloquence, as many of the auctioneers of Boston are. The occasion seemed to warrant, and his duty urged him to make a display. He addressed his audience as follows: "The estate, gentlemen, which we offer you this day, was once the property of a family now extinct. It has escheated to the Commonwealth for want of heirs. Lest any one of you should be deterred from bidding on so large an estate as this, for fear of a disputed title, I am authorised by the Solicitor General to proclaim that the purchaser shall have the best of all titles, a warrantee deed from the Commonwealth. I state this, gentlemen, because I know there is an idle rumor in this vicinity, that one Peter Rugg, the original owner of this estate, is still living. This rumor, gentlemen, has no foundation, and can have no foundation in the nature of things. It originated about two years since, from the incredible story of one Jonathan Dunwell of New-York. Mrs. Croft, indeed, whose husband I see present, and whose mouth waters for this estate, has countenanced this fiction. But, gentlemen, was it ever known, that any estate, especially an estate of this value, lay unclaimed for nearly half a century, if any heir, ever so remote, was existing? For, gentlemen, all agree, that old Peter Rugg, if living, would be at least, one hundred years of age. It is said that he and his daughter, with a horse and chaise, were missed more than half a century ago; and because they never returned home, forsooth, they must be now living, and will, some day, come and claim this great estate. Such logic, gentlemen, never led to a good investment. Let not this idle story cross the noble purpose of consigning these ruins to the genius of architecture. If such a contingency could check the spirit of enterprise, farewell to all mercantile excitement. Your surplus money, instead of refreshing your sleep with the golden dreams of new sources of speculation, would turn to the nightmare. A man's money, if not employed, serves only to disturb his rest. Look, then, to the prospect before you. Here is half an acre of land, more than twenty thousand square feet, a corner lot, with wonderful capabilities; none of your contracted lots of forty feet by fifty, where, in dog days, you can breathe only through your scuttles. On the contrary, an architect cannot contemplate this extensive lot without rapture, for here is room enough for his genius to shame the temple of Solomon. Then, the prospect, how commanding! To the East, so near to the Atlantic, that Neptune freighted with the select treasures of the whole earth can knock at your door with his trident. From the West, all the produce of the river of paradise, the Connecticut, will soon, by the blessings of steam, railways, and canals, pass under your windows; and thus, on this spot, Neptune shall marry Ceres, and Pomona from Roxbury, and Flora from Cambridge, shall dance at the wedding.

"Gentlemen of science, men of taste, ye, of the Literary Emporium; for I perceive many of you present; to you, this is holy ground. If the spot over which, in times past, a hero left only the print of a footstep, is now sacred, of what price is the birth place of one, who, all the world knows, was born in Middle-street, directly opposite to this lot; and who, if his birth place was not well known, would now be claimed by more than seven cities. To you, then, the value of these premises must be inestimable. For, ere long, there will arise in front view of the edifice to be erected here, a monument, the wonder and veneration of the world. A column shall spring to the clouds; and on that column will be engraven one word, that will convey all that is wise in intellect, useful in science, good in morals, prudent in counsel, and benevolent in principle; a name, when living, the patron of the poor, the delight of the cottage, and the admiration of kings; now dead, worth the whole seven wise men of Greece. Need I tell you his name? He fixed the thunder, and guided the lightning.

"Men of the North End! Need I appeal to your patriotism, in order to enhance the value of this lot? The earth affords no such scenery as this; there, around that corner, lived James Otis; here, Samuel Adams—there, Joseph Warren—and around that other corner, Josiah Quincy. Here, was the birth place of Freedom; here, Liberty was born, and nursed, and grew to manhood. Here, man was new created. Here is the nursery of American Independence—I am too modest—here commenced the emancipation of the world; a thousand generations hence, millions of men will cross the Atlantic, just to look at the North End of Boston. Your fathers,—what do I say? Yourselves, yes, this moment, I behold several attending this auction who lent a hand to rock the cradle of Independence.

"Men of speculation! Ye who are deaf to every thing except the sound of money, you, I know, will give me both of your ears, when I tell you the city of Boston must have a piece of this estate in order to widen Ann-street. Do you hear me; do you all hear me? I say the city must have a large piece of this land in order to widen Ann-street. What a chance! The city scorns to take a man's land for nothing. If they seize your property, they are generous beyond the dreams of avarice. The only oppression is, you are in danger of being smothered under a load of wealth. Witness the old lady who lately died of a broken heart, when the Mayor paid her for a piece of her kitchen garden. All the Faculty agreed that the sight of the treasure, which the Mayor incautiously paid her in dazzling dollars, warm from the mint, sped joyfully all the blood of her body into her heart, and rent it in raptures. Therefore, let him who purchases this estate, fear his good fortune, and not Peter Rugg. Bid then liberally, and do not let the name of Rugg damp your ardor. How much will you give per foot for this estate?" Thus spoke the auctioneer, and gracefully waved his ivory hammer. From fifty to seventy-five cents per foot, were offered in a few moments. It labored from seventy-five to ninety. At length one dollar was offered. The auctioneer seemed satisfied; and looking at his watch, said he would knock off the estate in five minutes, if no one offered more. There was a deep silence, during this short period. While the hammer was suspended, a strange rumbling noise was heard, which arrested the attention of every one. Presently, it was like the sound of many shipwrights driving home the bolts of a seventy-four. As the sound approached nearer, some exclaimed, "the buildings in the new market are falling in promiscuous ruin." Others said, "no; it is an earthquake, we perceive the earth joggle." Others said "not so; the sound proceeds from Hanover-street, and approaches nearer;" and this proved true, for presently Peter Rugg was in the midst of us.

"Alas, Jenny," said Peter, "I am ruined; our house has been burnt, and here are all our neighbours around the ruins. Heaven grant your mother, dame Rugg, is safe." "They don't look like our neighbours," said Jenny, "but sure enough our house is burnt, and nothing left but the door stone, and old cedar post—do ask where mother is?"

In the mean time, more than a thousand men had surrounded Rugg, and his horse and chair: Yet neither Rugg, personally, nor his horse and carriage attracted more attention than the auctioneer. The confident look and searching eyes of Rugg, to every one present, carried more conviction, that the estate was his, than could any parchment or paper with signature and seal. The impression which the auctioneer had just made on the company was effaced in a moment: and although the latter words of the auctioneer were, "fear not Peter Rugg," the moment the auctioneer met the eye of Rugg, his occupation was gone, his arm fell down to his hips, his late lively hammer hung heavy in his hand, and the auction was forgotten. The black horse, too, gave his evidence. He knew his journey was ended, for he stretched himself into a horse and a half, rested his cheek bone over the cedar post, and whinneyed thrice, causing his harness to tremble from headstall to crupper. Rugg then stood upright in his chair, and asked with some authority, "Who has demolished my house, in my absence, for I see no signs of a conflagration? I demand, by what accident this has happened; and wherefore this collection of strange people has assembled before my doorstep? I thought I knew every man in Boston, but you appear to me a new generation of men. Yet I am familiar with many of the countenances here present, and I can call some of you by name; but in truth I do not recollect, that before this moment, I ever saw any one of you. There, I am certain, is a Winslow, and here a Sargent; there stands a Sewall, and next to him a Dudley. Will none of you speak to me? Or is this all a delusion? I see, indeed, many forms of men, and no want of eyes, but of motion, speech, and hearing you seem to be destitute. Strange! will no one inform me who has demolished my house?" Then spake a voice from the crowd, but whence it came I could not discern. "There is nothing strange here, but yourself, Mr. Rugg. Time, which destroys and renews all things, has dilapidated your house, and placed us here. You have suffered many years under an illusion. The tempest which you profanely defied at Menotomy has at length subsided; but you will never see home; for your house and wife and neighbors have all disappeared. Your estate, indeed, remains, but no home. You were cut off from the last age, and you can never be fitted to the present. Your home is gone, and you can never have another home in this world."

J. DUNWELL.

1824–27

# JAMES KIRKE PAULDING

(1778–1860)

---

## *The End of the World*

### *A Vision*

HAPPENING, the other day, to meet with an account of a mighty gathering of the disciples of a certain great prophet, who, I believe, has, in spite of the proverb, rather more honor in his own country than any other, I fell upon a train of reflections on the probability of this world coming to an end the first of April next, as predicted by that venerable seer. That it will come to an end, some time or other, is certain, for nothing created can last forever; and that this event may happen to-morrow, is, for aught we know, just as likely as that it will take place an hundred or a thousand years hence. The precise hour is, however, wisely hidden from all but the eyes of our inspired prophet, and the first of April is quite as probable as any other, although, for the credit of the prediction, I could wish it had been fixed for some other day than that so specially consecrated to making fools.

It appeared to me, however, on due consideration, that there were many startling indications that this world of ours was pretty well worn thread-bare, and that it was high time to lay it aside, or get rid of it altogether, by a summary process, like the Bankrupt Law. Nor am I alone, among very discreet reflecting persons, in this opinion. I was lately conversing with an old gentleman, of great experience and sagacity, who has predicted several hard winters, and who assured me he did not see how it was possible for this world to last much longer. "In the first place," said he, "it has grown a great deal too wise to be honest, and common sense, like a specie currency, become the most uncommon of all commodities. Now, I maintain that, without the ballast of common sense, the world must inevitably turn upside down, or, at least, fall on its beam-ends, and all the passengers tumble overboard. In the second place, it is perfectly apparent that the balance-wheel which regulates the machine, and keeps all its functions in equilibrium, is almost worn out, if not entirely destroyed. There is now no medium in any thing. The love of money has become a raging passion, a mania equally destructive to morals and happiness. So with every other pursuit and passion of our nature. Every man is "like a beggar on horseback," and the old proverb will tell where he rides. All spur away, until they break down, ride over a precipice, or tumble into the mire. If a man, as every man does now-a-days, pines for riches, instead of seeking them in the good old fashioned way of industry, prudence and economy, he plunges heels over head in mad, extravagant and visionary schemes, that lead inevitably, not only to his own ruin, but that of others, and in all probability, in the end, leave him as destitute of character as of fortune. Or, if he is smitten with a desire to benefit his fellow creatures, he carries his philanthropy into the camp of the enemy, that is, to the opposite extreme of vice. His sympathies for one class of human suffering entirely shut his eyes and his heart to the claims and rights of others, and he would sacrifice the world to an atom. His pity for the guilty degenerates into the encouragement of crime, and instead of an avenger, he becomes an accomplice. No man, it would seem, in this most enlightened of all ages, appears to be aware of what is irrefragably true, that an honest abhorrence of guilt is one of the most powerful preservatives of human virtue; and that one of the most effectual modes of engendering vice in our own hearts, is to accustom ourselves to view it merely as an object of pity and forgiveness. It seems to be a growing opinion, that the punishment of crime is an usurpation of society, a despotic exercise of power over individuals, and, in short, 'a relic of the dark ages.'"

My excellent old friend is a great talker, when he gets on a favorite subject—though he rails by the hour at members of Congress for their long speeches—and proceeded, after stopping to take breath, as follows:—"There are other pregnant indications of this world being on its last legs, in the fashionable cant"—so my friend called it, most irreverently—"of ascribing almost all the great conservative principles of the social state to 'the dark ages.' The laws, indispensable to the security of property, the restraint of imprudence and extravagance, the safety of persons, and the punishment of their transgressors—those laws, in short, that constitute the great pillars of society, and without which barbarity and violence would again overrun the world, are, forsooth, traced by the advocates of 'progress' to those very dark ages, whose ignorance and barbarism they contributed more than all other causes to dissipate and destroy. An honest man who resorts to those laws which are founded in the first principles of justice, for the recovery of that which is necessary to his comfort, perhaps his very existence, or for the purpose of punishing some profligate spendthrift for defrauding him, is now denounced by philanthropic legislators, and mawkish moralists, as a dealer in human flesh, a Shylock demanding his pound of flesh, and whetting his knife for performing the sacrifice. The murderer—the cool, premeditated murderer—is delicately denominated 'an unfortunate man,' lest we should hurt his fine feelings. Our sympathies are invoked when he is called upon to pay the penalty of his crime, while the poor victims, living and dead, are left, the one without pity, the other without relief.

"Not only this," continued the worthy old gentleman, who gradually waxed warmer and warmer as he proceeded—"not only this, but as if to give the last most unequivocal evidence of dotage, we have become puffed up with the idea of this being the most enlightened of all the ages of the world, for no other reason, that I can perceive, than that we are become very great mechanics, and have, in consequence of the wonderful perfection to which machinery has been brought, depreciated the value of human labor, until it has become insufficient for human support, and beggared ourselves and our posterity, in making canals for frogs to spawn in, and railroads from interminable forests to flourishing towns that never had existence. It is perfectly evident to me, that matters are speedily coming to a crisis, and that a world, in which there is no other pursuit but money, where all sympathy is monopolized by guilt, and where common sense and common honesty are considered relics of the dark ages, cannot last much longer, unless," added he, with a peculiar expression of his eye, "unless Congress takes it in hand, and brings about a radical reform, by speechification. The truth is, it owes so much more than it can pay, that the sooner it winds up its concerns the better."

Saying this, my worthy and excellent friend, after predicting a hard winter, left me to cogitate alone in my old arm chair, very much inclined to a nap, as I generally am after listening to a long harangue. It was in a quiet back room, where I could see nothing but the smoke of my opposite neighbor's chimney; nothing disturbed me but a fly, which, notwithstanding the world was wide enough for us both, I should have utterly exterminated, if I could; and I continued to ponder over the subject, till, by degrees, sleep overpowered me, and the following vision passed over my bewildered brain.

Methought the eve of the first of April had come, and with it every indication that the prediction of the prophet was about to be fulfilled. The waters of the rivers, brooks and springs became gradually warmer and warmer, until some of them began to boil; hot currents of air issued from the fissures of the earth, whose surface became heated so that the bare-footed urchins rather danced than walked upon it; a thick, dun-colored vapor, by degrees, involved the world from the horizon to the skies, and there prevailed a dead, oppressive calm, without a single stirring breath of air. The earth became, as it were, one vast heated oven. The air was dry and parching; the turkeys lay sprawling on their breasts, with expanded wings; the dogs strolled wistfully around, seeking some cool retreat, panting and lolling out their tongues; the little birds hid themselves in the recesses of the woods, and ceased to sing; the leaves of the trees and flowers wilted and shriveled up under the excessive heat of the burning sun—and the world ceased to revolve, either from a suspension of the laws of nature, or for fear of dissolving in a profuse perspiration.

Other fearful auguries proclaimed that the hour had come. The sun was like a red ball of living fire; the whole firmament rocked and trembled, as if panting with the throes of suffocation; ever and anon, long flashes of zigzag lightning shot athwart the heavens in dead silence, for no thunder followed; and all nature, rational and irrational, animate and inanimate, seemed awaiting in death-like silence the hour of their final dissolution, as predicted by the prophet.

Methought I wandered about in that unhappy and distracted state of mind which generally ensues when we are haunted by some dim, half visible spectre of undefined misery, whose presence we feel, but whose persecutions we cannot avoid. It seemed that I strolled to the river side, in the hope of inhaling the cool, refreshing breezes from its bosom, but it sent forth nothing but a scalding vapor, like that from a steam-engine. The fishes lay sprawling and panting, and dying on its surface; and a hungry hawk, that had plunged down for his prey, being exhausted by the consuming heat, lay fluttering helplessly on the waters. From the mountains of the opposite shore, columns of blood-red smoke and flashes of sulphurous fire issued with an angry roaring vehemency; and in some of the deep fissures of the rocks, methought I could see the raging fires, as through the bars of a furnace. Then came rolling out of the bowels of the earth torrents of liquid flame; then came on the dread struggle of the rebel elements, released from the guiding hand of their Great Master. The dissolving earth rushed into the waters; a noise, like the hissing of millions of serpents, succeeded, and when I looked again the river was dry.

I fled from the appalling spectacle, and sought the city, where all was dismay and confusion. Some were shrieking and tearing their hair, in guilty apprehension of the horrors of death, and the sufferings of the world to come. Others sat in mute despair, awaiting in numb insensibility the fate of all the rest of their race; while others, impelled by the instinct of self-preservation, and forgetful of the inevitable doom that awaited them, were devising various expedients for escaping, and securing their most valuable articles about their persons. A little love-sick maiden had hung the picture of her lover about her snowy neck; an anxious mother sat weeping and wringing her hands by the side of a cradle, where lay a little laughing cherub playing with a kitten; while another was rushing madly about, with a child in her arms, which she had squeezed to death in her convulsive writhings. Thousands of scenes like these occurred all around, but I delight not to dwell on horrors, and will proceed to state what I saw of the exhibitions of the various modes of grief, disappointment and despair, which served to convince me that the ruling passion will struggle in the last agonies of existence, and triumph at the moment of the dissolution of nature herself.

In the course of my wanderings, methought I encountered the celebrated Fire-King, who was sitting at home, quietly smoking his cigar, and calculating that being the destined survivor of all his race, he would succeed to an immense landed estate, and become lord proprietor of the whole earth. Having agreed upon the terms, he furnished me with an antidote against the heat of the most raging anthracite furnace, and being now assured of safety, I made my observations with more coolness and precision. Being of rather a prying disposition, I conceived that as every thing was in a state of utter confusion, the doors and windows all open, and no police officers on duty, there was no occasion to stand upon ceremony.

I accordingly made my way into the most private recesses of various habitations, where I saw many things which I would not disclose, were it not that all this is nothing but a dream. Entering a handsome house, rather splendidly furnished, I saw an old man of upwards of fourscore, who was bitterly complaining of being thus suddenly cut off, without time to make his will, and repent of his sins; while an elderly woman, whom I took to be one of Job's comforters, was upbraiding him for not taking her advice, and attending to these matters long ago. In another miserable house, without furniture, and destitute of every comfort of life, I discovered a shriveled, cadaverous spectre, hugging a bag of gold, and lamenting the hardship of being called away just the day before the interest became payable on his bank stocks. I met in another place a speculator, with the perspiration rolling down his face in torrents, who was calculating the immense profits he might have made if he had only foreseen this sudden catastrophe. A little farther on, I saw a glutton devouring a pair of canvass backs, and heard him at intervals mumbling to himself—"They sha n't cheat me of my dinner." The next person I particularly noticed, was a stanch believer in "progress," who was terribly out of humor that the world should be destroyed just as it was on the high-road to perfectibility. He had an essay in his hand, which he was rolling up to enclose in a bottle, hermetically sealed, in the hope that it might float down to posterity, and make him immortal, forgetting, as I supposed, that the world was now about to perish by fire, and not by water. In the course of my farther peregrinations, I fell in with a father, very busy in making a will, dividing his property among his children; and another disinheriting his son for marrying against his wishes. A usurer was lamenting that he was not aware of what was coming, as he would certainly have borrowed a good round sum, and thus escaped paying the interest. A worthy dealer in political haberdashery, who had been seeking office, I believe, ever since the flood, was exclaiming against fate for casting him off, now that he had actually received a promise of succeeding a gentleman who was only five years younger than himself, immediately on his death. This example, by the way, brought to my recollection a circumstance that actually happened in real life, and within my own knowledge, where an old man of upwards of threescore and ten actually hanged himself on the marriage of his daughter, to whose fortune he looked forward to becoming heir, provided she died without issue. It is somewhat singular that people always calculate on outliving those by whose deaths they expect to be benefitted.

In the course of my peregrinations, I encountered some of the disciples of the prophet, who, one might have supposed, would have been prepared for the event they had so long confidently anticipated. But it seemed they were as much taken by surprise as their unbelieving neighbors, and were running to and fro in great consternation, or preparing in all haste for what they had been expecting at leisure, according to the ways of the wise people of this world, who see farther into futurity than their neighbors. Entering the chamber of a middle-aged widow, a stanch follower of the prophet, who had retreated somewhere, I found an open letter, not quite finished, which purported to be an answer to a proposal of marriage from another disciple, and in which the prudent dame very judiciously postponed her final decision until after the first of April. I own I proceeded to other unwarrantable indulgences of curiosity, only pardonable in a person fast asleep, in the course of which I made certain discoveries, which, now that I am awake, I scorn to disclose to the world. All I will venture to say is, that I saw enough to convince me that if the widow really believed in the approaching dissolution of the world, she had determined to make the most of it while it lasted. It is impossible to say what other discoveries I might have achieved if I had not heard footsteps approaching; and apprehending it might be the lady herself, I retreated with considerable precipitation, in doing which I encountered, and overthrew, a fat cook maid, who was coming up in great haste to apprize her mistress that the kitchen was so hot she could not breathe in it any longer, and who, notwithstanding the solemnity of the occasion, gave me a most awful benediction.

The next house I entered was that of a notorious usurer, who was never known to do a kindness to any human being. He had accumulated millions by a rigid, inflexible system of preying upon the wants of his fellow creatures, and denying himself the common necessaries of life, except on rare occasions, when his vanity got the better of his avarice; and he would give some great party, or ostentatious feast, in order to excite the envy of his neighbors, and get puffed in the newspapers, always making himself amends for this prodigality by squeezing additional sums out of his unfortunate clients. I found him busily employed in making his will, and talking to himself by fits and starts, from which I gathered there was a great contest going on between the ruling passion and the fear of the future, which prompted him to make reparation, as far as possible, for his past transgressions. From what I could gather, he had come to a determination to restore the principal of all the money he had screwed from his debtors by his usurious practices, but could not bring himself to give back the interest on these exactions, which he said would utterly ruin him. As the heat became more intense, he seemed gradually to relax; but the moment it subsided a little, relapsed again. This happened several times, until at length the old man quieted his conscience by leaving his whole estate for the purpose of erecting a hospital for the reception of the families of all those he had reduced to beggary by his frauds and inhumanity, at the same time saying to himself, "I shall go down to posterity as a great public benefactor." As I looked over his shoulder, I, however, observed that the bequest was conditional on the fulfillment of the prophecy.

Leaving the house of this repentant sinner, I proceeded on my way without any definite object, and met a fellow in irons, who had taken advantage of the confusion which reigned every where around, to make his escape from prison. He had committed a wanton and atrocious murder; and his execution was fixed for the next day. He seemed so elated at his escape, that I could not forbear reminding him that he had only got out of the frying-pan into the fire. He briskly replied, "O, but you forget I have escaped the disgrace of hanging." On my reminding him that the disgrace was in the crime, not the punishment, he answered, "I differ with you entirely in this matter," and proceeded on, rattling his chains as if in triumph.

My next encounter was with a person who had distinguished himself in several controversies on questions which, admitting of no demonstration either of facts or arguments, afford the finest scope for interminable discussion. He had written more than one dissertation to prove that the prophet knew nothing about what he had predicted, and gone nigh to convince his readers that he was in the same predicament. I was proceeding to converse with him on the unexpected catastrophe so rapidly approaching, when he impatiently interrupted me: "Unexpected, indeed!" said he, "I have been so busy in proving it to be all humbug, that I am sorry to say I am altogether unprepared. But that is not the worst. The most provoking part of the business is, that this old blockhead should be right, and I wrong. My reputation is entirely ruined; and I shall go down to posterity as a teacher of false doctrines, and a bad reasoner." "Do n't be uneasy on that score," I replied, "posterity will know nothing of the matter." Upon which he left me in a great passion, affirming that I had reflected on himself and his works, which, upon my honor, was not my intention.

The philosopher had scarcely left me, when there approached an old man of rather venerable appearance, who seemed an exception to the rest of the world—being evidently elated at what filled all others with horror and dismay. He was rubbing his hands in great glee, ever and anon exclaiming, "I told them so; I predicted all this years ago, but the blockheads would n't believe me. They have got it now, and may laugh as much as they please." Anxious to know the meaning of all this, I ventured to ask an explanation: "What!" said he, "do n't you know I am the prophet who foretold the destruction of the world by fire, the first of April, 1843? The clergy preached against me in their pulpits; the philosophers laughed; and the would-be wise ones hooted at me as a fool, or an impostor. But they have got it now—they have got it now—ha! ha! ha!" and the worthy old prophet went his way delighted at the fulfillment of his prediction. He had not proceeded far, however, when he came in sight of the bed of the river, which was now one vast volcano of consuming fires, and encountered such a scorching blast from that quarter, that he turned round and approached me again with great precipitation. On inquiring where he was going in such a hurry, he replied, "Going? why to make preparation for this awful catastrophe, which, to tell you the truth, I have entirely neglected, being altogether taken up with predicting it. Bless my soul! I had no idea it would be so hot!" At that moment it seemed that he took fire, and in a few moments was consumed to ashes, exclaiming to the last, "Well, well, it matters not, I shall go down to posterity as the last of the prophets!"

The last person I recollect meeting, was the worthy old gentleman who railed against the world so copiously at the commencement of this vision. He was puffing and blowing, and fanning himself with his hat at a prodigious rate. "Well, my friend," said I, very coolly and quietly, "well, my friend, you were quite right in your opinion that the world was pretty well worn out, and on its last legs. It is, in truth, an old, superannuated concern, not worth mending; and as you truly stated, so over head and ears in debt, that the sooner it winds up its affairs, and calls its creditors together, the better." The old gentleman, however, did not seem altogether to agree with me in this opinion. He hesitated, wiped his brow, and at length replied: "Why, ay—yes—to be sure! I confess, I thought so yesterday, but had no idea it was going to happen so soon; and, besides, really when one comes to consider the matter coolly," and then he puffed and panted as if almost roasted to death; "when one, I say, considers the matter coolly, this world, after all is said and done, is not so bad but that an honest man might have made up his mind to live in it a little longer. It might have been mended so as to be tolerable; and considering the pains every body is taking to make it better, I do n't think the case was altogether desperate. Really, it has scarcely had a fair trial, and with a few scores of years more, what with the great improvements in machinery; the wonderful facilities in traveling; and the exertions of a comprehensive philanthropy, I see no reason to despair of the millennium. But it is all over now; the advocates of 'progress,' will never know whether they were dreaming or awake; and I shall die without ever predicting another hard winter."

How much farther my good old friend would have carried his recantation, can never be known; for just at this critical moment, methought he blew up with a prodigious explosion; a glare of light, so intensely brilliant as to be beyond endurance, flashed before my eyes, and a sense of suffocation came over me, with such overwhelming force, that I struggled myself awake; and the first sounds I heard in the street, were those of the little boys crying out "April fool! April fool!"

1843

# WASHINGTON IRVING

(1783–1859)

---

## *The Little Man in Black*

THE FOLLOWING story has been handed down by family tradition for more than a century. It is one on which my cousin Christopher dwells with more than usual prolixity; and, being in some measure connected with a personage often quoted in our work, I have thought it worthy of being laid before my readers.

Soon after my grandfather, mr. Lemuel Cockloft, had quietly settled himself at the hall, and just about the time that the gossips of the neighbourhood, tired of prying into his affairs, were anxious for some new tea-table topick, the busy community of our little village was thrown into a grand turmoil of curiosity and conjecture; (a situation very common to little gossiping villages) by the sudden and unaccountable appearance of a mysterious individual.

The object of this solicitude was a little black looking man of a foreign aspect, who took possession of an old building, which having long had the reputation of being haunted, was in a state of ruinous desolation, and an object of fear to all true believers in ghosts. He usually wore a high sugar-loaf hat, with a narrow brim, and a little black cloak, which, short as he was, scarcely reached below his knees. He sought no intimacy or acquaintance with any one; appeared to take no interest in the pleasures or the little broils of the village, nor ever talked; except sometimes to himself in an outlandish tongue. He commonly carried a large book, covered with sheepskin, under his arm; appeared always to be lost in meditation, and was often met by the peasantry, sometimes watching the dawning of day, sometimes at noon seated under a tree poring over his volume, and sometimes at evening, gazing with a look of sober tranquility at the sun as it gradually sunk below the horizon.

The good people of the vicinity beheld something prodigiously singular in all this—a profound mystery seemed to hang about the stranger, which, with all their sagacity they could not penetrate, and in the excess of worldly charity they pronounced it a sure sign "that he was no better than he should be"—a phrase innocent enough in itself, but which, as applied in common, signifies nearly every thing that is bad. The young people thought him a gloomy misanthrope, because he never joined in their sports—the old men thought still more hardly of him, because he followed no trade, nor even seemed ambitious of earning a farthing—and as to the old gossips, baffled by the inflexible taciturnity of the stranger, they unanimously decreed that a man who could not or would not talk, was no better than a dumb beast. The little man in black, careless of their opinions, seemed resolved to maintain the liberty of keeping his own secret; and the consequence was that, in a little while, the whole village was in an uproar—for in little communities of this description, the members have always the privilege of being thoroughly versed, and even of meddling in all the affairs of each other.

A confidential conference was held one Sunday morning after sermon, at the door of the village church, and the character of the unknown fully investigated. The schoolmaster gave as his opinion that he was the wandering Jew—the sexton was certain that he must be a free-mason from his silence—a third maintained, with great obstinacy, that he was a high german doctor, and that the book which he carried about with him, contained the secrets of the black art; but the most prevailing opinion seemed to be that he was a *witch*—a race of beings at that time abounding in those parts; and a sagacious old matron from Connecticut proposed to ascertain the fact by sousing him into a kettle of hot water.

Suspicion, when once afloat, goes with wind and tide, and soon becomes certainty. Many a stormy night was the little man in black seen by the flashes of lightning, frisking and curveting in the air upon a broomstick; and it was always observed that at those times the storm did more mischief than at any other. The old lady in particular, who suggested the humane ordeal of the boiling kettle, lost on one of these occasions a fine brindled cow; which accident was entirely ascribed to the vengeance of the little man in black. If ever a mischievous hireling rode his master's favourite horse to a distant frolick, and the animal was observed to be lame and jaded in the morning—the little man in black was sure to be at the bottom of the affair, nor could a high wind howl through the village at night, but the old women shrugged up their shoulders and observed "the little man in black was in his *tantrums*." In short he became the bugbear of every house, and was as effectual in frightening little children into obedience and hystericks, as the redoubtable Raw-head-and-bloody-bones himself; nor could a house-wife of the village sleep in peace, except under the guardianship of a horse-shoe nailed to the door.

The object of these direful suspicions remained for some time totally ignorant of the wonderful quandary he had occasioned, but he was soon doomed to feel its effects. An individual who is once so unfortunate as to incur the odium of a village, is in a great measure outlawed and proscribed; and becomes a mark for injury and insult—particularly if he has not the power or the disposition to recriminate. The little venomous passions, which in the great world are dissipated and weakened by being widely diffused, act in the narrow limits of a country town with collected vigour, and become rancorous in proportion as they are confined in their sphere of action. The little man in black experienced the truth of this—every mischievous urchin returning from school, had full liberty to break his windows; and this was considered as a most daring exploit, for, in such awe did they stand of him, that the most adventurous schoolboy was never seen to approach his threshold, and at night would prefer going round by the cross-roads, where a traveller had been murdered by the indians, rather than pass by the door of his forlorn habitation.

The only living creature that seemed to have any care or affection for this deserted being, was an old turnspit—the companion of his lonely mansion and his solitary wanderings—the sharer of his scanty meals, and, sorry am I to say it—the sharer of his persecutions. The turnspit, like his master, was peaceable and inoffensive; never known to bark at a horse, to growl at a traveller, or to quarrel with the dogs of the neighbourhood. He followed close at his master's heels when he went out, and when he returned stretched himself in the sunbeams at the door, demeaning himself in all things like a civil and well disposed turnspit. But notwithstanding his exemplary deportment he fell likewise under the ill report of the village, as being the familiar of the little man in black, and the evil spirit that presided at his incantations. The old hovel was considered as the scene of their unhallowed rites, and its harmless tenants regarded with a detestation, which their inoffensive conduct never merited. Though pelted and jeered at by the brats of the village, and frequently abused by their parents, the little man in black never turned to rebuke them, and his faithful dog, when wantonly assaulted, looked up wistfully in his master's face, and there learned a lesson of patience and forbearance.

The movements of this inscrutable being had long been the subject of speculation at Cockloft-hall, for its inmates were full as much given to *wondering* as their descendants. The patience with which he bore his persecutions, particularly surprised them—for patience is a virtue but little known in the Cockloft family. My grandmother, who it appears was rather superstitious, saw in this humility nothing but the gloomy sullenness of a wizard, who restrained himself for the present, in hopes of midnight vengeance—the parson of the village, who was a man of some reading, pronounced it the stubborn insensibility of a stoick philosopher:—my grandfather, who, worthy soul, seldom wandered abroad in search of conclusions, took a data from his own excellent heart, and regarded it as the humble forgiveness of a christian. But however different were their opinions as to the character of the stranger, they agreed in one particular, namely, in never intruding upon his solitude; and my grandmother, who was at that time nursing my mother, never left the room, without wisely putting the large family bible in the cradle—a sure talisman, in her opinion, against witchcraft and necromancy.

One stormy winter night, when a bleak north-east wind moaned about the cottages, and howled around the village steeple, my grandfather was returning from club, preceded by a servant with a lantern. Just as he arrived opposite the desolate abode of the little man in black, he was arrested by the piteous howling of a dog which, heard in the pauses of the storm, was exquisitely mournful; and he fancied now and then, that he caught the low and broken groans of some one in distress. He stopped for some minutes, hesitating between the benevolence of his heart and a sensation of genuine delicacy, which in spite of his eccentricity he fully possessed—and which forbade him to pry into the concerns of his neighbours. Perhaps too, this hesitation might have been strengthened by a little taint of superstition; for surely, if the unknown had been addicted to witchcraft, this was a most propitious night for his vagaries. At length the old gentleman's philanthropy predominated; he approached the hovel and pushing open the door—for poverty has no occasion for locks and keys—beheld, by the light of the lantern, a scene that smote his generous heart to the core.

On a miserable bed, with pallid and emaciated visage and hollow eyes—in a room destitute of every convenience—without fire to warm, or friend to console him, lay this helpless mortal who had been so long the terror and wonder of the village. His dog was crouching on the scanty coverlet, and shivering with cold. My grandfather stepped softly and hesitatingly to the bed side, and accosted the forlorn sufferer in his usual accents of kindness. The little man in black seemed recalled by the tones of compassion from the lethargy into which he had fallen; for, though his heart was almost frozen, there was yet one chord that answered to the call of the good old man who bent over him—the tones of sympathy, so novel to his ear, called back his wandering senses and acted like a restorative to his solitary feelings.

He raised his eyes, but they were vacant and haggard—he put forth his hand, but it was cold—he essayed to speak, but the sound died away in his throat—he pointed to his mouth with an expression of dreadful meaning, and, sad to relate! my grandfather understood that the harmless stranger, deserted by society, was perishing with hunger!—With the quick impulse of humanity he dispatched the servant to the hall for refreshment. A little warm nourishment renovated him for a short time—but not long; it was evident his pilgrimage was drawing to a close, and he was about entering that peaceful asylum, where "the wicked cease from troubling."

His tale of misery was short and quickly told; infirmities had stolen upon him, heightened by the rigours of the season: he had taken to his bed without strength to rise and ask for assistance—"and if I had," said he, in a tone of bitter despondency, "to whom should I have applied? I have no friend that I know of in the world!—the villagers avoid me as something loathsome and dangerous; and here, in the midst of christians, should I have perished without a fellow-being to soothe the last moments of existence, and close my dying eyes, had not the howlings of my faithful dog excited your attention."

He seemed deeply sensible of the kindness of my grandfather, and at one time as he looked up into his old benefactor's face, a solitary tear was observed to steal adown the parched furrows of his cheek—poor outcast!—it was the last tear he shed—but I warrant it was not the first by millions! My grandfather watched by him all night. Towards morning he gradually declined, and as the rising sun gleamed through the window, he begged to be raised in his bed that he might look at it for the last time. He contemplated it for a moment with a kind of religious enthusiasm, and his lips moved as if engaged in prayer. The strange conjectures concerning him rushed on my grandfather's mind: "he is an idolator!" thought he, "and is worshipping the sun!"—He listened a moment and blushed at his own uncharitable suspicion—he was only engaged in the pious devotions of a christian. His simple orison being finished, the little man in black withdrew his eyes from the east, and taking my grandfather's hand in one of his, and making a motion with the other, towards the sun—"I love to contemplate it," said he, "tis an emblem of the universal benevolence of a true christian—and it is the most glorious work of him, who is philanthropy itself!" My grandfather blushed still deeper at his ungenerous surmises; he had pitied the stranger at first, but now he revered him—he turned once more to regard him, but his countenance had undergone a change—the holy enthusiasm that had lighted up each feature had given place to an expression of mysterious import—a gleam of grandeur seemed to steal across his gothick visage, and he appeared full of some mighty secret which he hesitated to impart. He raised the tattered nightcap that had sunk almost over his eyes, and waving his withered hand with a slow and feeble expression of dignity,—"In me," said he, with laconick solemnity—"In me you behold the last descendant of the renowned Linkum Fidelius!" My grandfather gazed at him with reverence, for though he had never heard of the illustrious personage thus pompously announced, yet there was a certain black-letter dignity in the name, that peculiarly struck his fancy and commanded his respect.

"You have been kind to me," continued the little man in black, after a momentary pause, "and richly will I requite your kindness, by making you heir to my treasures! In yonder large deal box are the volumes of my illustrious ancestor, of which I alone am the fortunate possessor. Inherit them—ponder over them—and be wise!" He grew faint with the exertion he had made, and sunk back almost breathless on his pillow. His hand, which, inspired with the importance of his subject, he had raised to my grandfather's arm, slipped from its hold and fell over the side of the bed, and his faithful dog licked it, as if anxious to soothe the last moments of his master, and testify his gratitude to the hand that had so often cherished him. The untaught caresses of the faithful animal were not lost upon his dying master—he raised his languid eyes—turned them on the dog, then on my grandfather, and having given this silent recommendation—closed them forever.

The remains of the little man in black, notwithstanding the objections of many pious people, were decently interred in the church-yard of the village, and his spirit, harmless as the body it once animated, has never been known to molest a living being. My grandfather complied as far as possible with his last request—he conveyed the volumes of Linkum Fidelius to his library—he pondered over them frequently—but whether he grew wiser the tradition does not mention. This much is certain, that his kindness to the poor descendant of Fidelius, was amply rewarded by the approbation of his own heart, and the devoted attachment of the old turnspit, who transferring his affection from his deceased master to his benefactor, became his constant attendant, and was father to a long line of runty curs that still flourish in the family. And thus was the Cockloft library first enriched by the invaluable folioes of the sage LINKUM FIDELIUS.

1807

# WASHINGTON IRVING

(1783–1859)

---

## *Rip Van Winkle*

The following Tale was found among the papers of the late Diedrich Knickerbocker, an old gentleman of New York, who was very curious in the Dutch history of the province, and the manners of the descendants from its primitive settlers. His historical researches, however, did not lie so much among books, as among men; for the former are lamentably scanty on his favourite topics; whereas he found the old burghers, and still more, their wives, rich in that legendary lore so invaluable to true history. Whenever, therefore, he happened upon a genuine Dutch family, snugly shut up in its low roofed farm house, under a spreading sycamore, he looked upon it as a little clasped volume of black letter, and studied it with the zeal of a bookworm.

The result of all these researches was a history of the province, during the reign of the Dutch governors, which he published some years since. There have been various opinions as to the literary character of his work and, to tell the truth, it is not a whit better than it should be. Its chief merit is its scrupulous accuracy, which indeed was a little questioned on its first appearance, but has since been completely established; and it is now admitted into all historical collections as a book of unquestionable authority.

The old gentleman died shortly after the publication of his work, and now that he is dead and gone, it cannot do much harm to his memory to say that his time might have been much better employed in weightier labours. He, however, was apt to ride his hobby his own way; and though it did now and then kick up the dust a little in the eyes of his neighbours, and grieve the spirit of some friends for whom he felt the truest deference and affection; yet his errors and follies are remembered "more in sorrow than in anger," and it begins to be suspected that he never intended to injure or offend. But however his memory may be appreciated by criticks, it is still held dear by many folk whose good opinion is well worth having; particularly by certain biscuit bakers, who have gone so far as to imprint his likeness on their new year cakes, and have thus given him a chance for immortality, almost equal to being stamped on a Waterloo medal, or a Queen Anne's farthing.

### *A Posthumous Writing of Diedrich Knickerbocker*

By Woden, God of Saxons,
From whence comes Wensday, that is Wodensday,
Truth is a thing that ever I will keep
Unto thylke day in which I creep into
My sepulchre—

*Cartwright*

WHOEVER HAS made a voyage up the Hudson must remember the Kaatskill mountains. They are a dismembered branch of the great Appalachian family, and are seen away to the west of the river swelling up to noble height and lording it over the surrounding country. Every change of season, every change of weather, indeed every hour of the day, produces some change in the magical hues and shapes of these mountains, and they are regarded by all the good wives far and near as perfect barometers. When the weather is fair and settled they are clothed in blue and purple, and print their bold outlines on the clear evening sky; but sometimes, when the rest of the landscape is cloudless, they will gather a hood of grey vapours about their summits, which, in the last rays of the setting sun, will glow and light up like a crown of glory.

At the foot of these fairy mountains the voyager may have descried the light smoke curling up from a village, whose shingle roofs gleam among the trees, just where the blue tints of the upland melt away into the fresh green of the nearer landscape. It is a little village of great antiquity, having been founded by some of the Dutch colonists in the early times of the province, just about the beginning of the government of the good Peter Stuyvesant, (may he rest in peace!) and there were some of the houses of the original settlers standing within a few years; built of small yellow bricks brought from Holland, having latticed windows and gable fronts, surmounted with weathercocks.

In that same village, and in one of these very houses (which to tell the precise truth was sadly time worn and weather beaten) there lived many years since, while the country was yet a province of Great Britain, a simple good natured fellow of the name of Rip Van Winkle. He was a descendant of the Van Winkles who figured so gallantly in the chivalrous days of Peter Stuyvesant, and accompanied him to the siege of Fort Christina. He inherited, however, but little of the martial character of his ancestors. I have observed that he was a simple good natured man; he was moreover a kind neighbour, and an obedient, henpecked husband. Indeed to the latter circumstance might be owing that meekness of spirit which gained him such universal popularity; for those men are most apt to be obsequious and conciliating abroad, who are under the discipline of shrews at home. Their tempers doubtless are rendered pliant and malleable in the fiery furnace of domestic tribulation, and a curtain lecture is worth all the sermons in the world for teaching the virtues of patience and long suffering. A termagant wife may therefore in some respects be considered a tolerable blessing—and if so, Rip Van Winkle was thrice blessed.

Certain it is that he was a great favourite among all the good wives of the village, who as usual with the amiable sex, took his part in all family squabbles, and never failed, whenever they talked those matters over in their evening gossippings, to lay all the blame on Dame Van Winkle. The children of the village too would shout with joy whenever he approached. He assisted at their sports, made their play things, taught them to fly kites and shoot marbles, and told them long stories of ghosts, witches and Indians. Whenever he went dodging about the village he was surrounded by a troop of them hanging on his skirts, clambering on his back and playing a thousand tricks on him with impunity; and not a dog would bark at him throughout the neighbourhood.

The great error in Rip's composition was an insuperable aversion to all kinds of profitable labour. It could not be from the want of assiduity or perseverance; for he would sit on a wet rock, with a rod as long and heavy as a Tartar's lance, and fish all day without a murmur, even though he should not be encouraged by a single nibble. He would carry a fowling piece on his shoulder for hours together, trudging through woods, and swamps and up hill and down dale, to shoot a few squirrels or wild pigeons; he would never refuse to assist a neighbour even in the roughest toil, and was a foremost man at all country frolicks for husking Indian corn, or building stone fences; the women of the village too used to employ him to run their errands and to do such little odd jobs as their less obliging husbands would not do for them—in a word Rip was ready to attend to any body's business but his own; but as to doing family duty, and keeping his farm in order, he found it impossible.

In fact he declared it was of no use to work on his farm; it was the most pestilent little piece of ground in the whole country; every thing about it went wrong and would go wrong in spite of him. His fences were continually falling to pieces; his cow would either go astray or get among the cabbages, weeds were sure to grow quicker in his fields than any where else; the rain always made a point of setting in just as he had some outdoor work to do. So that though his patrimonial estate had dwindled away under his management, acre by acre until there was little more left than a mere patch of Indian corn and potatoes, yet it was the worst conditioned farm in the neighbourhood.

His children too were as ragged and wild as if they belonged to nobody. His son Rip, an urchin begotten in his own likeness, promised to inherit the habits with the old clothes of his father. He was generally seen trooping like a colt at his mother's heels, equipped in a pair of his father's cast off galligaskins, which he had much ado to hold up with one hand, as a fine lady does her train in bad weather.

Rip Van Winkle, however, was one of those happy mortals of foolish, well oiled dispositions, who take the world easy, eat white bread or brown, whichever can be got with least thought or trouble, and would rather starve on a penny than work for a pound. If left to himself, he would have whistled life away in perfect contentment, but his wife kept continually dinning in his ears about his idleness, his carelessness and the ruin he was bringing on his family. Morning noon and night her tongue was incessantly going, and every thing he said or did was sure to produce a torrent of household eloquence. Rip had but one way of replying to all lectures of the kind, and that by frequent use had grown into a habit. He shrugged his shoulders, shook his head, cast up his eyes, but said nothing. This, however, always provoked a fresh volley from his wife, so that he was fain to draw off his forces and take to the outside of the house—the only side which in truth belongs to a henpecked husband.

Rip's sole domestic adherent was his dog Wolf who was as much henpecked as his master, for Dame Van Winkle regarded them as companions in idleness, and even looked upon Wolf with an evil eye as the cause of his master's going so often astray. True it is, in all points of spirit befitting an honourable dog, he was as courageous an animal as ever scoured the woods—but what courage can withstand the ever during and all besetting terrors of a woman's tongue? The moment Wolf entered the house his crest fell, his tail drooped to the ground or curled between his legs, he sneaked about with a gallows air, casting many a sidelong glance at Dame Van Winkle, and at the least flourish of a broomstick or ladle he would fly to the door with yelping precipitation.

Times grew worse and worse with Rip Van Winkle as years of matrimony rolled on; a tart temper never mellows with age, and a sharp tongue is the only edged tool that grows keener with constant use. For a long while he used to console himself when driven from home, by frequenting a kind of perpetual club of the sages, philosophers and other idle personages of the village which held its sessions on a bench before a small inn, designated by a rubicund portrait of his majesty George the Third. Here they used to sit in the shade, through a long lazy summer's day, talking listlessly over village gossip, or telling endless sleepy stories about nothing. But it would have been worth any statesman's money to have heard the profound discussions that sometimes took place, when by chance an old newspaper fell into their hands from some passing traveller. How solemnly they would listen to the contents as drawled out by Derrick Van Bummel the schoolmaster, a dapper, learned little man, who was not to be daunted by the most gigantic word in the dictionary; and how sagely they would deliberate upon public events some months after they had taken place.

The opinions of this junto were completely controlled by Nicholaus Vedder, a patriarch of the village, and landlord of the inn, at the door of which he took his seat from morning till night, just moving sufficiently to avoid the sun and keep in the shade of a large tree; so that the neighbours could tell the hour by his movements as accurately as by a sun dial. It is true he was rarely heard to speak, but smoked his pipe incessantly. His adherents, however (for every great man has his adherents), perfectly understood him and knew how to gather his opinions. When any thing that was read or related displeased him, he was observed to smoke his pipe vehemently and to send forth short, frequent and angry puffs; but when pleased he would inhale the smoke slowly and tranquilly and emit it in light and placid clouds, and sometimes taking the pipe from his mouth and letting the fragrant vapour curl about his nose, would gravely nod his head in token of perfect approbation.

From even this strong hold the unlucky Rip was at length routed by his termagant wife who would suddenly break in upon the tranquility of the assemblage and call the members all to naught; nor was that august personage Nicholaus Vedder himself sacred from the daring tongue of this terrible virago, who charged him outright with encouraging her husband in habits of idleness.

Poor Rip was at last reduced almost to despair; and his only alternative to escape from the labour of the farm and the clamour of his wife, was to take gun in hand and stroll away into the woods. Here he would sometimes seat himself at the foot of a tree and share the contents of his wallet with Wolf, with whom he sympathised as a fellow sufferer in persecution. "Poor Wolf," he would say, "thy mistress leads thee a dog's life of it, but never mind my lad, whilst I live thou shalt never want a friend to stand by thee!" Wolf would wag his tail, look wistfully in his master's face, and if dogs can feel pity I verily believe he reciprocated the sentiment with all his heart.

In a long ramble of the kind on a fine autumnal day, Rip had unconsciously scrambled to one of the highest parts of the Kaatskill mountains. He was after his favourite sport of squirrel shooting and the still solitudes had echoed and reechoed with the reports of his gun. Panting and fatigued he threw himself, late in the afternoon, on a green knoll, covered with mountain herbage, that crowned the brow of a precipice. From an opening between the trees he could overlook all the lower country for many a mile of rich woodland. He saw at a distance the lordly Hudson, far, far below him, moving on its silent but majestic course, with the reflection of a purple cloud, or the sail of a lagging bark here and there sleeping on its glassy bosom, and at last losing itself in the blue highlands.

On the other side he looked down into a deep mountain glen, wild, lonely and shagged, the bottom filled with fragments from the impending cliffs and scarcely lighted by the reflected rays of the setting sun. For some time Rip lay musing on this scene, evening was gradually advancing, the mountains began to throw their long blue shadows over the valleys, he saw that it would be dark, long before he could reach the village, and he heaved a heavy sigh when he thought of encountering the terrors of Dame Van Winkle.

As he was about to descend he heard a voice from a distance hallooing "Rip Van Winkle! Rip Van Winkle!" He looked around, but could see nothing but a crow winging its solitary flight across the mountain. He thought his fancy must have deceived him and turned again to descend, when he heard the same cry ring through the still evening air: "Rip Van Winkle! Rip Van Winkle!"—at the same time Wolf bristled up his back and giving a low growl, skulked to his master's side, looking fearfully down into the glen. Rip now felt a vague apprehension stealing over him; he looked anxiously in the same direction and perceived a strange figure slowly toiling up the rocks and bending under the weight of something he carried on his back. He was surprised to see any human being in this lonely and unfrequented place, but supposing it to be some one of the neighbourhood in need of his assistance he hastened down to yield it.

On nearer approach he was still more surprised at the singularity of the stranger's appearance. He was a short, square built old fellow, with thick bushy hair and a grizzled beard. His dress was of the antique Dutch fashion, a cloth jerkin strapped round the waist, several pair of breeches, the outer one of ample volume decorated with rows of buttons down the sides and bunches at the knees. He bore on his shoulder a stout keg that seemed full of liquor, and made signs for Rip to approach and assist him with the load. Though rather shy and distrustful of this new acquaintance Rip complied with his usual alacrity, and mutually relieving each other they clambered up a narrow gully apparently the dry bed of a mountain torrent. As they ascended Rip every now and then heard long rolling peals like distant thunder, that seemed to issue out of a deep ravine or rather cleft between lofty rocks, toward which their rugged path conducted.

He paused for an instant, but supposing it to be the muttering of one of those transient thunder showers which often take place in mountain heights, he proceeded. Passing through the ravine they came to a hollow like a small amphitheatre, surrounded by perpendicular precipices, over the brinks of which impending trees shot their branches, so that you only caught glimpses of the azure sky and the bright evening cloud. During the whole time Rip and his companion had laboured on in silence, for though the former marvelled greatly what could be the object of carrying a keg of liquor up this wild mountain, yet there was something strange and incomprehensible about the unknown, that inspired awe and checked familiarity.

On entering the amphitheatre new objects of wonder presented themselves. On a level spot in the centre was a company of odd looking personages playing at ninepins. They were dressed in a quaint outlandish fashion—some wore short doublets, others jerkins with long knives in their belts and most of them had enormous breeches of similar style with that of the guide's. Their visages too were peculiar. One had a large head, broad face and small piggish eyes. The face of another seemed to consist entirely of nose, and was surmounted by a white sugarloaf hat, set off with a little red cock's tail. They all had beards of various shapes and colours. There was one who seemed to be the Commander. He was a stout old gentleman, with a weather-beaten countenance. He wore a laced doublet, broad belt and hanger, high crowned hat and feather, red stockings and high heel'd shoes with roses in them. The whole group reminded Rip of the figures in an old Flemish painting, in the parlour of Dominie Van Schaick the village parson, and which had been brought over from Holland at the time of the settlement.

What seemed particularly odd to Rip was, that though these folks were evidently amusing themselves, yet they maintained the gravest faces, the most mysterious silence, and were, withal, the most melancholy party of pleasure he had ever witnessed. Nothing interrupted the stillness of the scene, but the noise of the balls, which, whenever they were rolled, echoed along the mountains like rumbling peals of thunder.

As Rip and his companion approached them they suddenly desisted from their play and stared at him with such fixed statue like gaze, and such strange uncouth, lack lustre countenances, that his heart turned within him, and his knees smote together. His companion now emptied the contents of the keg into large flagons and made signs to him to wait upon the company. He obeyed with fear and trembling; they quaffed the liquor in profound silence and then returned to their game.

By degrees Rip's awe and apprehension subsided. He even ventured, when no eye was fixed upon him, to taste the beverage, which he found had much of the flavour of excellent hollands. He was naturally a thirsty soul and was soon tempted to repeat the draught. One taste provoked another, and he reiterated his visits to the flagon so often that at length his senses were overpowered, his eyes swam in his head—his head gradually declined and he fell into a deep sleep.

On awaking he found himself on the green knoll from whence he had first seen the old man of the glen. He rubbed his eyes—it was a bright, sunny morning. The birds were hopping and twittering among the bushes, and the eagle was wheeling aloft and breasting the pure mountain breeze. "Surely," thought Rip, "I have not slept here all night." He recalled the occurrences before he fell asleep. The strange man with a keg of liquor—the mountain ravine—the wild retreat among the rocks—the woe begone party at ninepins—the flagon—"ah! that flagon! that wicked flagon!" thought Rip—"what excuse shall I make to Dame Van Winkle?"

He looked round for his gun, but in place of the clean well oiled fowling piece he found an old firelock lying by him, the barrel encrusted with rust; the lock falling off and the stock worm eaten. He now suspected that the grave roysters of the mountain had put a trick upon him, and having dosed him with liquor, had robbed him of his gun. Wolf too had disappeared, but he might have strayed away after a squirrel or partridge. He whistled after him and shouted his name—but all in vain; the echoes repeated his whistle and shout, but no dog was to be seen.

He determined to revisit the scene of the last evening's gambol, and if he met with any of the party, to demand his dog and gun. As he arose to walk he found himself stiff in the joints and wanting in his usual activity. "These mountain beds do not agree with me," thought Rip, "and if this frolick should lay me up with a fit of the rheumatism, I shall have a blessed time with

Dame Van Winkle." With some difficulty he got down into the glen; he found the gully up which he and his companion had ascended the preceding evening, but to his astonishment a mountain stream was now foaming down it; leaping from rock to rock, and filling the glen with babbling murmurs. He, however, made shift to scramble up its sides working his toilsome way through thickets of birch, sassafras and witch hazel, and sometimes tripped up or entangled by the wild grape vines that twisted their coils and tendrils from tree to tree, and spread a kind of net work in his path.

At length he reached to where the ravine had opened through the cliffs, to the amphitheatre—but no traces of such opening remained. The rocks presented a high impenetrable wall over which the torrent came tumbling in a sheet of feathery foam, and fell into a broad deep basin black from the shadows of the surrounding forest. Here then poor Rip was brought to a stand. He again called and whistled after his dog—he was only answered by the cawing of a flock of idle crows, sporting high in air about a dry tree that overhung a sunny precipice; and who, secure in their elevation seemed to look down and scoff at the poor man's perplexities.

What was to be done? The morning was passing away and Rip felt famished for want of his breakfast. He grieved to give up his dog and gun; he dreaded to meet his wife; but it would not do to starve among the mountains. He shook his head, shouldered the rusty fire lock and with a heart full of trouble and anxiety, turned his steps homeward.

As he approached the village he met a number of people, but none whom he knew, which somewhat surprised him, for he had thought himself acquainted with every one in the country round. Their dress too was of a different fashion from that to which he was accustomed. They all stared at him with equal marks of surprise, and whenever they cast their eyes upon him, invariably stroked their chins. The constant recurrence of this gesture induced Rip involuntarily to do the same, when to his astonishment he found his beard had grown a foot long!

He had now entered the skirts of the village. A troop of strange children ran at his heels, hooting after him and pointing at his grey beard. The dogs too, not one of which he recognized for an old acquaintance, barked at him as he passed. The very village was altered—it was larger and more populous. There were rows of houses which he had never seen before, and those which had been his familiar haunts had disappeared. Strange names were over the doors—strange faces at the windows—every thing was strange. His mind now misgave him; he began to doubt whether both he and the world around him were not bewitched. Surely this was his native village which he had left but the day before. There stood the Kaatskill mountains—there ran the silver Hudson at a distance—there was every hill and dale precisely as it had always been—Rip was sorely perplexed—"That flagon last night," thought he, "has addled my poor head sadly!"

It was with some difficulty that he found the way to his own house, which he approached with silent awe, expecting every moment to hear the shrill voice of Dame Van Winkle. He found the house gone to decay—the roof fallen in, the windows shattered and the doors off the hinges. A half starved dog that looked like Wolf was skulking about it. Rip called him by name but the cur snarled, shewed his teeth and passed on. This was an unkind cut indeed—"My very dog," sighed poor Rip, "has forgotten me!"

He entered the house, which, to tell the truth, Dame Van Winkle had always kept in neat order. It was empty, forlorn and apparently abandoned. This desolateness overcame all his connubial fears—he called loudly for his wife and children—the lonely chambers rung for a moment with his voice, and then all again was silence.

He now hurried forth and hastened to his old resort, the village inn—but it too was gone. A large, ricketty wooden building stood in its place, with great gaping windows, some of them broken, and mended with old hats and petticoats, and over the door was printed "The Union Hotel, by Jonathan Doolittle." Instead of the great tree, that used to shelter the quiet little Dutch inn of yore, there now was reared a tall naked pole with something on top that looked like a red night cap, and from it was fluttering a flag on which was a singular assemblage of stars and stripes—all this was strange and incomprehensible. He recognized on the sign, however, the ruby face of King George under which he had smoked so many a peaceful pipe, but even this was singularly metamorphosed. The red coat was changed for one of blue and buff; a sword was held in the hand instead of a sceptre; the head was decorated with a cocked hat, and underneath was printed in large characters GENERAL WASHINGTON.

There was as usual a crowd of folk about the door; but none that Rip recollected. The very character of the people seemed changed. There was a busy, bustling disputatious tone about it, instead of the accustomed phlegm and drowsy tranquility. He looked in vain for the sage Nicholaus Vedder with his broad face, double chin and fair long pipe, uttering clouds of tobacco smoke instead of idle speeches. Or Van Bummel the schoolmaster doling forth the contents of an ancient newspaper. In place of these a lean bilious looking fellow with his pockets full of hand bills, was haranguing vehemently about rights of citizens—elections—members of Congress—liberty—Bunker's hill—heroes of seventy six—and other words which were a perfect babylonish jargon to the bewildered Van Winkle.

The appearance of Rip with his long grizzled beard, his rusty fowling piece, his uncouth dress and an army of women and children at his heels soon attracted the attention of the tavern politicians. They crowded around him eying him from head to foot, with great curiosity. The orator bustled up to him, and drawing him partly aside, enquired "on which side he voted?"—Rip stared in vacant stupidity. Another short but busy little fellow, pulled him by the arm and rising on tiptoe, enquired in his ear "whether he was Federal or Democrat?"—Rip was equally at a loss to comprehend the question—when a knowing, self important old gentleman, in a sharp cocked hat, made his way through the crowd, putting them to the right and left with his elbows as he passed, and planting himself before Van Winkle, with one arm akimbo, the other resting on his cane, his keen eyes and sharp hat penetrating as it were into his very soul, demanded in an austere tone—"what brought him to the election with a gun on his shoulder and a mob at his heels, and whether he meant to breed a riot in the village?"—"Alas gentlemen," cried Rip, somewhat dismayed, "I am a poor quiet man, a native of the place, and a loyal subject of the King—God bless him!"

Here a general shout burst from the byestanders—"A tory! a tory! a spy! a Refugee! hustle him! away with him!"—It was with great difficulty that the self important man in the cocked hat restored order; and having assumed a ten fold austerity of brow demanded again of the unknown culprit, what he came there for and whom he was seeking. The poor man humbly assured him that he meant no harm; but merely came there in search of some of his neighbours, who used to keep about the tavern.

"—Well—who are they?—name them."

Rip bethought himself a moment and enquired, "Where's Nicholaus Vedder?"

There was a silence for a little while, when an old man replied, in a thin, piping voice, "Nicholaus Vedder? why he is dead and gone these eighteen years! There was a wooden tombstone in the church yard that used to tell all about him, but that's rotted and gone too."

"Where's Brom Dutcher?"

"Oh he went off to the army in the beginning of the war; some say he was killed at the storming of Stoney Point—others say he was drowned in a squall at the foot of Antony's Nose—I don't know—he never came back again."

"Where's Van Bummel the schoolmaster?"

"He went off to the wars too—was a great militia general, and is now in Congress."

Rip's heart died away at hearing of these sad changes in his home and friends, and finding himself thus alone in the world—every answer puzzled him too by treating of such enormous lapses of time and of matters which he could not understand—war—Congress, Stoney Point—he had no courage to ask after any more friends, but cried out in despair, "Does nobody here know Rip Van Winkle?"

"Oh. Rip Van Winkle?" exclaimed two or three—"oh to be sure!—that's Rip Van Winkle—yonder—leaning against the tree."

Rip looked and beheld a precise counterpart of himself, as he went up the mountain: apparently as lazy and certainly as ragged! The poor fellow was now completely confounded. He doubted his own identity, and whether he was himself or another man. In the midst of his bewilderment the man in the cocked hat demanded who he was,—what was his name?

"God knows," exclaimed he, at his wit's end, "I'm not myself.—I'm somebody else—that's me yonder—no—that's somebody else got into my shoes—I was myself last night; but I fell asleep on the mountain—and they've changed my gun—and every thing's changed—and I'm changed—and I can't tell what's my name, or who I am!"

The byestanders began now to look at each other, nod, wink significantly and tap their fingers against their foreheads. There was a whisper also about securing the gun, and keeping the old fellow from doing mischief—at the very suggestion of which, the self important man in the cocked hat retired with some precipitation. At this critical moment a fresh likely looking woman pressed through the throng to get a peep at the greybearded man. She had a chubby child in her arms, which frightened at his looks began to cry. "Hush Rip," cried she, "hush you little fool, the old man won't hurt you." The name of the child, the air of the mother, the tone of her voice all awakened a train of recollections in his mind. "What is your name my good woman?" asked he.

"Judith Gardenier."

"And your father's name?"

"Ah, poor man, Rip Van Winkle was his name, but it's twenty years since he went away from home with his gun and never has been heard of since—his dog came home without him—but whether he shot himself, or was carried away by the Indians no body can tell. I was then but a little girl."

Rip had but one question more to ask, but he put it with a faltering voice—

"Where's your mother?"—

Oh she too had died but a short time since—she broke a blood vessel in a fit of passion at a New England pedlar.—

There was a drop of comfort at least in this intelligence. The honest man could contain himself no longer—he caught his daughter and her child in his arms.—"I am your father!" cried he—"Young Rip Van Winkle once—old Rip Van Winkle now!—does nobody know poor Rip Van Winkle!"

All stood amazed, until an old woman tottering out from among the crowd put her hand to her brow and peering under it in his face for a moment exclaimed—"Sure enough!—it is Rip Van Winkle—it is himself—welcome home again old neighbour—why, where have you been these twenty long years?"

Rip's story was soon told, for the whole twenty years had been to him but as one night. The neighbours stared when they heard it; some were seen to wink at each other and put their tongues in their cheeks, and the self important man in the cocked hat, who when the alarm was over had returned to the field, screwed down the corners of his mouth and shook his head—upon which there was a general shaking of the head throughout the assemblage.

It was determined, however, to take the opinion of old Peter Vanderdonk, who was seen slowly advancing up the road. He was a descendant of the historian of that name, who wrote one of the earliest accounts of the province. Peter was the most ancient inhabitant of the village and well versed in all the wonderful events and traditions of the neighbourhood. He recollected Rip at once, and corroborated his story in the most satisfactory manner. He assured the company that it was a fact handed down from his ancestor the historian, that the Kaatskill mountains had always been haunted by strange beings. That it was affirmed that the great Hendrick Hudson, the first discoverer of the river and country, kept a kind of vigil there every twenty years, with his crew of the Half Moon—being permitted in this way to revisit the scenes of his enterprize and keep a guardian eye upon the river and the great city called by his name. That his father had once seen them in their old Dutch dresses playing at nine pins in a hollow of the mountain; and that he himself had heard one summer afternoon the sound of their balls, like distant peals of thunder.

To make a long story short—the company broke up, and returned to the more important concerns of the election. Rip's daughter took him home to live with her; she had a snug well furnished house, and a stout cheery farmer for a husband whom Rip recollected for one of the urchins that used to climb upon his back. As to Rip's son and heir, who was the ditto of himself seen leaning against the tree; he was employed to work on the farm; but evinced an hereditary disposition to attend to any thing else but his business.

Rip now resumed his old walks and habits; he soon found many of his former cronies, though all rather the worse for the wear and tear of time; and preferred making friends among the rising generation, with whom he soon grew into great favour.

Having nothing to do at home, and being arrived at that happy age when a man can be idle, with impunity, he took his place once more on the bench at the inn door and was reverenced as one of the patriarchs of the village and a chronicle of the old times "before the war." It was some time before he could get into the regular track of gossip, or could be made to comprehend the strange events that had taken place during his torpor. How that there had been a revolutionary war—that the country had thrown off the yoke of Old England and that instead of being a subject of his majesty George the Third, he was now a free citizen of the United States. Rip in fact was no politician; the changes of states and empires made but little impression on him; but there was one species of despotism under which he had long groaned and that was petticoat government. Happily that was at an end—he had got his neck out of the yoke of matrimony, and could go in and out whenever he pleased without dreading the tyranny of Dame Van Winkle. Whenever her name was mentioned, however, he shook his head, shrugged his shoulders and cast up his eyes; which might pass either for an expression of resignation to his fate or joy at his deliverance.

He used to tell his story to every stranger that arrived at Mr. Doolittle's Hotel. He was observed at first to vary on some points, every time he told it, which was doubtless owing to his having so recently awaked. It at last settled down precisely to the tale I have related and not a man woman or child in the neighbourhood but knew it by heart. Some always pretended to doubt the reality of it, and insisted that Rip had been out of his head, and that this was one point on which he always remained flighty. The old Dutch inhabitants, however, almost universally gave it full credit—Even to this day they never hear a thunder storm of a summer afternoon about the Kaatskill, but they say Hendrick Hudson and his crew are at their game of nine pins; and it is a common wish of all henpecked husbands in the neighbourhood, when life hangs heavy on their hands, that they might have a quieting draught out of Rip Van Winkle's flagon.

## NOTE

The foregoing tale one would suspect had been suggested to Mr. Knickerbocker by a little German superstition about the emperor Frederick *der Rothbart* and the Kypphauser Mountain; the subjoined note, however, which he had appended to the tale, shews that it is an absolute fact, narrated with his usual fidelity.—

"The story of Rip Van Winkle may seem incredible to many, but nevertheless I give it my full belief, for I know the vicinity of our old Dutch settlements to have been very subject to marvellous events and appearances. Indeed I have heard many stranger stories than this, in the villages along the Hudson; all of which were too well authenticated to admit of a doubt. I have even talked with Rip Van Winkle myself, who when last I saw him was a very venerable old man and so perfectly rational and consistent on every other point, that I think no conscientious person could refuse to take this into the bargain—nay I have seen a certificate on the subject taken before a country justice and signed with a cross in the justice's own hand writing. The story therefore is beyond the possibility of doubt.

D.K."

## POSTSCRIPT

The following are travelling notes from a memorandum book of Mr. Knickerbocker.

The Kaatsberg or Catskill mountains have always been a region full of fable. The Indians considered them the abode of spirits who influenced the weather, spreading sunshine or clouds over the landscape and sending good or bad hunting seasons. They were ruled by an old squaw spirit, said to be their mother. She dwelt on the highest peak of the Catskills and had charge of the doors of day and night to open and shut them at the proper hour. She hung up the new moons in the skies and cut up the old ones into stars. In times of drought, if properly propitiated, she would spin light summer clouds out of cobwebs and morning dew, and send them off, from the crest of the mountain, flake after flake, like flakes of carded cotton to float in the air: until, dissolved by the heat of the sun, they would fall in gentle showers, causing the grass to spring, the fruits to ripen and the corn to grow an inch an hour. If displeased, however, she would brew up clouds black as ink, sitting in the midst of them like a bottle bellied spider in the midst of its web; and when these clouds broke—woe betide the valleys!

In old times say the Indian traditions, there was a kind of Manitou or Spirit, who kept about the wildest recesses of the Catskill mountains, and took a mischievous pleasure in wreak-ing all kinds of evils and vexations upon the red men. Sometimes he would assume the form of a bear a panther or a deer, lead the bewildered hunter a weary chace through tangled forests and among rugged rocks; and then spring off with a loud ho! ho! leaving him aghast on the brink of a beetling precipice or raging torrent.

The favorite abode of this Manitou is still shewn. It is a great rock or cliff in the loneliest part of the mountains, and, from the flowering vines which clamber about it, and the wild flowers which abound in its neighborhood, is known by the name of the Garden Rock. Near the foot of it is a small lake the haunt of the solitary bittern, with water snakes basking in the sun on the leaves of the pond lillies which lie on the surface. This place was held in great awe by the Indians, insomuch that the boldest hunter would not pursue his game within its precincts. Once upon a time, however, a hunter who had lost his way, penetrated to the garden rock where he beheld a number of gourds placed in the crotches of trees. One of these he seized and made off with it, but in the hurry of his retreat he let it fall among the rocks, when a great stream gushed forth which washed him away and swept him down precipices where he was dashed to pieces, and the stream made its way to the Hudson and continues to flow to the present day; being the identical stream known by the name of the Kaaters-kill.

1819

# WASHINGTON IRVING

(1783–1859)

---

## *The Legend of Sleepy Hollow*

### *(Found among the Papers of the late Diedrich Knickerbocker)*

A pleasing land of drowsy head it was,
Of dreams that wave before the half-shut eye;
And of gay castles in the clouds that pass,
Forever flushing round a summer sky.

*Castle of Indolence*

In the bosom of one of those spacious coves which indent the eastern shore of the Hudson, at that broad expansion of the river denominated by the ancient Dutch navigators the Tappaan Zee, and where they always prudently shortened sail, and implored the protection of St. Nicholas when they crossed, there lies a small market town or rural port, which by some is called Greensburgh, but which is more generally and properly known by the name of Tarry Town. This name was given, we are told, in former days, by the good housewives of the adjacent country, from the inveterate propensity of their husbands to linger about the village tavern on market days. Be that as it may, I do not vouch for the fact, but merely advert to it, for the sake of being precise and authentic. Not far from this village, perhaps about two miles, there is a little valley, or rather lap of land among high hills, which is one of the quietest places in the whole world. A small brook glides through it, with just murmur enough to lull one to repose, and the occasional whistle of a quail, or tapping of a woodpecker, is almost the only sound that ever breaks in upon the uniform tranquillity.

I recollect that when a stripling, my first exploit in squirrel shooting was in a grove of tall walnut trees that shades one side of the valley. I had wandered into it at noon time, when all nature is peculiarly quiet, and was startled by the roar of my own gun, as it broke the sabbath stillness around, and was prolonged and reverberated by the angry echoes. If ever I should wish for a retreat, whither I might steal from the world and its distractions, and dream quietly away the remnant of a troubled life, I know of none more promising than this little valley.

From the listless repose of the place, and the peculiar character of its inhabitants, who are descendants from the original Dutch settlers, this sequestered glen has long been known by the name of SLEEPY HOLLOW, and its rustic lads are called the Sleepy Hollow Boys throughout all the neighbouring country. A drowsy, dreamy influence seems to hang over the land, and to pervade the very atmosphere. Some say that the place was bewitched by a high German doctor during the early days of the settlement; others, that an old Indian chief, the prophet or wizard of his tribe, held his powwows there before the country was discovered by Master Hendrick Hudson. Certain it is, the place still continues under the sway of some witching power, that holds a spell over the minds of the good people, causing them to walk in a continual reverie. They are given to all kinds of marvellous beliefs; are subject to trances and visions, and frequently see strange sights, and hear music and voices in the air. The whole neighbourhood abounds with local tales, haunted spots, and twilight superstitions; stars shoot and meteors glare oftener across the valley than in any other part of the country, and the night mare, with her whole nine fold, seems to make it the favourite scene of her gambols.

The dominant spirit, however, that haunts this enchanted region, and seems to be commander in chief of all the powers of the air, is the apparition of a figure on horseback without a head. It is said by some to be the ghost of a Hessian trooper, whose head had been carried away by a cannon ball, in some nameless battle during the revolutionary war, and who is ever and anon seen by the country folk, hurrying along in the gloom of night, as if on the wings of the wind. His haunts are not confined to the valley, but extend at times to the adjacent roads, and especially to the vicinity of a church at no great distance. Indeed, certain of the most authentic historians of those parts, who have been careful in collecting and collating the floating facts concerning this spectre, allege, that the body of the trooper having been buried in the church yard, the ghost rides forth to the scene of battle in nightly quest of his head, and that the rushing speed with which he sometimes passes along the hollow, like a midnight blast, is owing to his being belated, and in a hurry to get back to the church yard before day break.

Such is the general purport of this legendary superstition, which has furnished materials for many a wild story in that region of shadows; and the spectre is known, at all the country firesides, by the name of The Headless Horseman of Sleepy Hollow.

It is remarkable, that the visionary propensity I have mentioned is not confined to the native inhabitants of the valley, but is unconsciously imbibed by every one who resides there for a time. However wide awake they may have been before they entered that sleepy region, they are sure, in a little time, to inhale the witching influence of the air, and begin to grow imaginative—to dream dreams, and see apparitions.

I mention this peaceful spot with all possible laud; for it is in such little retired Dutch valleys, found here and there embosomed in the great state of New York, that population, manners, and customs, remain fixed, while the great torrent of migration and improvement, which is making such incessant changes in other parts of this restless country, sweeps by them unobserved. They are like those little nooks of still water, which border a rapid stream, where we may see the straw and bubble riding quietly at anchor, or slowly revolving in their mimic harbour, undisturbed by the rush of the passing current. Though many years have elapsed since I trod the drowsy shades of Sleepy Hollow, yet I question whether I should not still find the same trees and the same families vegetating in its sheltered bosom.

In this by place of nature there abode, in a remote period of American history, that is to say, some thirty years since, a worthy wight of the name of Ichabod Crane, who sojourned, or, as he expressed it, "tarried," in Sleepy Hollow, for the purpose of instructing the children of the vicinity. He was a native of Connecticut, a state which supplies the Union with pioneers for the mind as well as for the forest, and sends forth yearly its legions of frontier woodmen and country schoolmasters. The cognomen of Crane was not inapplicable to his person. He was tall, but exceedingly lank, with narrow shoulders, long arms and legs, hands that dangled a mile out of his sleeves, feet that might have served for shovels, and his whole frame most loosely hung together. His head was small, and flat at top, with huge ears, large green glassy eyes, and a long snipe nose, so that it looked like a weathercock perched upon his spindle neck, to tell which way the wind blew. To see him striding along the profile of a hill on a windy day, with his clothes bagging and fluttering about him, one might have mistaken him for the genius of famine descending upon the earth, or some scarecrow eloped from a cornfield.

His school house was a low building of one large room, rudely constructed of logs; the windows partly glazed, and partly patched with leaves of old copy books. It was most ingeniously secured at vacant hours, by a withe twisted in the handle of the door, and stakes set against the window shutters; so that though a thief might get in with perfect ease, he would find some embarrassment in getting out; an idea most probably borrowed by the architect, Yost Van Houten, from the mystery of an eelpot. The school house stood in a rather lonely but pleasant situation, just at the foot of a woody hill, with a brook running close by, and a formidable birch tree growing at one end of it. From hence the low murmur of his pupils' voices conning over their lessons, might be heard of a drowsy summer's day, like the hum of a bee hive; interrupted now and then by the authoritative voice of the master, in the tone of menace or command, or peradventure, by the appalling sound of the birch, as he urged some tardy loiterer along the flowery path of knowledge. Truth to say, he was a conscientious man, and ever bore in mind the golden maxim, "spare the rod and spoil the child."—Ichabod Crane's scholars certainly were not spoiled.

I would not have it imagined, however, that he was one of those cruel potentates of the school, who joy in the smart of their subjects; on the contrary, he administered justice with discrimination rather than severity; taking the burthen off the backs of the weak, and laying it on those of the strong. Your mere puny stripling, that winced at the least flourish of the rod, was passed by with indulgence; but the claims of justice were satisfied, by inflicting a double portion on some little, tough, wrong headed, broad skirted Dutch urchin, who sulked and swelled and grew dogged and sullen beneath the birch. All this he called "doing his duty by their parents;" and he never inflicted a chastisement without following it by the assurance, so consolatory to the smarting urchin, that "he would remember it and thank him for it the longest day he had to live."

When school hours were over, he was even the companion and playmate of the larger boys; and on holyday afternoons would convoy some of the smaller ones home, who happened to have pretty sisters, or good housewives for mothers, noted for the comforts of the cupboard. Indeed, it behooved him to keep on good terms with his pupils. The revenue arising from his school was small, and would have been scarcely sufficient to furnish him with daily bread, for he was a huge feeder, and though lank, had the dilating powers of an Anaconda; but to help out his maintenance, he was, according to country custom in those parts, boarded and lodged at the houses of the farmers, whose children he instructed. With these he lived successively a week at a time, thus going the rounds of the neighbourhood, with all his worldly effects tied up in a cotton handkerchief.

That all this might not be too onerous on the purses of his rustic patrons, who are apt to consider the costs of schooling a grievous burthen, and schoolmasters as mere drones, he had various ways of rendering himself both useful and agreeable. He assisted the farmers occasionally in the lighter labours of their farms, helped to make hay, mended the fences, took the horses to water, drove the cows from pasture, and cut wood for the winter fire. He laid aside, too, all the dominant dignity and absolute sway, with which he lorded it in his little empire, the school, and became wonderfully gentle and ingratiating. He found favour in the eyes of the mothers, by petting the children, particularly the youngest, and like the lion bold, which whilome so magnanimously the lamb did hold, he would sit with a child on one knee, and rock a cradle with his foot, for whole hours together.

In addition to his other vocations, he was the singing master of the neighbourhood, and picked up many bright shillings by instructing the young folks in psalmody. It was a matter of no little vanity to him on Sundays, to take his station in front of the church gallery, with a band of chosen singers; where, in his own mind, he completely carried away the palm from the parson. Certain it is, his voice resounded far above all the rest of the congregation, and there are peculiar quavers still to be heard in that church, and which may even be heard half a mile off, quite to the opposite side of the mill pond, of a still Sunday morning, which are said to be legitimately descended from the nose of Ichabod Crane. Thus, by diverse little make shifts, in that ingenious way which is commonly denominated "by hook and by crook," the worthy pedagogue got on tolerably enough, and was thought, by all who understood nothing of the labour of headwork, to have a wonderfully easy life of it.

The schoolmaster is generally a man of some importance in the female circle of a rural neighbourhood, being considered a kind of idle gentleman like personage, of vastly superior taste and accomplishments to the rough country swains, and, indeed, inferior in learning only to the parson. His appearance, therefore, is apt to occasion some little stir at the tea table of a farm house, and the addition of a supernumerary dish of cakes or sweetmeats, or, peradventure, the parade of a silver tea pot. Our man of letters, therefore, was peculiarly happy in the smiles of all the country damsels. How he would figure among them in the church yard, between services on Sundays; gathering grapes for them from the wild vines that overrun the surrounding trees; reciting for their amusement all the epitaphs on the tombstones, or sauntering, with a whole bevy of them, along the banks of the adjacent mill pond; while the more bashful country bumpkins hung sheepishly back, envying his superior elegance and address.

From his half itinerant life, also, he was a kind of travelling gazette, carrying the whole budget of local gossip from house to house; so that his appearance was always greeted with satisfaction. He was, moreover, esteemed by the women as a man of great erudition, for he had read several books quite through, and was a perfect master of Cotton Mather's History of New England Witchcraft, in which, by the way, he most firmly and potently believed.

He was, in fact, an odd mixture of small shrewdness and simple credulity. His appetite for the marvellous, and his powers of digesting it, were equally extraordinary; and both had been increased by his residence in this spell bound region. No tale was too gross or monstrous for his capacious swallow. It was often his delight, after his school was dismissed of an afternoon, to stretch himself on the rich bed of clover, bordering the little brook that whimpered by his school house, and there con over old Mather's direful tales, until the gathering dusk of evening made the printed page a mere mist before his eyes. Then, as he wended his way, by swamp and stream and awful woodland, to the farm house where he happened to be quartered, every sound of nature, at that witching hour, fluttered his excited imagination: the moan of the whip-poor-will* from the hill side; the boding cry of the tree toad, that harbinger of storm; the dreary hooting of the screech owl; or the sudden rustling in the thicket, of birds frightened from their roost. The fire flies, too, which sparkled most vividly in the darkest places, now and then startled him, as one of uncommon brightness would stream across his path; and if, by chance, a huge blockhead of a beetle came winging his blundering flight against him, the poor varlet was ready to give up the ghost, with the idea that he was struck with a witch's token. His only resource on such occasions, either to drown thought, or drive away evil spirits, was to sing psalm tunes;—and the good people of Sleepy Hollow, as they sat by their doors of an evening, were often filled with awe, at hearing his nasal melody, "in linked sweetness long drawn out," floating from the distant hill, or along the dusky road.

Another of his sources of fearful pleasure was, to pass long winter evenings with the old Dutch wives, as they sat spinning by the fire, with a row of apples roasting and sputtering along the hearth, and listen to their marvellous tales of ghosts and goblins, and haunted fields and haunted brooks, and haunted bridges and haunted houses, and particularly of the headless horseman, or galloping Hessian of the Hollow, as they sometimes called him. He would delight them equally by his anecdotes of witchcraft, and of the direful omens and portentous sights and sounds in the air, which prevailed in the earlier times of Connecticut; and would frighten them wofully with speculations upon comets and shooting stars, and with the alarming fact that the world did absolutely turn round, and that they were half the time topsy-turvy!

*The whip-poor-will is a bird which is only heard at night. It receives its name from its note which is thought to resemble those words.

But if there was a pleasure in all this, while snugly cuddling in the chimney corner of a chamber that was all of a ruddy glow from the crackling wood fire, and where, of course, no spectre dared to show its face, it was dearly purchased by the terrors of his subsequent walk homewards. What fearful shapes and shadows beset his path, amidst the dim and ghastly glare of a snowy night!—With what wistful look did he eye every trembling ray of light streaming across the waste fields from some distant window!—How often was he appalled by some shrub covered with snow, which like a sheeted spectre beset his very path!—How often did he shrink with curdling awe at the sound of his own steps on the frosty crust beneath his feet; and dread to look over his shoulder, lest he should behold some uncouth being tramping close behind him!—and how often was he thrown into complete dismay by some rushing blast, howling among the trees, in the idea that it was the gallopping Hessian on one of his nightly scourings.

All these, however, were mere terrors of the night, phantoms of the mind, that walk in darkness; and though he had seen many spectres in his time, and been more than once beset by Satan in diverse shapes, in his lonely perambulations, yet daylight put an end to all these evils; and he would have passed a pleasant life of it, in despite of the Devil and all his works, if his path had not been crossed by a being that causes more perplexity to mortal man, than ghosts, goblins, and the whole race of witches put together, and that was—a woman.

Among the musical disciples who assembled, one evening in each week, to receive his instructions in psalmody, was Katrina Van Tassel, the daughter and only child of a substantial Dutch farmer. She was a blooming lass of fresh eighteen; plump as a partridge; ripe and melting and rosy cheeked as one of her father's peaches, and universally famed, not merely for her beauty, but her vast expectations. She was withal a little of a coquette, as might be perceived even in her dress, which was a mixture of ancient and modern fashions, as most suited to set off her charms. She wore the ornaments of pure yellow gold, which her great great grandmother had brought over from Saardam; the tempting stomacher of the olden time, and withal a provokingly short petticoat, to display the prettiest foot and ankle in the country round.

Ichabod Crane had a soft and foolish heart toward the sex; and it is not to be wondered at, that so tempting a morsel soon found favour in his eyes, more especially after he had visited her in her paternal mansion. Old Baltus Van Tassel was a perfect picture of a thriving, contented, liberal hearted farmer. He seldom, it is true, sent either his eyes or his thoughts beyond the boundaries of his own farm; but within those every thing was snug, happy, and well conditioned. He was satisfied with his wealth, but not proud of it, and piqued himself upon the hearty abundance, rather than the style in which he lived. His strong hold was situated on the banks of the Hudson, in one of those green, sheltered, fertile nooks, in which the Dutch farmers are so fond of nestling. A great elm tree spread its broad branches over it, at the foot of which bubbled up a spring of the softest and sweetest water, in a little well, formed of a barrel, and then stole sparkling away through the grass, to a neighbouring brook, that babbled along among elders and dwarf willows. Hard by the farm house was a vast barn, that might have served for a church; every window and crevice of which seemed bursting forth with the treasures of the farm; the flail was busily resounding within it from morning to night; swallows and martins skimmed twittering about the eaves, and rows of pigeons, some with one eye turned up, as if watching the weather, some with their heads under their wings, or buried in their bosoms, and others, swelling, and cooing, and bowing about their dames, were enjoying the sunshine on the roof. Sleek unwieldy porkers were grunting in the repose and abundance of their pens, from whence sallied forth, now and then, troops of sucking pigs, as if to snuff the air. A stately squadron of snowy geese were riding in an adjoining pond, convoying whole fleets of ducks; regiments of turkeys were gobbling through the farm yard, and guinea fowls fretting about it like ill tempered housewives, with their peevish discontented cry. Before the barn door strutted the gallant cock, that pattern of a husband, a warrior, and a fine gentleman, clapping his burnished wings, and crowing in the pride and gladness of his heart—sometimes tearing up the earth with his feet, and then generously calling his ever hungry family of wives and children to enjoy the rich morsel which he had discovered.

The pedagogue's mouth watered, as he looked upon this sumptuous promise of luxurious winter fare. In his devouring mind's eye, he pictured to himself every roasting pig running about with a pudding in his belly, and an apple in his mouth; the pigeons were snugly put to bed in a comfortable pie, and tucked in with a coverlet of crust; the geese were swimming in their own gravy; and the ducks pairing cosily in dishes, like snug married couples, with a decent competency of onion sauce; in the porkers he saw carved out the future sleek side of bacon, and juicy relishing ham; not a turkey, but he beheld daintily trussed up, with its gizzard under its wing, and, peradventure, a necklace of savoury sausages; and even bright chanticleer himself lay sprawling on his back, in a side dish, with uplifted claws, as if craving that quarter, which his chivalrous spirit disdained to ask while living.

As the enraptured Ichabod fancied all this, and as he rolled his great green eyes over the fat meadow lands, the rich fields of wheat, of rye, of buckwheat, and Indian corn, and the orchards burthened with ruddy fruit, which surrounded the warm tenement of Van Tassel, his heart yearned after the damsel who was to inherit these domains, and his imagination expanded with the idea, how they might be readily turned into cash, and the money invested in immense tracts of wild land, and shingle palaces in the wilderness. Nay, his busy fancy already realized his hopes, and presented to him the blooming Katrina, with a whole family of children, mounted on the top of a waggon loaded with household trumpery, with pots and kettles dangling beneath; and he beheld himself bestriding a pacing mare, with a colt at her heels, setting out for Kentucky, Tennessee, or the Lord knows where!

When he entered the house, the conquest of his heart was complete. It was one of those spacious farm houses, with high ridged, but lowly sloping roofs, built in the style handed down from the first Dutch settlers. The low, projecting eaves formed a piazza along the front, capable of being closed up in bad weather. Under this were hung flails, harness, various utensils of husbandry, and nets for fishing in the neighbouring river. Benches were built along the sides for summer use; and a great spinning wheel at one end, and a churn at the other, showed the various uses to which this important porch might be devoted. From this piazza the wondering Ichabod entered the hall, which formed the centre of the mansion, and the place of usual residence. Here, rows of resplendent pewter, ranged on a long dresser, dazzled his eyes. In one corner stood a huge bag of wool ready to be spun; in another a quantity of linsey-woolsey just from the loom; ears of Indian corn, and strings of dried apples and peaches, hung in gay festoons along the walls, mingled with the gaud of red peppers; and a door left ajar, gave him a peep into the best parlour, where the claw footed chairs, and dark mahogany tables, shone like mirrors; andirons, with their accompanying shovel and tongs, glistened from their covert of asparagus tops; mock oranges and conch shells decorated the mantlepiece; strings of various coloured birds' eggs were suspended above it; a great ostrich egg was hung from the centre of the room, and a corner cupboard, knowingly left open, displayed immense treasures of old silver and well mended china.

From the moment Ichabod laid his eyes upon these regions of delight, the peace of his mind was at an end, and his only study was how to gain the affections of the peerless daughter of Van Tassel. In this enterprize, however, he had more real difficulties than generally fell to the lot of a knight errant of yore, who seldom had any thing but giants, enchanters, fiery dragons, and such like easily conquered adversaries, to contend with; and had to make his way merely through gates of iron and brass, and walls of adamant, to the castle keep, where the lady of his heart was confined; all which he achieved as easily as a man would carve his way to the centre of a Christmas pie, and then the lady gave him her hand as a matter of course. Ichabod, on the contrary, had to win his way to the heart of a country coquette, beset with a labyrinth of whims and caprices, which were for ever presenting new difficulties and impediments, and he had to encounter a host of fearful adversaries of real flesh and blood, the numerous rustic admirers, who beset every portal to her heart, keeping a watchful and angry eye upon each other, but ready to fly out in the common cause against any new competitor.

Among these, the most formidable, was a burly, roaring, roystering blade, of the name of Abraham, or, according to the Dutch abbreviation, Brom Van Brunt, the hero of the country round, which rung with his feats of strength and hardihood. He was broad shouldered and double jointed, with short curly black hair, and a bluff, but not unpleasant countenance, having a mingled air of fun and arrogance. From his Herculean frame and great powers of limb, he had received the nick name of Brom Bones, by which he was universally known. He was famed for great knowledge and skill in horsemanship, being as dexterous on horseback as a Tartar. He was foremost at all races and cock fights, and with the ascendancy which bodily strength acquires in rustic life, was the umpire in all disputes, setting his hat on one side, and giving his decisions with an air and tone admitting of no gainsay or appeal. He was always ready for either a fight or a frolick; but had more mischief than ill will in his composition; and with all his overbearing roughness, there was a strong dash of waggish good humour at bottom. He had three or four boon companions, who regarded him as their model, and at the head of whom he scoured the country, attending every scene of feud or merriment for miles round. In cold weather he was distinguished by a fur cap, surmounted with a flaunting fox's tail, and when the folks at a country gathering descried this well known crest at a distance, whisking about among a squad of hard riders, they always stood by for a squall. Sometimes his crew would be heard dashing along past the farm houses at midnight, with whoop and halloo, like a troop of Don Cossacks, and the old dames, startled out of their sleep, would listen for a moment till the hurry scurry had clattered by, and then exclaim, "aye, there goes Brom Bones and his gang!" The neighbours looked upon him with a mixture of awe, admiration, and good will; and when any mad cap prank, or rustic brawl, occurred in the vicinity, always shook their heads, and warranted Brom Bones was at the bottom of it.

This rantipole hero had for some time singled out the blooming Katrina for the object of his uncouth gallantries, and though his amorous toyings were something like the gentle caresses and endearments of a bear, yet it was whispered that she did not altogether discourage his hopes. Certain it is, his advances were signals for rival candidates to retire, who felt no inclination to cross a lion in his amours; insomuch, that when his horse was seen tied to Van Tassel's paling, of a Sunday night, (a sure sign that his master was courting, or, as it is termed, "sparking," within,) all other suitors passed by in despair, and carried the war into other quarters.

Such was the formidable rival with whom Ichabod Crane had to contend, and, considering all things, a stouter man than he would have shrunk from the competition, and a wiser man would have despaired. He had, however, a happy mixture of pliability and perseverance in his nature; he was in form and spirit like a supple jack—yielding, but tough; though he bent, he never broke; and though he bowed beneath the slightest pressure, yet, the moment it was away—jerk!—he was as erect, and carried his head as high as ever.

To have taken the field openly against his rival, would have been madness; for he was not a man to be thwarted in his amours, any more than that stormy lover, Achilles. Ichabod, therefore, made his advances in a quiet and gently insinuating manner. Under cover of his character of singing master, he made frequent visits at the farm house; not that he had any thing to apprehend from the meddlesome interference of parents, which is so often a stumbling block in the path of lovers. Balt Van Tassel was an easy indulgent soul; he loved his daughter better even than his pipe, and like a reasonable man, and an excellent father, let her have her way in every thing. His notable little wife too, had enough to do to attend to her housekeeping and manage her poultry, for, as she sagely observed, ducks and geese are foolish things, and must be looked after, but girls can take care of themselves. Thus while the busy dame bustled about the house, or plied her spinning wheel at one end of the piazza, honest Balt would sit smoking his evening pipe at the other, watching the achievements of a little wooden warrior, who, armed with a sword in each hand, was most valiantly fighting the wind on the pinnacle of the barn. In the mean time, Ichabod would carry on his suit with the daughter by the side of the spring under the great elm, or sauntering along in the twilight, that hour so favourable to the lover's eloquence.

I profess not to know how women's hearts are wooed and won. To me they have always been matters of riddle and admiration. Some seem to have but one vulnerable point, or door of access; while others have a thousand avenues, and may be captured in a thousand different ways. It is a great triumph of skill to gain the former, but a still greater proof of generalship to maintain possession of the latter, for a man must battle for his fortress at every door and window. He who wins a thousand common hearts, is therefore entitled to some renown; but he who keeps undisputed sway over the heart of a coquette, is indeed a hero. Certain it is, this was not the case with the redoutable Brom Bones; and from the moment Ichabod Crane made his advances, the interests of the former evidently declined; his horse was no longer seen tied at the palings on Sunday nights, and a deadly feud gradually arose between him and the preceptor of Sleepy Hollow.

Brom, who had a degree of rough chivalry in his nature, would fain have carried matters to open warfare, and have settled their pretensions to the lady, according to the mode of those most concise and simple reasoners, the knights errant of yore—by single combat; but Ichabod was too conscious of the superior might of his adversary to enter the lists against him; he had overheard a boast of Bones, that he would "double the schoolmaster up, and lay him on a shelf of his own school house;" and he was too wary to give him an opportunity. There was something extremely provoking in this obstinately pacific system; it left Brom no alternative but to draw upon the funds of rustic waggery in his disposition, and to play off boorish practical jokes upon his rival. Ichabod became the object of whimsical persecution to Bones, and his gang of rough riders. They harried his hitherto peaceful domains; smoked out his singing school, by stopping up the chimney; broke into the school house at night, in spite of its formidable fastenings of withe and window stakes, and turned every thing topsy-turvy, so that the poor schoolmaster began to think all the witches in the country held their meetings there. But what was still more annoying, Brom took all opportunities of turning him into ridicule in presence of his mistress, and had a scoundrel dog, whom he taught to whine in the most ludicrous manner, and introduced as a rival of Ichabod's, to instruct her in psalmody.

In this way, matters went on for some time, without producing any material effect on the relative situations of the contending powers. On a fine autumnal afternoon, Ichabod, in pensive mood, sat enthroned on the lofty stool from whence he usually watched all the concerns of his little literary realm. In his hand he swayed a ferule, that sceptre of despotic power; the birch of justice reposed on three nails, behind the throne, a constant terror to evil doers; while on the desk before him might be seen sundry contraband articles and prohibited weapons, detected upon the persons of idle urchins, such as half munched apples, popguns, whirligigs, fly cages, and whole legions of rampant little paper game cocks. Apparently there had been some appalling act of justice recently inflicted, for his scholars were all busily intent upon their books, or slyly whispering behind them with one eye kept upon the master; and a kind of buzzing stillness reigned throughout the school room. It was suddenly interrupted by the appearance of a negro in tow cloth jacket and trowsers, a round crowned fragment of a hat, like the cap of Mercury, and mounted on the back of a ragged, wild, half broken colt, which he managed with a rope by way of halter. He came clattering up to the school door with an invitation to Ichabod to attend a merry making, or "quilting frolick," to be held that evening at Mynheer Van Tassel's, and having delivered his message with that air of importance, and effort at fine language, which a negro is apt to display on petty embassies of the kind, he dashed over the brook, and was seen scampering away up the hollow, full of the importance and hurry of his mission.

All was now bustle and hubbub in the late quiet school room. The scholars were hurried through their lessons, without stopping at trifles; those who were nimble, skipped over half with impunity, and those who were tardy, had a smart application now and then in the rear, to quicken their speed, or help them over a tall word. Books were flung aside, without being put away on the shelves; inkstands were overturned, benches thrown down, and the whole school was turned loose an hour before the usual time; bursting forth like a legion of young imps, yelping and racketing about the green, in joy at their early emancipation.

The gallant Ichabod now spent at least an extra half hour at his toilet, brushing and furbishing up his best, and indeed only suit of rusty black, and arranging his looks by a bit of broken looking glass, that hung up in the school house. That he might make his appearance before his mistress in the true style of a cavalier, he borrowed a horse from the farmer with whom he was domiciliated, a choleric old Dutchman, of the name of Hans

Van Ripper, and thus gallantly mounted, issued forth like a knight errant in quest of adventures. But it is meet I should, in the true spirit of romantic story, give some account of the looks and equipments of my hero and his steed. The animal he bestrode was a broken down plough horse, that had outlived almost every thing but his viciousness. He was gaunt and shagged, with a ewe neck and a head like a hammer; his rusty mane and tail were tangled and knotted with burrs; one eye had lost its pupil, and was glaring and spectral, but the other had the gleam of a genuine devil in it. Still he must have had fire and mettle in his day, if we may judge from the name he bore of Gunpowder. He had, in fact, been a favourite steed of his master's, the cholerick Van Ripper, who was a furious rider, and had infused, very probably, some of his own spirit into the animal, for, old and broken down as he looked, there was more of the lurking devil in him than in any young filly in the country.

Ichabod was a suitable figure for such a steed. He rode with short stirrups, which brought his knees nearly up to the pommel of the saddle; his sharp elbows stuck out like grasshoppers'; he carried his whip perpendicularly in his hand, like a sceptre, and as his horse jogged on, the motion of his arms was not unlike the flapping of a pair of wings. A small wool hat rested on the top of his nose, for so his scanty strip of forehead might be called, and the skirts of his black coat fluttered out almost to the horse's tail. Such was the appearance of Ichabod and his steed, as they shambled out of the gate of Hans Van Ripper, and it was altogether such an apparition as is seldom to be met with in broad day light.

It was, as I have said, a fine autumnal day, the sky was clear and serene, and nature wore that rich and golden livery which we always associate with the idea of abundance. The forests had put on their sober brown and yellow, while some trees of the tenderer kind had been nipped by the frosts into brilliant dyes of orange, purple, and scarlet. Streaming files of wild ducks began to make their appearance high in the air; the bark of the squirrel might be heard from the groves of beech and hickory nuts, and the pensive whistle of the quail at intervals from the neighbouring stubble field.

The small birds were taking their farewell banquets. In the fullness of their revelry, they fluttered, chirping and frolicking, from bush to bush, and tree to tree, capricious from the very profusion and variety around them. There was the honest cock robin, the favourite game of stripling sportsmen, with its loud querulous note; and the twittering blackbirds flying in sable clouds; and the golden winged woodpecker, with his crimson crest, his broad black gorget, and splendid plumage; and the cedar bird, with its red tipt wings and yellow tipt tail, and its little monteiro cap of feathers; and the blue jay, that noisy coxcomb, in his gay light blue coat and white under clothes, screaming and chattering, nodding, and bobbing, and bowing, and pretending to be on good terms with every songster of the grove.

As Ichabod jogged slowly on his way, his eye, ever open to every symptom of culinary abundance, ranged with delight over the treasures of jolly autumn. On all sides he beheld vast store of apples, some hanging in oppressive opulence on the trees, some gathered into baskets and barrels for the market, others heaped up in rich piles for the cider press. Further on he beheld great fields of Indian corn, with its golden ears peeping from their leafy coverts, and holding out the promise of cakes and hasty pudding; and the yellow pumpkins lying beneath them, turning up their fair round bellies to the sun, and giving ample prospects of the most luxurious of pies; and anon he passed the fragrant buckwheat fields, breathing the odour of the bee hive, and as he beheld them, soft anticipations stole over his mind of dainty slap jacks, well buttered, and garnished with honey or treacle, by the delicate little dimpled hand of Katrina Van Tassel.

Thus feeding his mind with many sweet thoughts and "sugared suppositions," he journeyed along the sides of a range of hills which look out upon some of the goodliest scenes of the mighty Hudson. The sun gradually wheeled his broad disk down into the west. The wide bosom of the Tappaan Zee lay motionless and glassy, excepting that here and there a gentle undulation waved and prolonged the blue shadow of the distant mountain: a few amber clouds floated in the sky, without a breath of air to move them. The horizon was of a fine golden tint, changing gradually into a pure apple green, and from that into the deep blue of the mid-heaven. A slanting ray lingered on the woody crests of the precipices that overhung some parts of the river, giving greater depth to the dark grey and purple of their rocky sides. A sloop was loitering in the distance, dropping slowly down with the tide, her sail hanging uselessly against the mast, and as the reflection of the sky gleamed along the still water, it seemed as if the vessel was suspended in the air.

It was toward evening that Ichabod arrived at the castle of the Heer Van Tassel, which he found thronged with the pride and flower of the adjacent country. Old farmers, a spare, leathern faced race, in homespun coats and breeches, blue stockings, huge shoes and magnificent pewter buckles. Their brisk withered little dames in close crimped caps, long waisted short gowns, homespun petticoats, with scissors and pincushions, and gay calico pockets, hanging on the outside. Buxom lasses, almost as antiquated as their mothers, excepting where a straw hat, a fine ribband, or perhaps a white frock, gave symptoms of city innovation. The sons, in short square skirted coats with rows of stupendous brass buttons, and their hair generally queued in the fashion of the times, especially if they could procure an eel skin for the purpose, it being esteemed throughout the country as a potent nourisher and strengthener of the hair.

Brom Bones, however, was the hero of the scene, having come to the gathering on his favourite steed Daredevil, a creature, like himself, full of mettle and mischief, and which no one but himself could manage. He was in fact noted for preferring vicious animals, given to all kinds of tricks, which kept the rider in constant risk of his neck, for he held a tractable well broken horse as unworthy of a lad of spirit.

Fain would I pause to dwell upon the world of charms that burst upon the enraptured gaze of my hero, as he entered the state parlour of Van Tassel's mansion. Not those of the bevy of buxom lasses, with their luxurious display of red and white: but the ample charms of a genuine Dutch country tea table, in the sumptuous time of autumn. Such heaped up platters of cakes of various and almost indescribable kinds, known only to experienced Dutch housewives. There was the doughty dough nut, the tenderer oly koek, and the crisp and crumbling cruller; sweet cakes and short cakes, ginger cakes and honey cakes, and the whole family of cakes. And then there were apple pies and peach pies and pumpkin pies; besides slices of ham and smoked beef; and moreover delectable dishes of preserved plums, and peaches, and pears, and quinces; not to mention broiled shad and roasted chickens; together with bowls of milk and cream, all mingled higgledy-piggledy, pretty much as I have enumerated them, with the motherly tea pot sending up its clouds of vapour from the midst—Heaven bless the mark! I want breath and time to discuss this banquet as it deserves, and am too eager to get on with my story. Happily, Ichabod Crane was not in so great a hurry as his historian, but did ample justice to every dainty.

He was a kind and thankful creature, whose heart dilated in proportion as his skin was filled with good cheer, and whose spirits rose with eating, as some men's do with drink. He could not help, too, rolling his large eyes round him as he ate, and chuckling with the possibility that he might one day be lord of all this scene of almost unimaginable luxury and splendour. Then, he thought, how soon he'd turn his back upon the old school house; snap his fingers in the face of Hans Van Ripper, and every other niggardly patron, and kick any itinerant pedagogue out of doors that should dare to call him comrade!

Old Baltus Van Tassel moved about among his guests with a face dilated with content and good humour, round and jolly as the harvest moon. His hospitable attentions were brief, but expressive, being confined to a shake of the hand, a slap on the shoulder, a loud laugh, and a pressing invitation to "fall to, and help themselves."

And now the sound of the music from the common room or hall, summoned to the dance. The musician was an old grey headed negro, who had been the itinerant orchestra of the neighbourhood for more than half a century. His instrument was as old and battered as himself. The greater part of the time he scraped away on two or three strings, accompanying every movement of the bow with a motion of the head; bowing almost to the ground, and stamping with his foot whenever a fresh couple were to start.

Ichabod prided himself upon his dancing as much as upon his vocal powers. Not a limb, not a fibre about him was idle, and to have seen his loosely hung frame in full motion, and clattering about the room, you would have thought Saint Vitus himself, that blessed patron of the dance, was figuring before you in person. He was the admiration of all the negroes, who, having gathered, of all ages and sizes, from the farm and the neighbourhood, stood forming a pyramid of shining black faces at every door and window, gazing with delight at the scene, rolling their white eye balls, and showing grinning rows of ivory from ear to ear. How could the flogger of urchins be otherwise than animated and joyous; the lady of his heart was his partner in the dance; and smiling graciously in reply to all his amorous oglings, while Brom Bones, sorely smitten with love and jealousy, sat brooding by himself in one corner.

When the dance was at an end, Ichabod was attracted to a knot of the sager folks, who, with old Van Tassel, sat smoking at one end of the piazza, gossipping over former times, and drawling out long stories about the war.

This neighbourhood, at the time of which I am speaking, was one of those highly favoured places which abound with chronicle and great men. The British and American line had run near it during the war; it had, therefore, been the scene of marauding, and been infested with refugees, cow boys, and all kinds of border chivalry. Just sufficient time had elapsed to enable each story teller to dress up his tale with a little becoming fiction, and in the indistinctness of his recollection, to make himself the hero of every exploit.

There was the story of Doffue Martling, a large, blue bearded Dutchman, who had nearly taken a British frigate with an old iron nine pounder from a mud breastwork, only that his gun burst at the sixth discharge. And there was an old gentleman who shall be nameless, being too rich a mynheer to be lightly mentioned, who in the battle of Whiteplains, being an excellent master of defence, parried a musket ball with a small sword, insomuch that he absolutely felt it whiz round the blade, and glance off at the hilt: in proof of which, he was ready at any time to show the sword, with the hilt a little bent. There were several more who had been equally great in the field, not one of whom but was persuaded that he had a considerable hand in bringing the war to a happy termination.

But all these were nothing to the tales of ghosts and apparitions that succeeded. The neighbourhood is rich in legendary treasures of the kind. Local tales and superstitions thrive best in these sheltered, long settled retreats; but are trampled under foot, by the shifting throng that forms the population of most of our country places. Besides, there is no encouragement for ghosts in most of our villages, for they have scarce had time to finish their first nap, and turn themselves in their graves, before their surviving friends have travelled away from the neighbourhood, so that when they turn out of a night to walk the rounds, they have no acquaintance left to call upon. This is perhaps the reason why we so seldom hear of ghosts except in our long established Dutch communities.

The immediate cause, however, of the prevalence of supernatural stories in these parts, was doubtless owing to the vicinity of Sleepy Hollow. There was a contagion in the very air that blew from that haunted region; it breathed forth an atmosphere of dreams and fancies infecting all the land. Several of the Sleepy Hollow people were present at Van Tassel's, and, as usual, were doling out their wild and wonderful legends. Many dismal tales were told about funeral trains, and mournful cries and wailings heard and seen about the great tree where the unfortunate Major André was taken, and which stood in the neighbourhood. Some mention was made also of the woman in white, that haunted the dark glen at Raven Rock, and was often heard to shriek on winter nights before a storm, having perished there in the snow. The chief part of the stories, however, turned upon the favourite spectre of Sleepy Hollow, the headless horseman, who had been heard several times of late, patroling the country; and it was said, tethered his horse nightly among the graves in the church yard.

The sequestered situation of this church seems always to have made it a favourite haunt of troubled spirits. It stands on a knoll, surrounded by locust trees and lofty elms, from among which its decent, whitewashed walls shine modestly forth, like Christian purity, beaming through the shades of retirement. A gentle slope descends from it to a silver sheet of water, bordered by high trees, between which, peeps may be caught at the blue hills of the Hudson. To look upon its grass grown yard, where the sunbeams seem to sleep so quietly, one would think that there at least the dead might rest in peace. On one side of the church extends a wide woody dell, along which raves a large brook among broken rocks and trunks of fallen trees. Over a deep black part of the stream, not far from the church, was formerly thrown a wooden bridge; the road that led to it, and the bridge itself, were thickly shaded by overhanging trees, which cast a gloom about it, even in the day time; but occasioned a fearful darkness at night. Such was one of the favourite haunts of the headless horseman, and the place where he was most frequently encountered. The tale was told of old Brouwer, a most heretical disbeliever in ghosts, how he met the horseman returning from his foray into Sleepy Hollow, and was obliged to get up behind him; how they gallopped over bush and brake, over hill and swamp, until they reached the bridge, when the horseman suddenly turned into a skeleton, threw old Brouwer into the brook, and sprang away over the tree tops with a clap of thunder.

This story was immediately matched by a thrice marvellous adventure of Brom Bones, who made light of the gallopping Hessian as an arrant jockey. He affirmed, that on returning one night from the neighbouring village of Sing-Sing, he had been overtaken by this midnight trooper; that he had offered to race with him for a bowl of punch, and should have won it too, for Daredevil beat the goblin horse all hollow, but just as they came to the church bridge, the Hessian bolted, and vanished in a flash of fire.

All these tales, told in that drowsy under tone with which men talk in the dark, the countenances of the listeners only now and then receiving a casual gleam from the glare of a pipe, sunk deep in the mind of Ichabod. He repaid them in kind with large extracts from his invaluable author, Cotton Mather, and added many very marvellous events that had taken place in his native state of Connecticut, and fearful sights which he had seen in his nightly walks about Sleepy Hollow.

The revel now gradually broke up. The old farmers gathered together their families in their wagons, and were heard for some time rattling along the hollow roads, and over the distant hills. Some of the damsels, mounted on pillions behind their favourite swains, and their light hearted laughter mingling with the clatter of hoofs, echoed along the silent woodlands, sounding fainter and fainter until they gradually died away—and the late scene of noise and frolick was all silent and deserted. Ichabod only lingered behind, according to the custom of country lovers, to have a tête-a-tête with the heiress; fully convinced that he was now on the high road to success.

What passed at this interview I will not pretend to say, for in fact I do not know. Something, however, I fear me, must have gone wrong, for he certainly sallied forth, after no very great interval, with an air quite desolate and chopfallen—Oh these women! these women! Could that girl have been playing off any of her coquettish tricks?—Was her encouragement of the poor pedagogue all a mere sham to secure her conquest of his rival?—Heaven only knows, not I!—Let it suffice to say, Ichabod stole forth with the air of one who had been sacking a hen roost, rather than a fair lady's heart. Without looking to the right or left to notice the scene of rural wealth, on which he had so often gloated, he went straight to the stable, and with several hearty cuffs and kicks, roused his steed most uncourteously from the comfortable quarters in which he was soundly sleeping, dreaming of mountains of corn and oats, and whole valleys of timothy and clover.

It was the very witching time of night that Ichabod, heavy hearted and crest fallen, pursued his travel homewards, along the sides of the lofty hills which rise above Tarry Town, and which he had traversed so cheerily in the afternoon. The hour was as dismal as himself. Far below him the Tappaan Zee spread its dusky and indistinct waste of waters, with here and there the tall mast of a sloop, riding quietly at anchor under the land. In the dead hush of midnight, he could even hear the barking of the watch dog from the opposite shore of the Hudson; but it was so vague and faint as only to give an idea of his distance from this faithful companion of man. Now and then, too, the long drawn crowing of a cock, accidentally awakened, would sound far, far off, from some farm house away among the hills—but it was like a dreaming sound in his ear. No signs of life occurred near him, but occasionally the melancholy chirp of a cricket, or perhaps the guttural twang of a bull frog, from a neighbouring marsh, as if sleeping uncomfortably, and turning suddenly in his bed.

All the stories of ghosts and goblins that he had heard in the afternoon, now came crowding upon his recollection. The night grew darker and darker; the stars seemed to sink deeper in the sky, and driving clouds occasionally hid them from his sight. He had never felt so lonely and dismal. He was, moreover, approaching the very place where many of the scenes of the ghost stories had been laid. In the centre of the road stood an enormous tulip tree, which towered like a giant above all the other trees of the neighbourhood, and formed a kind of land mark. Its limbs were gnarled, and fantastic, large enough to form trunks for ordinary trees, twisting down almost to the earth, and rising again into the air. It was connected with the tragical story of the unfortunate André, who had been taken prisoner hard by; and was universally known by the name of Major André's tree. The common people regarded it with a mixture of respect and superstition, partly out of sympathy for the fate of its ill starred namesake, and partly from the tales of strange sights, and doleful lamentations, told concerning it.

As Ichabod approached this fearful tree, he began to whistle; he thought his whistle was answered: it was but a blast sweeping sharply through the dry branches. As he approached a little nearer, he thought he saw something white, hanging in the midst of the tree: he paused and ceased whistling; but on looking more narrowly, perceived that it was a place where the tree had been scathed by lightning, and the white wood laid bare. Suddenly he heard a groan—his teeth chattered, and his knees smote against the saddle: it was but the rubbing of one huge bough upon another, as they were swayed about by the breeze. He passed the tree in safety, but new perils lay before him.

About two hundred yards from the tree, a small brook crossed the road, and ran into a marshy and thickly wooded glen, known by the name of Wiley's Swamp. A few rough logs, laid side by side, served for a bridge over this stream. On that side of the road where the brook entered the wood, a group of oaks and chestnuts, matted thick with wild grape vines, threw a cavernous gloom over it. To pass this bridge, was the severest trial. It was at this identical spot that the unfortunate André was captured, and under the covert of those chestnuts and vines were the sturdy yeomen concealed who surprised him. This has ever since been considered a haunted stream, and fearful are the feelings of the schoolboy who has to pass it alone after dark.

As he approached the stream, his heart began to thump; he, however, summoned up all his resolution, gave his horse half a score of kicks in the ribs, and attempted to dash briskly across the bridge; but instead of starting forward, the perverse old animal made a lateral movement, and ran broadside against the fence. Ichabod, whose fears increased with the delay, jerked the reins on the other side, and kicked lustily with the contrary foot: it was all in vain; his steed started, it is true, but it was only to plunge to the opposite side of the road into a thicket of brambles and alder bushes. The schoolmaster now bestowed both whip and heel upon the starvelling ribs of old Gunpowder, who dashed forward, snuffling and snorting, but came to a stand just by the bridge with a suddenness that had nearly sent his rider sprawling over his head. Just at this moment a plashy tramp by the side of the bridge caught the sensitive ear of Ichabod. In the dark shadow of the grove, on the margin of the brook, he beheld something huge, misshapen, black and towering. It stirred not, but seemed gathered up in the gloom, like some gigantic monster ready to spring upon the traveller.

The hair of the affrighted pedagogue rose upon his head with terror. What was to be done? To turn and fly was now too late; and besides, what chance was there of escaping ghost or goblin, if such it was, which could ride upon the wings of the wind? Summoning up, therefore, a show of courage, he demanded in stammering accents—"who are you?" He received no reply. He repeated his demand in a still more agitated voice.—Still there was no answer. Once more he cudgelled the sides of the inflexible Gunpowder, and shutting his eyes, broke forth with involuntary fervour into a psalm tune. Just then the shadowy object of alarm put itself in motion, and with a scramble and a bound, stood at once in the middle of the road. Though the night was dark and dismal, yet the form of the unknown might now in some degree be ascertained. He appeared to be a horseman of large dimensions, and mounted on a black horse of powerful frame. He made no offer of molestation or sociability, but kept aloof on one side of the road, jogging along on the blind side of old Gunpowder, who had now got over his fright and waywardness.

Ichabod, who had no relish for this strange midnight companion, and bethought himself of the adventure of Brom Bones with the gallopping Hessian, now quickened his steed, in hopes of leaving him behind. The stranger, however, quickened his horse to an equal pace; Ichabod pulled up, and fell into a walk, thinking to lag behind—the other did the same.

His heart began to sink within him; he endeavoured to resume his psalm tune, but his parched tongue clove to the roof of his mouth, and he could not utter a stave. There was something in the moody and dogged silence of this pertinacious companion, that was mysterious and appalling. It was soon fearfully accounted for. On mounting a rising ground, which brought the figure of his fellow traveller in relief against the sky, gigantic in height, and muffled in a cloak, Ichabod was horror struck, on perceiving that he was headless! but his horror was still more increased, on observing, that the head, which should have rested on his shoulders, was carried before him on the pommel of the saddle! His terror rose to desperation; he rained a shower of kicks and blows upon Gunpowder, hoping, by a sudden movement, to give his companion the slip—but the spectre started full jump with him. Away, then, they dashed, through thick and thin; stones flying, and sparks flashing, at every bound. Ichabod's flimsy garments fluttered in the air, as he stretched his long lank body away over his horse's head, in the eagerness of his flight.

They had now reached the road which turns off to Sleepy Hollow; but Gunpowder, who seemed possessed with a demon, instead of keeping up it, made an opposite turn, and plunged headlong down hill to the left. This road leads through a sandy hollow shaded by trees for about a quarter of a mile, where it crosses the bridge famous in goblin story, and just beyond swells the green knoll on which stands the whitewashed church.

As yet the panic of the steed had given his unskilful rider an apparent advantage in the chace, but just as he had got half way through the hollow, the girths of the saddle gave way, and he felt it slipping from under him; he seized it by the pommel, and endeavoured to hold it firm, but in vain; and had just time to save himself by clasping old Gunpowder round the neck, when the saddle fell to the earth, and he heard it trampled under foot by his pursuer. For a moment the terror of Hans Van Ripper's wrath passed across his mind—for it was his Sunday saddle; but this was no time for petty fears: the goblin was hard on his haunches; and (unskilful rider that he was!) he had much ado to maintain his seat; sometimes slipping on one side, sometimes on another, and sometimes jolted on the high ridge of his horse's back bone, with a violence that he verily feared would cleave him asunder.

An opening in the trees now cheered him with the hopes that the Church Bridge was at hand. The wavering reflection of a silver star in the bosom of the brook told him that he was not mistaken. He saw the walls of the church dimly glaring under the trees beyond. He recollected the place where Brom Bones' ghostly competitor had disappeared. "If I can but reach that bridge," thought Ichabod, "I am safe." Just then he heard the black steed panting and blowing close behind him; he even fancied that he felt his hot breath. Another convulsive kick in the ribs, and old Gunpowder sprung upon the bridge; he thundered over the resounding planks; he gained the opposite side, and now Ichabod cast a look behind to see if his pursuer should vanish, according to rule, in a flash of fire and brimstone. Just then he saw the goblin rising in his stirrups, and in the very act of hurling his head at him. Ichabod endeavoured to dodge the horrible missile, but too late. It encountered his cranium with a tremendous crash—he was tumbled headlong into the dust, and Gunpowder, the black steed, and the goblin rider, passed by like a whirlwind.——

The next morning the old horse was found without his saddle, and with the bridle under his feet, soberly cropping the grass at his master's gate. Ichabod did not make his appearance at breakfast—dinner hour came, but no Ichabod. The boys assembled at the schoolhouse, and strolled idly about the banks of the brook; but no schoolmaster. Hans Van Ripper now began to feel some uneasiness about the fate of poor Ichabod, and his saddle. An inquiry was set on foot, and after diligent investigation they came upon his traces. In one part of the road leading to the church, was found the saddle trampled in the dirt; the tracks of horses' hoofs deeply dented in the road, and evidently at furious speed, were traced to the bridge, beyond which, on the bank of a broad part of the brook, where the water ran deep and black, was found the hat of the unfortunate Ichabod, and close beside it a shattered pumpkin.

The brook was searched, but the body of the schoolmaster was not to be discovered. Hans Van Ripper, as executor of his estate, examined the bundle which contained all his worldly effects. They consisted of two shirts and a half; two stocks for the neck; a pair or two of worsted stockings; an old pair of corduroy small clothes; a rusty razor; a book of psalm tunes, full of dog's ears; and a broken pitch pipe. As to the books and furniture of the schoolhouse, they belonged to the community, excepting Cotton Mather's History of Witchcraft, a New England Almanack, and a book of dreams and fortune telling, in which last was a sheet of foolscap much scribbled and blotted, in several fruitless attempts to make a copy of verses in honour of the heiress of Van Tassel. These magic books and the poetic scrawl were forthwith consigned to the flames by Hans Van Ripper, who from that time forward determined to send his children no more to school, observing, that he never knew any good come of this same reading and writing. Whatever money the schoolmaster possessed, and he had received his quarter's pay but a day or two before, he must have had about his person at the time of his disappearance.

The mysterious event caused much speculation at the Church on the following Sunday. Knots of gazers and gossips were collected in the church yard, at the bridge, and at the spot where the hat and pumpkin had been found. The stories of Brouwer, of Bones, and a whole budget of others, were called to mind; and when they had diligently considered them all, and compared them with the symptoms of the present case, they shook their heads, and came to the conclusion, that Ichabod had been carried off by the gallopping Hessian. As he was a bachelor, and in nobody's debt, nobody troubled his head any more about him, the school was removed to a different quarter of the hollow, and another pedagogue reigned in his stead.

It is true, an old farmer, who had been down to New York on a visit several years after, and from whom this account of the ghostly adventure was received, brought home the intelligence that Ichabod Crane was still alive; that he had left the neighbourhood partly through fear of the goblin and Hans Van Ripper, and partly in mortification at having been suddenly dismissed by the heiress; that he had changed his quarters to a distant part of the country; had kept school and studied law at the same time; had been admitted to the bar, turned politician, electioneered, written for the newspapers, and finally had been made a Justice of the Ten Pound Court. Brom Bones too, who, shortly after his rival's disappearance, conducted the blooming Katrina in triumph to the altar, was observed to look exceedingly knowing whenever the story of Ichabod was related, and always burst into a hearty laugh at the mention of the pumpkin; which led some to suspect that he knew more about the matter than he chose to tell.

The old country wives, however, who are the best judges of these matters, maintain to this day, that Ichabod was spirited away by supernatural means; and it is a favourite story often told about the neighbourhood round the winter evening fire. The bridge became more than ever an object of superstitious awe, and that may be the reason why the road has been altered of late years, so as to approach the church by the border of the millpond. The schoolhouse being deserted, soon fell to decay, and was reported to be haunted by the ghost of the unfortunate pedagogue; and the plough boy, loitering homeward of a still summer evening, has often fancied his voice at a distance, chanting a melancholy psalm tune among the tranquil solitudes of Sleepy Hollow.

## POSTSCRIPT

### *Found in the Handwriting of Mr. Knickerbocker*

The preceding Tale is given, almost in the precise words in which I heard it related at a corporation meeting of the ancient city of Manhattoes, at which were present many of its sagest and most illustrious burghers. The narrator was a pleasant, shabby, gentlemanly old fellow, in pepper and salt clothes, with a sadly humourous face, and one whom I strongly suspected of being poor, he made such efforts to be entertaining. When his story was concluded, there was much laughter and approbation, particularly from two or three deputy aldermen, who had been asleep the greater part of the time. There was, however, one tall, dry looking old gentleman, with beetling eye brows, who maintained a grave and rather severe face throughout; now and then folding his arms, inclining his head, and looking down upon the floor, as if turning a doubt over in his mind. He was one of your wary men, who never laugh but upon good grounds—when they have reason and the law on their side. When the mirth of the rest of the company had subsided, and silence was restored, he leaned one arm on the elbow of his chair, and sticking the other akimbo, demanded, with a slight, but exceedingly sage motion of the head, and contraction of the brow, what was the moral of the story, and what it went to prove.

The story teller, who was just putting a glass of wine to his lips, as a refreshment after his toils, paused for a moment, looked at his inquirer with an air of infinite deference, and lowering the glass slowly to the table, observed, that the story was intended most logically to prove,

"That there is no situation in life but has its advantages and pleasures, provided we will but take a joke as we find it:

"That, therefore, he that runs races with goblin troopers, is likely to have rough riding of it:

"Ergo, for a country schoolmaster to be refused the hand of a Dutch heiress, is a certain step to high preferment in the state."

The cautious old gentleman knit his brows tenfold closer after this explanation, being sorely puzzled by the ratiocination of the syllogism; while methought the one in pepper and salt eyed him with something of a triumphant leer. At length he observed, that all this was very well, but still he thought the story a little on the extravagant—there were one or two points on which he had his doubts.

"Faith, sir," replied the story teller, "as to that matter, I don't believe one half of it myself."

D.K.

1820

# WASHINGTON IRVING

(1783–1859)

## *The Devil and Tom Walker*

A FEW MILES from Boston, in Massachusetts, there is a deep inlet winding several miles into the interior of the country from Charles Bay, and terminating in a thickly wooded swamp, or morass. On one side of this inlet is a beautiful dark grove; on the opposite side the land rises abruptly from the water's edge, into a high ridge on which grow a few scattered oaks of great age and immense size. Under one of these gigantic trees, according to old stories, there was a great amount of treasure buried by Kidd the pirate. The inlet allowed a facility to bring the money in a boat secretly and at night to the very foot of the hill. The elevation of the place permitted a good look out to be kept that no one was at hand, while the remarkable trees formed good landmarks by which the place might easily be found again. The old stories add, moreover, that the devil presided at the hiding of the money, and took it under his guardianship; but this, it is well known, he always does with buried treasure, particularly when it has been ill gotten. Be that as it may, Kidd never returned to recover his wealth; being shortly after seized at Boston, sent out to England, and there hanged for a pirate.

About the year 1727, just at the time when earthquakes were prevalent in New England, and shook many tall sinners down upon their knees, there lived near this place a meagre miserly fellow of the name of Tom Walker. He had a wife as miserly as himself; they were so miserly that they even conspired to cheat each other. Whatever the woman could lay hands on she hid away: a hen could not cackle but she was on the alert to secure the new laid egg. Her husband was continually prying about to detect her secret hoards, and many and fierce were the conflicts that took place about what ought to have been common property. They lived in a forlorn looking house, that stood alone and had an air of starvation. A few straggling savin trees, emblems of sterility, grew near it; no smoke ever curled from its chimney; no traveller stopped at its door. A miserable horse, whose ribs were as articulate as the bars of a gridiron, stalked about a field where a thin carpet of moss, scarcely covering the ragged beds of pudding stone, tantalized and balked his hunger; and sometimes he would lean his head over the fence, look piteously at the passer by, and seem to petition deliverance from this land of famine. The house and its inmates had altogether a bad name. Tom's wife was a tall termagant, fierce of temper, loud of tongue, and strong of arm. Her voice was often heard in wordy warfare with her husband; and his face sometimes showed signs that their conflicts were not confined to words. No one ventured, however, to interfere between them; the lonely wayfarer shrank within himself at the horrid clamour and clapper clawing; eyed the den of discord askance, and hurried on his way, rejoicing, if a bachelor, in his celibacy.

One day that Tom Walker had been to a distant part of the neighbourhood, he took what he considered a short cut homewards through the swamp. Like most short cuts, it was an ill chosen route. The swamp was thickly grown with great gloomy pines and hemlocks, some of them ninety feet high; which made it dark at noonday, and a retreat for all the owls of the neighbourhood. It was full of pits and quagmires, partly covered with weeds and mosses; where the green surface often betrayed the traveller into a gulf of black smothering mud; there were also dark and stagnant pools, the abodes of the tadpole, the bull frog, and the water snake, where the trunks of pines and hemlocks lay half drowned, half rotting, looking like alligators, sleeping in the mire.

Tom had long been picking his way cautiously through this treacherous forest; stepping from tuft to tuft of rushes and roots which afforded precarious footholds among deep sloughs; or pacing carefully, like a cat, along the prostrate trunks of trees; startled now and then by the sudden screaming of the bittern, or the quacking of a wild duck, rising on the wing from some solitary pool. At length he arrived at a piece of firm ground, which ran out like a peninsula into the deep bosom of the swamp. It had been one of the strong holds of the Indians during their wars with the first colonists. Here they had thrown up a kind of fort which they had looked upon as almost impregnable, and had used as a place of refuge for their squaws and children. Nothing remained of the old Indian fort but a few embankments gradually sinking to the level of the surrounding earth, and already overgrown in part by oaks and other forest trees, the foliage of which formed a contrast to the dark pines and hemlocks of the swamp.

It was late in the dusk of evening when Tom Walker reached the old fort, and he paused there for a while to rest himself. Any one but he would have felt unwilling to linger in this lonely melancholy place, for the common people had a bad opinion of it from the stories handed down from the time of the Indian wars; when it was asserted that the savages held incantations here and made sacrifices to the evil spirit. Tom Walker, however, was not a man to be troubled with any fears of the kind.

He reposed himself for some time on the trunk of a fallen hemlock, listening to the boding cry of the tree toad, and delving with his walking staff into a mound of black mould at his feet. As he turned up the soil unconsciously, his staff struck against something hard. He raked it out of the vegetable mould, and lo! a cloven skull with an Indian tomahawk buried deep in it, lay before him. The rust on the weapon showed the time that had elapsed since this death blow had been given. It was a dreary memento of the fierce struggle that had taken place in this last foothold of the Indian warriors.

"Humph!" said Tom Walker, as he gave the skull a kick to shake the dirt from it.

"Let that skull alone!" said a gruff voice.

Tom lifted up his eyes and beheld a great black man, seated directly opposite him on the stump of a tree. He was exceedingly surprised, having neither seen nor heard any one approach, and he was still more perplexed on observing, as well as the gathering gloom would permit, that the stranger was neither negro nor Indian. It is true, he was dressed in a rude, half Indian garb, and had a red belt or sash swathed round his body, but his face was neither black nor copper colour, but swarthy and dingy and begrimed with soot, as if he had been accustomed to toil among fires and forges. He had a shock of coarse black hair, that stood out from his head in all directions; and bore an axe on his shoulder.

He scowled for a moment at Tom with a pair of great red eyes.

"What are you doing on my grounds?" said the black man, with a hoarse growling voice.

"Your grounds?" said Tom, with a sneer; "no more your grounds than mine: they belong to Deacon Peabody."

"Deacon Peabody be d——d," said the stranger, "as I flatter myself he will be, if he does not look more to his own sins and less to those of his neighbours. Look yonder, and see how Deacon Peabody is faring."

Tom looked in the direction that the stranger pointed, and beheld one of the great trees, fair and flourishing without, but rotten at the core, and saw that it had been nearly hewn through, so that the first high wind was likely to blow it down. On the bark of the tree was scored the name of Deacon Peabody, an eminent man, who had waxed wealthy by driving shrewd bargains with the Indians. He now looked round and found most of the tall trees marked with the name of some great man of the colony, and all more or less scored by the axe. The one on which he had been seated, and which had evidently just been hewn down, bore the name of Crowninshield; and he recollected a mighty rich man of that name, who made a vulgar display of wealth, which it was whispered he had acquired by buccaneering.

"He's just ready for burning!" said the black man, with a growl of triumph. "You see I am likely to have a good stock of firewood for winter."

"But what right have you," said Tom, "to cut down Deacon Peabody's timber?"

"The right of prior claim," said the other. "This woodland belonged to me long before one of your white faced race put foot upon the soil."

"And pray, who are you, if I may be so bold?" said Tom.

"Oh, I go by various names. I am the Wild Huntsman in some countries; the Black Miner in others. In this neighbourhood I am known by the name of the Black Woodsman. I am he to whom the red men consecrated this spot, and in honour of whom they now and then roasted a white man by way of sweet smelling sacrifice. Since the red men have been exterminated by you white savages, I amuse myself by presiding at the persecutions of quakers and anabaptists; I am the great patron and prompter of slave dealers, and the grand master of the Salem witches."

"The upshot of all which is, that, if I mistake not," said Tom, sturdily, "you are he commonly called Old Scratch."

"The same at your service!" replied the black man, with a half civil nod.

Such was the opening of this interview, according to the old story, though it has almost too familiar an air to be credited. One would think that to meet with such a singular personage in this wild lonely place, would have shaken any man's nerves: but Tom was a hard minded fellow, not easily daunted, and he had lived so long with a termagant wife, that he did not even fear the devil.

It is said that after this commencement, they had a long and earnest conversation together, as Tom returned homewards. The black man told him of great sums of money buried by Kidd the pirate, under the oak trees on the high ridge not far from the morass. All these were under his command and protected by his power, so that none could find them but such as propitiated his favour. These he offered to place within Tom Walker's reach, having conceived an especial kindness for him: but they were to be had only on certain conditions. What these conditions were, may easily be surmised, though Tom never disclosed them publicly. They must have been very hard, for he required time to think of them, and he was not a man to stick at trifles where money was in view. When they had reached the edge of the swamp the stranger paused.

"What proof have I that all you have been telling me is true?" said Tom.

"There is my signature," said the black man, pressing his finger on Tom's forehead. So saying, he turned off among the thickets of the swamp, and seemed, as Tom said, to go down, down, down, into the earth, until nothing but his head and shoulders could be seen, and so on until he totally disappeared.

When Tom reached home he found the black print of a finger burnt, as it were, into his forehead, which nothing could obliterate.

The first news his wife had to tell him was the sudden death of Absalom Crowninshield the rich buccaneer. It was announced in the papers with the usual flourish, that "a great man had fallen in Israel."

Tom recollected the tree which his black friend had just hewn down, and which was ready for burning. "Let the free-booter roast," said Tom, "who cares!" He now felt convinced that all he had heard and seen was no illusion.

He was not prone to let his wife into his confidence; but as this was an uneasy secret, he willingly shared it with her. All her avarice was awakened at the mention of hidden gold, and she urged her husband to comply with the black man's terms and secure what would make them wealthy for life. However Tom might have felt disposed to sell himself to the devil, he was determined not to do so to oblige his wife; so he flatly refused out of the mere spirit of contradiction. Many and bitter were the quarrels they had on the subject, but the more she talked the more resolute was Tom not to be damned to please her. At length she determined to drive the bargain on her own account, and if she succeeded, to keep all the gain to herself.

Being of the same fearless temper as her husband, she set off for the old Indian fort towards the close of a summer's day. She was many hours absent. When she came back she was reserved and sullen in her replies. She spoke something of a black man whom she had met about twilight, hewing at the root of a tall tree. He was sulky, however, and would not come to terms; she was to go again with a propitiatory offering, but what it was she forbore to say.

The next evening she set off again for the swamp, with her apron heavily laden. Tom waited and waited for her, but in vain: midnight came, but she did not make her appearance; morning, noon, night returned, but still she did not come. Tom now grew uneasy for her safety; especially as he found she had carried off in her apron the silver teapot and spoons and every portable article of value. Another night elapsed, another morning came; but no wife. In a word, she was never heard of more.

What was her real fate nobody knows, in consequence of so many pretending to know. It is one of those facts which have become confounded by a variety of historians. Some asserted that she lost her way among the tangled mazes of the swamp and sank into some pit or slough; others, more uncharitable, hinted that she had eloped with the household booty, and made off to some other province; while others assert that the tempter had decoyed her into a dismal quagmire on top of which her hat was found lying. In confirmation of this, it was said a great black man with an axe on his shoulder was seen late that very evening coming out of the swamp, carrying a bundle tied in a check apron, with an air of surly triumph.

The most current and probable story, however, observes that Tom Walker grew so anxious about the fate of his wife and his property that he set out at length to seek them both at the Indian fort. During a long summer's afternoon he searched about the gloomy place, but no wife was to be seen. He called her name repeatedly, but she was no where to be heard. The bittern alone responded to his voice, as he flew screaming by; or the bull frog croaked dolefully from a neighbouring pool. At length, it is said, just in the brown hour of twilight, when the owls began to hoot and the bats to flit about, his attention was attracted by the clamour of carrion crows hovering about a cypress tree. He looked up and beheld a bundle tied in a check apron and hanging in the branches of the tree; with a great vulture perched hard by, as if keeping watch upon it. He leaped with joy, for he recognized his wife's apron, and supposed it to contain the household valuables.

"Let us get hold of the property," said he, consolingly to himself, "and we will endeavour to do without the woman."

As he scrambled up the tree the vulture spread its wide wings, and sailed off screaming into the deep shadows of the forest. Tom seized the check apron, but, woful sight! found nothing but a heart and liver tied up in it.

Such, according to the most authentic old story, was all that was to be found of Tom's wife. She had probably attempted to deal with the black man as she had been accustomed to deal with her husband; but though a female scold is generally considered a match for the devil, yet in this instance she appears to have had the worst of it. She must have died game however; for it is said Tom noticed many prints of cloven feet deeply stamped about the tree, and found handsful of hair, that looked as if they had been plucked from the coarse black shock of the woodsman. Tom knew his wife's prowess by experience.

He shrugged his shoulders as he looked at the signs of a fierce clapper clawing. "Egad," said he to himself, "Old Scratch must have had a tough time of it!"

Tom consoled himself for the loss of his property with the loss of his wife; for he was a man of fortitude. He even felt something like gratitude towards the black woodsman, who he considered had done him a kindness. He sought, therefore, to cultivate a further acquaintance with him, but for some time without success; the old black legs played shy, for whatever people may think, he is not always to be had for calling for; he knows how to play his cards when pretty sure of his game.

At length, it is said, when delay had whetted Tom's eagerness to the quick, and prepared him to agree to any thing rather than not gain the promised treasure, he met the black man one evening in his usual woodman dress, with his axe on his shoulder, sauntering along the edge of the swamp, and humming a tune. He affected to receive Tom's advances with great indifference, made brief replies, and went on humming his tune.

By degrees, however, Tom brought him to business, and they began to haggle about the terms on which the former was to have the pirate's treasure. There was one condition which need not be mentioned, being generally understood in all cases where the devil grants favours; but there were others about which, though of less importance, he was inflexibly obstinate. He insisted that the money found through his means should be employed in his service. He proposed, therefore, that Tom should employ it in the black traffick; that is to say, that he should fit out a slave ship. This, however, Tom resolutely refused; he was bad enough in all conscience; but the devil himself could not tempt him to turn slave dealer.

Finding Tom so squeamish on this point, he did not insist upon it, but proposed instead that he should turn usurer; the devil being extremely anxious for the increase of usurers, looking upon them as his peculiar people.

To this no objections were made, for it was just to Tom's taste.

"You shall open a broker's shop in Boston next month," said the black man.

"I'll do it tomorrow, if you wish," said Tom Walker.

"You shall lend money at two per cent. a month."

"Egad, I'll charge four!" replied Tom Walker.

"You shall extort bonds, foreclose mortgages, drive the merchant to bankruptcy——"

"I'll drive him to the d——l," cried Tom Walker, eagerly.

"You are the usurer for my money!" said the black legs, with delight. "When will you want the rhino?"

"This very night."

"Done!" said the devil.

"Done!" said Tom Walker.—So they shook hands, and struck a bargain.

A few days' time saw Tom Walker seated behind his desk in a counting house in Boston. His reputation for a ready moneyed man, who would lend money out for a good consideration, soon spread abroad. Every body remembers the days of Governor Belcher, when money was particularly scarce. It was a time of paper credit. The country had been deluged with government bills; the famous Land Bank had been established; there had been a rage for speculating; the people had run mad with schemes for new settlements; for building cities in the wilderness; land jobbers went about with maps of grants, and townships, and Eldorados, lying nobody knew where, but which every body was ready to purchase. In a word, the great speculating fever which breaks out every now and then in the country, had raged to an alarming degree, and every body was dreaming of making sudden fortunes from nothing. As usual the fever had subsided; the dream had gone off, and the imaginary fortunes with it; the patients were left in doleful plight, and the whole country resounded with the consequent cry of "hard times."

At this propitious time of public distress did Tom Walker set up as a usurer in Boston. His door was soon thronged by customers. The needy and the adventurous; the gambling speculator; the dreaming land jobber; the thriftless tradesman; the merchant with cracked credit; in short, every one driven to raise money by desperate means and desperate sacrifices, hurried to Tom Walker.

Thus Tom was the universal friend of the needy, and he acted like a "friend in need;" that is to say, he always exacted good pay and good security. In proportion to the distress of the applicant was the hardness of his terms. He accumulated bonds and mortgages; gradually squeezed his customers closer and closer; and sent them at length, dry as a sponge from his door.

In this way he made money hand over hand; became a rich and mighty man, and exalted his cocked hat upon change. He built himself, as usual, a vast house, out of ostentation; but left the greater part of it unfinished and unfurnished out of parsimony. He even set up a carriage in the fullness of his vain glory, though he nearly starved the horses which drew it; and as the ungreased wheels groaned and screeched on the axle trees, you would have thought you heard the souls of the poor debtors he was squeezing.

As Tom waxed old, however, he grew thoughtful. Having secured the good things of this world, he began to feel anxious about those of the next. He thought with regret on the bargain he had made with his black friend, and set his wits to work to cheat him out of the conditions. He became, therefore, all of a sudden, a violent church goer. He prayed loudly and strenuously as if heaven were to be taken by force of lungs. Indeed, one might always tell when he had sinned most during the week, by the clamour of his Sunday devotion. The quiet christians who had been modestly and steadfastly travelling Zionward, were struck with self reproach at seeing themselves so suddenly outstripped in their career by this new made convert. Tom was as rigid in religious, as in money matters; he was a stern supervisor and censurer of his neighbours, and seemed to think every sin entered up to their account became a credit on his own side of the page. He even talked of the expediency of reviving the persecution of quakers and anabaptists. In a word, Tom's zeal became as notorious as his riches.

Still, in spite of all this strenuous attention to forms, Tom had a lurking dread that the devil, after all, would have his due. That he might not be taken unawares, therefore, it is said he always carried a small bible in his coat pocket. He had also a great folio bible on his counting house desk, and would frequently be found reading it when people called on business; on such occasions he would lay his green spectacles in the book, to mark the place, while he turned round to drive some usurious bargain.

Some say that Tom grew a little crack brained in his old days, and that fancying his end approaching, he had his horse new shod, saddled and bridled, and buried with his feet uppermost;

because he supposed that at the last day the world would be turned upside down; in which case he should find his horse standing ready for mounting, and he was determined at the worst to give his old friend a run for it. This, however, is probably a mere old wives' fable. If he really did take such a precaution it was totally superfluous; at least so says the authentic old legend which closes his story in the following manner.

One hot afternoon in the dog days, just as a terrible black thundergust was coming up, Tom sat in his counting house in his white linen cap and India silk morning gown. He was on the point of foreclosing a mortgage, by which he would complete the ruin of an unlucky land speculator for whom he had professed the greatest friendship. The poor land jobber begged him to grant a few months' indulgence. Tom had grown testy and irritated and refused another day.

"My family will be ruined and brought upon the parish," said the land jobber. "Charity begins at home," replied Tom, "I must take care of myself in these hard times."

"You have made so much money out of me," said the speculator.

Tom lost his patience and his piety—"The devil take me," said he, "if I have made a farthing!"

Just then there were three loud knocks at the street door. He stepped out to see who was there. A black man was holding a black horse which neighed and stamped with impatience.

"Tom, you're come for!" said the black fellow, gruffly. Tom shrunk back, but too late. He had left his little bible at the bottom of his coat pocket, and his big bible on the desk buried under the mortgage he was about to foreclose: never was sinner taken more unawares. The black man whisked him like a child into the saddle, gave the horse a lash, and away he galloped, with Tom on his back, in the midst of a thunder storm. The clerks stuck their pens behind their ears and stared after him from the windows. Away went Tom Walker, dashing down the streets; his white cap bobbing up and down; his morning gown fluttering in the wind, and his steed striking fire out of the pavement at every bound. When the clerks turned to look for the black man he had disappeared.

Tom Walker never returned to foreclose the mortgage. A countryman who lived on the border of the swamp, reported that in the height of the thunder gust he had heard a great clattering of hoofs and a howling along the road, and running to the window caught sight of a figure, such as I have described, on a horse that galloped like mad across the fields, over the hills and down into the black hemlock swamp towards the old Indian fort; and that shortly after a thunderbolt falling in that direction seemed to set the whole forest in a blaze.

The good people of Boston shook their heads and shrugged their shoulders, but had been so much accustomed to witches and goblins and tricks of the devil in all kinds of shapes from the first settlement of the colony, that they were not so much horror struck as might have been expected. Trustees were appointed to take charge of Tom's effects. There was nothing, however, to administer upon. On searching his coffers all his bonds and mortgages were found reduced to cinders. In place of gold and silver his iron chest was filled with chips and shavings; two skeletons lay in his stable instead of his half starved horses, and the very next day his great house took fire and was burnt to the ground.

Such was the end of Tom Walker and his ill gotten wealth. Let all griping money brokers lay this story to heart. The truth of it is not to be doubted. The very hole under the oak trees, whence he dug Kidd's money is to be seen to this day; and the neighbouring swamp and old Indian fort are often haunted in stormy nights by a figure on horseback, in a morning gown and white cap, which is doubtless the troubled spirit of the usurer. In fact, the story has resolved itself into a proverb, and is the origin of that popular saying, prevalent throughout New England, of "The Devil and Tom Walker."

1824

# CATHARINE MARIA SEDGWICK

(1789–1867)

---

## *Cacoethes Scribendi*

Glory and gain the industrious tribe provoke.—*Pope.*

THE LITTLE secluded and quiet village of H. lies at no great distance from our "literary emporium." It was never remarked or remarkable for any thing, save one mournful pre-eminence, to those who sojourned within its borders—it was duller even than common villages. The young men of the better class all emigrated. The most daring spirits adventured on the sea. Some went to Boston; some to the south; and some to the west; and left a community of women who lived like nuns, with the advantage of more liberty and fresh air, but without the consolation and excitement of a religious vow. Literally, there was not a single young gentleman in the village—nothing in manly shape to which these desperate circumstances could give the form and quality and uses of a beau. Some dashing city blades, who once strayed from the turnpike to this sequestered spot, averred that the girls stared at them as if, like Miranda, they would have exclaimed—

"What is't? a spirit?
Lord, how it looks about! Believe me, sir,
It carries a brave form:—But 'tis a spirit."

A peculiar fatality hung over this devoted place. If death seized on either head of a family, he was sure to take the husband; every woman in H. was a widow or maiden; and it is a sad fact, that when the holiest office of the church was celebrated, they were compelled to borrow deacons from an adjacent village. But, incredible as it may be, there was no great diminution of happiness in consequence of the absence of the nobler sex. Mothers were occupied with their children and housewifery, and the young ladies read their books with as much interest as if they had lovers to discuss them with, and worked their frills and capes as diligently, and wore them as complacently, as if they were to be seen by manly eyes. Never was there pleasanter gatherings or parties (for that was the word even in their nomenclature) than those of the young girls of H. There was no mincing—no affectation—no hope of passing for what they were not—no envy of the pretty and fortunate—no insolent triumph over the plain and demure and neglected,—but all was good will and good humour. They were a pretty circle of girls—a garland of bright fresh flowers. Never were there more sparkling glances,—never sweeter smiles—nor more of them. Their present was all health and cheerfulness; and their future, not the gloomy perspective of dreary singleness, for somewhere in the passage of life they were sure to be mated. Most of the young men who had abandoned their native soil, as soon as they found themselves *getting along*, loyally returned to lay their fortunes at the feet of the companions of their childhood.

The girls made occasional visits to Boston, and occasional journeys to various parts of the country, for they were all enterprising and independent, and had the characteristic New England avidity for seizing a "privilege;" and in these various ways, to borrow a phrase of their good grandames, "a door was opened for them," and in due time they fulfilled the destiny of women.

We spoke strictly, and literally, when we said that in the village of H. there was not a single *beau*. But on the outskirts of the town, at a pleasant farm, embracing hill and valley, upland and meadow land; in a neat house, looking to the south, with true economy of sunshine and comfort, and overlooking the prettiest winding stream that ever sent up its sparkling beauty to the eye, and flanked on the north by a rich maple grove, beautiful in spring and summer, and glorious in autumn, and the kindest defence in winter;—on this farm and in this house dwelt a youth, to fame unknown, but known and loved by every inhabitant of H., old and young, grave and gay, lively and severe. Ralph Hepburn was one of nature's favourites. He had a figure that would have adorned courts and cities; and a face that adorned human nature, for it was full of good humour, kind-heartedness, spirit, and intelligence; and driving the plough or wielding the scythe, his cheek flushed with manly and profitable exercise, he looked as if he had been moulded in a poet's fancy—as farmers look in Georgics and Pastorals. His gifts were by no means all external. He wrote verses in every album in the village, and very pretty album verses they were, and numerous too—for the number of albums was equivalent to the whole female population. He was admirable at pencil sketches; and once with a little paint, the refuse of a house painting, he achieved an admirable portrait of his grandmother and her cat. There was, to be sure, a striking likeness between the two figures, but he was limited to the same colours for both; and besides, it was not out of nature, for the old lady and her cat had purred together in the chimney corner, till their physiognomies bore an obvious resemblance to each other. Ralph had a talent for music too. His voice was the sweetest of all the Sunday choir, and one would have fancied, from the bright eyes that were turned on him from the long line and double lines of treble and counter singers, that Ralph Hepburn was a note book, or that the girls listened with their eyes as well as their ears. Ralph did not restrict himself to psalmody. He had an ear so exquisitely susceptible to the "touches of sweet harmony," that he discovered, by the stroke of his axe, the musical capacities of certain species of wood, and he made himself a violin of chesnut, and drew strains from it, that if they could not create a soul under the ribs of death, could make the prettiest feet and the lightest hearts dance, an achievement far more to Ralph's taste than the aforesaid miracle. In short, it seemed as if nature, in her love of compensation, had showered on Ralph all the gifts that are usually diffused through a community of beaux. Yet Ralph was no prodigy; none of his talents were in excess, but all in moderate degree. No genius was ever so good humoured, so useful, so practical; and though, in his small and modest way, a Crichton, he was not, like most universal geniuses, good for nothing for any particular office in life. His farm was not a pattern farm—a prize farm for an agricultural society, but in wonderful order *considering*—his miscellaneous pursuits. He was the delight of his grandfather for his sagacity in hunting bees—the old man's favourite, in truth his only pursuit. He was so skilled in woodcraft that the report of his gun was as certain a signal of death as the tolling of a church bell. The fish always caught at his bait. He manufactured half his farming utensils, improved upon old inventions, and struck out some new ones; tamed partridges—the most untameable of all the feathered tribe; domesticated squirrels; rivalled Scheherazade herself in telling stories, strange and long—the latter quality being essential at a country fireside; and, in short, Ralph made a perpetual holiday of a life of labour.

Every girl in the village street knew when Ralph's wagon or sleigh traversed it; indeed, there was scarcely a house to which the horses did not, as if by instinct, turn up while their master greeted its fair tenants. This state of affairs had continued for two winters and two summers since Ralph came to his majority and, by the death of his father, to the sole proprietorship of the "Hepburn farm,"—the name his patrimonial acres had obtained from the singular circumstance (in our *moving* country) of their having remained in the same family for four generations. Never was the matrimonial destiny of a young lord, or heir just come to his estate, more thoroughly canvassed than young Hepburn's by mothers, aunts, daughters, and nieces. But Ralph, perhaps from sheer good heartedness, seemed reluctant to give to "a party what was meant for mankind," to give one the heart that diffused rays of sunshine through the whole village.

With all decent people he eschewed the doctrines of a certain erratic female lecturer on the odious monopoly of marriage, yet Ralph, like a tender hearted judge, hesitated to place on a single brow the crown matrimonial which so many deserved, and which, though Ralph was far enough from a coxcomb, he could not but see so many coveted.

Whether our hero perceived that his mind was becoming elated or distracted with this general favour, or that he observed a dawning of rivalry among the fair competitors, or whatever was the cause, the fact was, that he by degrees circumscribed his visits, and finally concentrated them in the family of his aunt Courland.

Mrs. Courland was a widow, and Ralph was the kindest of nephews to her, and the kindest of cousins to her children. To their mother he seemed their guardian angel. That the five lawless, daring litle urchins did not drown themselves when they were swimming, nor shoot themselves when they were shooting, was, in her eyes, Ralph's merit; and then "he was so attentive to Alice, her only daughter—a brother could not be kinder." But who would not be kind to Alice? she was a sweet girl of seventeen, not beautiful, not handsome perhaps,—but pretty enough—with soft hazel eyes, a profusion of light brown hair, always in the neatest trim, and a mouth that could not but be lovely and loveable, for all kind and tender affections were playing about it. Though Alice was the only daughter of a doting mother, the only sister of five loving boys, the only niece of three single, fond aunts, and, last and greatest, the only cousin of our only beau, Ralph Hepburn, no girl of seventeen was ever more disinterested, unassuming, unostentatious, and unspoiled. Ralph and Alice had always lived on terms of cousinly affection—an affection of a neutral tint that they never thought of being shaded into the deep dye of a more tender passion. Ralph rendered her all cousinly offices. If he had twenty damsels to escort, not an uncommon case, he never forgot Alice. When he returned from any little excursion, he always brought some graceful offering to Alice.

He had lately paid a visit to Boston. It was at the season of the periodical inundation of annuals. He brought two of the prettiest to Alice, Ah! little did she think they were to prove Pandora's box to her, Poor simple girl! she sat down to read them, as if an annual were meant to be read, and she was honestly interested and charmed. Her mother observed her delight. "What have you there, Alice?" she asked. "Oh the prettiest story, mamma!—two such tried faithful lovers, and married at last! It ends beautifully: I hate love stories that don't end in marriage."

"And so do I, Alice," exclaimed Ralph, who entered at the moment, and for the first time Alice felt her cheeks tingle at his approach. He had brought a basket, containing a choice plant he had obtained for her, and she laid down the annual and went with him to the garden to see it set by his own hand.

Mrs. Courland seized upon the annual with avidity. She had imbibed a literary taste in Boston, where the best and happiest years of her life were passed. She had some literary ambition too. She read the North American Review from beginning to end, and she fancied no conversation could be sensible or improving that was not about books. But she had been effectually prevented, by the necessities of a narrow income, and by the unceasing wants of five teasing boys, from indulging her literary inclinations; for Mrs. Courland, like all New England women, had been taught to consider domestic duties as the first temporal duties of her sex. She had recently seen some of the native productions with which the press is daily teeming, and which certainly have a tendency to dispel our early illusions about the craft of authorship. She had even felt some obscure intimations, within her secret soul, that she might herself become an author. The annual was destined to fix her fate. She opened it—the publisher had written the names of the authors of the anonymous pieces against their productions. Among them she found some of the familiar friends of her childhood and youth.

If, by a sudden gift of second sight, she had seen them enthroned as kings and queens, she would not have been more astonished. She turned to their pieces, and read them, as perchance no one else ever did, from beginning to end—faithfully. Not a sentence—a sentence! not a word was skipped. She paused to consider commas, colons, and dashes. All the art and magic of authorship were made level to her comprehension, and when she closed the book, she *felt a call* to become an author, and before she retired to bed she obeyed the call, as if it had been in truth, a divinity stirring within her. In the morning she presented an article to *her* public, consisting of her own family and a few select friends. All applauded, and every voice, save one, was unanimous for publication—that one was Alice. She was a modest, prudent girl; she feared failure, and feared notoriety still more. Her mother laughed at her childish scruples. The piece was sent off, and in due time graced the pages of an annual. Mrs. Courland's fate was now decided. She had, to use her own phrase, started in the career of letters, and she was no Atalanta to be seduced from her straight onward way. She was a social, sympathetic, good hearted creature too, and she could not bear to go forth in the golden field to reap alone.

She was, besides, a prudent woman, as most of her countrywomen are, and the little pecuniary equivalent for this delightful exercise of talents was not overlooked. Mrs. Courland, as we have somewhere said, had three single sisters—worthy women they were—but nobody ever dreamed of their taking to authorship. She, however, held them all in sisterly estimation. Their talents were magnified as the talents of persons who live in a circumscribed sphere are apt to be, particularly if seen through the dilating medium of affection.

Miss Anne, the oldest, was fond of flowers, a successful cultivator, and a diligent student of the science of botany. All this taste and knowledge, Mrs. Courland thought, might be turned to excellent account; and she persuaded Miss Anne to write a little book entitled "Familiar Dialogues on Botany." The second sister, Miss Ruth, had a turn for education ("bachelor's wives and maid's children are always well taught,") and Miss Ruth undertook a popular treatise on that subject. Miss Sally, the youngest, was the saint of the family, and she doubted about the propriety of a literary occupation, till her scruples were overcome by the fortunate suggestion that her coup d'essai should be a Saturday night book entitled "Solemn Hours,"—and solemn hours they were to their unhappy readers. Mrs. Courland next besieged her old mother. "You know, mamma," she said, "you have such a precious fund of anecdotes of the revolution and the French war, and you talk just like the 'Annals of the Parish,' and I am certain you can write a book fully as good."

"My child, you are distracted! I write a dreadful poor hand, and I never learned to spell—no girls did in my time."

"Spell! that is not of the least consequence—the printers correct the spelling."

But the honest old lady would not be tempted on the crusade, and her daughter consoled herself with the reflection that if she would not write, she was an admirable subject to be written about, and her diligent fingers worked off three distinct stories in which the old lady figured.

Mrs. Courland's ambition, of course, embraced within its widening circle her favourite nephew Ralph. She had always thought him a genius, and genius in her estimation was the philosopher's stone. In his youth she had laboured to persuade his father to send him to Cambridge, but the old man uniformly replied that Ralph "was a smart lad on the farm, and steady, and by that he knew he was no genius." As Ralph's character was developed, and talent after talent broke forth, his aunt renewed her lamentations over his ignoble destiny. That Ralph was useful, good, and happy—the most difficult and rare results achieved in life—was nothing, so long as he was but a farmer in H. Once she did half persuade him to turn painter, but his good sense and filial duty triumphed over her eloquence, and suppressed the hankerings after distinction that are innate in every human breast from the little ragged chimneysweep that hopes to be a *boss*, to the political aspirant whose bright goal is the presidential chair.

Now Mrs. Courland fancied Ralph might climb the steep of fame without quitting his farm; occasional authorship was compatible with his vocation. But alas! she could not persuade Ralph to pluck the laurels that she saw ready grown to his hand. She was not offended, for she was the best natured woman in the world, but she heartily pitied him, and seldom mentioned his name without repeating that stanza of Gray's, inspired for the consolation of hopeless obscurity:

"Full many a gem of purest ray serene," &c.

Poor Alice's sorrows we have reserved to the last, for they were heaviest. "Alice," her mother said, "was gifted; she was well educated, well informed; she was every thing necessary to be an author." But Alice resisted; and, though the gentlest, most complying of all good daughters, she would have resisted to the death—she would as soon have stood in a pillory as appeared in print. Her mother, Mrs. Courland, was not an obstinate woman, and gave up in despair. But still our poor heroine was destined to be the victim of this *cacoethes scribendi*; for Mrs. Courland divided the world into two classes, or rather parts—authors and subjects for authors; the one active, the other passive. At first blush one would have thought the village of H. rather a barren field for such a reaper as Mrs. Courland, but her zeal and indefatigableness worked wonders. She converted the stern scholastic divine of H. into as much of a La Roche as she could describe; a tall wrinkled bony old woman, who reminded her of Meg Merrilies, sat for a witch; the school master for an Ichabod Crane; a poor half witted boy was made to utter as much pathos and sentiment and wit as she could put into his lips; and a crazy vagrant was a God-send to her. Then every "wide spreading elm," "blasted pine," or "gnarled oak," flourished on her pages. The village church and school house stood there according to their actual dimensions. One old *pilgrim* house was as prolific as haunted tower or ruined abbey. It was surveyed outside, ransacked inside, and again made habitable for the reimbodied spirits of its founders.

The most kind hearted of woman, Mrs. Courland's interests came to be so at variance with the prosperity of the little community of H. that a sudden calamity, a death, a funeral, were fortunate events to her. To do her justice she felt them in a twofold capacity. She wept as a woman, and exulted as an author. The days of the calamities of authors have passed by. We have all wept over Otway and shivered at the thought of Tasso. But times are changed. The lean sheaf is devouring the full one. A new class of sufferers has arisen, and there is nothing more touching in all the memoirs Mr. D'Israeli has collected, than the trials of poor Alice, tragi-comic though they were. Mrs. Courland's new passion ran most naturally in the worn channel of maternal affection. Her boys were too purely boys for her art—but Alice, her sweet Alice, was pre-eminently lovely in the new light in which she now placed every object. Not an incident of her life but was inscribed on her mother's memory, and thence transferred to her pages, by way of precept, or example, or pathetic or ludicrous circumstance. She regretted now, for the first time, that Alice had no lover whom she might introduce among her dramatis personæ. Once her thoughts did glance on Ralph, but she had not quite merged the woman in the author; she knew instinctively that Alice would be particularly offended at being thus paired with Ralph. But Alice's *public life* was not limited to her mother's productions. She was the darling niece of her three aunts. She had studied botany with the eldest, and Miss Anne had recorded in her private diary all her favourite's clever remarks during their progress in the science. This diary was now a mine of gold to her, and faithfully worked up for a circulating medium. But, most trying of all to poor Alice, was the attitude in which she appeared in her aunt Sally's "solemn hours." Every aspiration of piety to which her young lips had given utterance was there *printed*. She felt as if she were condemned to say her prayers in the market place. Every act of kindness, every deed of charity, she had ever performed, were produced to the public. Alice would have been consoled if she had known how small that public was; but, as it was, she felt like a modest country girl when she first enters an apartment hung on every side with mirrors, when, shrinking from observation, she sees in every direction her image multiplied and often distorted; for, notwithstanding Alice's dutiful respect for her good aunts, and her consciousness of their affectionate intentions, she could not but perceive that they were unskilled painters. She grew afraid to speak or to act, and from being the most artless, frank, and, at home, social little creature in the world, she became as silent and as stiff as a statue. And, in the circle of her young associates, her natural gaiety was constantly checked by their winks and smiles, and broader allusions to her multiplied portraits; for they had instantly recognized them through the thin veil of feigned names of persons and places. They called her a blue stocking too; for they had the vulgar notion that every body must be tinged that lived under the same roof with an author. Our poor victim was afraid to speak of a book—worse than that, she was afraid to touch one, and the last Waverley novel actually lay in the house a month before she opened it. She avoided wearing even a blue ribbon, as fearfully as a forsaken damsel shuns the colour of green.

It was during the height of this literary fever in the Courland family, that Ralph Hepburn, as has been mentioned, concentrated all his visiting there. He was of a compassionate disposition, and he knew Alice was, unless relieved by him, in solitary possession of their once social parlour, while her mother and aunts were driving their quills in their several apartments.

Oh! what a changed place was that parlour! Not the tower of Babel, after the builders had forsaken it, exhibited a sadder reverse; not a Lancaster school, when the boys have left it, a more striking contrast. Mrs. Courland and her sisters were all "talking women," and too generous to encroach on one another's rights and happiness. They had acquired the power to hear and speak simultaneously. Their parlour was the general gathering place, a sort of village exchange, where all the innocent gossips, old and young, met together. "There are tongues in trees," and surely there seemed to be tongues in the very walls of that vocal parlour. Every thing there had a social aspect. There was something agreeable and conversable in the litter of netting and knitting work, of sewing implements, and all the signs and shows of happy female occupation.

Now, all was as orderly as a town drawing room in company hours. Not a sound was heard there save Ralph's and Alice's voices, mingling in soft and suppressed murmurs, as if afraid of breaking the chain of their aunt's ideas, or, perchance, of too rudely jarring a tenderer chain. One evening, after tea, Mrs. Courland remained with her daughter, instead of retiring, as usual, to her writing desk.—"Alice, my dear," said the good mother, "I have noticed for a few days past that you look out of spirits. You will listen to nothing I say on that subject; but if you would try it, my dear, if you would only try it, you would find there is nothing so tranquillizing as the occupation of writing."

"I shall never try it, mamma."

"You are afraid of being called a blue stocking. Ah! Ralph, how are you?"—Ralph entered at this moment.—"Ralph, tell me honestly, do you not think it a weakness in Alice to be so afraid of blue stockings?"

"It would be a pity, aunt, to put blue stockings on such pretty feet as Alice's."

Alice blushed and smiled, and her mother said—"Nonsense, Ralph; you should bear in mind the celebrated saying of the Edinburgh wit—'no matter how blue the stockings are, if the petticoats are long enough to hide them.'"

"Hide Alice's feet! Oh aunt, worse and worse!"

"Better hide her feet, Ralph, than her talents—that is a sin for which both she and you will have to answer. Oh! you and Alice need not exchange such significant glances! You are doing yourselves and the public injustice, and you have no idea how easy writing is."

"Easy writing, but hard reading, aunt."

"That's false modesty, Ralph. If I had but your opportunities to collect materials"—Mrs. Courland did not know that in literature, as in some species of manufacture, the most exquisite productions are wrought from the smallest quantity of raw material—"There's your journey to New York, Ralph," she continued, "you might have made three capital articles out of that. The revolutionary officer would have worked up for the 'Legendary;' the mysterious lady for the 'Token;' and the man in black for the 'Remember Me;'—all founded on fact, all romantic and pathetic."

"But mamma," said Alice, expressing in words what Ralph's arch smile expressed almost as plainly, "you know the officer drank too much; and the mysterious lady turned out to be a runaway milliner; and the man in black—oh! what a theme for a pathetic story!—the man in black was a widower, on his way to Newhaven, where he was to select his third wife from three *recommended* candidates."

"Pshaw! Alice: do you suppose it is necessary to tell things precisely as they are?"

"Alice is wrong, aunt, and you are right; and if she will open her writing desk for me, I will sit down this moment, and write a story—a true story—true from beginning to end; and if it moves you, my dear aunt, if it meets your approbation, my destiny is decided."

Mrs. Courland was delighted; she had slain the giant, and she saw fame and fortune smiling on her favourite. She arranged the desk for him herself; she prepared a folio sheet of paper, folded the ominous margins; and was so absorbed in her bright visions, that she did not hear a little by-talk between Ralph and Alice, nor see the tell-tale flush on their cheeks, nor notice the perturbation with which Alice walked first to one window and then to another, and finally settled herself to that best of all sedatives—hemming a ruffle. Ralph chewed off the end of his quill, mended his pen twice, though his aunt assured him "printers did not mind the penmanship," and had achieved a single line when Mrs. Courland's vigilant eye was averted by the entrance of her servant girl, who put a packet into her hands. She looked at the direction, cut the string, broke the seals, and took out a periodical fresh from the publisher. She opened at the first article—a strangely mingled current of maternal pride and literary triumph rushed through her heart and brightened her face. She whispered to the servant a summons to all her sisters to the parlour, and an intimation, sufficiently intelligible to them, of her joyful reason for interrupting them.

Our readers will sympathize with her, and with Alice too, when we disclose to them the secret of her joy. The article in question was a clever composition written by our devoted Alice when she was at school. One of her fond aunts had preserved it, and aunts and mother had combined in the pious fraud of giving it to the public, unknown to Alice. They were perfectly aware of her determination never to be an author. But they fancied it was the mere timidity of an unfledged bird; and that when, by their innocent artifice, she found that her pinions could soar in a literary atmosphere, she would realize the sweet fluttering sensations they had experienced at their first flight. The good souls all hurried to the parlour, eager to witness the *coup de theatre.* Miss Sally's pen stood emblematically erect in her turban; Miss Ruth, in her haste, had overset her inkstand, and the drops were trickling down her white dressing, or, as she now called it, writing-gown; and Miss Anne had a wild flower in her hand, as she hoped, of an undescribed species, which, in her joyful agitation, she most unluckily picked to pieces. All bit their lips to retain their impatient congratulations. Ralph was so intent on his writing, and Alice on her hemming, that neither noticed the irruption; and Mrs. Courland was obliged twice to speak to her daughter before she could draw her attention.

"Alice, look here—Alice, my dear."

"What is it, mamma? something new of yours?"

"No; guess again, Alice."

"Of one of my aunts, of course?"

"Neither, dear, neither. Come and look for yourself, and see if you can then tell whose it is."

Alice dutifully laid aside her work, approached and took the book. The moment her eye glanced on the fatal page, all her apathy vanished—deep crimson overspread her cheeks, brow, and neck. She burst into tears of irrepressible vexation, and threw the book into the blazing fire.

The gentle Alice! Never had she been guilty of such an ebullition of temper. Her poor dismayed aunts retreated; her mother looked at her in mute astonishment; and Ralph, struck with her emotion, started from the desk, and would have asked an explanation, but Alice exclaimed—"Don't say any thing about it, mamma—I cannot bear it now."

Mrs. Courland knew instinctively that Ralph would sympathize entirely with Alice, and quite willing to avoid an explanation, she said—"Some other time, Ralph, I'll tell you the whole. Show me now what you have written. How have you begun?"

Ralph handed her the paper with a novice's trembling hand.

"Oh! how very little! and so scratched and interlined! but never mind—'c'est le premier pas qui coute.'"

While making these general observations, the good mother was getting out and opening her spectacles, and Alice and Ralph had retreated behind her. Alice rested her head on his shoulder, and Ralph's lips were not far from her ear. Whether he was soothing her ruffled spirit, or what he was doing, is not recorded. Mrs. Courland read and re-read the sentence. She dropped a tear on it. She forgot her literary aspirations for Ralph and Alice—forgot she was herself an author—forgot every thing but the mother; and rising, embraced them both as her dear children, and expressed, in her raised and moistened eye, consent to their union, which Ralph had dutifully and prettily asked in that short and true story of his love for his sweet cousin Alice.

—

In due time the village of H. was animated with the celebration of Alice's nuptials: and when her mother and aunts saw her the happy mistress of the Hepburn farm, and the happiest of wives, they relinquished, without a sigh, the hope of ever seeing her an AUTHOR.

1830

# LYDIA MARIA CHILD

(1802–1880)

---

## *Hilda Silfverling*

### *A Fantasy*

"Thou hast nor youth nor age;
But, as it were, an after dinner's sleep,
Dreaming on both."—*Measure for Measure.*

HILDA GYLLENLOF was the daughter of a poor Swedish clergyman. Her mother died before she had counted five summers. The good father did his best to supply the loss of maternal tenderness; nor were kind neighbors wanting, with friendly words, and many a small gift for the pretty little one. But at the age of thirteen, Hilda lost her father also, just as she was receiving rapidly from his affectionate teachings as much culture as his own education and means afforded. The unfortunate girl had no other resource than to go to distant relatives, who were poor, and could not well conceal that the destitute orphan was a burden. At the end of a year, Hilda, in sadness and weariness of spirit, went to Stockholm, to avail herself of an opportunity to earn her living by her needle, and some light services about the house.

She was then in the first blush of maidenhood, with a clear innocent look, and exceedingly fair complexion. Her beauty soon attracted the attention of Magnus Andersen, mate of a Danish vessel then lying at the wharves of Stockholm. He could not be otherwise than fascinated with her budding loveliness; and alone as she was in the world, she was naturally prone to listen to the first words of warm affection she had heard since her father's death. What followed is the old story, which will continue to be told as long as there are human passions and human laws. To do the young man justice, though selfish, he was not deliberately unkind; for he did not mean to be treacherous to the friendless young creature who trusted him. He sailed from Sweden with the honest intention to return and make her his wife; but he was lost in a storm at sea, and the earth saw him no more.

Hilda never heard the sad tidings; but, for another cause, her heart was soon oppressed with shame and sorrow. If she had had a mother's bosom on which to lean her aching head, and confess all her faults and all her grief, much misery might have been saved. But there was none to whom she dared to speak of her anxiety and shame. Her extreme melancholy attracted the attention of a poor old woman, to whom she sometimes carried clothes for washing. The good Virika, after manifesting her sympathy in various ways, at last ventured to ask outright why one so young was so very sad. The poor child threw herself on the friendly bosom, and confessed all her wretchedness. After that, they had frequent confidential conversations; and the kind-hearted peasant did her utmost to console and cheer the desolate orphan. She said she must soon return to her native village in the Norwegian valley of Westfjordalen; and as she was alone in the world, and wanted something to love, she would gladly take the babe, and adopt it for her own.

Poor Hilda, thankful for any chance to keep her disgrace a secret, gratefully accepted the offer. When the babe was ten days old, she allowed the good Virika to carry it away; though not without bitter tears, and the oft-repeated promise that her little one might be reclaimed, whenever Magnus returned and fulfilled his promise of marriage.

But though these arrangements were managed with great caution, the young mother did not escape suspicion. It chanced, very unfortunately, that soon after Virika's departure, an infant was found in the water, strangled with a sash very like one Hilda had been accustomed to wear. A train of circumstantial evidence seemed to connect the child with her, and she was arrested. For some time, she contented herself with assertions of innocence, and obstinately refused to tell anything more. But at last, having the fear of death before her eyes, she acknowledged that she had given birth to a daughter, which had been carried away by Virika Gjetter, to her native place, in the parish of Tind, in the Valley of Westfjordalen. Inquiries were accordingly made in Norway, but the answer obtained was that Virika had not been heard of in her native valley, for many years. Through weary months, Hilda lingered in prison, waiting in vain for favourable testimony; and at last, on strong circumstantial evidence, she was condemned to die.

It chanced there was at that time a very learned chemist in Stockholm; a man whose thoughts were all gas, and his hours marked only by combinations and explosions. He had discovered a process of artificial cold, by which he could suspend animation in living creatures, and restore it at any prescribed time. He had in one apartment of his laboratory a bear that had been in a torpid state five years, a wolf two years, and so on. This of course excited a good deal of attention in the scientific world. A metaphysician suggested how extremely interesting it would be to put a human being asleep thus, and watch the reunion of soul and body, after the lapse of a hundred years. The chemist was half wild with the magnificence of this idea; and he forthwith petitioned that Hilda, instead of being beheaded, might be delivered to him, to be frozen for a century. He urged that her extreme youth demanded pity; that his mode of execution would be a very gentle one, and, being so strictly private, would be far less painful to the poor young creature than exposure to the public gaze.

His request, being seconded by several men of science, was granted by the government; for no one suggested a doubt of its divine right to freeze human hearts, instead of chopping off human heads, or choking human lungs. This change in the mode of death was much lauded as an act of clemency, and poor Hilda tried to be as grateful as she was told she ought to be.

On the day of execution, the chaplain came to pray with her, but found himself rather embarrassed in using the customary form. He could not well allude to her going in a few hours to meet her final judge; for the chemist said she would come back in a hundred years, and where her soul would be meantime was more than theology could teach. Under these novel circumstances, the old nursery prayer seemed to be the only appropriate one for her to repeat:

"Now I lay me down to sleep,
I pray the Lord my soul to keep:
If I should die before I wake,
I pray the Lord my soul to take."

The subject of this curious experiment was conveyed in a close carriage from the prison to the laboratory. A shudder ran through soul and body, as she entered the apartment assigned her. It was built entirely of stone, and rendered intensely cold by an artificial process. The light was dim and spectral, being admitted from above through a small circle of blue glass. Around the sides of the room, were tiers of massive stone shelves, on which reposed various objects in a torpid state. A huge bear lay on his back, with paws crossed on his breast, as devoutly as some pious knight of the fourteenth century. There was in fact no inconsiderable resemblance in the proceedings by which both these characters gained their worldly possessions; they were equally based on the maxim that "might makes right." It is true, the Christian obtained a better name, inasmuch as he paid a tithe of his gettings to the holy church, which the bear never had the grace to do. But then it must be remembered that the bear had no soul to save, and the Christian knight would have been very unlikely to pay fees to the ferryman, if he likewise had had nothing to send over.

The two public functionaries, who had attended the prisoner, to make sure that justice was not defrauded of its due, soon begged leave to retire, complaining of the unearthly cold. The pale face of the maiden became still paler, as she saw them depart. She seized the arm of the old chemist, and said, imploringly, "You will not go away, too, and leave me with these dreadful creatures?"

He replied, not without some touch of compassion in his tones, "You will be sound asleep, my dear, and will not know whether I am here or not. Drink this; it will soon make you drowsy."

"But what if that great bear should wake up?" asked she, trembling.

"Never fear. He cannot wake up," was the brief reply.

"And what if I should wake up, all alone here?"

"Don't disturb yourself," said he, "I tell you that you will not wake up. Come, my dear, drink quick; for I am getting chilly myself."

The poor girl cast another despairing glance round the tomb-like apartment, and did as she was requested. "And now," said the chemist, "let us shake hands, and say farewell; for you will never see me again."

"Why, won't you come to wake me up?" inquired the prisoner; not reflecting on all the peculiar circumstances of her condition.

"My great-grandson may," replied he, with a smile. "Adieu, my dear. It is a great deal pleasanter than being beheaded. You will fall asleep as easily as a babe in his cradle."

She gazed in his face, with a bewildered drowsy look, and big tears rolled down her cheeks. "Just step up here, my poor child," said he; and he offered her his hand.

"Oh, don't lay me so near the crocodile!" she exclaimed. "If he *should* wake up!"

"You wouldn't know it, if he did," rejoined the patient chemist; "but never mind. Step up to this other shelf, if you like it better."

He handed her up very politely, gathered her garments about her feet, crossed her arms below her breast, and told her to be perfectly still. He then covered his face with a mask, let some gasses escape from an apparatus in the centre of the room, and immediately went out, locking the door after him.

The next day, the public functionaries looked in, and expressed themselves well satisfied to find the maiden lying as rigid and motionless as the bear, the wolf, and the snake. On the edge of the shelf where she lay was pasted an inscription: "Put to sleep for infanticide, Feb. 10, 1740, by order of the king. To be wakened Feb. 10, 1840."

The earth whirled round on its axis, carrying with it the Alps and the Andes, the bear, the crocodile, and the maiden. Summer and winter came and went; America took place among the nations; Bonaparte played out his great game, with kingdoms for pawns; and still the Swedish damsel slept on her stone shelf with the bear and the crocodile.

When ninety-five years had passed, the bear, having fulfilled his prescribed century, was waked according to agreement. The curious flocked round him, to see him eat, and hear whether he could growl as well as other bears. Not liking such close observation, he broke his chain one night, and made off for the hills. How he seemed to his comrades, and what mistakes he made in his recollections, there were never any means of ascertaining. But bears, being more strictly conservative than men, happily escape the influence of French revolutions, German philosophy, Fourier theories, and reforms of all sorts; therefore Bruin doubtless found less change in *his* fellow citizens, than an old knight or viking might have done, had he chanced to sleep so long.

At last, came the maiden's turn to be resuscitated. The populace had forgotten her and her story long ago; but a select scientific few were present at the ceremony, by special invitation. The old chemist and his children all "slept the sleep that knows no waking." But carefully written orders had been transmitted from generation to generation; and the duty finally devolved on a great grandson, himself a chemist of no mean reputation.

Life returned very slowly; at first by almost imperceptible degrees, then by a visible shivering through the nerves. When the eyes opened, it was as if by the movement of pulleys, and there was something painfully strange in their marble gaze. But the lamp within the inner shrine lighted up, and gradually shone through them, giving assurance of the presence of a soul. As consciousness returned, she looked in the faces round her, as if seeking for some one; for her first dim recollection was of the old chemist. For several days, there was a general sluggishness of soul and body; an overpowering inertia, which made all exertion difficult, and prevented memory from rushing back in too tumultuous a tide.

For some time, she was very quiet and patient; but the numbers who came to look at her, their perpetual questions how things seemed to her, what was the state of her appetite and her memory, made her restless and irritable. Still worse was it when she went into the street. Her numerous visitors pointed her out to others, who ran to doors and windows to stare at her, and this soon attracted the attention of boys and lads. To escape such annoyances, she one day walked into a little shop, bearing the name of a woman she had formerly known. It was now kept by her grand-daughter, an aged woman, who was evidently as afraid of Hilda, as if she had been a witch or a ghost.

This state of things became perfectly unendurable. After a few weeks, the forlorn being made her escape from the city, at dawn of day, and with money which had been given her by charitable people, she obtained a passage to her native village, under the new name of Hilda Silfverling. But to stand, in the bloom of sixteen, among well-remembered hills and streams, and not recognise a single human face, or know a single human voice, this was the most mournful of all; far worse than loneliness in a foreign land; sadder than sunshine on a ruined city. And all these suffocating emotions must be crowded back on her own heart; for if she revealed them to any one, she would assuredly be considered insane or bewitched.

As the thought became familiar to her that even the little children she had known were all dead long ago, her eyes assumed an indescribably perplexed and mournful expression, which gave them an appearance of supernatural depth. She was seized with an inexpressible longing to go where no one had ever heard of her, and among scenes she had never looked upon. Her thoughts often reverted fondly to old Virika Gjetter, and the babe for whose sake she had suffered so much; and her heart yearned for Norway. But then she was chilled by the remembrance that even if her child had lived to the usual age of mortals, she must have been long since dead; and if she had left descendants, what would they know of *her*? Overwhelmed by the complete desolation of her lot on earth, she wept bitterly. But she was never utterly hopeless; for in the midst of her anguish, something prophetic seemed to beckon through the clouds, and call her into Norway.

In Stockholm, there was a white-haired old clergyman, who had been peculiarly kind, when he came to see her, after her centennial slumber. She resolved to go to him, to tell him how oppressively dreary was her restored existence, and how earnestly she desired to go, under a new name, to some secluded village in Norway, where none would be likely to learn her history, and where there would be nothing to remind her of the gloomy past. The good old man entered at once into her feelings, and approved her plan. He had been in that country himself, and had staid a few days at the house of a kind old man, named Eystein Hansen. He furnished Hilda with means for the journey, and gave her an affectionate letter of introduction, in which he described her as a Swedish orphan, who had suffered much, and would be glad to earn her living in any honest way that could be pointed out to her.

It was the middle of June when Hilda arrived at the house of Eystein Hanson. He was a stout, clumsy, red-visaged old man, with wide mouth, and big nose, hooked like an eagle's beak; but there was a right friendly expression in his large eyes, and when he had read the letter, he greeted the young stranger with such cordiality, she felt at once that she had found a father. She must come in his boat, he said, and he would take her at once to his island-home, where his good woman would give her a hearty welcome. She always loved the friendless; and especially would she love the Swedish orphan, because her last and youngest daughter had died the year before. On his way to the boat, the worthy man introduced her to several people, and when he told her story, old men and young maidens took her by the hand, and spoke as if they thought Heaven had sent them a daughter and a sister. The good Brenda received her with open arms, as her husband had said she would. She was an old weather-beaten woman, but there was a whole heart full of sunshine in her honest eyes.

And this new home looked so pleasant under the light of the summer sky! The house was embowered in the shrubbery of a small island, in the midst of a fiord, the steep shores of which were thickly covered with pine, fir, and juniper, down to the water's edge. The fiord went twisting and turning about, from promontory to promontory, as if the Nereides, dancing up from the sea, had sportively chased each other into nooks and corners, now hiding away behind some bold projection of rock, and now peeping out suddenly, with a broad sunny smile. Directly in front of the island, the fiord expanded into a broad bay, on the shores of which was a little primitive romantic-looking village. Here and there a sloop was at anchor, and picturesque little boats tacked off and on from cape to cape, their white sails glancing in the sun. A range of lofty blue mountains closed in the distance. One giant, higher than all the rest, went up perpendicularly into the clouds, wearing a perpetual crown of glittering snow. As the maiden gazed on this sublime and beautiful scenery, a new and warmer tide seemed to flow through her stagnant heart. Ah, how happy might life be here among these mountain homes, with a people of such patriarchal simplicity, so brave and free, so hospitable, frank and hearty!

The house of Eystein Hansen was built of pine logs, neatly white-washed. The roof was covered with grass, and bore a crop of large bushes. A vine, tangled among these, fell in heavy festoons that waved at every touch of the wind. The door was painted with flowers in gay colours, and surmounted with fantastic carving. The interior of the dwelling was ornamented with many little grotesque images, boxes, bowls, ladles, &c., curiously carved in the close-grained and beautifully white wood of the Norwegian fir. This was a common amusement with the peasantry, and Eystein being a great favourite among them, received many such presents during his frequent visits in the surrounding parishes.

But nothing so much attracted Hilda's attention as a kind of long trumpet, made of two hollow half cylinders of wood, bound tightly together with birch bark. The only instrument of the kind she had ever seen was in the possession of Virika Gjetter, who called it a *luhr*, and said it was used to call the cows home in her native village, in Upper Tellemarken. She showed how it was used, and Hilda, having a quick ear, soon learned to play upon it with considerable facility.

And here in her new home, this rude instrument reappeared; forming the only visible link between her present life and that dreamy past! With strange feelings, she took up the pipe, and began to play one of the old tunes. At first, the tones flitted like phantoms in and out of her brain; but at last, they all came back, and took their places rank and file. Old Brenda said it was a pleasant tune, and asked her to play it again; but to Hilda it seemed awfully solemn, like a voice warbling from the grave. She would learn other tunes to please the good mother, she said; but this she would play no more; it made her too sad, for she had heard it in her youth.

"Thy youth!" said Brenda, smiling. "One sees well that must have been a long time ago. To hear thee talk, one might suppose thou wert an old autumn leaf, just ready to drop from the bough, like myself."

Hilda blushed, and said she felt old, because she had had much trouble.

"Poor child," responded the good Brenda: "I hope thou hast had thy share."

"I feel as if nothing could trouble me here," replied Hilda, with a grateful smile; "all seems so kind and peaceful." She breathed a few notes through the *luhr*, as she laid it away on the shelf where she had found it. "But, my good mother," said she, "how clear and soft are these tones! The pipe I used to hear was far more harsh."

"The wood is very old," rejoined Brenda: "They say it is more than a hundred years. Alerik Thorild gave it to me, to call my good man when he is out in the boat. Ah, he was such a Berserker* of a boy! and in truth he was not much more sober when he was here three years ago. But no matter what he did; one could never help loving him."

"And who is Alerik?" asked the maiden.

Brenda pointed to an old house, seen in the distance, on the declivity of one of the opposite hills. It overlooked the broad bright bay, with its picturesque little islands, and was sheltered in the rear by a noble pine forest. A water-fall came down from the hillside, glancing in and out among the trees; and when the sun kissed it as he went away, it lighted up with a smile of rainbows.

"That house," said Brenda, "was built by Alerik's grandfather. He was the richest man in the village. But his only son was away among the wars for a long time, and the old place has been going to decay. But they say Alerik is coming back to live among us; and he will soon give it a different look. He has been away to Germany and Paris, and other outlandish parts, for a long time. Ah! the rogue! there was no mischief he didn't think of. He was always tying cats together under the windows, and barking in the middle of the night, till he set all the dogs in the neighbourhood a howling. But as long as it was Alerik that did it, it was all well enough: for everybody loved him, and he always made one believe just what he liked. If he wanted to make thee think thy hair was as black as Noeck's† mane, he *would* make thee think so."

*A warrior famous in the Northern Sagas for his stormy and untamable character.

†An elfish spirit, which, according to popular tradition in Norway, appears in the form of a coal black horse.

Hilda smiled as she glanced at her flaxen hair, with here and there a gleam of paly gold, where the sun touched it. "I think it would be hard to prove *this* was black," said she.

"Nevertheless," rejoined Brenda, "if Alerik undertook it, he would do it. He always has his say, and does what he will. One may as well give in to him first as last."

This account of the unknown youth carried with it that species of fascination, which the idea of uncommon power always has over the human heart. The secluded maiden seldom touched the *luhr* without thinking of the giver; and not unfrequently she found herself conjecturing when this wonderful Alerik would come home.

Meanwhile, constant but not excessive labour, the mountain air, the quiet life, and the kindly hearts around her, restored to Hilda more than her original loveliness. In her large blue eyes, the inward-looking sadness of experience now mingled in strange beauty with the out-looking clearness of youth. Her fair complexion was tinged with the glow of health, and her motions had the airy buoyancy of the mountain breeze. When she went to the mainland, to attend church, or rustic festival, the hearts of young and old greeted her like a May blossom. Thus with calm cheerfulness her hours went by, making no noise in their flight, and leaving no impress. But here was an unsatisfied want! She sighed for hours that did leave a mark behind them. She thought of the Danish youth, who had first spoken to her of love; and plaintively came the tones from her *luhr*, as she gazed on the opposite hills, and wondered whether the Alerik they talked of so much, was indeed so very superior to other young men.

Father Hansen often came home at twilight with a boat full of juniper boughs, to be strewed over the floors, that they might diffuse a balmy odour, inviting to sleep. One evening, when Hilda saw him coming with his verdant load, she hastened down to the water's edge to take an armful of the fragrant boughs. She had scarcely appeared in sight, before he called out, "I do believe Alerik has come! I heard the organ up in the old house. Somebody was playing on it like a Northeast storm; and surely, said I, that must be Alerik."

"Is there an organ there?" asked the damsel, in surprise.

"Yes. He built it himself, when he was here three years ago. He can make anything he chooses. An organ, or a basket cut from a cherry stone, is all one to him."

When Hilda returned to the cottage, she of course repeated the news to Brenda, who exclaimed joyfully, "Ah, then we shall see him soon! If he does not come before, we shall certainly see him at the weddings in the church to-morrow."

"And plenty of tricks we shall have now," said Father Hansen, shaking his head with a good-natured smile. "There will be no telling which end of the world is uppermost, while he is here."

"Oh yes, there will, my friend," answered Brenda, laughing; "for it will certainly be whichever end Alerik stands on. The handsome little Berserker! How I should like to see him!"

The next day there was a sound of lively music on the waters; for two young couples from neighbouring islands were coming up the fiord, to be married at the church in the opposite village. Their boats were ornamented with gay little banners, friends and neighbours accompanied them, playing on musical instruments, and the rowers had their hats decorated with garlands. As the rustic band floated thus gayly over the bright waters, they were joined by Father Hansen, with Brenda and Hilda in his boat.

Friendly villagers had already decked the simple little church with ever-greens and flowers, in honour of the bridal train. As they entered, Father Hansen observed that two young men stood at the door with clarinets in their hands. But he thought no more of it, till, according to immemorial custom, he, as clergy man's assistant, began to sing the first lines of the hymn that was given out. The very first note he sounded, up struck the clarinets at the door. The louder they played, the louder the old man bawled; but the instruments gained the victory. When he essayed to give out the lines of the next verse, the merciless clarinets brayed louder than before. His stentorian voice had become vociferous and rough, from thirty years of halloing across the water, and singing of psalms in four village churches. He exerted it to the utmost, till the perspiration poured down his rubicund visage; but it was of no use. His rivals had strong lungs, and they played on clarinets in F. If the whole village had screamed fire, to the shrill accompaniment of rail-road whistles, they would have over-topped them all.

Father Hansen was vexed at heart, and it was plain enough that he was so. The congregation held down their heads with suppressed laughter; all except one tall vigorous young man, who sat up very serious and dignified, as if he were reverently listening to some new manifestation of musical genius. When the people left church, Hilda saw this young stranger approaching toward them, as fast as numerous handshakings by the way would permit. She had time to observe him closely. His noble figure, his vigorous agile motions, his expressive countenance, hazel eyes with strongly marked brows, and abundant brown hair, tossed aside with a careless grace, left no doubt in her mind that this was the famous Alerik Thorild; but what made her heart beat more wildly was his strong resemblance to Magnus the Dane. He went up to Brenda and kissed her, and threw his arms about Father Hansen's neck, with expressions of joyful recognition. The kind old man, vexed as he was, received these affectionate demonstrations with great friendliness. "Ah, Alerik," said he, after the first salutations were over, "that was not kind of thee."

"Me! What!" exclaimed the young man, with well-feigned astonishment.

"To put up those confounded clarinets to drown my voice," rejoined he bluntly. "When a man has led the singing thirty years in four parishes, I can assure thee it is not a pleasant joke to be treated in that style. I know the young men are tired of my voice, and think they could do things in better fashion, as young fools always do; but I may thank thee for putting it into their heads to bring those cursed clarinets."

"Oh, dear Father Hansen," replied the young man, in the most coaxing tones, and with the most caressing manner, "you *couldn't* think I would do such a thing!"

"On the contrary, it is just the thing I think thou couldst do," answered the old man: "Thou need not think to cheat me out of my eye-teeth, this time. Thou hast often enough made me believe the moon was made of green cheese. But I know thy tricks. I shall be on my guard now; and mind thee, I am not going to be bamboozled by thee again."

Alerik smiled mischievously; for he, in common with all the villagers, knew it was the easiest thing in the world to gull the simple-hearted old man. "Well, come, Father Hansen," said he, "shake hands and be friends. When you come over to the village, to-morrow, we will drink a mug of ale together, at the Wolf's Head."

"Oh yes, and be played some trick for his pains," said Brenda.

"No, no," answered Alerik, with great gravity; "he is on his guard now, and I cannot bamboozle him again." With a friendly nod and smile, he bounded off, to greet some one whom he recognised. Hilda had stepped back to hide herself from observation. She was a little afraid of the handsome Berserker; and his resemblance to the Magnus of her youthful recollections made her sad.

The next afternoon, Alerik met his old friend, and reminded him of the agreement to drink ale at the Wolf's Head. On the way, he invited several young companions. The ale was excellent, and Alerik told stories and sang songs, which filled the little tavern with roars of laughter. In one of the intervals of merriment, he turned suddenly to the honest old man, and said, "Father Hansen, among the many things I have learned and done in foreign countries, did I ever tell you I had made a league with the devil, and am shot-proof?"

"One might easily believe thou hadst made a league with the devil, before thou wert born," replied Eystein, with a grin at his own wit; "but as for being shot-proof, that is another affair."

"Try and see," rejoined Alerik. "These friends are witnesses that I tell you it is perfectly safe to try. Come, I will stand here; fire your pistol, and you will soon see that the Evil One will keep the bargain he made with me."

"Be done with thy nonsense, Alerik," rejoined his old friend.

"Ah, I see how it is," replied Alerik, turning towards the young men. "Father Hansen used to be a famous shot. Nobody was more expert in the bear or the wolf-hunt than he; but old eyes grow dim, and old hands will tremble. No wonder he does not like to have us see how much he fails."

This was attacking honest Eystein Hansen on his weak side. He was proud of his strength and skill in shooting, and he did not like to admit that he was growing old. "I not hit a mark!"

exclaimed he, with indignation: "When did I ever miss a thing I aimed at?"

"Never, when you were young," answered one of the company; "but it is no wonder you are afraid to try now."

"Afraid!" exclaimed the old hunter, impatiently. "Who the devil said I was afraid?"

Alerik shrugged his shoulders, and replied carelessly, "It is natural enough that these young men should think so, when they see you refuse to aim at me, though I assure you that I am shot-proof, and that I will stand perfectly still."

"But art thou really shot-proof?" inquired the guileless old man. "The devil has helped thee to do so many strange things, that one never knows what he will help thee to do next."

"Really, Father Hansen, I speak in earnest. Take up your pistol and try, and you will soon see with your own eyes that I am shot-proof."

Eystein looked round upon the company like one perplexed. His wits, never very bright, were somewhat muddled by the ale. "What shall I do with this wild fellow?" inquired he. "You see he *will* be shot."

"Try him, try him," was the general response. "He has assured you he is shot-proof; what more do you need?"

The old man hesitated awhile, but after some further parley, took up his pistol and examined it. "Before we proceed to business," said Alerik, "let me tell you that if you do *not* shoot me, you shall have a gallon of the best ale you ever drank in your life. Come and taste it, Father Hansen, and satisfy yourself that it is good."

While they were discussing the merits of the ale, one of the young men took the ball from the pistol. "I am ready now," said Alerik: "Here I stand. Now don't lose your name for a good marksman."

The old man fired, and Alerik fell back with a deadly groan. Poor Eystein stood like a stone image of terror. His arms adhered rigidly to his sides, his jaw dropped, and his great eyes seemed starting from their sockets. "Oh, Father Hansen, how *could* you do it!" exclaimed the young men.

The poor horrified dupe stared at them wildly, and gasping and stammering replied, "Why he said he was shot-proof; and you all told me to do it."

"Oh yes," said they; "but we supposed you would have sense enough to know it was all in fun. But don't take it too much to heart. You will probably forfeit your life; for the government will of course consider it a poor excuse, when you tell them that you fired at a man merely to oblige him, and because he said he was shot-proof. But don't be too much cast down, Father Hansen. We must all meet death in some way; and if worst comes to worst, it will be a great comfort to you and your good Brenda that you did not intend to commit murder."

The poor old man gazed at them with an expression of such extreme suffering, that they became alarmed, and said, "Cheer up, cheer up. Come, you must drink something to make you feel better." They took him by the shoulders, but as they led him out, he continued to look back wistfully on the body.

The instant he left the apartment, Alerik sprang up and darted out of the opposite door; and when Father Hansen entered the other room, there he sat, as composedly as possible, reading a paper, and smoking his pipe.

"There he is!" shrieked the old man, turning paler than ever.

"Who is there?" inquired the young men.

"Don't you see Alerik Thorild?" exclaimed he, pointing, with an expression of intense horror.

They turned to the landlord, and remarked, in a compassionate tone, "Poor Father Hansen has shot Alerik Thorild, whom he loved so well; and the dreadful accident has so affected his brain, that he imagines he sees him."

The old man pressed his broad hand hard against his forehead, and again groaned out, "Oh, don't you see him?"

The tones indicated such agony, that Alerik had not the heart to prolong the scene. He sprang on his feet, and exclaimed, "Now for your gallon of ale, Father Hansen! You see the devil did keep his bargain with me."

"And *are* you alive?" shouted the old man.

The mischievous fellow soon convinced him of that, by a slap on the shoulder, that made his bones ache.

Eystein Hansen capered like a dancing bear. He hugged Alerik, and jumped about, and clapped his hands, and was altogether beside himself. He drank unknown quantities of ale, and this time sang loud enough to drown a brace of clarinets in F.

The night was far advanced when he went on board his boat to return to his island home. He pulled the oars vigorously, and the boat shot swiftly across the moon-lighted waters. But on arriving at the customary landing, he could discover no vestige of his white-washed cottage. Not knowing that Alerik, in the full tide of his mischief, had sent men to paint the house with a dark brown wash, he thought he must have made a mistake in the landing; so he rowed round to the other side of the island, but with no better success. Ashamed to return to the mainland, to inquire for a house that had absconded, and a little suspicious that the ale had hung some cobwebs in his brain, he continued to row hither and thither, till his strong muscular arms fairly ached with exertion. But the moon was going down, and all the landscape settling into darkness; and he at last reluctantly concluded that it was best to go back to the village inn.

Alerik, who had expected this result much sooner, had waited there to receive him. When he had kept him knocking a sufficient time, he put his head out of the window, and inquired who was there.

"Eystein Hansen," was the disconsolate reply. "For the love of mercy let me come in and get a few minutes sleep, before morning. I have been rowing about the bay these four hours, and I can't find my house any where."

"This is a very bad sign," replied Alerik, solemnly. "Houses don't run away, except from drunken men. Ah, Father Hansen! Father Hansen! what *will* the minister say?"

He did not have a chance to persecute the weary old man much longer; for scarcely had he come under the shelter of the house, before he was snoring in a profound sleep.

Early the next day, Alerik sought his old friends in their brown-washed cottage. He found it not so easy to conciliate them as usual. They were really grieved; and Brenda even said she believed he wanted to be the death of her old man. But he had brought them presents, which he knew they would like particularly well; and he kissed their hands, and talked over his boyish days, till at last he made them laugh. "Ah now," said he, "you have forgiven me, my dear old friends. And you see, father, it was all your own fault. You put the mischief into me, by boasting before all those young men that I could never bamboozle you again."

"Ah thou incorrigible rogue!" answered the old man. "I believe thou hast indeed made a league with the devil; and he gives thee the power to make every body love thee, do what thou wilt."

Alerik's smile seemed to express that he always had a pleasant consciousness of such power. The *luhr* lay on the table beside him, and as he took it up, he asked, "Who plays on this? Yesterday, when I was out in my boat, I heard very wild pretty little variations on some of my old favourite airs."

Brenda, instead of answering, called, "Hilda! Hilda!" and the young girl came from the next room, blushing as she entered. Alerik looked at her with evident surprise. "Surely, this is not your Gunilda?" said he.

"No," replied Brenda, "She is a Swedish orphan, whom the all-kind Father sent to take the place of our Gunilda, when she was called hence."

After some words of friendly greeting, the visitor asked Hilda if it was she who played so sweetly on the *luhr*. She answered timidly, without looking up. Her heart was throbbing; for the tones of his voice were like Magnus the Dane.

The acquaintance thus begun, was not likely to languish on the part of such an admirer of beauty as was Alerik Thorild. The more he saw of Hilda, during the long evenings of the following winter, the more he was charmed with her natural refinement of look, voice, and manner. There was, as we have said, a peculiarity in her beauty, which gave it a higher character than mere rustic loveliness. A deep, mystic, plaintive expression in her eyes; a sort of graceful bewilderment in her countenance, and at times in the carriage of her head, and the motions of her body; as if her spirit had lost its way, and was listening intently. It was not strange that he was charmed by her spiritual beauty, her simple untutored modesty. No wonder she was delighted with his frank strong exterior, his cordial caressing manner, his expressive eyes, now tender and earnest, and now sparkling with merriment, and his "smile most musical," because always so in harmony with the inward feeling, whether of sadness, fun, or tenderness. Then his moods were so bewitchingly various. Now powerful as the organ, now bright as the flute, now *naive* as the oboe. Brenda said every thing he did seemed to be alive.

He carved a wolf's head on her old man's cane, and she was always afraid it would bite her.

Brenda, in her simplicity, perhaps gave as good a description of genius as *could* be given, when she said everything it did seemed to be alive. Hilda thought it certainly was so with Alerik's music. Sometimes all went madly with it, as if fairies danced on the grass, and ugly gnomes came and made faces at them, and shrieked, and clutched at their garments; the fairies pelted them off with flowers, and then all died away to sleep in the moonlight. Sometimes, when he played on flute, or violin, the sounds came mournfully as the midnight wind through ruined towers; and they stirred up such sorrowful memories of the past, that Hilda pressed her hand upon her swelling heart, and said, "Oh, not such strains as that, dear Alerik." But when his soul overflowed with love and happiness, oh, then how the music gushed and nestled!

> "The lark could scarce get out his notes for joy,
> But shook his song together, as he neared
> His happy home, the ground."

The old *luhr* was a great favourite with Alerik; not for its musical capabilities, but because it was entwined with the earliest recollections of his childhood. "Until I heard thee play upon it," said he, "I half repented having given it to the good Brenda. It has been in our family for several generations, and my nurse used to play upon it when I was in my cradle. They tell me my grandmother was a foundling. She was brought to my great-grandfather's house by an old peasant woman, on her way to the valley of Westfjordalen. She died there, leaving the babe and the *luhr* in my great-grandmother's keeping. They could never find out to whom the babe belonged; but she grew up very beautiful, and my grandfather married her."

"What was the old woman's name?" asked Hilda; and her voice was so deep and suppressed, that it made Alerik start.

"Virika Gjetter, they have always told me," he replied. "But my dearest one, what *is* the matter?"

Hilda, pale and fainting, made no answer. But when he placed her head upon his bosom, and kissed her forehead, and spoke soothingly, her glazed eyes softened, and she burst into tears. All his entreaties, however, could obtain no information at that time. "Go home now," she said, in tones of deep despondency. "To-morrow I will tell thee all. I have had many unhappy hours; for I have long felt that I ought to tell thee all my past history; but I was afraid to do it, for I thought thou wouldst not love me any more; and that would be worse than death. But come to-morrow, and I will tell thee all."

"Well, dearest Hilda, I will wait," replied Alerik; "but what my grandmother, who died long before I was born, can have to do with my love for thee, is more than I can imagine."

The next day, when Hilda saw Alerik coming to claim the fulfilment of her promise, it seemed almost like her death-warrant. "He will not love me any more," thought she, "he will never again look at me so tenderly; and then what can I do, but die?"

With much embarrassment, and many delays, she at last began her strange story. He listened to the first part very attentively, and with a gathering frown; but as she went on, the muscles of his face relaxed into a smile; and when she ended by saying, with the most melancholy seriousness, "So thou seest, dear Alerik, we cannot be married; because it is very likely that I am thy great-grandmother"—he burst into immoderate peals of laughter.

When his mirth had somewhat subsided, he replied, "Likely as not thou art my great-grandmother, dear Hilda; and just as likely I was thy grandfather, in the first place. A great German scholar* teaches that our souls keep coming back again and again into new bodies. An old Greek philosopher is said to have come back for the fourth time, under the name of Pythagoras. If these things are so, how the deuce is a man ever to tell whether he marries his grandmother or not?"

"But, dearest Alerik, I am not jesting," rejoined she. "What I have told thee is really true. They did put me to sleep for a hundred years."

"Oh, yes," answered he, laughing, "I remember reading about it in the Swedish papers; and I thought it a capital joke. I will tell thee how it is with thee, my precious one. The elves

* Lessing.

sometimes seize people, to carry them down into their subterranean caves; but if the mortals run away from them, they, out of spite, forever after fill their heads with gloomy insane notions. A man in Drontheim ran away from them, and they made him believe he was an earthen coffee-pot. He sat curled up in a corner all the time, for fear somebody would break his nose off."

"Nay, now thou art joking, Alerik; but really"—

"No, I tell thee, as thou hast told me, it was no joke at all," he replied. "The man himself told me he was a coffee-pot."

"But be serious, Alerik," said she, "and tell me, dost thou not believe that some learned men can put people to sleep for a hundred years?"

"I don't doubt some of my college professors could," rejoined he; "provided their tongues could hold out so long."

"But, Alerik, dost thou not think it possible that people may be alive, and yet not alive?"

"Of course I do," he replied; "the greater part of the world are in that condition."

"Oh, Alerik, what a tease thou art! I mean, is it not possible that there are people now living, or staying somewhere, who were moving about on this earth ages ago?"

"Nothing more likely," answered he; "for instance, who knows what people there may be under the ice-sea of Folgefond? They say the cocks are heard crowing down there, to this day. How a fowl of any feather got there is a curious question; and what kind of atmosphere he has to crow in, is another puzzle. Perhaps they are poor ghosts, without sense of shame, crowing over the recollections of sins committed in the human body. The ancient Egyptians thought the soul was obliged to live three thousand years, in a succession of different animals, before it could attain to the regions of the blest. I am pretty sure I have already been a lion and a nightingale. What I shall be next, the Egyptians know as well as I do. One of their sculptors made a stone image, half woman and half lioness. Doubtless his mother had been a lioness, and had transmitted to him some dim recollection of it. But I am glad, dearest, they sent thee back in the form of a lovely maiden; for if thou hadst come as a wolf, I might have shot thee; and I shouldn't like to shoot my—great-grandmother. Or if thou hadst come as a red herring, Father Hansen might have eaten thee in his soup; and then I should have had no Hilda Silfverling."

Hilda smiled, as she said, half reproachfully, "I see well that thou dost not believe one word I say."

"Oh yes, I do, dearest," rejoined he, very seriously. "I have no doubt the fairies carried thee off some summer's night and made thee verily believe thou hadst slept for a hundred years. They do the strangest things. Sometimes they change babies in the cradle; leave an imp, and carry off the human to the metal mines, where he hears only clink! clink! Then the fairies bring him back, and put him in some other cradle. When he grows up, how he does hurry skurry after the silver! He is obliged to work all his life, as if the devil drove him. The poor miser never knows what is the matter with him; but it is all because the gnomes brought him up in the mines, and he could never get the clink out of his head. A more poetic kind of fairies sometimes carry a babe to Æolian caves, full of wild dreamy sounds; and when he is brought back to upper earth, ghosts of sweet echoes keep beating time in some corner of his brain, to something which *they* hear, but which nobody else is the wiser for. I know that is true; for I was brought up in those caves myself."

Hilda remained silent for a few minutes, as he sat looking in her face with comic gravity. "Thou wilt do nothing but make fun of me," at last she said. "I do wish I could persuade thee to be serious. What I told thee was no fairy story. It really happened. I remember it as distinctly as I do our sail round the islands yesterday. I seem to see that great bear now, with his paws folded up, on the shelf opposite to me."

"He must have been a great bear to have staid there," replied Alerik, with eyes full of roguery. "If I had been in his skin, may I be shot if all the drugs and gasses in the world would have kept *me* there, with my paws folded on my breast."

Seeing a slight blush pass over her cheek, he added, more seriously, "After all, I ought to thank that wicked elf, whoever he was, for turning thee into a stone image; for otherwise thou wouldst have been in the world a hundred years too soon for me, and so I should have missed my life's best blossom."

Feeling her tears on his hand, he again started off into a vein of merriment. "Thy case was not so very peculiar," said he. "There was a Greek lady, named Niobe, who was changed to stone. The Greek gods changed women into trees, and fountains, and all manner of things. A man couldn't chop a walking-stick in those days, without danger of cutting off some lady's finger. The tree might be—his great-grandmother; and she of course would take it very unkindly of him."

"All these things are like the stories about Odin and Frigga," rejoined Hilda. "They are not true, like the Christian religion. When I tell thee a true story, why dost thou always meet me with fairies and fictions?"

"But tell me, best Hilda," said he, "what the Christian religion has to do with penning up young maidens with bears and crocodiles? In its marriage ceremonies, I grant that it sometimes does things not very unlike that, only omitting the important part of freezing the maiden's heart. But since thou hast mentioned the Christian religion, I may as well give thee a bit of consolation from that quarter. I have read in my mother's big Bible, that a man must not marry his grandmother; but I do not remember that it said a single word against his marrying his *great*-grandmother."

Hilda laughed, in spite of herself. But after a pause, she looked at him earnestly, and said, "Dost thou indeed think there would be no harm in marrying, under these circumstances, if I were really thy great-grandmother? Is it thy earnest? Do be serious for once, dear Alerik!"

"Certainly there would be no harm," answered he. "Physicians have agreed that the body changes entirely once in seven years. That must be because the soul outgrows its clothes; which proves that the soul changes every seven years, also. Therefore, in the course of one hundred years, thou must have had fourteen complete changes of soul and body. It is therefore as plain as daylight, that if thou wert my great-grandmother when thou fell asleep, thou couldst not have been my great-grandmother when they waked thee up."

"Ah, Alerik," she replied, "it is as the good Brenda says, there is no use in talking with thee. One might as well try to twist a string that is not fastened at either end."

He looked up merrily in her face. The wind was playing with her ringlets, and freshened the colour on her cheeks. "I only wish I had a mirror to hold before thee," said he; "that thou couldst see how very like thou art to a—great grandmother."

"Laugh at me as thou wilt," answered she; "but I assure thee I have strange thoughts about myself sometimes. Dost thou know," added she, almost in a whisper, "I am not always quite certain that I have not died, and am now in heaven?"

A ringing shout of laughter burst from the light-hearted lover. "Oh, I like that! I like that!" exclaimed he. "That is good! That a Swede coming to Norway does not know certainly whether she is in heaven or not."

"Do be serious, Alerik," said she imploringly. "Don't carry thy jests too far."

"Serious? I am serious. If Norway is not heaven, one sees plainly enough that it must have been the scaling place, where the old giants got up to heaven; for they have left their ladders standing. Where else wilt thou find clusters of mountains running up perpendicularly thousands of feet right into the sky? If thou wast to see some of them, thou couldst tell whether Norway is a good climbing place into heaven."

"Ah, dearest Alerik, thou hast taught me that already," she replied, with a glance full of affection; "so a truce with thy joking. Truly one never knows how to take thee. Thy talk sets everything *in* the world, and *above* it, and *below* it, dancing together in the strangest fashion."

"Because they all do dance together," rejoined the perverse man.

"Oh, be done! be done, Alerik!" she said, putting her hand playfully over his mouth. "Thou wilt tie my poor brain all up into knots."

He seized her hand and kissed it, then busied himself with braiding the wild spring flowers into a garland for her fair hair. As she gazed on him earnestly, her eyes beaming with love and happiness, he drew her to his breast, and exclaimed fervently, "Oh, thou art beautiful as an angel; and here or elsewhere, with thee by my side, it seemeth heaven."

They spoke no more for a long time. The birds now and then serenaded the silent lovers with little twittering gushes of song. The setting sun, as he went away over the hills, threw diamonds on the bay, and a rainbow ribbon across the distant waterfall. Their hearts were in harmony with the peaceful beauty of Nature. As he kissed her drowsy eyes, she murmured, "Oh, it was well worth a hundred years with bears and crocodiles, to fall asleep thus on thy heart."

* * * * *

The next autumn, a year and a half after Hilda's arrival in Norway, there was another procession of boats, with banners, music and garlands. The little church was again decorated with evergreens; but no clarinet players stood at the door to annoy good Father Hansen. The worthy man had in fact taken the hint, though somewhat reluctantly, and had good-naturedly ceased to disturb modern ears with his clamorous vociferation of the hymns. He and his kind-hearted Brenda were happy beyond measure at Hilda's good fortune. But when she told her husband anything he did not choose to believe, they could never rightly make out what he meant by looking at her so slily, and saying, "Pooh! Pooh! tell that to my——great-grandmother."

1845

# NATHANIEL HAWTHORNE

(1804–1864)

## *Young Goodman Brown*

YOUNG GOODMAN BROWN came forth, at sunset, into the street of Salem village, but put his head back, after crossing the threshold, to exchange a parting kiss with his young wife. And Faith, as the wife was aptly named, thrust her own pretty head into the street, letting the wind play with the pink ribbons of her cap, while she called to Goodman Brown.

'Dearest heart,' whispered she, softly and rather sadly, when her lips were close to his ear, 'pr'y thee, put off your journey until sunrise, and sleep in your own bed to-night. A lone woman is troubled with such dreams and such thoughts, that she's afeard of herself, sometimes. Pray, tarry with me this night, dear husband, of all nights in the year!'

'My love and my Faith,' replied young Goodman Brown, 'of all nights in the year, this one night must I tarry away from thee. My journey, as thou callest it, forth and back again, must needs be done 'twixt now and sunrise. What, my sweet, pretty wife, dost thou doubt me already, and we but three months married!'

'Then, God bless you!' said Faith, with the pink ribbons, 'and may you find all well, when you come back.'

'Amen!' cried Goodman Brown. 'Say thy prayers, dear Faith, and go to bed at dusk, and no harm will come to thee.'

So they parted; and the young man pursued his way, until, being about to turn the corner by the meeting-house, he looked back, and saw the head of Faith still peeping after him, with a melancholy air, in spite of her pink ribbons.

'Poor little Faith!' thought he, for his heart smote him. 'What a wretch am I, to leave her on such an errand! She talks of dreams, too. Methought, as she spoke, there was trouble in her face, as if a dream had warned her what work is to be done to-night. But, no, no! 'twould kill her to think it. Well; she's a blessed angel on earth; and after this one night, I'll cling to her skirts and follow her to Heaven.'

With this excellent resolve for the future, Goodman Brown felt himself justified in making more haste on his present evil purpose. He had taken a dreary road, darkened by all the gloomiest trees of the forest, which barely stood aside to let the narrow path creep through, and closed immediately behind. It was all as lonely as could be; and there is this peculiarity in such a solitude, that the traveller knows not who may be concealed by the innumerable trunks and the thick boughs overhead; so that, with lonely footsteps, he may yet be passing through an unseen multitude.

'There may be a devilish Indian behind every tree,' said Goodman Brown, to himself; and he glanced fearfully behind him, as he added, 'What if the devil himself should be at my very elbow!'

His head being turned back, he passed a crook of the road, and looking forward again, beheld the figure of a man, in grave and decent attire, seated at the foot of an old tree. He arose, at Goodman Brown's approach, and walked onward, side by side with him.

'You are late, Goodman Brown,' said he. 'The clock of the Old South was striking as I came through Boston; and that is full fifteen minutes agone.'

'Faith kept me back awhile,' replied the young man, with a tremor in his voice, caused by the sudden appearance of his companion, though not wholly unexpected.

It was now deep dusk in the forest, and deepest in that part of it where these two were journeying. As nearly as could be discerned, the second traveller was about fifty years old, apparently in the same rank of life as Goodman Brown, and bearing a considerable resemblance to him, though perhaps more in expression than features. Still, they might have been taken for father and son. And yet, though the elder person was as simply clad as the younger, and as simple in manner too, he had an indescribable air of one who knew the world, and would not have felt abashed at the governor's dinner-table, or in King William's court, were it possible that his affairs should call him thither. But the only thing about him, that could be fixed upon as remarkable, was his staff, which bore the likeness of a great black snake, so curiously wrought, that it might almost be seen to twist and wriggle itself, like a living serpent. This, of course, must have been an ocular deception, assisted by the uncertain light.

'Come, Goodman Brown!' cried his fellow-traveller, 'this is a dull pace for the beginning of a journey. Take my staff, if you are so soon weary.'

'Friend,' said the other, exchanging his slow pace for a full stop, 'having kept covenant by meeting thee here, it is my purpose now to return whence I came. I have scruples, touching the matter thou wot'st of.'

'Sayest thou so?' replied he of the serpent, smiling apart. 'Let us walk on, nevertheless, reasoning as we go, and if I convince thee not, thou shalt turn back. We are but a little way in the forest, yet.'

'Too far, too far!' exclaimed the goodman, unconsciously resuming his walk. 'My father never went into the woods on such an errand, nor his father before him. We have been a race of honest men and good Christians, since the days of the martyrs. And shall I be the first of the name of Brown, that ever took this path, and kept—'

'Such company, thou wouldst say,' observed the elder person, interpreting his pause. 'Well said, Goodman Brown! I have been as well acquainted with your family as with ever a one among the Puritans; and that's no trifle to say. I helped your grandfather, the constable, when he lashed the Quaker woman so smartly through the streets of Salem. And it was I that brought your father a pitch-pine knot, kindled at my own hearth, to set fire to an Indian village, in King Philip's war. They were my good friends, both; and many a pleasant walk have we had along this path, and returned merrily after midnight. I would fain be friends with you, for their sake.'

'If it be as thou sayest,' replied Goodman Brown, 'I marvel they never spoke of these matters. Or, verily, I marvel not, seeing that the least rumor of the sort would have driven them from New-England. We are a people of prayer, and good works, to boot, and abide no such wickedness.'

'Wickedness or not,' said the traveller with the twisted staff, 'I have a very general acquaintance here in New-England. The deacons of many a church have drunk the communion wine with me; the selectmen, of divers towns, make me their chairman; and a majority of the Great and General Court are firm supporters of my interest. The governor and I, too—but these are state-secrets.'

'Can this be so!' cried Goodman Brown, with a stare of amazement at his undisturbed companion. 'Howbeit, I have nothing to do with the governor and council; they have their own ways, and are no rule for a simple husbandman, like me. But, were I to go on with thee, how should I meet the eye of that good old man, our minister, at Salem village? Oh, his voice would make me tremble, both Sabbath-day and lecture-day!'

Thus far, the elder traveller had listened with due gravity, but now burst into a fit of irrepressible mirth, shaking himself so violently, that his snake-like staff actually seemed to wriggle in sympathy.

'Ha! ha! ha!' shouted he, again and again; then composing himself, 'Well, go on, Goodman Brown, go on; but pr'y thee, don't kill me with laughing!'

'Well, then, to end the matter at once,' said Goodman Brown, considerably nettled, 'there is my wife, Faith. It would break her dear little heart; and I'd rather break my own!'

'Nay, if that be the case,' answered the other, 'e'en go thy ways, Goodman Brown. I would not, for twenty old women like the one hobbling before us, that Faith should come to any harm.'

As he spoke, he pointed his staff at a female figure on the path, in whom Goodman Brown recognized a very pious and exemplary dame, who had taught him his catechism, in youth, and was still his moral and spiritual adviser, jointly with the minister and Deacon Gookin.

'A marvel, truly, that Goody Cloyse should be so far in the wilderness, at night-fall!' said he. 'But, with your leave, friend, I shall take a cut through the woods, until we have left this Christian woman behind. Being a stranger to you, she might ask whom I was consorting with, and whither I was going.'

'Be it so,' said his fellow-traveller. 'Betake you to the woods, and let me keep the path.'

Accordingly, the young man turned aside, but took care to watch his companion, who advanced softly along the road, until he had come within a staff's length of the old dame. She, meanwhile, was making the best of her way, with singular speed for so aged a woman, and mumbling some indistinct words, a prayer, doubtless, as she went. The traveller put forth his staff, and touched her withered neck with what seemed the serpent's tail.

'The devil!' screamed the pious old lady.

'Then Goody Cloyse knows her old friend?' observed the traveller, confronting her, and leaning on his writhing stick.

'Ah, forsooth, and is it your worship, indeed?' cried the good dame. 'Yea, truly is it, and in the very image of my old gossip, Goodman Brown, the grandfather of the silly fellow that now is. But—would your worship believe it?—my broomstick hath strangely disappeared, stolen, as I suspect, by that unhanged witch, Goody Cory, and that, too, when I was all anointed with the juice of smallage and cinque-foil and wolf's-bane—'

'Mingled with fine wheat and the fat of a new-born babe,' said the shape of old Goodman Brown.

'Ah, your worship knows the receipt,' cried the old lady, cackling aloud. 'So, as I was saying, being all ready for the meeting, and no horse to ride on, I made up my mind to foot it; for they tell me, there is a nice young man to be taken into communion to-night. But now your good worship will lend me your arm, and we shall be there in a twinkling.'

'That can hardly be,' answered her friend. 'I may not spare you my arm, Goody Cloyse, but here is my staff, if you will.'

So saying, he threw it down at her feet, where, perhaps, it assumed life, being one of the rods which its owner had formerly lent to the Egyptian Magi. Of this fact, however, Goodman Brown could not take cognizance. He had cast up his eyes in astonishment, and looking down again, beheld neither Goody Cloyse nor the serpentine staff, but his fellow-traveller alone, who waited for him as calmly as if nothing had happened.

'That old woman taught me my catechism!' said the young man; and there was a world of meaning in this simple comment.

They continued to walk onward, while the elder traveller exhorted his companion to make good speed and persevere in the path, discoursing so aptly, that his arguments seemed rather to spring up in the bosom of his auditor, than to be suggested by himself. As they went, he plucked a branch of maple, to serve for a walking-stick, and began to strip it of the twigs and little boughs, which were wet with evening dew. The moment his fingers touched them, they became strangely withered and dried up, as with a week's sunshine. Thus the pair proceeded, at a good free pace, until suddenly, in a gloomy hollow of the road, Goodman Brown sat himself down on the stump of a tree, and refused to go any farther.

'Friend,' said he, stubbornly, 'my mind is made up. Not another step will I budge on this errand. What if a wretched old woman do choose to go to the devil, when I thought she was going to Heaven! Is that any reason why I should quit my dear Faith, and go after her?'

'You will think better of this, by-and-by,' said his acquaintance, composedly. 'Sit here and rest yourself awhile; and when you feel like moving again, there is my staff to help you along.'

Without more words, he threw his companion the maple stick, and was as speedily out of sight, as if he had vanished into the deepening gloom. The young man sat a few moments, by the road-side, applauding himself greatly, and thinking with how clear a conscience he should meet the minister, in his morning-walk, nor shrink from the eye of good old Deacon Gookin. And what calm sleep would be his, that very night, which was to have been spent so wickedly, but purely and sweetly now, in the arms of Faith! Amidst these pleasant and praiseworthy meditations, Goodman Brown heard the tramp of horses along the road, and deemed it advisable to conceal himself within the verge of the forest, conscious of the guilty purpose that had brought him thither, though now so happily turned from it.

On came the hoof-tramps and the voices of the riders, two grave old voices, conversing soberly as they drew near. These mingled sounds appeared to pass along the road, within a few yards of the young man's hiding-place; but owing, doubtless, to the depth of the gloom, at that particular spot, neither the travellers nor their steeds were visible. Though their figures brushed the small boughs by the way-side, it could not be seen that they intercepted, even for a moment, the faint gleam from the strip of bright sky, athwart which they must have passed. Goodman Brown alternately crouched and stood on tip-toe, pulling aside the branches, and thrusting forth his head as far as he durst, without discerning so much as a shadow. It vexed him the more, because he could have sworn, were such a thing possible, that he recognized the voices of the minister and Deacon Gookin, jogging along quietly, as they were wont to do, when bound to some ordination or ecclesiastical council. While yet within hearing, one of the riders stopped to pluck a switch.

'Of the two, reverend Sir,' said the voice like the deacon's, 'I had rather miss an ordination-dinner than to-night's meeting. They tell me that some of our community are to be here from Falmouth and beyond, and others from Connecticut and Rhode-Island; besides several of the Indian powows, who, after their fashion, know almost as much deviltry as the best of us. Moreover, there is a goodly young woman to be taken into communion.'

'Mighty well, Deacon Gookin!' replied the solemn old tones of the minister. 'Spur up, or we shall be late. Nothing can be done, you know, until I get on the ground.'

The hoofs clattered again, and the voices, talking so strangely in the empty air, passed on through the forest, where no church had ever been gathered, nor solitary Christian prayed. Whither, then, could these holy men be journeying, so deep into the heathen wilderness? Young Goodman Brown caught hold of a tree, for support, being ready to sink down on the ground, faint and overburthened with the heavy sickness of his heart. He looked up to the sky, doubting whether there really was a Heaven above him. Yet, there was the blue arch, and the stars brightening in it.

'With Heaven above, and Faith below, I will yet stand firm against the devil!' cried Goodman Brown.

While he still gazed upward, into the deep arch of the firmament, and had lifted his hands to pray, a cloud, though no wind was stirring, hurried across the zenith, and hid the brightening stars. The blue sky was still visible, except directly overhead, where this black mass of cloud was sweeping swiftly northward. Aloft in the air, as if from the depths of the cloud, came a confused and doubtful sound of voices. Once, the listener fancied that he could distinguish the accents of town's-people of his own, men and women, both pious and ungodly, many of whom he had met at the communion-table, and had seen others rioting at the tavern. The next moment, so indistinct were the sounds, he doubted whether he had heard aught but the murmur of the old forest, whispering without a wind. Then came a stronger swell of those familiar tones, heard daily in the sunshine, at Salem village, but never, until now, from a cloud of night. There was one voice, of a young woman, uttering lamentations, yet with an uncertain sorrow, and entreating for some favor, which, perhaps, it would grieve her to obtain. And all the unseen multitude, both saints and sinners, seemed to encourage her onward.

'Faith!' shouted Goodman Brown, in a voice of agony and desperation; and the echoes of the forest mocked him, crying—'Faith! Faith!' as if bewildered wretches were seeking her, all through the wilderness.

The cry of grief, rage, and terror, was yet piercing the night, when the unhappy husband held his breath for a response. There was a scream, drowned immediately in a louder murmur of voices, fading into far-off laughter, as the dark cloud swept away, leaving the clear and silent sky above Goodman Brown. But something fluttered lightly down through the air, and caught on the branch of a tree. The young man seized it, and beheld a pink ribbon.

'My Faith is gone!' cried he, after one stupefied moment. 'There is no good on earth; and sin is but a name. Come, devil! for to thee is this world given.'

And maddened with despair, so that he laughed loud and long, did Goodman Brown grasp his staff and set forth again, at such a rate, that he seemed to fly along the forest-path, rather than to walk or run. The road grew wilder and drearier, and more faintly traced, and vanished at length, leaving him in the heart of the dark wilderness, still rushing onward, with the instinct that guides mortal man to evil. The whole forest was peopled with frightful sounds; the creaking of the trees, the howling of wild beasts, and the yell of Indians; while, sometimes, the wind tolled like a distant church-bell, and sometimes gave a broad roar around the traveller, as if all Nature were laughing him to scorn. But he was himself the chief horror of the scene, and shrank not from its other horrors.

'Ha! ha! ha!' roared Goodman Brown, when the wind laughed at him. 'Let us hear which will laugh loudest! Think not to frighten me with your deviltry! Come witch, come wizard, come Indian powow, come devil himself! and here comes Goodman Brown. You may as well fear him as he fear you!'

In truth, all through the haunted forest, there could be nothing more frightful than the figure of Goodman Brown. On he flew, among the black pines, brandishing his staff with frenzied gestures, now giving vent to an inspiration of horrid blasphemy, and now shouting forth such laughter, as set all the echoes of the forest laughing like demons around him. The fiend in his own shape is less hideous, than when he rages in the breast of man. Thus sped the demoniac on his course, until, quivering among the trees, he saw a red light before him, as when the felled trunks and branches of a clearing have been set on fire, and throw up their lurid blaze against the sky, at the hour of midnight. He paused, in a lull of the tempest that had driven him onward, and heard the swell of what seemed a hymn, rolling solemnly from a distance, with the weight of many voices. He knew the tune; it was a familiar one in the choir of the village meeting-house. The verse died heavily away, and was lengthened by a chorus, not of human voices, but of all the sounds of the benighted wilderness, pealing in awful harmony together. Goodman Brown cried out; and his cry was lost to his own ear, by its unison with the cry of the desert.

In the interval of silence, he stole forward, until the light glared full upon his eyes. At one extremity of an open space, hemmed in by the dark wall of the forest, arose a rock, bearing some rude, natural resemblance either to an altar or a pulpit, and surrounded by four blazing pines, their tops aflame, their stems untouched, like candles at an evening meeting. The mass of foliage, that had overgrown the summit of the rock, was all on fire, blazing high into the night, and fitfully illuminating the whole field. Each pendent twig and leafy festoon was in a blaze. As the red light arose and fell, a numerous congregation alternately shone forth, then disappeared in shadow, and again grew, as it were, out of the darkness, peopling the heart of the solitary woods at once.

'A grave and dark-clad company!' quoth Goodman Brown.

In truth, they were such. Among them, quivering to-and-fro, between gloom and splendor, appeared faces that would be seen, next day, at the council-board of the province, and others which, Sabbath after Sabbath, looked devoutly heavenward, and benignantly over the crowded pews, from the holiest pulpits in the land. Some affirm, that the lady of the governor was there. At least, there were high dames well known to her, and wives of honored husbands, and widows, a great multitude, and ancient maidens, all of excellent repute, and fair young girls, who trembled, lest their mothers should espy them. Either the sudden gleams of light, flashing over the obscure field, bedazzled Goodman Brown, or he recognized a score of the church-members of Salem village, famous for their especial sanctity. Good old Deacon Gookin had arrived, and waited at the skirts of that venerable saint, his revered pastor. But, irreverently consorting with these grave, reputable, and pious people, these elders of the church, these chaste dames and dewy virgins, there were men of dissolute lives and women of spotted fame, wretches given over to all mean and filthy vice, and suspected even of horrid crimes. It was strange to see, that the good shrank not from the wicked, nor were the sinners abashed by the saints. Scattered, also, among their pale-faced enemies, were the Indian priests, or powows, who had often scared their native forest with more hideous incantations than any known to English witchcraft.

'But, where is Faith?' thought Goodman Brown; and, as hope came into his heart, he trembled.

Another verse of the hymn arose, a slow and mournful strain, such as the pious love, but joined to words which expressed all that our nature can conceive of sin, and darkly hinted at far more. Unfathomable to mere mortals is the lore of fiends. Verse after verse was sung, and still the chorus of the desert swelled between, like the deepest tone of a mighty organ. And, with the final peal of that dreadful anthem, there came a sound, as if the roaring wind, the rushing streams, the howling beasts, and every other voice of the unconverted wilderness, were mingling and according with the voice of guilty man, in homage to the prince of all. The four blazing pines threw up a loftier flame, and obscurely discovered shapes and visages of horror on the smoke-wreaths, above the impious assembly. At the same moment, the fire on the rock shot redly forth, and formed a glowing arch above its base, where now appeared a figure. With reverence be it spoken, the figure bore no slight similitude, both in garb and manner, to some grave divine of the New-England churches.

'Bring forth the converts!' cried a voice, that echoed through the field and rolled into the forest.

At the word, Goodman Brown stept forth from the shadow of the trees, and approached the congregation, with whom he felt a loathful brotherhood, by the sympathy of all that was wicked in his heart. He could have well nigh sworn, that the shape of his own dead father beckoned him to advance, looking downward from a smoke-wreath, while a woman, with dim features of despair, threw out her hand to warn him back. Was it his mother? But he had no power to retreat one step, nor to resist, even in thought, when the minister and good old Deacon Gookin seized his arms, and led him to the blazing rock. Thither came also the slender form of a veiled female, led between Goody Cloyse, that pious teacher of the catechism, and Martha Carrier, who had received the devil's promise to be queen of hell. A rampant hag was she! And there stood the proselytes, beneath the canopy of fire.

'Welcome, my children,' said the dark figure, 'to the communion of your race! Ye have found, thus young, your nature and your destiny. My children, look behind you!'

They turned; and flashing forth, as it were, in a sheet of flame, the fiend-worshippers were seen; the smile of welcome gleamed darkly on every visage.

'There,' resumed the sable form, 'are all whom ye have reverenced from youth. Ye deemed them holier than yourselves, and shrank from your own sin, contrasting it with their lives of righteousness, and prayerful aspirations heavenward. Yet, here are they all, in my worshipping assembly! This night it shall be granted you to know their secret deeds; how hoary-bearded elders of the church have whispered wanton words to the young maids of their households; how many a woman, eager for widow's weeds, has given her husband a drink at bed-time, and let him sleep his last sleep in her bosom; how beardless youths have made haste to inherit their fathers' wealth; and how fair damsels—blush not, sweet ones!—have dug little graves in the garden, and bidden me, the sole guest, to an infant's funeral. By the sympathy of your human hearts for sin, ye shall scent out all the places—whether in church, bed-chamber, street, field, or forest—where crime has been committed, and shall exult to behold the whole earth one stain of guilt, one mighty blood-spot. Far more than this! It shall be yours to penetrate, in every bosom, the deep mystery of sin, the fountain of all wicked arts, and which inexhaustibly supplies more evil impulses than human power—than my power, at its utmost!—can make manifest in deeds. And now, my children, look upon each other.'

They did so; and, by the blaze of the hell-kindled torches, the wretched man beheld his Faith, and the wife her husband, trembling before that unhallowed altar.

'Lo! there ye stand, my children,' said the figure, in a deep and solemn tone, almost sad, with its despairing awfulness, as if his once angelic nature could yet mourn for our miserable race. 'Depending upon one another's hearts, ye had still hoped, that virtue were not all a dream. Now are ye undeceived! Evil is the nature of mankind. Evil must be your only happiness. Welcome, again, my children, to the communion of your race!'

'Welcome!' repeated the fiend-worshippers, in one cry of despair and triumph.

And there they stood, the only pair, as it seemed, who were yet hesitating on the verge of wickedness, in this dark world. A basin was hollowed, naturally, in the rock. Did it contain water, reddened by the lurid light? or was it blood? or, perchance, a liquid flame? Herein did the Shape of Evil dip his hand, and prepare to lay the mark of baptism upon their foreheads, that they might be partakers of the mystery of sin, more conscious of the secret guilt of others, both in deed and thought, than they could now be of their own. The husband cast one look at his pale wife, and Faith at him. What polluted wretches would the next glance shew them to each other, shuddering alike at what they disclosed and what they saw!

'Faith! Faith!' cried the husband. 'Look up to Heaven, and resist the Wicked One!'

Whether Faith obeyed, he knew not. Hardly had he spoken, when he found himself amid calm night and solitude, listening to a roar of the wind, which died heavily away through the forest. He staggered against the rock and felt it chill and damp, while a hanging twig, that had been all on fire, besprinkled his cheek with the coldest dew.

The next morning, young Goodman Brown came slowly into the street of Salem village, staring around him like a bewildered man. The good old minister was taking a walk along the grave-yard, to get an appetite for breakfast and meditate his sermon, and bestowed a blessing, as he passed, on Goodman Brown. He shrank from the venerable saint, as if to avoid an anathema. Old Deacon Gookin was at domestic worship, and the holy words of his prayer were heard through the open window. 'What God doth the wizard pray to?' quoth Goodman Brown. Goody Cloyse, that excellent old Christian, stood in the early sunshine, at her own lattice, catechising a little girl, who had brought her a pint of morning's milk. Goodman Brown snatched away the child, as from the grasp of the fiend himself. Turning the corner by the meeting-house, he spied the head of Faith, with the pink ribbons, gazing anxiously forth, and bursting into such joy at sight of him, that she skipt along the street, and almost kissed her husband before the whole village. But, Goodman Brown looked sternly and sadly into her face, and passed on without a greeting.

Had Goodman Brown fallen asleep in the forest, and only dreamed a wild dream of a witch-meeting?

Be it so, if you will. But, alas! it was a dream of evil omen for young Goodman Brown. A stern, a sad, a darkly meditative, a distrustful, if not a desperate man, did he become, from the night of that fearful dream. On the Sabbath-day, when the congregation were singing a holy psalm, he could not listen, because an anthem of sin rushed loudly upon his ear, and drowned all the blessed strain. When the minister spoke from the pulpit, with power and fervid eloquence, and, with his hand on the open Bible, of the sacred truths of our religion, and of saint-like lives and triumphant deaths, and of future bliss or misery unutterable, then did Goodman Brown turn pale, dreading, lest the roof should thunder down upon the gray blasphemer and his hearers. Often, awakening suddenly at midnight, he shrank from the bosom of Faith, and at morning or eventide, when the family knelt down at prayer, he scowled, and muttered to himself, and gazed sternly at his wife, and turned away. And when he had lived long, and was borne to his grave, a hoary corpse, followed by Faith, an aged woman, and children and grand-children, a goodly procession, besides neighbors, not a few, they carved no hopeful verse upon his tomb-stone; for his dying hour was gloom.

1835

# NATHANIEL HAWTHORNE

(1804–1864)

## *Wakefield*

IN SOME old magazine or newspaper, I recollect a story, told as truth, of a man—let us call him Wakefield—who absented himself for a long time, from his wife. The fact, thus abstractedly stated, is not very uncommon, nor—without a proper distinction of circumstances—to be condemned either as naughty or nonsensical. Howbeit, this, though far from the most aggravated, is perhaps the strangest instance, on record, of marital delinquency; and, moreover, as remarkable a freak as may be found in the whole list of human oddities. The wedded couple lived in London. The man, under pretence of going a journey, took lodgings in the next street to his own house, and there, unheard of by his wife or friends, and without the shadow of a reason for such self-banishment, dwelt upwards of twenty years. During that period, he beheld his home every day, and frequently the forlorn Mrs. Wakefield. And after so great a gap in his matrimonial felicity—when his death was reckoned certain, his estate settled, his name dismissed from memory, and his wife, long, long ago, resigned to her autumnal widowhood—he entered the door one evening, quietly, as from a day's absence, and became a loving spouse till death.

This outline is all that I remember. But the incident, though of the purest originality, unexampled, and probably never to be repeated, is one, I think, which appeals to the general sympathies of mankind. We know, each for himself, that none of us would perpetrate such a folly, yet feel as if some other might. To my own contemplations, at least, it has often recurred, always exciting wonder, but with a sense that the story must be true, and a conception of its hero's character. Whenever any subject so forcibly affects the mind, time is well spent in thinking of it. If the reader choose, let him do his own meditation; or if he prefer to ramble with me through the twenty years of Wakefield's vagary, I bid him welcome; trusting that there will be a pervading spirit and a moral, even should we fail to find them, done up neatly, and condensed into the final sentence. Thought has always its efficacy, and every striking incident its moral.

What sort of a man was Wakefield? We are free to shape out our own idea, and call it by his name. He was now in the meridian of life; his matrimonial affections, never violent, were sobered into a calm, habitual sentiment; of all husbands, he was likely to be the most constant, because a certain sluggishness would keep his heart at rest, wherever it might be placed. He was intellectual, but not actively so; his mind occupied itself in long and lazy musings, that tended to no purpose, or had not vigor to attain it; his thoughts were seldom so energetic as to seize hold of words. Imagination, in the proper meaning of the term, made no part of Wakefield's gifts. With a cold, but not depraved nor wandering heart, and a mind never feverish with riotous thoughts, nor perplexed with originality, who could have anticipated, that our friend would entitle himself to a foremost place among the doers of eccentric deeds? Had his acquaintances been asked, who was the man in London, the surest to perform nothing to-day which should be remembered on the morrow, they would have thought of Wakefield. Only the wife of his bosom might have hesitated. She, without having analyzed his character, was partly aware of a quiet selfishness, that had rusted into his inactive mind—of a peculiar sort of vanity, the most uneasy attribute about him—of a disposition to craft, which had seldom produced more positive effects than the keeping of petty secrets, hardly worth revealing—and, lastly, of what she called a little strangeness, sometimes, in the good man. This latter quality is indefinable, and perhaps non-existent.

Let us now imagine Wakefield bidding adieu to his wife. It is the dusk of an October evening. His equipment is a drab greatcoat, a hat covered with an oil-cloth, top-boots, an umbrella in one hand and a small portmanteau in the other. He has informed Mrs. Wakefield that he is to take the night-coach into the country. She would fain inquire the length of his journey, its object, and the probable time of his return; but, indulgent to his harmless love of mystery, interrogates him only by a look. He tells her not to expect him positively by the return coach, nor to be alarmed should he tarry three or four days; but, at all events, to look for him at supper on Friday evening. Wakefield himself, be it considered, has no suspicion of what is before him. He holds out his hand; she gives her own, and meets his parting kiss, in the matter-of-course way of a ten years' matrimony; and forth goes the middle-aged Mr. Wakefield, almost resolved to perplex his good lady by a whole week's absence. After the door has closed behind him, she perceives it thrust partly open, and a vision of her husband's face, through the aperture, smiling on her, and gone in a moment. For the time, this little incident is dismissed without a thought. But, long afterwards, when she has been more years a widow than a wife, that smile recurs, and flickers across all her reminiscences of Wakefield's visage. In her many musings, she surrounds the original smile with a multitude of fantasies, which make it strange and awful; as, for instance, if she imagines him in a coffin, that parting look is frozen on his pale features; or, if she dreams of him in Heaven, still his blessed spirit wears a quiet and crafty smile. Yet, for its sake, when all others have given him up for dead, she sometimes doubts whether she is a widow.

But, our business is with the husband. We must hurry after him, along the street, ere he lose his individuality, and melt into the great mass of London life. It would be vain searching for him there. Let us follow close at his heels, therefore, until, after several superfluous turns and doublings, we find him comfortably established by the fireside of a small apartment, previously bespoken. He is in the next street to his own, and at his journey's end. He can scarcely trust his good fortune, in having got thither unperceived—recollecting that, at one time, he was delayed by the throng, in the very focus of a lighted lantern; and, again, there were footsteps, that seemed to tread behind his own, distinct from the multitudinous tramp around him; and, anon, he heard a voice shouting afar, and fancied that it called his name. Doubtless, a dozen busy-bodies had been watching him, and told his wife the whole affair. Poor Wakefield! Little knowest thou thine own insignificance in this great world! No mortal eye but mine has traced thee. Go quietly to thy bed, foolish man; and, on the morrow, if thou wilt be wise, get thee home to good Mrs. Wakefield, and tell her the truth. Remove not thyself, even for a little week, from thy place in her chaste bosom. Were she, for a single moment, to deem thee dead, or lost, or lastingly divided from her, thou wouldst be woefully conscious of a change in thy true wife, forever after. It is perilous to make a chasm in human affections; not that they gape so long and wide—but so quickly close again!

Almost repenting of his frolic, or whatever it may be termed, Wakefield lies down betimes, and starting from his first nap, spreads forth his arms into the wide and solitary waste of the unaccustomed bed. 'No'—thinks he, gathering the bed-clothes about him—'I will not sleep alone another night.'

In the morning, he rises earlier than usual, and sets himself to consider what he really means to do. Such are his loose and rambling modes of thought, that he has taken this very singular step, with the consciousness of a purpose, indeed, but without being able to define it sufficiently for his own contemplation. The vagueness of the project, and the convulsive effort with which he plunges into the execution of it, are equally characteristic of a feeble-minded man. Wakefield sifts his ideas, however, as minutely as he may, and finds himself curious to know the progress of matters at home—how his exemplary wife will endure her widowhood, of a week; and, briefly, how the little sphere of creatures and circumstances, in which he was a central object, will be affected by his removal. A morbid vanity, therefore, lies nearest the bottom of the affair. But, how is he to attain his ends? Not, certainly, by keeping close in this comfortable lodging, where, though he slept and awoke in the next street to his home, he is as effectually abroad, as if the stage-coach had been whirling him away all night. Yet, should he reappear, the whole project is knocked in the head. His poor brains being hopelessly puzzled with this dilemma, he at length ventures out, partly resolving to cross the head of the street, and send one hasty glance towards his forsaken domicile. Habit—for he is a man of habits—takes him by the hand, and guides him, wholly unaware, to his own door, where, just at the critical moment, he is aroused by the scraping of his foot upon the step. Wakefield! whither are you going?

At that instant, his fate was turning on the pivot. Little dreaming of the doom to which his first backward step devotes him, he hurries away, breathless with agitation hitherto unfelt, and hardly dares turn his head, at the distant corner. Can it be, that nobody caught sight of him? Will not the whole household—the decent Mrs. Wakefield, the smart maid-servant, and the dirty little foot-boy—raise a hue-and-cry, through London streets, in pursuit of their fugitive lord and master? Wonderful escape! He gathers courage to pause and look homeward, but is perplexed with a sense of change about the familiar edifice, such as affects us all, when, after a separation of months or years, we again see some hill or lake, or work of art, with which we were friends, of old. In ordinary cases, this indescribable impression is caused by the comparison and contrast between our imperfect reminiscences and the reality. In Wakefield, the magic of a single night has wrought a similar transformation, because, in that brief period, a great moral change has been effected. But this is a secret from himself. Before leaving the spot, he catches a far and momentary glimpse of his wife, passing athwart the front window, with her face turned towards the head of the street. The crafty nincompoop takes to his heels, scared with the idea, that, among a thousand such atoms of mortality, her eye must have detected him. Right glad is his heart, though his brain be somewhat dizzy, when he finds himself by the coalfire of his lodgings.

So much for the commencement of this long whim-wham. After the initial conception, and the stirring up of the man's sluggish temperament to put it in practice, the whole matter evolves itself in a natural train. We may suppose him, as the result of deep deliberation, buying a new wig, of reddish hair, and selecting sundry garments, in a fashion unlike his customary suit of brown, from a Jew's old-clothes bag. It is accomplished. Wakefield is another man. The new system being now established, a retrograde movement to the old would be almost as difficult as the step that placed him in his unparalleled position. Furthermore, he is rendered obstinate by a sulkiness, occasionally incident to his temper, and brought on, at present, by the inadequate sensation which he conceives to have been produced in the bosom of Mrs. Wakefield. He will not go back until she be frightened half to death. Well, twice or thrice has she passed before his sight, each time with a heavier step, a paler cheek, and more anxious brow; and, in the third week of his non-appearance, he detects a portent of evil entering the house, in the guise of an apothecary. Next day, the knocker is muffled. Towards nightfall, comes the chariot of a physician, and deposits its big-wigged and solemn burthen at Wakefield's door, whence, after a quarter of an hour's visit, he emerges, perchance the herald of a funeral. Dear woman! Will she die? By this time, Wakefield is excited to something like energy of feeling, but still lingers away from his wife's bedside, pleading with his conscience, that she must not be disturbed at such a juncture. If aught else restrains him, he does not know it. In the course of a few weeks, she gradually recovers; the crisis is over; her heart is sad, perhaps, but quiet; and, let him return soon or late, it will never be feverish for him again. Such ideas glimmer through the mist of Wakefield's mind, and render him indistinctly conscious, that an almost impassable gulf divides his hired apartment from his former home. 'It is but in the next street!' he sometimes says. Fool! it is in another world. Hitherto, he has put off his return from one particular day to another; henceforward, he leaves the precise time undetermined. Not to-morrow—probably next week—pretty soon. Poor man! The dead have nearly as much chance of re-visiting their earthly homes, as the self-banished Wakefield.

Would that I had a folio to write, instead of an article of a dozen pages! Then might I exemplify how an influence, beyond our control, lays its strong hand on every deed which we do, and weaves its consequences into an iron tissue of necessity. Wakefield is spell-bound. We must leave him, for ten years or so, to haunt around his house, without once crossing the threshold, and to be faithful to his wife, with all the affection of which his heart is capable, while he is slowly fading out of hers. Long since, it must be remarked, he has lost the perception of singularity in his conduct.

Now for a scene! Amid the throng of a London street, we distinguish a man, now waxing elderly, with few characteristics to attract careless observers, yet bearing, in his whole aspect, the hand-writing of no common fate, for such as have the skill to read it. He is meagre; his low and narrow forehead is deeply wrinkled; his eyes, small and lustreless, sometimes wander apprehensively about him, but oftener seem to look inward. He bends his head, but moves with an indescribable obliquity of gait, as if unwilling to display his full front to the world. Watch him, long enough to see what we have described, and you will allow, that circumstances—which often produce remarkable men from nature's ordinary handiwork—have produced one such here. Next, leaving him to sidle along the foot-walk, cast your eyes in the opposite direction, where a portly female, considerably in the wane of life, with a prayer-book in her hand, is proceeding to yonder church. She has the placid mien of settled widowhood. Her regrets have either died away, or have become so essential to her heart, that they would be poorly exchanged for joy. Just as the lean man and well conditioned woman are passing, a slight obstruction occurs, and brings these two figures directly in contact. Their hands touch; the pressure of the crowd forces her bosom against his shoulder; they stand, face to face, staring into each other's eyes. After a ten years' separation, thus Wakefield meets his wife!

The throng eddies away, and carries them asunder. The sober widow, resuming her former pace, proceeds to church, but pauses in the portal, and throws a perplexed glance along the street. She passes in, however, opening her prayer-book as she goes. And the man? With so wild a face, that busy and selfish London stands to gaze after him, he hurries to his lodgings, bolts the door, and throws himself upon the bed. The latent feelings of years break out; his feeble mind acquires a brief energy from their strength; all the miserable strangeness of his life is revealed to him at a glance; and he cries out, passionately—'Wakefield! Wakefield! You are mad!'

Perhaps he was so. The singularity of his situation must have so moulded him to itself, that, considered in regard to his fellow-creatures and the business of life, he could not be said to possess his right mind. He had contrived, or rather he had happened, to dissever himself from the world—to vanish—to give up his place and privileges with living men, without being admitted among the dead. The life of a hermit is nowise parallel to his. He was in the bustle of the city, as of old; but the crowd swept by, and saw him not; he was, we may figuratively say, always beside his wife, and at his hearth, yet must never feel the warmth of the one, nor the affection of the other. It was Wakefield's unprecedented fate, to retain his original share of human sympathies, and to be still involved in human interests, while he had lost his reciprocal influence on them. It would be a most curious speculation, to trace out the effect of such circumstances on his heart and intellect, separately, and in unison. Yet, changed as he was, he would seldom be conscious of it, but deem himself the same man as ever; glimpses of the truth, indeed, would come, but only for the moment; and still he would keep saying—'I shall soon go back!'—nor reflect, that he had been saying so for twenty years.

I conceive, also, that these twenty years would appear, in the retrospect, scarcely longer than the week to which Wakefield had at first limited his absence. He would look on the affair as no more than an interlude in the main business of his life. When, after a little while more, he should deem it time to re-enter his parlor, his wife would clap her hands for joy, on beholding the middle-aged Mr. Wakefield. Alas, what a mistake! Would Time but await the close of our favorite follies, we should be young men, all of us, and till Doom's Day.

One evening, in the twentieth year since he vanished, Wakefield is taking his customary walk towards the dwelling which he still calls his own. It is a gusty night of autumn, with frequent showers, that patter down upon the pavement, and are gone, before a man can put up his umbrella. Pausing near the house, Wakefield discerns, through the parlor-windows of the second floor, the red glow, and the glimmer and fitful flash, of a comfortable fire. On the ceiling, appears a grotesque shadow of good Mrs. Wakefield. The cap, the nose and chin, and the broad waist, form an admirable caricature, which dances, moreover, with the up-flickering and down-sinking blaze, almost too merrily for the shade of an elderly widow. At this instant, a shower chances to fall, and is driven, by the unmannerly gust, full into Wakefield's face and bosom. He is quite penetrated with its autumnal chill. Shall he stand, wet and shivering here, when his own hearth has a good fire to warm him, and his own wife will run to fetch the gray coat and small-clothes, which, doubtless, she has kept carefully in the closet of their bedchamber? No! Wakefield is no such fool. He ascends the steps—heavily!—for twenty years have stiffened his legs, since he came down—but he knows it not. Stay, Wakefield! Would you go to the sole home that is left you? Then step into your grave! The door opens. As he passes in, we have a parting glimpse of his visage, and recognize the crafty smile, which was the precursor of the little joke, that he has ever since been playing off at his wife's expense. How unmercifully has he quizzed the poor woman! Well; a good night's rest to Wakefield!

This happy event—supposing it to be such—could only have occurred at an unpremeditated moment. We will not follow our friend across the threshold. He has left us much food for thought, a portion of which shall lend its wisdom to a moral; and be shaped into a figure. Amid the seeming confusion of our mysterious world, individuals are so nicely adjusted to a system, and systems to one another, and to a whole, that, by stepping aside for a moment, a man exposes himself to a fearful risk of losing his place forever. Like Wakefield, he may become, as it were, the Outcast of the Universe.

1835

# NATHANIEL HAWTHORNE

(1804–1864)

## *The Minister's Black Veil*

### *A Parable**

THE sexton stood in the porch of Milford meeting-house, pulling lustily at the bell-rope. The old people of the village came stooping along the street. Children, with bright faces, tript merrily beside their parents, or mimicked a graver gait, in the conscious dignity of their Sunday clothes. Spruce bachelors looked sidelong at the pretty maidens, and fancied that the Sabbath sunshine made them prettier than on weekdays. When the throng had mostly streamed into the porch, the sexton began to toll the bell, keeping his eye on the Reverend Mr. Hooper's door. The first glimpse of the clergyman's figure was the signal for the bell to cease its summons.

'But what has good Parson Hooper got upon his face?' cried the sexton in astonishment.

All within hearing immediately turned about, and beheld the semblance of Mr. Hooper, pacing slowly his meditative way towards the meeting-house. With one accord they started, expressing more wonder than if some strange minister were coming to dust the cushions of Mr. Hooper's pulpit.

'Are you sure it is our parson?' inquired Goodman Gray of the sexton.

'Of a certainty it is good Mr. Hooper,' replied the sexton. 'He was to have exchanged pulpits with Parson Shute of Westbury; but Parson Shute sent to excuse himself yesterday, being to preach a funeral sermon.'

* Another clergyman in New England, Mr. Joseph Moody, of York, Maine, who died about eighty years since, made himself remarkable by the same eccentricity that is here related of the Reverend Mr. Hooper. In his case, however, the symbol had a different import. In early life he had accidentally killed a beloved friend; and from that day till the hour of his own death, he hid his face from men.

The cause of so much amazement may appear sufficiently slight. Mr. Hooper, a gentlemanly person of about thirty, though still a bachelor, was dressed with due clerical neatness, as if a careful wife had starched his band, and brushed the weekly dust from his Sunday's garb. There was but one thing remarkable in his appearance. Swathed about his forehead, and hanging down over his face, so low as to be shaken by his breath, Mr. Hooper had on a black veil. On a nearer view, it seemed to consist of two folds of crape, which entirely concealed his features, except the mouth and chin, but probably did not intercept his sight, farther than to give a darkened aspect to all living and inanimate things. With this gloomy shade before him, good Mr. Hooper walked onward, at a slow and quiet pace, stooping somewhat and looking on the ground, as is customary with abstracted men, yet nodding kindly to those of his parishioners who still waited on the meeting-house steps. But so wonderstruck were they, that his greeting hardly met with a return.

'I can't really feel as if good Mr. Hooper's face was behind that piece of crape,' said the sexton.

'I don't like it,' muttered an old woman, as she hobbled into the meeting-house. 'He has changed himself into something awful, only by hiding his face.'

'Our parson has gone mad!' cried Goodman Gray, following him across the threshold.

A rumor of some unaccountable phenomenon had preceded Mr. Hooper into the meeting-house, and set all the congregation astir. Few could refrain from twisting their heads towards the door; many stood upright, and turned directly about; while several little boys clambered upon the seats, and came down again with a terrible racket. There was a general bustle, a rustling of the women's gowns and shuffling of the men's feet, greatly at variance with that hushed repose which should attend the entrance of the minister. But Mr. Hooper appeared not to notice the perturbation of his people. He entered with an almost noiseless step, bent his head mildly to the pews on each side, and bowed as he passed his oldest parishioner, a white-haired great-grandsire, who occupied an arm-chair in the centre of the aisle. It was strange to observe, how slowly this venerable man became conscious of something singular in the appearance of his pastor. He seemed not fully to partake of the prevailing wonder, till Mr. Hooper had ascended the stairs, and showed himself in the pulpit, face to face with his congregation, except for the black veil. That mysterious emblem was never once withdrawn. It shook with his measured breath as he gave out the psalm; it threw its obscurity between him and the holy page, as he read the Scriptures; and while he prayed, the veil lay heavily on his uplifted countenance. Did he seek to hide it from the dread Being whom he was addressing?

Such was the effect of this simple piece of crape, that more than one woman of delicate nerves was forced to leave the meeting-house. Yet perhaps the pale-faced congregation was almost as fearful a sight to the minister, as his black veil to them.

Mr. Hooper had the reputation of a good preacher, but not an energetic one: he strove to win his people heavenward, by mild persuasive influences, rather than to drive them thither, by the thunders of the Word. The sermon which he now delivered, was marked by the same characteristics of style and manner, as the general series of his pulpit oratory. But there was something, either in the sentiment of the discourse itself, or in the imagination of the auditors, which made it greatly the most powerful effort that they had ever heard from their pastor's lips. It was tinged, rather more darkly than usual, with the gentle gloom of Mr. Hooper's temperament. The subject had reference to secret sin, and those sad mysteries which we hide from our nearest and dearest, and would fain conceal from our own consciousness, even forgetting that the Omniscient can detect them. A subtle power was breathed into his words. Each member of the congregation, the most innocent girl, and the man of hardened breast, felt as if the preacher had crept upon them, behind his awful veil, and discovered their hoarded iniquity of deed or thought. Many spread their clasped hands on their bosoms. There was nothing terrible in what Mr. Hooper said; at least, no violence; and yet, with every tremor of his melancholy voice, the hearers quaked. An unsought pathos came hand in hand with awe. So sensible were the audience of some unwonted attribute in their minister, that they longed for a breath of wind to blow aside the veil, almost believing that a stranger's visage would be discovered, though the form, gesture, and voice were those of Mr. Hooper.

At the close of the services, the people hurried out with indecorous confusion, eager to communicate their pent-up amazement, and conscious of lighter spirits, the moment they lost sight of the black veil. Some gathered in little circles, huddled closely together, with their mouths all whispering in the centre; some went homeward alone, wrapt in silent meditation; some talked loudly, and profaned the Sabbath-day with ostentatious laughter. A few shook their sagacious heads, intimating that they could penetrate the mystery; while one or two affirmed that there was no mystery at all, but only that Mr. Hooper's eyes were so weakened by the midnight lamp, as to require a shade. After a brief interval, forth came good Mr. Hooper also, in the rear of his flock. Turning his veiled face from one group to another, he paid due reverence to the hoary heads, saluted the middle-aged with kind dignity, as their friend and spiritual guide, greeted the young with mingled authority and love, and laid his hands on the little children's heads to bless them. Such was always his custom on the Sabbath-day. Strange and bewildered looks repaid him for his courtesy. None, as on former occasions, aspired to the honor of walking by their pastor's side. Old Squire Saunders, doubtless by an accidental lapse of memory, neglected to invite Mr. Hooper to his table, where the good clergyman had been wont to bless the food, almost every Sunday since his settlement. He returned, therefore, to the parsonage, and, at the moment of closing the door, was observed to look back upon the people, all of whom had their eyes fixed upon the minister. A sad smile gleamed faintly from beneath the black veil, and flickered about his mouth, glimmering as he disappeared.

'How strange,' said a lady, 'that a simple black veil, such as any woman might wear on her bonnet, should become such a terrible thing on Mr. Hooper's face!'

'Something must surely be amiss with Mr. Hooper's intellects,' observed her husband, the physician of the village. 'But the strangest part of the affair is the effect of this vagary, even on a sober-minded man like myself. The black veil, though it covers only our pastor's face, throws its influence over his whole person, and makes him ghost-like from head to foot. Do you not feel it so?'

'Truly do I,' replied the lady; 'and I would not be alone with him for the world. I wonder he is not afraid to be alone with himself!'

'Men sometimes are so,' said her husband.

The afternoon service was attended with similar circumstances. At its conclusion, the bell tolled for the funeral of a young lady. The relatives and friends were assembled in the house, and the more distant acquaintances stood about the door, speaking of the good qualities of the deceased, when their talk was interrupted by the appearance of Mr. Hooper, still covered with his black veil. It was now an appropriate emblem. The clergyman stepped into the room where the corpse was laid, and bent over the coffin, to take a last farewell of his deceased parishioner. As he stooped, the veil hung straight down from his forehead, so that, if her eye-lids had not been closed for ever, the dead maiden might have seen his face. Could Mr. Hooper be fearful of her glance, that he so hastily caught back the black veil? A person, who watched the interview between the dead and living, scrupled not to affirm, that, at the instant when the clergyman's features were disclosed, the corpse had slightly shuddered, rustling the shroud and muslin cap, though the countenance retained the composure of death. A superstitious old woman was the only witness of this prodigy. From the coffin, Mr. Hooper passed into the chamber of the mourners, and thence to the head of the staircase, to make the funeral prayer. It was a tender and heart-dissolving prayer, full of sorrow, yet so imbued with celestial hopes, that the music of a heavenly harp, swept by the fingers of the dead, seemed faintly to be heard among the saddest accents of the minister. The people trembled, though they but darkly understood him, when he prayed that they, and himself, and all of mortal race, might be ready, as he trusted this young maiden had been, for the dreadful hour that should snatch the veil from their faces. The bearers went heavily forth, and the mourners followed, saddening all the street, with the dead before them, and Mr. Hooper in his black veil behind.

'Why do you look back?' said one in the procession to his partner.

'I had a fancy,' replied she, 'that the minister and the maiden's spirit were walking hand in hand.'

'And so had I, at the same moment,' said the other.

That night, the handsomest couple in Milford village were to be joined in wedlock. Though reckoned a melancholy man, Mr. Hooper had a placid cheerfulness for such occasions, which often excited a sympathetic smile, where livelier merriment would have been thrown away. There was no quality of his disposition which made him more beloved than this. The company at the wedding awaited his arrival with impatience, trusting that the strange awe, which had gathered over him throughout the day, would now be dispelled. But such was not the result. When Mr. Hooper came, the first thing that their eyes rested on was the same horrible black veil, which had added deeper gloom to the funeral, and could portend nothing but evil to the wedding. Such was its immediate effect on the guests, that a cloud seemed to have rolled duskily from beneath the black crape, and dimmed the light of the candles. The bridal pair stood up before the minister. But the bride's cold fingers quivered in the tremulous hand of the bridegroom, and her death-like paleness caused a whisper, that the maiden who had been buried a few hours before, was come from her grave to be married. If ever another wedding were so dismal, it was that famous one, where they tolled the wedding-knell. After performing the ceremony, Mr. Hooper raised a glass of wine to his lips, wishing happiness to the new-married couple, in a strain of mild pleasantry that ought to have brightened the features of the guests, like a cheerful gleam from the hearth. At that instant, catching a glimpse of his figure in the looking-glass, the black veil involved his own spirit in the horror with which it overwhelmed all others. His frame shuddered—his lips grew white—he spilt the untasted wine upon the carpet—and rushed forth into the darkness. For the Earth, too, had on her Black Veil.

The next day, the whole village of Milford talked of little else than Parson Hooper's black veil. That, and the mystery concealed behind it, supplied a topic for discussion between acquaintances meeting in the street, and good women gossiping at their open windows. It was the first item of news that the tavern-keeper told to his guests. The children babbled of it on their way to school. One imitative little imp covered his face with an old black handkerchief, thereby so affrighting his playmates, that the panic seized himself, and he well nigh lost his wits by his own waggery.

It was remarkable, that, of all the busy-bodies and impertinent people in the parish, not one ventured to put the plain question to Mr. Hooper, wherefore he did this thing. Hitherto, whenever there appeared the slightest call for such interference, he had never lacked advisers, nor shown himself averse to be guided by their judgment. If he erred at all, it was by so painful a degree of self-distrust, that even the mildest censure would lead him to consider an indifferent action as a crime. Yet, though so well acquainted with this amiable weakness, no individual among his parishioners chose to make the black veil a subject of friendly remonstrance. There was a feeling of dread, neither plainly confessed nor carefully concealed, which caused each to shift the responsibility upon another, till at length it was found expedient to send a deputation of the church, in order to deal with Mr. Hooper about the mystery, before it should grow into a scandal. Never did an embassy so ill discharge its duties. The minister received them with friendly courtesy, but became silent, after they were seated, leaving to his visiters the whole burthen of introducing their important business. The topic, it might be supposed, was obvious enough. There was the black veil, swathed round Mr. Hooper's forehead, and concealing every feature above his placid mouth, on which, at times, they could perceive the glimmering of a melancholy smile. But that piece of crape, to their imagination, seemed to hang down before his heart, the symbol of a fearful secret between him and them. Were the veil but cast aside, they might speak freely of it, but not till then. Thus they sat a considerable time, speechless, confused, and shrinking uneasily from Mr. Hooper's eye, which they felt to be fixed upon them with an invisible glance. Finally, the deputies returned abashed to their constituents, pronouncing the matter too weighty to be handled, except by a council of the churches, if, indeed, it might not require a general synod.

But there was one person in the village, unappalled by the awe with which the black veil had impressed all beside herself. When the deputies returned without an explanation, or even venturing to demand one, she, with the calm energy of her character, determined to chase away the strange cloud that appeared to be settling round Mr. Hooper, every moment more darkly than before. As his plighted wife, it should be her privilege to know what the black veil concealed. At the minister's first visit, therefore, she entered upon the subject, with a direct simplicity, which made the task easier both for him and her. After he had seated himself, she fixed her eyes steadfastly upon the veil, but could discern nothing of the dreadful gloom that had so overawed the multitude: it was but a double fold of crape, hanging down from his forehead to his mouth, and slightly stirring with his breath.

'No,' said she aloud, and smiling, 'there is nothing terrible in this piece of crape, except that it hides a face which I am always glad to look upon. Come, good sir, let the sun shine from behind the cloud. First lay aside your black veil: then tell me why you put it on.'

Mr. Hooper's smile glimmered faintly.

'There is an hour to come,' said he, 'when all of us shall cast aside our veils. Take it not amiss, beloved friend, if I wear this piece of crape till then.'

'Your words are a mystery too,' returned the young lady. 'Take away the veil from them, at least.'

'Elizabeth, I will,' said he, 'so far as my vow may suffer me. Know, then, this veil is a type and a symbol, and I am bound to wear it ever, both in light and darkness, in solitude and before the gaze of multitudes, and as with strangers, so with my familiar friends. No mortal eye will see it withdrawn. This dismal shade must separate me from the world: even you, Elizabeth, can never come behind it!'

'What grievous affliction hath befallen you,' she earnestly inquired, 'that you should thus darken your eyes for ever?'

'If it be a sign of mourning,' replied Mr. Hooper, 'I, perhaps, like most other mortals, have sorrows dark enough to be typified by a black veil.'

'But what if the world will not believe that it is the type of an innocent sorrow?' urged Elizabeth. 'Beloved and respected as you are, there may be whispers, that you hide your face under the consciousness of secret sin. For the sake of your holy office, do away this scandal!'

The color rose into her cheeks, as she intimated the nature of the rumors that were already abroad in the village. But Mr. Hooper's mildness did not forsake him. He even smiled again—that same sad smile, which always appeared like a faint glimmering of light, proceeding from the obscurity beneath the veil.

'If I hide my face for sorrow, there is cause enough,' he merely replied; 'and if I cover it for secret sin, what mortal might not do the same?'

And with this gentle, but unconquerable obstinacy, did he resist all her entreaties. At length Elizabeth sat silent. For a few moments she appeared lost in thought, considering, probably, what new methods might be tried, to withdraw her lover from so dark a fantasy, which, if it had no other meaning, was perhaps a symptom of mental disease. Though of a firmer character than his own, the tears rolled down her cheeks. But, in an instant, as it were, a new feeling took the place of sorrow: her eyes were fixed insensibly on the black veil, when, like a sudden twilight in the air, its terrors fell around her. She arose, and stood trembling before him.

'And do you feel it then at last?' said he mournfully.

She made no reply, but covered her eyes with her hand, and turned to leave the room. He rushed forward and caught her arm.

'Have patience with me, Elizabeth!' cried he passionately. 'Do not desert me, though this veil must be between us here on earth. Be mine, and hereafter there shall be no veil over my face, no darkness between our souls! It is but a mortal veil—it is not for eternity! Oh! you know not how lonely I am, and how frightened to be alone behind my black veil. Do not leave me in this miserable obscurity for ever!'

'Lift the veil but once, and look me in the face,' said she.

'Never! It cannot be!' replied Mr. Hooper.

'Then, farewell!' said Elizabeth.

She withdrew her arm from his grasp, and slowly departed, pausing at the door, to give one long, shuddering gaze, that seemed almost to penetrate the mystery of the black veil. But, even amid his grief, Mr. Hooper smiled to think that only a material emblem had separated him from happiness, though the horrors which it shadowed forth, must be drawn darkly between the fondest of lovers.

From that time no attempts were made to remove Mr. Hooper's black veil, or, by a direct appeal, to discover the secret which it was supposed to hide. By persons who claimed a superiority to popular prejudice, it was reckoned merely an eccentric whim, such as often mingles with the sober actions of men otherwise rational, and tinges them all with its own semblance of insanity. But with the multitude, good Mr. Hooper was irreparably a bugbear. He could not walk the streets with any peace of mind, so conscious was he that the gentle and timid would turn aside to avoid him, and that others would make it a point of hardihood to throw themselves in his way. The impertinence of the latter class compelled him to give up his customary walk, at sunset, to the burial ground, for when he leaned pensively over the gate, there would always be faces behind the grave-stones, peeping at his black veil. A fable went the rounds, that the stare of the dead people drove him thence. It grieved him, to the very depth of his kind heart, to observe how the children fled from his approach, breaking up their merriest sports, while his melancholy figure was yet afar off. Their instinctive dread caused him to feel, more strongly than aught else, that a preternatural horror was interwoven with the threads of the black crape. In truth, his own antipathy to the veil was known to be so great, that he never willingly passed before a mirror, nor stooped to drink at a still fountain, lest, in its peaceful bosom, he should be affrighted by himself. This was what gave plausibility to the whispers, that Mr. Hooper's conscience tortured him for some great crime, too horrible to be entirely concealed, or otherwise than so obscurely intimated. Thus, from beneath the black veil, there rolled a cloud into the sunshine, an ambiguity of sin or sorrow, which enveloped the poor minister, so that love or sympathy could never reach him. It was said, that ghost and fiend consorted with him there. With self-shudderings and outward terrors, he walked continually in its shadow, groping darkly within his own soul, or gazing through a medium that saddened the whole world. Even the lawless wind, it was believed, respected his dreadful secret, and never blew aside the veil. But still good Mr. Hooper sadly smiled, at the pale visages of the worldly throng as he passed by.

Among all its bad influences, the black veil had the one desirable effect, of making its wearer a very efficient clergyman. By the aid of his mysterious emblem—for there was no other apparent cause—he became a man of awful power, over souls that were in agony for sin. His converts always regarded him with a dread peculiar to themselves, affirming, though but figuratively, that, before he brought them to celestial light, they had been with him behind the black veil. Its gloom, indeed, enabled him to sympathize with all dark affections. Dying sinners cried aloud for Mr. Hooper, and would not yield their breath till he appeared; though ever, as he stooped to whisper consolation, they shuddered at the veiled face so near their own. Such were the terrors of the black veil, even when Death had bared his visage! Strangers came long distances to attend service at his church, with the mere idle purpose of gazing at his figure, because it was forbidden them to behold his face. But many were made to quake ere they departed! Once, during Governor Belcher's administration, Mr. Hooper was appointed to preach the election sermon. Covered with his black veil, he stood before the chief magistrate, the council, and the representatives, and wrought so deep an impression, that the legislative measures of that year, were characterized by all the gloom and piety of our earliest ancestral sway.

In this manner Mr. Hooper spent a long life, irreproachable in outward act, yet shrouded in dismal suspicions; kind and loving, though unloved, and dimly feared; a man apart from men, shunned in their health and joy, but ever summoned to their aid in mortal anguish. As years wore on, shedding their snows above his sable veil, he acquired a name throughout the New-England churches, and they called him Father Hooper. Nearly all his parishioners, who were of mature age when he was settled, had been borne away by many a funeral: he had one congregation in the church, and a more crowded one in the church-yard; and having wrought so late into the evening, and done his work so well, it was now good Father Hooper's turn to rest.

Several persons were visible by the shaded candlelight, in the death-chamber of the old clergyman. Natural connections he had none. But there was the decorously grave, though unmoved physician, seeking only to mitigate the last pangs of the patient whom he could not save. There were the deacons, and other eminently pious members of his church. There, also, was the Reverend Mr. Clark, of Westbury, a young and zealous divine, who had ridden in haste to pray by the bedside of the expiring minister. There was the nurse, no hired handmaiden of death, but one whose calm affection had endured thus long, in secresy, in solitude, amid the chill of age, and would not perish, even at the dying hour. Who, but Elizabeth! And there lay the hoary head of good Father Hooper upon the death-pillow, with the black veil still swathed about his brow and reaching down over his face, so that each more difficult gasp of his faint breath caused it to stir. All through life that piece of crape had hung between him and the world: it had separated him from cheerful brotherhood and woman's love, and kept him in that saddest of all prisons, his own heart; and still it lay upon his face, as if to deepen the gloom of his darksome chamber, and shade him from the sunshine of eternity.

For some time previous, his mind had been confused, wavering doubtfully between the past and the present, and hovering forward, as it were, at intervals, into the indistinctness of the world to come. There had been feverish turns, which tossed him from side to side, and wore away what little strength he had. But in his most convulsive struggles, and in the wildest vagaries of his intellect, when no other thought retained its sober influence, he still showed an awful solicitude lest the black veil should slip aside. Even if his bewildered soul could have forgotten, there was a faithful woman at his pillow, who, with averted eyes, would have covered that aged face, which she had last beheld in the comeliness of manhood. At length the death-stricken old man lay quietly in the torpor of mental and bodily exhaustion, with an imperceptible pulse, and breath that grew fainter and fainter, except when a long, deep, and irregular inspiration seemed to prelude the flight of his spirit.

The minister of Westbury approached the bedside.

'Venerable Father Hooper,' said he, 'the moment of your release is at hand. Are you ready for the lifting of the veil, that shuts in time from eternity?'

Father Hooper at first replied merely by a feeble motion of his head; then, apprehensive, perhaps, that his meaning might be doubtful, he exerted himself to speak.

'Yea,' said he, in faint accents, 'my soul hath a patient weariness until that veil be lifted.'

'And is it fitting,' resumed the Reverend Mr. Clark, 'that a man so given to prayer, of such a blameless example, holy in deed and thought, so far as mortal judgment may pronounce; is it fitting that a father in the church should leave a shadow on his memory, that may seem to blacken a life so pure? I pray you, my venerable brother, let not this thing be! Suffer us to be gladdened by your triumphant aspect, as you go to your reward. Before the veil of eternity be lifted, let me cast aside this black veil from your face!'

And thus speaking, the Reverend Mr. Clark bent forward to reveal the mystery of so many years. But, exerting a sudden energy, that made all the beholders stand aghast, Father Hooper snatched both his hands from beneath the bedclothes, and pressed them strongly on the black veil, resolute to struggle, if the minister of Westbury would contend with a dying man.

'Never!' cried the veiled clergyman. 'On earth, never!'

'Dark old man!' exclaimed the affrighted minister, 'with what horrible crime upon your soul are you now passing to the judgment?'

Father Hooper's breath heaved; it rattled in his throat; but, with a mighty effort, grasping forward with his hands, he caught hold of life, and held it back till he should speak. He even raised himself in bed; and there he sat, shivering with the arms of death around him, while the black veil hung down, awful, at that last moment, in the gathered terrors of a life-time. And yet the faint, sad smile, so often there, now seemed to glimmer from its obscurity, and linger on Father Hooper's lips.

'Why do you tremble at me alone?' cried he, turning his veiled face round the circle of pale spectators. 'Tremble also at each other! Have men avoided me, and women shown no pity, and children screamed and fled, only for my black veil? What, but the mystery which it obscurely typifies, has made this piece of crape so awful? When the friend shows his inmost heart to his friend; the lover to his best-beloved; when man does not vainly shrink from the eye of his Creator, loathsomely treasuring up the secret of his sin; then deem me a monster, for the symbol beneath which I have lived, and die! I look around me, and, lo! on every visage a Black Veil!'

While his auditors shrank from one another, in mutual affright, Father Hooper fell back upon his pillow, a veiled corpse, with a faint smile lingering on the lips. Still veiled, they laid him in his coffin, and a veiled corpse they bore him to the grave. The grass of many years has sprung up and withered on that grave, the burial-stone is moss-grown, and good Mr. Hooper's face is dust; but awful is still the thought, that it mouldered beneath the Black Veil!

1836

# NATHANIEL HAWTHORNE

(1804–1864)

## *Rappaccini's Daughter*

### *From the Writings of Aubépine*

We do not remember to have seen any translated specimens of the productions of M. de l'Aubépine; a fact the less to be wondered at, as his very name is unknown to many of his own countrymen, as well as to the student of foreign literature. As a writer, he seems to occupy an unfortunate position between the Transcendentalists (who, under one name or another, have their share in all the current literature of the world), and the great body of pen-and-ink men who address the intellect and sympathies of the multitude. If not too refined, at all events too remote, too shadowy and unsubstantial in his modes of development, to suit the taste of the latter class, and yet too popular to satisfy the spiritual or metaphysical requisitions of the former, he must necessarily find himself without an audience; except here and there an individual, or possibly an isolated clique. His writings, to do them justice, are not altogether destitute of fancy and originality; they might have won him greater reputation but for an inveterate love of allegory, which is apt to invest his plots and characters with the aspect of scenery and people in the clouds, and to steal away the human warmth out of his conceptions. His fictions are sometimes historical, sometimes of the present day, and sometimes, so far as can be discovered, have little or no reference either to time or space. In any case, he generally contents himself with a very slight embroidery of outward manners,—the faintest possible counterfeit of real life,—and endeavors to create an interest by some less obvious peculiarity of the subject. Occasionally, a breath of nature, a rain-drop of pathos and tenderness, or a gleam of humor, will find its way into the midst of his fantastic imagery, and make us feel as if, after all, we were yet within the limits of our native earth. We will only add to this very cursory notice, that M. de l'Aubépine's productions, if the reader chance to take them in precisely the proper point of view, may amuse a leisure hour as well as those of a brighter man; if otherwise, they can hardly fail to look excessively like nonsense.

Our author is voluminous; he continues to write and publish with as much praiseworthy and indefatigable prolixity, as if his efforts were crowned with the brilliant success that so justly attends those of Eugene Sue. His first appearance was by a collection of stories, in a long series of volumes, entitled "*Contes deux fois racontées.*" The titles of some of his more recent works (we quote from memory) are as follows:—"*Le Voyage Céleste à Chemin de Fer,*" 3 tom. 1838. "*Le nouveau Père Adam et la nouvelle Mère Eve,*" 2 tom. 1839. "*Roderic; ou le Serpent à l'estomac,*" 2 tom. 1840. "*Le Culte du Feu,*" a folio volume of ponderous research into the religion and ritual of the old Persian Ghebers, published in 1841. "*La Soirée du Chateau en Espagne,*" 1 tom. 8vo. 1842; and "*L'Artiste du Beau; ou le Papillon Mécanique,*" 5 tom. 4to. 1843. Our somewhat wearisome perusal of this startling catalogue of volumes has left behind it a certain personal affection and sympathy, though by no means admiration, for M. de l'Aubépine; and we would fain do the little in our power towards introducing him favorably to the American public. The ensuing tale is a translation of his "*Beatrice; ou la Belle Empoisonneuse,*" recently published in "*La Revue Anti-Aristocratique.*" This journal, edited by the Comte de Bearhaven, has, for some years past, led the defence of liberal principles and popular rights, with a faithfulness and ability worthy of all praise.

A young man, named Giovanni Guasconti, came, very long ago, from the more southern region of Italy, to pursue his studies at the University of Padua. Giovanni, who had but a scanty supply of gold ducats in his pocket, took lodgings in a high and gloomy chamber of an old edifice, which looked not unworthy to have been the palace of a Paduan noble, and which, in fact, exhibited over its entrance the armorial bearings of a family long since extinct. The young stranger, who was not unstudied in the great poem of his country, recollected that one of the ancestors of this family, and perhaps an occupant of this very mansion, had been pictured by Dante as a partaker of the immortal agonies of his Inferno. These reminiscences and associations, together with the tendency to heart-break natural to a young man for the first time out of his native sphere, caused Giovanni to sigh heavily, as he looked around the desolate and ill-furnished apartment.

"Holy Virgin, Signor," cried old dame Lisabetta, who, won by the youth's remarkable beauty of person, was kindly endeavoring to give the chamber a habitable air, "what a sigh was that to come out of a young man's heart! Do you find this old mansion gloomy? For the love of heaven, then, put your head out of the window, and you will see as bright sunshine as you have left in Naples."

Guasconti mechanically did as the old woman advised, but could not quite agree with her that the Paduan sunshine was as cheerful as that of southern Italy. Such as it was, however, it fell upon a garden beneath the window, and expended its fostering influences on a variety of plants, which seemed to have been cultivated with exceeding care.

"Does this garden belong to the house?" asked Giovanni.

"Heaven forbid, Signor!—unless it were fruitful of better potherbs than any that grow there now," answered old Lisabetta. "No; that garden is cultivated by the own hands of Signor Giacomo Rappaccini, the famous Doctor, who, I warrant him, has been heard of as far as Naples. It is said that he distils these plants into medicines that are as potent as a charm. Oftentimes you may see the Signor Doctor at work, and perchance the Signora his daughter, too, gathering the strange flowers that grow in the garden."

The old woman had now done what she could for the aspect of the chamber, and, commending the young man to the protection of the saints, took her departure.

Giovanni still found no better occupation than to look down into the garden beneath his window. From its appearance, he judged it to be one of those botanic gardens, which were of earlier date in Padua than elsewhere in Italy, or in the world. Or, not improbably, it might once have been the pleasure-place of an opulent family; for there was the ruin of a marble fountain in the centre, sculptured with rare art, but so wofully shattered that it was impossible to trace the original design from the chaos of remaining fragments. The water, however, continued to gush and sparkle into the sunbeams as cheerfully as ever. A little gurgling sound ascended to the young man's window, and made him feel as if the fountain were an immortal spirit, that sung its song unceasingly, and without heeding the vicissitudes around it; while one century embodied it in marble, and another scattered the perishable garniture on the soil. All about the pool into which the water subsided, grew various plants, that seemed to require a plentiful supply of moisture for the nourishment of gigantic leaves, and, in some instances, flowers gorgeously magnificent. There was one shrub in particular, set in a marble vase in the midst of the pool, that bore a profusion of purple blossoms, each of which had the lustre and richness of a gem; and the whole together made a show so resplendent that it seemed enough to illuminate the garden, even had there been no sunshine. Every portion of the soil was peopled with plants and herbs, which, if less beautiful, still bore tokens of assiduous care; as if all had their individual virtues, known to the scientific mind that fostered them. Some were placed in urns, rich with old carving, and others in common garden-pots; some crept serpent-like along the ground, or climbed on high, using whatever means of ascent was offered them. One plant had wreathed itself round a statue of Vertumnus, which was thus quite veiled and shrouded in a drapery of hanging foliage, so happily arranged that it might have served a sculptor for a study.

While Giovanni stood at the window, he heard a rustling behind a screen of leaves, and became aware that a person was at work in the garden. His figure soon emerged into view, and showed itself to be that of no common laborer, but a tall, emaciated, sallow, and sickly-looking man, dressed in a scholar's garb of black. He was beyond the middle term of life, with grey hair, a thin grey beard, and a face singularly marked with intellect and cultivation, but which could never, even in his more youthful days, have expressed much warmth of heart.

Nothing could exceed the intentness with which this scientific gardener examined every shrub which grew in his path; it seemed as if he was looking into their inmost nature, making observations in regard to their creative essence, and discovering why one leaf grew in this shape, and another in that, and wherefore such and such flowers differed among themselves in hue and perfume. Nevertheless, in spite of this deep intelligence on his part, there was no approach to intimacy between himself and these vegetable existences. On the contrary, he avoided their actual touch, or the direct inhaling of their odors, with a caution that impressed Giovanni most disagreeably; for the man's demeanor was that of one walking among malignant influences, such as savage beasts, or deadly snakes, or evil spirits, which, should he allow them one moment of license, would wreak upon him some terrible fatality. It was strangely frightful to the young man's imagination, to see this air of insecurity in a person cultivating a garden, that most simple and innocent of human toils, and which had been alike the joy and labor of the unfallen parents of the race. Was this garden, then, the Eden of the present world?—and this man, with such a perception of harm in what his own hands caused to grow, was he the Adam?

The distrustful gardener, while plucking away the dead leaves or pruning the too luxuriant growth of the shrubs, defended his hands with a pair of thick gloves. Nor were these his only armor. When, in his walk through the garden, he came to the magnificent plant that hung its purple gems beside the marble fountain, he placed a kind of mask over his mouth and nostrils, as if all this beauty did but conceal a deadlier malice. But finding his task still too dangerous, he drew back, removed the mask, and called loudly, but in the infirm voice of a person affected with inward disease:

"Beatrice!—Beatrice!"

"Here am I, my father! What would you?" cried a rich and youthful voice from the window of the opposite house; a voice as rich as a tropical sunset, and which made Giovanni, though he knew not why, think of deep hues of purple or crimson, and of perfumes heavily delectable.—"Are you in the garden?"

"Yes, Beatrice," answered the gardener, "and I need your help."

Soon there emerged from under a sculptured portal the figure of a young girl, arrayed with as much richness of taste as the most splendid of the flowers, beautiful as the day, and with a bloom so deep and vivid that one shade more would have been too much. She looked redundant with life, health, and energy; all of which attributes were bound down and compressed, as it were, and girdled tensely, in their luxuriance, by her virgin zone. Yet Giovanni's fancy must have grown morbid, while he looked down into the garden; for the impression which the fair stranger made upon him was as if here were another flower, the human sister of those vegetable ones, as beautiful as they—more beautiful than the richest of them—but still to be touched only with a glove, nor to be approached without a mask. As Beatrice came down the garden path, it was observable that she handled and inhaled the odor of several of the plants, which her father had most sedulously avoided.

"Here, Beatrice," said the latter,—"see how many needful offices require to be done to our chief treasure. Yet, shattered as I am, my life might pay the penalty of approaching it so closely as circumstances demand. Henceforth, I fear, this plant must be consigned to your sole charge."

"And gladly will I undertake it," cried again the rich tones of the young lady, as she bent towards the magnificent plant, and opened her arms as if to embrace it. "Yes, my sister, my splendor, it shall be Beatrice's task to nurse and serve thee; and thou shalt reward her with thy kisses and perfumed breath, which to her is as the breath of life!"

Then, with all the tenderness in her manner that was so strikingly expressed in her words, she busied herself with such attentions as the plant seemed to require; and Giovanni, at his lofty window, rubbed his eyes, and almost doubted whether it were a girl tending her favorite flower, or one sister performing the duties of affection to another. The scene soon terminated. Whether Doctor Rappaccini had finished his labors in the garden, or that his watchful eye had caught the stranger's face, he now took his daughter's arm and retired. Night was already closing in; oppressive exhalations seemed to proceed from the plants, and steal upward past the open window; and Giovanni, closing the lattice, went to his couch, and dreamed of a rich flower and beautiful girl. Flower and maiden were different and yet the same, and fraught with some strange peril in either shape.

But there is an influence in the light of morning that tends to rectify whatever errors of fancy, or even of judgment, we may have incurred during the sun's decline, or among the shadows of the night, or in the less wholesome glow of moonshine. Giovanni's first movement on starting from sleep, was to throw open the window, and gaze down into the garden which his dreams had made so fertile of mysteries. He was surprised, and a little ashamed, to find how real and matter-of-fact an affair it proved to be, in the first rays of the sun, which gilded the dew-drops that hung upon leaf and blossom, and, while giving a brighter beauty to each rare flower, brought everything within the limits of ordinary experience. The young man rejoiced, that, in the heart of the barren city, he had the privilege of overlooking this spot of lovely and luxuriant vegetation. It would serve, he said to himself, as a symbolic language, to keep him in communion with Nature. Neither the sickly and thought-worn Doctor Giacomo Rappaccini, it is true, nor his brilliant daughter, were now visible; so that Giovanni could not determine how much of the singularity which he attributed to both, was due to their own qualities, and how much to his wonder-working fancy. But he was inclined to take a most rational view of the whole matter.

In the course of the day, he paid his respects to Signor Pietro Baglioni, professor of medicine in the University, a physician of eminent repute, to whom Giovanni had brought a letter of introduction. The Professor was an elderly personage, apparently of genial nature, and habits that might almost be called jovial; he kept the young man to dinner, and made himself very agreeable by the freedom and liveliness of his conversation, especially when warmed by a flask or two of Tuscan wine. Giovanni, conceiving that men of science, inhabitants of the same city, must needs be on familiar terms with one another, took an opportunity to mention the name of Doctor Rappaccini. But the Professor did not respond with so much cordiality as he had anticipated.

"Ill would it become a teacher of the divine art of medicine," said Professor Pietro Baglioni, in answer to a question of Giovanni, "to withhold due and well-considered praise of a physician so eminently skilled as Rappaccini. But, on the other hand, I should answer it but scantily to my conscience, were I to permit a worthy youth like yourself, Signor Giovanni, the son of an ancient friend, to imbibe erroneous ideas respecting a man who might hereafter chance to hold your life and death in his hands. The truth is, our worshipful Doctor Rappaccini has as much science as any member of the faculty—with perhaps one single exception—in Padua, or all Italy. But there are certain grave objections to his professional character."

"And what are they?" asked the young man.

"Has my friend Giovanni any disease of body or heart, that he is so inquisitive about physicians?" said the Professor, with a smile. "But as for Rappaccini, it is said of him—and I, who know the man well, can answer for its truth—that he cares infinitely more for science than for mankind. His patients are interesting to him only as subjects for some new experiment. He would sacrifice human life, his own among the rest, or whatever else was dearest to him, for the sake of adding so much as a grain of mustard-seed to the great heap of his accumulated knowledge."

"Methinks he is an awful man, indeed," remarked Guasconti, mentally recalling the cold and purely intellectual aspect of Rappaccini. "And yet, worshipful Professor, is it not a noble spirit? Are there many men capable of so spiritual a love of science?"

"God forbid," answered the Professor, somewhat testily—"at least, unless they take sounder views of the healing art than those adopted by Rappaccini. It is his theory, that all medicinal virtues are comprised within those substances which we term vegetable poisons. These he cultivates with his own hands, and is said even to have produced new varieties of poison, more horribly deleterious than Nature, without the assistance of this learned person, would ever have plagued the world withal. That the Signor Doctor does less mischief than might be expected, with such dangerous substances, is undeniable. Now and then, it must be owned, he has effected—or seemed to effect—a marvellous cure. But, to tell you my private mind, Signor Giovanni, he should receive little credit for such instances of success—they being probably the work of chance—but should be held strictly accountable for his failures, which may justly be considered his own work."

The youth might have taken Baglioni's opinions with many grains of allowance, had he known that there was a professional warfare of long continuance between him and Doctor Rappaccini, in which the latter was generally thought to have gained the advantage. If the reader be inclined to judge for himself, we refer him to certain black-letter tracts on both sides, preserved in the medical department of the University of Padua.

"I know not, most learned Professor," returned Giovanni, after musing on what had been said of Rappaccini's exclusive zeal for science—"I know not how dearly this physician may love his art; but surely there is one object more dear to him. He has a daughter."

"Aha!" cried the Professor with a laugh. "So now our friend Giovanni's secret is out. You have heard of this daughter, whom all the young men in Padua are wild about, though not half a dozen have ever had the good hap to see her face. I know little of the Signora Beatrice, save that Rappaccini is said to have instructed her deeply in his science, and that, young and beautiful as fame reports her, she is already qualified to fill a professor's chair. Perchance her father destines her for mine! Other absurd rumors there be, not worth talking about, or listening to. So now, Signor Giovanni, drink off your glass of Lacryma."

Guasconti returned to his lodgings somewhat heated with the wine he had quaffed, and which caused his brain to swim with strange fantasies in reference to Doctor Rappaccini and the beautiful Beatrice. On his way, happening to pass by a florist's, he bought a fresh bouquet of flowers.

Ascending to his chamber, he seated himself near the window, but within the shadow thrown by the depth of the wall, so that he could look down into the garden with little risk of being discovered. All beneath his eye was a solitude. The strange plants were basking in the sunshine, and now and then nodding gently to one another, as if in acknowledgment of sympathy and kindred. In the midst, by the shattered fountain, grew the magnificent shrub, with its purple gems clustering all over it; they glowed in the air, and gleamed back again out of the depths of the pool, which thus seemed to overflow with colored radiance from the rich reflection that was steeped in it. At first, as we have said, the garden was a solitude. Soon, however,—as Giovanni had half-hoped, half-feared, would be the case,—a figure appeared beneath the antique sculptured portal, and came down between the rows of plants, inhaling their various perfumes, as if she were one of those beings of old classic fable, that lived upon sweet odors. On again beholding Beatrice, the young man was even startled to perceive how much her beauty exceeded his recollection of it; so brilliant, so vivid was its character, that she glowed amid the sunlight, and, as Giovanni whispered to himself, positively illuminated the more shadowy intervals of the garden path. Her face being now more revealed than on the former occasion, he was struck by its expression of simplicity and sweetness; qualities that had not entered into his idea of her character, and which made him ask anew, what manner of mortal she might be. Nor did he fail again to observe, or imagine, an analogy between the beautiful girl and the gorgeous shrub that hung its gem-like flowers over the fountain; a resemblance which Beatrice seemed to have indulged a fantastic humor in heightening, both by the arrangement of her dress and the selection of its hues.

Approaching the shrub, she threw open her arms, as with a passionate ardor, and drew its branches into an intimate embrace; so intimate, that her features were hidden in its leafy bosom, and her glistening ringlets all intermingled with the flowers.

"Give me thy breath, my sister," exclaimed Beatrice; "for I am faint with common air! And give me this flower of thine, which I separate with gentlest fingers from the stem, and place it close beside my heart."

With these words, the beautiful daughter of Rappaccini plucked one of the richest blossoms of the shrub, and was about to fasten it in her bosom. But now, unless Giovanni's draughts of wine had bewildered his senses, a singular incident occurred. A small orange-colored reptile, of the lizard or chameleon species, chanced to be creeping along the path, just at the feet of Beatrice. It appeared to Giovanni—but, at the distance from which he gazed, he could scarcely have seen anything so minute—it appeared to him, however, that a drop or two of moisture from the broken stem of the flower descended upon the lizard's head. For an instant, the reptile contorted itself violently, and then lay motionless in the sunshine. Beatrice observed this remarkable phenomenon, and crossed herself, sadly, but without surprise; nor did she therefore hesitate to arrange the fatal flower in her bosom. There it blushed, and almost glimmered with the dazzling effect of a precious stone, adding to her dress and aspect the one appropriate charm, which nothing else in the world could have supplied. But Giovanni, out of the shadow of his window, bent forward and shrank back, and murmured and trembled.

"Am I awake? Have I my senses?" said he to himself. "What is this being?—beautiful, shall I call her?—or inexpressibly terrible?"

Beatrice now strayed carelessly through the garden, approaching closer beneath Giovanni's window, so that he was compelled to thrust his head quite out of its concealment in order to gratify the intense and painful curiosity which she excited. At this moment, there came a beautiful insect over the garden wall; it had perhaps wandered through the city and found no flowers nor verdure among those antique haunts of men, until the heavy perfumes of Doctor Rappaccini's shrubs had lured it from afar. Without alighting on the flowers, this winged brightness seemed to be attracted by Beatrice, and lingered in the air and fluttered about her head. Now, here it could not be but that Giovanni Guasconti's eyes deceived him. Be that as it might, he fancied that while Beatrice was gazing at the insect with childish delight, it grew faint and fell at her feet;—its bright wings shivered; it was dead—from no cause that he could discern, unless it were the atmosphere of her breath. Again Beatrice crossed herself and sighed heavily, as she bent over the dead insect.

An impulsive movement of Giovanni drew her eyes to the window. There she beheld the beautiful head of the young man—rather a Grecian than an Italian head, with fair, regular features, and a glistening of gold among his ringlets—gazing down upon her like a being that hovered in midair. Scarcely knowing what he did, Giovanni threw down the bouquet which he had hitherto held in his hand.

"Signora," said he, "there are pure and healthful flowers. Wear them for the sake of Giovanni Guasconti!"

"Thanks, Signor," replied Beatrice, with her rich voice, that came forth as it were like a gush of music; and with a mirthful expression half childish and half woman-like. "I accept your gift, and would fain recompense it with this precious purple flower; but if I toss it into the air, it will not reach you. So Signor Guasconti must even content himself with my thanks."

She lifted the bouquet from the ground, and then as if inwardly ashamed at having stepped aside from her maidenly reserve to respond to a stranger's greeting, passed swiftly homeward through the garden. But, few as the moments were, it seemed to Giovanni when she was on the point of vanishing beneath the sculptured portal, that his beautiful bouquet was already beginning to wither in her grasp. It was an idle thought; there could be no possibility of distinguishing a faded flower from a fresh one at so great a distance.

For many days after this incident, the young man avoided the window that looked into Doctor Rappaccini's garden, as if something ugly and monstrous would have blasted his eyesight, had he been betrayed into a glance. He felt conscious of having put himself, to a certain extent, within the influence of an unintelligible power, by the communication which he had opened with Beatrice. The wisest course would have been, if his heart were in any real danger, to quit his lodgings and Padua itself, at once; the next wiser, to have accustomed himself, as far as possible, to the familiar and day-light view of Beatrice; thus bringing her rigidly and systematically within the limits of ordinary experience. Least of all, while avoiding her sight, ought Giovanni to have remained so near this extraordinary being, that the proximity and possibility even of intercourse, should give a kind of substance and reality to the wild vagaries which his imagination ran riot continually in producing. Guasconti had not a deep heart—or at all events, its depths were not sounded now—but he had a quick fancy, and an ardent southern temperament, which rose every instant to a higher fever-pitch. Whether or no Beatrice possessed those terrible attributes—that fatal breath—the affinity with those so beautiful and deadly flowers—which were indicated by what Giovanni had witnessed, she had at least instilled a fierce and subtle poison into his system. It was not love, although her rich beauty was a madness to him; nor horror, even while he fancied her spirit to be imbued with the same baneful essence that seemed to pervade her physical frame; but a wild offspring of both love and horror that had each parent in it, and burned like one and shivered like the other. Giovanni knew not what to dread; still less did he know what to hope; yet hope and dread kept a continual warfare in his breast, alternately vanquishing one another and starting up afresh to renew the contest. Blessed are all simple emotions, be they dark or bright! It is the lurid intermixture of the two that produces the illuminating blaze of the infernal regions.

Sometimes he endeavored to assuage the fever of his spirit by a rapid walk through the streets of Padua, or beyond its gates; his footsteps kept time with the throbbings of his brain, so that the walk was apt to accelerate itself to a race. One day, he found himself arrested; his arm was seized by a portly personage who had turned back on recognizing the young man, and expended much breath in overtaking him.

"Signor Giovanni!—stay, my young friend!" cried he. "Have you forgotten me? That might well be the case, if I were as much altered as yourself."

It was Baglioni, whom Giovanni had avoided, ever since their first meeting, from a doubt that the Professor's sagacity would look too deeply into his secrets. Endeavoring to recover himself, he stared forth wildly from his inner world into the outer one, and spoke like a man in a dream:

"Yes; I am Giovanni Guasconti. You are Professor Pietro Baglioni. Now let me pass!"

"Not yet—not yet, Signor Giovanni Guasconti," said the Professor, smiling, but at the same time scrutinizing the youth with an earnest glance.—"What; did I grow up side by side with your father, and shall his son pass me like a stranger, in these old streets of Padua? Stand still, Signor Giovanni; for we must have a word or two, before we part."

"Speedily, then, most worshipful Professor, speedily!" said Giovanni, with feverish impatience. "Does not your worship see that I am in haste?"

Now, while he was speaking, there came a man in black along the street, stooping and moving feebly, like a person in inferior health. His face was all overspread with a most sickly and sallow hue, but yet so pervaded with an expression of piercing and active intellect, that an observer might easily have overlooked the merely physical attributes, and have seen only this wonderful energy. As he passed, this person exchanged a cold and distant salutation with Baglioni, but fixed his eyes upon Giovanni with an intentness that seemed to bring out whatever was within him worthy of notice. Nevertheless, there was a peculiar quietness in the look, as if taking merely a speculative, not a human, interest in the young man.

"It is Doctor Rappaccini!" whispered the Professor, when the stranger had passed.—"Has he ever seen your face before?"

"Not that I know," answered Giovanni, starting at the name.

"He *has* seen you!—he must have seen you!" said Baglioni, hastily. "For some purpose or other, this man of science is making a study of you. I know that look of his! It is the same that coldly illuminates his face, as he bends over a bird, a mouse, or a butterfly, which, in pursuance of some experiment, he has killed by the perfume of a flower;—a look as deep as Nature itself, but without Nature's warmth of love. Signor Giovanni, I will stake my life upon it, you are the subject of one of Rappaccini's experiments!"

"Will you make a fool of me?" cried Giovanni, passionately. "*That*, Signor Professor, were an untoward experiment."

"Patience, patience!" replied the imperturbable Professor.—"I tell thee, my poor Giovanni, that Rappaccini has a scientific interest in thee. Thou hast fallen into fearful hands! And the Signora Beatrice? What part does she act in this mystery?"

But Guasconti, finding Baglioni's pertinacity intolerable, here broke away, and was gone before the Professor could again seize his arm. He looked after the young man intently, and shook his head.

"This must not be," said Baglioni to himself. "The youth is the son of my old friend, and shall not come to any harm from which the arcana of medical science can preserve him. Besides, it is too insufferable an impertinence in Rappaccini, thus to snatch the lad out of my own hands, as I may say, and make use of him for his infernal experiments. This daughter of his! It shall be looked to. Perchance, most learned Rappaccini, I may foil you where you little dream of it!"

Meanwhile, Giovanni had pursued a circuitous route, and at length found himself at the door of his lodgings. As he crossed the threshold, he was met by old Lisabetta, who smirked and smiled, and was evidently desirous to attract his attention; vainly, however, as the ebullition of his feelings had momentarily subsided into a cold and dull vacuity. He turned his eyes full upon the withered face that was puckering itself into a smile, but seemed to behold it not. The old dame, therefore, laid her grasp upon his cloak.

"Signor!—Signor!" whispered she, still with a smile over the whole breadth of her visage, so that it looked not unlike a grotesque carving in wood, darkened by centuries—"Listen, Signor! There is a private entrance into the garden!"

"What do you say?" exclaimed Giovanni, turning quickly about, as if an inanimate thing should start into feverish life.—"A private entrance into Doctor Rappaccini's garden!"

"Hush! hush!—not so loud!" whispered Lisabetta, putting her hand over his mouth. "Yes; into the worshipful Doctor's garden, where you may see all his fine shrubbery. Many a young man in Padua would give gold to be admitted among those flowers."

Giovanni put a piece of gold into her hand.

"Show me the way," said he.

A surmise, probably excited by his conversation with Baglioni, crossed his mind, that this interposition of old Lisabetta might perchance be connected with the intrigue, whatever were its nature, in which the Professor seemed to suppose that Doctor Rappaccini was involving him. But such a suspicion, though it disturbed Giovanni, was inadequate to restrain him. The instant that he was aware of the possibility of approaching Beatrice, it seemed an absolute necessity of his existence to do so. It mattered not whether she were angel or demon; he was irrevocably within her sphere, and must obey the law that whirled him onward, in ever lessening circles, towards a result which he did not attempt to foreshadow. And yet, strange to say, there came across him a sudden doubt, whether this intense interest on his part were not delusory—whether it were really of so deep and positive a nature as to justify him in now thrusting himself into an incalculable position—whether it were not merely the fantasy of a young man's brain, only slightly, or not at all, connected with his heart!

He paused—hesitated—turned half about—but again went on. His withered guide led him along several obscure passages, and finally undid a door, through which, as it was opened, there came the sight and sound of rustling leaves, with the broken sunshine glimmering among them. Giovanni stepped forth, and forcing himself through the entanglement of a shrub that wreathed its tendrils over the hidden entrance, he stood beneath his own window, in the open area of Doctor Rappaccini's garden.

How often is it the case, that, when impossibilities have come to pass, and dreams have condensed their misty substance into tangible realities, we find ourselves calm, and even coldly self-possessed, amid circumstances which it would have been a delirium of joy or agony to anticipate! Fate delights to thwart us thus. Passion will choose his own time to rush upon the scene, and lingers sluggishly behind, when an appropriate adjustment of events would seem to summon his appearance. So was it now with Giovanni. Day after day, his pulses had throbbed with feverish blood, at the improbable idea of an interview with Beatrice, and of standing with her, face to face, in this very garden, basking in the Oriental sunshine of her beauty, and snatching from her full gaze the mystery which he deemed the riddle of his own existence. But now there was a singular and untimely equanimity within his breast. He threw a glance around the garden to discover if Beatrice or her father were present, and perceiving that he was alone, began a critical observation of the plants.

The aspect of one and all of them dissatisfied him; their gorgeousness seemed fierce, passionate, and even unnatural. There was hardly an individual shrub which a wanderer, straying by himself through a forest, would not have been startled to find growing wild, as if an unearthly face had glared at him out of the thicket. Several, also, would have shocked a delicate instinct by an appearance of artificialness, indicating that there had been such commixture, and, as it were, adultery of various vegetable species, that the production was no longer of God's making, but the monstrous offspring of man's depraved fancy, glowing with only an evil mockery of beauty. They were probably the result of experiment, which, in one or two cases, had succeeded in mingling plants individually lovely into a compound possessing the questionable and ominous character that distinguished the whole growth of the garden. In fine, Giovanni recognized but two or three plants in the collection, and those of a kind that he well knew to be poisonous. While busy with these contemplations, he heard the rustling of a silken garment, and turning, beheld Beatrice emerging from beneath the sculptured portal.

Giovanni had not considered with himself what should be his deportment; whether he should apologize for his intrusion into the garden, or assume that he was there with the privity, at least, if not by the desire, of Doctor Rappaccini or his daughter. But Beatrice's manner placed him at his ease, though leaving him still in doubt by what agency he had gained admittance. She came lightly along the path, and met him near the broken fountain. There was surprise in her face, but brightened by a simple and kind expression of pleasure.

"You are a connoisseur in flowers, Signor," said Beatrice with a smile, alluding to the bouquet which he had flung her from the window. "It is no marvel, therefore, if the sight of my father's rare collection has tempted you to take a nearer view. If he were here, he could tell you many strange and interesting facts as to the nature and habits of these shrubs, for he has spent a life-time in such studies, and this garden is his world."

"And yourself, lady"—observed Giovanni—"if fame says true—you, likewise, are deeply skilled in the virtues indicated by these rich blossoms, and these spicy perfumes. Would you deign to be my instructress, I should prove an apter scholar than if taught by Signor Rappaccini himself."

"Are there such idle rumors?" asked Beatrice, with the music of a pleasant laugh. "Do people say that I am skilled in my father's science of plants? What a jest is there! No; though I have grown up among these flowers, I know no more of them than their hues and perfume; and sometimes, methinks I would fain rid myself of even that small knowledge. There are many flowers here, and those not the least brilliant, that shock and offend me, when they meet my eye. But, pray, Signor, do not believe these stories about my science. Believe nothing of me save what you see with your own eyes."

"And must I believe all that I have seen with my own eyes?" asked Giovanni pointedly, while the recollection of former scenes made him shrink. "No, Signora, you demand too little of me. Bid me believe nothing, save what comes from your own lips."

It would appear that Beatrice understood him. There came a deep flush to her cheek; but she looked full into Giovanni's eyes, and responded to his gaze of uneasy suspicion with a queen-like haughtiness.

"I do so bid you, Signor!" she replied. "Forget whatever you may have fancied in regard to me. If true to the outward senses, still it may be false in its essence. But the words of Beatrice Rappaccini's lips are true from the depths of the heart outward. Those you may believe!"

A fervor glowed in her whole aspect, and beamed upon Giovanni's consciousness like the light of truth itself. But while she spoke, there was a fragrance in the atmosphere around her, rich and delightful, though evanescent, yet which the young man, from an indefinable reluctance, scarcely dared to draw into his lungs. It might be the odor of the flowers. Could it be Beatrice's breath, which thus embalmed her words with a strange richness, as if by steeping them in her heart? A faintness passed like a shadow over Giovanni, and flitted away; he seemed to gaze through the beautiful girl's eyes into her transparent soul, and felt no more doubt or fear.

The tinge of passion that had colored Beatrice's manner vanished; she became gay, and appeared to derive a pure delight from her communion with the youth, not unlike what the maiden of a lonely island might have felt, conversing with a voyager from the civilized world. Evidently her experience of life had been confined within the limits of that garden. She talked now about matters as simple as the day-light or summer-clouds, and now asked questions in reference to the city, or Giovanni's distant home, his friends, his mother, and his sisters; questions indicating such seclusion, and such lack of familiarity with modes and forms, that Giovanni responded as if to an infant. Her spirit gushed out before him like a fresh rill, that was just catching its first glimpse of the sunlight, and wondering at the reflections of earth and sky which were flung into its bosom. There came thoughts, too, from a deep source, and fantasies of a gem-like brilliancy, as if diamonds and rubies sparkled upward among the bubbles of the fountain. Ever and anon, there gleamed across the young man's mind a sense of wonder, that he should be walking side by side with the being who had so wrought upon his imagination—whom he had idealized in such hues of terror—in whom he had positively witnessed such manifestations of dreadful attributes—that he should be conversing with Beatrice like a brother, and should find her so human and so maiden-like. But such reflections were only momentary; the effect of her character was too real, not to make itself familiar at once.

In this free intercourse, they had strayed through the garden, and now, after many turns among its avenues, were come to the shattered fountain, beside which grew the magnificent shrub with its treasury of glowing blossoms. A fragrance was diffused from it, which Giovanni recognized as identical with that which he had attributed to Beatrice's breath, but incomparably more powerful. As her eyes fell upon it, Giovanni beheld her press her hand to her bosom, as if her heart were throbbing suddenly and painfully.

"For the first time in my life," murmured she, addressing the shrub, "I had forgotten thee!"

"I remember, Signora," said Giovanni, "that you once promised to reward me with one of these living gems for the bouquet, which I had the happy boldness to fling to your feet. Permit me now to pluck it as a memorial of this interview."

He made a step towards the shrub, with extended hand. But Beatrice darted forward, uttering a shriek that went through his heart like a dagger. She caught his hand, and drew it back with the whole force of her slender figure. Giovanni felt her touch thrilling through his fibres.

"Touch it not!" exclaimed she, in a voice of agony. "Not for thy life! It is fatal!"

Then, hiding her face, she fled from him, and vanished beneath the sculptured portal. As Giovanni followed her with his eyes, he beheld the emaciated figure and pale intelligence of Doctor Rappaccini, who had been watching the scene, he knew not how long, within the shadow of the entrance.

No sooner was Guasconti alone in his chamber, than the image of Beatrice came back to his passionate musings, invested with all the witchery that had been gathering around it ever since his first glimpse of her, and now likewise imbued with a tender warmth of girlish womanhood. She was human: her nature was endowed with all gentle and feminine qualities; she was worthiest to be worshipped; she was capable, surely, on her part, of the height and heroism of love. Those tokens, which he had hitherto considered as proofs of a frightful peculiarity in her physical and moral system, were now either forgotten, or, by the subtle sophistry of passion, transmuted into a golden crown of enchantment, rendering Beatrice the more admirable, by so much as she was the more unique. Whatever had looked ugly, was now beautiful; or, if incapable of such a change, it stole away and hid itself among those shapeless half-ideas, which throng the dim region beyond the daylight of our perfect consciousness. Thus did he spend the night, nor fell asleep, until the dawn had begun to awake the slumbering flowers in Doctor Rappaccini's garden, whither Giovanni's dreams doubtless led him. Up rose the sun in his due season, and flinging his beams upon the young man's eyelids, awoke him to a sense of pain. When thoroughly aroused, he became sensible of a burning and tingling agony in his hand—in his right hand—the very hand which Beatrice had grasped in her own, when he was on the point of plucking one of the gem-like flowers. On the back of that hand there was now a purple print, like that of four small fingers, and the likeness of a slender thumb upon his wrist.

Oh, how stubbornly does love—or even that cunning semblance of love which flourishes in the imagination, but strikes no depth of root into the heart—how stubbornly does it hold its faith, until the moment come, when it is doomed to vanish into thin mist! Giovanni wrapt a handkerchief about his hand, and wondered what evil thing had stung him, and soon forgot his pain in a reverie of Beatrice.

After the first interview, a second was in the inevitable course of what we call fate. A third; a fourth; and a meeting with Beatrice in the garden was no longer an incident in Giovanni's daily life, but the whole space in which he might be said to live; for the anticipation and memory of that ecstatic hour made up the remainder. Nor was it otherwise with the daughter of Rappaccini. She watched for the youth's appearance, and flew to his side with confidence as unreserved as if they had been playmates from early infancy—as if they were such playmates still. If, by any unwonted chance, he failed to come at the appointed moment, she stood beneath the window, and sent up the rich sweetness of her tones to float around him in his chamber, and echo and reverberate throughout his heart—"Giovanni! Giovanni! Why tarriest thou? Come down!"—And down he hastened into that Eden of poisonous flowers.

But, with all this intimate familiarity, there was still a reserve in Beatrice's demeanor, so rigidly and invariably sustained, that the idea of infringing it scarcely occurred to his imagination. By all appreciable signs, they loved; they had looked love, with eyes that conveyed the holy secret from the depths of one soul into the depths of the other, as if it were too sacred to be whispered by the way; they had even spoken love, in those gushes of passion when their spirits darted forth in articulated breath, like tongues of long-hidden flame; and yet there had been no seal of lips, no clasp of hands, nor any slightest caress, such as love claims and hallows. He had never touched one of the gleaming ringlets of her hair; her garment—so marked was the physical barrier between them—had never been waved against him by a breeze. On the few occasions when Giovanni had seemed tempted to overstep the limit, Beatrice grew so sad, so stern, and withal wore such a look of desolate separation, shuddering at itself, that not a spoken word was requisite to repel him. At such times, he was startled at the horrible suspicions that rose, monster-like, out of the caverns of his heart, and stared him in the face; his love grew thin and faint as the morning-mist; his doubts alone had substance. But when Beatrice's face brightened again, after the momentary shadow, she was transformed at once from the mysterious, questionable being, whom he had watched with so much awe and horror; she was now the beautiful and unsophisticated girl, whom he felt that his spirit knew with a certainty beyond all other knowledge.

A considerable time had now passed since Giovanni's last meeting with Baglioni. One morning, however, he was disagreeably surprised by a visit from the Professor, whom he had scarcely thought of for whole weeks, and would willingly have forgotten still longer. Given up, as he had long been, to a pervading excitement, he could tolerate no companions, except upon condition of their perfect sympathy with his present state of feeling. Such sympathy was not to be expected from Professor Baglioni.

The visitor chatted carelessly, for a few moments, about the gossip of the city and the University, and then took up another topic.

"I have been reading an old classic author lately," said he, "and met with a story that strangely interested me. Possibly you may remember it. It is of an Indian prince, who sent a beautiful woman as a present to Alexander the Great. She was as lovely as the dawn, and gorgeous as the sunset; but what especially distinguished her was a certain rich perfume in her breath—richer than a garden of Persian roses. Alexander, as was natural to a youthful conqueror, fell in love at first sight with this magnificent stranger. But a certain sage physician, happening to be present, discovered a terrible secret in regard to her."

"And what was that?" asked Giovanni, turning his eyes downward to avoid those of the Professor.

"That this lovely woman," continued Baglioni, with emphasis, "had been nourished with poisons from her birth upward, until her whole nature was so imbued with them, that she herself had become the deadliest poison in existence. Poison was her element of life. With that rich perfume of her breath, she blasted the very air. Her love would have been poison!—her embrace death! Is not this a marvelous tale?"

"A childish fable," answered Giovanni, nervously starting from his chair. "I marvel how your worship finds time to read such nonsense, among your graver studies."

"By the bye," said the Professor, looking uneasily about him, "what singular fragrance is this in your apartment? Is it the perfume of your gloves? It is faint, but delicious, and yet, after all, by no means agreeable. Were I to breathe it long, methinks it would make me ill. It is like the breath of a flower—but I see no flowers in the chamber."

"Nor are there any," replied Giovanni, who had turned pale as the Professor spoke; "nor, I think, is there any fragrance, except in your worship's imagination. Odors, being a sort of element combined of the sensual and the spiritual, are apt to deceive us in this manner. The recollection of a perfume—the bare idea of it—may easily be mistaken for a present reality."

"Aye; but my sober imagination does not often play such tricks," said Baglioni; "and were I to fancy any kind of odor, it would be that of some vile apothecary drug, wherewith my fingers are likely enough to be imbued. Our worshipful friend Rappaccini, as I have heard, tinctures his medicaments with odors richer than those of Araby. Doubtless, likewise, the fair and learned Signora Beatrice would minister to her patients with draughts as sweet as a maiden's breath. But wo to him that sips them!"

Giovanni's face evinced many contending emotions. The tone in which the Professor alluded to the pure and lovely daughter of Rappaccini was a torture to his soul; and yet, the intimation of a view of her character, opposite to his own, gave instantaneous distinctness to a thousand dim suspicions, which now grinned at him like so many demons. But he strove hard to quell them, and to respond to Baglioni with a true lover's perfect faith.

"Signor Professor," said he, "you were my father's friend—perchance, too, it is your purpose to act a friendly part towards his son. I would fain feel nothing towards you, save respect and deference. But I pray you to observe, Signor, that there is one subject on which we must not speak. You know not the Signora Beatrice. You cannot, therefore, estimate the wrong—the blasphemy, I may even say—that is offered to her character by a light or injurious word."

"Giovanni!—my poor Giovanni!" answered the Professor, with a calm expression of pity, "I know this wretched girl far better than yourself. You shall hear the truth in respect to the poisoner Rappaccini, and his poisonous daughter. Yes; poisonous as she is beautiful! Listen; for even should you do violence to my grey hairs, it shall not silence me. That old fable of the Indian woman has become a truth, by the deep and deadly science of Rappaccini, and in the person of the lovely Beatrice!"

Giovanni groaned and hid his face.

"Her father," continued Baglioni, "was not restrained by natural affection from offering up his child, in this horrible manner, as the victim of his insane zeal for science. For—let us do him justice—he is as true a man of science as ever distilled his own heart in an alembic. What, then, will be your fate? Beyond a doubt, you are selected as the material of some new experiment. Perhaps the result is to be death—perhaps a fate more awful still! Rappaccini, with what he calls the interest of science before his eyes, will hesitate at nothing."

"It is a dream!" muttered Giovanni to himself, "surely it is a dream!"

"But," resumed the Professor, "be of good cheer, son of my friend! It is not yet too late for the rescue. Possibly, we may even succeed in bringing back this miserable child within the limits of ordinary nature, from which her father's madness has estranged her. Behold this little silver vase! It was wrought by the hands of the renowned Benvenuto Cellini, and is well worthy to be a love-gift to the fairest dame in Italy. But its contents are invaluable. One little sip of this antidote would have rendered the most virulent poisons of the Borgias innocuous. Doubt not that it will be as efficacious against those of Rappaccini. Bestow the vase, and the precious liquid within it, on your Beatrice, and hopefully await the result."

Baglioni laid a small, exquisitely wrought silver phial on the table, and withdrew, leaving what he had said to produce its effect upon the young man's mind.

"We will thwart Rappaccini yet!" thought he, chuckling to himself, as he descended the stairs. "But, let us confess the truth of him, he is a wonderful man!—a wonderful man indeed! A vile empiric, however, in his practice, and therefore not to be tolerated by those who respect the good old rules of the medical profession!"

Throughout Giovanni's whole acquaintance with Beatrice, he had occasionally, as we have said, been haunted by dark surmises as to her character. Yet, so thoroughly had she made herself felt by him as a simple, natural, most affectionate and guileless creature, that the image now held up by Professor Baglioni, looked as strange and incredible, as if it were not in accordance with his own original conception. True, there were ugly recollections connected with his first glimpses of the beautiful girl; he could not quite forget the bouquet that withered in her grasp, and the insect that perished amid the sunny air, by no ostensible agency, save the fragrance of her breath. These incidents, however, dissolving in the pure light of her character, had no longer the efficacy of facts, but were acknowledged as mistaken fantasies, by whatever testimony of the senses they might appear to be substantiated. There is something truer and more real, than what we can see with the eyes, and touch with the finger. On such better evidence, had Giovanni founded his confidence in Beatrice, though rather by the necessary force of her high attributes, than by any deep and generous faith, on his part. But, now, his spirit was incapable of sustaining itself at the height to which the early enthusiasm of passion had exalted it; he fell down, grovelling among earthly doubts, and defiled therewith the pure whiteness of Beatrice's image. Not that he gave her up; he did but distrust. He resolved to institute some decisive test that should satisfy him, once for all, whether there were those dreadful peculiarities in her physical nature, which could not be supposed to exist without some corresponding monstrosity of soul. His eyes, gazing down afar, might have deceived him as to the lizard, the insect, and the flowers. But if he could witness, at the distance of a few paces, the sudden blight of one fresh and healthful flower in Beatrice's hand, there would be room for no further question. With this idea, he hastened to the florist's, and purchased a bouquet that was still gemmed with the morning dew-drops.

It was now the customary hour of his daily interview with Beatrice. Before descending into the garden, Giovanni failed not to look at his figure in the mirror; a vanity to be expected in a beautiful young man, yet, as displaying itself at that troubled and feverish moment, the token of a certain shallowness of feeling and insincerity of character. He did gaze, however, and said to himself, that his features had never before possessed so rich a grace, nor his eyes such vivacity, nor his cheeks so warm a hue of superabundant life.

"At least," thought he, "her poison has not yet insinuated itself into my system. I am no flower to perish in her grasp!"

With that thought, he turned his eyes on the bouquet, which he had never once laid aside from his hand. A thrill of indefinable horror shot through his frame, on perceiving that those dewy flowers were already beginning to droop; they wore the aspect of things that had been fresh and lovely, yesterday. Giovanni grew white as marble, and stood motionless before the mirror, staring at his own reflection there, as at the likeness of something frightful. He remembered Baglioni's remark about the fragrance that seemed to pervade the chamber. It must have been the poison in his breath! Then he shuddered—shuddered at himself! Recovering from his stupor, he began to watch, with curious eye, a spider that was busily at work, hanging its web from the antique cornice of the apartment, crossing and recrossing the artful system of interwoven lines, as vigorous and active a spider as ever dangled from an old ceiling. Giovanni bent towards the insect, and emitted a deep, long breath. The spider suddenly ceased its toil; the web vibrated with a tremor originating in the body of the small artizan. Again Giovanni sent forth a breath, deeper, longer, and imbued with a venomous feeling out of his heart; he knew not whether he were wicked or only desperate. The spider made a convulsive gripe with his limbs, and hung dead across the window.

"Accursed! Accursed!" muttered Giovanni, addressing himself. "Hast thou grown so poisonous, that this deadly insect perishes by thy breath?"

At that moment, a rich, sweet voice came floating up from the garden:—

"Giovanni! Giovanni! It is past the hour! Why tarriest thou! Come down!"

"Yes," muttered Giovanni again. "She is the only being whom my breath may not slay! Would that it might!"

He rushed down, and in an instant, was standing before the bright and loving eyes of Beatrice. A moment ago, his wrath and despair had been so fierce that he could have desired nothing so much as to wither her by a glance. But, with her actual presence, there came influences which had too real an existence to be at once shaken off; recollections of the delicate and benign power of her feminine nature, which had so often enveloped him in a religious calm; recollections of many a holy and passionate outgush of her heart, when the pure fountain had been unsealed from its depths, and made visible in its transparency to his mental eye; recollections which, had Giovanni known how to estimate them, would have assured him that all this ugly mystery was but an earthly illusion, and that, whatever mist of evil might seem to have gathered over her, the real Beatrice was a heavenly angel. Incapable as he was of such high faith, still her presence had not utterly lost its magic. Giovanni's rage was quelled into an aspect of sullen insensibility. Beatrice, with a quick spiritual sense, immediately felt that there was a gulf of blackness between them, which neither he nor she could pass. They walked on together, sad and silent, and came thus to the marble fountain, and to its pool of water on the ground, in the midst of which grew the shrub that bore gem-like blossoms. Giovanni was affrighted at the eager enjoyment—the appetite, as it were—with which he found himself inhaling the fragrance of the flowers.

"Beatrice," asked he abruptly, "whence came this shrub?"

"My father created it," answered she, with simplicity.

"Created it! created it!" repeated Giovanni. "What mean you, Beatrice?"

"He is a man fearfully acquainted with the secrets of nature," replied Beatrice; "and, at the hour when I first drew breath, this plant sprang from the soil, the offspring of his science, of his intellect, while I was but his earthly child. Approach it not!"

continued she, observing with terror that Giovanni was drawing nearer to the shrub. "It has qualities that you little dream of. But I, dearest Giovanni,—I grew up and blossomed with the plant, and was nourished with its breath. It was my sister, and I loved it with a human affection: for—alas! hast thou not suspected it? there was an awful doom."

Here Giovanni frowned so darkly upon her that Beatrice paused and trembled. But her faith in his tenderness reassured her, and made her blush that she had doubted for an instant.

"There was an awful doom," she continued,—"the effect of my father's fatal love of science—which estranged me from all society of my kind. Until Heaven sent thee, dearest Giovanni, Oh! how lonely was thy poor Beatrice!"

"Was it a hard doom?" asked Giovanni, fixing his eyes upon her.

"Only of late have I known how hard it was," answered she tenderly. "Oh, yes; but my heart was torpid, and therefore quiet."

Giovanni's rage broke forth from his sullen gloom like a lightning-flash out of a dark cloud.

"Accursed one!" cried he, with venomous scorn and anger. "And finding thy solitude wearisome, thou hast severed me, likewise, from all the warmth of life, and enticed me into thy region of unspeakable horror!"

"Giovanni!" exclaimed Beatrice, turning her large bright eyes upon his face. The force of his words had not found its way into her mind; she was merely thunder-struck.

"Yes, poisonous thing!" repeated Giovanni, beside himself with passion. "Thou hast done it! Thou hast blasted me! Thou hast filled my veins with poison! Thou hast made me as hateful, as ugly, as loathsome and deadly a creature as thyself,—a world's wonder of hideous monstrosity! Now—if our breath be happily as fatal to ourselves as to all others—let us join our lips in one kiss of unutterable hatred, and so die!"

"What has befallen me?" murmured Beatrice, with a low moan out of her heart. "Holy Virgin pity me, a poor heart-broken child!"

"Thou! Dost thou pray?" cried Giovanni, still with the same fiendish scorn. "Thy very prayers, as they come from thy lips, taint the atmosphere with death. Yes, yes; let us pray! Let us to church, and dip our fingers in the holy water at the portal! They that come after us will perish as by a pestilence. Let us sign crosses in the air! It will be scattering curses abroad in the likeness of holy symbols!"

"Giovanni," said Beatrice calmly, for her grief was beyond passion, "why dost thou join thyself with me thus in those terrible words? I, it is true, am the horrible thing thou namest me. But thou!—what hast thou to do, save with one other shudder at my hideous misery, to go forth out of the garden and mingle with thy race, and forget that there ever crawled on earth such a monster as poor Beatrice?"

"Dost thou pretend ignorance?" asked Giovanni, scowling upon her. "Behold! This power have I gained from the pure daughter of Rappaccini!"

There was a swarm of summer-insects flitting through the air, in search of the food promised by the flower-odors of the fatal garden. They circled round Giovanni's head, and were evidently attracted towards him by the same influence which had drawn them, for an instant, within the sphere of several of the shrubs. He sent forth a breath among them, and smiled bitterly at Beatrice, as at least a score of the insects fell dead upon the ground.

"I see it! I see it!" shrieked Beatrice. "It is my father's fatal science! No, no, Giovanni; it was not I! Never, never! I dreamed only to love thee, and be with thee a little time, and so to let thee pass away, leaving but thine image in mine heart. For, Giovanni—believe it—though my body be nourished with poison, my spirit is God's creature, and craves love as its daily food. But my father!—he has united us in this fearful sympathy. Yes; spurn me!—tread upon me!—kill me! Oh, what is death, after such words as thine? But it was not I! Not for a world of bliss would I have done it!"

Giovanni's passion had exhausted itself in its outburst from his lips. There now came across him a sense, mournful, and not without tenderness, of the intimate and peculiar relationship between Beatrice and himself. They stood, as it were, in an utter solitude, which would be made none the less solitary by the densest throng of human life. Ought not, then, the desert of humanity around them to press this insulated pair closer together? If they should be cruel to one another, who was there to be kind to them? Besides, thought Giovanni, might there not still be a hope of his returning within the limits of ordinary nature, and leading Beatrice—the redeemed Beatrice—by the hand? Oh, weak, and selfish, and unworthy spirit, that could dream of an earthly union and earthly happiness as possible, after such deep love had been so bitterly wronged as was Beatrice's love by Giovanni's blighting words! No, no; there could be no such hope. She must pass heavily, with that broken heart, across the borders of Time—she must bathe her hurts in some fount of Paradise, and forget her grief in the light of immortality—and *there* be well!

But Giovanni did not know it.

"Dear Beatrice," said he, approaching her, while she shrank away, as always at his approach, but now with a different impulse—"dearest Beatrice, our fate is not yet so desperate. Behold! There is a medicine, potent, as a wise physician has assured me, and almost divine in its efficacy. It is composed of ingredients the most opposite to those by which thy awful father has brought this calamity upon thee and me. It is distilled of blessed herbs. Shall we not quaff it together, and thus be purified from evil?"

"Give it me!" said Beatrice, extending her hand to receive the little silver phial which Giovanni took from his bosom. She added, with a peculiar emphasis: "I will drink—but do thou await the result."

She put Baglioni's antidote to her lips; and, at the same moment, the figure of Rappaccini emerged from the portal, and came slowly towards the marble fountain. As he drew near, the pale man of science seemed to gaze with a triumphant expression at the beautiful youth and maiden, as might an artist who should spend his life in achieving a picture or a group of statuary, and finally be satisfied with his success. He paused—his bent form grew erect with conscious power, he spread out his hands over them, in the attitude of a father imploring a blessing upon his children. But those were the same hands that had thrown poison into the stream of their lives! Giovanni trembled. Beatrice shuddered nervously, and pressed her hand upon her heart.

"My daughter," said Rappaccini, "thou art no longer lonely in the world! Pluck one of those precious gems from thy sister shrub, and bid thy bridegroom wear it in his bosom. It will not harm him now! My science, and the sympathy between thee and him, have so wrought within his system, that he now stands apart from common men, as thou dost, daughter of my pride and triumph, from ordinary women. Pass on, then, through the world, most dear to one another, and dreadful to all besides!"

"My father," said Beatrice, feebly—and still, as she spoke, she kept her hand upon her heart—"wherefore didst thou inflict this miserable doom upon thy child?"

"Miserable!" exclaimed Rappaccini. "What mean you, foolish girl? Dost thou deem it misery to be endowed with marvellous gifts, against which no power nor strength could avail an enemy? Misery, to be able to quell the mightiest with a breath? Misery, to be as terrible as thou art beautiful? Wouldst thou, then, have preferred the condition of a weak woman, exposed to all evil, and capable of none?"

"I would fain have been loved, not feared," murmured Beatrice, sinking down upon the ground.—"But now it matters not; I am going, father, where the evil, which thou hast striven to mingle with my being, will pass away like a dream—like the fragrance of these poisonous flowers, which will no longer taint my breath among the flowers of Eden. Farewell, Giovanni! Thy words of hatred are like lead within my heart—but they, too, will fall away as I ascend. Oh, was there not, from the first, more poison in thy nature than in mine?"

To Beatrice—so radically had her earthly part been wrought upon by Rappaccini's skill—as poison had been life, so the powerful antidote was death. And thus the poor victim of man's ingenuity and of thwarted nature, and of the fatality that attends all such efforts of perverted wisdom, perished there, at the feet of her father and Giovanni. Just at that moment, Professor Pietro Baglioni looked forth from the window, and called loudly, in a tone of triumph mixed with horror, to the thunder-stricken man of science:

"Rappaccini! Rappaccini! And is *this* the upshot of your experiment?"

1844

# NATHANIEL PARKER WILLIS

(1806–1867)

---

## *The Lunatic's Skate*

I HAVE ONLY, in my life, known one *lunatic*—properly so called. In the days when I carried a satchel on the banks of the Shawsheen, (a river whose half-lovely, half-wild scenery is tied like a silver thread about my heart,) Larry Wynn and myself were the farthest boarders from school, in a solitary farm-house on the edge of a lake of some miles square, called by the undignified title of Pomp's Pond. An old negro, who was believed by the boys to have come over with Christopher Columbus, was the only other human being within any thing like a neighbourhood of the lake, (it took its name from him,) and the only approaches to its waters, girded in as it was by an almost impenetrable forest, were the path through old Pomp's clearing, and that by our own door. Out of school, Larry and I were inseparable. He was a pale, sad-faced boy, and, in the first days of our intimacy, he had confided a secret to me which, from its uncommon nature, and the excessive caution with which he kept it from every one else, bound me to him with more than the common ties of schoolfellow attachment. We built wigwams together in the woods, had our tomahawks made of the same fashion, united our property in fox-traps, and played Indians with perfect contentment in each other's approbation.

I had found out, soon after my arrival at school, that Larry never slept on a moonlight night. With the first slender horn that dropped its silver and graceful shape behind the hills, his uneasiness commenced, and by the time its full and perfect orb poured a flood of radiance over vale and mountain, he was like one haunted by a pursuing demon. At early twilight he closed the shutters, stuffing every crevice that could admit a ray; and then, lighting as many candles as he could beg or steal from our thrifty landlord, he sat down with his book, in moody silence, or paced the room with an uneven step, and a solemn melancholy in his fine countenance, of which, with all my familiarity with him, I was almost afraid. Violent exercise seemed the only relief, and when the candles burnt low after midnight, and the stillness around the lone farm-house became too absolute to endure, he would throw up the window, and, leaping desperately out into the moonlight, rush up the hill into the depths of the wild forest, and walk on with supernatural excitement till the day dawned. Faint and pale he would then creep into his bed, and, begging me to make his very common and always credited excuse of illness, sleep soundly till I returned from school. I soon became used to his way, ceased to follow him, as I had once or twice endeavoured to do, into the forest, and never attempted to break in on the fixed and rapt silence which seemed to transform his lips to marble. And for all this Larry loved me.

Our preparatory studies were completed, and, to our mutual despair, we were destined to different universities. Larry's father was a disciple of the great Channing, and mine a Trinitarian of uncommon zeal; and the two institutions of Yale and Harvard were in the hands of most eminent men of either persuasion, and few are the minds that could resist a four years' ordeal in either. A student was as certain to come forth a Unitarian from one as a Calvinist from the other; and in the New-England States these two sects are bitterly hostile. So, to the glittering atmosphere of Channing and Everett went poor Larry, lonely and dispirited; and I was committed to the sincere zealots of Connecticut, some two hundred miles off, to learn Latin and Greek, if it pleased Heaven, but the mysteries of "election and free grace," whether or no.

Time crept, ambled, and galloped by turns, as we were *in* love or *out*, moping in term-time, or revelling in vacation, and gradually, I know not why, our correspondence had dropped, and the four years had come to their successive deaths, and we had never met. I grieved over it; for in those days I believed with a school-boy's fatuity,

> "That two, or one, are almost what they seem;"

and I loved Larry Wynn, as I hope I may never love man or woman again—with a pain at my heart. I wrote one or two reproachful letters in my senior years, but his answers were overstrained, and too full of protestations by half; and seeing that absence had done its usual work on him, I gave it up, and wrote an epitaph on a departed friendship. I do not know, by the way, why I am detaining you with all this, for it has nothing to do with my story; but let it pass as an evidence that it is a true one. The climax of things in real life has not the regular procession of incidents in a tragedy.

Some two or three years after we had taken "the irrevocable yoke" of life upon us, (not matrimony, but money-making,) a winter occurred of uncommonly fine sleighing—*sledging*, you call it in England. At such times the American world is all abroad, either for business or pleasure. The roads are passable at any rate of velocity of which a horse is capable; smooth as *montagnes Russes*, and hard as is good for hoofs; and a hundred miles is diminished to ten in facility of locomotion. The hunter brings down his venison to the cities, the western trader takes his family a hundred leagues to buy calicoes and tracts, and parties of all kinds scour the country, drinking mulled wine and "flip," and shaking the very nests out of the fir-trees with the ringing of their horses' bells. You would think death and sorrow were buried in the snow with the leaves of the last autumn.

I do not know why I undertook, at this time, a journey to the west; certainly not for scenery, for it was a world of waste, desolate, and dazzling whiteness, for a thousand unbroken miles. The trees were weighed down with snow, and the houses were thatched and half-buried in it, and the mountains and valleys were like the vast waves of an illimitable sea, congealed with its yesty foam in the wildest hour of a tempest. The eye lost its powers in gazing on it. The "spirit-bird" that spread his refreshing green wings before the pained eyes of Thalaba would have been an inestimable fellow-traveller. The worth of the eyesight lay in the purchase of a pair of green goggles.

In the course of a week or two, after skimming over the buried scenery of half a dozen states, each as large as Great Britain, (more or less,) I found myself in a small town on the border of one of our western lakes. It was some twenty years since the bears had found it thinly settled enough for their purposes, and now it contained perhaps twenty thousand souls. The oldest inhabitant, born in the town, was a youth in his minority. With the usual precocity of new settlements, it had already most of the peculiarities of an old metropolis. The burnt stumps still stood about among the houses, but there was a fashionable circle, at the head of which were the lawyer's wife and the member of Congress's daughter; and people ate their peas with silver forks, and drank their tea with scandal, and forgave men's *many* sins and refused to forgive woman's *one*, very much as in towns whose history is written in black letter. I dare say there were not more than one or two offences against the moral and Levitical law, fashionable on this side the water, which had not been committed, with the authentic aggravations, in the town of ——; I would mention the name if this were not a true story.

Larry Wynn (now Lawrence Wynn, Esq.) lived here. He had, as they say in the United States, "hung out a shingle" (*Londonicé*, put up a sign) as attorney at law, and to all the twenty thousand innocent inhabitants of the place, he was the oracle and the squire. He was besides colonel of militia, churchwarden, and canal commissioner; appointments which speak volumes for the prospects of "rising young men" in our flourishing republic.

Larry was glad to see me—very. I was more glad to see *him*. I have a soft heart, and forgive a wrong generally, if it touches neither my vanity nor my purse. I forgot his neglect, and called him "Larry." By the same token he did *not* call me "Phil." (There are very few that love me, patient reader; but those who do, thus abbreviate my pleasant name of Philip. I was called after the Indian Sachem of that name, whose blood runs in this tawny hand.) Larry looked upon me as a *man*. I looked on him, with all his dignities and changes, through the sweet vista of memory—as a *boy*. His mouth had acquired the pinched corners of caution and mistrust common to those who know their fellow men; but I never saw it unless when speculating as I am now. He was to me the pale-faced and melancholy friend of my boyhood; and I could have slept, as I used to do, with my arm around his neck, and feared to stir lest I should wake him. Had my last earthly hope lain in the palm of my hand, I could have given it to him, had he needed it, but to make him sleep; and yet he thought of me but as a stranger under his roof, and added, in his warmest moments, a "Mr." to my name! There is but one circumstance in my life that has wounded me more. Memory, avaunt!

Why should there be no unchangeableness in the world? why no friendship? or why am I, and you, gentle reader, (for by your continuing to pore over these idle musings, you have a heart too,) gifted with this useless and restless organ beating in our bosoms, if its thirst for love is never to be slaked, and its aching self-fulness never to find flow or utterance? I would positively sell my whole stock of affections for three farthings. Will you say "*two*?"

"You are come in good time," said Larry one morning, with a half-smile, "and shall be groomsman to me. I am going to be married."

"Married?"

"Married."

I repeated the word after him, for I was surprised. He had never opened his lips about his unhappy lunacy since my arrival, and I had felt hurt at this apparent unwillingness to renew our ancient confidence, but had felt a repugnance to any forcing of the topic upon him, and could only hope that he had outgrown or overcome it. I argued, immediately on this information of his intended marriage, that it must be so. No man in his senses, I thought, would link an impending madness to the fate of a confiding and lovely woman.

He took me into his sleigh, and we drove to her father's house. She was a flower in the wilderness. Of a delicate form, as all my countrywomen are, and lovely, as *quite* all certainly are not, large-eyed, soft in her manners, and yet less timid than confiding and sister-like, with a shade of melancholy in her smile, caught, perhaps, with the "trick of sadness" from himself, and a patrician slightness of reserve, or pride, which Nature sometimes, in very mockery of high birth, teaches her most secluded child,—the bride elect was, as I said before, a flower in the wilderness. She was one of those women we sigh to look upon as they pass by, as if there went a fragment of the wreck of some blessed dream.

The day arrived for the wedding, and the sleigh-bells jingled merrily into the village. The morning was as soft and genial as June, and the light snow on the surface of the lake melted, and lay on the breast of the solid ice beneath, giving it the effect of one white silver mirror, stretching to the edge of the horizon. It was exquisitely beautiful, and I was standing at the window in the afternoon, looking off upon the shining expanse, when Larry approached, and laid his hand familiarly on my shoulder.

"What glorious skating we shall have," said I, "if this smooth water freezes to-night!"

I turned the next moment to look at him; for we had not skated together since I went out, at his earnest entreaty, at midnight, to skim the little lake where we had passed our boyhood, and drive away the fever from his brain, under the light of a full moon.

He remembered it, and so did I; and I put my arm behind him, for the colour fled from his face, and I thought he would have sunk to the floor.

"The moon is full to-night," said he, recovering instantly to a cold self-possession.

I took hold of his hand firmly, and, in as kind a tone as I could summon, spoke of our early friendship, and apologizing thus for the freedom, asked if he had quite overcome his melancholy disease. His face worked with emotion, and he tried to withdraw his hand from my clasp, and evidently wished to avoid an answer.

"Tell me, dear Larry," said I.

"Oh God! *No!*" said he, breaking violently from me, and throwing himself with his face downwards upon the sofa. The tears streamed through his fingers upon the silken cushion.

"Not cured? And does *she* know it?"

"No! no! thank God! not yet!"

I remained silent a few minutes, listening to his suppressed moans, (for he seemed heart-broken with the confession,) and pitying while I inwardly condemned him. And then the picture of that lovely and fond woman rose up before me, and the impossibility of concealing his fearful malady from his wife, and the fixed insanity in which it must end, and the whole wreck of her hopes and his own prospects and happiness,—and my heart grew sick.

I sat down by him, and, as it was too late to remonstrate on the injustice he was committing toward her, I asked how he came to appoint the night of a full moon for his wedding. He gave up his reserve, calmed himself, and talked of it at last as if he were relieved by the communication. Never shall I forget the doomed pallor, the straining eye, and feverish hand of my poor friend during that half hour.

Since he had left college he had striven with the whole energy of his soul against it. He had plunged into business,—he had kept his bed resolutely night after night, till his brain seemed on the verge of frenzy with the effort,—he had taken opium to secure to himself an artificial sleep;—but he had never dared to confide it to any one, and he had no friend to sustain him in his fearful and lonely hours; and it grew upon him rather than diminished. He described to me with the most touching pathos how he had concealed it for years,—how he had stolen out like a thief to give vent to his insane restlessness in the silent streets of the city at midnight, and in the more silent solitudes of the forest,—how he had prayed, and wrestled, and wept over it,—and finally, how he had come to believe that there was no hope for him except in the assistance and constant presence of some one who would devote life to him in love and pity. Poor Larry! I put up a silent prayer in my heart that the desperate experiment might not end in agony and death.

The sun set, and, according to my prediction, the wind changed suddenly to the north, and the whole surface of the lake in a couple of hours became of the lustre of polished steel. It was intensely cold.

The fires blazed in every room of the bride's paternal mansion, and I was there early to fulfil my office of master of ceremonies at the bridal. My heart was weighed down with a sad boding, but I shook off at least the appearance of it, and superintended the concoction of a huge bowl of punch with a merriment which communicated itself in the shape of most joyous hilarity to a troop of juvenile relations. The house resounded with their shouts of laughter.

In the midst of our noise in the small inner room entered Larry. I started back, for he looked more like a demon possessed than a Christian man. He had walked to the house alone in the moonlight, not daring to trust himself in company. I turned out the turbulent troop about me, and tried to dispel his gloom, for a face like his at that moment would have put to flight the rudest bridal party ever assembled on holy ground. He seized on the bowl of strong spirits which I had mixed for a set of hardy farmers, and before I could tear it from his lips had drunk a quantity which, in an ordinary mood, would have intoxicated him helplessly in an hour. He then sat down with his face buried in his hands, and in a few minutes rose, his eyes sparkling with excitement, and the whole character of his face utterly changed. I thought he had gone wild.

"Now, Phil," said he; "now for my bride!" And with an unbecoming levity he threw open the door, and went half dancing into the room where the friends were already assembled to witness the ceremony.

I followed with fear and anxiety. He took his place by the side of the fair creature on whom he had placed his hopes of life, and, though sobered somewhat by the impressiveness of the scene, the wild sparkle still danced in his eyes, and I could see that every nerve in his frame was excited to the last pitch of tension. If he had fallen a gibbering maniac on the floor, I should not have been astonished.

The ceremony proceeded, and the first tone of his voice in the response startled even the bride. If it had rung from the depths of a cavern, it could not have been more sepulchral. I looked at him with a shudder. His lips were curled with an exulting expression, mixed with an indefinable fear; and all the blood in his face seemed settled about his eyes, which were so bloodshot and fiery, that I have ever since wondered he was not, at the first glance, suspected of insanity. But oh! the heavenly sweetness with which that loveliest of creatures promised to love and cherish him, in sickness and in health! I never go to a bridal but it half breaks my heart; and as the soft voice of that beautiful girl fell with its eloquent meaning on my ear, and I looked at her, with lips calm and eyes moistened, vowing a love which I knew to be stronger than death, to one who, I feared, was to bring only pain and sorrow into her bosom, my eyes warmed with irrepressible tears, and I wept.

The stir in the room as the clergyman closed his prayer seemed to awake him from a trance. He looked around with a troubled face for a moment; and then, fixing his eyes on his bride, he suddenly clasped his arms about her, and straining her violently to his bosom, broke into an hysterical passion of tears and laughter. Then suddenly resuming his self-command, he apologized for the over-excitement of his feelings, and behaved with forced and gentle propriety till the guests departed.

There was an apprehensive gloom over the spirits of the small bridal party left in the lighted rooms; and, as they gathered round the fire, I approached, and endeavoured to take a gay farewell. Larry was sitting with his arm about his wife, and he wrung my hand in silence as I said, "Good night," and dropped his head upon her shoulder. I made some futile attempt to rally him, but it jarred on the general feeling, and I left the house.

It was a glorious night. The clear piercing air had a vitreous brilliancy, which I have never seen in any other climate, the rays of the moonlight almost visibly splintering with the keenness of the frost. The moon herself was in the zenith, and there seemed nothing between her and the earth but palpable and glittering cold.

I hurried home: it was but eleven o'clock; and, heaping up the wood in the large fire-place, I took a volume of "Ivanhoe," which had just then appeared, and endeavoured to rid myself of my unpleasant thoughts. I read on till midnight; and then, in a pause of the story, I rose to look out upon the night, hoping, for poor Larry's sake, that the moon was buried in clouds. The house was near the edge of the lake: and as I looked down upon the glassy waste, spreading away from the land, I saw the dark figure of a man kneeling directly in the path of the moon's rays. In another moment he rose to his feet, and the tall, slight form of my poor friend was distinctly visible, as, with long and powerful strokes, he sped away upon his skates along the shore.

To take my own Hollanders, put a collar of fur around my mouth, and hurry after him, was the work of but a minute. My straps were soon fastened; and, following in the marks of the sharp irons at the top of my speed, I gained sight of him in about half an hour, and with great effort neared him sufficiently to shout his name with a hope of being heard.

"Larry! Larry!"

The lofty mountain-shore gave back the cry in repeated echoes; but he redoubled his strokes, and sped on faster than before. At my utmost speed I followed on; and when, at last, I could almost lay my hand on his shoulder, I summoned my strength to my breathless lungs, and shouted again—"Larry! Larry!"

He half looked back, and the full moon at that instant streamed full into his eyes. I have thought since that he could not have seen me for its dazzling brightness; but I saw every line of *his* features with the distinctness of daylight, and I shall never forget them. A line of white foam ran through his half-parted lips; his hair streamed wildly over his forehead, on which the perspiration glittered in large drops; and every lineament of his expressive face was stamped with unutterable and awful horror. He looked back no more; but, increasing his speed with an energy of which I did not think his slender frame capable, he began gradually to outstrip me. Trees, rocks, and hills fled back like magic. My limbs began to grow numb; my fingers had lost all feeling, but a strong north-east wind was behind us, and the ice smoother than a mirror; and I struck out my feet mechanically, and still sped on.

For two hours we had kept along the shore. The branches of the trees were reflected in the polished ice, and the hills seemed hanging in the air, and floating past us with the velocity of storm-clouds. Far down the lake, however, there glimmered the just visible light of a fire, and I was thanking God that we were probably approaching some human succour, when, to my horror, the retreating figure before me suddenly darted off to the left, and made swifter than before toward the centre of the icy waste. Oh, God! what feelings were mine at that moment. Follow him far I dared not; for, the sight of land once lost, as it would be almost instantly with our tremendous speed, we perished, without a possibility of relief.

He was far beyond my voice, and to overtake him was the only hope. I summoned my last nerve for the effort, and, keeping him in my eye, struck across at a sharper angle, with the advantage of the wind full in my back. I had taken note of the mountains, and knew that we were already forty miles from home, a distance it would be impossible to retrace against the wind; and the thought of freezing to death, even if I could overtake him, forced itself appallingly upon me.

Away I flew, despair giving new force to my limbs, and soon gained on the poor lunatic, whose efforts seemed flagging and faint. I neared him. Another struggle! I could have dropped down where I was, and slept, if there were death in the first minute, so stiff and drowsy was every muscle in my frame.

"Larry!" I shouted. "Larry!"

He started at the sound, and I could hear a smothered and breathless shriek, as, with supernatural strength, he straightened up his bending figure, and, leaning forward again, sped away from me like a phantom on the blast.

I could follow no longer. I stood stiff on my skates, still going on rapidly before the wind, and tried to look after him, but the frost had stiffened my eyes, and there was a mist before them, and they felt like glass. Nothing was visible around me but moonlight and ice, and dimly and slowly I began to retrace the slight path of semicircles toward the shore. It was painful work. The wind seemed to divide the very fibres of the skin upon my face. Violent exercise no longer warmed my body, and I felt the cold shoot sharply into my loins, and bind across my breast like a chain of ice; and, with the utmost strength of mind at my command, I could just resist the terrible inclination to lie down and sleep. I forgot poor Larry. Life—dear life!—was now my only thought! So selfish are we in our extremity!

With difficulty I at last reached the shore, and then, unbuttoning my coat, and spreading it wide for a sail, I set my feet together, and went slowly down before the wind, till the fire which I had before noticed began to blaze cheerily in the distance. It seemed an eternity in my slow progress. Tree after tree threw the shadow of its naked branches across the way; hill after hill glided slowly backward; but my knees seemed frozen together, and my joints fixed in ice; and if my life had depended on striking out my feet, I should have died powerless. My jaws were locked, my shoulders drawn half down to my knees, and in a few minutes more, I am well convinced, the blood would have thickened in my veins, and stood still, for ever.

I could see the tongues of the flames—I counted the burning faggots—a form passed between me and the fire—I struck, and fell prostrate on the snow; and I remember no more.

The sun was darting a slant beam through the trees when I awoke. The genial warmth of a large bed of embers played on my cheek, a thick blanket enveloped me, and beneath my head was a soft cushion of withered leaves. On the opposite side of the fire lay four Indians wrapped in their blankets, and, with her head on her knees, and her hands clasped over her ankles, sat an Indian woman, who had apparently fallen asleep upon her watch. The stir I made aroused her, and, as she piled on fresh faggots, and kindled them to a bright blaze with a handful of leaves, drowsiness came over me again, and I wrapped the blanket about me more closely, and shut my eyes to sleep.

I awoke refreshed. It must have been ten o'clock by the sun. The Indians were about, occupied in various avocations, and the woman was broiling a slice of deer's flesh on the coals. She offered it to me as I rose; and having eaten part of it with a piece of a cake made of meal, I requested her to call in the men, and with offers of reward, easily induced them to go with me in search of my lost friend.

We found him, as I had anticipated, frozen to death, far out on the lake. The Indians tracked him by the marks of his skate-irons, and from their appearance he had sunk quietly down, probably drowsy and exhausted, and had died of course without pain. His last act seemed to have been under the influence of his strange madness, for he lay on his face, turned from the quarter of the setting moon.

We carried him home to his bride. Even the Indians were affected by her uncontrollable agony. I cannot describe that scene, familiar as I am with pictures of horror.

I made inquiries with respect to the position of his bridal chamber. There were no shutters, and the moon streamed broadly into it, and after kissing his shrinking bride with the violence of a madman, he sprang out of the room with a terrific scream, and she saw him no more till he lay dead on his bridal bed.

1834

# EDGAR ALLAN POE

(1809–1849)

---

## *Ligeia*

> And the will therein lieth, which dieth not. Who knoweth the mysteries of the will, with its vigor? For God is but a great will pervading all things by nature of its intentness. Man doth not yield himself to the angels, nor unto death utterly, save only through the weakness of his feeble will.
>
> *Joseph Glanvill*

I CANNOT, for my soul, remember how, when, or even precisely where, I first became acquainted with the lady Ligeia. Long years have since elapsed, and my memory is feeble through much suffering. Or, perhaps, I cannot *now* bring these points to mind, because, in truth, the character of my beloved, her rare learning, her singular yet placid cast of beauty, and the thrilling and enthralling eloquence of her low musical language, made their way into my heart by paces so steadily and stealthily progressive that they have been unnoticed and unknown. Yet I believe that I met her first and most frequently in some large, old, decaying city near the Rhine. Of her family—I have surely heard her speak. That it is of a remotely ancient date cannot be doubted. Ligeia! Ligeia! Buried in studies of a nature more than all else adapted to deaden impressions of the outward world, it is by that sweet word alone—by Ligeia—that I bring before mine eyes in fancy the image of her who is no more. And now, while I write, a recollection flashes upon me that I have *never known* the paternal name of her who was my friend and my betrothed, and who became the partner of my studies, and finally the wife of my bosom. Was it a playful charge on the part of my Ligeia? or was it a test of my strength of affection, that I should institute no inquiries upon this point? or was it rather a caprice of my own—a wildly romantic offering on the shrine of the most passionate devotion? I but indistinctly recall the fact itself—what wonder that I have utterly forgotten the circumstances which originated or attended it? And, indeed, if ever that spirit which is entitled *Romance*—if ever she, the wan and the misty-winged *Ashtophet* of idolatrous Egypt, presided, as they tell, over marriages ill-omened, then most surely she presided over mine.

There is one dear topic, however, on which my memory fails me not. It is the *person* of Ligeia. In stature she was tall, somewhat slender, and, in her latter days, even emaciated. I would in vain attempt to portray the majesty, the quiet ease, of her demeanor, or the incomprehensible lightness and elasticity of her footfall. She came and departed as a shadow. I was never made aware of her entrance into my closed study save by the dear music of her low sweet voice, as she placed her marble hand upon my shoulder. In beauty of face no maiden ever equalled her. It was the radiance of an opium dream—an airy and spirit-lifting vision more wildly divine than the phantasies which hovered about the slumbering souls of the daughters of Delos. Yet her features were not of that regular mould which we have been falsely taught to worship in the classical labors of the heathen. "There is no exquisite beauty," says Bacon, Lord Verulam, speaking truly of all the forms and *genera* of beauty, "without some *strangeness* in the proportion." Yet, although I saw that the features of Ligeia were not of a classic regularity—although I perceived that her loveliness was indeed "exquisite," and felt that there was much of "strangeness" pervading it, yet I have tried in vain to detect the irregularity and to trace home my own perception of "the strange." I examined the contour of the lofty and pale forehead—it was faultless—how cold indeed that word when applied to a majesty so divine!—the skin rivalling the purest ivory, the commanding extent and repose, the gentle prominence of the regions above the temples; and then the raven-black, the glossy, the luxuriant and naturally-curling tresses, setting forth the full force of the Homeric epithet, "hyacinthine!" I looked at the delicate outlines of the nose—and nowhere but in the graceful medallions of the Hebrews had I beheld a similar perfection. There were the same luxurious smoothness of surface, the same scarcely perceptible tendency to the aquiline, the same harmoniously curved nostrils speaking the free spirit. I regarded the sweet mouth. Here was indeed the triumph of all things heavenly—the magnificent turn of the short upper lip—the soft, voluptuous slumber of the under—the dimples which sported, and the color which spoke—the teeth glancing back, with a brilliancy almost startling, every ray of the holy light which fell upon them in her serene and placid, yet most exultingly radiant of all smiles. I scrutinized the formation of the chin—and here, too, I found the gentleness of breadth, the softness and the majesty, the fullness and the spirituality, of the Greek—the contour which the God Apollo revealed but in a dream, to Cleomenes, the son of the Athenian. And then I peered into the large eyes of Ligeia.

For eyes we have no models in the remotely antique. It might have been, too, that in these eyes of my beloved lay the secret to which Lord Verulam alludes. They were, I must believe, far larger than the ordinary eyes of our own race. They were even fuller than the fullest of the gazelle eyes of the tribe of the valley of Nourjahad. Yet it was only at intervals—in moments of intense excitement—that this peculiarity became more than slightly noticeable in Ligeia. And at such moments was her beauty—in my heated fancy thus it appeared perhaps—the beauty of beings either above or apart from the earth—the beauty of the fabulous Houri of the Turk. The hue of the orbs was the most brilliant of black, and, far over them, hung jetty lashes of great length. The brows, slightly irregular in outline, had the same tint. The "strangeness," however, which I found in the eyes, was of a nature distinct from the formation, or the color, or the brilliancy of the features, and must, after all, be referred to the *expression*. Ah, word of no meaning! behind whose vast latitude of mere sound we intrench our ignorance of so much of the spiritual. The expression of the eyes of Ligeia! How for long hours have I pondered upon it! How have I, through the whole of a midsummer night, struggled to fathom it! What was it—that something more profound than the well of Democritus—which lay far within the pupils of my beloved? What *was* it? I was possessed with a passion to discover. Those eyes! those large, those shining, those divine orbs! they became to me twin stars of Leda, and I to them devoutest of astrologers.

There is no point, among the many incomprehensible anomalies of the science of mind, more thrillingly exciting than the fact—never, I believe, noticed in the schools—that, in our endeavors to recall to memory something long forgotten, we often find ourselves *upon the very verge* of remembrance, without being able, in the end, to remember. And thus how frequently, in my intense scrutiny of Ligeia's eyes, have I felt approaching the full knowledge of their expression—felt it approaching—yet not quite be mine—and so at length entirely depart! And (strange, oh strangest mystery of all!) I found, in the commonest objects of the universe, a circle of analogies to that expression. I mean to say that, subsequently to the period when Ligeia's beauty passed into my spirit, there dwelling as in a shrine, I derived, from many existences in the material world, a sentiment such as I felt always aroused within me by her large and luminous orbs. Yet not the more could I define that sentiment, or analyze, or even steadily view it. I recognized it, let me repeat, sometimes in the survey of a rapidly-growing vine—in the contemplation of a moth, a butterfly, a chrysalis, a stream of running water. I have felt it in the ocean; in the falling of a meteor. I have felt it in the glances of unusually aged people. And there are one or two stars in heaven—(one especially, a star of the sixth magnitude, double and changeable, to be found near the large star in Lyra) in a telescopic scrutiny of which I have been made aware of the feeling. I have been filled with it by certain sounds from stringed instruments, and not unfrequently by passages from books. Among innumerable other instances, I well remember something in a volume of Joseph Glanvill, which (perhaps merely from its quaintness—who shall say?) never failed to inspire me with the sentiment;—"And the will therein lieth, which dieth not. Who knoweth the mysteries of the will, with its vigor? For God is but a great will pervading all things by nature of its intentness. Man doth not yield him to the angels, nor unto death utterly, save only through the weakness of his feeble will."

Length of years, and subsequent reflection, have enabled me to trace, indeed, some remote connection between this passage in the English moralist and a portion of the character of Ligeia. An *intensity* in thought, action, or speech, was possibly, in her, a result, or at least an index, of that gigantic volition which, during our long intercourse, failed to give other and more immediate evidence of its existence. Of all the women whom I have ever known, she, the outwardly calm, the ever-placid Ligeia, was the most violently a prey to the tumultuous vultures of stern passion. And of such passion I could form no estimate, save by the miraculous expansion of those eyes which at once so delighted and appalled me—by the almost magical melody, modulation, distinctness and placidity of her very low voice—and by the fierce energy (rendered doubly effective by contrast with her manner of utterance) of the wild words which she habitually uttered.

I have spoken of the learning of Ligeia: it was immense—such as I have never known in woman. In the classical tongues was she deeply proficient, and as far as my own acquaintance extended in regard to the modern dialects of Europe, I have never known her at fault. Indeed upon any theme of the most admired, because simply the most abstruse of the boasted erudition of the academy, have I *ever* found Ligeia at fault? How singularly—how thrillingly, this one point in the nature of my wife has forced itself, at this late period only, upon my attention! I said her knowledge was such as I have never known in woman—but where breathes the man who has traversed, and successfully, *all* the wide areas of moral, physical, and mathematical science? I saw not then what I now clearly perceive, that the acquisitions of Ligeia were gigantic, were astounding; yet I was sufficiently aware of her infinite supremacy to resign myself, with a child-like confidence, to her guidance through the chaotic world of metaphysical investigation at which I was most busily occupied during the earlier years of our marriage. With how vast a triumph—with how vivid a delight—with how much of all that is ethereal in hope—did I *feel,* as she bent over me in studies but little sought—but less known—that delicious vista by slow degrees expanding before me, down whose long, gorgeous, and all untrodden path, I might at length pass onward to the goal of a wisdom too divinely precious not to be forbidden!

How poignant, then, must have been the grief with which, after some years, I beheld my well-grounded expectations take wings to themselves and fly away! Without Ligeia I was but as a child groping benighted. Her presence, her readings alone, rendered vividly luminous the many mysteries of the transcendentalism in which we were immersed. Wanting the radiant lustre of her eyes, letters, lambent and golden, grew duller than

Saturnian lead. And now those eyes shone less and less frequently upon the pages over which I pored. Ligeia grew ill. The wild eyes blazed with a too—too glorious effulgence; the pale fingers became of the transparent waxen hue of the grave, and the blue veins upon the lofty forehead swelled and sank impetuously with the tides of the most gentle emotion. I saw that she must die—and I struggled desperately in spirit with the grim Azrael. And the struggles of the passionate wife were, to my astonishment, even more energetic than my own. There had been much in her stern nature to impress me with the belief that, to her, death would have come without its terrors;—but not so. Words are impotent to convey any just idea of the fierceness of resistance with which she wrestled with the Shadow. I groaned in anguish at the pitiable spectacle. I would have soothed—I would have reasoned; but, in the intensity of her wild desire for life,—for life—*but* for life—solace and reason were alike the uttermost of folly. Yet not until the last instance, amid the most convulsive writhings of her fierce spirit, was shaken the external placidity of her demeanor. Her voice grew more gentle—grew more low—yet I would not wish to dwell upon the wild meaning of the quietly uttered words. My brain reeled as I hearkened, entranced, to a melody more than mortal—to assumptions and aspirations which mortality had never before known.

That she loved me I should not have doubted; and I might have been easily aware that, in a bosom such as hers, love would have reigned no ordinary passion. But in death only, was I fully impressed with the strength of her affection. For long hours, detaining my hand, would she pour out before me the overflowing of a heart whose more than passionate devotion amounted to idolatry. How had I deserved to be so blessed by such confessions?—how had I deserved to be so cursed with the removal of my beloved in the hour of her making them? But upon this subject I cannot bear to dilate. Let me say only, that in Ligeia's more than womanly abandonment to a love, alas! all unmerited, all unworthily bestowed, I at length recognized the principle of her longing with so wildly earnest a desire for the life which was now fleeing so rapidly away. It is this wild longing—it is this eager vehemence of desire for life—*but* for life—that I have no power to portray—no utterance capable of expressing.

At high noon of the night in which she departed, beckoning me, peremptorily, to her side, she bade me repeat certain verses composed by herself not many days before. I obeyed her.—They were these:

Lo! 'tis a gala night
  Within the lonesome latter years!
An angel throng, bewinged, bedight
  In veils, and drowned in tears,
Sit in a theatre, to see
  A play of hopes and fears,
While the orchestra breathes fitfully
  The music of the spheres.

Mimes, in the form of God on high,
  Mutter and mumble low,
And hither and thither fly—
  Mere puppets they, who come and go
At bidding of vast formless things
  That shift the scenery to and fro,
Flapping from out their Condor wings
  Invisible Wo!

That motley drama!—oh, be sure
  It shall not be forgot!
With its Phantom chased forevermore,
  By a crowd that seize it not,
Through a circle that ever returneth in
  To the self-same spot,
And much of Madness and more of Sin,
  And Horror the soul of the plot.

But see, amid the mimic rout,
  A crawling shape intrude!
A blood-red thing that writhes from out
  The scenic solitude!
It writhes!—it writhes!—with mortal pangs
  The mimes become its food,
And the seraphs sob at vermin fangs
  In human gore imbued.

Out—out are the lights—out all!
  And over each quivering form,
The curtain, a funeral pall,
  Comes down with the rush of a storm,
And the angels, all pallid and wan,
  Uprising, unveiling, affirm
That the play is the tragedy, "Man,"
  And its hero the Conqueror Worm.

"O God!" half shrieked Ligeia, leaping to her feet and extending her arms aloft with a spasmodic movement, as I made an end of these lines—"O God! O Divine Father!—shall these things be undeviatingly so?—shall this Conqueror be not once conquered? Are we not part and parcel in Thee? Who—who knoweth the mysteries of the will with its vigor? Man doth not yield him to the angels, *nor unto death utterly*, save only through the weakness of his feeble will."

And now, as if exhausted with emotion, she suffered her white arms to fall, and returned solemnly to her bed of Death. And as she breathed her last sighs, there came mingled with them a low murmur from her lips. I bent to them my ear and distinguished, again, the concluding words of the passage in Glanvill—"*Man doth not yield him to the angels, nor unto death utterly, save only through the weakness of his feeble will.*"

She died;—and I, crushed into the very dust with sorrow, could no longer endure the lonely desolation of my dwelling in the dim and decaying city by the Rhine. I had no lack of what the world calls wealth. Ligeia had brought me far more, very far more than ordinarily falls to the lot of mortals. After a few months, therefore, of weary and aimless wandering, I purchased, and put in some repair, an abbey, which I shall not name, in one of the wildest and least frequented portions of fair England. The gloomy and dreary grandeur of the building, the almost savage aspect of the domain, the many melancholy and time-honored memories connected with both, had much in unison with the feelings of utter abandonment which had driven me into that remote and unsocial region of the country. Yet although the external abbey, with its verdant decay hanging about it, suffered but little alteration, I gave way, with a child-like perversity, and perchance with a faint hope of alleviating my sorrows, to a display of more than regal magnificence within. For such follies, even in childhood, I had imbibed a taste, and now they came back to me as if in the dotage of grief. Alas, I feel how much even of incipient madness might have been discovered in the gorgeous and fantastic draperies, in the solemn carvings of Egypt, in the wild cornices and furniture, in the Bedlam patterns of the carpets of tufted gold! I had become a bounden slave in the trammels of opium, and my labors and my orders had taken a coloring from my dreams. But these absurdities I must not pause to detail. Let me speak only of that one chamber, ever accursed, whither in a moment of mental alienation, I led from the altar as my bride—as the successor of the unforgotten Ligeia—the fair-haired and blue-eyed Lady Rowena Trevanion, of Tremaine.

There is no individual portion of the architecture and decoration of that bridal chamber which is not now visibly before me. Where were the souls of the haughty family of the bride, when, through thirst of gold, they permitted to pass the threshold of an apartment *so* bedecked, a maiden and a daughter so beloved? I have said that I minutely remember the details of the chamber—yet I am sadly forgetful on topics of deep moment—and here there was no system, no keeping, in the fantastic display, to take hold upon the memory. The room lay in a high turret of the castellated abbey, was pentagonal in shape, and of capacious size. Occupying the whole southern face of the pentagon was the sole window—an immense sheet of unbroken glass from Venice—a single pane, and tinted of a leaden hue, so that the rays of either the sun or moon, passing through it, fell with a ghastly lustre on the objects within. Over the upper portion of this huge window, extended the trellice-work of an aged vine, which clambered up the massy walls of the turret. The ceiling, of gloomy-looking oak, was excessively lofty, vaulted, and elaborately fretted with the wildest and most grotesque specimens of a semi-Gothic, semi-Druidical device. From out the most central recess of this melancholy vaulting, depended, by a single chain of gold with long links, a huge censer of the same metal, Saracenic in pattern, and with many perforations so contrived that there writhed in and out of them, as if endued with a serpent vitality, a continual succession of particolored fires.

Some few ottomans and golden candelabra, of Eastern figure, were in various stations about—and there was the couch, too—the bridal couch—of an Indian model, and low, and sculptured of solid ebony, with a pall-like canopy above. In each of the angles of the chamber stood on end a gigantic sarcophagus of black granite, from the tombs of the kings over against Luxor, with their aged lids full of immemorial sculpture. But in the draping of the apartment lay, alas! the chief phantasy of all. The lofty walls, gigantic in height—even unproportionably so—were hung from summit to foot, in vast folds, with a heavy and massive-looking tapestry—tapestry of a material which was found alike as a carpet on the floor, as a covering for the ottomans and the ebony bed, as a canopy for the bed, and as the gorgeous volutes of the curtains which partially shaded the window. The material was the richest cloth of gold. It was spotted all over, at irregular intervals, with arabesque figures, about a foot in diameter, and wrought upon the cloth in patterns of the most jetty black. But these figures partook of the true character of the arabesque only when regarded from a single point of view. By a contrivance now common, and indeed traceable to a very remote period of antiquity, they were made changeable in aspect. To one entering the room, they bore the appearance of simple monstrosities; but upon a farther advance, this appearance gradually departed; and step by step, as the visiter moved his station in the chamber, he saw himself surrounded by an endless succession of the ghastly forms which belong to the superstition of the Norman, or arise in the guilty slumbers of the monk. The phantasmagoric effect was vastly heightened by the artificial introduction of a strong continual current of wind behind the draperies—giving a hideous and uneasy animation to the whole.

In halls such as these—in a bridal chamber such as this—I passed, with the Lady of Tremaine, the unhallowed hours of the first month of our marriage—passed them with but little disquietude. That my wife dreaded the fierce moodiness of my temper—that she shunned me and loved me but little—I could not help perceiving; but it gave me rather pleasure than otherwise. I loathed her with a hatred belonging more to demon than to man. My memory flew back, (oh, with what intensity of regret!) to Ligeia, the beloved, the august, the beautiful, the entombed. I revelled in recollections of her purity, of her wisdom, of her lofty, her ethereal nature, of her passionate, her idolatrous love. Now, then, did my spirit fully and freely burn with more than all the fires of her own. In the excitement of my opium dreams (for I was habitually fettered in the shackles of the drug) I would call aloud upon her name, during the silence of the night, or among the sheltered recesses of the glens by day, as if, through the wild eagerness, the solemn passion, the consuming ardor of my longing for the departed, I could restore her to the pathway she had abandoned—ah, *could* it be forever?—upon the earth.

About the commencement of the second month of the marriage, the Lady Rowena was attacked with sudden illness, from which her recovery was slow. The fever which consumed her rendered her nights uneasy; and in her perturbed state of half-slumber, she spoke of sounds, and of motions, in and about the chamber of the turret, which I concluded had no origin save in the distemper of her fancy, or perhaps in the phantasmagoric influences of the chamber itself. She became at length convalescent—finally well. Yet but a brief period elapsed, ere a second more violent disorder again threw her upon a bed of suffering; and from this attack her frame, at all times feeble, never altogether recovered. Her illnesses were, after this epoch, of alarming character, and of more alarming recurrence, defying alike the knowledge and the great exertions of her physicians. With the increase of the chronic disease which had thus, apparently, taken too sure hold upon her constitution to be eradicated by human means, I could not fail to observe a similar increase in the nervous irritation of her temperament, and in her excitability by trivial causes of fear. She spoke again, and now more frequently and pertinaciously, of the sounds—of the slight sounds—and of the unusual motions among the tapestries, to which she had formerly alluded.

One night, near the closing in of September, she pressed this distressing subject with more than usual emphasis upon my attention. She had just awakened from an unquiet slumber, and I had been watching, with feelings half of anxiety, half of a vague terror, the workings of her emaciated countenance. I sat by the side of her ebony bed, upon one of the ottomans of India. She partly arose, and spoke, in an earnest low whisper, of sounds which she *then* heard, but which I could not hear—of motions which she *then* saw, but which I could not perceive. The wind was rushing hurriedly behind the tapestries, and I wished to show her (what, let me confess it, I could not *all* believe) that those almost inarticulate breathings, and those very gentle variations of the figures upon the wall, were but the natural effects of that customary rushing of the wind. But a deadly pallor, over-spreading her face, had proved to me that my exertions to reassure her would be fruitless. She appeared to be fainting, and no attendants were within call. I remembered where was deposited a decanter of light wine which had been ordered by her physicians, and hastened across the chamber to procure it. But, as I stepped beneath the light of the censer, two circumstances of a startling nature attracted my attention. I had felt that some palpable although invisible object had passed lightly by my person; and I saw that there lay upon the golden carpet, in the very middle of the rich lustre thrown from the censer, a shadow—a faint, indefinite shadow of angelic aspect—such as might be fancied for the shadow of a shade. But I was wild with the excitement of an immoderate dose of opium, and heeded these things but little, nor spoke of them to Rowena. Having found the wine, I recrossed the chamber, and poured out a goblet-ful, which I held to the lips of the fainting lady. She had now partially recovered, however, and took the vessel herself, while I sank upon an ottoman near me, with my eyes fastened upon her person. It was then that I became distinctly aware of a gentle foot-fall upon the carpet, and near the couch; and in a second thereafter, as Rowena was in the act of raising the wine to her lips, I saw, or may have dreamed that I saw, fall within the goblet, as if from some invisible spring in the atmosphere of the room, three or four large drops of a brilliant and ruby colored fluid. If this I saw—not so Rowena. She swallowed the wine unhesitatingly, and I forbore to speak to her of a circumstance which must, after all, I considered, have been but the suggestion of a vivid imagination, rendered morbidly active by the terror of the lady, by the opium, and by the hour.

Yet I cannot conceal it from my own perception that, immediately subsequent to the fall of the ruby-drops, a rapid change for the worse took place in the disorder of my wife; so that, on the third subsequent night, the hands of her menials prepared her for the tomb, and on the fourth, I sat alone, with her shrouded body, in that fantastic chamber which had received her as my bride. Wild visions, opium-engendered, flitted, shadow-like, before me. I gazed with unquiet eye upon the sarcophagi in the angles of the room, upon the varying figures of the drapery, and upon the writhing of the parti-colored fires in the censer overhead. My eyes then fell, as I called to mind the circumstances of a former night, to the spot beneath the glare of the censer where I had seen the faint traces of the shadow. It was there, however, no longer; and breathing with greater freedom, I turned my glances to the pallid and rigid figure upon the bed. Then rushed upon me a thousand memories of Ligeia—and then came back upon my heart, with the turbulent violence of a flood, the whole of that unutterable wo with which I had regarded *her* thus enshrouded. The night waned; and still, with a bosom full of bitter thoughts of the one only and supremely beloved, I remained gazing upon the body of Rowena.

It might have been midnight, or perhaps earlier, or later, for I had taken no note of time, when a sob, low, gentle, but very distinct, startled me from my revery. I *felt* that it came from the bed of ebony—the bed of death. I listened in an agony of superstitious terror—but there was no repetition of the sound. I strained my vision to detect any motion in the corpse—but there was not the slightest perceptible. Yet I could not have been deceived. I *had* heard the noise, however faint, and my soul was awakened within me. I resolutely and perseveringly kept my attention riveted upon the body. Many minutes elapsed before any circumstance occurred tending to throw light upon the mystery. At length it became evident that a slight, a very feeble, and barely noticeable tinge of color had flushed up within the cheeks, and along the sunken small veins of the eyelids. Through a species of unutterable horror and awe, for which the language of mortality has no sufficiently energetic expression, I felt my heart cease to beat, my limbs grow rigid where I sat. Yet a sense of duty finally operated to restore my self-possession. I could no longer doubt that we had been precipitate in our preparations—that Rowena still lived. It was necessary that some immediate exertion be made; yet the turret was altogether apart from the portion of the abbey tenanted by the servants—there were none within call—I had no means of summoning them to my aid without leaving the room for many minutes—and this I could not venture to do. I therefore struggled alone in my endeavors to call back the spirit still hovering. In a short period it was certain, however, that a relapse had taken place; the color disappeared from both eyelid and cheek, leaving a wanness even more than that of marble; the lips became doubly shrivelled and pinched up in the ghastly expression of death; a repulsive clamminess and coldness overspread rapidly the surface of the body; and all the usual rigorous stiffness immediately supervened. I fell back with a shudder upon the couch from which I had been so startlingly aroused, and again gave myself up to passionate waking visions of Ligeia.

An hour thus elapsed when (could it be possible?) I was a second time aware of some vague sound issuing from the region of the bed. I listened—in extremity of horror. The sound came again—it was a sigh. Rushing to the corpse, I saw—distinctly saw—a tremor upon the lips. In a minute afterward they relaxed, disclosing a bright line of the pearly teeth. Amazement now struggled in my bosom with the profound awe which had hitherto reigned there alone. I felt that my vision grew dim, that my reason wandered; and it was only by a violent effort that I at length succeeded in nerving myself to the task which duty thus once more had pointed out. There was now a partial glow upon the forehead and upon the cheek and throat; a perceptible warmth pervaded the whole frame; there was even a slight pulsation at the heart. The lady *lived*; and with redoubled ardor I betook myself to the task of restoration. I chafed and bathed the temples and the hands, and used every exertion which experience, and no little medical reading, could suggest. But in vain. Suddenly, the color fled, the pulsation ceased, the lips resumed the expression of the dead, and, in an instant afterward, the whole body took upon itself the icy chilliness, the livid hue, the intense rigidity, the sunken outline, and all the loathsome peculiarities of that which has been, for many days, a tenant of the tomb.

And again I sunk into visions of Ligeia—and again, (what marvel that I shudder while I write?) *again* there reached my ears a low sob from the region of the ebony bed. But why shall I minutely detail the unspeakable horrors of that night? Why shall I pause to relate how, time after time, until near the period of the gray dawn, this hideous drama of revivification was repeated; how each terrific relapse was only into a sterner and apparently more irredeemable death; how each agony wore the aspect of a struggle with some invisible foe; and how each struggle was succeeded by I know not what of wild change in the personal appearance of the corpse? Let me hurry to a conclusion.

The greater part of the fearful night had worn away, and she who had been dead, once again stirred—and now more vigorously than hitherto, although arousing from a dissolution more appalling in its utter hopelessness than any. I had long ceased to struggle or to move, and remained sitting rigidly upon the ottoman, a helpless prey to a whirl of violent emotions, of which extreme awe was perhaps the least terrible, the least consuming. The corpse, I repeat, stirred, and now more vigorously than before. The hues of life flushed up with unwonted energy into the countenance—the limbs relaxed—and, save that the eyelids were yet pressed heavily together, and that the bandages and draperies of the grave still imparted their charnel character to the figure, I might have dreamed that Rowena had indeed shaken off, utterly, the fetters of Death. But if this idea was not, even then, altogether adopted, I could at least doubt no longer, when, arising from the bed, tottering, with feeble steps, with closed eyes, and with the manner of one bewildered in a dream, the thing that was enshrouded advanced bodily and palpably into the middle of the apartment.

I trembled not—I stirred not—for a crowd of unutterable fancies connected with the air, the stature, the demeanor of the figure, rushing hurriedly through my brain, had paralyzed—had chilled me into stone. I stirred not—but gazed upon the apparition. There was a mad disorder in my thoughts—a tumult unappeasable. Could it, indeed, be the *living* Rowena who confronted me? Could it indeed be Rowena *at all*—the fair-haired, the blue-eyed Lady Rowena Trevanion of Tremaine? Why, *why* should I doubt it? The bandage lay heavily about the mouth—but then might it not be the mouth of the breathing Lady of Tremaine? And the cheeks—there were the roses as in her noon of life—yes, these might indeed be the fair cheeks of the living Lady of Tremaine. And the chin, with its dimples, as in health, might it not be hers?—but *had she then grown taller since her malady*? What inexpressible madness seized me with that thought? One bound, and I had reached her feet! Shrinking from my touch, she let fall from her head the ghastly cerements which had confined it, and there streamed forth, into the rushing atmosphere of the chamber, huge masses of long and dishevelled hair; *it was blacker than the wings of the midnight*! And now slowly opened *the eyes* of the figure which stood before me. "Here then, at least," I shrieked aloud, "can I never—can I never be mistaken—these are the full, and the black, and the wild eyes—of my lost love—of the lady—of the LADY LIGEIA!"

1838

# EDGAR ALLAN POE

(1809–1849)

---

## *The Fall of the House of Usher*

Son cœur est un luth suspendu;
Sitôt qu'on le touche il résonne.
*De Béranger*

DURING THE whole of a dull, dark, and soundless day in the autumn of the year, when the clouds hung oppressively low in the heavens, I had been passing alone, on horseback, through a singularly dreary tract of country; and at length found myself, as the shades of the evening drew on, within view of the melancholy House of Usher. I know not how it was—but, with the first glimpse of the building, a sense of insufferable gloom pervaded my spirit. I say insufferable; for the feeling was unrelieved by any of that half-pleasurable, because poetic, sentiment, with which the mind usually receives even the sternest natural images of the desolate or terrible. I looked upon the scene before me—upon the mere house, and the simple landscape features of the domain—upon the bleak walls—upon the vacant eye-like windows—upon a few rank sedges—and upon a few white trunks of decayed trees—with an utter depression of soul which I can compare to no earthly sensation more properly than to the after-dream of the reveller upon opium—the bitter lapse into everyday life—the hideous dropping off of the veil. There was an iciness, a sinking, a sickening of the heart—an unredeemed dreariness of thought which no goading of the imagination could torture into aught of the sublime. What was it—I paused to think—what was it that so unnerved me in the contemplation of the House of Usher? It was a mystery all insoluble; nor could I grapple with the shadowy fancies that crowded upon me as I pondered. I was forced to fall back upon the unsatisfactory conclusion, that while, beyond doubt, there *are* combinations of very simple natural objects which have the power of thus affecting us, still the analysis of this power lies among considerations beyond our depth. It was possible,

I reflected, that a mere different arrangement of the particulars of the scene, of the details of the picture, would be sufficient to modify, or perhaps to annihilate its capacity for sorrowful impression; and, acting upon this idea, I reined my horse to the precipitous brink of a black and lurid tarn that lay in unruffled lustre by the dwelling, and gazed down—but with a shudder even more thrilling than before—upon the remodelled and inverted images of the gray sedge, and the ghastly tree-stems, and the vacant and eye-like windows.

Nevertheless, in this mansion of gloom I now proposed to myself a sojourn of some weeks. Its proprietor, Roderick Usher, had been one of my boon companions in boyhood; but many years had elapsed since our last meeting. A letter, however, had lately reached me in a distant part of the country—a letter from him—which, in its wildly importunate nature, had admitted of no other than a personal reply. The MS. gave evidence of nervous agitation. The writer spoke of acute bodily illness—of a mental disorder which oppressed him—and of an earnest desire to see me, as his best, and indeed his only personal friend, with a view of attempting, by the cheerfulness of my society, some alleviation of his malady. It was the manner in which all this, and much more, was said—it was the apparent *heart* that went with his request—which allowed me no room for hesitation; and I accordingly obeyed forthwith what I still considered a very singular summons.

Although, as boys, we had been even intimate associates, yet I really knew little of my friend. His reserve had been always excessive and habitual. I was aware, however, that his very ancient family had been noted, time out of mind, for a peculiar sensibility of temperament, displaying itself, through long ages, in many works of exalted art, and manifested, of late, in repeated deeds of munificent yet unobtrusive charity, as well as in a passionate devotion to the intricacies, perhaps even more than to the orthodox and easily recognisable beauties, of musical science. I had learned, too, the very remarkable fact, that the stem of the Usher race, all time-honored as it was, had put forth, at no period, any enduring branch; in other words, that the entire family lay in the direct line of descent, and had always, with very trifling and very temporary variation, so lain. It was this deficiency, I considered, while running over in thought the perfect keeping of the character of the premises with the accredited character of the people, and while speculating upon the possible influence which the one, in the long lapse of centuries, might have exercised upon the other—it was this deficiency, perhaps, of collateral issue, and the consequent undeviating transmission, from sire to son, of the patrimony with the name, which had, at length, so identified the two as to merge the original title of the estate in the quaint and equivocal appellation of the "House of Usher"—an appellation which seemed to include, in the minds of the peasantry who used it, both the family and the family mansion.

I have said that the sole effect of my somewhat childish experiment—that of looking down within the tarn—had been to deepen the first singular impression. There can be no doubt that the consciousness of the rapid increase of my superstition—for why should I not so term it?—served mainly to accelerate the increase itself. Such, I have long known, is the paradoxical law of all sentiments having terror as a basis. And it might have been for this reason only, that, when I again uplifted my eyes to the house itself, from its image in the pool, there grew in my mind a strange fancy—a fancy so ridiculous, indeed, that I but mention it to show the vivid force of the sensations which oppressed me. I had so worked upon my imagination as really to believe that about the whole mansion and domain there hung an atmosphere peculiar to themselves and their immediate vicinity—an atmosphere which had no affinity with the air of heaven, but which had reeked up from the decayed trees, and the gray wall, and the silent tarn—a pestilent and mystic vapor, dull, sluggish, faintly discernible, and leaden-hued.

Shaking off from my spirit what *must* have been a dream, I scanned more narrowly the real aspect of the building. Its principal feature seemed to be that of an excessive antiquity. The discoloration of ages had been great. Minute fungi overspread the whole exterior, hanging in a fine tangled web-work from the eaves. Yet all this was apart from any extraordinary dilapidation. No portion of the masonry had fallen; and there appeared to be a wild inconsistency between its still perfect adaptation of parts, and the crumbling condition of the individual stones. In this there was much that reminded me of the specious totality of old wood-work which has rotted for long years in some neglected vault, with no disturbance from the breath of the external air. Beyond this indication of extensive decay, however, the fabric gave little token of instability. Perhaps the eye of a scrutinizing observer might have discovered a barely perceptible fissure, which, extending from the roof of the building in front, made its way down the wall in a zigzag direction, until it became lost in the sullen waters of the tarn.

Noticing these things, I rode over a short causeway to the house. A servant in waiting took my horse, and I entered the Gothic archway of the hall. A valet, of stealthy step, thence conducted me, in silence, through many dark and intricate passages in my progress to the *studio* of his master. Much that I encountered on the way contributed, I know not how, to heighten the vague sentiments of which I have already spoken. While the objects around me—while the carvings of the ceilings, the sombre tapestries of the walls, the ebon blackness of the floors, and the phantasmagoric armorial trophies which rattled as I strode, were but matters to which, or to such as which, I had been accustomed from my infancy—while I hesitated not to acknowledge how familiar was all this—I still wondered to find how unfamiliar were the fancies which ordinary images were stirring up. On one of the staircases, I met the physician of the family. His countenance, I thought, wore a mingled expression of low cunning and perplexity. He accosted me with trepidation and passed on. The valet now threw open a door and ushered me into the presence of his master.

The room in which I found myself was very large and lofty. The windows were long, narrow, and pointed, and at so vast a distance from the black oaken floor as to be altogether inaccessible from within. Feeble gleams of encrimsoned light made their way through the trellissed panes, and served to render sufficiently distinct the more prominent objects around; the eye, however, struggled in vain to reach the remoter angles of the chamber, or the recesses of the vaulted and fretted ceiling. Dark draperies hung upon the walls. The general furniture was profuse, comfortless, antique, and tattered. Many books and musical instruments lay scattered about, but failed to give any vitality to the scene. I felt that I breathed an atmosphere of sorrow. An air of stern, deep, and irredeemable gloom hung over and pervaded all.

Upon my entrance, Usher arose from a sofa on which he had been lying at full length, and greeted me with a vivacious warmth which had much in it, I at first thought, of an overdone cordiality—of the constrained effort of the *ennuyé* man of the world. A glance, however, at his countenance, convinced me of his perfect sincerity. We sat down; and for some moments, while he spoke not, I gazed upon him with a feeling half of pity, half of awe. Surely, man had never before so terribly altered, in so brief a period, as had Roderick Usher! It was with difficulty that I could bring myself to admit the identity of the wan being before me with the companion of my early boyhood. Yet the character of his face had been at all times remarkable. A cadaverousness of complexion; an eye large, liquid, and luminous beyond comparison; lips somewhat thin and very pallid, but of a surpassingly beautiful curve; a nose of a delicate Hebrew model, but with a breadth of nostril unusual in similar formations; a finely moulded chin, speaking, in its want of prominence, of a want of moral energy; hair of a more than web-like softness and tenuity; these features, with an inordinate expansion above the regions of the temple, made up altogether a countenance not easily to be forgotten. And now in the mere exaggeration of the prevailing character of these features, and of the expression they were wont to convey, lay so much of change that I doubted to whom I spoke. The now ghastly pallor of the skin, and the now miraculous lustre of the eye, above all things startled and even awed me. The silken hair, too, had been suffered to grow all unheeded, and as, in its wild gossamer texture, it floated rather than fell about the face, I could not, even with effort, connect its Arabesque expression with any idea of simple humanity.

In the manner of my friend I was at once struck with an incoherence—an inconsistency; and I soon found this to arise from a series of feeble and futile struggles to overcome an habitual trepidancy—an excessive nervous agitation. For something of this nature I had indeed been prepared, no less by his letter, than by reminiscences of certain boyish traits, and by conclusions deduced from his peculiar physical conformation and temperament. His action was alternately vivacious and sullen. His voice varied rapidly from a tremulous indecision (when the animal spirits seemed utterly in abeyance) to that species of energetic concision—that abrupt, weighty, unhurried, and hollow-sounding enunciation—that leaden, self-balanced and perfectly modulated guttural utterance, which may be observed in the lost drunkard, or the irreclaimable eater of opium, during the periods of his most intense excitement.

It was thus that he spoke of the object of my visit, of his earnest desire to see me, and of the solace he expected me to afford him. He entered, at some length, into what he conceived to be the nature of his malady. It was, he said, a constitutional and a family evil, and one for which he despaired to find a remedy—a mere nervous affection, he immediately added, which would undoubtedly soon pass off. It displayed itself in a host of unnatural sensations. Some of these, as he detailed them, interested and bewildered me; although, perhaps, the terms, and the general manner of the narration had their weight. He suffered much from a morbid acuteness of the senses; the most insipid food was alone endurable; he could wear only garments of certain texture; the odors of all flowers were oppressive; his eyes were tortured by even a faint light; and there were but peculiar sounds, and these from stringed instruments, which did not inspire him with horror.

To an anomalous species of terror I found him a bounden slave. "I shall perish," said he, "I *must* perish in this deplorable folly. Thus, thus, and not otherwise, shall I be lost. I dread the events of the future, not in themselves, but in their results. I shudder at the thought of any, even the most trivial, incident, which may operate upon this intolerable agitation of soul. I have, indeed, no abhorrence of danger, except in its absolute effect—in terror. In this unnerved—in this pitiable condition—I feel that the period will sooner or later arrive when I must abandon life and reason together, in some struggle with the grim phantasm, FEAR."

I learned, moreover, at intervals, and through broken and equivocal hints, another singular feature of his mental condition. He was enchained by certain superstitious impressions in regard to the dwelling which he tenanted, and whence, for many years, he had never ventured forth—in regard to an influence whose supposititious force was conveyed in terms too shadowy here to be re-stated—an influence which some peculiarities in the mere form and substance of his family mansion, had, by dint of long sufferance, he said, obtained over his spirit—an effect which the *physique* of the gray walls and turrets, and of the dim tarn into which they all looked down, had, at length, brought about upon the *morale* of his existence.

He admitted, however, although with hesitation, that much of the peculiar gloom which thus afflicted him could be traced to a more natural and far more palpable origin—to the severe and long-continued illness—indeed to the evidently approaching dissolution—of a tenderly beloved sister—his sole companion for long years—his last and only relative on earth. "Her decease," he said, with a bitterness which I can never forget, "would leave him (him the hopeless and the frail) the last of the ancient race of the Ushers." While he spoke, the lady Madeline (for so was she called) passed slowly through a remote portion of the apartment, and, without having noticed my presence, disappeared. I regarded her with an utter astonishment not unmingled with dread—and yet I found it impossible to account for such feelings. A sensation of stupor oppressed me, as my eyes followed her retreating steps. When a door, at length, closed upon her, my glance sought instinctively and eagerly the countenance of the brother—but he had buried his face in his hands, and I could only perceive that a far more than ordinary wanness had overspread the emaciated fingers through which trickled many passionate tears.

The disease of the lady Madeline had long baffled the skill of her physicians. A settled apathy, a gradual wasting away of the person, and frequent although transient affections of a partially cataleptical character, were the unusual diagnosis. Hitherto she had steadily borne up against the pressure of her malady, and had not betaken herself finally to bed; but, on the closing in of the evening of my arrival at the house, she succumbed (as her brother told me at night with inexpressible agitation) to the prostrating power of the destroyer; and I learned that the glimpse I had obtained of her person would thus probably be the last I should obtain—that the lady, at least while living, would be seen by me no more.

For several days ensuing, her name was unmentioned by either Usher or myself: and during this period I was busied in earnest endeavors to alleviate the melancholy of my friend. We painted and read together; or I listened, as if in a dream, to the wild improvisations of his speaking guitar. And thus, as a closer and still closer intimacy admitted me more unreservedly into the recesses of his spirit, the more bitterly did I perceive the futility of all attempt at cheering a mind from which darkness, as if an inherent positive quality, poured forth upon all objects of the moral and physical universe, in one unceasing radiation of gloom.

I shall ever bear about me a memory of the many solemn hours I thus spent alone with the master of the House of Usher. Yet I should fail in any attempt to convey an idea of the exact character of the studies, or of the occupations, in which he involved me, or led me the way. An excited and highly distempered ideality threw a sulphureous lustre over all. His long improvised dirges will ring forever in my ears. Among other things, I hold painfully in mind a certain singular perversion and amplification of the wild air of the last waltz of Von Weber. From the paintings over which his elaborate fancy brooded, and which grew, touch by touch, into vaguenesses at which I shuddered the more thrillingly, because I shuddered knowing not why;—from these paintings (vivid as their images now are before me) I would in vain endeavor to educe more than a small portion which should lie within the compass of merely written words. By the utter simplicity, by the nakedness of his designs, he arrested and overawed attention. If ever mortal painted an idea, that mortal was Roderick Usher. For me at least—in the circumstances then surrounding me—there arose out of the pure abstractions which the hypochondriac contrived to throw upon his canvass, an intensity of intolerable awe, no shadow of which felt I ever yet in the contemplation of the certainly glowing yet too concrete reveries of Fuseli.

One of the phantasmagoric conceptions of my friend, partaking not so rigidly of the spirit of abstraction, may be shadowed forth, although feebly, in words. A small picture presented the interior of an immensely long and rectangular vault or tunnel, with low walls, smooth, white, and without interruption or device. Certain accessory points of the design served well to convey the idea that this excavation lay at an exceeding depth below the surface of the earth. No outlet was observed in any portion of its vast extent, and no torch, or other artificial source of light was discernible; yet a flood of intense rays rolled throughout, and bathed the whole in a ghastly and inappropriate splendor.

I have just spoken of that morbid condition of the auditory nerve which rendered all music intolerable to the sufferer, with the exception of certain effects of stringed instruments. It was, perhaps, the narrow limits to which he thus confined himself upon the guitar, which gave birth, in great measure, to the fantastic character of his performances. But the fervid *facility* of his *impromptus* could not be so accounted for. They must have been, and were, in the notes, as well as in the words of his wild fantasias (for he not unfrequently accompanied himself with rhymed verbal improvisations), the result of that intense mental collectedness and concentration to which I have previously alluded as observable only in particular moments of the highest artificial excitement. The words of one of these rhapsodies I have easily remembered. I was, perhaps, the more forcibly impressed with it, as he gave it, because, in the under or mystic current of its meaning, I fancied that I perceived, and for the first time, a full consciousness on the part of Usher, of the tottering of his lofty reason upon her throne. The verses, which were entitled "The Haunted Palace," ran very nearly, if not accurately, thus:

I

In the greenest of our valleys,
  By good angels tenanted,
Once a fair and stately palace—
  Radiant palace—reared its head.
In the monarch Thought's dominion—
  It stood there!
Never seraph spread a pinion
  Over fabric half so fair.

II

Banners yellow, glorious, golden,
  On its roof did float and flow;
(This—all this—was in the olden
  Time long ago)
And every gentle air that dallied,
  In that sweet day,

Along the ramparts plumed and pallid,
  A winged odor went away.

III

Wanderers in that happy valley
  Through two luminous windows saw
Spirits moving musically
  To a lute's well-tunéd law,
Round about a throne, where sitting
  (Porphyrogene!)
In state his glory well befitting,
  The ruler of the realm was seen.

IV

And all with pearl and ruby glowing
  Was the fair palace door,
Through which came flowing, flowing, flowing,
  And sparkling evermore,
A troop of Echoes whose sweet duty
  Was but to sing,
In voices of surpassing beauty,
  The wit and wisdom of their king.

V

But evil things, in robes of sorrow,
  Assailed the monarch's high estate;
(Ah, let us mourn, for never morrow
  Shall dawn upon him, desolate!)
And, round about his home, the glory
  That blushed and bloomed
Is but a dim-remembered story
  Of the old time entombed.

VI

And travellers now within that valley,
  Through the red-litten windows, see
Vast forms that move fantastically
  To a discordant melody;
While, like a rapid ghastly river,
  Through the pale door,
A hideous throng rush out forever,
  And laugh—but smile no more.

I well remember that suggestions arising from this ballad, led us into a train of thought wherein there became manifest an opinion of Usher's which I mention not so much on account of its novelty, (for other men* have thought thus,) as on account of the pertinacity with which he maintained it. This opinion, in its general form, was that of the sentience of all vegetable things. But, in his disordered fancy, the idea had assumed a more daring character, and trespassed, under certain conditions, upon the kingdom of inorganization. I lack words to express the full extent, or the earnest *abandon* of his persuasion. The belief, however, was connected (as I have previously hinted) with the gray stones of the home of his forefathers. The conditions of the sentience had been here, he imagined, fulfilled in the method of collocation of these stones—in the order of their arrangement, as well as in that of the many *fungi* which overspread them, and of the decayed trees which stood around—above all, in the long undisturbed endurance of this arrangement, and in its reduplication in the still waters of the tarn. Its evidence—the evidence of the sentience—was to be seen, he said, (and I here started as he spoke,) in the gradual yet certain condensation of an atmosphere of their own about the waters and the walls. The result was discoverable, he added, in that silent, yet importunate and terrible influence which for centuries had moulded the destinies of his family, and which made *him* what I now saw him—what he was. Such opinions need no comment, and I will make none.

Our books—the books which, for years, had formed no small portion of the mental existence of the invalid—were, as might be supposed, in strict keeping with this character of phantasm. We pored together over such works as the Ververt et Chartreuse of Gresset; the Belphegor of Machiavelli; the Heaven and Hell of Swedenborg; the Subterranean Voyage of Nicholas Klimm by Holberg; the Chiromancy of Robert Flud, of Jean D'Indaginé, and of De la Chambre; the Journey into the Blue Distance of Tieck; and the City of the Sun of Campanella. One favorite volume was a small octavo edition of the *Directorium Inquisitorium,* by the Dominican Eymeric de Gironne; and

*Watson, Dr. Percival, Spallanzani, and especially the Bishop of Landaff.—See "Chemical Essays," vol. v.

there were passages in Pomponius Mela, about the old African Satyrs and Œgipans, over which Usher would sit dreaming for hours. His chief delight, however, was found in the perusal of an exceedingly rare and curious book in quarto Gothic—the manual of a forgotten church—the *Vigiliae Mortuorum secundum Chorum Ecclesiae Maguntinae.*

I could not help thinking of the wild ritual of this work, and of its probable influence upon the hypochondriac, when, one evening, having informed me abruptly that the lady Madeline was no more, he stated his intention of preserving her corpse for a fortnight, (previously to its final interment,) in one of the numerous vaults within the main walls of the building. The worldly reason, however, assigned for this singular proceeding, was one which I did not feel at liberty to dispute. The brother had been led to his resolution (so he told me) by consideration of the unusual character of the malady of the deceased, of certain obtrusive and eager inquiries on the part of her medical men, and of the remote and exposed situation of the burial-ground of the family. I will not deny that when I called to mind the sinister countenance of the person whom I met upon the staircase, on the day of my arrival at the house, I had no desire to oppose what I regarded as at best but a harmless, and by no means an unnatural, precaution.

At the request of Usher, I personally aided him in the arrangements for the temporary entombment. The body having been encoffined, we two alone bore it to its rest. The vault in which we placed it (and which had been so long unopened that our torches, half smothered in its oppressive atmosphere, gave us little opportunity for investigation) was small, damp, and entirely without means of admission for light; lying, at great depth, immediately beneath that portion of the building in which was my own sleeping apartment. It had been used, apparently, in remote feudal times, for the worst purposes of a donjon-keep, and, in later days, as a place of deposit for powder, or some other highly combustible substance, as a portion of its floor, and the whole interior of a long archway through which we reached it, were carefully sheathed with copper. The door, of massive iron, had been, also, similarly protected. Its immense weight caused an unusually sharp grating sound, as it moved upon its hinges.

Having deposited our mournful burden upon tressels within this region of horror, we partially turned aside the yet unscrewed lid of the coffin, and looked upon the face of the tenant. A striking similitude between the brother and sister now first arrested my attention; and Usher, divining, perhaps, my thoughts, murmured out some few words from which I learned that the deceased and himself had been twins, and that sympathies of a scarcely intelligible nature had always existed between them. Our glances, however, rested not long upon the dead—for we could not regard her unawed. The disease which had thus entombed the lady in the maturity of youth, had left, as usual in all maladies of a strictly cataleptical character, the mockery of a faint blush upon the bosom and the face, and that suspiciously lingering smile upon the lip which is so terrible in death. We replaced and screwed down the lid, and, having secured the door of iron, made our way, with toil, into the scarcely less gloomy apartments of the upper portion of the house.

And now, some days of bitter grief having elapsed, an observable change came over the features of the mental disorder of my friend. His ordinary manner had vanished. His ordinary occupations were neglected or forgotten. He roamed from chamber to chamber with hurried, unequal, and objectless step. The pallor of his countenance had assumed, if possible, a more ghastly hue—but the luminousness of his eye had utterly gone out. The once occasional huskiness of his tone was heard no more; and a tremulous quaver, as if of extreme terror, habitually characterized his utterance. There were times, indeed, when I thought his unceasingly agitated mind was laboring with some oppressive secret, to divulge which he struggled for the necessary courage. At times, again, I was obliged to resolve all into the mere inexplicable vagaries of madness, for I beheld him gazing upon vacancy for long hours, in an attitude of the profoundest attention, as if listening to some imaginary sound. It was no wonder that his condition terrified—that it infected me. I felt creeping upon me, by slow yet certain degrees, the wild influences of his own fantastic yet impressive superstitions.

It was, especially, upon retiring to bed late in the night of the seventh or eighth day after the placing of the lady Madeline within the donjon, that I experienced the full power of such feelings. Sleep came not near my couch—while the hours waned and waned away. I struggled to reason off the nervousness which had dominion over me. I endeavored to believe that much, if not all of what I felt, was due to the bewildering influence of the gloomy furniture of the room—of the dark and tattered draperies, which, tortured into motion by the breath of a rising tempest, swayed fitfully to and fro upon the walls, and rustled uneasily about the decorations of the bed. But my efforts were fruitless. An irrepressible tremor gradually pervaded my frame; and, at length, there sat upon my very heart an incubus of utterly causeless alarm. Shaking this off with a gasp and a struggle, I uplifted myself upon the pillows, and, peering earnestly within the intense darkness of the chamber, harkened—I know not why, except that an instinctive spirit prompted me—to certain low and indefinite sounds which came, through the pauses of the storm, at long intervals, I knew not whence. Overpowered by an intense sentiment of horror, unaccountable yet unendurable, I threw on my clothes with haste (for I felt that I should sleep no more during the night), and endeavored to arouse myself from the pitiable condition into which I had fallen, by pacing rapidly to and fro through the apartment.

I had taken but few turns in this manner, when a light step on an adjoining staircase arrested my attention. I presently recognised it as that of Usher. In an instant afterward he rapped, with a gentle touch, at my door, and entered, bearing a lamp. His countenance was, as usual, cadaverously wan—but, moreover, there was a species of mad hilarity in his eyes—an evidently restrained *hysteria* in his whole demeanor. His air appalled me—but anything was preferable to the solitude which I had so long endured, and I even welcomed his presence as a relief.

"And you have not seen it?" he said abruptly, after having stared about him for some moments in silence—"you have not then seen it?—but, stay! you shall." Thus speaking, and having carefully shaded his lamp, he hurried to one of the casements, and threw it freely open to the storm.

The impetuous fury of the entering gust nearly lifted us from our feet. It was, indeed, a tempestuous yet sternly beautiful night, and one wildly singular in its terror and its beauty. A whirlwind had apparently collected its force in our vicinity; for there were frequent and violent alterations in the direction of the wind; and the exceeding density of the clouds (which hung so low as to press upon the turrets of the house) did not prevent our perceiving the life-like velocity with which they flew careering from all points against each other, without passing away into the distance. I say that even their exceeding density did not prevent our perceiving this—yet we had no glimpse of the moon or stars—nor was there any flashing forth of the lightning. But the under surfaces of the huge masses of agitated vapor, as well as all terrestrial objects immediately around us, were glowing in the unnatural light of a faintly luminous and distinctly visible gaseous exhalation which hung about and enshrouded the mansion.

"You must not—you shall not behold this!" said I, shudderingly, to Usher, as I led him, with a gentle violence, from the window to a seat. "These appearances, which bewilder you, are merely electrical phenomena not uncommon—or it may be that they have their ghastly origin in the rank miasma of the tarn. Let us close this casement;—the air is chilling and dangerous to your frame. Here is one of your favorite romances. I will read, and you shall listen;—and so we will pass away this terrible night together."

The antique volume which I had taken up was the "Mad Trist" of Sir Launcelot Canning; but I had called it a favorite of Usher's more in sad jest than in earnest; for, in truth, there is little in its uncouth and unimaginative prolixity which could have had interest for the lofty and spiritual ideality of my friend. It was, however, the only book immediately at hand; and I indulged a vague hope that the excitement which now agitated the hypochondriac, might find relief (for the history of mental disorder is full of similar anomalies) even in the extremeness of the folly which I should read. Could I have judged, indeed, by the wild overstrained air of vivacity with which he harkened, or apparently harkened, to the words of the tale, I might well have congratulated myself upon the success of my design.

I had arrived at that well-known portion of the story where Ethelred, the hero of the Trist, having sought in vain for peaceable admission into the dwelling of the hermit, proceeds to make good an entrance by force. Here, it will be remembered, the words of the narrative run thus:

"And Ethelred, who was by nature of a doughty heart, and who was now mighty withal, on account of the powerfulness of the wine which he had drunken, waited no longer to hold parley with the hermit, who, in sooth, was of an obstinate and maliceful turn, but, feeling the rain upon his shoulders, and fearing the rising of the tempest, uplifted his mace outright, and, with blows, made quickly room in the plankings of the door for his gauntleted hand; and now pulling therewith sturdily, he so cracked, and ripped, and tore all asunder, that the noise of the dry and hollow-sounding wood alarummed and reverberated throughout the forest."

At the termination of this sentence I started, and for a moment, paused; for it appeared to me (although I at once concluded that my excited fancy had deceived me)—it appeared to me that, from some very remote portion of the mansion, there came, indistinctly, to my ears, what might have been, in its exact similarity of character, the echo (but a stifled and dull one certainly) of the very cracking and ripping sound which Sir Launcelot had so particularly described. It was, beyond doubt, the coincidence alone which had arrested my attention; for, amid the rattling of the sashes of the casements, and the ordinary commingled noises of the still increasing storm, the sound, in itself, had nothing, surely, which should have interested or disturbed me. I continued the story:

"But the good champion Ethelred, now entering within the door, was sore enraged and amazed to perceive no signal of the maliceful hermit; but, in the stead thereof, a dragon of a scaly and prodigious demeanor, and of a fiery tongue, which sate in guard before a palace of gold, with a floor of silver; and upon the wall there hung a shield of shining brass with this legend enwritten—

Who entereth herein, a conqueror hath bin;
Who slayeth the dragon, the shield he shall win;

And Ethelred uplifted his mace, and struck upon the head of the dragon, which fell before him, and gave up his pesty breath, with a shriek so horrid and harsh, and withal so piercing, that Ethelred had fain to close his ears with his hands against the dreadful noise of it, the like whereof was never before heard."

Here again I paused abruptly, and now with a feeling of wild amazement—for there could be no doubt whatever that, in this instance, I did actually hear (although from what direction it proceeded I found it impossible to say) a low and apparently distant, but harsh, protracted, and most unusual screaming or grating sound—the exact counterpart of what my fancy had already conjured up for the dragon's unnatural shriek as described by the romancer.

Oppressed, as I certainly was, upon the occurrence of this second and most extraordinary coincidence, by a thousand conflicting sensations, in which wonder and extreme terror were predominant, I still retained sufficient presence of mind to avoid exciting, by any observation, the sensitive nervousness of my companion. I was by no means certain that he had noticed the sounds in question; although, assuredly, a strange alteration had, during the last few minutes, taken place in his demeanor. From a position fronting my own, he had gradually brought round his chair, so as to sit with his face to the door of the chamber; and thus I could but partially perceive his features, although I saw that his lips trembled as if he were murmuring inaudibly. His head had dropped upon his breast—yet I knew that he was not asleep, from the wide and rigid opening of the eye as I caught a glance of it in profile. The motion of his body, too, was at variance with this idea—for he rocked from side to side with a gentle yet constant and uniform sway. Having rapidly taken notice of all this, I resumed the narrative of Sir Launcelot, which thus proceeded:

"And now, the champion, having escaped from the terrible fury of the dragon, bethinking himself of the brazen shield, and of the breaking up of the enchantment which was upon it, removed the carcass from out of the way before him, and approached valorously over the silver pavement of the castle to where the shield was upon the wall; which in sooth tarried not for his full coming, but fell down at his feet upon the silver floor, with a mighty great and terrible ringing sound."

No sooner had these syllables passed my lips, than—as if a shield of brass had indeed, at the moment, fallen heavily upon a floor of silver—I became aware of a distinct, hollow, metallic, and clangorous, yet apparently muffled reverberation. Completely unnerved, I leaped to my feet; but the measured rocking movement of Usher was undisturbed. I rushed to the chair in which he sat. His eyes were bent fixedly before him, and throughout his whole countenance there reigned a stony rigidity. But, as I placed my hand upon his shoulder, there came a strong shudder over his whole person; a sickly smile quivered about his lips; and I saw that he spoke in a low, hurried, and gibbering murmur, as if unconscious of my presence. Bending closely over him, I at length drank in the hideous import of his words.

"Not hear it?—yes, I hear it, and *have* heard it. Long—long—long—many minutes, many hours, many days, have I heard it—yet I dared not—oh, pity me, miserable wretch that I am!—I dared not—I *dared* not speak! *We have put her living in the tomb!* Said I not that my senses were acute? I *now* tell you that I heard her first feeble movements in the hollow coffin. I heard them—many, many days ago—yet I dared not—*I dared not speak!* And now—to-night—Ethelred—ha! ha!—the breaking of the hermit's door, and the death-cry of the dragon, and the clangor of the shield!—say, rather, the rending of her coffin, and the grating of the iron hinges of her prison, and her struggles within the coppered archway of the vault! Oh whither shall I fly? Will she not be here anon? Is she not hurrying to upbraid me for my haste? Have I not heard her footstep on the stair? Do I not distinguish that heavy and horrible beating of her heart? Madman!"—here he sprang furiously to his feet, and shrieked out his syllables, as if in the effort he were giving up his soul—"*Madman! I tell you that she now stands without the door!*"

As if in the superhuman energy of his utterance there had been found the potency of a spell—the huge antique pannels to which the speaker pointed, threw slowly back, upon the instant, their ponderous and ebony jaws. It was the work of the rushing gust—but then without those doors there *did* stand the lofty and enshrouded figure of the lady Madeline of Usher. There was blood upon her white robes, and the evidence of some bitter struggle upon every portion of her emaciated frame. For a moment she remained trembling and reeling to and fro upon the threshold—then, with a low moaning cry, fell heavily inward upon the person of her brother, and in her violent and now final death-agonies, bore him to the floor a corpse, and a victim to the terrors he had anticipated.

From that chamber, and from that mansion, I fled aghast. The storm was still abroad in all its wrath as I found myself crossing the old causeway. Suddenly there shot along the path a wild light, and I turned to see whence a gleam so unusual could have issued; for the vast house and its shadows were alone behind me. The radiance was that of the full, setting, and blood-red moon, which now shone vividly through that once barely-discernible fissure, of which I have before spoken as extending from the roof of the building, in a zigzag direction, to the base. While I gazed, this fissure rapidly widened—there came a fierce breath of the whirlwind—the entire orb of the satellite burst at once upon my sight—my brain reeled as I saw the mighty walls rushing asunder—there was a long tumultuous shouting sound like the voice of a thousand waters—and the deep and dank tarn at my feet closed sullenly and silently over the fragments of the "*House of Usher.*"

1839

# EDGAR ALLAN POE

(1809–1849)

## *The Man of the Crowd*

Ce grand malheur, de ne pouvoir être seul.
*La Bruyère*

IT WAS WELL SAID of a certain German book that "*er lasst sich nicht lesen*"—it does not permit itself to be read. There are some secrets which do not permit themselves to be told. Men die nightly in their beds, wringing the hands of ghostly confessors, and looking them piteously in the eyes—die with despair of heart and convulsion of throat, on account of the hideousness of mysteries which will not *suffer themselves* to be revealed. Now and then, alas, the conscience of man takes up a burthen so heavy in horror that it can be thrown down only into the grave. And thus the essence of all crime is undivulged.

Not long ago, about the closing in of an evening in autumn, I sat at the large bow window of the D—— Coffee-House in London. For some months I had been ill in health, but was now convalescent, and, with returning strength, found myself in one of those happy moods which are so precisely the converse of *ennui*—moods of the keenest appetency, when the film from the mental vision departs—the αχλυς ος πριν επηεν—and the intellect, electrified, surpasses as greatly its every-day condition, as does the vivid yet candid reason of Leibnitz, the mad and flimsy rhetoric of Gorgias. Merely to breathe was enjoyment; and I derived positive pleasure even from many of the legitimate sources of pain. I felt a calm but inquisitive interest in every thing. With a cigar in my mouth and a newspaper in my lap, I had been amusing myself for the greater part of the afternoon, now in poring over advertisements, now in observing the promiscuous company in the room, and now in peering through the smoky panes into the street.

This latter is one of the principal thoroughfares of the city, and had been very much crowded during the whole day. But, as the darkness came on, the throng momently increased; and, by the time the lamps were well lighted, two dense and continuous tides of population were rushing past the door. At this particular period of the evening I had never before been in a similar situation, and the tumultuous sea of human heads filled me, therefore, with a delicious novelty of emotion. I gave up, at length, all care of things within the hotel, and became absorbed in contemplation of the scene without.

At first my observations took an abstract and generalizing turn. I looked at the passengers in masses, and thought of them in their aggregate relations. Soon, however, I descended to details, and regarded with minute interest the innumerable varieties of figure, dress, air, gait, visage, and expression of countenance.

By far the greater number of those who went by had a satisfied business-like demeanor, and seemed to be thinking only of making their way through the press. Their brows were knit, and their eyes rolled quickly; when pushed against by fellow-wayfarers they evinced no symptom of impatience, but adjusted their clothes and hurried on. Others, still a numerous class, were restless in their movements, had flushed faces, and talked and gesticulated to themselves, as if feeling in solitude on account of the very denseness of the company around. When impeded in their progress, these people suddenly ceased muttering, but redoubled their gesticulations, and awaited, with an absent and overdone smile upon the lips, the course of the persons impeding them. If jostled, they bowed profusely to the jostlers, and appeared overwhelmed with confusion.—There was nothing very distinctive about these two large classes beyond what I have noted. Their habiliments belonged to that order which is pointedly termed the decent. They were undoubtedly noblemen, merchants, attorneys, tradesmen, stock-jobbers—the Eupatrids and the common-places of society—men of leisure and men actively engaged in affairs of their own—conducting business upon their own responsibility. They did not greatly excite my attention.

The tribe of clerks was an obvious one and here I discerned two remarkable divisions. There were the junior clerks of flash houses—young gentlemen with tight coats, bright boots, well-oiled hair, and supercilious lips. Setting aside a certain dapperness of carriage, which may be termed *deskism* for want of a better word, the manner of these persons seemed to me an exact fac-simile of what had been the perfection of *bon ton* about twelve or eighteen months before. They wore the cast-off graces of the gentry;—and this, I believe, involves the best definition of the class.

The division of the upper clerks of staunch firms, or of the "steady old fellows," it was not possible to mistake. These were known by their coats and pantaloons of black or brown, made to sit comfortably, with white cravats and waistcoats, broad solid-looking shoes, and thick hose or gaiters.—They had all slightly bald heads, from which the right ears, long used to pen-holding, had an odd habit of standing off on end. I observed that they always removed or settled their hats with both hands, and wore watches, with short gold chains of a substantial and ancient pattern. Theirs was the affectation of respectability;—if indeed there be an affectation so honorable.

There were many individuals of dashing appearance, whom I easily understood as belonging to the race of swell pickpockets, with which all great cities are infested. I watched these gentry with much inquisitiveness, and found it difficult to imagine how they should ever be mistaken for gentlemen by gentlemen themselves. Their voluminousness of wristband, with an air of excessive frankness, should betray them at once.

The gamblers, of whom I descried not a few, were still more easily recognisable. They wore every variety of dress, from that of the desperate thimble-rig bully, with velvet waistcoat, fancy neckerchief, gilt chains, and filagreed buttons, to that of the scrupulously inornate clergyman, than which nothing could be less liable to suspicion. Still all were distinguished by a certain sodden swarthiness of complexion, a filmy dimness of eye, and pallor and compression of lip. There were two other traits, moreover, by which I could always detect them;—a guarded lowness of tone in conversation, and a more than ordinary extension of the thumb in a direction at right angles with the fingers.—Very often, in company with these sharpers, I observed an order of men somewhat different in habits, but still birds of a kindred feather. They may be defined as the gentlemen who live by their wits. They seem to prey upon the public in two battalions—that of the dandies and that of the military men. Of the first grade the leading features are long locks and smiles; of the second frogged coats and frowns.

Descending in the scale of what is termed gentility, I found darker and deeper themes for speculation. I saw Jew pedlars, with hawk eyes flashing from countenances whose every other feature wore only an expression of abject humility; sturdy professional street beggars scowling upon mendicants of a better stamp, whom despair alone had driven forth into the night for charity; feeble and ghastly invalids, upon whom death had placed a sure hand, and who sidled and tottered through the mob, looking every one beseechingly in the face, as if in search of some chance consolation, some lost hope; modest young girls returning from long and late labor to a cheerless home, and shrinking more tearfully than indignantly from the glances of ruffians, whose direct contact, even, could not be avoided; women of the town of all kinds and of all ages—the unequivocal beauty in the prime of her womanhood, putting one in mind of the statue in Lucian, with the surface of Parian marble, and the interior filled with filth—the loathsome and utterly lost leper in rags—the wrinkled, bejewelled and paint-begrimed beldame, making a last effort at youth—the mere child of immature form, yet, from long association, an adept in the dreadful coquetries of her trade, and burning with a rabid ambition to be ranked the equal of her elders in vice; drunkards innumerable and indescribable—some in shreds and patches, reeling, inarticulate, with bruised visage and lack-lustre eyes—some in whole although filthy garments, with a slightly unsteady swagger, thick sensual lips, and hearty-looking rubicund faces—others clothed in materials which had once been good, and which even now were scrupulously well brushed—men who walked with a more than naturally firm and springy step, but whose countenances were fearfully pale, whose eyes hideously wild and red, and who clutched with quivering fingers, as they strode through the crowd, at every object which came within their reach; beside these, pie-men, porters, coal-heavers, sweeps; organ-grinders, monkey-exhibiters and ballad mongers, those who vended with those who sang; ragged artizans and exhausted laborers of every description, and all full of a noisy and inordinate vivacity which jarred discordantly upon the ear, and gave an aching sensation to the eye.

As the night deepened, so deepened to me the interest of the scene; for not only did the general character of the crowd materially alter (its gentler features retiring in the gradual withdrawal of the more orderly portion of the people, and its harsher ones coming out into bolder relief, as the late hour brought forth every species of infamy from its den,) but the rays of the gas-lamps, feeble at first in their struggle with the dying day, had now at length gained ascendancy, and threw over every thing a fitful and garish lustre. All was dark yet splendid—as that ebony to which has been likened the style of Tertullian.

The wild effects of the light enchained me to an examination of individual faces; and although the rapidity with which the world of light flitted before the window, prevented me from casting more than a glance upon each visage, still it seemed that, in my then peculiar mental state, I could frequently read, even in that brief interval of a glance, the history of long years.

With my brow to the glass, I was thus occupied in scrutinizing the mob, when suddenly there came into view a countenance (that of a decrepid old man, some sixty-five or seventy years of age,)—a countenance which at once arrested and absorbed my whole attention, on account of the absolute idiosyncracy of its expression. Any thing even remotely resembling that expression I had never seen before. I well remember that my first thought, upon beholding it, was that Retzch, had he viewed it, would have greatly preferred it to his own pictural incarnations of the fiend. As I endeavored, during the brief minute of my original survey, to form some analysis of the meaning conveyed, there arose confusedly and paradoxically within my mind, the ideas of vast mental power, of caution, of penuriousness, of avarice, of coolness, of malice, of blood-thirstiness, of triumph, of merriment, of excessive terror, of intense—of supreme despair. I felt singularly aroused, startled, fascinated. "How wild a history," I said to myself, "is written within that bosom!" Then came a craving desire to keep the man in view—to know more of him. Hurriedly putting on an overcoat, and seizing my hat and cane, I made my way into the street, and pushed through the crowd in the direction which I had seen him take; for he had already disappeared. With some little difficulty I at length came within sight of him, approached, and followed him closely, yet cautiously, so as not to attract his attention.

I had now a good opportunity of examining his person. He was short in stature, very thin, and apparently very feeble. His clothes, generally, were filthy and ragged; but as he came, now and then, within the strong glare of a lamp, I perceived that his linen, although dirty, was of beautiful texture; and my vision deceived me, or, through a rent in a closely-buttoned and evidently second-handed *roquelaire* which enveloped him, I caught a glimpse both of a diamond and of a dagger. These observations heightened my curiosity, and I resolved to follow the stranger whithersoever he should go.

It was now fully night-fall, and a thick humid fog hung over the city, soon ending in a settled and heavy rain. This change of weather had an odd effect upon the crowd, the whole of which was at once put into new commotion, and overshadowed by a world of umbrellas. The waver, the jostle, and the hum increased in a tenfold degree. For my own part I did not much regard the rain—the lurking of an old fever in my system rendering the moisture somewhat too dangerously pleasant. Tying a handkerchief about my mouth, I kept on. For half an hour the old man held his way with difficulty along the great thoroughfare; and I here walked close at his elbow through fear of losing sight of him. Never once turning his head to look back, he did not observe me. By and bye he passed into a cross street, which, although densely filled with people, was not quite so much thronged as the main one he had quitted. Here a change in his demeanor became evident. He walked more slowly and with less object than before—more hesitatingly. He crossed and re-crossed the way repeatedly without apparent aim; and the press was still so thick that, at every such movement, I was obliged to follow him closely. The street was a narrow and long one, and his course lay within it for nearly an hour, during which the passengers had gradually diminished to about that number which is ordinarily seen at noon in Broadway near the Park—so vast a difference is there between a London populace and that of the most frequented American city. A second turn brought us into a square, brilliantly lighted, and overflowing with life. The old manner of the stranger re-appeared. His chin fell upon his breast, while his eyes rolled wildly from under his knit brows, in every direction, upon those who hemmed him in. He urged his way steadily and perseveringly. I was surprised, however, to find, upon his having made the circuit of the square, that he turned and retraced his steps. Still more was I astonished to see him repeat the same walk several times—once nearly detecting me as he came round with a sudden movement.

In this exercise he spent another hour, at the end of which we met with far less interruption from passengers than at first. The rain fell fast; the air grew cool; and the people were retiring to their homes. With a gesture of impatience, the wanderer passed into a bye-street comparatively deserted. Down this, some quarter of a mile long, he rushed with an activity I could not have dreamed of seeing in one so aged, and which put me to much trouble in pursuit. A few minutes brought us to a large and busy bazaar, with the localities of which the stranger appeared well acquainted, and where his original demeanor again became apparent, as he forced his way to and fro, without aim, among the host of buyers and sellers.

During the hour and a half, or thereabouts, which we passed in this place, it required much caution on my part to keep him within reach without attracting his observation. Luckily I wore a pair of caoutchouc over-shoes, and could move about in perfect silence. At no moment did he see that I watched him. He entered shop after shop, priced nothing, spoke no word, and looked at all objects with a wild and vacant stare. I was now utterly amazed at his behaviour, and firmly resolved that we should not part until I had satisfied myself in some measure respecting him.

A loud-toned clock struck eleven, and the company were fast deserting the bazaar. A shop-keeper, in putting up a shutter, jostled the old man, and at the instant I saw a strong shudder come over his frame. He hurried into the street, looked anxiously around him for an instant, and then ran with incredible swiftness through many crooked and peopleless lanes, until we emerged once more upon the great thoroughfare whence we had started—the street of the D—— Hotel. It no longer wore, however, the same aspect. It was still brilliant with gas; but the rain fell fiercely, and there were few persons to be seen. The stranger grew pale. He walked moodily some paces up the once populous avenue, then, with a heavy sigh, turned in the direction of the river, and, plunging through a great variety of devious ways, came out, at length, in view of one of the principal theatres. It was about being closed, and the audience were thronging from the doors. I saw the old man gasp as if for breath while he threw himself amid the crowd; but I thought that the intense agony of his countenance had, in some measure, abated. His head again fell upon his breast; he appeared as I had seen him at first. I observed that he now took the course in which had gone the greater number of the audience—but, upon the whole, I was at a loss to comprehend the waywardness of his actions.

As he proceeded, the company grew more scattered, and his old uneasiness and vacillation were resumed. For some time he followed closely a party of some ten or twelve roisterers; but from this number one by one dropped off, until three only remained together, in a narrow and gloomy lane little frequented. The stranger paused, and, for a moment, seemed lost in thought; then, with every mark of agitation, pursued rapidly a route which brought us to the verge of the city, amid regions very different from those we had hitherto traversed. It was the most noisome quarter of London, where every thing wore the worst impress of the most deplorable poverty, and of the most desperate crime. By the dim light of an accidental lamp, tall, antique, worm-eaten, wooden tenements were seen tottering to their fall, in directions so many and capricious that scarce the semblance of a passage was discernible between them. The paving-stones lay at random, displaced from their beds by the rankly-growing grass. Horrible filth festered in the dammed-up gutters. The whole atmosphere teemed with desolation. Yet, as we proceeded, the sounds of human life revived by sure degrees, and at length large bands of the most abandoned of a London populace were seen reeling to and fro. The spirits of the old man again flickered up, as a lamp which is near its death-hour. Once more he strode onward with elastic tread. Suddenly a corner was turned, a blaze of light burst upon our sight, and we stood before one of the huge suburban temples of Intemperance—one of the palaces of the fiend, Gin.

It was now nearly day-break; but a number of wretched inebriates still pressed in and out of the flaunting entrance. With a half shriek of joy the old man forced a passage within, resumed at once his original bearing, and stalked backward and forward, without apparent object, among the throng. He had not been thus long occupied, however, before a rush to the doors gave token that the host was closing them for the night. It was something even more intense than despair that I then observed upon the countenance of the singular being whom I had watched so pertinaciously. Yet he did not hesitate in his career, but, with a mad energy, retraced his steps at once, to the heart of the mighty London. Long and swiftly he fled, while I followed him in the wildest amazement, resolute not to abandon a scrutiny in which I now felt an interest all-absorbing. The sun arose while we proceeded, and, when we had once again reached that most thronged mart of the populous town, the street of the D—— Hotel, it presented an appearance of human bustle and activity scarcely inferior to what I had seen on the evening before. And here, long, amid the momently increasing confusion, did I persist in my pursuit of the stranger. But, as usual, he walked to and fro, and during the day did not pass from out the turmoil of that street. And, as the shades of the second evening came on, I grew wearied unto death, and, stopping fully in front of the wanderer, gazed at him steadfastly in the face. He noticed me not, but resumed his solemn walk, while I, ceasing to follow, remained absorbed in contemplation. "This old man," I said at length, "is the type and the genius of deep crime. He refuses to be alone. *He is the man of the crowd.* It will be in vain to follow; for I shall learn no more of him, nor of his deeds. The worst heart of the world is a grosser book than the 'Hortulus Animæ,'* and perhaps it is but one of the great mercies of God that '*er lasst sich nicht lesen.*'"

1840

*The "*Hortulus Animæ cum Oratiunculis Aliquibus Superadditis*" of Grünninger.

# EDGAR ALLAN POE

(1809–1849)

---

## *The Masque of the Red Death*

THE "RED DEATH" had long devastated the country. No pestilence had ever been so fatal, or so hideous. Blood was its Avatar and its seal—the redness and the horror of blood. There were sharp pains, and sudden dizziness, and then profuse bleeding at the pores, with dissolution. The scarlet stains upon the body and especially upon the face of the victim, were the pest ban which shut him out from the aid and from the sympathy of his fellow-men. And the whole seizure, progress and termination of the disease, were the incidents of half an hour.

But the Prince Prospero was happy and dauntless and sagacious. When his dominions were half depopulated, he summoned to his presence a thousand hale and light-hearted friends from among the knights and dames of his court, and with these retired to the deep seclusion of one of his castellated abbeys. This was an extensive and magnificent structure, the creation of the prince's own eccentric yet august taste. A strong and lofty wall girdled it in. This wall had gates of iron. The courtiers, having entered, brought furnaces and massy hammers and welded the bolts. They resolved to leave means neither of ingress or egress to the sudden impulses of despair or of frenzy from within. The abbey was amply provisioned. With such precautions the courtiers might bid defiance to contagion. The external world could take care of itself. In the meantime it was folly to grieve, or to think. The prince had provided all the appliances of pleasure. There were buffoons, there were improvisatori, there were ballet-dancers, there were musicians, there was Beauty, there was wine. All these and security were within. Without was the "Red Death."

It was toward the close of the fifth or sixth month of his seclusion, and while the pestilence raged most furiously abroad, that the Prince Prospero entertained his thousand friends at a masked ball of the most unusual magnificence.

It was a voluptuous scene, that masquerade. But first let me tell of the rooms in which it was held. There were seven—an imperial suite. In many palaces, however, such suites form a long and straight vista, while the folding doors slide back nearly to the walls on either hand, so that the view of the whole extent is scarcely impeded. Here the case was very different; as might have been expected from the duke's love of the *bizarre*. The apartments were so irregularly disposed that the vision embraced but little more than one at a time. There was a sharp turn at every twenty or thirty yards, and at each turn a novel effect. To the right and left, in the middle of each wall, a tall and narrow Gothic window looked out upon a closed corridor which pursued the windings of the suite. These windows were of stained glass whose color varied in accordance with the prevailing hue of the decorations of the chamber into which it opened. That at the eastern extremity was hung, for example, in blue—and vividly blue were its windows. The second chamber was purple in its ornaments and tapestries, and here the panes were purple. The third was green throughout, and so were the casements. The fourth was furnished and lighted with orange—the fifth with white—the sixth with violet. The seventh apartment was closely shrouded in black velvet tapestries that hung all over the ceiling and down the walls, falling in heavy folds upon a carpet of the same material and hue. But in this chamber only, the color of the windows failed to correspond with the decorations. The panes here were scarlet—a deep blood color. Now in no one of the seven apartments was there any lamp or candelabrum, amid the profusion of golden ornaments that lay scattered to and fro or depended from the roof. There was no light of any kind emanating from lamp or candle within the suite of chambers. But in the corridors that followed the suite, there stood, opposite to each window, a heavy tripod, bearing a brazier of fire that projected its rays through the tinted glass and so glaringly illumined the room. And thus were produced a multitude of gaudy and fantastic appearances. But in the western or black chamber the effect of the fire-light that streamed upon the dark hangings through the blood-tinted panes, was ghastly in the extreme, and produced so wild a look upon the countenances of those who entered, that there were few of the company bold enough to set foot within its precincts at all.

It was in this apartment, also, that there stood against the western wall, a gigantic clock of ebony. Its pendulum swung to and fro with a dull, heavy, monotonous clang; and when the minute-hand made the circuit of the face, and the hour was to be stricken, there came from the brazen lungs of the clock a sound which was clear and loud and deep and exceedingly musical, but of so peculiar a note and emphasis that, at each lapse of an hour, the musicians of the orchestra were constrained to pause, momentarily, in their performance, to harken to the sound; and thus the waltzers perforce ceased their evolutions; and there was a brief disconcert of the whole gay company; and, while the chimes of the clock yet rang, it was observed that the giddiest grew pale, and the more aged and sedate passed their hands over their brows as if in confused reverie or meditation. But when the echoes had fully ceased, a light laughter at once pervaded the assembly; the musicians looked at each other and smiled as if at their own nervousness and folly, and made whispering vows, each to the other, that the next chiming of the clock should produce in them no similar emotion; and then, after the lapse of sixty minutes, (which embrace three thousand and six hundred seconds of the Time that flies,) there came yet another chiming of the clock, and then were the same disconcert and tremulousness and meditation as before.

But, in spite of these things, it was a gay and magnificent revel. The tastes of the duke were peculiar. He had a fine eye for colors and effects. He disregarded the *decora* of mere fashion. His plans were bold and fiery, and his conceptions glowed with barbaric lustre. There are some who would have thought him mad. His followers felt that he was not. It was necessary to hear and see and touch him to be *sure* that he was not.

He had directed, in great part, the moveable embellishments of the seven chambers, upon occasion of this great *fête*; and it was his own guiding taste which had given character to the masqueraders. Be sure they were grotesque. There were much glare and glitter and piquancy and phantasm—much of what has been since seen in "Hernani." There were arabesque figures with unsuited limbs and appointments. There were delirious fancies such as the madman fashions. There was much of the beautiful, much of the wanton, much of the *bizarre*, something of the terrible, and not a little of that which might have excited disgust. To and fro in the seven chambers there stalked, in fact, a multitude of dreams. And these—the dreams—writhed in and about, taking hue from the rooms, and causing the wild music of the orchestra to seem as the echo of their steps. And, anon, there strikes the ebony clock which stands in the hall of the velvet. And then, for a moment, all is still, and all is silent save the voice of the clock. The dreams are stiff-frozen as they stand. But the echoes of the chime die away—they have endured but an instant—and a light, half-subdued laughter floats after them as they depart. And now again the music swells, and the dreams live, and writhe to and fro more merrily than ever, taking hue from the many tinted windows through which stream the rays from the tripods. But to the chamber which lies most westwardly of the seven, there are now none of the maskers who venture: for the night is waning away; and there flows a ruddier light through the blood-colored panes; and the blackness of the sable drapery appals; and to him whose foot falls upon the sable carpet, there comes from the near clock of ebony a muffled peal more solemnly emphatic than any which reaches *their* ears who indulge in the more remote gaieties of the other apartments.

But these other apartments were densely crowded, and in them beat feverishly the heart of life. And the revel went whirlingly on, until at length there commenced the sounding of midnight upon the clock. And then the music ceased, as I have told; and the evolutions of the waltzers were quieted; and there was an uneasy cessation of all things as before. But now there were twelve strokes to be sounded by the bell of the clock; and thus it happened, perhaps, that more of thought crept, with more of time, into the meditations of the thoughtful among those who revelled. And thus, too, it happened, perhaps, that before the last echoes of the last chime had utterly sunk into silence, there were many individuals in the crowd who had found leisure to become aware of the presence of a masked figure which had arrested the attention of no single individual before. And the rumor of this new presence having spread itself whisperingly around, there arose at length from the whole company a buzz, or murmur, expressive of disapprobation and surprise—then, finally, of terror, of horror, and of disgust.

In an assembly of phantasms such as I have painted, it may well be supposed that no ordinary appearance could have excited such sensation. In truth the masquerade license of the night was nearly unlimited; but the figure in question had out-Heroded Herod, and gone beyond the bounds of even the prince's indefinite decorum. There are chords in the hearts of the most reckless which cannot be touched without emotion. Even with the utterly lost, to whom life and death are equally jests, there are matters of which no jest can be made. The whole company, indeed, seemed now deeply to feel that in the costume and bearing of the stranger neither wit nor propriety existed. The figure was tall and gaunt, and shrouded from head to foot in the habiliments of the grave. The mask which concealed the visage was made so nearly to resemble the countenance of a stiffened corpse that the closest scrutiny must have had difficulty in detecting the cheat. And yet all this might have been endured, if not approved, by the mad revellers around. But the mummer had gone so far as to assume the type of the Red Death. His vesture was dabbled in *blood*—and his broad brow, with all the features of the face, was besprinkled with the scarlet horror.

When the eyes of Prince Prospero fell upon this spectral image (which with a slow and solemn movement, as if more fully to sustain its *rôle*, stalked to and fro among the waltzers) he was seen to be convulsed, in the first moment with a strong shudder either of terror or distaste; but, in the next, his brow reddened with rage.

"Who dares?" he demanded hoarsely of the courtiers who stood near him—"who dares insult us with this blasphemous mockery? Seize him and unmask him—that we may know whom we have to hang at sunrise, from the battlements!"

It was in the eastern or blue chamber in which stood the Prince Prospero as he uttered these words. They rang throughout the seven rooms loudly and clearly—for the prince was a bold and robust man, and the music had become hushed at the waving of his hand.

It was in the blue room where stood the prince, with a group of pale courtiers by his side. At first, as he spoke, there was a slight rushing movement of this group in the direction of the intruder, who at the moment was also near at hand, and now, with deliberate and stately step, made closer approach to the speaker. But from a certain nameless awe with which the mad assumptions of the mummer had inspired the whole party, there were found none who put forth hand to seize him; so that, unimpeded, he passed within a yard of the prince's person; and, while the vast assembly, as if with one impulse, shrank from the centres of the rooms to the walls, he made his way uninterruptedly, but with the same solemn and measured step which had distinguished him from the first, through the blue chamber to the purple—through the purple to the green—through the green to the orange—through this again to the white—and even thence to the violet, ere a decided movement had been made to arrest him. It was then, however, that the Prince Prospero, maddening with rage and the shame of his own momentary cowardice, rushed hurriedly through the six chambers, while none followed him on account of a deadly terror that had seized upon all. He bore aloft a drawn dagger, and had approached, in rapid impetuosity, to within three or four feet of the retreating figure, when the latter, having attained the extremity of the velvet apartment, turned suddenly and confronted his pursuer. There was a sharp cry—and the dagger dropped gleaming upon the sable carpet, upon which, instantly afterwards, fell prostrate in death the Prince Prospero. Then, summoning the wild courage of despair, a throng of the revellers at once threw themselves into the black apartment, and, seizing the mummer, whose tall figure stood erect and motionless within the shadow of the ebony clock, gasped in unutterable horror at finding the grave-cerements and corpse-like mask which they handled with so violent a rudeness, untenanted by any tangible form.

And now was acknowledged the presence of the Red Death. He had come like a thief in the night. And one by one dropped the revellers in the blood-bedewed halls of their revel, and died each in the despairing posture of his fall. And the life of the ebony clock went out with that of the last of the gay. And the flames of the tripods expired. And Darkness and Decay and the Red Death held illimitable dominion over all.

1842

# EDGAR ALLAN POE

(1809–1849)

## *The Purloined Letter*

Nil sapientiae odiosius acumine nimio.
*Seneca*

AT PARIS, just after dark one gusty evening in the autumn of 18—, I was enjoying the twofold luxury of meditation and a meerschaum, in company with my friend C. Auguste Dupin, in his little back library, or book-closet, *au troisième, No. 33, Rue Dunôt, Faubourg St. Germain.* For one hour at least we had maintained a profound silence; while each, to any casual observer, might have seemed intently and exclusively occupied with the curling eddies of smoke that oppressed the atmosphere of the chamber. For myself, however, I was mentally discussing certain topics which had formed matter for conversation between us at an earlier period of the evening; I mean the affair of the Rue Morgue, and the mystery attending the murder of Marie Rogêt. I looked upon it, therefore, as something of a coincidence, when the door of our apartment was thrown open and admitted our old acquaintance, Monsieur G——, the Prefect of the Parisian police.

We gave him a hearty welcome; for there was nearly half as much of the entertaining as of the contemptible about the man, and we had not seen him for several years. We had been sitting in the dark, and Dupin now arose for the purpose of lighting a lamp, but sat down again, without doing so, upon G.'s saying that he had called to consult us, or rather to ask the opinion of my friend, about some official business which had occasioned a great deal of trouble.

"If it is any point requiring reflection," observed Dupin, as he forebore to enkindle the wick, "we shall examine it to better purpose in the dark."

"That is another of your odd notions," said the Prefect, who had a fashion of calling every thing "odd" that was beyond his comprehension, and thus lived amid an absolute legion of "oddities."

"Very true," said Dupin, as he supplied his visiter with a pipe, and rolled towards him a comfortable chair.

"And what is the difficulty now?" I asked. "Nothing more in the assassination way, I hope?"

"Oh no; nothing of that nature. The fact is, the business is *very* simple indeed, and I make no doubt that we can manage it sufficiently well ourselves; but then I thought Dupin would like to hear the details of it, because it is so excessively *odd*."

"Simple and odd," said Dupin.

"Why, yes; and not exactly that, either. The fact is, we have all been a good deal puzzled because the affair *is* so simple, and yet baffles us altogether."

"Perhaps it is the very simplicity of the thing which puts you at fault," said my friend.

"What nonsense you *do* talk!" replied the Prefect, laughing heartily.

"Perhaps the mystery is a little *too* plain," said Dupin.

"Oh, good heavens! who ever heard of such an idea?"

"A little *too* self-evident."

"Ha! ha! ha!—ha! ha! ha!—ho! ho! ho!" roared our visiter, profoundly amused, "oh, Dupin, you will be the death of me yet!"

"And what, after all, *is* the matter on hand?" I asked.

"Why, I will tell you," replied the Prefect, as he gave a long, steady, and contemplative puff, and settled himself in his chair. "I will tell you in a few words; but, before I begin, let me caution you that this is an affair demanding the greatest secrecy, and that I should most probably lose the position I now hold, were it known that I confided it to any one."

"Proceed," said I.

"Or not," said Dupin.

"Well, then; I have received personal information, from a very high quarter, that a certain document of the last importance, has been purloined from the royal apartments. The individual who purloined it is known; this beyond a doubt; he was seen to take it. It is known, also, that it still remains in his possession."

"How is this known?" asked Dupin.

"It is clearly inferred," replied the Prefect, "from the nature of the document, and from the non-appearance of certain results which would at once arise from its passing *out* of the robber's possession;—that is to say, from his employing it as he must design in the end to employ it."

"Be a little more explicit," I said.

"Well, I may venture so far as to say that the paper gives its holder a certain power in a certain quarter where such power is immensely valuable." The Prefect was fond of the cant of diplomacy.

"Still I do not quite understand," said Dupin.

"No? Well; the disclosure of the document to a third person, who shall be nameless, would bring in question the honor of a personage of most exalted station; and this fact gives the holder of the document an ascendancy over the illustrious personage whose honor and peace are so jeopardized."

"But this ascendancy," I interposed, "would depend upon the robber's knowledge of the loser's knowledge of the robber. Who would dare—"

"The thief," said G., "is the Minister D——, who dares all things, those unbecoming as well as those becoming a man. The method of the theft was not less ingenious than bold. The document in question—a letter, to be frank—had been received by the personage robbed while alone in the royal *boudoir*. During its perusal she was suddenly interrupted by the entrance of the other exalted personage from whom especially it was her wish to conceal it. After a hurried and vain endeavor to thrust it in a drawer, she was forced to place it, open as it was, upon a table. The address, however, was uppermost, and, the contents thus unexposed, the letter escaped notice. At this juncture enters the Minister D——. His lynx eye immediately perceives the paper, recognises the handwriting of the address, observes the confusion of the personage addressed, and fathoms her secret. After some business transactions, hurried through in his ordinary manner, he produces a letter somewhat similar to the one in question, opens it, pretends to read it, and then places it in close juxtaposition to the other. Again he converses, for some fifteen minutes, upon the public affairs. At length, in taking leave, he takes also from the table the letter to which he had no claim. Its rightful owner saw, but, of course, dared not call attention to the act, in the presence of the third personage who stood at her elbow. The minister decamped; leaving his own letter—one of no importance—upon the table."

"Here, then," said Dupin to me, "you have precisely what you demand to make the ascendancy complete—the robber's knowledge of the loser's knowledge of the robber."

"Yes," replied the Prefect; "and the power thus attained has, for some months past, been wielded, for political purposes, to a very dangerous extent. The personage robbed is more thoroughly convinced, every day, of the necessity of reclaiming her letter. But this, of course, cannot be done openly. In fine, driven to despair, she has committed the matter to me."

"Than whom," said Dupin, amid a perfect whirlwind of smoke, "no more sagacious agent could, I suppose, be desired, or even imagined."

"You flatter me," replied the Prefect; "but it is possible that some such opinion may have been entertained."

"It is clear," said I, "as you observe, that the letter is still in possession of the minister; since it is this possession, and not any employment of the letter, which bestows the power. With the employment the power departs."

"True," said G.; "and upon this conviction I proceeded. My first care was to make thorough search of the minister's hotel; and here my chief embarrassment lay in the necessity of searching without his knowledge. Beyond all things, I have been warned of the danger which would result from giving him reason to suspect our design."

"But," said I, "you are quite *au fait* in these investigations. The Parisian police have done this thing often before."

"O yes; and for this reason I did not despair. The habits of the minister gave me, too, a great advantage. He is frequently absent from home all night. His servants are by no means numerous. They sleep at a distance from their master's apartment, and, being chiefly Neapolitans, are readily made drunk. I have keys, as you know, with which I can open any chamber or cabinet in Paris. For three months a night has not passed, during the greater part of which I have not been engaged, personally, in ransacking the D—— Hotel. My honor is interested, and, to mention a great secret, the reward is enormous. So I did not abandon the search until I had become fully satisfied that the thief is a more astute man than myself. I fancy that I have investigated every nook and corner of the premises in which it is possible that the paper can be concealed."

"But is it not possible," I suggested, "that although the letter may be in possession of the minister, as it unquestionably is, he may have concealed it elsewhere than upon his own premises?"

"This is barely possible," said Dupin. "The present peculiar condition of affairs at court, and especially of those intrigues in which D—— is known to be involved, would render the instant availability of the document—its susceptibility of being produced at a moment's notice—a point of nearly equal importance with its possession."

"Its susceptibility of being produced?" said I.

"That is to say, of being *destroyed*," said Dupin.

"True," I observed; "the paper is clearly then upon the premises. As for its being upon the person of the minister, we may consider that as out of the question."

"Entirely," said the Prefect. "He has been twice waylaid, as if by footpads, and his person rigorously searched under my own inspection."

"You might have spared yourself this trouble," said Dupin. "D——, I presume, is not altogether a fool, and, if not, must have anticipated these waylayings, as a matter of course."

"Not *altogether* a fool," said G., "but then he's a poet, which I take to be only one remove from a fool."

"True," said Dupin, after a long and thoughtful whiff from his meerschaum, "although I have been guilty of certain doggrel myself."

"Suppose you detail," said I, "the particulars of your search."

"Why the fact is, we took our time, and we searched *every where*. I have had long experience in these affairs. I took the entire building, room by room; devoting the nights of a whole week to each. We examined, first, the furniture of each apartment. We opened every possible drawer; and I presume you know that, to a properly trained police agent, such a thing as a *secret* drawer is impossible. Any man is a dolt who permits a 'secret' drawer to escape him in a search of this kind. The thing is *so* plain. There is a certain amount of bulk—of space—to be accounted for in every cabinet. Then we have accurate rules. The fiftieth part of a line could not escape us. After the cabinets we took the chairs. The cushions we probed with the fine long needles you have seen me employ. From the tables we removed the tops."

"Why so?"

"Sometimes the top of a table, or other similarly arranged piece of furniture, is removed by the person wishing to conceal an article; then the leg is excavated, the article deposited within the cavity, and the top replaced. The bottoms and tops of bed-posts are employed in the same way."

"But could not the cavity be detected by sounding?" I asked.

"By no means, if, when the article is deposited, a sufficient wadding of cotton be placed around it. Besides, in our case, we were obliged to proceed without noise."

"But you could not have removed—you could not have taken to pieces *all* articles of furniture in which it would have been possible to make a deposit in the manner you mention. A letter may be compressed into a thin spiral roll, not differing much in shape or bulk from a large knitting-needle, and in this form it might be inserted into the rung of a chair, for example. You did not take to pieces all the chairs?"

"Certainly not; but we did better—we examined the rungs of every chair in the hotel, and, indeed, the jointings of every description of furniture, by the aid of a most powerful microscope. Had there been any traces of recent disturbance we should not have failed to detect it instantly. A single grain of gimlet-dust, for example, would have been as obvious as an apple. Any disorder in the glueing—any unusual gaping in the joints—would have sufficed to insure detection."

"I presume you looked to the mirrors, between the boards and the plates, and you probed the beds and the bed-clothes, as well as the curtains and carpets."

"That of course; and when we had absolutely completed every particle of the furniture in this way, then we examined the house itself. We divided its entire surface into compartments, which we numbered, so that none might be missed; then we scrutinized each individual square inch throughout the premises, including the two houses immediately adjoining, with the microscope, as before."

"The two houses adjoining!" I exclaimed; "you must have had a great deal of trouble."

"We had; but the reward offered is prodigious."

"You include the *grounds* about the houses?"

"All the grounds are paved with brick. They gave us comparatively little trouble. We examined the moss between the bricks, and found it undisturbed."

"You looked among D——'s papers, of course, and into the books of the library?"

"Certainly; we opened every package and parcel; we not only opened every book, but we turned over every leaf in each volume, not contenting ourselves with a mere shake, according to the fashion of some of our police officers. We also measured the thickness of every book-*cover*, with the most accurate admeasurement, and applied to each the most jealous scrutiny of the microscope. Had any of the bindings been recently meddled with, it would have been utterly impossible that the fact should have escaped observation. Some five or six volumes, just from the hands of the binder, we carefully probed, longitudinally, with the needles."

"You explored the floors beneath the carpets?"

"Beyond doubt. We removed every carpet, and examined the boards with the microscope."

"And the paper on the walls?"

"Yes."

"You looked into the cellars?"

"We did."

"Then," I said, "you have been making a miscalculation, and the letter is *not* upon the premises, as you suppose."

"I fear you are right there," said the Prefect. "And now, Dupin, what would you advise me to do?"

"To make a thorough re-search of the premises."

"That is absolutely needless," replied G——. "I am not more sure that I breathe than I am that the letter is not at the Hotel."

"I have no better advice to give you," said Dupin. "You have, of course, an accurate description of the letter?"

"Oh yes!"—And here the Prefect, producing a memorandum-book, proceeded to read aloud a minute account of the internal, and especially of the external appearance of the missing document. Soon after finishing the perusal of this description, he took his departure, more entirely depressed in spirits than I had ever known the good gentleman before.

In about a month afterwards he paid us another visit, and found us occupied very nearly as before. He took a pipe and a chair and entered into some ordinary conversation. At length I said,—

"Well, but G——, what of the purloined letter? I presume you have at last made up your mind that there is no such thing as overreaching the Minister?"

"Confound him, say I—yes; I made the re-examination, however, as Dupin suggested—but it was all labor lost, as I knew it would be."

"How much was the reward offered, did you say?" asked Dupin.

"Why, a very great deal—a *very* liberal reward—I don't like to say how much, precisely; but one thing I *will* say, that I wouldn't mind giving my individual check for fifty thousand francs to any one who could obtain me that letter. The fact is, it is becoming of more and more importance every day; and the reward has been lately doubled. If it were trebled, however, I could do no more than I have done."

"Why, yes," said Dupin, drawlingly, between the whiffs of his meerschaum, "I really—think, G——, you have not exerted yourself—to the utmost in this matter. You might—do a little more, I think, eh?"

"How?—in what way?"

"Why—puff, puff—you might—puff, puff—employ counsel in the matter, eh?—puff, puff, puff. Do you remember the story they tell of Abernethy?"

"No; hang Abernethy!"

"To be sure! hang him and welcome. But, once upon a time, a certain rich miser conceived the design of spunging upon this Abernethy for a medical opinion. Getting up, for this purpose, an ordinary conversation in a private company, he insinuated his case to the physician, as that of an imaginary individual.

"'We will suppose,' said the miser, 'that his symptoms are such and such; now, doctor, what would *you* have directed him to take?'

"'Take!' said Abernethy, 'why, take *advice*, to be sure.'"

"But," said the Prefect, a little discomposed, "*I* am *perfectly* willing to take advice, and to pay for it. I would *really* give fifty thousand francs to any one who would aid me in the matter."

"In that case," replied Dupin, opening a drawer, and producing a check-book, "you may as well fill me up a check for the amount mentioned. When you have signed it, I will hand you the letter."

I was astounded. The Prefect appeared absolutely thunderstricken. For some minutes he remained speechless and motionless, looking incredulously at my friend with open mouth, and eyes that seemed starting from their sockets; then, apparently recovering himself in some measure, he seized a pen, and after several pauses and vacant stares, finally filled up and signed a check for fifty thousand francs, and handed it across the table to Dupin. The latter examined it carefully and deposited it in his pocket-book; then, unlocking an *escritoire*, took thence a letter and gave it to the Prefect. This functionary grasped it in a perfect agony of joy, opened it with a trembling hand, cast a rapid glance at its contents, and then, scrambling and struggling to the door, rushed at length unceremoniously from the room and from the house, without having uttered a syllable since Dupin had requested him to fill up the check.

When he had gone, my friend entered into some explanations.

"The Parisian police," he said, "are exceedingly able in their way. They are persevering, ingenious, cunning, and thoroughly versed in the knowledge which their duties seem chiefly to demand. Thus, when G—— detailed to us his mode of searching the premises at the Hotel D——, I felt entire confidence in his having made a satisfactory investigation—so far as his labors extended."

"So far as his labors extended?" said I.

"Yes," said Dupin. "The measures adopted were not only the best of their kind, but carried out to absolute perfection. Had the letter been deposited within the range of their search, these fellows would, beyond a question, have found it."

I merely laughed—but he seemed quite serious in all that he said.

"The measures, then," he continued, "were good in their kind, and well executed; their defect lay in their being inapplicable to the case, and to the man. A certain set of highly ingenious resources are, with the Prefect, a sort of Procrustean bed, to which he forcibly adapts his designs. But he perpetually errs by being too deep or too shallow, for the matter in hand; and many a schoolboy is a better reasoner than he. I knew one about eight years of age, whose success at guessing in the game of 'even and odd' attracted universal admiration. This game is simple, and is played with marbles. One player holds in his hand a number of these toys, and demands of another whether that number is even or odd. If the guess is right, the guesser wins one; if wrong, he loses one. The boy to whom I allude won all the marbles of the school. Of course he had some principle of guessing; and this lay in mere observation and admeasurement of the astuteness of his opponents. For example, an arrant simpleton is his opponent, and, holding up his closed hand, asks, 'are they even or odd?' Our schoolboy replies, 'odd,' and loses; but upon the second trial he wins, for he then says to himself, "the simpleton had them even upon the first trial, and his amount of cunning is just sufficient to make him have them odd upon the second; I will therefore guess odd;—he guesses odd, and wins. Now, with a simpleton a degree above the first, he would have reasoned thus: 'This fellow finds that in the first instance I guessed odd, and, in the second, he will propose to himself, upon the first impulse, a simple variation from even to odd, as did the first simpleton; but then a second thought will suggest that this is too simple a variation, and finally he will decide upon putting it even as before. I will therefore guess even;'—he guesses even, and wins. Now this mode of reasoning in the schoolboy, whom his fellows termed 'lucky,'—what, in its last analysis, is it?"

"It is merely," I said, "an identification of the reasoner's intellect with that of his opponent."

"It is," said Dupin; "and, upon inquiring of the boy by what means he effected the *thorough* identification in which his success consisted, I received answer as follows: 'When I wish to find out how wise, or how stupid, or how good, or how wicked is any one, or what are his thoughts at the moment, I fashion the expression of my face, as accurately as possible, in accordance with the expression of his, and then wait to see what thoughts or sentiments arise in my mind or heart, as if to match or correspond with the expression.' This response of the schoolboy lies at the bottom of all the spurious profundity which has been attributed to Rochefoucault, to La Bruyère, to Machiavelli, and to Campanella."

"And the identification," I said, "of the reasoner's intellect with that of his opponent, depends, if I understand you aright, upon the accuracy with which the opponent's intellect is admeasured."

"For its practical value it depends upon this," replied Dupin; "and the Prefect and his cohort fail so frequently, first, by default of this identification, and, secondly, by ill-admeasurement, or rather through non-admeasurement, of the intellect with which they are engaged. They consider only their *own* ideas of ingenuity; and, in searching for anything hidden, advert only to the modes in which *they* would have hidden it. They are right in this much—that their own ingenuity is a faithful representative of that of *the mass*; but when the cunning of the individual felon is diverse in character from their own, the felon foils them, of course. This always happens when it is above their own, and very usually when it is below. They have no variation of principle in their investigations; at best, when urged by some unusual emergency—by some extraordinary reward—they extend or exaggerate their old modes of *practice*, without touching their principles. What, for example, in this case of D——, has been done to vary the principle of action? What is all this boring, and probing, and sounding, and scrutinizing with the microscope, and dividing the surface of the building into registered square inches—what is it all but an exaggeration *of the application* of the one principle or set of principles of search, which are based upon the one set of notions regarding human ingenuity, to which the Prefect, in the long routine of his duty, has been accustomed? Do you not see he has taken it for granted that *all* men proceed to conceal a letter,—not exactly in a gimlet-hole bored in a chair-leg—but, at least, in *some* out-of-the-way hole or corner suggested by the same tenor of thought which would urge a man to secrete a letter in a gimlet-hole bored in a chair-leg? And do you not see also, that such *recherchés* nooks for concealment are adapted only for ordinary occasions, and would be adopted only by ordinary intellects; for, in all cases of concealment, a disposal of the article concealed—a disposal of it in this *recherché* manner,—is, in the very first instance, presumable and presumed; and thus its discovery depends, not at all upon the acumen, but altogether upon the mere care, patience, and determination of the seekers; and where the case is of importance—or, what amounts to the same thing in the policial eyes, when the reward is of magnitude,—the qualities in question have *never* been known to fail. You will now understand what I meant in suggesting that, had the purloined letter been hidden any where within the limits of the Prefect's examination—in other words, had the principle of its concealment been comprehended within the principles of the Prefect—its discovery would have been a matter altogether beyond question. This functionary, however, has been thoroughly mystified; and the remote source of his defeat lies in the supposition that the Minister is a fool, because he has acquired renown as a poet. All fools are poets; this the Prefect *feels*; and he is merely guilty of a *non distributio medii* in thence inferring that all poets are fools."

"But is this really the poet?" I asked. "There are two brothers, I know; and both have attained reputation in letters. The Minister I believe has written learnedly on the Differential Calculus. He is a mathematician, and no poet."

"You are mistaken; I know him well; he is both. As poet *and* mathematician, he would reason well; as mere mathematician, he could not have reasoned at all, and thus would have been at the mercy of the Prefect."

"You surprise me," I said, "by these opinions, which have been contradicted by the voice of the world. You do not mean to set at naught the well-digested idea of centuries. The mathematical reason has long been regarded as *the* reason *par excellence.*"

"'*Il y a à parier,*'" replied Dupin, quoting from Chamfort, "'*que toute idée publique, toute convention reçue, est une sottise, car elle a convenu au plus grand nombre.*' The mathematicians, I grant you, have done their best to promulgate the popular error to which you allude, and which is none the less an error for its promulgation as truth. With an art worthy a better cause, for example, they have insinuated the term 'analysis' into application to algebra. The French are the originators of this particular deception; but if a term is of any importance—if words derive any value from applicability—then 'analysis' conveys 'algebra' about as much as, in Latin, '*ambitus*' implies 'ambition,' '*religio*' 'religion,' or '*homines honesti*,' a set of *honorable* men."

"You have a quarrel on hand, I see," said I, "with some of the algebraists of Paris; but proceed."

"I dispute the availability, and thus the value, of that reason which is cultivated in any especial form other than the abstractly logical. I dispute, in particular, the reason educed by mathematical study. The mathematics are the science of form and quantity; mathematical reasoning is merely logic applied to observation upon form and quantity. The great error lies in supposing that even the truths of what is called *pure* algebra, are abstract or general truths. And this error is so egregious that I am confounded at the universality with which it has been received. Mathematical axioms are *not* axioms of general truth. What is true of *relation*—of form and quantity—is often grossly false in regard to morals, for example. In this latter science it is very usually *un*true that the aggregated parts are equal to the whole. In chemistry also the axiom fails. In the consideration of motive it fails; for two motives, each of a given value, have not, necessarily, a value when united, equal to the sum of their values apart. There are numerous other mathematical truths which are only truths within the limits of *relation*. But the mathematician argues, from his *finite truths*, through habit, as if they were of an absolutely general applicability—as the world indeed imagines them to be. Bryant, in his very learned 'Mythology,' mentions an analogous source of error, when he says that 'although the Pagan fables are not believed, yet we forget ourselves continually, and make inferences from them as existing realities.' With the algebraists, however, who are Pagans themselves, the 'Pagan fables' *are* believed, and the inferences are made, not so much through lapse of memory, as through an unaccountable addling of the brains. In short, I never yet encountered the mere mathematician who could be trusted out of equal roots, or one who did not clandestinely hold it as a point of his faith that $x^2+px$ was absolutely and unconditionally equal to $q$. Say to one of these gentlemen, by way of experiment, if you please, that you believe occasions may occur where $x^2+px$ is *not* altogether equal to $q$, and, having made him understand what you mean, get out of his reach as speedily as convenient, for, beyond doubt, he will endeavor to knock you down.

"I mean to say," continued Dupin, while I merely laughed at his last observations, "that if the Minister had been no more than a mathematician, the Prefect would have been under no necessity of giving me this check. I knew him, however, as both mathematician and poet, and my measures were adapted to his capacity, with reference to the circumstances by which he was surrounded. I knew him as a courtier, too, and as a bold *intriguant*. Such a man, I considered, could not fail to be aware of the ordinary policial modes of action. He could not have failed to anticipate—and events have proved that he did not fail to anticipate—the waylayings to which he was subjected. He must have foreseen, I reflected, the secret investigations of his premises. His frequent absences from home at night, which were hailed by the Prefect as certain aids to his success, I regarded only as *ruses*, to afford opportunity for thorough search to the police, and thus the sooner to impress them with the conviction to which G——, in fact, did finally arrive—the conviction that the letter was not upon the premises. I felt, also, that the whole train of thought, which I was at some pains in detailing to you just now, concerning the invariable principle of policial action in searches for articles concealed—I felt that this whole train of thought would necessarily pass through the mind of the Minister. It would imperatively lead him to despise all the ordinary *nooks* of concealment. *He* could not, I reflected, be so weak as not to see that the most intricate and remote recess of his hotel would be as open as his commonest closets to the eyes, to the probes, to the gimlets, and to the microscopes of the Prefect. I saw, in fine, that he would be driven, as a matter of course, to *simplicity*, if not deliberately induced to it as a matter of choice. You will remember, perhaps, how desperately the Prefect laughed when I suggested, upon our first interview, that it was just possible this mystery troubled him so much on account of its being so *very* self-evident."

"Yes," said I, "I remember his merriment well. I really thought he would have fallen into convulsions."

"The material world," continued Dupin, "abounds with very strict analogies to the immaterial; and thus some color of truth has been given to the rhetorical dogma, that metaphor, or simile, may be made to strengthen an argument, as well as to embellish a description. The principle of the *vis inertiæ*, for example, seems to be identical in physics and metaphysics. It is not more true in the former, that a large body is with more difficulty set in motion than a smaller one, and that its subsequent *momentum* is commensurate with this difficulty, than it is, in the latter, that intellects of the vaster capacity, while more forcible, more constant, and more eventful in their movements than those of inferior grade, are yet the less readily moved, and more embarrassed and full of hesitation in the first few steps of their progress. Again: have you ever noticed which of the street signs, over the shop-doors, are the most attractive of attention?"

"I have never given the matter a thought," I said.

"There is a game of puzzles," he resumed, "which is played upon a map. One party playing requires another to find a given word—the name of town, river, state or empire—any word, in short, upon the motley and perplexed surface of the chart. A novice in the game generally seeks to embarrass his opponents by giving them the most minutely lettered names; but the adept selects such words as stretch, in large characters, from one end of the chart to the other. These, like the over-largely lettered signs and placards of the street, escape observation by dint of being excessively obvious; and here the physical oversight is precisely analogous with the moral inapprehension by which the intellect suffers to pass unnoticed those considerations which are too obtrusively and too palpably self-evident. But this is a point, it appears, somewhat above or beneath the understanding of the Prefect. He never once thought it probable, or possible, that the Minister had deposited the letter immediately beneath the nose of the whole world, by way of best preventing any portion of that world from perceiving it.

"But the more I reflected upon the daring, dashing, and discriminating ingenuity of D——; upon the fact that the document must always have been *at hand*, if he intended to use it to good purpose; and upon the decisive evidence, obtained by the Prefect, that it was not hidden within the limits of that dignitary's ordinary search—the more satisfied I became that, to conceal this letter, the Minister had resorted to the comprehensive and sagacious expedient of not attempting to conceal it at all.

"Full of these ideas, I prepared myself with a pair of green spectacles, and called one fine morning, quite by accident, at the

Ministerial hotel. I found D—— at home, yawning, lounging, and dawdling, as usual, and pretending to be in the last extremity of *ennui*. He is, perhaps, the most really energetic human being now alive—but that is only when nobody sees him.

"To be even with him, I complained of my weak eyes, and lamented the necessity of the spectacles, under cover of which I cautiously and thoroughly surveyed the apartment, while seemingly intent only upon the conversation of my host.

"I paid especial attention to a large writing-table near which he sat, and upon which lay confusedly, some miscellaneous letters and other papers, with one or two musical instruments and a few books. Here, however, after a long and very deliberate scrutiny, I saw nothing to excite particular suspicion.

"At length my eyes, in going the circuit of the room, fell upon a trumpery fillagree card-rack of pasteboard, that hung dangling by a dirty blue ribbon from a little brass knob just beneath the middle of the mantel-piece. In this rack, which had three or four compartments, were five or six visiting cards and a solitary letter. This last was much soiled and crumpled. It was torn nearly in two, across the middle—as if a design, in the first instance, to tear it entirely up as worthless, had been altered, or stayed, in the second. It had a large black seal, bearing the D—— cipher *very* conspicuously, and was addressed, in a diminutive female hand, to D——, the minister, himself. It was thrust carelessly, and even, as it seemed, contemptuously, into one of the upper divisions of the rack.

"No sooner had I glanced at this letter, than I concluded it to be that of which I was in search. To be sure, it was, to all appearance, radically different from the one of which the Prefect had read us so minute a description. Here the seal was large and black, with the D—— cipher; there it was small and red, with the ducal arms of the S—— family. Here, the address, to the Minister, was diminutive and feminine; there the superscription, to a certain royal personage, was markedly bold and decided; the size alone formed a point of correspondence. But, then, the *radicalness* of these differences, which was excessive; the dirt; the soiled and torn condition of the paper, so inconsistent with the *true* methodical habits of D——, and so suggestive of a design to delude the beholder into an idea of the worthlessness of the document; these things, together with the hyperobtrusive situation of this document, full in the view of every visiter, and thus exactly in accordance with the conclusions to which I had previously arrived; these things, I say, were strongly corroborative of suspicion, in one who came with the intention to suspect.

"I protracted my visit as long as possible, and, while I maintained a most animated discussion with the Minister, on a topic which I knew well had never failed to interest and excite him, I kept my attention really riveted upon the letter. In this examination, I committed to memory its external appearance and arrangement in the rack; and also fell, at length, upon a discovery which set at rest whatever trivial doubt I might have entertained. In scrutinizing the edges of the paper, I observed them to be more *chafed* than seemed necessary. They presented the *broken* appearance which is manifested when a stiff paper, having been once folded and pressed with a folder, is refolded in a reversed direction, in the same creases or edges which had formed the original fold. This discovery was sufficient. It was clear to me that the letter had been turned, as a glove, inside out, re-directed, and re-sealed. I bade the Minister good morning, and took my departure at once, leaving a gold snuff-box upon the table.

"The next morning I called for the snuff-box, when we resumed, quite eagerly, the conversation of the preceding day. While thus engaged, however, a loud report, as if of a pistol, was heard immediately beneath the windows of the hotel, and was succeeded by a series of fearful screams, and the shoutings of a mob. D—— rushed to a casement, threw it open, and looked out. In the meantime, I stepped to the card-rack, took the letter, put it in my pocket, and replaced it by a *fac-simile*, (so far as regards externals,) which I had carefully prepared at my lodgings; imitating the D—— cipher, very readily, by means of a seal formed of bread.

"The disturbance in the street had been occasioned by the frantic behavior of a man with a musket. He had fired it among a crowd of women and children. It proved, however, to have been without ball, and the fellow was suffered to go his way as a lunatic or a drunkard. When he had gone, D—— came from the window, whither I had followed him immediately upon securing the object in view. Soon afterwards I bade him farewell. The pretended lunatic was a man in my own pay."

"But what purpose had you," I asked, "in replacing the letter by a *fac-simile*? Would it not have been better, at the first visit, to have seized it openly, and departed?"

"D——," replied Dupin, "is a desperate man, and a man of nerve. His hotel, too, is not without attendants devoted to his interests. Had I made the wild attempt you suggest, I might never have left the Ministerial presence alive. The good people of Paris might have heard of me no more. But I had an object apart from these considerations. You know my political prepossessions. In this matter, I act as a partisan of the lady concerned. For eighteen months the Minister has had her in his power. She has now him in hers; since, being unaware that the letter is not in his possession, he will proceed with his exactions as if it was. Thus will he inevitably commit himself, at once, to his political destruction. His downfall, too, will not be more precipitate than awkward. It is all very well to talk about the *facilis descensus Averni*; but in all kinds of climbing, as Catalani said of singing, it is far more easy to get up than to come down. In the present instance I have no sympathy—at least no pity—for him who descends. He is that ***monstrum horrendum***, an unprincipled man of genius. I confess, however, that I should like very well to know the precise character of his thoughts, when, being defied by her whom the Prefect terms 'a certain personage,' he is reduced to opening the letter which I left for him in the card-rack."

"How? did you put any thing particular in it?"

"Why—it did not seem altogether right to leave the interior blank—that would have been insulting. D——, at Vienna once, did me an evil turn, which I told him, quite good-humoredly, that I should remember. So, as I knew he would feel some curiosity in regard to the identity of the person who had outwitted him, I thought it a pity not to give him a clue. He is well acquainted with my MS., and I just copied into the middle of the blank sheet the words—

——Un dessein si funeste,
S'il n'est digne d'Atrée, est digne de Thyeste.

They are to be found in Crébillon's 'Atrée.'"

1844

# HARRIET BEECHER STOWE

(1811–1896)

---

## *The Minister's Housekeeper*

SCENE.—The shady side of a blueberry-pasture.—Sam Lawson with the boys, picking blueberries.—Sam, *loq.*

WAL, YOU SEE, boys, 'twas just here,—Parson Carryl's wife, she died along in the forepart o' March: my cousin Huldy, she undertook to keep house for him. The way on't was, that Huldy, she went to take care o' Mis' Carryl in the fust on't, when she fust took sick. Huldy was a tailoress by trade; but then she was one o' these 'ere facultised persons that has a gift for most any thing, and that was how Mis' Carryl come to set sech store by her, that, when she was sick, nothin' would do for her but she must have Huldy round all the time: and the minister, he said he'd make it good to her all the same, and she shouldn't lose nothin' by it. And so Huldy, she staid with Mis' Carryl full three months afore she died, and got to seein' to every thing pretty much round the place.

"Wal, arter Mis' Carryl died, Parson Carryl, he'd got so kind o' used to hevin' on her 'round, takin' care o' things, that he wanted her to stay along a spell; and so Huldy, she staid along a spell, and poured out his tea, and mended his close, and made pies and cakes, and cooked and washed and ironed, and kep' every thing as neat as a pin. Huldy was a dreffful chipper sort o' gal; and work sort o' rolled off from her like water off a duck's back. There warn't no gal in Sherburne that could put sich a sight o' work through as Huldy; and yet, Sunday mornin', she always come out in the singers' seat like one o' these 'ere June roses, lookin' so fresh and smilin', and her voice was jest as clear and sweet as a meadow lark's—Lordy massy! I 'member how she used to sing some o' them 'are places where the treble and counter used to go together: her voice kind o' trembled a little, and it sort o' went thro' and thro' a feller! tuck him right where he lived!"

Here Sam leaned contemplatively back with his head in a clump of sweet fern, and refreshed himself with a chew of young wintergreen. "This 'ere young wintergreen, boys, is jest like a feller's thoughts o' things that happened when he was young: it comes up jest so fresh and tender every year, the longest time you hev to live; and you can't help chawin' on't tho' 'tis sort o' stingin'. I don't never get over likin' young wintergreen."

"But about Huldah, Sam?"

"Oh, yes! about Huldy. Lordy massy! when a feller is Indianin' round, these 'ere pleasant summer days, a feller's thoughts gits like a flock o' young partridges: they's up and down and everywhere; 'cause one place is jest about as good as another, when they's all so kind o' comfortable and nice. Wal, about Huldy,—as I was a sayin'. She was jest as handsome a gal to look at as a feller could have; and I think a nice, well-behaved young gal in the singers' seat of a Sunday is a means o' grace: it's sort o' drawin' to the unregenerate, you know. Why, boys, in them days, I've walked ten miles over to Sherburne of a Sunday mornin', jest to play the bass-viol in the same singers' seat with Huldy. She was very much respected, Huldy was; and, when she went out to tailorin', she was allers bespoke six months ahead, and sent for in waggins up and down for ten miles round; for the young fellers was allers 'mazin' anxious to be sent after Huldy, and was quite free to offer to go for her. Wal, after Mis' Carryl died, Huldy got to be sort o' housekeeper at the minister's, and saw to every thing, and did every thing: so that there warn't a pin out o' the way.

"But you know how 'tis in parishes: there allers is women that thinks the minister's affairs belongs to them, and they ought to have the rulin' and guidin' of 'em; and, if a minister's wife dies, there's folks that allers has their eyes open on providences,—lookin' out who's to be the next one.

"Now, there was Mis' Amaziah Pipperidge, a widder with snappin' black eyes, and a hook nose,—kind o' like a hawk; and she was one o' them up-and-down commandin' sort o' women, that feel that they have a call to be seein' to every thing that goes on in the parish, and 'specially to the minister.

"Folks did say that Mis' Pipperidge sort o' sot her eye on the parson for herself: wal, now that 'are might a been, or it might not. Some folks thought it was a very suitable connection. You see she hed a good property of her own, right nigh to the minister's lot, and was allers kind o' active and busy; so, takin' one thing with another, I shouldn't wonder if Mis' Pipperidge should a thought that Providence p'inted that way. At any rate, she went up to Deakin Blodgett's wife, and they two sort o' put their heads together a mournin' and condolin' about the way things was likely to go on at the minister's now Mis' Carryl was dead. Ye see, the parson's wife, she was one of them women who hed their eyes everywhere and on every thing. She was a little thin woman, but tough as Inger rubber, and smart as a steel trap; and there warn't a hen laid an egg, or cackled, but Mis' Carryl was right there to see about it; and she hed the garden made in the spring, and the medders mowed in summer, and the cider made, and the corn husked, and the apples got in the fall; and the doctor, he hedn't nothin' to do but jest sit stock still a meditatin' on Jerusalem and Jericho and them things that ministers think about. But Lordy massy! he didn't know nothin' about where any thing he eat or drunk or wore come from or went to: his wife jest led him 'round in temporal things and took care on him like a baby.

"Wal, to be sure, Mis' Carryl looked up to him in spirituals, and thought all the world on him; for there warn't a smarter minister no where 'round. Why, when he preached on decrees and election, they used to come clear over from South Parish, and West Sherburne, and Old Town to hear him; and there was sich a row o' waggins tied along by the meetin'-house that the stables was all full, and all the hitchin'-posts was full clean up to the tavern, so that folks said the doctor made the town look like a gineral trainin'-day a Sunday.

"He was gret on texts, the doctor was. When he hed a p'int to prove, he'd jest go thro' the Bible, and drive all the texts ahead o' him like a flock o' sheep; and then, if there was a text that seemed agin him, why, he'd come out with his Greek and Hebrew, and kind o' chase it 'round a spell, jest as ye see a fellar chase a contrary bell-wether, and make him jump the fence arter the rest. I tell you, there wa'n't no text in the Bible that could stand agin the doctor when his blood was up. The year arter the doctor was app'inted to preach the 'lection sermon in Boston, he made such a figger that the Brattlestreet Church sent a committee right down to see if they couldn't get him to Boston; and then the Sherburne folks, they up and raised his salary; ye see, there ain't nothin' wakes folks up like somebody else's wantin' what you've got. Wal, that fall they made him a Doctor o' Divinity at Cambridge College, and so they sot more by him than ever. Wal, you see, the doctor, of course he felt kind o' lonesome and afflicted when Mis' Carryl was gone; but railly and truly, Huldy was so up to every thing about house, that the doctor didn't miss nothin' in a temporal way. His shirt-bosoms was pleated finer than they ever was, and them ruffles 'round his wrists was kep' like the driven snow; and there warn't a brack in his silk stockin's, and his shoe buckles was kep' polished up, and his coats brushed; and then there warn't no bread and biscuit like Huldy's; and her butter was like solid lumps o' gold; and there wern't no pies to equal hers; and so the doctor never felt the loss o' Miss Carryl at table. Then there was Huldy allers oppisite to him, with her blue eyes and her cheeks like two fresh peaches. She was kind o' pleasant to look at; and the more the doctor looked at her the better he liked her; and so things seemed to be goin' on quite quiet and comfortable ef it hadn't been that Mis' Pipperidge and Mis' Deakin Blodgett and Mis' Sawin got their heads together a talkin' about things.

"'Poor man,' says Mis' Pipperidge, 'what can that child that he's got there do towards takin' the care of all that place? It takes a mature woman,' she says, 'to tread in Mis' Carryl's shoes.'

"'That it does,' said Mis' Blodgett; 'and, when things once get to runnin' down hill, there ain't no stoppin' on 'em,' says she.

"Then Mis' Sawin she took it up. (Ye see, Mis' Sawin used to go out to dress-makin', and was sort o' jealous, 'cause folks sot more by Huldy than they did by her). 'Well,' says she, 'Huldy Peters is well enough at her trade. I never denied that, though I do say I never did believe in her way o' makin' button-holes; and I must say, if 'twas the dearest friend I hed, that I thought Huldy tryin' to fit Mis' Kittridge's plumb-colored silk was a clear piece o' presumption; the silk was jist spiled, so 'twarn't fit to come into the meetin'-house. I must say, Huldy's a gal that's always too ventersome about takin' 'sponsibilities she don't know nothin' about.'

"'Of course she don't,' said Mis' Deakin Blodgett. 'What does she know about all the lookin' and seein' to that there ought to be in guidin' the minister's house. Huldy's well meanin', and she's good at her work, and good in the singers' seat; but Lordy massy! she hain't got no experience. Parson Carryl ought to have an experienced woman to keep house for him. There's the spring house-cleanin' and the fall house-cleanin' to be seen to, and the things to be put away from the moths; and then the gettin' ready for the association and all the ministers' meetin's; and the makin' the soap and the candles, and settin' the hens and turkeys, watchin' the calves, and seein' after the hired men and the garden; and there that 'are blessed man jist sets there at home as serene, and has nobody 'round but that 'are gal, and don't even know how things must be a runnin' to waste!'

"Wal, the upshot on't was, they fussed and fuzzled and wuzzled till they'd drinked up all the tea in the teapot; and then they went down and called on the parson, and wuzzled him all up talkin' about this, that, and t'other that wanted lookin' to, and that it was no way to leave every thing to a young chit like Huldy, and that he ought to be lookin' about for an experienced woman. The parson he thanked 'em kindly, and said he believed their motives was good, but he didn't go no further. He didn't ask Mis' Pipperidge to come and stay there and help him, nor nothin' o' that kind; but he said he'd attend to matters himself. The fact was, the parson had got such a likin' for havin' Huldy 'round, that he couldn't think o' such a thing as swappin' her off for the Widder Pipperidge.

"But he thought to himself, 'Huldy is a good girl; but I oughtn't to be a leavin' every thing to her,—it's too hard on her. I ought to be instructin' and guidin' and helpin' of her; 'cause 'tain't everybody could be expected to know and do what Mis' Carryl did;' and so at it he went; and Lordy massy! didn't Huldy hev a time on't when the minister began to come out of his study, and want to tew 'round and see to things? Huldy, you see, thought all the world of the minister, and she was 'most afraid to laugh; but she told me she couldn't, for the life of her, help it when his back was turned, for he wuzzled things up in the most singular way. But Huldy she'd jest say 'Yes, sir,' and get him off into his study, and go on her own way.

"'Huldy,' says the minister one day, 'you ain't experienced out doors; and, when you want to know any thing, you must come to me.'

"'Yes, sir,' says Huldy.

"'Now, Huldy,' says the parson, 'you must be sure to save the turkey-eggs, so that we can have a lot of turkeys for Thanksgiving.'

"'Yes, sir,' says Huldy; and she opened the pantry-door, and showed him a nice dishful she'd been a savin' up. Wal, the very next day the parson's hen-turkey was found killed up to old Jim Scroggs's barn. Folks said Scroggs killed it; though Scroggs, he stood to it he didn't: at any rate, the Scroggses, they made a meal on't, and Huldy, she felt bad about it 'cause she'd set her heart on raisin' the turkeys; and says she, 'Oh, dear! I don't know what I shall do. I was just ready to see her.'

"'Do, Huldy?' says the parson: 'why, there's the other turkey, out there by the door; and a fine bird, too, he is.'

"Sure enough, there was the old tom-turkey a struttin' and a sidlin' and a quitterin,' and a floutin' his tail-feathers in the sun, like a lively young widower, all ready to begin life over agin.

"'But,' says Huldy, 'you know *he* can't set on eggs.'

"'He can't? I'd like to know why,' says the parson. 'He *shall* set on eggs, and hatch 'em too.'

"'O doctor!' says Huldy, all in a tremble; 'cause, you know, she didn't want to contradict the minister, and she was afraid she should laugh,—'I never heard that a tom-turkey would set on eggs.'

"'Why, they ought to,' said the parson, getting quite 'arnest: 'what else be they good for? you just bring out the eggs, now, and put 'em in the nest, and I'll make him set on 'em.'

"So Huldy she thought there wern't no way to convince him but to let him try: so she took the eggs out, and fixed 'em all nice in the nest; and then she come back and found old Tom a skirmishin' with the parson pretty lively, I tell ye. Ye see, old Tom he didn't take the idee at all; and he flopped and gobbled, and fit the parson; and the parson's wig got 'round so that his cue stuck straight out over his ear, but he'd got his blood up. Ye see, the old doctor was used to carryin' his p'ints o' doctrine; and he hadn't fit the Arminians and Socinians to be beat by a tom-turkey; so finally he made a dive, and ketched him by the neck in spite o' his floppin', and stroked him down, and put Huldy's apron 'round him.

"'There, Huldy,' he says, quite red in the face, 'we've got him now;' and he travelled off to the barn with him as lively as a cricket.

"Huldy came behind jist chokin' with laugh, and afraid the minister would look 'round and see her.

"'Now, Huldy, we'll crook his legs, and set him down,' says the parson, when they got him to the nest: 'you see he is getting quiet, and he'll set there all right.'

"And the parson, he sot him down; and old Tom he sot there solemn enough, and held his head down all droopin', lookin' like a rail pious old cock, as long as the parson sot by him.

"'There: you see how still he sets,' says the parson to Huldy.

"Huldy was 'most dyin' for fear she should laugh. 'I'm afraid he'll get up,' says she, 'when you do.'

"'Oh, no, he won't!' says the parson, quite confident. 'There, there,' says he, layin' his hands on him, as if pronouncin' a blessin'. But when the parson riz up, old Tom he riz up too, and began to march over the eggs.

"'Stop, now!' says the parson. 'I'll make him get down agin: hand me that corn-basket; we'll put that over him.'

"So he crooked old Tom's legs, and got him down agin; and they put the corn-basket over him, and then they both stood and waited.

"'That'll do the thing, Huldy,' said the parson.

"'I don't know about it,' says Huldy.

"'Oh, yes, it will, child! I understand,' says he.

"Just as he spoke, the basket riz right up and stood, and they could see old Tom's long legs.

"'I'll make him stay down, confound him,' says the parson; for, ye see, parsons is men, like the rest on us, and the doctor had got his spunk up.

"'You jist hold him a minute, and I'll get something that'll make him stay, I guess;' and out he went to the fence, and brought in a long, thin, flat stone, and laid it on old Tom's back.

"Old Tom he wilted down considerable under this, and looked railly as if he was goin' to give in. He staid still there a good long spell, and the minister and Huldy left him there and come up to the house; but they hadn't more than got in the door before they see old Tom a hippin' along, as high-steppin' as ever, sayin' 'Talk! talk! and quitter! quitter!' and struttin' and gobblin' as if he'd come through the Red Sea, and got the victory.

"'Oh, my eggs!' says Huldy. 'I'm afraid he's smashed 'em!'

"And sure enough, there they was, smashed flat enough under the stone.

"'I'll have him killed,' said the parson: 'we won't have such a critter 'round.'

"But the parson, he slep' on't, and then didn't do it: he only come out next Sunday with a tip-top sermon on the ''Riginal Cuss' that was pronounced on things in gineral, when Adam fell, and showed how every thing was allowed to go contrary ever since. There was pig-weed, and pusley, and Canady thistles, cut-worms, and bag-worms, and canker-worms, to say nothin' of rattlesnakes. The doctor made it very impressive and sort o' improvin'; but Huldy, she told me, goin' home, that she hardly could keep from laughin' two or three times in the sermon when she thought of old Tom a standin' up with the corn-basket on his back.

"Wal, next week Huldy she jist borrowed the minister's horse and side-saddle, and rode over to South Parish to her Aunt Bascome's,—Widder Bascome's, you know, that lives there by the trout-brook,—and got a lot o' turkey-eggs o' her, and come back and set a hen on 'em, and said nothin'; and in good time there was as nice a lot o' turkey-chicks as ever ye see.

"Huldy never said a word to the minister about his experiment, and he never said a word to her; but he sort o' kep' more to his books, and didn't take it on him to advise so much.

"But not long arter he took it into his head that Huldy ought to have a pig to be a fattin' with the buttermilk. Mis' Pipperidge set him up to it; and jist then old Tim Bigelow, out to Juniper Hill, told him if he'd call over he'd give him a little pig.

"So he sent for a man, and told him to build a pig-pen right out by the well, and have it all ready when he came home with his pig.

"Huldy she said she wished he might put a curb round the well out there, because in the dark, sometimes, a body might stumble into it; and the parson, he told him he might do that.

"Wal, old Aikin, the carpenter, he didn't come till most the middle of the arternoon; and then he sort o' idled, so that he didn't get up the well-curb till sundown; and then he went off and said he'd come and do the pig-pen next day.

"Wal, arter dark, Parson Carryl he driv into the yard, full chizel, with his pig. He'd tied up his mouth to keep him from squeelin'; and he see what he thought was the pig-pen,—he was rather near-sighted,—and so he ran and threw piggy over; and down he dropped into the water, and the minister put out his horse and pranced off into the house quite delighted.

"'There, Huldy, I've got you a nice little pig.'

"'Dear me!' says Huldy: 'where have you put him?'

"'Why, out there in the pig-pen, to be sure.'

"'Oh, dear me!' says Huldy: 'that's the well-curb; there ain't no pig-pen built,' says she.

"'Lordy massy!' says the parson: 'then I've thrown the pig in the well!'

"Wal, Huldy she worked and worked, and finally she fished piggy out in the bucket, but he was dead as a door-nail; and she got him out o' the way quietly, and didn't say much; and the parson, he took to a great Hebrew book in his study; and says he, 'Huldy, I ain't much in temporals,' says he. Huldy says she kind o' felt her heart go out to him, he was so sort o' meek and helpless and larned; and says she, 'Wal, Parson Carryl, don't trouble your head no more about it; I'll see to things;' and sure enough, a week arter there was a nice pen, all ship-shape, and two little white pigs that Huldy bought with the money for the butter she sold at the store.

"'Wal, Huldy,' said the parson, 'you are a most amazin' child: you don't say nothin', but you do more than most folks.'

"Arter that the parson set sich store by Huldy that he come to her and asked her about every thing, and it was amazin' how every thing she put her hand to prospered. Huldy planted marigolds and larkspurs, pinks and carnations, all up and down the path to the front door, and trained up mornin' glories and scarlet-runners round the windows. And she was always a gettin' a root here, and a sprig there, and a seed from somebody else: for Huldy was one o' them that has the gift, so that ef you jist give 'em the leastest sprig of any thing they make a great bush out of it right away; so that in six months Huldy had roses and geraniums and lilies, sich as it would a took a gardener to raise. The parson, he took no notice at fust; but when the yard was all ablaze with flowers he used to come and stand in a kind o' maze at the front door, and say, 'Beautiful, beautiful: why, Huldy, I never see any thing like it.' And then when her work was done arternoons, Huldy would sit with her sewin' in the porch, and sing and trill away till she'd draw the meadow-larks and the bobolinks, and the orioles to answer her, and the great big elm-tree overhead would get perfectly rackety with the birds; and the parson, settin' there in his study, would git to kind o' dreamin' about the angels, and golden harps, and the New Jerusalem; but he wouldn't speak a word, 'cause Huldy she was jist like them wood-thrushes, she never could sing so well when she thought folks was hearin'. Folks noticed, about this time, that the parson's sermons got to be like Aaron's rod, that budded and blossomed: there was things in 'em about flowers and birds, and more 'special about the music o' heaven. And Huldy she noticed, that ef there was a hymn run in her head while she was 'round a workin' the minister was sure to give it out next Sunday. You see, Huldy was jist like a bee: she always sung when she was workin', and you could hear her trillin', now down in the corn-patch, while she was pickin' the corn; and now in the buttery, while she was workin' the butter; and now she'd go singin' down cellar, and then she'd be singin' up over head, so that she seemed to fill a house chock full o' music.

"Huldy was so sort o' chipper and fair spoken, that she got the hired men all under her thumb: they come to her and took her orders jist as meek as so many calves; and she traded at the store, and kep' the accounts, and she hed her eyes everywhere, and tied up all the ends so tight that there want no gettin' 'round her. She wouldn't let nobody put nothin' off on Parson Carryl, 'cause he was a minister. Huldy was allers up to anybody that wanted to make a hard bargain; and, afore he knew jist what he was about, she'd got the best end of it, and everybody said that Huldy was the most capable gal that they'd ever traded with.

"Wal, come to the meetin' of the Association, Mis' Deakin Blodgett and Mis' Pipperidge come callin' up to the parson's, all in a stew, and offerin' their services to get the house ready; but the doctor, he jist thanked 'em quite quiet, and turned 'em over to Huldy; and Huldy she told 'em that she'd got every thing ready, and showed 'em her pantries, and her cakes and her pies and her puddin's, and took 'em all over the house; and they went peekin' and pokin', openin' cupboard-doors, and lookin' into drawers; and they couldn't find so much as a thread out o' the way, from garret to cellar, and so they went off quite discontented. Arter that the women set a new trouble a brewin'. Then they begun to talk that it was a year now since Mis' Carryl died; and it r'ally wasn't proper such a young gal to be stayin' there, who everybody could see was a settin' her cap for the minister.

"Mis' Pipperidge said, that, so long as she looked on Huldy as the hired gal, she hadn't thought much about it; but Huldy was railly takin' on airs as an equal, and appearin' as mistress o' the house in a way that would make talk if it went on. And Mis' Pipperidge she driv 'round up to Deakin Abner Snow's, and down to Mis' 'Lijah Perry's, and asked them if they wasn't afraid that the way the parson and Huldy was a goin' on might make talk. And they said they hadn't thought on't before, but now, come to think on't, they was sure it would; and they all went and talked with somebody else, and asked them if they didn't think it would make talk. So come Sunday, between meetin's there warn't nothin' else talked about; and Huldy saw folks a noddin' and a winkin', and a lookin' arter her, and she begun to feel drefful sort o' disagreeable. Finally Mis' Sawin she says to her, 'My dear, didn't you, never think folk would talk about you and the minister?'

"'No: why should they?' says Huldy, quite innocent.

"'Wal, dear,' says she, 'I think it's a shame; but they say you're tryin' to catch him, and that it's so bold and improper for you to be courtin' of him right in his own house,—you know folks will talk,—I thought I'd tell you 'cause I think so much of you,' says she.

"Huldy was a gal of spirit, and she despised the talk, but it made her drefful uncomfortable; and when she got home at night she sat down in the mornin'-glory porch, quite quiet, and didn't sing a word.

"The minister he had heard the same thing from one of his deakins that day; and, when he saw Huldy so kind o' silent, he says to her, 'Why don't you sing, my child?'

"He hed a pleasant sort o' way with him, the minister had, and Huldy had got to likin' to be with him; and it all come over her that perhaps she ought to go away; and her throat kind o' filled up so she couldn't hardly speak; and, says she, 'I can't sing to-night.'

"Says he, 'You don't know how much good you're singin' has done me, nor how much good *you* have done me in all ways, Huldy. I wish I knew how to show my gratitude.'

"'O sir!' says Huldy, '*is* it improper for me to be here?'

"'No, dear,' says the minister, 'but ill-natured folks will talk; but there is one way we can stop it, Huldy—if you will marry me. You'll make me very happy, and I'll do all I can to make you happy. Will you?'

"Wal, Huldy never told me jist what she said to the minister,—gals never does give you the particulars of them 'are things jist as you'd like 'em,—only I know the upshot and the hull on't was, that Huldy she did a consid'able lot o' clear starchin' and ironin' the next two days; and the Friday o' next week the minister and she rode over together to Dr. Lothrop's in Old Town; and the doctor, he jist made 'em man and wife, 'spite of envy of the Jews,' as the hymn says. Wal, you'd better believe there was a starin' and a wonderin' next Sunday mornin' when the second bell was a tollin', and the minister walked up the broad aisle with Huldy, all in white, arm in arm with him, and he opened the minister's pew, and handed her in as if she was a princess; for, you see, Parson Carryl come of a good family, and was a born gentleman, and had a sort o' grand way o' bein' polite to women-folks. Wal, I guess there was a rus'lin' among the bunnets. Mis' Pipperidge gin a great bounce, like corn poppin' on a shovel, and her eyes glared through her glasses at Huldy as if they'd a sot her afire; and everybody in the meetin' house was a starin', I tell *yew*. But they couldn't none of 'em say nothin' agin Huldy's looks; for there wa'n't a crimp nor a frill about her that wa'n't jis' *so*; and her frock was white as the driven snow, and she had her bunnet all trimmed up with white ribbins; and all the fellows said the old doctor had stole a march, and got the handsomest gal in the parish.

"Wal, arter meetin' they all come 'round the parson and Huldy at the door, shakin' hands and laughin'; for by that time they was about agreed that they'd got to let putty well alone.

"'Why, Parson Carryl,' says Mis' Deakin Blodgett, 'how you've come it over us.'

"'Yes,' says the parson, with a kind o' twinkle in his eye. 'I thought,' says he, 'as folks wanted to talk about Huldy and me, I'd give 'em somethin' wuth talkin' about.'"

1872

# JAMES MCCUNE SMITH

(1813–1865)

## *Heads of the Colored People.—No. 3*

### *The Washerwoman*

SATURDAY NIGHT! *Dunk!* goes the smoothing-iron, then a swift gliding sound as it passes smoothly over starched bosom and collar, and wrist-bands, of one of the many dozen shirts that hang round the room on horses, chairs, lines and every other thing capable of being hanged on. *Dunk! dunk!* goes the iron, sadly, wearily, but steadily, as if the very heart of toil were throbbing its penultimate beats! *Dunk! dunk!* and that small and delicately formed hand and wrist swell up with knotted muscles and bursting veins! And the eye and brow, chiselled out for stern resolve and high thought, the one now dull and haggard, and the other, seamed and blistered with deep furrows and great drops of sweat wrung out by over toil.

The apartment is small, hot as an oven, the air in it thick and misty with the steam rising from the ironing table; in the corners, under the tables, and in all out-of-the-way places, are stowed tubs of various sizes, some empty, some full of clothes soaking for next-week's labor. On the walls hang pictures of old Pappy Thompson, or Brother Paul, or Sammy Cornish: in one corner of the room, a newly varnished mahogany table is partly filled with books—Bunyan's Pilgrim's Progress, Watts' Hymns, the Life of Christ, and a nice "greasy novel" just in from the circulating library; between the windows stand an old bureau, the big drawer of which is the larder, containing sundry slices of cold meat, second handed toast, "with butter on it," and the carcase of a turkey, the return cargo of a basket of clothes sent down town that morning. But even this food is untasted; for, the Sabbath approaches, and old Zion, and the vivid doses of hell fire ready to be showered from the pulpit, on all who "do labor" (saving the parson, who *does* pound the reading board in a style which, to the unsanctified, looks like hard work) on the Day of Rest. *Dunk! dunk!!* goes the smoothing-iron, the frame of the washerwoman bends again to her task, her mind is "far away" in the sunny South, with her sisters and their children who toil as hard but without any pay! And she fancies the smiles which will gladden their faces, when receiving the things she sent them in a box by the last Georgetown packet. *Dunk! dunk!! dunk!!!* goes the iron, this time right swift and cheerily, shot away and back, under thy smile, Oh Freedom! No *Prie Dieu*, in reverential corner, no crucifix and lugubrious beads pendent from the sidewall, no outward and visible sign, but the great impulse of progressive humanity has touched her heart as with flame, and her tired muscles forget all weariness, the iron flies as a weaver's shuttle, shirts appear and disappear with rapidity from the heated blanket and at a quarter to twelve, the groaning table is cleared, and the poor washerwoman sinks upon her knees in prayer for them, that they also may soon partake of that freedom which, however toilsome, is yet so sweet.

Once lighted up, the imagination ranges over the possibilities of their enfranchisement. Each one of her three sisters had been brought North with the white family, and went back, for their children's sake, into bondage. She alone had remained North, from her girlhood, as a slave, until one day, when she had reached woman's years, her so-called master, with much bustle, with whip in hand, had called her up stairs for punishment. The scene was short and decisive; the tall, stout man had raised his arm to strike—"see here!" fiercely exclaimed the frail being before him, "if you dare touch me with that lash, I will tear you to pieces!" The whipper, whipped, dropt his uplifted arm, and quietly slunk down stairs. There had been, unseen by either of them, a silent witness of the scene, who, looking through a glass door, ready to stay the arm of his uncle, had felt a terrible fear, and a terrible triumph. * * *

Yes! well, I had forgotten to say, that, alongside the ironing table, was a good-for-nothing looking quarter grown, bushy-headed boy, a shade or two lighter than his mother, so intent upon "Aladdin; or, the Wonderful Lamp," that he had to be called three or four times before he sprang to put fresh wood on the fire, or light another candle, or bring a pail of water. A boy there, but no evidence around the room, that he called any one father, nor had he, ever, except the unseen, universal "our Father, which art in Heaven." A sort of social Pariah, he had come into the world, after the fashion which so stirs up Ethiop's pious honor. And yet, genial, forgiving Nature, with a healthy forgetfulness of priests and the rituals, had stamped this boy's face with no lineament particularly hideous, nor yet remarkable, except a "laughing devil" in his eye that seemed ready to "face the devil" without Burn's prophylactic.

*Sunday evening!* Can it be the same apartment? No sign of toil is there; everything tidy, neat and clean; all the signs of the hard week's work stowed away in drawers or in the celler. The washerwoman dressed up in neat, even expensive, garments; and her boy with his Sunday go-to-meetin's on, one of the pockets stuffed with sixpence worth of "pieces," (candy,) which he had made Stuart the Confectioner (corner of Chamber and Greenwich, father of the present millionaires) rouse up, at day light, and sell him, as he came back from carrying home clothes, that morning. * * *

But I must break off this sketch halfway, lest Ethiop should "tire" wading through it. . . .

Yours,
Communipaw.

1852

# JAMES MCCUNE SMITH

(1813–1865)

## *Heads of the Colored People.—No. 4*

### *The Sexton*

YEARS AGO, when the idea of turning church and churchyard into houses and lots would have brought down a volley of oaths in low Dutch, French and English, all along Nassau street, there lived and flourished the most remarkable of New York sextons.—All the sextons in those days were colored men; John Mace and a thousand other funerals were *nondum*. Our hero was of gigantic height, with broad double-jointed shoulders, bowed legs and a head to match: he seemed to have grown up under the church, part of its support, one of its under-ground pillars, so much a part of it, that whenever he crept out of the vaults into the open air, it seemed clear that he must have braced up a huge stone pillar, to take his place "until his return," else *that* side of the edifice must have caved in. His mother must have brooded in charnel houses, fascinated with vampire fancies, or he never would have come into the world with that huge, misshapen head! His eyes were large, prominent and staring, with the whites visible all round, and seemed to have been placed at different times and unsymmetrical places in his head; they were no more a pair than if they had belonged to different persons. His hair, on week days, lay close to his head, carefully done up in five closely plaited pig-tails which lay close to the scalp, from the natural disposition to "grow in again," manifested by "each partic'lar hair." But on Sundays, his whole scalp passed from the grub to the butterfly state—the pig-tails expanded into whirls, elaborately combed out, into prow, *alae*, *naviculum*, in short, decidedly papilionaceous; thus affording a tempting subject for urchin's laughter, and for the minister's illustration of the doctrine of euthanasia. Such was

> "The sexton he, whose strenuous arm
> Dug all the graves, and tolled the bell,"

All else appeared to him as dead,
Awaiting but the shroud and pall,
It seemed that to himself he said,
"I soon shall dig the graves of all."

He held a plurality of offices; sexton to the French church, and grave-digger to St. Philips. On Sundays, he assisted the French minister in robing, and about mid-sermon, walked softly up the aisle to whisper a word to Dr. P——, one of the church wardens: the Doctor would hasten out, hat in hand, under the earnest gaze of half the congregation, then in a little while would return, with a peculiar beam of satisfaction in his face, that allayed all anxiety about the "danger of the case." It happened so regularly, that inquiry was set on foot, when it was discovered that the patient was in the doctor's own stomach first, then in the sexton's, for they both had visited Niblo's coffee house, then located just over the way.

But it was in the old Chrystie street grave-yard that our sexton most did flourish. There he had buried all the colored population for quarter of a century; at first with the aid of two assistants, but latterly, as the ground grew full, alone. People enough were buried there every six months to fill any ground of the same area, but our sexton's sharp spade, and skill in packing, made room for more.—With a huge wall, or pestle, and a convenient corner in the vault, skulls and other bones not quite dry, were hastened in the process of turning it to dust. His labors extended far into the night, and there are persons living who attest that they have seen him crawl out of the old Chrystie street yard, at crow of cock, licking his chops, and with suspicious bits of flesh adhering to his frowsy garments; and one lady bought a bureau the veneering of which she was sure was the exact grain of the lid of her husband's coffin! When they built the tallow melting establishment next door to the grave-yard, coffins were found shoved under the old foundations like drawers in a druggist's store. And most strange to say, when this establishment went into operation, the grave-yard grew more roomy, whilst the odor from the bone boiling-factory grew horridly human.

Fierce rumors grew apace, and even reached the dull ears of the vestry of St. Philips, in the shape of threats; but that stolid body quietly looked at the account-book, found that the grave-yard yielded them plenty of money, which being all they wanted from live niggers, was all they could expect from dead ones. "Was not the liturgy read?—Was not the minister paid? What further had the vestry to do with the matter?"—"This grumbling must be the doing of envious outsiders who wished to disturb the peace of the church." Such were the replies of the vestry.

Our sexton was a public man of some note. He helped to organize the New York African Society for mutual relief in 1809: on the occurrence of the first death in that body, he, along with a loading sweep-master, kept watch over the corpse the first night.—As these two compared notes and reckoned profits in business, towards midnight they heard a series of raps! One went to the door, called, but no one answered nor appeared. They resumed talking when the raps came again! Again going to the door, and finding no one, the sweep-master locked the door and laid the key on the table.

The raps occurred again and again, as horror crept through the bones of the two setters up! Finding one of the eyes of the sexton resting on the sheet-covered corpse, saw the linen rise and fall as the raps came; with a shriek and howl he pointed to the spot, when the sweep-master also caught sight, and both made for the chimney, the sweep-master up first and the other clenching to his heels. Their uproar stirred the neighbors, who, finding the door locked, burst it open, sure (from his reputation that way) to find the sexton feasting on the corpse! Some one snatched the sheet from the body and found—the deceased man's favorite spaniel—the cause of the rappings sadly crouched near his dead master's remains.

The rumors against our sexton at length reached the ears of the corporation of the city of New York. He was notified that on a certain day, the city Inspector would visit the grave-yard in Chrystie street; on the morning of that day at daylight, the sexton's wife missed him from her side, (he always came home at cock crowing,) and he has never been heard of since. Rewards were offered, the city and the vaults ransacked, and although everybody knew him, no one had witnessed his exit. About twenty years after, in 1850, a man came to my house, hardly over the fright, for he declared that he had seen and spoken to this very sexton in Detroit, in a barber's shop. But the sexton's wife, yet living, did not believe him, the vestry of St. Philips *did* believe him, and *that* is regarded as proof that the man must have been mistaken.

Yours lengthily,
Communipaw

1852

# THOMAS BANGS THORPE

(1815–1878)

---

## *The Big Bear of Arkansas*

A STEAMBOAT ON the Mississippi, frequently, in making her regular trips, carries between places varying from one to two thousand miles apart; and, as these boats advertise to land passengers and freight at "all intermediate landings," the heterogeneous character of the passengers of one of these up-country boats can scarcely be imagined by one who has never seen it with his own eyes.

Starting from New Orleans in one of these boats, you will find yourself associated with men from every State in the Union, and from every portion of the globe; and a man of observation need not lack for amusement or instruction in such a crowd, if he will take the trouble to read the great book of character so favorably opened before him.

Here may be seen, jostling together, the wealthy Southern planter and the pedler of tin-ware from New England—the Northern merchant and the Southern jockey—a venerable bishop, and a desperate gambler—the land speculator, and the honest farmer—professional men of all creeds and characters—Wolvereens, Suckers, Hoosiers, Buckeyes, and Corncrackers, beside a "plentiful sprinkling" of the half-horse and half-alligator species of men, who are peculiar to "old Mississippi," and who appear to gain a livelihood by simply going up and down the river. In the pursuit of pleasure or business, I have frequently found myself in such a crowd.

On one occasion, when in New Orleans, I had occasion to take a trip of a few miles up the Mississippi, and I hurried on board the well-known "high-pressure-and-beat-every-thing" steamboat "Invincible," just as the last note of the last bell was sounding; and when the confusion and bustle that is natural to a boat's getting under way had subsided, I discovered that I was associated in as heterogeneous a crowd as was ever got together. As my trip was to be of a few hours' duration only, I made no endeavors to become acquainted with my fellow-passengers, most of whom would be together many days. Instead of this, I took out of my pocket the "latest paper," and more critically than usual examined its contents; my fellow-passengers, at the same time, disposed of themselves in little groups.

While I was thus busily employed in reading, and my companions were more busily still employed, in discussing such subjects as suited their humors best, we were most unexpectedly startled by a loud Indian whoop, uttered in the "social hall," that part of the cabin fitted off for a bar; then was to be heard a loud crowing, which would not have continued to interest us—such sounds being quite common in that *place of spirits*—had not the hero of these windy accomplishments stuck his head into the cabin, and hallooed out, "Hurra for the Big B*e*ar of Arkansaw!"

Then might be heard a confused hum of voices, unintelligible, save in such broken sentences as "horse," "screamer," "lightning is slow," &c.

As might have been expected, this continued interruption, attracted the attention of every one in the cabin; all conversation ceased, and in the midst of this surprise, the "Big B*e*ar" walked into the cabin, took a chair, put his feet on the stove, and looking back over his shoulder, passed the general and familiar salute—"Strangers, how are you?"

He then expressed himself as much at home as if he had been at "the Forks of Cypress," and "prehaps a little more so."

Some of the company at this familiarity looked a little angry, and some astonished; but in a moment every face was wreathed in a smile. There was something about the intruder that won the heart on sight. He appeared to be a man enjoying perfect health and contentment; his eyes were as sparkling as diamonds and good-natured to simplicity. Then his perfect confidence in himself was irresistibly droll.

"Prehaps," said he, "gentlemen," running on without a person interrupting, "prehaps you have been to New Orleans often; I never made *the first visit before*, and I don't intend to make another in a crow's life. I am thrown away in that ar place, and useless, that ar a fact. Some of the gentlemen thar called me *green*—well, prehaps I am, said I, *but I arn't so at home*; and if I aint off my trail much, the heads of them perlite chaps themselves wern't much the hardest; for according to my notion, they were *real know-nothings*, green as a pumpkin-vine—

couldn't, in farming, I'll bet, raise a crop of turnips; and as for shooting, they'd miss a barn if the door was swinging, and that, too, with the best rifle in the country. And then they talked to me 'bout hunting, and laughed at my calling the principal game in Arkansaw poker, and high-low-jack.

"'Prehaps,' said I, 'you prefer checkers and roulette;' at this they laughed harder than ever, and asked me if I lived in the woods, and didn't know what *game* was?

"At this, I rather think *I* laughed.

"'Yes,' I roared, and says, I, 'Strangers, if you'd asked me *how we got our meat* in Arkansaw, I'd a told you at once, and given you a list of varmints that would make a caravan, beginning with the bar, and ending off with the cat; that's *meat* though, not game.

"Game, indeed,—that's what city folks call it; and with them it means chippen-birds and shite-pokes; may be such trash live in my diggins, but I arn't noticed them yet: a bird anyway is too trifling. I never did shoot at but one, and I'd never forgiven myself for that, had it weighed less than forty pounds. I wouldn't draw a rifle on any thing less heavy than that; and when I meet with another wild turkey of the same size, I will drap him."

"A wild turkey weighing forty pounds!" exclaimed twenty voices in the cabin at once.

"Yes, strangers, and wasn't it a whopper? You see, the thing was so fat that it couldn't fly far; and when he fell out of the tree, after I shot him, on striking the ground he bust open behind, and the way the pound gobs of tallow rolled out of the opening was perfectly beautiful."

"Where did all that happen?" asked a cynical-looking Hoosier.

"Happen! happened in Arkansaw: where else could it have happened, but in the creation State, the finishing-up country—a State where the *sile* runs down to the centre of the 'arth, and government gives you a title to every inch of it? Then its airs—just breathe them, and they will make you snort like a horse. It's a State without a fault, it is."

"Excepting mosquitoes," cried the Hoosier.

"Well, stranger, except them; for it ar a fact that they are rather *enormous*, and do push themselves in somewhat troublesome. But, stranger, they never stick twice in the same place;

and give them a fair chance for a few months, and you will get as much above noticing them as an alligator. They can't hurt my feelings, for they lay under the skin; and I never knew but one case of injury resulting from them, and that was to a Yankee: and they take worse to foreigners, any how, than they do to natives. But the way they used that fellow up! first they punched him until he swelled up and busted; then he sup-per-a-ted, as the doctor called it, until he was as raw as beef; then, owing to the warm weather, he tuck the ager, and finally he tuck a steamboat and left the country. He was the only man that ever tuck mosquitoes at heart that I knowd of.

"But mosquitoes is natur, and I never find fault with her. If they ar large, Arkansaw is large, her varmints ar large, her trees ar large, her rivers ar large, and a small mosquito would be of no more use in Arkansaw than preaching in a cane-brake."

This knock-down argument in favor of big mosquitoes used the Hoosier up, and the logician started on a new track, to explain how numerous bear were in his "diggins," where he represented them to be "about as plenty as blackberries, and a little plentifuller."

Upon the utterance of this assertion, a timid little man near me inquired, if the bear in Arkansaw ever attacked the settlers in numbers?

"No," said our hero, warming with the subject, "no, stranger, for you see it ain't the natur of b*e*ar to go in droves; but the way they squander about in pairs and single ones is edifying.

"And then the way I hunt them—the old black rascals know the crack of my gun as well as they know a pig's squealing. They grow thin in our parts, it frightens them so, and they do take the noise dreadfully, poor things. That gun of mine is a perfect *epidemic among bear*: if not watched closely, it will go off as quick on a warm scent as my dog Bowieknife will: and then that dog—whew! why the fellow thinks that the world is full of b*e*ar, he finds them so easy. It's lucky he don't talk as well as think; for with his natural modesty, if he should suddenly learn how much he is acknowledged to be ahead of all other dogs in the universe, he would be astonished to death in two minutes.

"Strangers, that dog knows a b*e*ar's way as well as a horse-jockey knows a woman's: he always barks at the right time, bites at the exact place, and whips without getting a scratch.

"I never could tell whether he was made expressly to hunt b*e*ar, or whether b*e*ar was made expressly for him to hunt; any way, I believe they were ordained to go together as naturally as Squire Jones says a man and woman is, when he moralizes in marrying a couple. In fact, Jones once said, said he, 'Marriage according to law is a civil contract of divine origin; it's common to all countries as well as Arkansaw, and people take to it as naturally as Jim Doggett's Bowieknife takes to b*e*ar.'"

"What season of the year do your hunts take place?" inquired a gentlemanly foreigner, who, from some peculiarities of his baggage, I suspected to be an Englishman, on some hunting expedition, probably at the foot of the Rocky Mountains.

"The season for b*e*ar hunting, stranger," said the man of Arkansaw, "is generally all the year round, and the hunts take place about as regular. I read in history that varmints have their fat season, and their lean season. That is not the case in Arkansaw, feeding as they do upon the *spontenacious* productions of the sile, they have one continued fat season the year round; though in winter things in this way is rather more greasy than in summer, I must admit. For that reason b*e*ar with us run in warm weather, but in winter they only waddle.

"Fat, fat! it's an enemy to speed; it tames every thing that has plenty of it. I have seen wild turkeys, from its influence, as gentle as chickens. Run a b*e*ar in this fat condition, and the way it improves the critter for eating is amazing; it sort of mixes the ile up with the meat, until you can't tell t'other from which. I've done this often.

"I recollect one perty morning in particular, of putting an old he fellow on the stretch, and considering the weight he carried, he run well. But the dogs soon tired him down, and when I came up with him wasn't he in a beautiful sweat—I might say fever; and then to see his tongue sticking out of his mouth a feet, and his sides sinking and opening like a bellows, and his cheeks so fat that he couldn't look cross. In this fix I blazed at him, and pitch me naked into a briar patch, if the steam didn't come out of the bullet-hole ten foot in a straight line. The fellow, I reckon, was made on the high-pressure system, and the lead sort of bust his biler."

"That column of steam was rather curious, or else the bear must have been very *warm*," observed the foreigner, with a laugh.

"Stranger, as you observe, that b*e*ar was WARM, and the blowing off of the steam show'd it, and also how hard the varmint had been run. I have no doubt if he had kept on two miles farther his insides would have been stewed; and I expect to meet with a varmint yet of extra bottom, that will run himself into a skinfull of b*e*ar's grease: it is possible; much onlikelier things have happened."

"Whereabouts are these bears so abundant?" inquired the foreigner, with increasing interest.

"Why, stranger, they inhabit the neighborhood of my settlement, one of the prettiest places on old Mississipp—a perfeet location, and no mistake; a place that had some defects until the river made the 'cut-off' at 'Shirt-tail bend,' and that remedied the evil, as it brought my cabin on the edge of the river—a great advantage in wet weather, I assure you, as you can now roll a barrel of whiskey into my yard in high water from a boat, as easy as falling off a log. It's a great improvement, as toting it by land in a jug, as I used to do, *evaporated* it too fast, and it became expensive.

"Just stop with me, stranger, a month or two, or a year, if you like, and you will appreciate my place. I can give you plenty to eat; for beside hog and hominy, you can have b*e*ar-ham, and b*e*ar-sausages, and a mattrass of b*e*ar-skins to sleep on, and a wildcat-skin, pulled off hull, stuffed with corn-shucks, for a pillow. That bed would put you to sleep if you had the rheumatics in every joint in your body. I call that ar bed, a *quietus.*

"Then look at my 'pre-emption'—the government aint got another like it to dispose of. Such timber, and such bottom land,—why you can't preserve any thing natural you plant in it unless you pick it young, things thar will grow out of shape so quick.

"I once planted in those diggins a few potatoes and beets; they took a fine start, and after that, an ox team couldn't have kept them from growing. About that time I went off to old Kaintuck on business, and did not hear from them things in three months, when I accidentally stumbled on a fellow who had drapped in at my place, with an idea of buying me out.

"'How did you like things?' said I.

"'Pretty well,' said he; 'the cabin is convenient, and the timber land is good; but that bottom land aint worth the first red cent.'"

"'Why?' said I.

"''Cause,' said he.

"''Cause what?' said I.

"''Cause it's full of cedar stumps and Indian mounds, and *can't be cleared.*'

"'Lord,' said I, 'them ar "cedar stumps" is beets, and them ar "Indian mounds" tater hills.'

"As I had expected, the crop was overgrown and useless: the sile is too rich, *and planting in Arkansaw is dangerous.*

"I had a good-sized sow killed in that same bottom-land. The old thief stole an ear of corn, and took it down to eat where she slept at night. Well, she left a grain or two on the ground, and lay down on them: before morning the corn shot up, and the percussion killed her dead. I don't plant any more: natur intended Arkansaw for a hunting ground, and I go according to natur."

The questioner, who had thus elicited the description of our hero's settlement, seemed to be perfectly satisfied, and said no more; but the "Big Bear of Arkansaw" rambled on from one thing to another with a volubility perfectly astonishing, occasionally disputing with those around him, particularly with a "live Sucker" from Illinois, who had the daring to say that our Arkansaw friend's stories "smelt rather tall."

The evening was nearly spent by the incidents we have detailed; and conscious that my own association with so singular a personage would probably end before morning, I asked him if he would not give me a description of some particular bear hunt; adding, that I took great interest in such things, though I was no sportsman. The desire seemed to please him, and he squared himself round towards me, saying, that he could give me an idea of a bear hunt that was never beat in this world, or in any other. His manner was so singular, that half of his story consisted in his excellent way of telling it, the great peculiarity of which was, the happy manner he had of emphasizing the prominent parts of his conversation. As near as I can recollect, I have italicized the words, and given the story in his own way.

"Stranger," said he, "in bear hunts *I am numerous*, and which particular one, as you say, I shall tell, puzzles me.

"There was the old she devil I shot at the Hurricane last fall—then there was the old hog thief I popped over at the Bloody Crossing, and then—Yes, I have it! I will give you an idea of a hunt, in which the greatest bear was killed that ever lived, *none excepted*; about an old fellow that I hunted, more or less, for two or three years; and if that aint a *particular bear hunt*, I ain't got one to tell.

"But in the first place, stranger, let me say, I am pleased with you, because you aint ashamed to gain information by asking and listening; and that's what I say to Countess's pups every day when I'm home; and I have got great hopes of them ar pups, because they are continually *nosing* about; and though they stick it sometimes in the wrong place, they gain experience any how, and may learn something useful to boot.

"Well, as I was saying about this big bear, you see when I and some more first settled in our region, we were drivin to hunting naturally; we soon liked it, and after that we found it an easy matter to make the thing our business. One old chap who had pioneered 'afore us, gave us to understand that we had settled in the right place. He dwelt upon its merits until it was affecting, and showed us, to prove his assertions, more scratches on the bark of the sassafras trees, than I ever saw chalk marks on a tavern door 'lection time.

"'Who keeps that ar reckoning?' said I.

"'The bear,' said he.

"'What for?' said I.

"'Can't tell,' said he; 'but so it is: the bear bite the bark and wood too, at the highest point from the ground they can reach, and you can tell, by the marks,' said he, 'the length of the bear to an inch.'

"'Enough,' said I; 'I've learned something here a'ready, and I'll put it in practice.'

"Well, stranger, just one month from that time I killed a bar, and told its exact length before I measured it, by those very marks; and when I did that, I swelled up considerably—I've been a prouder man ever since.

"So I went on, larning something every day, until I was reckoned a buster, and allowed to be decidedly the best bear hunter in my district; and that is a reputation as much harder to earn than to be reckoned first man in Congress, as an iron ramrod is harder than a toadstool.

"Do the varmints grow over-cunning by being fooled with by greenhorn hunters, and by this means get troublesome, they send for me, as a matter of course; and thus I do my own hunting, and most of my neighbors'. I walk into the varmints though, and it has become about as much the same to me as drinking. It is told in two sentences—

"A b*ear* is started, and he is killed.

"The thing is somewhat monotonous now—I know just how much they will run, where they will tire, how much they will growl, and what a thundering time I will have in getting their meat home. I could give you the history of the chase with all the particulars at the commencement, I know the signs so well—*Stranger, I'm certain.* Once I met with a match, though, and I will tell you about it; for a common hunt would not be worth relating.

"On a fine fall day, long time ago, I was trailing about for b*ear*, and what should I see but fresh marks on the sassafras trees, about eight inches above any in the forests that I knew of. Says I, 'Them marks is a hoax, or it indicates the d——t b*ear* that was ever grown.' In fact, stranger, I couldn't believe it was real, and I went on. Again I saw the same marks, at the same height, and *I knew the thing lived.* That conviction came home to my soul like an earthquake.

"Says I, 'Here is something a-purpose for me: that b*ear* is mine, or I give up the hunting business.' The very next morning, what should I see but a number of buzzards hovering over my corn-field. 'The rascal has been there,' said I, 'for that sign is certain:' and, sure enough, on examining, I found the bones of what had been as beautiful a hog the day before, as was ever raised by a Buckeye. Then I tracked the critter out of the field to the woods, and all the marks he left behind, showed me that he was *the bear.*

"Well, stranger, the first fair chase I ever had with that big critter, I saw him no less than three distinct times at a distance: the dogs run him over eighteen miles and broke down, my horse gave out, and I was as nearly used up as a man can be, made on *my* principle, *which is patent.*

"Before this adventure, such things were unknown to me as possible; but, strange as it was, that b*ea*r got me used to it before I was done with him; for he got so at last, that he would leave me on a long chase *quite easy*. How he did it, I never could understand.

"That a b*ea*r runs at all, is puzzling; but how this one could tire down and bust up a pack of hounds and a horse, that were used to overhauling every thing they started after in no time, was past my understanding. Well, stranger, that b*ea*r finally got so sassy, that he used to help himself to a hog off my premises whenever he wanted one; the buzzards followed after what he left, and so, between *bear and buzzard*, I rather think I got *out of pork*.

"Well, missing that b*ea*r so often took hold of my vitals, and I wasted away. The thing had been carried too far, and it reduced me in flesh faster than an ager. I would see that b*ea*r in every thing I did: *he hunted me*, and that, too, like a devil, which I began to think he was.

"While in this shaky fix, I made preparations to give him a last brush, and be done with it. Having completed every thing to my satisfaction, I started at sunrise, and to my great joy, I discovered from the way the dogs run, that they were near him. Finding his trail was nothing, for that had become as plain to the pack as a turnpike road.

"On we went, and coming to an open country, what should I see but the b*ea*r very leisurely ascending a hill, and the dogs close at his heels, either a match for him this time in speed, or else he did not care to get out of their way—I don't know which. But wasn't he a beauty, though! I loved him like a brother.

"On he went, until he came to a tree, the limbs of which formed a crotch about six feet from the ground. Into this crotch he got and seated himself, the dogs yelling all around it; and there he sat eyeing them as quiet as a pond in low water.

"A greenhorn friend of mine, in company, reached shooting distance before me, and blazed away, hitting the critter in the centre of his forehead. The b*ea*r shook his head as the ball struck it, and then walked down from that tree, as gently as a lady would from a carriage.

"'Twas a beautiful sight to see him do that—he was in such a rage, that he seemed to be as little afraid of the dogs as if they had been sucking pigs; and the dogs warn't slow in making a ring around him at a respectful distance, I tell you; even Bowieknife himself, stood off. Then the way his eyes flashed!—why the fire of them would have singed a cat's hair; in fact, that bear was in a *wrath all over.* Only one pup came near him, and he was brushed out so totally with the bear's left paw, that he entirely disappeared; and that made the old dogs more cautious still. In the mean time, I came up, and taking deliberate aim, as a man should do, at his side, just back of his foreleg, *if my gun did not snap*, call me a coward, and I won't take it personal.

"Yes, stranger, *it snapped*, and I could not find a cap about my person. While in this predicament, I turned round to my fool friend—'Bill,' says I, 'you're an ass—you're a fool—you might as well have tried to kill that bear by barking the tree under his belly, as to have done it by hitting him in the head. Your shot has made a tiger of him; and blast me, if a dog gets killed or wounded when they come to blows, I will stick my knife into your liver, I will ——.' My wrath was up. I had lost my caps, my gun had snapped, the fellow with me had fired at the bear's head, and I expected every moment to see him close in with the dogs and kill a dozen of them at least. In this thing I was mistaken; for the bear leaped over the ring formed by the dogs, and giving a fierce growl, was off—the pack, of course, in full cry after him. The run this time was short, for coming to the edge of a lake, the varmint jumped in, and swam to a little island in the lake, which it reached, just a moment before the dogs.

"'I'll have him now,' said I, for I had found my caps in the *lining of my coat*—so, rolling a log into the lake, I paddled myself across to the island, just as the dogs had cornered the bear in a thicket. I rushed up and fired—at the same time the critter leaped over the dogs and came within three feet of me, running like mad; he jumped into the lake, and tried to mount the log I had just deserted, but every time he got half his body on it, it would roll over and send him under; the dogs, too, got around him, and pulled him about, and finally Bowieknife clenched with him, and they sunk into the lake together.

"Stranger, about this time I was excited, and I stripped off my coat, drew my knife, and intended to have taken a part with Bowieknife myself, when the bear rose to the surface. But the varmint staid under—Bowieknife came up alone, more dead than alive, and with the pack came ashore.

"'Thank God!' said I, 'the old villain has got his deserts at last.'

"Determined to have the body, I cut a grape-vine for a rope, and dove down where I could see the bear in the water, fastened my rope to his leg, and fished him, with great difficulty, ashore. Stranger, may I be chawed to death by young alligators, if the thing I looked at wasn't a *she bear, and not the old critter after all.*

"The way matters got mixed on that island was onaccountably curious, and thinking of it made me more than ever convinced that I was hunting the devil himself. I went home that night and took to my bed—the thing was killing me. The entire team of Arkansaw in bear-hunting acknowledged himself used up, and the fact sunk into my feelings as a snagged boat will in the Mississippi. I grew as cross as a bear with two cubs and a sore tail. The thing got out 'mong my neighbors, and I was asked how come on that individ-u-al that never lost a bear when once started? and if that same individ-u-al didn't wear telescopes when he turned a she-bear, of ordinary size, into an old he one, a little larger than a horse?

"'Prehaps,' said I, 'friends'—getting wrathy—'prehaps you want to call somebody a liar?'

"'Oh, no,' said they, 'we only heard of such things being *rather common* of late, but we don't believe one word of it; oh, no,'—and then they would ride off, and laugh like so many hyenas over a dead nigger.

It was too much, and I determined to catch that bear, go to Texas, or die,—and I made my preparations accordin'.

"I had the pack shut up and rested. I took my rifle to pieces, and iled it.

"I put caps in every pocket about my person, *for fear of the lining.*

"I then told my neighbors, that on Monday morning—naming the day—I would start THAT BEAR, and bring him home with me, or they might divide my settlement among them, the owner having disappeared.

"Well, stranger, on the morning previous to the great day of my hunting expedition, I went into the woods near my house, taking my gun and Bowieknife along, just *from habit*, and there sitting down, also from habit, what should I see, getting over my fence, but *the bear*! Yes, the old varmint was within a hundred yards of me, and the way he walked *over that fence*—stranger; he loomed up like a *black mist*, he seemed so large, and he walked right towards me.

"I raised myself, took deliberate aim, and fired. Instantly the varmint wheeled, gave a yell, and *walked through the fence*, as easy as a falling tree would through a cobweb.

"I started after, but was tripped up by my inexpressibles, which, either from habit or the excitement of the moment, were about my heels, and before I had really gathered myself up, I heard the old varmint groaning, like a thousand sinners, in a thicket near by, and, by the time I reached him, he was a corpse.

"Stranger, it took five niggers and myself to put that carcass on a mule's back, and old long-ears waddled under his load, as if he was foundered in every leg of his body; and with a common whopper of a b*ear*, he would have trotted off, and enjoyed himself.

"'Twould astonish you to know how big he was: I made a *bed-spread of his skin*, and the way it used to cover my b*ear* mattress, and leave several feet on each side to tuck up, would have delighted you. It was, in fact, a creation b*ear*, and if it had lived in Samson's time, and had met him in a fair fight, he would have licked him in the twinkling of a dice-box.

"But, stranger, I never liked the way I hunted him, *and missed him*. There is something curious about it, that I never could understand,—and I never was satisfied at his giving in so *easy at last*. Prehaps he had heard of my preparations to hunt him the next day, so he jist guv up, like Captain Scott's coon, to save his wind to grunt with in dying; but that ain't likely. My private opinion is, that that bear was an *unhuntable bear, and died when his time come*."

When this story was ended, our hero sat some minutes with his auditors, in a grave silence; I saw there was a mystery to him connected with the bear whose death he had just related, that had evidently made a strong impression on his mind. It was also evident that there was some superstitious awe connected with the affair,—a feeling common with all "children of the wood," when they meet with any thing out of their everyday experience.

He was the first one, however, to break the silence, and, jumping up, he asked all present to "liquor" before going to bed,—a thing which he did, with a number of companions, evidently to his heart's content.

Long before day, I was put ashore at my place of destination, and I can only follow with the reader, in imagination, our Arkansas friend, in his adventures at the "Forks of Cypress," on the Mississippi.

1841

# FREDERICK DOUGLASS

(1818–1895)

---

## *The Heroic Slave*

### Part I.

Oh! child of grief, why weepest thou?
Why droops thy sad and mournful brow?
Why is thy look so like despair?
What deep, sad sorrow lingers there?

THE STATE of Virginia is famous in American annals for the multitudinous array of her statesmen and heroes. She has been dignified by some the mother of statesmen. History has not been sparing in recording their names, or in blazoning their deeds. Her high position in this respect, has given her an enviable distinction among her sister States. With Virginia for his birth-place, even a man of ordinary parts, on account of the general partiality for her sons, easily rises to eminent stations. Men, not great enough to attract special attention in their native States, have, like a certain distinguished citizen in the State of New York, sighed and repined that they were not born in Virginia. Yet not all the great ones of the Old Dominion have, by the fact of their birth-place, escaped undeserved obscurity. By some strange neglect, *one* of the truest, manliest, and bravest of her children,—one who, in after years, will, I think, command the pen of genius to set his merits forth, holds now no higher place in the records of that grand old Commonwealth than is held by a horse or an ox. Let those account for it who can, but there stands the fact, that a man who loved liberty as well as did Patrick Henry,—who deserved it as much as Thomas Jefferson,—and who fought for it with a valor as high, an arm as strong, and against odds as great, as he who led all the armies of the American colonies through the great war for freedom and independence, lives now only in the chattel records of his native State.

Glimpses of this great character are all that can now be presented. He is brought to view only by a few transient incidents, and these afford but partial satisfaction. Like a guiding star on a stormy night, he is seen through the parted clouds and the howling tempests; or, like the gray peak of a menacing rock on a perilous coast, he is seen by the quivering flash of angry lightning, and he again disappears covered with mystery.

Curiously, earnestly, anxiously we peer into the dark, and wish even for the blinding flash, or the light of northern skies to reveal him. But alas! he is still enveloped in darkness, and we return from the pursuit like a wearied and disheartened mother, (after a tedious and unsuccessful search for a lost child,) who returns weighed down with disappointment and sorrow. Speaking of marks, traces, possibles, and probabilities, we come before our readers.

In the spring of 1835, on a Sabbath morning, within hearing of the solemn peals of the church bells at a distant village, a Northern traveller through the State of Virginia drew up his horse to drink at a sparkling brook, near the edge of a dark pine forest. While his weary and thirsty steed drew in the grateful water, the rider caught the sound of a human voice, apparently engaged in earnest conversation.

Following the direction of the sound, he descried, among the tall pines, the man whose voice had arrested his attention. "To whom can he be speaking?" thought the traveller. "He seems to be alone." The circumstance interested him much, and he became intensely curious to know what thoughts and feelings, or, it might be, high aspirations, guided those rich and mellow accents. Tieing his horse at a short distance from the brook, he stealthily drew near the solitary speaker; and, concealing himself by the side of a huge fallen tree, he distinctly heard the following soliloquy:—

"What, then, is life to me? it is aimless and worthless, and worse than worthless. Those birds, perched on yon swinging boughs, in friendly conclave, sounding forth their merry notes in seeming worship of the rising sun, though liable to the sportsman's fowling-piece, are still my superiors. They *live free*, though they may die slaves. They fly where they list by day, and retire in freedom at night. But what is freedom to me, or I to it? I am a *slave*,—born a slave, an abject slave,—even before I made part of this breathing world, the scourge was platted for my back; the fetters were forged for my limbs. How mean a thing am I. That accursed and crawling snake, that miserable reptile, that has just glided into its slimy home, is freer and better off than I. He escaped my blow, and is safe. But here am I, a man,—yes, *a man*!—with thoughts and wishes, with powers and faculties as far as angel's flight above that hated reptile,—yet he is my superior, and scorns to own me as his master, or to stop to take my blows. When he saw my uplifted arm, he darted beyond my reach, and turned to give me battle. I dare not do as much as that. I neither run nor fight, but do meanly stand, answering each heavy blow of a cruel master with doleful wails and piteous cries. I am galled with irons; but even these are more tolerable than the consciousness, the *galling* consciousness of cowardice and indecision. Can it be that I *dare* not run away? *Perish the thought*, I *dare* do any thing which may be done by another. When that young man struggled with the waves *for life*, and others stood back appalled in helpless horror, did I not plunge in, forgetful of life, to save his? The raging bull from whom all others fled, pale with fright, did I not keep at bay with a single pitchfork? Could a coward do that? *No*,—*no*,—I wrong myself,—I am no coward. *Liberty* I will have, or die in the attempt to gain it. This working that others may live in idleness! This cringing submission to insolence and curses! This living under the constant dread and apprehension of being sold and transferred, like a mere brute, is *too* much for me. I will stand it no longer. What others have done, I will do. These trusty legs, or these sinewy arms shall place me among the free. Tom escaped; so can I. The North Star will not be less kind to me than to him. I will follow it. I will at least make the trial. I have nothing to lose. If I am caught, I shall only be a slave. If I am shot, I shall only lose a life which is a burden and a curse. If I get clear, (as something tells me I shall,) liberty, the inalienable birth-right of every man, precious and priceless, will be mine. My resolution is fixed. *I shall be free*."

At these words the traveller raised his head cautiously and noiselessly, and caught, from his hiding-place, a full view of the unsuspecting speaker. Madison (for that was the name of our hero) was standing erect, a smile of satisfaction rippled upon his expressive countenance, like that which plays upon the face of one who has but just solved a difficult problem, or vanquished a malignant foe; for at that moment he was free, at least in spirit. The future gleamed brightly before him, and his fetters lay broken at his feet. His air was triumphant.

Madison was of manly form. Tall, symmetrical, round, and strong. In his movements he seemed to combine, with the strength of the lion, the lion's elasticity. His torn sleeves disclosed arms like polished iron. His face was "black, but comely." His eye, lit with emotion, kept guard under a brow as dark and as glossy as the raven's wing. His whole appearance betokened Herculean strength; yet there was nothing savage or forbidding in his aspect. A child might play in his arms, or dance on his shoulders. A giant's strength, but not a giant's heart was in him. His broad mouth and nose spoke only of good nature and kindness. But his voice, that unfailing index of the soul, though full and melodious, had that in it which could terrify as well as charm. He was just the man you would choose when hardships were to be endured, or danger to be encountered,—intelligent and brave. He had the head to conceive, and the hand to execute. In a word, he was one to be sought as a friend, but to be dreaded as an enemy.

As our traveller gazed upon him, he almost trembled at the thought of his dangerous intrusion. Still he could not quit the place. He had long desired to sound the mysterious depths of the thoughts and feelings of a slave. He was not, therefore, disposed to allow so providential an opportunity to pass unimproved. He resolved to hear more; so he listened again for those mellow and mournful accents which, he says, made such an impression upon him as can never be erased. He did not have to wait long. There came another gush from the same full fountain; now bitter, and now sweet. Scathing denunciations of the cruelty and injustice of slavery; heart-touching narrations of his own personal suffering, intermingled with prayers to the God of the oppressed for help and deliverance, were followed by presentations of the dangers and difficulties of escape, and formed the burden of his eloquent utterances; but his high resolution clung to him,—for he ended each speech by an emphatic declaration of his purpose to be free. It seemed that the very repetition of this, imparted a glow to his countenance. The hope of freedom seemed to sweeten, for a season, the bitter cup of slavery, and to make it, for a time, tolerable; for when in the very whirlwind of anguish,—when his heart's cord seemed screwed up to snapping tension, hope sprung up and soothed his troubled spirit. Fitfully he would exclaim, "How can I leave her? Poor thing! What can she do when I am gone? Oh! oh! 'tis impossible that I can leave poor Susan!"

A brief pause intervened. Our traveller raised his head, and saw again the sorrow-smitten slave. His eye was fixed upon the ground. The strong man staggered under a heavy load. Recovering himself, he argued thus aloud: "All is uncertain here. To-morrow's sun may not rise before I am sold, and separated from her I love. What, then, could I do for her? I should be in more hopeless slavery, and she no nearer to liberty,—whereas if I were free,—my arms my own,—I might devise the means to rescue her."

This said, Madison cast around a searching glance, as if the thought of being overheard had flashed across his mind. He said no more, but, with measured steps, walked away, and was lost to the eye of our traveller amidst the wildering woods.

Long after Madison had left the ground, Mr. Listwell (our traveller) remained in motionless silence, meditating on the extraordinary revelations to which he had listened. He seemed fastened to the spot, and stood half hoping, half fearing the return of the sable preacher to his solitary temple. The speech of Madison rung through the chambers of his soul, and vibrated through his entire frame. "Here is indeed a man," thought he, "of rare endowments,—a child of God,—guilty of no crime but the color of his skin,—hiding away from the face of humanity, and pouring out his thoughts and feelings, his hopes and resolutions to the lonely woods; to him those distant church bells have no grateful music. He shuns the church, the altar, and the great congregation of christian worshippers, and wanders away to the gloomy forest, to utter in the vacant air complaints and griefs, which the religion of his times and his country can neither console nor relieve. Goaded almost to madness by the sense of the injustice done him, he resorts hither to give vent to his pent up feelings, and to debate with himself the feasibility of plans, plans of his own invention, for his own deliverance. From this hour I am an abolitionist. I have seen enough and heard enough, and I shall go to my home in Ohio resolved to atone for my past indifference to this ill-starred race, by making such exertions as I shall be able to do, for the speedy emancipation of every slave in the land."

## Part II.

"The gaudy, blabbing and remorseful day  
Is crept into the bosom of the sea;  
And now loud-howling wolves arouse the jades  
That drag the tragic melancholy night;  
Who with their drowsy, slow, and flagging wings  
Clip dead men's graves, and from their misty jaws  
Breathe foul contagions, darkness in the air."

*Shakspeare.*

Five years after the foregoing singular occurrence, in the winter of 1840, Mr. and Mrs. Listwell sat together by the fireside of their own happy home, in the State of Ohio. The children were all gone to bed. A single lamp burnt brightly on the centre-table. All was still and comfortable within; but the night was cold and dark; a heavy wind sighed and moaned sorrowfully around the house and barn, occasionally bringing against the clattering windows a stray leaf from the large oak trees that embowered their dwelling. It was a night for strange noises and for strange fancies. A whole wilderness of thought might pass through one's mind during such an evening. The smouldering embers, partaking of the spirit of the restless night, became fruitful of varied and fantastic pictures, and revived many bygone scenes and old impressions. The happy pair seemed to sit in silent fascination, gazing on the fire. Suddenly this *reverie* was interrupted by a heavy growl. Ordinarily such an occurrence would have scarcely provoked a single word, or excited the least apprehension. But there are certain seasons when the slightest sound sends a jar through all the subtle chambers of the mind; and such a season was this. The happy pair started up, as if some sudden danger had come upon them. The growl was from their trusty watch-dog.

"What can it mean? certainly no one can be out on such a night as this," said Mrs. Listwell.

"The wind has deceived the dog, my dear; he has mistaken the noise of falling branches, brought down by the wind, for that of the footsteps of persons coming to the house. I have several times to-night thought that I heard the sound of footsteps. I am sure, however, that it was but the wind. Friends would not be likely to come out at such an hour, or such a night; and thieves are too lazy and self-indulgent to expose themselves to this biting frost; but should there be any one about, our brave old Monte, who is on the lookout, will not be slow in sounding the alarm."

Saying this they quietly left the window, whither they had gone to learn the cause of the menacing growl, and re-seated themselves by the fire, as if reluctant to leave the slowly expiring embers, although the hour was late. A few minutes only intervened after resuming their seats, when again their sober meditations were disturbed. Their faithful dog now growled and barked furiously, as if assailed by an advancing foe. Simultaneously the good couple arose, and stood in mute expectation. The contest without seemed fierce and violent. It was, however, soon over,—the barking ceased, for, with true canine instinct, Monte quickly discovered that a friend, not an enemy of the family, was coming to the house, and instead of rushing to repel the supposed intruder, he was now at the door, whimpering and dancing for the admission of himself and his newly made friend.

Mr. Listwell knew by this movement that all was well; he advanced and opened the door, and saw by the light that streamed out into the darkness, a tall man advancing slowly towards the house, with a stick in one hand, and a small bundle in the other. "It is a traveller," thought he, "who has missed his way, and is coming to inquire the road. I am glad we did not go to bed earlier,—I have felt all the evening as if somebody would be here to-night."

The man had now halted a short distance from the door, and looked prepared alike for flight or battle. "Come in, sir, don't be alarmed, you have probably lost your way."

Slightly hesitating, the traveller walked in; not, however, without regarding his host with a scrutinizing glance. "No, sir," said he, "I have come to ask you a greater favor."

Instantly Mr. Listwell exclaimed, (as the recollection of the Virginia forest scene flashed upon him,) "Oh, sir, I know not your name, but I have seen your face, and heard your voice before. I am glad to see you. *I know all.* You are flying for your liberty,—be seated,—be seated,—banish all fear. You are safe under my roof."

This recognition, so unexpected, rather disconcerted and disquieted the noble fugitive. The timidity and suspicion of persons escaping from slavery are easily awakened, and often what is intended to dispel the one, and to allay the other, has precisely the opposite effect. It was so in this case. Quickly observing the unhappy impression made by his words and action, Mr. Listwell assumed a more quiet and inquiring aspect, and finally succeeded in removing the apprehensions which his very natural and generous salutation had aroused.

Thus assured, the stranger said, "Sir, you have rightly guessed, I am, indeed, a fugitive from slavery. My name is Madison,—Madison Washington my mother used to call me. I am on my way to Canada, where I learn that persons of my color are protected in all the rights of men; and my object in calling upon you was, to beg the privilege of resting my weary limbs for the night in your barn. It was my purpose to have continued my journey till morning; but the piercing cold, and the frowning darkness compelled me to seek shelter; and, seeing a light through the lattice of your window, I was encouraged to come here to beg the privilege named. You will do me a great favor by affording me shelter for the night."

"A resting-place, indeed, sir, you shall have; not, however, in my barn, but in the best room of my house. Consider yourself, if you please, under the roof of a friend; for such I am to you, and to all your deeply injured race."

While this introductory conversation was going on, the kind lady had revived the fire, and was diligently preparing supper; for she, not less than her husband, felt for the sorrows of the oppressed and hunted ones of the earth, and was always glad of an opportunity to do them a service. A bountiful repast was quickly prepared, and the hungry and toil-worn bondman was cordially invited to partake thereof. Gratefully he acknowledged the favor of his benevolent benefactress; but appeared scarcely to understand what such hospitality could mean. It was the first time in his life that he had met so humane and friendly a greeting at the hands of persons whose color was unlike his own; yet it was impossible for him to doubt the charitableness of his new friends, or the genuineness of the welcome so freely given; and he therefore, with many thanks, took his seat at the table with Mr. and Mrs. Listwell, who, desirous to make him feel at home, took a cup of tea themselves, while urging upon Madison the best that the house could afford.

Supper over, all doubts and apprehensions banished, the three drew around the blazing fire, and a conversation commenced which lasted till long after midnight.

"Now," said Madison to Mr. Listwell, "I was a little surprised and alarmed when I came in, by what you said; do tell me, sir, *why* you thought you had seen my face before, and by what you knew me to be a fugitive from slavery; for I am sure that I never was before in this neighborhood, and I certainly sought to conceal what I supposed to be the manner of a fugitive slave."

Mr. Listwell at once frankly disclosed the secret; describing the place where he first saw him; rehearsing the language which he (Madison) had used; referring to the effect which his manner and speech had made upon him; declaring the resolution he there formed to be an abolitionist; telling how often he had spoken of the circumstance, and the deep concern he had ever since felt to know what had become of him; and whether he had carried out the purpose to make his escape, as in the woods he declared he would do.

"Ever since that morning," said Mr. Listwell, "you have seldom been absent from my mind, and though now I did not dare to hope that I should ever see you again, I have often wished that such might be my fortune; for, from that hour, your face seemed to be daguerreotyped on my memory."

Madison looked quite astonished, and felt amazed at the narration to which he had listened. After recovering himself he said, "I well remember that morning, and the bitter anguish that wrung my heart; I will state the occasion of it. I had, on the previous Saturday, suffered a cruel lashing; had been tied up to the limb of a tree, with my feet chained together, and a heavy iron bar placed between my ankles. Thus suspended, I received on my naked back forty stripes, and was kept in this distressing position three or four hours, and was then let down, only to have my torture increased; for my bleeding back, gashed by the cow-skin, was washed by the overseer with old brine, partly to augment my suffering, and partly, as he said, to prevent inflammation. My crime was that I had stayed longer at the mill, the day previous, than it was thought I ought to have done, which, I assured my master and the overseer, was no fault of mine; but no excuses were allowed. 'Hold your tongue, you impudent rascal,' met my every explanation. Slave-holders are so imperious when their passions are excited, as to construe every word of the slave into insolence. I could do nothing but submit to the agonizing infliction. Smarting still from the wounds, as well as from the consciousness of being whipt for no cause, I took advantage of the absence of my master, who had gone to church, to spend the time in the woods, and brood over my wretched lot. Oh, sir, I remember it well,—and can never forget it."

"But this was five years ago; where have you been since?"

"I will try to tell you," said Madison. "Just four weeks after that Sabbath morning, I gathered up the few rags of clothing I had, and started, as I supposed, for the North and for freedom. I must not stop to describe my feelings on taking this step. It seemed like taking a leap into the dark. The thought of leaving my poor wife and two little children caused me indescribable anguish; but consoling myself with the reflection that once free, I could, possibly, devise ways and means to gain their freedom also, I nerved myself up to make the attempt. I started, but ill-luck attended me; for after being out a whole week, strange to say, I still found myself on my master's grounds; the third night after being out, a season of clouds and rain set in, wholly preventing me from seeing the North Star, which I had trusted as my guide, not dreaming that clouds might intervene between us.

"This circumstance was fatal to my project, for in losing my star, I lost my way; so when I supposed I was far towards the North, and had almost gained my freedom, I discovered myself at the very point from which I had started. It was a severe trial, for I arrived at home in great destitution; my feet were sore, and in travelling in the dark, I had dashed my foot against a stump, and started a nail, and lamed myself. I was wet and cold; one week had exhausted all my stores; and when I landed on my master's plantation, with all my work to do over again,—hungry, tired, lame, and bewildered,—I almost cursed the day that I was born. In this extremity I approached the quarters. I did so stealthily, although in my desperation I hardly cared whether I was discovered or not. Peeping through the rents of the quarters, I saw my fellow-slaves seated by a warm fire, merrily passing away the time, as though their hearts knew no sorrow. Although I envied their seeming contentment, all wretched as I was, I despised the cowardly acquiescence in their own degradation which it implied, and felt a kind of pride and glory in my own desperate lot. I dared not enter the quarters,—for where there is seeming contentment with slavery, there is certain treachery to freedom. I proceeded towards the great house, in the hope of catching a glimpse of my poor wife, whom I knew might be trusted with my secrets even on the scaffold. Just as I reached the fence which divided the field from the garden, I saw a woman in the yard, who in the darkness I took to be my wife; but a nearer approach told me it was not she. I was about to speak; had I done so, I would not have been here this night; for an alarm would have been sounded, and the hunters been put on my track. Here were hunger, cold, thirst, disappointment, and chagrin, confronted only by the dim hope of liberty. I tremble to think of that dreadful hour. To face the deadly cannon's mouth in warm blood unterrified, is, I think, a small achievement, compared with a conflict like this with gaunt starvation. The gnawings of hunger conquers by degrees, till all that a man has he would give in exchange for a single crust of bread. Thank God, I was not quite reduced to this extremity.

"Happily for me, before the fatal moment of utter despair, my good wife made her appearance in the yard. It was she; I knew her step. All was well now. I was, however, afraid to speak lest I should frighten her. Yet speak I did; and, to my great joy, my voice was known. Our meeting can be more easily imagined than described. For a time hunger, thirst, weariness, and lameness were forgotten. But it was soon necessary for her to return to the house. She being a house-servant, her absence from the kitchen, if discovered, might have excited suspicion. Our parting was like tearing the flesh from my bones; yet it was the part of wisdom for her to go. She left me with the purpose of meeting me at midnight in the very forest where you last saw me. She knew the place well, as one of my melancholy resorts, and could easily find it, though the night was dark.

"I hastened away, therefore, and concealed myself, to await the arrival of my good angel. As I lay there among the leaves, I was strongly tempted to return again to the house of my master and give myself up; but remembering my solemn pledge on that memorable Sunday morning, I was able to linger out the two long hours between ten and midnight. I may well call them long hours. I have endured much hardship; I have encountered many perils; but the anxiety of those two hours, was the bitterest I ever experienced. True to her word, my wife came laden with provisions, and we sat down on the side of a log, at that dark and lonesome hour of the night. I cannot say we talked; our feelings were too great for that; yet we came to an understanding that I should make the woods my home, for if I gave myself up, I should be whipped and sold away; and if I started for the North, I should leave a wife doubly dear to me. We mutually determined, therefore, that I should remain in the vicinity. In the dismal swamps I lived, sir, five long years,—a cave for my home during the day. I wandered about at night with the wolf and the bear,—sustained by the promise that my good Susan would meet me in the pine woods at least once a week. This promise was redeemed, I assure you, to the letter, greatly to my relief. I had partly become contented with my mode of life, and had made up my mind to spend my days there; but the wilderness that sheltered me thus long took fire, and refused longer to be my hiding-place.

"I will not harrow up your feelings by portraying the terrific scene of this awful conflagration. There is nothing to which I can liken it. It was horribly and indescribably grand. The whole world seemed on fire, and it appeared to me that the day of judgment had come; that the burning bowels of the earth had burst forth, and that the end of all things was at hand. Bears and wolves, scorched from their mysterious hiding-places in the earth, and all the wild inhabitants of the untrodden forest, filled with a common dismay, ran forth, yelling, howling, bewildered amidst the smoke and flame. The very heavens seemed to rain down fire through the towering trees; it was by the merest chance that I escaped the devouring element. Running before it, and stopping occasionally to take breath, I looked back to behold its frightful ravages, and to drink in its savage magnificence. It was awful, thrilling, solemn, beyond compare. When aided by the fitful wind, the merciless tempest of fire swept on, sparkling, creaking, cracking, curling, roaring, out-doing in its dreadful splendor a thousand thunderstorms at once. From tree to tree it leaped, swallowing them up in its lurid, baleful glare; and leaving them leafless, limbless, charred, and lifeless behind. The scene was overwhelming, stunning,—nothing was spared,—cattle, tame and wild, herds of swine and of deer, wild beasts of every name and kind,—huge night-birds, bats, and owls, that had retired to their homes in lofty tree-tops to rest, perished in that fiery storm. The long-winged buzzard and croaking raven mingled their dismal cries with those of the countless myriads of small birds that rose up to the skies, and were lost to the sight in clouds of smoke and flame. Oh, I shudder when I think of it! Many a poor wandering fugitive, who, like myself, had sought among wild beasts the mercy denied by our fellow men, saw, in helpless consternation, his dwelling-place and city of refuge reduced to ashes forever. It was this grand conflagration that drove me hither; I ran alike from fire and from slavery."

After a slight pause, (for both speaker and hearers were deeply moved by the above recital,) Mr. Listwell, addressing Madison, said, "If it does not weary you too much, do tell us something of your journeyings since this disastrous burning,—we are deeply interested in everything which can throw light on the hardships of persons escaping from slavery; we could hear you talk all night; are there no incidents that you could relate of your travels hither? or are they such that you do not like to mention them?"

"For the most part, sir, my course has been uninterrupted; and, considering the circumstances, at times even pleasant. I have suffered little for want of food; but I need not tell you how I got it. Your moral code may differ from mine, as your customs and usages are different. The fact is, sir, during my flight, I felt myself robbed by society of all my just rights; that I was in an enemy's land, who sought both my life and my liberty. They had transformed me into a brute; made merchandise of my body, and, for all the purposes of my flight, turned day into night,—and guided by my own necessities, and in contempt of their conventionalities, I did not scruple to take bread where I could get it."

"And just there you were right," said Mr. Listwell; "I once had doubts on this point myself, but a conversation with Gerrit Smith, (a man, by the way, that I wish you could see, for he is a devoted friend of your race, and I know he would receive you gladly,) put an end to all my doubts on this point. But do not let me interrupt you."

"I had but one narrow escape during my whole journey," said Madison.

"Do let us hear of it," said Mr. Listwell.

"Two weeks ago," continued Madison, "after travelling all night, I was overtaken by daybreak, in what seemed to me an almost interminable wood. I deemed it unsafe to go farther, and, as usual, I looked around for a suitable tree in which to spend the day. I liked one with a bushy top, and found one just to my mind. Up I climbed, and hiding myself as well as I could, I, with this strap, (pulling one out of his old coat-pocket,) lashed myself to a bough, and flattered myself that I should get a *good night's* sleep that day; but in this I was soon disappointed. I had scarcely got fastened to my natural hammock, when I heard the voices of a number of persons, apparently approaching the part of the woods where I was. Upon my word, sir, I dreaded more these human voices than I should have done those of wild beasts. I was at a loss to know what to do. If I descended, I should probably be discovered by the men; and if they had dogs I should, doubtless, be '*treed*.' It was an anxious moment, but hardships and dangers have been the accompaniments of my life; and have, perhaps, imparted to me a certain hardness of character, which, to some extent, adapts me to them. In my present predicament, I decided to hold my place in the tree-top, and abide the consequences. But here I must disappoint you; for the men, who were all colored, halted at least a hundred yards from me, and began with their axes, in right good earnest, to attack the trees. The sound of their laughing axes was like the report of as many well-charged pistols. By and by there came down at least a dozen trees with a terrible crash. They leaped upon the fallen trees with an air of victory. I could see no dog with them, and felt myself comparatively safe, though I could not forget the possibility that some freak or fancy might bring the axe a little nearer my dwelling than comported with my safety.

"There was no sleep for me that day, and I wished for night. You may imagine that the thought of having the tree attacked under me was far from agreeable, and that it very easily kept me on the lookout. The day was not without diversion. The men at work seemed to be a gay set; and they would often make the woods resound with that uncontrolled laughter for which we, as a race, are remarkable. I held my place in the tree till sunset,—saw the men put on their jackets to be off. I observed that all left the ground except one, whom I saw sitting on the side of a stump, with his head bowed, and his eyes apparently fixed on the ground. I became interested in him. After sitting in the position to which I have alluded ten or fifteen minutes, he left the stump, walked directly towards the tree in which I was secreted, and halted almost under the same. He stood for a moment and looked around, deliberately and reverently took off his hat, by which I saw that he was a man in the evening of life, slightly bald and quite gray. After laying down his hat carefully, he knelt and prayed aloud, and such a prayer, the most fervent, earnest, and solemn, to which I think I ever listened. After reverently addressing the Almighty, as the all-wise, all-good, and the common Father of all mankind, he besought God for grace, for strength, to bear up under, and to endure, as a good soldier, all the hardships and trials which beset the journey of life, and to enable him to live in a manner which accorded with the gospel of Christ. His soul now broke out in humble supplication for deliverance from bondage. 'O thou,' said he, 'that hearest the raven's cry, take pity on poor me! O deliver me! O deliver me! in mercy, O God, deliver me from the chains and manifold hardships of slavery! With thee, O Father, all things are possible. Thou canst stand and measure the earth. Thou hast beheld and drove asunder the nations,—all power is in thy hand,—thou didst say of old, "I have seen the affliction of my people, and am come to deliver them,"—Oh look down upon our afflictions, and have mercy upon us.' But I cannot repeat his prayer, nor can I give you an idea of its deep pathos. I had given but little attention to religion, and had but little faith in it; yet, as the old man prayed, I felt almost like coming down and kneel by his side, and mingle my broken complaint with his.

"He had already gained my confidence; as how could it be otherwise? I knew enough of religion to know that the man who prays in secret is far more likely to be sincere than he who loves to pray standing in the street, or in the great congregation. When he arose from his knees, like another Zacheus, I came down from the tree. He seemed a little alarmed at first, but I told him my story, and the good man embraced me in his arms, and assured me of his sympathy.

"I was now about out of provisions, and thought I might safely ask him to help me replenish my store. He said he had no money; but if he had, he would freely give it me. I told him I had *one dollar*; it was all the money I had in the world. I gave it to him, and asked him to purchase some crackers and cheese, and to kindly bring me the balance; that I would remain in or near that place, and would come to him on his return, if he would whistle. He was gone only about an hour. Meanwhile, from some cause or other, I know not what, (but as you shall see very wisely,) I changed my place. On his return I started to meet him; but it seemed as if the shadow of approaching danger fell upon my spirit, and checked my progress. In a very few minutes, closely on the heels of the old man, I distinctly saw *fourteen men*, with something like guns in their hands."

"Oh! the old wretch!" exclaimed Mrs. Listwell, "he had betrayed you, had he?"

"I think not," said Madison, "I cannot believe that the old man was to blame. He probably went into a store, asked for the articles for which I sent, and presented the bill I gave him; and it is so unusual for slaves in the country to have money, that fact, doubtless, excited suspicion, and gave rise to inquiry. I can easily believe that the truthfulness of the old man's character compelled him to disclose the facts; and thus were these bloodthirsty men put on my track. Of course I did not present myself; but hugged my hiding-place securely. If discovered and attacked, I resolved to sell my life as dearly as possible.

"After searching about the woods silently for a time, the whole company gathered around the old man; one charged him with lying, and called him an old villain; said he was a thief; charged him with stealing money; said if he did not instantly tell where he got it, they would take the shirt from his old back, and give him thirty-nine lashes.

"'I did *not* steal the money,' said the old man, 'it was given me, as I told you at the store; and if the man who gave it me is not here, it is not my fault.'

"'Hush! you lying old rascal; we'll make you smart for it. You shall not leave this spot until you have told where you got that money.'

"They now took hold of him, and began to strip him; while others went to get sticks with which to beat him. I felt, at the moment, like rushing out in the midst of them; but considering that the old man would be whipped the more for having aided a fugitive slave, and that, perhaps, in the *melée* he might be killed outright, I disobeyed this impulse. They tied him to a tree, and began to whip him. My own flesh crept at every blow, and I seem to hear the old man's piteous cries even now. They laid thirty-nine lashes on his bare back, and were going to repeat that number, when one of the company besought his comrades to desist. 'You'll kill the d——d old scoundrel! You've already whipt a dollar's worth out of him, even if he stole it!' 'O yes,' said another, 'let him down. He'll never tell us another lie, I'll warrant ye!' With this, one of the company untied the old man, and bid him go about his business.

"The old man left, but the company remained as much as an hour, scouring the woods. Round and round they went, turning up the underbrush, and peering about like so many bloodhounds. Two or three times they came within six feet of where I lay. I tell you I held my stick with a firmer grasp than I did in coming up to your house to-night. I expected to level one of them at least. Fortunately, however, I eluded their pursuit, and they left me alone in the woods.

"My last dollar was now gone, and you may well suppose I felt the loss of it; but the thought of being once again free to pursue my journey, prevented that depression which a sense of destitution causes; so swinging my little bundle on my back, I caught a glimpse of the *Great Bear* (which ever points the way to my beloved star,) and I started again on my journey. What I lost in money I made up at a hen-roost that same night, upon which I fortunately came."

"But you did'nt eat your food raw? How did you cook it?" said Mrs. Listwell.

"O no, Madam," said Madison, turning to his little bundle;—"I had the means of cooking." Here he took out of his bundle an old-fashioned tinder-box, and taking up a piece of a file, which he brought with him, he struck it with a heavy flint, and brought out at least a dozen sparks at once. "I have had this old box," said he, "more than five years. It is the *only* property saved from the fire in the dismal swamp. It has done me good service. It has given me the means of broiling many a chicken!"

It seemed quite a relief to Mrs. Listwell to know that Madison had, at least, lived upon cooked food. Women have a perfect horror of eating uncooked food.

By this time thoughts of what was best to be done about getting Madison to Canada, began to trouble Mr. Listwell; for the laws of Ohio were very stringent against any one who should aid, or who were found aiding a slave to escape through that State. A citizen, for the simple act of taking a fugitive slave in his carriage, had just been stripped of all his property, and thrown penniless upon the world. Notwithstanding this, Mr. Listwell was determined to see Madison safely on his way to Canada. "Give yourself no uneasiness," said he to Madison, "for if it cost my farm, I shall see you safely out of the States, and on your way to a land of liberty. Thank God that there is *such* a land so near us! You will spend to-morrow with us, and to-morrow night I will take you in my carriage to the Lake. Once upon that, and you are safe."

"Thank you! thank you," said the fugitive; "I will commit myself to your care."

For the *first* time during *five* years, Madison enjoyed the luxury of resting his limbs on a comfortable bed, and inside a human habitation. Looking at the white sheets, he said to Mr. Listwell, "What, sir! you don't mean that I shall sleep in that bed?"

"Oh yes, oh yes."

After Mr. Listwell left the room, Madison said he really hesitated whether or not he should lie on the floor; for that was *far* more comfortable and inviting than any bed to which he had been used.

We pass over the thoughts and feelings, the hopes and fears, the plans and purposes, that revolved in the mind of Madison during the day that he was secreted at the house of Mr. Listwell.

The reader will be content to know that nothing occurred to endanger his liberty, or to excite alarm. Many were the little attentions bestowed upon him in his quiet retreat and hiding-place. In the evening, Mr. Listwell, after treating Madison to a new suit of winter clothes, and replenishing his exhausted purse with five dollars, all in silver, brought out his two-horse wagon, well provided with buffaloes, and silently started off with him to Cleveland. They arrived there without interruption, a few minutes before sunrise the next morning. Fortunately the steamer Admiral lay at the wharf, and was to start for Canada at nine o'clock. Here the last anticipated danger was surmounted. It was feared that just at this point the hunters of men might be on the look-out, and, possibly, pounce upon their victim. Mr. Listwell saw the captain of the boat; cautiously sounded him on the matter of carrying liberty-loving passengers, before he introduced his precious charge. This done, Madison was conducted on board. With usual generosity this true subject of the emancipating queen welcomed Madison, and assured him that he should be safely landed in Canada, free of charge. Madison now felt himself no more a piece of merchandise, but a passenger, and, like any other passenger, going about his business, carrying with him what belonged to him, and nothing which rightfully belonged to anybody else.

Wrapped in his new winter suit, snug and comfortable, a pocket full of silver, safe from his pursuers, embarked for a free country, Madison gave every sign of sincere gratitude, and bade his kind benefactor farewell, with such a grip of the hand as bespoke a heart full of honest manliness, and a soul that knew how to appreciate kindness. It need scarcely be said that Mr. Listwell was deeply moved by the gratitude and friendship he had excited in a nature so noble as that of the fugitive. He went to his home that day with a joy and gratification which knew no bounds. He had done something "to deliver the spoiled out of the hands of the spoiler," he had given bread to the hungry, and clothes to the naked; he had befriended a man to whom the laws of his country forbade all friendship,—and in proportion to the odds against his righteous deed, was the delightful satisfaction that gladdened his heart. On reaching home, he exclaimed, "*He is safe,—he is safe,—he is safe,*"—and the cup of his joy was shared by his excellent lady. The following letter was received from Madison a few days after:

"WINDSOR, CANADA WEST, DEC. 16, 1840.

My dear Friend,—for such you truly are:—

Madison is out of the woods at last; I nestle in the mane of the British lion, protected by his mighty paw from the talons and the beak of the American eagle. I AM FREE, and breathe an atmosphere too pure for *slaves*, slave-hunters, or slave-holders. My heart is full. As many thanks to you, sir, and to your kind lady, as there are pebbles on the shores of Lake Erie; and may the blessing of God rest upon you both. You will never be forgotten by your profoundly grateful friend,

MADISON WASHINGTON."

## Part III.

—His head was with his heart,
And that was far away!
*Childe Harold.*

Just upon the edge of the great road from Petersburg, Virginia, to Richmond, and only about fifteen miles from the latter place, there stands a somewhat ancient and famous public tavern, quite notorious in its better days, as being the grand resort for most of the leading gamblers, horse-racers, cock-fighters, and slave-traders from all the country round about. This old rookery, the nucleus of all sorts of birds, mostly those of ill omen, has, like everything else peculiar to Virginia, lost much of its ancient consequence and splendor; yet it keeps up some appearance of gaiety and high life, and is still frequented, even by respectable travellers, who are unacquainted with its past history and present condition. Its fine old portico looks well at a distance, and gives the building an air of grandeur. A nearer view, however, does little to sustain this pretension. The house is large, and its style imposing, but time and dissipation, unfailing in their results, have made ineffaceable marks upon it, and it must, in the common course of events, soon be numbered with the things that were. The gloomy mantle of ruin is, already, out-spread to envelop it, and its remains, even but now remind one of a human skull, after the flesh has mingled with the earth. Old hats and rags fill the places in the upper windows once occupied by large panes of glass, and the moulding boards along the roofing have dropped off from their places, leaving holes and crevices in the rented wall for bats and swallows to build their nests in. The platform of the portico, which fronts the highway is a rickety affair, its planks are loose, and in some places entirely gone, leaving effective man-traps in their stead for nocturnal ramblers. The wooden pillars, which once supported it, but which now hang as encumbrances, are all rotten, and tremble with the touch. A part of the stable, a fine old structure in its day, which has given comfortable shelter to hundreds of the noblest steeds of "the Old Dominion" at once, was blown down many years ago, and never has been, and probably never will be, rebuilt. The doors of the barn are in wretched condition; they will shut with a little human strength to help their worn out hinges, but not otherwise. The side of the great building seen from the road is much discolored in sundry places by slops poured from the upper windows, rendering it unsightly and offensive in other respects. Three or four great dogs, looking as dull and gloomy as the mansion itself, lie stretched out along the door-sills under the portico; and double the number of loafers, some of them completely rum-ripe, and others ripening, dispose themselves like so many sentinels about the front of the house. These latter understand the science of scraping acquaintance to perfection. They know every-body, and almost every-body knows them. Of course, as their title implies, they have no regular employment. They are (to use an expressive phrase) *hangers on*, or still better, they are what sailors would denominate *holders-on to the slack, in every-body's mess, and in no-body's watch.* They are, however, as good as the newspaper for the events of the day, and they sell their knowledge almost as cheap. Money they seldom have; yet they always have capital the most reliable. They make their way with a succeeding traveller by intelligence gained from a preceding one. All the great names of Virginia they know by heart, and have seen their owners often. The history of the house is folded in their lips, and they rattle off stories in connection with it, equal to the guides at Dryburgh Abbey. He must be a shrewd man, and well skilled in the art of evasion, who gets out of the hands of these fellows without being at the expense of a treat.

It was at this old tavern, while on a second visit to the State of Virginia in 1841, that Mr. Listwell, unacquainted with the fame of the place, turned aside, about sunset, to pass the night. Riding up to the house, he had scarcely dismounted, when one of the half dozen bar-room fraternity met and addressed him in a manner exceedingly bland and accommodating.

"Fine evening, sir."

"Very fine," said Mr. Listwell. "This is a tavern, I believe?"

"O yes, sir, yes; although you may think it looks a little the worse for wear, it was once as good a house as any in Virginy. I make no doubt if ye spend the night here, you'll think it a good house yet; for there aint a more accommodating man in the country than you'll find the landlord."

*Listwell.* "The most I want is a good bed for myself, and a full manger for my horse. If I get these, I shall be quite satisfied."

*Loafer.* "Well, I alloys like to hear a gentleman talk for his horse; and just becase the horse can't talk for itself. A man that don't care about his beast, and don't look arter it when he's travelling, aint much in my eye anyhow. Now, sir, I likes a horse, and I'll guarantee your horse will be taken good care on here. That old stable, for all you see it looks so shabby now, once sheltered the great *Eclipse*, when he run here agin *Batchelor* and *Jumping Jemmy*. Them was fast horses, but he beat 'em both."

*Listwell.* "Indeed."

*Loafer.* "Well, I rather reckon you've travelled a right smart distance to-day, from the look of your horse?"

*Listwell.* "Forty miles only."

*Loafer.* "Well! I'll be darned if that aint a pretty good *only*. Mister, that beast of yours is a singed cat, I warrant you. I never see'd a creature like that that was'nt good on the road. You've come about forty miles, then?"

*Listwell.* "Yes, yes, and a pretty good pace at that."

*Loafer.* "You're somewhat in a hurry, then, I make no doubt? I reckon I could guess if I would, what you're going to Richmond for? It would'nt be much of a guess either; for it's rumored hereabouts, that there's to be the greatest sale of niggers at Richmond to-morrow that has taken place there in a long time; and I'll be bound you're a going there to have a hand in it."

*Listwell.* "Why, you must think, then, that there's money to be made at that business?"

*Loafer.* "Well, 'pon my honor, sir, I never made any that way myself; but it stands to reason that it's a money making business; for almost all other business in Virginia is dropped to engage in this. One thing is sartain, I never see'd a nigger-buyer yet that had'nt a plenty of money, and he was'nt as free with it as water. I has known one on 'em to treat as high as twenty times in a night; and, ginerally speaking, they's men of edication, and knows all about the government. The fact is, sir, I alloys like to hear 'em talk, bekase I alloys can learn something from them."

*Listwell.* "What may I call your name, sir?"

*Loafer.* "Well, now, they calls me Wilkes. I'm known all around by the gentlemen that comes here. They all knows old Wilkes."

*Listwell.* "Well, Wilkes, you seem to be acquainted here, and I see you have a strong liking for a horse. Be so good as to speak a kind word for mine to the hostler to-night, and you'll not lose anything by it."

*Loafer.* "Well, sir, I see you don't say much, but you've got an insight into things. It's alloys wise to get the good will of them that's acquainted about a tavern; for a man don't know when he goes into a house what may happen, or how much he may need a friend." Here the loafer gave Mr. Listwell a significant grin, which expressed a sort of triumphant pleasure at having, as he supposed, by his tact succeeded in placing so fine appearing a gentleman under obligations to him.

The pleasure, however, was mutual; for there was something so insinuating in the glance of this loquacious customer, that Mr. Listwell was very glad to get quit of him, and to do so more successfully, he ordered his supper to be brought to him in his private room, private to the eye, but not to the ear. This room was directly over the bar, and the plastering being off, nothing but pine boards and naked laths separated him from the disagreeable company below,—he could easily hear what was said in the bar-room, and was rather glad of the advantage it afforded, for, as you shall see, it furnished him important hints as to the manner and deportment he should assume during his stay at that tavern.

Mr. Listwell says he had got into his room but a few moments, when he heard the officious Wilkes below, in a tone of disappointment, exclaim, "Whar's that gentleman?" Wilkes was evidently expecting to meet with his friend at the bar-room, on his return, and had no doubt of his doing the handsome thing. "He has gone to his room," answered the landlord, "and has ordered his supper to be brought to him."

Here some one shouted out, "Who is he, Wilkes? Where's he going?"

"Well, now, I'll be hanged if I know; but I'm willing to make any man a bet of this old hat agin a five dollar bill, that that gent is as full of money as a dog is of fleas. He's going down to Richmond to buy niggers, I make no doubt. He's no fool, I warrant ye."

"Well, he acts d——d strange," said another, "anyhow. I likes to see a man, when he comes up to a tavern, to come straight into the bar-room, and show that he's a man among men. Nobody was going to bite him."

"Now, I don't blame him a bit for not coming in here. That man knows his business, and means to take care on his money," answered Wilkes.

"Wilkes, you're a fool. You only say that, becase you hope to get a few coppers out on him."

"You only measure my corn by your half-bushel, I won't say that you're only mad becase I got the chance of speaking to him first."

"O Wilkes! you're known here. You'll praise up any body that will give you a copper; besides, 'tis my opinion that that fellow who took his long slab-sides up stairs, for all the world just like a half-scared woman, afraid to look honest men in the face, is a *Northerner*, and as mean as dish-water."

"Now what will you bet of that," said Wilkes.

The speaker said, "I make no bets with you, 'kase you can get that fellow up stairs there to say anything."

"Well," said Wilkes, "I am willing to bet any man in the company that *that* gentleman is a *nigger*-buyer. He did'nt tell me so right down, but I reckon I knows enough about men to give a pretty clean guess as to what they are arter."

The dispute as to *who* Mr. Listwell was, what his business, where he was going, etc., was kept up with much animation for some time, and more than once threatened a serious disturbance of the peace. Wilkes had his friends as well as his opponents. After this sharp debate, the company amused themselves by drinking whiskey, and telling stories. The latter consisting of quarrels, fights, *rencontres*, and duels, in which distinguished persons of that neighborhood, and frequenters of that house, had been actors. Some of these stories were frightful enough, and were told, too, with a relish which bespoke the pleasure of the parties with the horrid scenes they portrayed. It would not be proper here to give the reader any idea of the vulgarity and dark profanity which rolled, as "a sweet morsel," under these corrupt tongues. A more brutal set of creatures, perhaps, never congregated.

Disgusted, and a little alarmed withal, Mr. Listwell, who was not accustomed to such entertainment, at length retired, but not to sleep. He was *too* much wrought upon by what he had heard to rest quietly, and what snatches of sleep he got, were interrupted by dreams which were anything than pleasant. At eleven o'clock, there seemed to be several hundreds of persons crowding into the house. A loud and confused clamour, cursing and cracking of whips, and the noise of chains startled him from his bed; for a moment he would have given the half of his farm in Ohio to have been at home. This uproar was kept up with undulating course, till near morning. There was loud laughing,—loud singing,—loud cursing,—and yet there seemed to be weeping and mourning in the midst of all. Mr. Listwell said he had heard enough during the forepart of the night to convince him that a buyer of men and women stood the best chance of being respected. And he, therefore, thought it best to say nothing which might undo the favorable opinion that had been formed of him in the bar-room by at least one of the fraternity that swarmed about it. While he would not avow himself a purchaser of slaves, he deemed it not prudent to disavow it. He felt that he might, properly, refuse to cast such a pearl before parties which, to him, were worse than swine. To reveal himself, and to impart a knowledge of his real character and sentiments would, to say the least, be imparting intelligence with the certainty of seeing it and himself both abused. Mr. Listwell confesses, that this reasoning did not altogether satisfy his conscience, for, hating slavery as he did, and regarding it to be the immediate duty of every man to cry out against it, "without compromise and without concealment," it was hard for him to admit to himself the possibility of circumstances wherein a man might, properly, hold his tongue on the subject. Having as little of the spirit of a martyr as Erasmus, he concluded, like the latter, that it was wiser to trust the mercy of God for his soul, than the humanity of slave-traders for his body. Bodily fear, not conscientious scruples, prevailed.

In this spirit he rose early in the morning, manifesting no surprise at what he had heard during the night. His quondam friend was soon at his elbow, boring him with all sorts of questions. All, however, directed to find out his character, business, residence, purposes, and destination. With the most perfect appearance of good nature and carelessness, Mr. Listwell evaded these meddlesome inquiries, and turned conversation to general topics, leaving himself and all that specially pertained to him, out of discussion. Disengaging himself from their troublesome companionship, he made his way towards an old bowling-alley, which was connected with the house, and which, like all the rest, was in very bad repair.

On reaching the alley Mr. Listwell saw, for the first time in his life, a slave-gang on their way to market. A sad sight truly. Here were one hundred and thirty human beings,—children of a common Creator—guilty of no crime—men and women, with hearts, minds, and deathless spirits, chained and fettered, and bound for the market, in a christian country,—in a country boasting of its liberty, independence, and high civilization! Humanity converted into merchandise, and linked in iron bands, with no regard to decency or humanity! All sizes, ages, and sexes, mothers, fathers, daughters, brothers, sisters,—all huddled together, on their way to market to be sold and separated from home, and from each other *forever.* And all to fill the pockets of men too lazy to work for an honest living, and who gain their fortune by plundering the helpless, and trafficking in the souls and sinews of men. As he gazed upon this revolting and heart-rending scene, our informant said he almost doubted the existence of a God of justice! And he stood wondering that the earth did not open and swallow up such wickedness.

In the midst of these reflections, and while running his eye up and down the fettered ranks, he met the glance of one whose face he thought he had seen before. To be resolved, he moved towards the spot. It was MADISON WASHINGTON! Here was a scene for the pencil! Had Mr. Listwell been confronted by one risen from the dead, he could not have been more appalled. He was completely stunned. A thunderbolt could not have struck him more dumb. He stood, for a few moments, as motionless as one petrified; collecting himself, he at length exclaimed, "*Madison! is that you?*"

The noble fugitive, but little less astonished than himself, answered cheerily, "O yes, sir, they've got me again."

Thoughtless of consequences for the moment, Mr. Listwell ran up to his old friend, placing his hands upon his shoulders, and looked him in the face! Speechless they stood gazing at each other as if to be doubly resolved that there was no mistake about the matter, till Madison motioned his friend away, intimating a fear lest the keepers should find him there, and suspect him of tampering with the slaves.

"They will soon be out to look after us. You can come when they go to breakfast, and I will tell you all."

Pleased with this arrangement, Mr. Listwell passed out of the alley; but only just in time to save himself, for, while near the door, he observed three men making their way to the alley. The thought occurred to him to await their arrival, as the best means of diverting the ever ready suspicions of the guilty.

While the scene between Mr. Listwell and his friend Madison was going on, the other slaves stood as mute spectators,—at a loss to know what all this could mean. As he left, he heard the man chained to Madison ask, "Who is that gentleman?"

"He is a friend of mine. I cannot tell you now. Suffice it to say he is a friend. You shall hear more of him before long, but mark me! whatever shall pass between that gentleman and me, in your hearing, I pray you will say nothing about it. We are all chained here together,—ours is a common lot; and that gentleman is not less *your* friend than *mine*." At these words, all mysterious as they were, the unhappy company gave signs of satisfaction and hope. It seems that Madison, by that mesmeric power which is the invariable accompaniment of genius, had already won the confidence of the gang, and was a sort of general-in-chief among them.

By this time the keepers arrived. A horrid trio, well fitted for their demoniacal work. Their uncombed hair came down over foreheads "*villainously low*," and with eyes, mouths, and noses to match. "Hallo! hallo!" they growled out as they entered. "Are you all there?"

"All here," said Madison.

"Well, well, that's right! your journey will soon be over. You'll be in Richmond by eleven to-day, and then you'll have an easy time on it."

"I say, gal, what in the devil are you crying about?" said one of them. "I'll give you something to cry about, if you don't mind." This was said to a girl, apparently not more than twelve years old, who had been weeping bitterly. She had, probably, left behind her a loving mother, affectionate sisters, brothers, and friends, and her tears were but the natural expression of her sorrow, and the only solace. But the dealers in human flesh have *no* respect for such sorrow. They look upon it as a protest against their cruel injustice, and they are prompt to punish it.

This is a puzzle not easily solved. *How* came he here? what can I do for him? may I not even now be in some way compromised in this affair? were thoughts that troubled Mr. Listwell, and made him eager for the promised opportunity of speaking to Madison.

The bell now sounded for breakfast, and keepers and drivers, with pistols and bowie-knives gleaming from their belts, hurried in, as if to get the best places. Taking the chance now afforded, Mr. Listwell hastened back to the bowling-alley. Reaching Madison, he said, "Now *do* tell me all about the matter. Do you know me?"

"Oh, yes," said Madison, "I know you well, and shall never forget you nor that cold and dreary night you gave me shelter. I must be short," he continued, "for they'll soon be out again. This, then, is the story in brief. On reaching Canada, and getting over the excitement of making my escape, sir, my thoughts turned to my poor wife, who had well deserved my love by her virtuous fidelity and undying affection for me. I could not bear the thought of leaving her in the cruel jaws of slavery, without making an effort to rescue her. First, I tried to get money to buy her; but oh! the process was *too slow.* I despaired of accomplishing it. She was in all my thoughts by day, and my dreams by night. At times I could almost hear her voice, saying, 'O Madison! Madison! will you then leave me here? can you leave me here to die? No! no! you will come! you will come!' I was wretched. I lost my appetite. I could neither work, eat, nor sleep, till I resolved to hazard my own liberty, to gain that of my wife! But I must be short. Six weeks ago I reached my old master's place. I laid about the neighborhood nearly a week, watching my chance, and, finally, I ventured upon the desperate attempt to reach my poor wife's room by means of a ladder. I reached the window, but the noise in raising it frightened my wife, and she screamed and fainted. I took her in my arms, and was descending the ladder, when the dogs began to bark furiously, and before I could get to the woods the white folks were roused. The cool night air soon restored my wife, and she readily recognized me. We made the best of our way to the woods, but it was now *too* late,—the dogs were after us as though they would have torn us to pieces. It was all over with me now! My old master and his two sons ran out with loaded rifles, and before we were out of gunshot, our ears were assailed with '*Stop! stop! or be shot down.*' Nevertheless we ran on. Seeing that we gave no heed to their calls, they fired, and my poor wife fell by my side dead, while I received but a slight flesh wound. I now became desperate, and stood my ground, and awaited their attack over her dead body. They rushed upon me, with their rifles in hand. I parried their blows, and fought them 'till I was knocked down and overpowered."

"Oh! it was madness to have returned," said Mr. Listwell.

"Sir, I could not be free with the galling thought that my poor wife was still a slave. With her in slavery, my body, not my spirit, was free. I was taken to the house,—chained to a ring-bolt,—my wounds dressed. I was kept there three days. All the slaves, for miles around, were brought to see me. Many slaveholders came with their slaves, using me as proof of the completeness of their power, and of the impossibility of slaves getting away. I was taunted, jeered at, and berated by them, in a manner that pierced me to the soul. Thank God, I was able to smother my rage, and to bear it all with seeming composure.

After my wounds were nearly healed, I was taken to a tree and stripped, and I received sixty lashes on my naked back. A few days after, I was sold to a slave-trader, and placed in this gang for the New Orleans market."

"Do you think your master would sell you to me?"

"O no, sir! I was sold on condition of my being taken South. Their motive is revenge."

"Then, then," said Mr. Listwell, "I fear I can do nothing for you. Put your trust in God, and bear your sad lot with the manly fortitude which becomes a man. I shall see you at Richmond, but don't recognize me." Saying this, Mr. Listwell handed Madison ten dollars; said a few words to the other slaves; received their hearty "God bless you," and made his way to the house.

Fearful of exciting suspicion by too long delay, our friend went to the breakfast table, with the air of one who half reproved the greediness of those who rushed in at the sound of the bell. A cup of coffee was all that he could manage. His feelings were too bitter and excited, and his heart was too full with the fate of poor Madison (whom he loved as well as admired) to relish his breakfast; and although he sat long after the company had left the table, he really did little more than change the position of his knife and fork. The strangeness of meeting again one whom he had met on two several occasions before, under extraordinary circumstances, was well calculated to suggest the idea that a supernatural power, a wakeful providence, or an inexorable fate, had linked their destiny together; and that no efforts of his could disentangle him from the mysterious web of circumstances which enfolded him.

On leaving the table, Mr. Listwell nerved himself up and walked firmly into the bar-room. He was at once greeted again by that talkative chatter-box, Mr. Wilkes.

"Them's a likely set of niggers in the alley there," said Wilkes.

"Yes, they're fine looking fellows, one of them I should like to purchase, and for him I would be willing to give a handsome sum."

Turning to one of his comrades, and with a grin of victory, Wilkes said, "Aha, Bill, did you hear that? I told you I know'd that gentleman wanted to buy niggers, and would bid as high as any purchaser in the market."

"Come, come," said Listwell, "don't be too loud in your praise, you are old enough to know that prices rise when purchasers are plenty."

"That's a fact," said Wilkes, "I see you knows the ropes—and there's not a man in old Virginy whom I'd rather help to make a good bargain than you, sir."

Mr. Listwell here threw a dollar at Wilkes, (which the latter caught with a dexterous hand,) saying, "Take that for your kind good will."

Wilkes held up the dollar to his right eye, with a grin of victory, and turned to the morose grumbler in the corner who had questioned the liberality of a man of whom he knew nothing.

Mr. Listwell now stood as well with the company as any other occupant of the bar-room.

We pass over the hurry and bustle, the brutal vociferations of the slave-drivers in getting their unhappy gang in motion for Richmond; and we need not narrate every application of the lash to those who faltered in the journey. Mr. Listwell followed the train at a long distance, with a sad heart; and on reaching Richmond, left his horse at a hotel, and made his way to the wharf in the direction of which he saw the slave-coffle driven. He was just in time to see the whole company embark for New Orleans. The thought struck him that, while mixing with the multitude, he might do his friend Madison one last service, and he stept into a hardware store and purchased three strong *files*. These he took with him, and standing near the small boat, which lay in waiting to bear the company by parcels to the side of the brig that lay in the stream, he managed, as Madison passed him, to slip the files into his pocket, and at once darted back among the crowd.

All the company now on board, the imperious voice of the captain sounded, and instantly a dozen hardy seamen were in the rigging, hurrying aloft to unfurl the broad canvas of our Baltimore built American Slaver. The sailors hung about the ropes, like so many black cats, now in the round-tops, now in the cross-trees, now on the yard-arms; all was bluster and activity. Soon the broad fore topsail, the royal and top gallant sail were spread to the breeze. Round went the heavy windlass, clank, clank went the fall-bit,—the anchors weighed,—

jibs, mainsails, and topsails hauled to the wind, and the long, low, black slaver, with her cargo of human flesh, careened and moved forward to the sea.

Mr. Listwell stood on the shore, and watched the slaver till the last speck of her upper sails faded from sight, and announced the limit of human vision. "Farewell! farewell! brave and true man! God grant that brighter skies may smile upon your future than have yet looked down upon your thorny pathway."

Saying this to himself, our friend lost no time in completing his business, and in making his way homewards, gladly shaking off from his feet the dust of Old Virginia.

## Part IV.

Oh, where's the slave so lowly
Condemn'd to chains unholy,
Who could he burst
His bonds at first
Would pine beneath them slowly?
*Moore.*

———Know ye not
Who would be free, *themselves* must strike the blow.
*Childe Harold.*

What a world of inconsistency, as well as of wickedness, is suggested by the smooth and gliding phrase, AMERICAN SLAVE TRADE; and how strange and perverse is that moral sentiment which loathes, execrates, and brands as piracy and as deserving of death the carrying away into captivity men, women, and children from the *African coast*; but which is neither shocked nor disturbed by a similar traffic, carried on with the same motives and purposes, and characterized by even *more* odious peculiarities on the coast of our MODEL REPUBLIC. We execrate and hang the wretch guilty of this crime on the coast of Guinea, while we respect and applaud the guilty participators in this murderous business on the enlightened shores of the Chesapeake. The inconsistency is so flagrant and glaring, that it would seem to cast a doubt on the doctrine of the innate moral sense of mankind.

Just two months after the sailing of the Virginia slave brig, which the reader has seen move off to sea so proudly with her human cargo for the New Orleans market, there chanced to meet, in the Marine Coffee-house at Richmond, a company of *ocean birds*, when the following conversation, which throws some light on the subsequent history, not only of Madison Washington, but of the hundred and thirty human beings with whom we last saw him chained.

"I say, shipmate, you had rather rough weather on your late passage to Orleans?" said Jack Williams, a regular old salt, tauntingly, to a trim, compact, manly looking person, who proved to be the first mate of the slave brig in question.

"Foul play, as well as foul weather," replied the firmly knit personage, evidently but little inclined to enter upon a subject which terminated so ingloriously to the captain and officers of the American slaver.

"Well, betwixt you and me," said Williams, "that whole affair on board of the *Creole* was miserably and disgracefully managed. Those black rascals got the upper hand of ye altogether; and, in my opinion, the whole disaster was the result of ignorance of the real character of *darkies* in general. With half a dozen *resolute* white men, (I say it not boastingly,) I could have had the rascals in irons in ten minutes, not because I'm so strong, but I know how to manage 'em. With my back against the *caboose*, I could, myself, have flogged a dozen of them; and had I been on board, by every monster of the deep, every black devil of 'em all would have had his neck stretched from the yard-arm. Ye made a mistake in yer manner of fighting 'em. All that is needed in dealing with a set of rebellious *darkies*, is to show that yer not afraid of 'em. For my own part, I would not honor a dozen niggers by pointing a gun at one on 'em,—a good stout whip, or a stiff rope's end, is better than all the guns at Old Point to quell a *nigger* insurrection. Why, sir, to take a gun to a *nigger* is the best way you can select to tell him you are afraid of him, and the best way of inviting his attack."

This speech made quite a sensation among the company, and a part of them indicated solicitude for the answer which might be made to it. Our first mate replied, "Mr. Williams, all that you've now said sounds very well *here* on shore, where, perhaps, you have studied negro character. I do not profess to understand the subject as well as yourself; but it strikes me, you apply the same rule in dissimilar cases. It is quite easy to talk of flogging niggers here on land, where you have the sympathy of the community, and the whole physical force of the government, State and national, at your command; and where, if a negro shall lift his hand against a white man, the whole community, with one accord, are ready to unite in shooting him down. I say, in such circumstances, it's easy to talk of flogging negroes and of negro cowardice; but, sir, I deny that the negro is, naturally, a coward, or that your theory of managing slaves will stand the test of *salt* water. It may do very well for an overseer, a contemptible hireling, to take advantage of fears already in existence, and which his presence has no power to inspire; to swagger about whip in hand, and discourse on the timidity and cowardice of negroes; for they have a smooth sea and a fair wind. It is one thing to manage a company of slaves on a Virginia plantation, and quite another thing to quell an insurrection on the lonely billows of the Atlantic, where every breeze speaks of courage and liberty. For the negro to act cowardly on shore, may be to act wisely; and I've some doubts whether *you*, Mr. Williams, would find it very convenient were you a slave in Algiers, to raise your hand against the bayonets of a whole government."

"By George, shipmate," said Williams, "you're coming rather *too* near. Either I've fallen very low in your estimation, or your notions of negro courage have got up a button-hole too high. Now I more than ever wish I'd been on board of that luckless craft. I'd have given ye practical evidence of the truth of my theory. I don't doubt there's some difference in being at sea. But a nigger's a nigger, on sea or land; and is a coward, find him where you will; a drop of blood from one on 'em will skeer a hundred. A knock on the nose, or a kick on the shin, will tame the wildest '*darkey*' you can fetch me. I say again, and will stand by it, I could, with half a dozen good men, put the whole nineteen on 'em in irons, and have carried them safe to New Orleans too. Mind, I don't blame you, but I do say, and every gentleman here will bear me out in it, that the fault was somewhere, or them niggers would never have got off as they have done. For my part I feel ashamed to have the idea go abroad, that a ship load of slaves can't be safely taken from Richmond to New Orleans. I should like, merely to redeem the character of Virginia sailors, to take charge of a ship load on 'em to-morrow."

Williams went on in this strain, occasionally casting an imploring glance at the company for applause for his wit, and sympathy for his contempt of negro courage. He had, evidently, however, waked up the wrong passenger; for besides being in the right, his opponent carried that in his eye which marked him a man not to be trifled with.

"Well, sir," said the sturdy mate, "you can select your own method for distinguishing yourself;—the path of ambition in this direction is quite open to you in Virginia, and I've no doubt that you will be highly appreciated and compensated for all your valiant achievements in that line; but for myself, while I do not profess to be a giant, I have resolved never to set my foot on the deck of a slave ship, either as officer, or common sailor again; I have got enough of it."

"Indeed! indeed!" exclaimed Williams, derisively.

"Yes, *indeed*," echoed the mate; "but don't misunderstand me. It is not the high value that I set upon my life that makes me say what I have said; yet I'm resolved never to endanger my life again in a cause which my conscience does not approve. I dare say *here* what many men *feel*, but *dare not speak*, that this whole slave-trading business is a disgrace and scandal to Old Virginia."

"Hold! hold on! shipmate," said Williams, "I hardly thought you'd have shown your colors so soon,—I'll be hanged if you're not as good an abolitionist as Garrison himself."

The mate now rose from his chair, manifesting some excitement. "What do you mean, sir," said he, in a commanding tone. "*That man does not live who shall offer me an insult with impunity*."

The effect of these words was marked; and the company clustered around. Williams, in an apologetic tone, said, "Shipmate! keep your temper. I mean't no insult. We all know that Tom Grant is no coward, and what I said about your being an abolitionist was simply this: you *might* have put down them black mutineers and murderers, but your conscience held you back."

"In that, too," said Grant, "you were mistaken. I did all that any man with equal strength and presence of mind could have done. The fact is, Mr. Williams, you underrate the courage as well as the skill of these negroes, and further, you do not seem to have been correctly informed about the case in hand at all."

"All I know about it is," said Williams, "that on the ninth day after you left Richmond, a dozen or two of the niggers ye had on board, came on deck and took the ship from you;—had her steered into a British port, where, by the by, every wooly head of them went ashore and was free. Now I take this to be a discreditable piece of business, and one demanding explanation."

"There are a great many discreditable things in the world," said Grant. "For a ship to go down under a calm sky is, upon the first flush of it, disgraceful either to sailors or caulkers. But when we learn, that by some mysterious disturbance in nature, the waters parted beneath, and swallowed the ship up, we lose our indignation and disgust in lamentation of the disaster, and in awe of the Power which controls the elements."

"Very true, very true," said Williams, "I should be very glad to have an explanation which would relieve the affair of its present discreditable features. I have desired to see you ever since you got home, and to learn from you a full statement of the facts in the case. To me the whole thing seems unaccountable. I cannot see how a dozen or two of ignorant negroes, not one of whom had ever been to sea before, and all of them were closely ironed between decks, should be able to get their fetters off, rush out of the hatchway in open daylight, kill two white men, the one the captain and the other their master, and then carry the ship into a British port, where every '*darkey*' of them was set free. There must have been great carelessness, or cowardice somewhere!"

The company which had listened in silence during most of this discussion, now became much excited. One said, I agree with Williams; and several said the thing looks black enough. After the temporary tumultuous exclamations had subsided,—

"I see," said Grant, "how you regard this case, and how difficult it will be for me to render our ship's company blameless in your eyes. Nevertheless, I will state the facts precisely as they came under my own observation. Mr. Williams speaks of 'ignorant negroes,' and, as a general rule, they are ignorant; but had he been on board the *Creole* as I was, he would have seen cause to admit that there are exceptions to this general rule. The leader of the mutiny in question was just as shrewd a fellow as ever I met in my life, and was as well fitted to lead in a dangerous enterprise as any one white man in ten thousand. The name of this man, strange to say, (ominous of greatness,) was MADISON WASHINGTON. In the short time he had been on board, he had secured the confidence of every officer. The negroes fairly worshipped him. His manner and bearing were such, that no one could suspect him of a murderous purpose. The only feeling with which we regarded him was, that he was a powerful, good-disposed negro. He seldom spake to any one, and when he did speak, it was with the utmost propriety. His words were well chosen, and his pronunciation equal to that of any schoolmaster. It was a mystery to us *where* he got his knowledge of language; but as little was said to him, none of us knew the extent of his intelligence and ability till it was too late. It seems he brought three files with him on board, and must have gone to work upon his fetters the first night out; and he must have worked well at that; for on the day of the rising, he got the irons *off eighteen* besides himself.

"The attack began just about twilight in the evening. Apprehending a squall, I had commanded the second mate to order all hands on deck, to take in sail. A few minutes before this I had seen Madison's head above the hatchway, looking out upon the white-capped waves at the leeward. I think I never saw him look more good-natured. I stood just about midship, on the larboard side. The captain was pacing the quarter-deck on the starboard side, in company with Mr. Jameson, the owner of most of the slaves on board. Both were armed. I had just told the men to lay aloft, and was looking to see my orders obeyed, when I heard the discharge of a pistol on the starboard side; and turning suddenly around, the very deck seemed covered with fiends from the pit. The nineteen negroes were all on deck, with their broken fetters in their hands, rushing in all directions. I put my hand quickly in my pocket to draw out my jack-knife; but before I could draw it, I was knocked senseless to the deck. When I came to myself, (which I did in a few minutes, I suppose, for it was yet quite light,) there was not a white man on deck. The sailors were all aloft in the rigging, and dared not come down. Captain Clarke and Mr. Jameson lay stretched on the quarter-deck,—both dying,—while Madison himself stood at the helm unhurt.

"I was completely weakened by the loss of blood, and had not recovered from the stunning blow which felled me to the deck; but it was a little too much for me, even in my prostrate condition, to see our good brig commanded by a *black murderer.* So I called out to the men to come down and take the ship, or die in the attempt. Suiting the action to the word, I started aft. You murderous villain, said I, to the imp at the helm, and rushed upon him to deal him a blow, when he pushed me back with his strong, black arm, as though I had been a boy of twelve. I looked around for the men. They were still in the rigging. Not one had come down. I started towards Madison again. The rascal now told me to stand back. 'Sir,' said he, 'your life is in my hands. I could have killed you a dozen times over during this last half hour, and could kill you now. You call me a *black murderer.* I am not a murderer. God is my witness that LIBERTY, not *malice*, is the motive for this night's work. I have done no more to those dead men yonder, than they would have done to me in like circumstances. We have struck for our freedom, and if a true man's heart be in you, you will honor us for the deed. We have done that which you applaud your fathers for doing, and if we are murderers, *so were they.*'

"I felt little disposition to reply to this impudent speech. By heaven, it disarmed me. The fellow loomed up before me. I forgot his blackness in the dignity of his manner, and the eloquence of his speech. It seemed as if the souls of both the great dead (whose names he bore) had entered him. To the sailors in the rigging he said: 'Men! the battle is over,—your captain is dead. I have complete command of this vessel. All resistance to my authority will be in vain. My men have won their liberty, with no other weapons but their own BROKEN FETTERS. We are nineteen in number. We do not thirst for your blood, we demand only our rightful freedom. Do not flatter yourselves that I am ignorant of chart or compass. I know both. We are now only about sixty miles from Nassau. Come down, and do your duty. Land us in Nassau, and not a hair of your heads shall be hurt.'

"I shouted, *Stay where you are, men*,—when a sturdy black fellow ran at me with a handspike, and would have split my head open, but for the interference of Madison, who darted between me and the blow. 'I know what you are up to,' said the latter to me. 'You want to navigate this brig into a slave port, where you would have us all hanged; but you'll miss it; before this brig shall touch a slave-cursed shore while I am on board, I will myself put a match to the magazine, and blow her, and be blown with her, into a thousand fragments. Now I have saved your life twice within these last twenty minutes,—for, when you lay helpless on deck, my men were about to kill you. I held them in check. And if you now (seeing I am your friend and not your enemy) persist in your resistance to my authority, I give you fair warning YOU SHALL DIE.'

"Saying this to me, he cast a glance into the rigging where the terror-stricken sailors were clinging, like so many frightened monkeys, and commanded them to come down, in a tone from which there was no appeal; for four men stood by with muskets in hand, ready at the word of command to shoot them down.

"I now became satisfied that resistance was out of the question; that my best policy was to put the brig into Nassau, and secure the assistance of the American consul at that port. I felt sure that the authorities would enable us to secure the murderers, and bring them to trial.

"By this time the apprehended squall had burst upon us. The wind howled furiously,—the ocean was white with foam, which, on account of the darkness, we could see only by the quick flashes of lightning that darted occasionally from the angry sky. All was alarm and confusion. Hideous cries came up from the slave women. Above the roaring billows a succession of heavy thunder rolled along, swelling the terrific din. Owing to the great darkness, and a sudden shift of the wind, we found ourselves in the trough of the sea. When shipping a heavy sea over the starboard bow, the bodies of the captain and Mr. Jameson were washed overboard. For awhile we had dearer interests to look after than slave property. A more savage thunder-gust never swept the ocean. Our brig rolled and creaked as if every bolt would be started, and every thread of oakum would be pressed out of the seams. To the pumps! to the pumps! I cried, but not a sailor would quit his grasp. Fortunately this squall soon passed over, or we must have been food for sharks.

"During all the storm, Madison stood firmly at the helm,—his keen eye fixed upon the binnacle. He was not indifferent to the dreadful hurricane; yet he met it with the equanimity of an old sailor. He was silent but not agitated. The first words he uttered after the storm had slightly subsided, were characteristic of the man. 'Mr. Mate, you cannot write the bloody laws of slavery on those restless billows. The ocean, if not the land, is free.' I confess, gentlemen, I felt myself in the presence of a superior man; one who, had he been a white man, I would have followed willingly and gladly in any honorable enterprise. Our difference of color was the only ground for difference of action. It was not that his principles were wrong in the abstract; for they are the principles of 1776. But I could not bring myself to recognize their application to one whom I deemed my inferior.

"But to my story. What happened now is soon told. Two hours after the frightful tempest had spent itself, we were plump at the wharf in Nassau. I sent two of our men immediately to our consul with a statement of facts, requesting his interference in our behalf. What he did, or whither he did anything, I don't know; but, by order of the authorities, a company of *black* soldiers came on board, for the purpose, as they said, of protecting the property. These impudent rascals, when I called on them to assist me in keeping the slaves on board, sheltered themselves adroitly under their instructions only to protect property,—and said they did not recognize *persons* as *property*. I told them that by the laws of Virginia and the laws of the United States, the slaves on board were as much property as the barrels of flour in the hold. At this the stupid blockheads showed their *ivory*, rolled up their white eyes in horror, as if the idea of putting men on a footing with merchandise were revolting to their humanity. When these instructions were understood among the negroes, it was impossible for us to keep them on board. They deliberately gathered up their baggage before our eyes, and, against our remonstrances, poured through the gangway,—formed themselves into a procession on the wharf,—bid farewell to all on board, and, uttering the wildest shouts of exultation, they marched, amidst the deafening cheers of a multitude of sympathizing spectators, under the triumphant leadership of their heroic chief and deliverer, MADISON WASHINGTON."

1853

# HERMAN MELVILLE

(1819–1891)

## *Bartleby, the Scrivener*

### *A Story of Wall-Street*

I AM A rather elderly man. The nature of my avocations for the last thirty years has brought me into more than ordinary contact with what would seem an interesting and somewhat singular set of men, of whom as yet nothing that I know of has ever been written:—I mean the law-copyists or scriveners. I have known very many of them, professionally and privately, and if I pleased, could relate divers histories, at which good-natured gentlemen might smile, and sentimental souls might weep. But I waive the biographies of all other scriveners for a few passages in the life of Bartleby, who was a scrivener the strangest I ever saw or heard of. While of other law-copyists I might write the complete life, of Bartleby nothing of that sort can be done. I believe that no materials exist for a full and satisfactory biography of this man. It is an irreparable loss to literature. Bartleby was one of those beings of whom nothing is ascertainable, except from the original sources, and in his case those are very small. What my own astonished eyes saw of Bartleby, *that* is all I know of him, except, indeed, one vague report which will appear in the sequel.

Ere introducing the scrivener, as he first appeared to me, it is fit I make some mention of myself, my *employés*, my business, my chambers, and general surroundings; because some such description is indispensable to an adequate understanding of the chief character about to be presented.

Imprimis: I am a man who, from his youth upwards, has been filled with a profound conviction that the easiest way of life is the best. Hence, though I belong to a profession proverbially energetic and nervous, even to turbulence, at times, yet nothing of that sort have I ever suffered to invade my peace. I am one of those unambitious lawyers who never addresses a jury, or in any way draws down public applause; but in the cool tranquillity of a snug retreat, do a snug business among rich men's bonds and mortgages and title-deeds. All who know me, consider me an eminently *safe* man. The late John Jacob Astor, a personage little given to poetic enthusiasm, had no hesitation in pronouncing my first grand point to be prudence; my next, method. I do not speak it in vanity, but simply record the fact, that I was not unemployed in my profession by the late John Jacob Astor; a name which, I admit, I love to repeat, for it hath a rounded and orbicular sound to it, and rings like unto bullion. I will freely add, that I was not insensible to the late John Jacob Astor's good opinion.

Some time prior to the period at which this little history begins, my avocations had been largely increased. The good old office, now extinct in the State of New-York, of a Master in Chancery, had been conferred upon me. It was not a very arduous office, but very pleasantly remunerative. I seldom lose my temper; much more seldom indulge in dangerous indignation at wrongs and outrages; but I must be permitted to be rash here and declare, that I consider the sudden and violent abrogation of the office of Master in Chancery, by the new Constitution, as a —— premature act; inasmuch as I had counted upon a life-lease of the profits, whereas I only received those of a few short years. But this is by the way.

My chambers were up stairs at No. — Wall-street. At one end they looked upon the white wall of the interior of a spacious sky-light shaft, penetrating the building from top to bottom. This view might have been considered rather tame than otherwise, deficient in what landscape painters call "life." But if so, the view from the other end of my chambers offered, at least, a contrast, if nothing more. In that direction my windows commanded an unobstructed view of a lofty brick wall, black by age and everlasting shade; which wall required no spyglass to bring out its lurking beauties, but for the benefit of all near-sighted spectators, was pushed up to within ten feet of my window panes. Owing to the great height of the surrounding buildings, and my chambers being on the second floor, the interval between this wall and mine not a little resembled a huge square cistern.

At the period just preceding the advent of Bartleby, I had two persons as copyists in my employment, and a promising lad as an office-boy. First, Turkey; second, Nippers; third, Ginger Nut. These may seem names, the like of which are not usually found in the Directory. In truth they were nicknames, mutually conferred upon each other by my three clerks, and were deemed expressive of their respective persons or characters. Turkey was a short, pursy Englishman of about my own age, that is, somewhere not far from sixty. In the morning, one might say, his face was of a fine florid hue, but after twelve o'clock, meridian—his dinner hour—it blazed like a grate full of Christmas coals; and continued blazing—but, as it were, with a gradual wane—till 6 o'clock, P.M. or thereabouts, after which I saw no more of the proprietor of the face, which gaining its meridian with the sun, seemed to set with it, to rise, culminate, and decline the following day, with the like regularity and undiminished glory. There are many singular coincidences I have known in the course of my life, not the least among which was the fact, that exactly when Turkey displayed his fullest beams from his red and radiant countenance, just then, too, at that critical moment, began the daily period when I considered his business capacities as seriously disturbed for the remainder of the twenty-four hours. Not that he was absolutely idle, or averse to business then; far from it. The difficulty was, he was apt to be altogether too energetic. There was a strange, inflamed, flurried, flighty recklessness of activity about him. He would be incautious in dipping his pen into his inkstand. All his blots upon my documents, were dropped there after twelve o'clock, meridian. Indeed, not only would he be reckless and sadly given to making blots in the afternoon, but some days he went further, and was rather noisy. At such times, too, his face flamed with augmented blazonry, as if cannel coal had been heaped on anthracite. He made an unpleasant racket with his chair; spilled his sand-box; in mending his pens, impatiently split them all to pieces, and threw them on the floor in a sudden passion; stood up and leaned over his table, boxing his papers about in a most indecorous manner, very sad to behold in an elderly man like him. Nevertheless, as he was in many ways a most valuable person to me, and all the time before twelve o'clock, meridian, was the quickest, steadiest creature too, accomplishing a great deal of work in a style not easy to be matched—for these reasons, I was willing to overlook his eccentricities, though indeed, occasionally, I remonstrated with him. I did this very gently, however, because, though the civilest, nay, the blandest and most reverential of men in the morning, yet in the afternoon he was disposed, upon provocation, to be slightly rash with his tongue, in fact, insolent. Now, valuing his morning services as I did, and resolved not to lose them; yet, at the same time made uncomfortable by his inflamed ways after twelve o'clock; and being a man of peace, unwilling by my admonitions to call forth unseemly retorts from him; I took upon me, one Saturday noon (he was always worse on Saturdays), to hint to him, very kindly, that perhaps now that he was growing old, it might be well to abridge his labors; in short, he need not come to my chambers after twelve o'clock, but, dinner over, had best go home to his lodgings and rest himself till tea-time. But no; he insisted upon his afternoon devotions. His countenance became intolerably fervid, as he oratorically assured me—gesticulating with a long ruler at the other end of the room—that if his services in the morning were useful, how indispensable, then, in the afternoon?

"With submission, sir," said Turkey on this occasion, "I consider myself your right-hand man. In the morning I but marshal and deploy my columns; but in the afternoon I put myself at their head, and gallantly charge the foe, thus!"—and he made a violent thrust with the ruler.

"But the blots, Turkey," intimated I.

"True,—but, with submission, sir, behold these hairs! I am getting old. Surely, sir, a blot or two of a warm afternoon is not to be severely urged against gray hairs. Old age—even if it blot the page—is honorable. With submission, sir, we *both* are getting old."

This appeal to my fellow-feeling was hardly to be resisted. At all events, I saw that go he would not. So I made up my mind to let him stay, resolving, nevertheless, to see to it, that during the afternoon he had to do with my less important papers.

Nippers, the second on my list, was a whiskered, sallow, and, upon the whole, rather piratical-looking young man of about five and twenty. I always deemed him the victim of two evil powers—ambition and indigestion. The ambition was evinced by a certain impatience of the duties of a mere copyist, an unwarrantable usurpation of strictly professional affairs, such as the original drawing up of legal documents. The indigestion seemed betokened in an occasional nervous testiness and grinning irritability, causing the teeth to audibly grind together over mistakes committed in copying; unnecessary maledictions, hissed, rather than spoken, in the heat of business; and especially by a continual discontent with the height of the table where he worked. Though of a very ingenious mechanical turn, Nippers could never get this table to suit him. He put chips under it, blocks of various sorts, bits of pasteboard, and at last went so far as to attempt an exquisite adjustment by final pieces of folded blotting-paper. But no invention would answer. If, for the sake of easing his back, he brought the table lid at a sharp angle well up towards his chin, and wrote there like a man using the steep roof of a Dutch house for his desk:—then he declared that it stopped the circulation in his arms. If now he lowered the table to his waistbands, and stooped over it in writing, then there was a sore aching in his back. In short, the truth of the matter was, Nippers knew not what he wanted. Or, if he wanted any thing, it was to be rid of a scrivener's table altogether. Among the manifestations of his diseased ambition was a fondness he had for receiving visits from certain ambiguous-looking fellows in seedy coats, whom he called his clients. Indeed I was aware that not only was he, at times, considerable of a ward-politician, but he occasionally did a little business at the Justices' courts, and was not unknown on the steps of the Tombs. I have good reason to believe, however, that one individual who called upon him at my chambers, and who, with a grand air, he insisted was his client, was no other than a dun, and the alleged title-deed, a bill. But with all his failings, and the annoyances he caused me, Nippers, like his compatriot Turkey, was a very useful man to me; wrote a neat, swift hand; and, when he chose, was not deficient in a gentlemanly sort of deportment. Added to this, he always dressed in a gentlemanly sort of way; and so, incidentally, reflected credit upon my chambers. Whereas with respect to Turkey, I had much ado to keep him from being a reproach to me. His clothes were apt to look oily and smell of eating-houses. He wore his pantaloons very loose and baggy in summer. His coats were execrable; his hat not to be handled. But while the hat was a thing of indifference to me, inasmuch as his natural civility and deference, as a dependent Englishman, always led him to doff it the moment he entered the room, yet his coat was another matter. Concerning his coats, I reasoned with him; but with no effect. The truth was, I suppose, that a man with so small an income, could not afford to sport such a lustrous face and a lustrous coat at one and the same time. As Nippers once observed, Turkey's money went chiefly for red ink. One winter day I presented Turkey with a highly-respectable looking coat of my own, a padded gray coat, of a most comfortable warmth, and which buttoned straight up from the knee to the neck. I thought Turkey would appreciate the favor, and abate his rashness and obstreperousness of afternoons. But no. I verily believe that buttoning himself up in so downy and blanket-like a coat had a pernicious effect upon him; upon the same principle that too much oats are bad for horses. In fact, precisely as a rash, restive horse is said to feel his oats, so Turkey felt his coat. It made him insolent. He was a man whom prosperity harmed.

Though concerning the self-indulgent habits of Turkey I had my own private surmises, yet touching Nippers I was well persuaded that whatever might be his faults in other respects, he was, at least, a temperate young man. But indeed, nature herself seemed to have been his vintner, and at his birth charged him so thoroughly with an irritable, brandy-like disposition, that all subsequent potations were needless. When I consider how, amid the stillness of my chambers, Nippers would sometimes impatiently rise from his seat, and stooping over his table, spread his arms wide apart, seize the whole desk, and move it, and jerk it, with a grim, grinding motion on the floor, as if the table were a perverse voluntary agent, intent on thwarting and vexing him; I plainly perceive that for Nippers, brandy and water were altogether superfluous.

It was fortunate for me that, owing to its peculiar cause—indigestion—the irritability and consequent nervousness of Nippers, were mainly observable in the morning, while in the afternoon he was comparatively mild. So that Turkey's paroxysms only coming on about twelve o'clock, I never had to do with their eccentricities at one time. Their fits relieved each other like guards. When Nippers' was on, Turkey's was off; and *vice versa.* This was a good natural arrangement under the circumstances.

Ginger Nut, the third on my list, was a lad some twelve years old. His father was a carman, ambitious of seeing his son on the bench instead of a cart, before he died. So he sent him to my office as student at law, errand boy, and cleaner and sweeper, at the rate of one dollar a week. He had a little desk to himself, but he did not use it much. Upon inspection, the drawer exhibited a great array of the shells of various sorts of nuts. Indeed, to this quick-witted youth the whole noble science of the law was contained in a nut-shell. Not the least among the employments of Ginger Nut, as well as one which he discharged with the most alacrity, was his duty as cake and apple purveyor for Turkey and Nippers. Copying law papers being proverbially a dry, husky sort of business, my two scriveners were fain to moisten their mouths very often with Spitzenbergs to be had at the numerous stalls nigh the Custom House and Post Office. Also, they sent Ginger Nut very frequently for that peculiar cake—small, flat, round, and very spicy—after which he had been named by them. Of a cold morning when business was but dull, Turkey would gobble up scores of these cakes, as if they were mere wafers—indeed they sell them at the rate of six or eight for a penny—the scrape of his pen blending with the crunching of the crisp particles in his mouth. Of all the fiery afternoon blunders and flurried rashnesses of Turkey, was his once moistening a ginger-cake between his lips, and clapping it on to a mortgage for a seal. I came within an ace of dismissing him then. But he mollified me by making an oriental bow, and saying—"With submission, sir, it was generous of me to find you in stationery on my own account."

Now my original business—that of a conveyancer and title hunter, and drawer-up of recondite documents of all sorts—was considerably increased by receiving the master's office. There was now great work for scriveners. Not only must I push the clerks already with me, but I must have additional help. In answer to my advertisement, a motionless young man one morning, stood upon my office threshold, the door being open, for it was summer. I can see that figure now—pallidly neat, pitiably respectable, incurably forlorn! It was Bartleby.

After a few words touching his qualifications, I engaged him, glad to have among my corps of copyists a man of so singularly sedate an aspect, which I thought might operate beneficially upon the flighty temper of Turkey, and the fiery one of Nippers.

I should have stated before that ground glass folding-doors divided my premises into two parts, one of which was occupied by my scriveners, the other by myself. According to my humor I threw open these doors, or closed them. I resolved to assign Bartleby a corner by the folding-doors, but on my side of them, so as to have this quiet man within easy call, in case any trifling thing was to be done. I placed his desk close up to a small side-window in that part of the room, a window which originally had afforded a lateral view of certain grimy back-yards and bricks, but which, owing to subsequent erections, commanded at present no view at all, though it gave some light. Within three feet of the panes was a wall, and the light came down from far above, between two lofty buildings, as from a very small opening in a dome. Still further to a satisfactory arrangement, I procured a high green folding screen, which might entirely isolate Bartleby from my sight, though not remove him from my voice. And thus, in a manner, privacy and society were conjoined.

At first Bartleby did an extraordinary quantity of writing. As if long famishing for something to copy, he seemed to gorge himself on my documents. There was no pause for digestion. He ran a day and night line, copying by sun-light and by candle-light. I should have been quite delighted with his application, had he been cheerfully industrious. But he wrote on silently, palely, mechanically.

It is, of course, an indispensable part of a scrivener's business to verify the accuracy of his copy, word by word. Where there are two or more scriveners in an office, they assist each other in this examination, one reading from the copy, the other holding the original. It is a very dull, wearisome, and lethargic affair. I can readily imagine that to some sanguine temperaments it would be altogether intolerable. For example, I cannot credit that the mettlesome poet Byron would have contentedly sat down with Bartleby to examine a law document of, say five hundred pages, closely written in a crimpy hand.

Now and then, in the haste of business, it had been my habit to assist in comparing some brief document myself, calling Turkey or Nippers for this purpose. One object I had in placing Bartleby so handy to me behind the screen, was to avail myself of his services on such trivial occasions. It was on the third day,

I think, of his being with me, and before any necessity had arisen for having his own writing examined, that, being much hurried to complete a small affair I had in hand, I abruptly called to Bartleby. In my haste and natural expectancy of instant compliance, I sat with my head bent over the original on my desk, and my right hand sideways, and somewhat nervously extended with the copy, so that immediately upon emerging from his retreat, Bartleby might snatch it and proceed to business without the least delay.

In this very attitude did I sit when I called to him, rapidly stating what it was I wanted him to do—namely, to examine a small paper with me. Imagine my surprise, nay, my consternation, when without moving from his privacy, Bartleby in a singularly mild, firm voice, replied, "I would prefer not to."

I sat awhile in perfect silence, rallying my stunned faculties. Immediately it occurred to me that my ears had deceived me, or Bartleby had entirely misunderstood my meaning. I repeated my request in the clearest tone I could assume. But in quite as clear a one came the previous reply, "I would prefer not to."

"Prefer not to," echoed I, rising in high excitement, and crossing the room with a stride. "What do you mean? Are you moon-struck? I want you to help me compare this sheet here—take it," and I thrust it towards him.

"I would prefer not to," said he.

I looked at him steadfastly. His face was leanly composed; his gray eye dimly calm. Not a wrinkle of agitation rippled him. Had there been the least uneasiness, anger, impatience or impertinence in his manner; in other words, had there been any thing ordinarily human about him, doubtless I should have violently dismissed him from the premises. But as it was, I should have as soon thought of turning my pale plaster-of-paris bust of Cicero out of doors. I stood gazing at him awhile, as he went on with his own writing, and then reseated myself at my desk. This is very strange, thought I. What had one best do? But my business hurried me. I concluded to forget the matter for the present, reserving it for my future leisure. So calling Nippers from the other room, the paper was speedily examined.

A few days after this, Bartleby concluded four lengthy documents, being quadruplicates of a week's testimony taken before me in my High Court of Chancery. It became necessary to examine them. It was an important suit, and great accuracy was imperative. Having all things arranged I called Turkey, Nippers and Ginger Nut from the next room, meaning to place the four copies in the hands of my four clerks, while I should read from the original. Accordingly Turkey, Nippers and Ginger Nut had taken their seats in a row, each with his document in hand, when I called to Bartleby to join this interesting group.

"Bartleby! quick, I am waiting."

I heard a slow scrape of his chair legs on the uncarpeted floor, and soon he appeared standing at the entrance of his hermitage.

"What is wanted?" said he mildly.

"The copies, the copies," said I hurriedly. "We are going to examine them. There"—and I held towards him the fourth quadruplicate.

"I would prefer not to," he said, and gently disappeared behind the screen.

For a few moments I was turned into a pillar of salt, standing at the head of my seated column of clerks. Recovering myself, I advanced towards the screen, and demanded the reason for such extraordinary conduct.

"*Why* do you refuse?"

"I would prefer not to."

With any other man I should have flown outright into a dreadful passion, scorned all further words, and thrust him ignominiously from my presence. But there was something about Bartleby that not only strangely disarmed me, but in a wonderful manner touched and disconcerted me. I began to reason with him.

"These are your own copies we are about to examine. It is labor saving to you, because one examination will answer for your four papers. It is common usage. Every copyist is bound to help examine his copy. Is it not so? Will you not speak? Answer!"

"I prefer not to," he replied in a flute-like tone. It seemed to me that while I had been addressing him, he carefully revolved every statement that I made; fully comprehended the meaning; could not gainsay the irresistible conclusion; but, at the same time, some paramount consideration prevailed with him to reply as he did.

"You are decided, then, not to comply with my request—a request made according to common usage and common sense?"

He briefly gave me to understand that on that point my judgment was sound. Yes: his decision was irreversible.

It is not seldom the case that when a man is browbeaten in some unprecedented and violently unreasonable way, he begins to stagger in his own plainest faith. He begins, as it were, vaguely to surmise that, wonderful as it may be, all the justice and all the reason is on the other side. Accordingly, if any disinterested persons are present, he turns to them for some reinforcement for his own faltering mind.

"Turkey," said I, "what do you think of this? Am I not right?"

"With submission, sir," said Turkey, with his blandest tone, "I think that you are."

"Nippers," said I, "what do *you* think of it?"

"I think I should kick him out of the office."

(The reader of nice perceptions will here perceive that, it being morning, Turkey's answer is couched in polite and tranquil terms, but Nippers replies in ill-tempered ones. Or, to repeat a previous sentence, Nippers's ugly mood was on duty, and Turkey's off.)

"Ginger Nut," said I, willing to enlist the smallest suffrage in my behalf, "what do *you* think of it?"

"I think, sir, he's a little *luny*," replied Ginger Nut, with a grin.

"You hear what they say," said I, turning towards the screen, "come forth and do your duty."

But he vouchsafed no reply. I pondered a moment in sore perplexity. But once more business hurried me. I determined again to postpone the consideration of this dilemma to my future leisure. With a little trouble we made out to examine the papers without Bartleby, though at every page or two, Turkey deferentially dropped his opinion that this proceeding was quite out of the common; while Nippers, twitching in his chair with a dyspeptic nervousness, ground out between his set teeth occasional hissing maledictions against the stubborn oaf behind the screen. And for his (Nippers's) part, this was the first and the last time he would do another man's business without pay.

Meanwhile Bartleby sat in his hermitage, oblivious to every thing but his own peculiar business there.

Some days passed, the scrivener being employed upon another lengthy work. His late remarkable conduct led me to regard his ways narrowly. I observed that he never went to dinner; indeed that he never went any where. As yet I had never of my personal knowledge known him to be outside of my office. He was a perpetual sentry in the corner. At about eleven o'clock though, in the morning, I noticed that Ginger Nut would advance toward the opening in Bartleby's screen, as if silently beckoned thither by a gesture invisible to me where I sat. The boy would then leave the office jingling a few pence, and reappear with a handful of ginger-nuts which he delivered in the hermitage, receiving two of the cakes for his trouble.

He lives, then, on ginger-nuts, thought I; never eats a dinner, properly speaking; he must be a vegetarian then; but no; he never eats even vegetables, he eats nothing but ginger-nuts. My mind then ran on in reveries concerning the probable effects upon the human constitution of living entirely on ginger-nuts. Ginger-nuts are so called because they contain ginger as one of their peculiar constituents, and the final flavoring one. Now what was ginger? A hot, spicy thing. Was Bartleby hot and spicy? Not at all. Ginger, then, had no effect upon Bartleby. Probably he preferred it should have none.

Nothing so aggravates an earnest person as a passive resistance. If the individual so resisted be of a not inhumane temper, and the resisting one perfectly harmless in his passivity; then, in the better moods of the former, he will endeavor charitably to construe to his imagination what proves impossible to be solved by his judgment. Even so, for the most part, I regarded Bartleby and his ways. Poor fellow! thought I, he means no mischief; it is plain he intends no insolence; his aspect sufficiently evinces that his eccentricities are involuntary. He is useful to me. I can get along with him. If I turn him away, the chances are he will fall in with some less indulgent employer, and then he will be rudely treated, and perhaps driven forth miserably to starve. Yes. Here I can cheaply purchase a delicious self-approval. To befriend Bartleby; to humor him in his strange wilfulness, will cost me little or nothing, while I lay up in my soul what will eventually prove a sweet morsel for my conscience. But this mood was not invariable with me. The passiveness of Bartleby sometimes irritated me. I felt strangely goaded on to encounter him in new opposition, to elicit some angry spark from him answerable to my own. But indeed I might as well have essayed to strike fire with my knuckles against a bit of Windsor soap. But one afternoon the evil impulse in me mastered me, and the following little scene ensued:

"Bartleby," said I, "when those papers are all copied, I will compare them with you."

"I would prefer not to."

"How? Surely you do not mean to persist in that mulish vagary?"

No answer.

I threw open the folding-doors near by, and turning upon Turkey and Nippers, exclaimed:

"Bartleby a second time says, he won't examine his papers. What do you think of it, Turkey?"

It was afternoon, be it remembered. Turkey sat glowing like a brass boiler, his bald head steaming, his hands reeling among his blotted papers.

"Think of it?" roared Turkey; "I think I'll just step behind his screen, and black his eyes for him!"

So saying, Turkey rose to his feet and threw his arms into a pugilistic position. He was hurrying away to make good his promise, when I detained him, alarmed at the effect of incautiously rousing Turkey's combativeness after dinner.

"Sit down, Turkey," said I, "and hear what Nippers has to say. What do you think of it, Nippers? Would I not be justified in immediately dismissing Bartleby?"

"Excuse me, that is for you to decide, sir. I think his conduct quite unusual, and indeed unjust, as regards Turkey and myself. But it may only be a passing whim."

"Ah," exclaimed I, "you have strangely changed your mind then—you speak very gently of him now."

"All beer," cried Turkey; "gentleness is effects of beer—Nippers and I dined together to-day. You see how gentle *I* am, sir. Shall I go and black his eyes?"

"You refer to Bartleby, I suppose. No, not to-day, Turkey," I replied; "pray, put up your fists."

I closed the doors, and again advanced towards Bartleby. I felt additional incentives tempting me to my fate. I burned to be rebelled against again. I remembered that Bartleby never left the office.

"Bartleby," said I, "Ginger Nut is away; just step round to the Post Office, won't you? (it was but a three minutes walk,) and see if there is any thing for me."

"I would prefer not to."

"You *will* not?"

"I *prefer* not."

I staggered to my desk, and sat there in a deep study. My blind inveteracy returned. Was there any other thing in which I could procure myself to be ignominiously repulsed by this lean, penniless wight?—my hired clerk? What added thing is there, perfectly reasonable, that he will be sure to refuse to do?

"Bartleby!"

No answer.

"Bartleby," in a louder tone.

No answer.

"Bartleby," I roared.

Like a very ghost, agreeably to the laws of magical invocation, at the third summons, he appeared at the entrance of his hermitage.

"Go to the next room, and tell Nippers to come to me."

"I prefer not to," he respectfully and slowly said, and mildly disappeared.

"Very good, Bartleby," said I, in a quiet sort of serenely severe self-possessed tone, intimating the unalterable purpose of some terrible retribution very close at hand. At the moment I half intended something of the kind. But upon the whole, as it was drawing towards my dinner-hour, I thought it best to put on my hat and walk home for the day, suffering much from perplexity and distress of mind.

Shall I acknowledge it? The conclusion of this whole business was, that it soon became a fixed fact of my chambers, that a pale young scrivener, by the name of Bartleby, had a desk there; that he copied for me at the usual rate of four cents a folio (one hundred words); but he was permanently exempt from examining the work done by him, that duty being transferred to Turkey and Nippers, out of compliment doubtless to their superior acuteness; moreover, said Bartleby was never on any account to be dispatched on the most trivial errand of any sort; and that even if entreated to take upon him such a matter, it was generally understood that he would prefer not to—in other words, that he would refuse point-blank.

As days passed on, I became considerably reconciled to Bartleby. His steadiness, his freedom from all dissipation, his incessant industry (except when he chose to throw himself into a standing revery behind his screen), his great stillness, his unalterableness of demeanor under all circumstances, made him a valuable acquisition. One prime thing was this,—*he was always there*;—first in the morning, continually through the day, and the last at night. I had a singular confidence in his honesty. I felt my most precious papers perfectly safe in his hands. Sometimes to be sure I could not, for the very soul of me, avoid falling into sudden spasmodic passions with him. For it was exceeding difficult to bear in mind all the time those strange peculiarities, privileges, and unheard of exemptions, forming the tacit stipulations on Bartleby's part under which he remained in my office. Now and then, in the eagerness of dispatching pressing business, I would inadvertently summon Bartleby, in a short, rapid tone, to put his finger, say, on the incipient tie of a bit of red tape with which I was about compressing some papers. Of course, from behind the screen the usual answer, "I prefer not to," was sure to come; and then, how could a human creature with the common infirmities of our nature, refrain from bitterly exclaiming upon such perverseness—such unreasonableness. However, every added repulse of this sort which I received only tended to lessen the probability of my repeating the inadvertence.

Here it must be said, that according to the custom of most legal gentlemen occupying chambers in densely-populated law buildings, there were several keys to my door. One was kept by a woman residing in the attic, which person weekly scrubbed and daily swept and dusted my apartments. Another was kept by Turkey for convenience sake. The third I sometimes carried in my own pocket. The fourth I knew not who had.

Now, one Sunday morning I happened to go to Trinity Church, to hear a celebrated preacher, and finding myself rather early on the ground, I thought I would walk round to my chambers for a while. Luckily I had my key with me; but upon applying it to the lock, I found it resisted by something inserted from the inside. Quite surprised, I called out; when to my consternation a key was turned from within; and thrusting his lean visage at me, and holding the door ajar, the apparition of Bartleby appeared, in his shirt sleeves, and otherwise in a strangely tattered dishabille, saying quietly that he was sorry, but he was deeply engaged just then, and—preferred not admitting me at present. In a brief word or two, he moreover added, that perhaps I had better walk round the block two or three times, and by that time he would probably have concluded his affairs.

Now, the utterly unsurmised appearance of Bartleby, tenanting my law-chambers of a Sunday morning, with his cadaverously gentlemanly *nonchalance*, yet withal firm and self-possessed, had such a strange effect upon me, that incontinently I slunk away from my own door, and did as desired. But not without sundry twinges of impotent rebellion against the mild effrontery of this unaccountable scrivener. Indeed, it was his wonderful mildness chiefly, which not only disarmed me, but unmanned me, as it were. For I consider that one, for the time, is a sort of unmanned when he tranquilly permits his hired clerk to dictate to him, and order him away from his own premises. Furthermore, I was full of uneasiness as to what Bartleby could possibly be doing in my office in his shirt sleeves, and in an otherwise dismantled condition of a Sunday morning. Was any thing amiss going on? Nay, that was out of the question. It was not to be thought of for a moment that Bartleby was an immoral person. But what could he be doing there?—copying? Nay again, whatever might be his eccentricities, Bartleby was an eminently decorous person. He would be the last man to sit down to his desk in any state approaching to nudity. Besides, it was Sunday; and there was something about Bartleby that forbade the supposition that he would by any secular occupation violate the proprieties of the day.

Nevertheless, my mind was not pacified; and full of a restless curiosity, at last I returned to the door. Without hindrance I inserted my key, opened it, and entered. Bartleby was not to be seen. I looked round anxiously, peeped behind his screen; but it was very plain that he was gone. Upon more closely examining the place, I surmised that for an indefinite period

Bartleby must have ate, dressed, and slept in my office, and that too without plate, mirror, or bed. The cushioned seat of a ricketty old sofa in one corner bore the faint impress of a lean, reclining form. Rolled away under his desk, I found a blanket; under the empty grate, a blacking box and brush; on a chair, a tin basin, with soap and a ragged towel; in a newspaper a few crumbs of ginger-nuts and a morsel of cheese. Yes, thought I, it is evident enough that Bartleby has been making his home here, keeping bachelor's hall all by himself. Immediately then the thought came sweeping across me, What miserable friendlessness and loneliness are here revealed! His poverty is great; but his solitude, how horrible! Think of it. Of a Sunday, Wall-street is deserted as Petra; and every night of every day it is an emptiness. This building too, which of week-days hums with industry and life, at nightfall echoes with sheer vacancy, and all through Sunday is forlorn. And here Bartleby makes his home; sole spectator of a solitude which he has seen all populous—a sort of innocent and transformed Marius brooding among the ruins of Carthage!

For the first time in my life a feeling of overpowering stinging melancholy seized me. Before, I had never experienced aught but a not-unpleasing sadness. The bond of a common humanity now drew me irresistibly to gloom. A fraternal melancholy! For both I and Bartleby were sons of Adam. I remembered the bright silks and sparkling faces I had seen that day, in gala trim, swan-like sailing down the Mississippi of Broadway; and I contrasted them with the pallid copyist, and thought to myself, Ah, happiness courts the light, so we deem the world is gay; but misery hides aloof, so we deem that misery there is none. These sad fancyings—chimeras, doubtless, of a sick and silly brain—led on to other and more special thoughts, concerning the eccentricities of Bartleby. Presentiments of strange discoveries hovered round me. The scrivener's pale form appeared to me laid out, among uncaring strangers, in its shivering winding sheet.

Suddenly I was attracted by Bartleby's closed desk, the key in open sight left in the lock.

I mean no mischief, seek the gratification of no heartless curiosity, thought I; besides, the desk is mine, and its contents too, so I will make bold to look within. Every thing was methodically arranged, the papers smoothly placed. The pigeon holes were deep, and removing the files of documents, I groped into their recesses. Presently I felt something there, and dragged it out. It was an old bandanna handkerchief, heavy and knotted. I opened it, and saw it was a savings' bank.

I now recalled all the quiet mysteries which I had noted in the man. I remembered that he never spoke but to answer; that though at intervals he had considerable time to himself, yet I had never seen him reading—no, not even a newspaper; that for long periods he would stand looking out, at his pale window behind the screen, upon the dead brick wall; I was quite sure he never visited any refectory or eating house; while his pale face clearly indicated that he never drank beer like Turkey, or tea and coffee even, like other men; that he never went any where in particular that I could learn; never went out for a walk, unless indeed that was the case at present; that he had declined telling who he was, or whence he came, or whether he had any relatives in the world; that though so thin and pale, he never complained of ill health. And more than all, I remembered a certain unconscious air of pallid—how shall I call it?—of pallid haughtiness, say, or rather an austere reserve about him, which had positively awed me into my tame compliance with his eccentricities, when I had feared to ask him to do the slightest incidental thing for me, even though I might know, from his long-continued motionlessness, that behind his screen he must be standing in one of those dead-wall reveries of his.

Revolving all these things, and coupling them with the recently discovered fact that he made my office his constant abiding place and home, and not forgetful of his morbid moodiness; revolving all these things, a prudential feeling began to steal over me. My first emotions had been those of pure melancholy and sincerest pity; but just in proportion as the forlornness of Bartleby grew and grew to my imagination, did that same melancholy merge into fear, that pity into repulsion. So true it is, and so terrible too, that up to a certain point the thought or sight of misery enlists our best affections; but, in certain special cases, beyond that point it does not. They err who would assert that invariably this is owing to the inherent selfishness of the human heart. It rather proceeds from a certain hopelessness of remedying excessive and organic ill. To a sensitive being, pity is not seldom pain. And when at last it is perceived that such pity cannot lead to effectual succor, common sense bids the soul be rid of it. What I saw that morning persuaded me that the scrivener was the victim of innate and incurable disorder. I might give alms to his body; but his body did not pain him; it was his soul that suffered, and his soul I could not reach.

I did not accomplish the purpose of going to Trinity Church that morning. Somehow, the things I had seen disqualified me for the time from church-going. I walked homeward, thinking what I would do with Bartleby. Finally, I resolved upon this;—I would put certain calm questions to him the next morning, touching his history, &c., and if he declined to answer them openly and unreservedly (and I supposed he would prefer not), then to give him a twenty dollar bill over and above whatever I might owe him, and tell him his services were no longer required; but that if in any other way I could assist him, I would be happy to do so, especially if he desired to return to his native place, wherever that might be, I would willingly help to defray the expenses. Moreover, if, after reaching home, he found himself at any time in want of aid, a letter from him would be sure of a reply.

The next morning came.

"Bartleby," said I, gently calling to him behind his screen.

No reply.

"Bartleby," said I, in a still gentler tone, "come here; I am not going to ask you to do any thing you would prefer not to do—I simply wish to speak to you."

Upon this he noiselessly slid into view.

"Will you tell me, Bartleby, where you were born?"

"I would prefer not to."

"Will you tell me *any thing* about yourself?"

"I would prefer not to."

"But what reasonable objection can you have to speak to me? I feel friendly towards you."

He did not look at me while I spoke, but kept his glance fixed upon my bust of Cicero, which as I then sat, was directly behind me, some six inches above my head.

"What is your answer, Bartleby?" said I, after waiting a considerable time for a reply, during which his countenance remained immovable, only there was the faintest conceivable tremor of the white attenuated mouth.

"At present I prefer to give no answer," he said, and retired into his hermitage.

It was rather weak in me I confess, but his manner on this occasion nettled me. Not only did there seem to lurk in it a certain calm disdain, but his perverseness seemed ungrateful, considering the undeniable good usage and indulgence he had received from me.

Again I sat ruminating what I should do. Mortified as I was at his behavior, and resolved as I had been to dismiss him when I entered my office, nevertheless I strangely felt something superstitious knocking at my heart, and forbidding me to carry out my purpose, and denouncing me for a villain if I dared to breathe one bitter word against this forlornest of mankind. At last, familiarly drawing my chair behind his screen, I sat down and said: "Bartleby, never mind then about revealing your history; but let me entreat you, as a friend, to comply as far as may be with the usages of this office. Say now you will help to examine papers to-morrow or next day: in short, say now that in a day or two you will begin to be a little reasonable:—say so, Bartleby."

"At present I would prefer not to be a little reasonable," was his mildly cadaverous reply.

Just then the folding-doors opened, and Nippers approached. He seemed suffering from an unusually bad night's rest, induced by severer indigestion than common. He overheard those final words of Bartleby.

"*Prefer not*, eh?" gritted Nippers—"I'd *prefer* him, if I were you, sir," addressing me—"I'd *prefer* him; I'd give him preferences, the stubborn mule! What is it, sir, pray, that he *prefers* not to do now?"

Bartleby moved not a limb.

"Mr. Nippers," said I, "I'd prefer that you would withdraw for the present."

Somehow, of late I had got into the way of involuntarily using this word "prefer" upon all sorts of not exactly suitable occasions. And I trembled to think that my contact with the scrivener had already and seriously affected me in a mental way. And what further and deeper aberration might it not yet produce? This apprehension had not been without efficacy in determining me to summary measures.

As Nippers, looking very sour and sulky, was departing, Turkey blandly and deferentially approached.

"With submission, sir," said he, "yesterday I was thinking about Bartleby here, and I think that if he would but prefer to take a quart of good ale every day, it would do much towards mending him, and enabling him to assist in examining his papers."

"So you have got the word too," said I, slightly excited.

"With submission, what word, sir," asked Turkey, respectfully crowding himself into the contracted space behind the screen, and by so doing, making me jostle the scrivener. "What word, sir?"

"I would prefer to be left alone here," said Bartleby, as if offended at being mobbed in his privacy.

"*That's* the word, Turkey," said I—"*that's* it."

"Oh, *prefer*? oh yes—queer word. I never use it myself. But, sir, as I was saying, if he would but prefer—"

"Turkey," interrupted I, "you will please withdraw."

"Oh certainly, sir, if you prefer that I should."

As he opened the folding-doors to retire, Nippers at his desk caught a glimpse of me, and asked whether I would prefer to have a certain paper copied on blue paper or white. He did not in the least roguishly accent the word prefer. It was plain that it involuntarily rolled from his tongue. I thought to myself, surely I must get rid of a demented man, who already has in some degree turned the tongues, if not the heads of myself and clerks. But I thought it prudent not to break the dismission at once.

The next day I noticed that Bartleby did nothing but stand at his window in his dead-wall revery. Upon asking him why he did not write, he said that he had decided upon doing no more writing.

"Why, how now? what next?" exclaimed I, "do no more writing?"

"No more."

"And what is the reason?"

"Do you not see the reason for yourself," he indifferently replied.

I looked steadfastly at him, and perceived that his eyes looked dull and glazed. Instantly it occurred to me, that his unexampled diligence in copying by his dim window for the first few weeks of his stay with me might have temporarily impaired his vision.

I was touched. I said something in condolence with him. I hinted that of course he did wisely in abstaining from writing for a while; and urged him to embrace that opportunity of taking wholesome exercise in the open air. This, however, he did not do. A few days after this, my other clerks being absent, and being in a great hurry to dispatch certain letters by the mail, I thought that, having nothing else earthly to do, Bartleby would surely be less inflexible than usual, and carry these letters to the post-office. But he blankly declined. So, much to my inconvenience, I went myself.

Still added days went by. Whether Bartleby's eyes improved or not, I could not say. To all appearance, I thought they did. But when I asked him if they did, he vouchsafed no answer. At all events, he would do no copying. At last, in reply to my urgings, he informed me that he had permanently given up copying.

"What!" exclaimed I; "suppose your eyes should get entirely well—better than ever before—would you not copy then?"

"I have given up copying," he answered, and slid aside.

He remained as ever, a fixture in my chamber. Nay—if that were possible—he became still more of a fixture than before. What was to be done? He would do nothing in the office: why should he stay there? In plain fact, he had now become a millstone to me, not only useless as a necklace, but afflictive to bear. Yet I was sorry for him. I speak less than truth when I say that, on his own account, he occasioned me uneasiness. If he would but have named a single relative or friend, I would instantly have written, and urged their taking the poor fellow away to some convenient retreat. But he seemed alone, absolutely alone in the universe. A bit of wreck in the mid Atlantic. At length, necessities connected with my business tyrannized over all other considerations. Decently as I could, I told Bartleby that in six days' time he must unconditionally leave the office. I warned him to take measures, in the interval, for procuring some other abode. I offered to assist him in this endeavor, if he himself would but take the first step towards a removal. "And when you finally quit me, Bartleby," added I, "I shall see that you go not away entirely unprovided. Six days from this hour, remember."

At the expiration of that period, I peeped behind the screen, and lo! Bartleby was there.

I buttoned up my coat, balanced myself; advanced slowly towards him, touched his shoulder, and said, "The time has come; you must quit this place; I am sorry for you; here is money; but you must go."

"I would prefer not," he replied, with his back still towards me.

"You *must*."

He remained silent.

Now I had an unbounded confidence in this man's common honesty. He had frequently restored to me sixpences and shillings carelessly dropped upon the floor, for I am apt to be very reckless in such shirt-button affairs. The proceeding then which followed will not be deemed extraordinary.

"Bartleby," said I, "I owe you twelve dollars on account; here are thirty-two; the odd twenty are yours.—Will you take it?" and I handed the bills towards him.

But he made no motion.

"I will leave them here then," putting them under a weight on the table. Then taking my hat and cane and going to the door I tranquilly turned and added—"After you have removed your things from these offices, Bartleby, you will of course lock the door—since every one is now gone for the day but you—and if you please, slip your key underneath the mat, so that I may have it in the morning. I shall not see you again; so good-bye to you. If hereafter in your new place of abode I can be of any service to you, do not fail to advise me by letter. Good-bye, Bartleby, and fare you well."

But he answered not a word; like the last column of some ruined temple, he remained standing mute and solitary in the middle of the otherwise deserted room.

As I walked home in a pensive mood, my vanity got the better of my pity. I could not but highly plume myself on my masterly management in getting rid of Bartleby. Masterly I call it, and such it must appear to any dispassionate thinker. The beauty of my procedure seemed to consist in its perfect quietness. There was no vulgar bullying, no bravado of any sort, no choleric hectoring, and striding to and fro across the apartment, jerking out vehement commands for Bartleby to bundle himself off with his beggarly traps. Nothing of the kind. Without loudly bidding Bartleby depart—as an inferior genius might have done—I *assumed* the ground that depart he must; and upon that assumption built all I had to say. The more I thought over my procedure, the more I was charmed with it. Nevertheless, next morning, upon awakening, I had my doubts,—I had somehow slept off the fumes of vanity. One of the coolest and wisest hours a man has, is just after he awakes in the morning. My procedure seemed as sagacious as ever,—but only in theory. How it would prove in practice—there was the rub. It was truly a beautiful thought to have assumed Bartleby's departure; but, after all, that assumption was simply my own, and none of Bartleby's. The great point was, not whether I had assumed that he would quit me, but whether he would prefer so to do. He was more a man of preferences than assumptions.

After breakfast, I walked down town, arguing the probabilities *pro* and *con*. One moment I thought it would prove a miserable failure, and Bartleby would be found all alive at my office as usual; the next moment it seemed certain that I should find his chair empty. And so I kept veering about. At the corner of Broadway and Canal-street, I saw quite an excited group of people standing in earnest conversation.

"I'll take odds he doesn't," said a voice as I passed.

"Doesn't go?—done!" said I, "put up your money."

I was instinctively putting my hand in my pocket to produce my own, when I remembered that this was an election day. The words I had overheard bore no reference to Bartleby, but to the success or non-success of some candidate for the mayoralty. In my intent frame of mind, I had, as it were, imagined that all Broadway shared in my excitement, and were debating the same question with me. I passed on, very thankful that the uproar of the street screened my momentary absent-mindedness.

As I had intended, I was earlier than usual at my office door. I stood listening for a moment. All was still. He must be gone.

I tried the knob. The door was locked. Yes, my procedure had worked to a charm; he indeed must be vanished. Yet a certain melancholy mixed with this: I was almost sorry for my brilliant success. I was fumbling under the door mat for the key, which Bartleby was to have left there for me, when accidentally my knee knocked against a panel, producing a summoning sound, and in response a voice came to me from within—"Not yet; I am occupied."

It was Bartleby.

I was thunderstruck. For an instant I stood like the man who, pipe in mouth, was killed one cloudless afternoon long ago in Virginia, by summer lightning; at his own warm open window he was killed, and remained leaning out there upon the dreamy afternoon, till some one touched him, when he fell.

"Not gone!" I murmured at last. But again obeying that wondrous ascendancy which the inscrutable scrivener had over me, and from which ascendency, for all my chafing, I could not completely escape, I slowly went down stairs and out into the street, and while walking round the block, considered what I should next do in this unheard-of perplexity. Turn the man out by an actual thrusting I could not; to drive him away by calling him hard names would not do; calling in the police was an unpleasant idea; and yet, permit him to enjoy his cadaverous triumph over me,—this too I could not think of. What was to be done? or, if nothing could be done, was there any thing further that I could *assume* in the matter? Yes, as before I had prospectively assumed that Bartleby would depart, so now I might retrospectively assume that departed he was. In the legitimate carrying out of this assumption, I might enter my office in a great hurry, and pretending not to see Bartleby at all, walk straight against him as if he were air. Such a proceeding would in a singular degree have the appearance of a home-thrust. It was hardly possible that Bartleby could withstand such an application of the doctrine of assumptions. But upon second thoughts the success of the plan seemed rather dubious. I resolved to argue the matter over with him again.

"Bartleby," said I, entering the office, with a quietly severe expression, "I am seriously displeased. I am pained, Bartleby. I had thought better of you. I had imagined you of such a gentlemanly organization, that in any delicate dilemma a slight hint would suffice—in short, an assumption. But it appears I am deceived. Why," I added, unaffectedly starting, "you have not even touched that money yet," pointing to it, just where I had left it the evening previous.

He answered nothing.

"Will you, or will you not, quit me?" I now demanded in a sudden passion, advancing close to him.

"I would prefer *not* to quit you," he replied, gently emphasizing the *not*.

"What earthly right have you to stay here? Do you pay any rent? Do you pay my taxes? Or is this property yours?"

He answered nothing.

"Are you ready to go on and write now? Are your eyes recovered? Could you copy a small paper for me this morning? or help examine a few lines? or step round to the post-office? In a word, will you do any thing at all, to give a coloring to your refusal to depart the premises?"

He silently retired into his hermitage.

I was now in such a state of nervous resentment that I thought it but prudent to check myself at present from further demonstrations. Bartleby and I were alone. I remembered the tragedy of the unfortunate Adams and the still more unfortunate Colt in the solitary office of the latter; and how poor Colt, being dreadfully incensed by Adams, and imprudently permitting himself to get wildly excited, was at unawares hurried into his fatal act—an act which certainly no man could possibly deplore more than the actor himself. Often it had occurred to me in my ponderings upon the subject, that had that altercation taken place in the public street, or at a private residence, it would not have terminated as it did. It was the circumstance of being alone in a solitary office, up stairs, of a building entirely unhallowed by humanizing domestic associations—an uncarpeted office, doubtless, of a dusty, haggard sort of appearance;—this it must have been, which greatly helped to enhance the irritable desperation of the hapless Colt.

But when this old Adam of resentment rose in me and tempted me concerning Bartleby, I grappled him and threw him. How? Why, simply by recalling the divine injunction: "A new commandment give I unto you, that ye love one another." Yes, this it was that saved me. Aside from higher considerations, charity often operates as a vastly wise and prudent principle—a great safeguard to its possessor. Men have committed murder for jealousy's sake, and anger's sake, and hatred's sake, and selfishness' sake, and spiritual pride's sake; but no man that ever I heard of, ever committed a diabolical murder for sweet charity's sake. Mere self-interest, then, if no better motive can be enlisted, should, especially with high-tempered men, prompt all beings to charity and philanthropy. At any rate, upon the occasion in question, I strove to drown my exasperated feelings towards the scrivener by benevolently construing his conduct. Poor fellow, poor fellow! thought I, he don't mean any thing; and besides, he has seen hard times, and ought to be indulged.

I endeavored also immediately to occupy myself, and at the same time to comfort my despondency. I tried to fancy that in the course of the morning, at such time as might prove agreeable to him, Bartleby, of his own free accord, would emerge from his hermitage, and take up some decided line of march in the direction of the door. But no. Half-past twelve o'clock came; Turkey began to glow in the face, overturn his inkstand, and become generally obstreperous; Nippers abated down into quietude and courtesy; Ginger Nut munched his noon apple; and Bartleby remained standing at his window in one of his profoundest dead-wall reveries. Will it be credited? Ought I to acknowledge it? That afternoon I left the office without saying one further word to him.

Some days now passed, during which, at leisure intervals I looked a little into "Edwards on the Will," and "Priestley on Necessity." Under the circumstances, those books induced a salutary feeling. Gradually I slid into the persuasion that these troubles of mine touching the scrivener, had been all predestinated from eternity, and Bartleby was billeted upon me for some mysterious purpose of an all-wise Providence, which it was not for a mere mortal like me to fathom. Yes, Bartleby, stay there behind your screen, thought I; I shall persecute you no more; you are harmless and noiseless as any of these old chairs; in short, I never feel so private as when I know you are here. At last I see it, I feel it; I penetrate to the predestinated purpose of my life. I am content. Others may have loftier parts to enact; but my mission in this world, Bartleby, is to furnish you with office-room for such period as you may see fit to remain.

I believe that this wise and blessed frame of mind would have continued with me, had it not been for the unsolicited and uncharitable remarks obtruded upon me by my professional friends who visited the rooms. But this it often is, that the constant friction of illiberal minds wears out at last the best resolves of the more generous. Though to be sure, when I reflected upon it, it was not strange that people entering my office should be struck by the peculiar aspect of the unaccountable Bartleby, and so be tempted to throw out some sinister observations concerning him. Sometimes an attorney having business with me, and calling at my office, and finding no one but the scrivener there, would undertake to obtain some sort of precise information from him touching my whereabouts; but without heeding his idle talk, Bartleby would remain standing immovable in the middle of the room. So after contemplating him in that position for a time, the attorney would depart, no wiser than he came.

Also, when a Reference was going on, and the room full of lawyers and witnesses and business was driving fast; some deeply occupied legal gentleman present, seeing Bartleby wholly unemployed, would request him to run round to his (the legal gentleman's) office and fetch some papers for him. Thereupon, Bartleby would tranquilly decline, and yet remain idle as before. Then the lawyer would give a great stare, and turn to me. And what could I say? At last I was made aware that all through the circle of my professional acquaintance, a whisper of wonder was running round, having reference to the strange creature I kept at my office. This worried me very much. And as the idea came upon me of his possibly turning out a long-lived man, and keep occupying my chambers, and denying my authority; and perplexing my visitors; and scandalizing my professional reputation; and casting a general gloom over the premises; keeping soul and body together to the last upon his savings (for doubtless he spent but half a dime a day), and in the end perhaps outlive me, and claim possession of my office by right of his perpetual occupancy: as all these dark anticipations crowded upon me more and more, and my friends continually intruded their relentless remarks upon the apparition in my room; a great change was wrought in me. I resolved to gather all my faculties together, and for ever rid me of this intolerable incubus.

Ere revolving any complicated project, however, adapted to this end, I first simply suggested to Bartleby the propriety of his permanent departure. In a calm and serious tone, I commended the idea to his careful and mature consideration. But having taken three days to meditate upon it, he apprised me that his original determination remained the same; in short, that he still preferred to abide with me.

What shall I do? I now said to myself, buttoning up my coat to the last button. What shall I do? what ought I to do? what does conscience say I *should* do with this man, or rather ghost? Rid myself of him, I must; go, he shall. But how? You will not thrust him, the poor, pale, passive mortal,—you will not thrust such a helpless creature out of your door? you will not dishonor yourself by such cruelty? No, I will not, I cannot do that. Rather would I let him live and die here, and then mason up his remains in the wall. What then will you do? For all your coaxing, he will not budge. Bribes he leaves under your own paperweight on your table; in short, it is quite plain that he prefers to cling to you.

Then something severe, something unusual must be done. What! surely you will not have him collared by a constable, and commit his innocent pallor to the common jail? And upon what ground could you procure such a thing to be done?—a vagrant, is he? What! he a vagrant, a wanderer, who refuses to budge? It is because he will *not* be a vagrant, then, that you seek to count him *as* a vagrant. That is too absurd. No visible means of support: there I have him. Wrong again: for indubitably he *does* support himself, and that is the only unanswerable proof that any man can show of his possessing the means so to do. No more then. Since he will not quit me, I must quit him. I will change my offices; I will move elsewhere; and give him fair notice, that if I find him on my new premises I will then proceed against him as a common trespasser.

Acting accordingly, next day I thus addressed him: "I find these chambers too far from the City Hall; the air is unwholesome. In a word, I propose to remove my offices next week, and shall no longer require your services. I tell you this now, in order that you may seek another place."

He made no reply, and nothing more was said.

On the appointed day I engaged carts and men, proceeded to my chambers, and having but little furniture, every thing was removed in a few hours. Throughout, the scrivener remained standing behind the screen, which I directed to be removed the last thing. It was withdrawn; and being folded up like a huge folio, left him the motionless occupant of a naked room. I stood in the entry watching him a moment, while something from within me upbraided me.

I re-entered, with my hand in my pocket—and—and my heart in my mouth.

"Good-bye, Bartleby; I am going—good-bye, and God some way bless you; and take that," slipping something in his hand. But it dropped upon the floor, and then,—strange to say—I tore myself from him whom I had so longed to be rid of.

Established in my new quarters, for a day or two I kept the door locked, and started at every footfall in the passages. When I returned to my rooms after any little absence, I would pause at the threshold for an instant, and attentively listen, ere applying my key. But these fears were needless. Bartleby never came nigh me.

I thought all was going well, when a perturbed looking stranger visited me, inquiring whether I was the person who had recently occupied rooms at No. — Wall-street.

Full of forebodings, I replied that I was.

"Then sir," said the stranger, who proved a lawyer, "you are responsible for the man you left there. He refuses to do any copying; he refuses to do any thing; he says he prefers not to; and he refuses to quit the premises."

"I am very sorry, sir," said I, with assumed tranquillity, but an inward tremor, "but, really, the man you allude to is nothing to me—he is no relation or apprentice of mine, that you should hold me responsible for him."

"In mercy's name, who is he?"

"I certainly cannot inform you. I know nothing about him. Formerly I employed him as a copyist; but he has done nothing for me now for some time past."

"I shall settle him then,—good morning, sir."

Several days passed, and I heard nothing more; and though I often felt a charitable prompting to call at the place and see poor Bartleby, yet a certain squeamishness of I know not what withheld me.

All is over with him, by this time, thought I at last, when through another week no further intelligence reached me. But coming to my room the day after, I found several persons waiting at my door in a high state of nervous excitement.

"That's the man—here he comes," cried the foremost one, whom I recognized as the lawyer who had previously called upon me alone.

"You must take him away, sir, at once," cried a portly person among them, advancing upon me, and whom I knew to be the landlord of No. — Wall-street. "These gentlemen, my tenants, cannot stand it any longer; Mr. B——" pointing to the lawyer, "has turned him out of his room, and he now persists in haunting the building generally, sitting upon the banisters of the stairs by day, and sleeping in the entry by night. Every body is concerned; clients are leaving the offices; some fears are entertained of a mob; something you must do, and that without delay."

Aghast at this torrent, I fell back before it, and would fain have locked myself in my new quarters. In vain I persisted that Bartleby was nothing to me—no more than to any one else. In vain:—I was the last person known to have any thing to do with him, and they held me to the terrible account. Fearful then of being exposed in the papers (as one person present obscurely threatened) I considered the matter, and at length said, that if the lawyer would give me a confidential interview with the scrivener, in his (the lawyer's) own room, I would that afternoon strive my best to rid them of the nuisance they complained of.

Going up stairs to my old haunt, there was Bartleby silently sitting upon the banister at the landing.

"What are you doing here, Bartleby?" said I.

"Sitting upon the banister," he mildly replied.

I motioned him into the lawyer's room, who then left us.

"Bartleby," said I, "are you aware that you are the cause of great tribulation to me, by persisting in occupying the entry after being dismissed from the office?"

No answer.

"Now one of two things must take place. Either you must do something, or something must be done to you. Now what sort of business would you like to engage in? Would you like to re-engage in copying for some one?"

"No; I would prefer not to make any change."

"Would you like a clerkship in a dry-goods store?"

"There is too much confinement about that. No, I would not like a clerkship; but I am not particular."

"Too much confinement," I cried, "why you keep yourself confined all the time!"

"I would prefer not to take a clerkship," he rejoined, as if to settle that little item at once.

"How would a bar-tender's business suit you? There is no trying of the eyesight in that."

"I would not like it at all; though, as I said before, I am not particular."

His unwonted wordiness inspirited me. I returned to the charge.

"Well then, would you like to travel through the country collecting bills for the merchants? That would improve your health."

"No, I would prefer to be doing something else."

"How then would going as a companion to Europe, to entertain some young gentleman with your conversation,—how would that suit you?"

"Not at all. It does not strike me that there is any thing definite about that. I like to be stationary. But I am not particular."

"Stationary you shall be then," I cried, now losing all patience, and for the first time in all my exasperating connection with him fairly flying into a passion. "If you do not go away from these premises before night, I shall feel bound—indeed I *am* bound—to—to—to quit the premises myself!" I rather absurdly concluded, knowing not with what possible threat to try to frighten his immobility into compliance. Despairing of all further efforts, I was precipitately leaving him, when a final thought occurred to me—one which had not been wholly unindulged before.

"Bartleby," said I, in the kindest tone I could assume under such exciting circumstances, "will you go home with me now—not to my office, but my dwelling—and remain there till we can conclude upon some convenient arrangement for you at our leisure? Come, let us start now, right away."

"No: at present I would prefer not to make any change at all."

I answered nothing; but effectually dodging every one by the suddenness and rapidity of my flight, rushed from the building, ran up Wall-street towards Broadway, and jumping into the first omnibus was soon removed from pursuit. As soon as tranquillity returned I distinctly perceived that I had now done all that I possibly could, both in respect to the demands of the landlord and his tenants, and with regard to my own desire and sense of duty, to benefit Bartleby, and shield him from rude persecution. I now strove to be entirely care-free and quiescent; and my conscience justified me in the attempt; though indeed it was not so successful as I could have wished. So fearful was I of being again hunted out by the incensed landlord and his exasperated tenants, that, surrendering my business to Nippers, for a few days I drove about the upper part of the town and through the suburbs, in my rockaway; crossed over to Jersey City and Hoboken, and paid fugitive visits to Manhattanville and Astoria. In fact I almost lived in my rockaway for the time.

When again I entered my office, lo, a note from the landlord lay upon the desk. I opened it with trembling hands. It informed me that the writer had sent to the police, and had Bartleby removed to the Tombs as a vagrant. Moreover, since I knew more about him than any one else, he wished me to appear at that place, and make a suitable statement of the facts. These tidings had a conflicting effect upon me. At first I was indignant; but at last almost approved. The landlord's energetic, summary disposition, had led him to adopt a procedure which I do not think I would have decided upon myself; and yet as a last resort, under such peculiar circumstances, it seemed the only plan.

As I afterwards learned, the poor scrivener, when told that he must be conducted to the Tombs, offered not the slightest obstacle, but in his pale unmoving way, silently acquiesced.

Some of the compassionate and curious bystanders joined the party; and headed by one of the constables arm in arm with Bartleby, the silent procession filed its way through all the noise, and heat, and joy of the roaring thoroughfares at noon.

The same day I received the note I went to the Tombs, or to speak more properly, the Halls of Justice. Seeking the right officer, I stated the purpose of my call, and was informed that the individual I described was indeed within. I then assured the functionary that Bartleby was a perfectly honest man, and greatly to be compassionated, however unaccountably eccentric. I narrated all I knew, and closed by suggesting the idea of letting him remain in as indulgent confinement as possible till something less harsh might be done—though indeed I hardly knew what. At all events, if nothing else could be decided upon, the alms-house must receive him. I then begged to have an interview.

Being under no disgraceful charge, and quite serene and harmless in all his ways, they had permitted him freely to wander about the prison, and especially in the inclosed grass-platted yards thereof. And so I found him there, standing all alone in the quietest of the yards, his face towards a high wall, while all around, from the narrow slits of the jail windows, I thought I saw peering out upon him the eyes of murderers and thieves.

"Bartleby!"

"I know you," he said, without looking round,—"and I want nothing to say to you."

"It was not I that brought you here, Bartleby," said I, keenly pained at his implied suspicion. "And to you, this should not be so vile a place. Nothing reproachful attaches to you by being here. And see, it is not so sad a place as one might think. Look, there is the sky, and here is the grass."

"I know where I am," he replied, but would say nothing more, and so I left him.

As I entered the corridor again, a broad meat-like man, in an apron, accosted me, and jerking his thumb over his shoulder said—"Is that your friend?"

"Yes."

"Does he want to starve? If he does, let him live on the prison fare, that's all."

"Who are you?" asked I, not knowing what to make of such an unofficially speaking person in such a place.

"I am the grub-man. Such gentlemen as have friends here, hire me to provide them with something good to eat."

"Is this so?" said I, turning to the turnkey.

He said it was.

"Well then," said I, slipping some silver into the grub-man's hands (for so they called him). "I want you to give particular attention to my friend there; let him have the best dinner you can get. And you must be as polite to him as possible."

"Introduce me, will you?" said the grub-man, looking at me with an expression which seemed to say he was all impatience for an opportunity to give a specimen of his breeding.

Thinking it would prove of benefit to the scrivener, I acquiesced; and asking the grub-man his name, went up with him to Bartleby.

"Bartleby, this is Mr. Cutlets; you will find him very useful to you."

"Your sarvant, sir, your sarvant," said the grub-man, making a low salutation behind his apron. "Hope you find it pleasant here, sir; nice grounds—cool apartments, sir—hope you'll stay with us some time—try to make it agreeable. May Mrs. Cutlets and I have the pleasure of your company to dinner, sir, in Mrs. Cutlets' private room?"

"I prefer not to dine to-day," said Bartleby, turning away. "It would disagree with me; I am unused to dinners." So saying he slowly moved to the other side of the inclosure, and took up a position fronting the dead-wall.

"How's this?" said the grub-man, addressing me with a stare of astonishment. "He's odd, aint he?"

"I think he is a little deranged," said I, sadly.

"Deranged? deranged is it? Well now, upon my word, I thought that friend of yourn was a gentleman forger; they are always pale and genteel-like, them forgers. I can't help pity 'em—can't help it, sir. Did you know Monroe Edwards?" he added touchingly, and paused. Then, laying his hand pityingly on my shoulder, sighed, "he died of consumption at Sing-Sing. So you weren't acquainted with Monroe?"

"No, I was never socially acquainted with any forgers. But I cannot stop longer. Look to my friend yonder. You will not lose by it. I will see you again."

Some few days after this, I again obtained admission to the Tombs, and went through the corridors in quest of Bartleby; but without finding him.

"I saw him coming from his cell not long ago," said a turnkey, "may be he's gone to loiter in the yards."

So I went in that direction.

"Are you looking for the silent man?" said another turnkey passing me. "Yonder he lies—sleeping in the yard there. 'Tis not twenty minutes since I saw him lie down."

The yard was entirely quiet. It was not accessible to the common prisoners. The surrounding walls, of amazing thickness, kept off all sounds behind them. The Egyptian character of the masonry weighed upon me with its gloom. But a soft imprisoned turf grew under foot. The heart of the eternal pyramids, it seemed, wherein, by some strange magic, through the clefts, grass-seed, dropped by birds, had sprung.

Strangely huddled at the base of the wall, his knees drawn up, and lying on his side, his head touching the cold stones, I saw the wasted Bartleby. But nothing stirred. I paused; then went close up to him; stooped over, and saw that his dim eyes were open; otherwise he seemed profoundly sleeping. Something prompted me to touch him. I felt his hand, when a tingling shiver ran up my arm and down my spine to my feet.

The round face of the grub-man peered upon me now. "His dinner is ready. Won't he dine to-day, either? Or does he live without dining?"

"Lives without dining," said I, and closed the eyes.

"Eh!—He's asleep, aint he?"

"With kings and counsellors," murmured I.

* * *

There would seem little need for proceeding further in this history. Imagination will readily supply the meagre recital of poor Bartleby's interment. But ere parting with the reader, let me say, that if this little narrative has sufficiently interested him, to awaken curiosity as to who Bartleby was, and what manner of life he led prior to the present narrator's making his acquaintance, I can only reply, that in such curiosity I fully share, but am wholly unable to gratify it. Yet here I hardly know whether I should divulge one little item of rumor, which came to my ear a few months after the scrivener's decease. Upon what basis it rested, I could never ascertain; and hence, how true it is I cannot now tell. But inasmuch as this vague report has not been without a certain strange suggestive interest to me, however sad, it may prove the same with some others; and so I will briefly mention it. The report was this: that Bartleby had been a subordinate clerk in the Dead Letter Office at Washington, from which he had been suddenly removed by a change in the administration. When I think over this rumor, hardly can I express the emotions which seize me. Dead letters! does it not sound like dead men? Conceive a man by nature and misfortune prone to a pallid hopelessness, can any business seem more fitted to heighten it than that of continually handling these dead letters, and assorting them for the flames? For by the cart-load they are annually burned. Sometimes from out the folded paper the pale clerk takes a ring:—the finger it was meant for, perhaps, moulders in the grave; a bank-note sent in swiftest charity:—he whom it would relieve, nor eats nor hungers any more; pardon for those who died despairing; hope for those who died unhoping; good tidings for those who died stifled by unrelieved calamities. On errands of life, these letters speed to death.

Ah Bartleby! Ah humanity!

1853

# HERMAN MELVILLE

(1819–1891)

---

## *The Two Temples*

### (Dedicated to Sheridan Knowles)

#### TEMPLE FIRST

"THIS IS TOO BAD," said I, "here have I tramped this blessed Sunday morning, all the way from the Battery, three long miles, for this express purpose, prayer-book under arm; here I am, I say, and, after all, I can't get in.

"Too bad. And how disdainful the great, fat-paunched, beadle-faced man looked, when in answer to my humble petition, he said they had no galleries. Just the same as if he'd said, they didn't entertain poor folks. But I'll wager something that had my new coat been done last night, as the false tailor promised, and had I, arrayed therein this bright morning, tickled the fat-paunched, beadle-faced man's palm with a bank-note, then, gallery or no gallery, I would have had a fine seat in this marble-buttressed, stained-glassed, spic-and-span new temple.

"Well, here I am in the porch, very politely bowed out of the nave. I suppose I'm excommunicated; excluded, anyway.—That's a noble string of flashing carriages drawn up along the curb; those champing horses too have a haughty curve to their foam-flaked necks. Property of those 'miserable sinners' inside, I presume. I dont a bit wonder they unreservedly confess to such misery as *that*.—See the gold hatbands too, and other gorgeous trimmings, on those glossy groups of low-voiced gossippers near by. If I were in England now, I should think those chaps a company of royal dukes, right honorable barons &c. As it is, though, I guess they are only lackeys.—By the way, here I dodge about, as if I wanted to get into their aristocratic circle. In fact, it looks a sort of lackeyish to be idly standing outside a fine temple, cooling your heels, during service.—I had best move back to the Battery again, peeping into my prayer-book as I go.—But hold; dont I see a small door? Just in there, to one side, if I dont mistake, is a very low and very narrow vaulted door. None seem to go that way. Ten to one, that identical door leads up into the tower. And now that I think of it, there is usually in these splendid, new-fashioned Gothic Temples, a curious little window high over the orchestra and everything else, away up among the gilded clouds of the ceiling's frescoes; and that little window, seems to me, if one could but get there, ought to command a glorious bird's-eye view of the entire field of operations below.—I guess I'll try it. No one in the porch now. The beadle-faced man is smoothing down some ladies' cushions, far up the broad aisle, I dare say. Softly now. If the small door ain't locked, I shall have stolen a march upon the beadle-faced man, and secured a humble seat in the sanctuary, in spite of him.—Good! Thanks for this! The door is not locked. Bell-ringer forgot to lock it, no doubt. Now, like any felt-footed grimalkin, up I steal among the leads."

Ascending some fifty stone steps along a very narrow curving stair-way, I found myself on a blank platform forming the second story of the huge square tower.

I seemed inside some magic-lantern. On three sides, three gigantic Gothic windows of richly dyed glass, filled the otherwise meagre place with all sorts of sun-rises and sun-sets, lunar and solar rainbows, falling stars, and other flaming fireworks and pyrotechnics. But after all, it was but a gorgeous dungeon; for I could n't look out, any more than if I had been the occupant of a basement cell in "the Tombs." With some pains, and care not to do any serious harm, I contrived to scratch a minute opening in a great purple star forming the center of the chief compartment of the middle window; when peeping through, as through goggles, I ducked my head in dismay. The beadle-faced man, with no hat on his head, was just in act of driving three ragged little boys into the middle of the street; and how could I help trembling at the apprehension of his discovering a rebellious caitiff like me peering down on him from the tower? For in stealing up here, I had set at nought his high authority. He whom he thought effectually ejected, had burglariously returned. For a moment I was almost ready to bide my chance, and get to the side walk again with all dispatch. But another Jacob's ladder of lofty steps,—wooden ones, this time—allured me to another and still higher flight,—in sole hopes of gaining that one secret window where I might, at distance, take part in the proceedings.

Presently I noticed something which owing to the first marvellous effulgence of the place, had remained unseen till now. Two strong ropes, dropping through holes in the rude ceiling high overhead, fell a sheer length of sixty feet, right through the center of the space, and dropped in coils upon the floor of the huge magic-lantern. Bell-ropes these, thought I, and quaked. For if the beadle-faced man should learn that a grimalkin was somewhere prowling about the edifice, how easy for him to ring the alarm. Hark!—ah, that's only the organ—yes—it's the "Venite, exultemus Domine". Though an insider in one respect, yet am I but an outsider in another. But for all that, I will not be defrauded of my natural rights. Uncovering my head, and taking out my book, I stood erect, midway up the tall Jacob's ladder, as if standing among the congregation; and in spirit, if not in place, participated in those devout exultings. That over, I continued my upward path; and after crossing sundry minor platforms and irregular landings, all the while on a general ascent, at last I was delighted by catching sight of a small round window in the otherwise dead-wall side of the tower, where the tower attached itself to the main building. In front of the window was a rude narrow gallery, used as a bridge to cross from the lower stairs on one side to the upper stairs on the opposite.

As I drew nigh the spot, I well knew from the added clearness with which the sound of worship came to me, that the window did indeed look down upon the entire interior. But I was hardly prepared to find that no pane of glass, stained or unstained, was to stand between me and the far-under aisles and altar. For the purpose of ventilation, doubtless, the opening had been left unsupplied with sash of any sort. But a sheet of fine-woven, gauzy wire-work was in place of that. When, all eagerness, and open book in hand, I first advanced to stand before the window, I involuntarily shrank, as from before the mouth of a furnace, upon suddenly feeling a forceful puff of strange, heated air, blown, as by a blacksmith's bellows, full into my face and lungs. Yes, thought I, this window is doubtless for ventilation. Nor is it quite so comfortable as I fancied it might be. But beggars must not be choosers. The furnace which makes the people below there feel so snug and cosy in their padded pews, is to me, who stand here upon the naked gallery, cause of grievous trouble. Besides, though my face is scorched, my back is frozen. But I wont complain. Thanks for this much, any way,—that by hollowing one hand to my ear, and standing a little sideways out of the more violent rush of the torrid current, I can at least hear the priest sufficiently to make my responses in the proper place. Little dream the good congregation away down there, that they have a faithful clerk away up here. Here too is a fitter place for sincere devotions, where, though I see, I remain unseen. Depend upon it, no Pharisee would have my pew. I like it, and admire it too, because it is so very high. Height, somehow, hath devotion in it. The archangelic anthems are raised in a lofty place. All the good shall go to such an one. Yes, Heaven is high.

As thus I mused, the glorious organ burst, like an earthquake, almost beneath my feet; and I heard the invoking cry—"Govern them and *lift* them up forever!" Then down I gazed upon the standing human mass, far, far below, whose heads, gleaming in the many-colored window-stains, showed like beds of spangled pebbles flashing in a Cuban sun. So at least, I knew they needs would look, if but the wire-woven screen were drawn aside. That wire-woven screen had the effect of casting crape upon all I saw. Only by making allowances for the crape, could I gain a right idea of the scene disclosed.

Surprising, most surprising, too, it was. As said before, the window was a circular one; the part of the tower where I stood was dusky-dark; its height above the congregation-floor could not have been less than ninety or a hundred feet; the whole interior temple was lit by nought but glass dimmed, yet glorified with all imaginable rich and russet hues; the approach to my strange look-out, through perfect solitude, and along rude and dusty ways, enhanced the theatric wonder of the populous spectacle of this sumptuous sanctuary. Book in hand, responses on my tongue, standing in the very posture of devotion, I could not rid my soul of the intrusive thought, that, through some necromancer's glass, I looked down upon some sly enchanter's show.

At length the lessons being read, the chants chanted, the white-robed priest, a noble-looking man, with a form like the incomparable Talma's, gave out from the reading-desk the hymn before the sermon, and then through a side door vanished from the scene. In good time I saw the same Talma-like and noble-looking man re-appear through the same side door, his white apparel wholly changed for black.

By the melodious tone and persuasive gesture of the speaker, and the all-approving attention of the throng, I knew the sermon must be eloquent, and well adapted to an opulent auditory; but owing to the priest's changed position from the reading-desk, to the pulpit, I could not so distinctly hear him now as in the previous rites. The text however,—repeated at the outset, and often after quoted,—I could not but plainly catch:—"Ye are the salt of the earth."

At length the benediction was pronounced over the mass of low-inclining foreheads; hushed silence, intense motionlessness followed for a moment, as if the congregation were one of buried, not of living men; when, suddenly, miraculously, like the general rising at the Resurrection, the whole host came to their feet, amid a simultaneous roll, like a great drum-beat from the enrapturing, overpowering organ. Then, in three freshets,—all gay sprightly nods and becks—the gilded brooks poured down the gilded aisles.

Time for me too to go, thought I, as snatching one last look upon the imposing scene, I clasped my book and put it in my pocket. The best thing I can do just now, is to slide out unperceived amid the general crowd. Hurrying down the great length of ladder, I soon found myself at the base of the last stone step of the final flight; but started aghast—the door was locked! The bell-ringer, or more probably that forever-prying suspicious-looking beadle-faced man has done this. He would not let me in at all at first, and now, with the greatest inconsistency, he will not let me out. But what is to be done? Shall I knock on the door? That will never do. It will only frighten the crowd streaming by, and no one can adequately respond to my summons, except the beadle-faced man; and if he see me, he will recognise me, and perhaps roundly rate me—poor, humble worshiper—before the entire public. No, I wont knock. But what then?

Long time I thought, and thought, till at last all was hushed again. Presently a clicking sound admonished me that the church was being closed. In sudden desperation, I gave a rap on the door. But too late. It was not heard. I was left alone and solitary in a temple which but a moment before was more populous than many villages.

A strange trepidation of gloom and loneliness gradually stole over me. Hardly conscious of what I did, I reascended the stone steps; higher and higher still, and only paused, when once more I felt the hot-air blast from the wire-woven screen. Snatching another peep down into the vast arena, I started at its hushed desertness. The long ranges of grouped columns down the nave, and clusterings of them into copses about the corners of the transept; together with the subdued, dim-streaming light from the autumnal glasses; all assumed a secluded and deep-wooded air. I seemed gazing from Pisgah into the forests of old Canaan. A Puseyitish painting of a Madonna and child, adorning a lower window, seemed showing to me the sole tenants of this painted wilderness—the true Hagar and her Ishmael.—

With added trepidation I stole softly back to the magic-lantern platform; and revived myself a little by peeping through the scratch, upon the unstained light of open day.—But what is to be done, thought I, again.

I descended to the door; listened there; heard nothing. A third time climbing the stone steps, once more I stood in the magic-lantern, while the full nature of the more than awkwardness of my position came over me.

The first persons who will reênter the temple, mused I, will doubtless be the beadle-faced man, and the bell-ringer. And the first man to come up here, where I am, will be the latter. Now what will be his natural impressions upon first descrying an unknown prowler here? Rather disadvantageous to said prowler's moral character. Explanations will be vain. Circumstances are against me. True, I may hide, till he retires again. But how do I know, that he will then leave the door unlocked? Besides, in a position of affairs like this, it is generally best, I think, to anticipate discovery, and by magnanimously announcing yourself, forestall an inglorious detection. But how announce myself? Already have I knocked, and no response. That moment, my eye, impatiently ranging roundabout, fell upon the bell-ropes. They suggested the usual signal made at dwelling-houses to convey tidings of a stranger's presence. But I was not an outside caller; alas, I was an inside prowler.—But one little touch of that bell-rope, would be sure to bring relief. I have an appointment at three o'clock. The beadle-faced man must naturally reside very close by the church. He well knows the peculiar ring of his own bell. The slightest possible hum would bring him flying to the rescue. Shall I, or shall I not?—But I may alarm the neighborhood. Oh no; the merest tingle, not by any means a loud vociferous peal. Shall I? Better voluntarily bring the beadle-faced man to me, than be involuntarily dragged out from this most suspicious hiding-place. I have to face him, first or last. Better now than later.—Shall I?—

No more. Creeping to the rope, I gave it a cautious twitch. No sound. A little less warily. All was dumb. Still more strongly. Horrors! my hands, instinctively clapped to my ears, only served to condense the appalling din. Some undreamed-of mechanism seemed to have been touched. The bell must have thrice revolved on its thunderous axis, multiplying the astounding reverberation.

My business is effectually done, this time, thought I, all in a tremble. Nothing will serve me now but the reckless confidence of innocence reduced to desperation.

In less than five minutes, I heard a running noise beneath me; the lock of the door clicked, and up rushed the beadle-faced man, the perspiration starting from his cheeks.

"You! Is it *you*? The man I turned away this very morning, skulking here? *You* dare to touch that bell? Scoundrel!"

And ere I could defend myself, seizing me irresistably in his powerful grasp, he tore me along by the collar, and dragging me down the stairs, thrust me into the arms of three policemen, who, attracted by the sudden toll of the bell, had gathered curiously about the porch.

All remonstrances were vain. The beadle-faced man was bigoted against me. Represented as a lawless violator, and a remorseless disturber of the Sunday peace, I was conducted to the Halls of Justice. Next morning, my rather gentlemanly appearance procured me a private hearing from the judge. But the beadle-faced man must have made a Sunday night call on him. Spite of my coolest explanations, the circumstances of the case were deemed so exceedingly suspicious, that only after paying a round fine, and receiving a stinging reprimand, was I permitted to go at large, and pardoned for having humbly indulged myself in the luxury of public worship.

## TEMPLE SECOND

A stranger in London on Saturday night, and without a copper! What hospitalities may such an one expect? What shall I do with myself this weary night? My landlady wont receive me in her parlor. I owe her money. She looks like flint on me. So in this monstrous rabblement must I crawl about till, say ten o'clock, and then slink home to my unlighted bed.

The case was this: The week following my inglorious expulsion from the transatlantic temple, I had packed up my trunks and damaged character, and repaired to the fraternal, loving town of Philadelphia. There chance threw into my way an interesting young orphan lady and her aunt-duenna; the lady rich as Cleopatra, but not as beautiful; the duenna lovely as Charmian, but not so young. For the lady's health, prolonged travel had been prescribed. Maternally connected in old England, the lady chose London for her primal port. But ere securing their passage, the two were looking round for some young physician, whose disengagement from pressing business, might induce him to accept, on a moderate salary, the post of private Esculapius and knightly companion to the otherwise unprotected fair. The more necessary was this, as not only the voyage to England was intended, but an extensive European tour, to follow.

Enough. I came; I saw; I was made the happy man. We sailed. We landed on the other side; when after two weeks of agonized attendance on the vacillations of the lady, I was very cavalierly dismissed, on the score, that the lady's maternal relations had persuaded her to try, through the winter, the salubrious climate of the foggy Isle of Wight, in preference to the fabulous blue atmosphere of the Ionian Isles. So much for national prejudice.

Nota Bene.—The lady was in a sad decline.—

Having ere sailing been obliged to anticipate nearly a quarter's pay to foot my outfit bills, I was dismally cut adrift in Fleet

Street without a solitary shilling. By disposing, at certain pawnbrokers, of some of my less indispensable apparel, I had managed to stave off the more slaughterous onsets of my landlady, while diligently looking about for any business that might providentially appear.

So on I drifted amid those indescribable crowds which every seventh night pour and roar through each main artery and block the bye-veins of great London, the Leviathan. Saturday Night it was; and the markets and the shops, and every stall and counter were crushed with the one unceasing tide. A whole Sunday's victualling for three millions of human bodies, was going on. Few of them equally hungry with my own, as through my spent lassitude, the unscrupulous human whirlpools eddied me aside at corners, as any straw is eddied in the Norway Maelstrom. What dire suckings into oblivion must such swirling billows know. Better perish mid myriad sharks in mid Atlantic, than die a penniless stranger in Babylonian London. Forlorn, outcast, without a friend, I staggered on through three millions of my own human kind. The fiendish gas-lights shooting their Tartarean rays across the muddy sticky streets, lit up the pitiless and pitiable scene.

Well, well, if this were but Sunday now, I might conciliate some kind female pew-opener, and rest me in some inn-like chapel, upon some stranger's outside bench. But it is Saturday night. The end of the weary week, and all but the end of weary me.

Disentangling myself at last from those skeins of Pandemonian lanes which snarl one part of the metropolis between Fleet street and Holborn, I found myself at last in a wide and far less noisy street, a short and shopless one, leading up from the Strand, and terminating at its junction with a crosswise avenue. The comparative quietude of the place was inexpressively soothing. It was like emerging upon the green enclosure surrounding some Cathedral church, where sanctity makes all things still. Two lofty brilliant lights attracted me in this tranquil street. Thinking it might prove some moral or religious meeting, I hurried towards the spot; but was surprised to see two tall placards announcing the appearance that night, of the stately Macready in the part of Cardinal Richelieu. Very few loiterers hung about the place, the hour being rather late, and the play-bill hawkers mostly departed, or keeping entirely quiet. This theatre indeed, as I afterwards discovered, was not only one of the best in point of acting, but likewise one of the most decorous in its general management, inside and out. In truth the whole neighborhood, as it seemed to me—issuing from the jam and uproar of those turbulent tides against which, or borne on irresistably by which, I had so long been swimming—the whole neighborhood, I say, of this pleasing street seemed in good keeping with the character imputed to its theatre.

Glad to find one blessed oasis of tranquility, I stood leaning against a column of the porch, and striving to lose my sadness in running over one of the huge placards. No one molested me. A tattered little girl, to be sure, approached, with a handbill extended, but marking me more narrowly, retreated; her strange skill in physiognomy at once enabling her to determine that I was penniless. As I read, and read—for the placard, of enormous dimensions, contained minute particulars of each successive scene in the enacted play—gradually a strong desire to witness this celebrated Macready in this his celebrated part stole over me. By one act, I might rest my jaded limbs, and more than jaded spirits. Where else could I go for rest, unless I crawled into my cold and lonely bed far up in an attic of Craven Street, looking down upon the muddy Phlegethon of the Thames. Besides, what I wanted was not merely rest, but cheer; the making one of many pleased and pleasing human faces; the getting into a genial humane assembly of my kind; such as, at its best and highest, is to be found in the unified multitude of a devout congregation. But no such assemblies were accessible that night, even if my unbefriended and rather shabby air would overcome the scruples of those fastidious gentry with red gowns and long gilded staves, who guard the portals of the first-class London tabernacles from all profanation of a poor forlorn and fainting wanderer like me. Not inns, but ecclesiastical hotels, where the pews are the rented chambers.

No use to ponder, thought I, at last; it is Saturday night, not Sunday; and so, a Theatre only can receive me. So powerfully in the end did the longing to get into the edifice come over me, that I almost began to think of pawning my overcoat for admittance. But from this last infatuation I was providentially with-held by a sudden cheery summons, in a voice unmistakably benevolent. I turned, and saw a man who seemed to be some sort of a working-man.

"Take it," said he, holding a plain red ticket towards me, full in the gas-light. "You want to go in; I know you do. Take it. I am suddenly called home. There—hope you'll enjoy yourself. Good-bye."

Blankly, and mechanically, I had suffered the ticket to be thrust into my hand, and now stood quite astonished, bewildered, and for the time, ashamed. The plain fact was, I had received charity; and for the first time in my life. Often in the course of my strange wanderings I had needed charity, but never had asked it, and certainly never, ere this blessed night, had been offered it. And a stranger; and in the very maw of the roaring London too! Next moment my sense of foolish shame departed, and I felt a queer feeling in my left eye, which, as sometimes is the case with people, was the weaker one; probably from being on the same side with the heart.

I glanced round eagerly. But the kind giver was no longer in sight. I looked upon the ticket. I understood. It was one of those checks given to persons inside a theatre when for any cause they desire to step out a moment. Its presentation ensures unquestioned readmittance.

Shall I use it? mused I.—What? It's charity.—But if it be gloriously right to do a charitable deed, can it be ingloriously wrong to receive its benefit?—No one knows you; go boldly in.—Charity.—Why these unvanquishable scruples? All your life, nought but charity sustains you, and all others in the world. Maternal charity nursed you as a babe; paternal charity fed you as a child; friendly charity got you your profession; and to the charity of every man you meet this night in London, are you indebted for your unattempted life. Any knife, any hand of all the millions of knives and hands in London, has you this night at its mercy. You, and all mortals, live but by sufferance of your charitable kind; charitable by omission, not performance.—Stush for your self-upbraidings, and pitiful, poor, shabby pride, you friendless man without a purse.—Go in.

Debate was over. Marking the direction from which the stranger had accosted me, I stepped that way; and soon saw a low-vaulted, inferior-looking door on one side of the edifice. Entering, I wandered on and up, and up and on again, through various doubling stairs and wedge-like, ill-lit passages, whose bare boards much reminded me of my ascent of the Gothic tower on the ocean's far other side. At last I gained a lofty platform, and saw a fixed human countenance facing me from a mysterious window of a sort of sentry-box or closet. Like some saint in a shrine, the countenance was illuminated by two smoky candles. I divined the man. I exhibited my diploma, and he nodded me to a little door beyond; while a sudden burst of orchestral music, admonished me I was now very near my destination, and also revived the memory of the organ-anthems I had heard while on the ladder of the tower at home.

Next moment, the wire-woven gauzy screen of the ventilating window in that same tower, seemed enchantedly reproduced before me. The same hot blast of stifling air once more rushed into my lungs. From the same dizzy altitude, through the same fine-spun, vapory crapey air; far, far down upon just such a packed mass of silent human beings; listening to just such grand harmonies; I stood within the topmost gallery of the temple. But hardly alone and silently as before. This time I had company. Not of the first circles, and certainly not of the dress-circle; but most acceptable, right welcome, cheery company, to otherwise uncompanioned me. Quiet, well-pleased working men, and their glad wives and sisters, with here and there an aproned urchin, with all-absorbed, bright face, vermillioned by the excitement and the heated air, hovering like a painted cherub over the vast human firmament below. The height of the gallery was in truth appalling. The rail was low. I thought of deep-sea-leads, and the mariner in the vessel's chains, drawing up the line, with his long-drawn musical accompaniment. And like beds of glittering coral, through the deep sea of azure smoke, there, far down, I saw the jewelled necks and white sparkling arms of crowds of ladies in the semicirque. But, in the interval of two acts, again the orchestra was heard; some inspiring national anthem now was played. As the volumed sound came undulating up, and broke in showery spray and foam of melody against our gallery rail, my head involuntarily was bowed, my hand instinctively sought my pocket. Only by a second thought, did I check my momentary lunacy and remind myself that this time I had no small morocco book with me, and that this was not the house of prayer.

Quickly was my wandering mind—preternaturally affected by the sudden translation from the desolate street, to this bewildering and blazing spectacle—arrested in its wanderings, by feeling at my elbow a meaning nudge; when turning suddenly, I saw a sort of coffee-pot, and pewter mug hospitably presented to me by a ragged, but good-natured looking boy.

"Thank you", said I, "I wont take any coffee, I guess."

"Coffee?—I guess?—Aint you a Yankee?"

"Aye, boy; true blue."

"Well dad's gone to Yankee-land, a seekin' of his fortin'; so take a penny mug of ale, do Yankee, for poor dad's sake."

Out from the tilted coffee-pot-looking can, came a coffee-colored stream, and a small mug of humming ale was in my hand.

"I dont want it, boy. The fact is, my boy, I have no penny by me. I happened to leave my purse at my lodgings."

"Never do you mind, Yankee; drink to honest dad."

"With all my heart, you generous boy; here's immortal life to him!"

He stared at my strange burst, smiled merrily, and left me, offering his coffee-pot in all directions, and not in vain.

'Tis not always poverty to be poor, mused I; one may fare well without a penny. A ragged boy may be a prince-like benefactor.

Because that unpurchased penny-worth of ale revived my drooping spirits strangely. Stuff was in that barley-malt; a most sweet bitterness in those blessed hops. God bless the glorious boy!

The more I looked about me in this lofty gallery, the more was I delighted with its occupants. It was not spacious. It was, if anything, rather contracted, being the very cheapest portion of the house, where very limited attendance was expected; embracing merely the very crown of the topmost semicircle; and so, commanding, with a sovereign outlook, and imperial downlook, the whole theatre, with the expanded stage directly opposite, though some hundred feet below. As at the tower, peeping into the transatlantic temple, so stood I here, at the very main-mast-head of all the interior edifice.

Such was the decorum of this special theatre, that nothing objectionable was admitted within its walls. With an unhurt eye of perfect love, I sat serenely in the gallery, gazing upon the pleasing scene, around me and below. Neither did it abate from my satisfaction, to remember, that Mr Macready, the chief actor of the night, was an amiable gentleman, combining the finest qualities of social and Christian respectability, with the highest excellence in his particular profession; for which last he had conscientiously done much, in many ways, to refine, elevate, and chasten.

But now the curtain rises, and the robed Cardinal advances. How marvellous this personal resemblance! He looks every inch to be the self-same, stately priest I saw irradiated by the glow-worm dies of the pictured windows from my high tower-pew. And shining as he does, in the rosy reflexes of these stained walls and gorgeous galleries, the mimic priest down there; he too seems lit by Gothic blazonings.—Hark! The same measured, courtly, noble tone. See! the same imposing attitude. Excellent actor is this Richelieu!

He disappears behind the scenes. He slips, no doubt, into the Green Room. He reappears somewhat changed in his habilaments. Do I dream, or is it genuine memory that recalls some similar thing seen through the woven wires?

The curtain falls. Starting to their feet, the enraptured thousands sound their responses, deafeningly; unmistakably sincere. Right from the undoubted heart. I have no duplicate in my memory of this. In earnestness of response, this second temple stands unmatched. And hath mere mimicry done this? What is it then to act a part?

But now the music surges up again, and borne by that rolling billow, I, and all the gladdened crowd, are harmoniously attended to the street.

I went home to my lonely lodging, and slept not much that night, for thinking of the First Temple and the Second Temple; and how that, a stranger in a strange land, I found sterling charity in the one; and at home, in my own land, was thrust out from the other.

[1854]

# HERMAN MELVILLE

(1819–1891)

---

## *Jimmy Rose*

A TIME AGO, no matter how long precisely, I, an old man, removed from the country to the city, having become unexpected heir to a great old house in a narrow street of one of the lower wards, once the haunt of style and fashion, full of gay parlors and bridal chambers; but now, for the most part, transformed into counting-rooms and warehouses. There bales and boxes usurp the place of sofas; day-books and ledgers are spread where once the delicious breakfast toast was buttered. In those old wards the glorious old soft-warfle days are over.

Nevertheless, in this old house of mine, so strangely spared, some monument of departed days survived. Nor was this the only one. Amidst the warehouse ranges some few other dwellings likewise stood. The street's transmutation was not yet complete. Like those old English friars and nuns, long haunting the ruins of their retreats after they had been despoiled, so some few strange old gentlemen and ladies still lingered in the neighborhood, and would not, could not, might not quit it. And I thought that when, one spring, emerging from my white-blossoming orchard, my own white hairs and white ivory-headed cane were added to their loitering census, that those poor old souls insanely fancied the ward was looking up—the tide of fashion setting back again.

For many years the old house had been unoccupied by an owner; those into whose hands it from time to time had passed having let it out to various shifting tenants; decayed old towns-people, mysterious recluses, or transient, ambiguous-looking foreigners.

While from certain cheap furbishings to which the exterior had been subjected, such as removing a fine old pulpit-like porch crowning the summit of six lofty steps, and set off with a broad-brimmed sounding-board overshadowing the whole, as well as replacing the original heavy window-shutters (each pierced with a crescent in the upper panel to admit an Oriental and moony light into the otherwise shut-up rooms of a sultry morning in July) with frippery Venetian blinds; while, I repeat, the front of the house hereby presented an incongruous aspect, as if the graft of modernness had not taken in its ancient stock; still, however it might fare without, within little or nothing had been altered. The cellars were full of great grim, arched bins of blackened brick, looking like the ancient tombs of Templars, while overhead were shown the first-floor timbers, huge, square, and massive, all red oak, and through long eld, of a rich and Indian color. So large were those timbers, and so thickly ranked, that to walk in those capacious cellars was much like walking along a line-of-battle ship's gun-deck.

All the rooms in each story remained just as they stood ninety years ago, with all their heavy-moulded, wooden cornices, paneled wainscots, and carved and inaccessible mantles of queer horticultural and zoological devices. Dim with longevity, the very covering of the walls still preserved the patterns of the times of Louis XVI. In the largest parlor (the drawing-room, my daughters called it, in distinction from two smaller parlors, though I did not think the distinction indispensable) the paper hangings were in the most gaudy style. Instantly we knew such paper could only have come from Paris—genuine Versailles paper—the sort of paper that might have hung in Marie Antoinette's boudoir. It was of great diamond lozenges, divided by massive festoons of roses (onions, Biddy the girl said they were, but my wife soon changed Biddy's mind on that head); and in those lozenges, one and all, as in an overarbored garden-cage, sat a grand series of gorgeous illustrations of the natural history of the most imposing Parisian-looking birds; parrots, macaws, and peacocks, but mostly peacocks. Real Prince Esterhazies of birds; all rubies, diamonds, and Orders of the Golden Fleece. But, alas! the north side of this old apartment presented a strange look; half mossy and half mildew; something as ancient forest trees on their north sides, to which particular side the moss most clings, and where, they say, internal decay first strikes. In short, the original resplendence of the peacocks had been sadly dimmed on that north side of the room, owing to a small leak in the eaves, from which the rain had slowly trickled its way down the wall, clean down to the first floor. This leak the irreverent tenants, at that period occupying the premises, did not see fit to stop, or rather, did not think it worth their while, seeing that they only kept their fuel and dried their clothes in the parlor of the peacocks. Hence many of the once glowing birds seemed as if they had their princely plumage bedraggled in a dusty shower. Most mournfully their starry trains were blurred. Yet so patiently and so pleasantly, nay, here and there so ruddily did they seem to bide their bitter doom, so much of real elegance still lingered in their shapes, and so full, too, seemed they of a sweet engaging pensiveness, meditating all day long, for years and years, among their faded bowers, that though my family repeatedly adjured me (especially my wife, who, I fear, was too young for me) to destroy the whole hen-roost, as Biddy called it, and cover the walls with a beautiful, nice, genteel, cream-colored paper, despite all entreaties, I could not be prevailed upon, however submissive in other things.

But chiefly would I permit no violation of the old parlor of the peacocks or room of roses (I call it by both names), on account of its long association in my mind with one of the original proprietors of the mansion—the gentle Jimmy Rose.

Poor Jimmy Rose!

He was among my earliest acquaintances. It is not many years since he died; and I and two other tottering old fellows took hack, and in sole procession followed him to his grave.

Jimmy was born a man of moderate fortune. In his prime he had an uncommonly handsome person; large and manly, with bright eyes of blue, brown curling hair, and cheeks that seemed painted with carmine; but it was health's genuine bloom, deepened by the joy of life. He was by nature a great ladies' man, and like most deep adorers of the sex, never tied up his freedom of general worship by making one willful sacrifice of himself at the altar.

Adding to his fortune by a large and princely business, something like that of the great Florentine trader, Cosmo the Magnificent, he was enabled to entertain on a grand scale. For a long time his dinners, suppers, and balls, were not to be surpassed by any given in the party-giving city of New York. His uncommon cheeriness; the splendor of his dress; his sparkling wit; radiant chandeliers; infinite fund of small-talk; French furniture;

glowing welcomes to his guests; his bounteous heart and board; his noble graces and his glorious wine; what wonder if all these drew crowds to Jimmy's hospitable abode? In the winter assemblies he figured first on the manager's list. James Rose, Esq., too, was the man to be found foremost in all presentations of plate to highly successful actors at the Park, or of swords and guns to highly successful generals in the field. Often, also, was he chosen to present the gift on account of his fine gift of finely saying fine things.

"Sir," said he, in a great drawing-room in Broadway, as he extended toward General G——— a brace of pistols set with turquois. "Sir," said Jimmy with a Castilian flourish and a rosy smile, "there would have been more turquois here set, had the names of your glorious victories left room."

Ah, Jimmy, Jimmy! Thou didst excel in compliments. But it was inwrought with thy inmost texture to be affluent in all things which give pleasure. And who shall reproach thee with borrowed wit on this occasion, though borrowed indeed it was? Plagiarize otherwise as they may, not often are the men of this world plagiarists in praise.

But times changed. Time, true plagiarist of the seasons.

Sudden and terrible reverses in business were made mortal by mad prodigality on all hands. When his affairs came to be scrutinized, it was found that Jimmy could not pay more than fifteen shillings in the pound. And yet in time the deficiency might have been made up—of course, leaving Jimmy penniless—had it not been that in one winter gale two vessels of his from China perished off Sandy Hook; perished at the threshold of their port.

Jimmy was a ruined man.

It was years ago. At that period I resided in the country, but happened to be in the city on one of my annual visits. It was but four or five days since seeing Jimmy at his house the centre of all eyes, and hearing him at the close of the entertainment toasted by a brocaded lady, in these well-remembered words: "Our noble host; the bloom on his cheek, may it last long as the bloom in his heart!" And they, the sweet ladies and gentlemen there, they drank that toast so gayly and frankly off; and Jimmy, such a kind, proud, grateful tear stood in his honest eye, angelically glancing round at the sparkling faces, and equally sparkling, and equally feeling, decanters.

Ah! poor, poor Jimmy—God guard us all—poor Jimmy Rose!

Well, it was but four or five days after this that I heard a clap of thunder—no, a clap of bad news. I was crossing the Bowling Green in a snow-storm not far from Jimmy's house on the Battery, when I saw a gentleman come sauntering along, whom I remembered at Jimmy's table as having been the first to spring to his feet in eager response to the lady's toast. Not more brimming the wine in his lifted glass than the moisture in his eye on that happy occasion.

Well, this good gentleman came sailing across the Bowling Green, swinging a silver-headed ratan; seeing me, he paused, "Ah, lad, that was rare wine Jimmy gave us the other night. Sha'n't get any more, though. Heard the news? Jimmy's burst. Clean smash, I assure you. Come along down to the Coffee-house and I'll tell you more. And if you say so, we'll arrange over a bottle of claret for a sleighing party to Cato's to-night. Come along."

"Thank you," said I, "I—I—I am engaged."

Straight as an arrow I went to Jimmy's. Upon inquiring for him, the man at the door told me that his master was not in; nor did he know where he was; nor had his master been in the house for forty-eight hours.

Walking up Broadway again, I questioned passing acquaintances; but though each man verified the report, no man could tell where Jimmy was, and no one seemed to care, until I encountered a merchant, who hinted that probably Jimmy, having scraped up from the wreck a snug lump of coin, had prudently betaken himself off to parts unknown. The next man I saw, a great nabob he was too, foamed at the mouth when I mentioned Jimmy's name. "Rascal; regular scamp, Sir, is Jimmy Rose! But there are keen fellows after him." I afterward heard that this indignant gentleman had lost the sum of seventy-five dollars and seventy-five cents indirectly through Jimmy's failure. And yet I dare say the share of the dinners he had eaten at Jimmy's might more than have balanced that sum, considering that he was something of a wine-bibber, and such wines as Jimmy imported cost a plum or two. Indeed, now that I bethink me, I recall how I had more than once observed this same middle-aged gentleman, and how that toward the close of one of Jimmy's dinners he would sit at the table pretending to be earnestly talking with beaming Jimmy, but all the while, with a half furtive sort of tremulous eagerness and hastiness, pour down glass after glass of noble wine, as if now, while Jimmy's bounteous sun was at meridian, was the time to make his selfish hay.

At last I met a person famed for his peculiar knowledge of whatever was secret or withdrawn in the histories and habits of noted people. When I inquired of this person where Jimmy could possibly be, he took me close to Trinity Church rail, out of the jostling of the crowd, and whispered me, that Jimmy had the evening before entered an old house of his (Jimmy's), in C——— Street, which old house had been for a time untenanted. The inference seemed to be that perhaps Jimmy might be lurking there now. So getting the precise locality, I bent my steps in that direction, and at last halted before the house containing the room of roses. The shutters were closed, and cobwebs were spun in their crescents. The whole place had a dreary, deserted air. The snow lay unswept, drifted in one billowy heap against the porch, no footprint tracking it. Whoever was within, surely that lonely man was an abandoned one. Few or no people were in the street; for even at that period the fashion of the street had departed from it, while trade had not as yet occupied what its rival had renounced.

Looking up and down the sidewalk a moment, I softly knocked at the door. No response. I knocked again, and louder. No one came. I knocked and rung both; still without effect. In despair I was going to quit the spot, when, as a last resource, I gave a prolonged summons, with my utmost strength, upon the heavy knocker, and then again stood still; while from various strange old windows up and down the street, various strange old heads were thrust out in wonder at so clamorous a stranger. As if now frightened from its silence, a hollow, husky voice addressed me through the keyhole.

"Who are you?" it said.

"A friend."

"Then shall you not come in," replied the voice, more hollowly than before.

"Great Heaven! this is not Jimmy Rose?" thought I, starting. This is the wrong house. I have been misdirected. But still, to make all sure, I spoke again.

"Is James Rose within there?"

No reply.

Once more I spoke:

"I am William Ford; let me in."

"Oh, I can not, I can not! I am afraid of every one."

It *was* Jimmy Rose!

"Let me in, Rose; let me in, man. I am your friend."

"I will not. I can trust no man now."

"Let me in, Rose; trust at least one, in me."

"Quit the spot, or—"

With that I heard a rattling against the huge lock, not made by any key, as if some small tube were being thrust into the keyhole. Horrified, I fled fast as feet could carry me.

I was a young man then, and Jimmy was not more than forty. It was five-and-twenty years ere I saw him again. And what a change. He whom I expected to behold—if behold at all—dry, shrunken, meagre, cadaverously fierce with misery and misanthropy—amazement! the old Parisian roses bloomed in his cheeks. And yet poor as any rat; poor in the last dregs of poverty; a pauper beyond alms-house pauperism; a promenading pauper in a thin, thread-bare, careful coat; a pauper with wealth of polished words; a courteous, smiling, shivering gentleman.

Ah, poor, poor Jimmy—God guard us all—poor Jimmy Rose!

Though at the first onset of his calamity, when creditors, once fast friends, pursued him as carrion for jails; though then, to avoid their hunt, as well as the human eye, he had gone and denned in the old abandoned house; and there, in his loneliness, had been driven half mad, yet time and tide had soothed him down to sanity. Perhaps at bottom Jimmy was too thoroughly good and kind to be made from any cause a man-hater. And doubtless it at last seemed irreligious to Jimmy even to shun mankind.

Sometimes sweet sense of duty will entice one to bitter doom. For what could be more bitter than now, in abject need, to be seen of those—nay, crawl and visit them in an humble sort, and be tolerated as an old eccentric, wandering in their parlors—who once had known him richest of the rich, and gayest of the gay? Yet this Jimmy did. Without rudely breaking him right down to it, fate slowly bent him more and more to the lowest deep. From an unknown quarter he received an income of some seventy dollars, more or less. The principal he would never touch, but, by various modes of eking it out, managed to live on the interest. He lived in an attic, where he supplied himself with food. He took but one regular repast a day—meal and milk—and nothing more, unless procured at others' tables. Often about the tea-hour he would drop in upon some old acquaintance, clad in his neat, forlorn frock coat, with worn velvet sewed upon the edges of the cuffs, and a similar device upon the hems of his pantaloons, to hide that dire look of having been grated off by rats. On Sunday he made a point of always dining at some fine house or other.

It is evident that no man could with impunity be allowed to lead this life unless regarded as one who, free from vice, was by fortune brought so low that the plummet of pity alone could reach him. Not much merit redounded to his entertainers because they did not thrust the starving gentleman forth when he came for his poor alms of tea and toast. Some merit had been theirs had they clubbed together and provided him, at small cost enough, with a sufficient income to make him, in point of necessaries, independent of the daily dole of charity; charity not sent to him either, but charity for which he had to trudge round to their doors.

But the most touching thing of all were those roses in his cheeks; those ruddy roses in his nipping winter. How they bloomed; whether meal and milk, and tea and toast could keep them flourishing; whether now he painted them; by what strange magic they were made to blossom so; no son of man might tell. But there they bloomed. And besides the roses, Jimmy was rich in smiles. He smiled ever. The lordly door which received him to his eleemosynary teas, knew no such smiling guest as Jimmy. In his prosperous days the smile of Jimmy was famous far and wide. It should have been trebly famous now.

Wherever he went to tea, he had all of the news of the town to tell. By frequenting the reading-rooms, as one privileged through harmlessness, he kept himself informed of European affairs and the last literature, foreign and domestic. And of this, when encouragement was given, he would largely talk. But encouragement was not always given. At certain houses, and not a few, Jimmy would drop in about ten minutes before the tea-hour, and drop out again about ten minutes after it; well knowing that his further presence was not indispensable to the contentment or felicity of his host.

How forlorn it was to see him so heartily drinking the generous tea, cup after cup, and eating the flavorous bread and butter, piece after piece, when, owing to the lateness of the dinner hour with the rest, and the abundance of that one grand meal with them, no one besides Jimmy touched the bread and butter, or exceeded a single cup of Souchong. And knowing all this very well, poor Jimmy would try to hide his hunger, and yet gratify it too, by striving hard to carry on a sprightly conversation with his hostess, and throwing in the eagerest mouthfuls with a sort of absent-minded air, as if he ate merely for custom's sake, and not starvation's.

Poor, poor Jimmy—God guard us all—poor Jimmy Rose!

Neither did Jimmy give up his courtly ways. Whenever there were ladies at the table, sure were they of some fine word; though, indeed, toward the close of Jimmy's life, the young ladies rather thought his compliments somewhat musty, smacking of cocked hats and small clothes—nay, of old pawnbrokers' shoulder-lace and sword belts. For there still lingered in Jimmy's address a subdued sort of martial air; he having in his palmy days been, among other things, a general of the State militia. There seems a fatality in these militia generalships. Alas! I can recall more than two or three gentlemen who from militia generals become paupers. I am afraid to think why this is so. Is it that this military leaning in a man of an unmilitary heart—that is, a gentle, peaceable heart—is an indication of some weak love of vain display? But ten to one it is not so. At any rate, it is unhandsome, if not unchristian, in the happy, too much to moralize on those who are not so.

So numerous were the houses that Jimmy visited, or so cautious was he in timing his less welcome calls, that at certain mansions he only dropped in about once a year or so. And annually upon seeing at that house the blooming Miss Frances or Miss Arabella, he would profoundly bow in his forlorn old coat, and with his soft, white hand take hers in gallant wise, saying, "Ah, Miss Arabella, these jewels here are bright upon these fingers; but brighter would they look were it not for those still brighter diamonds of your eyes!"

Though in thy own need thou hadst no pence to give the poor, thou, Jimmy, still hadst alms to give the rich. For not the beggar chattering at the corner pines more after bread than the vain heart after compliment. The rich in their craving glut, as the poor in their craving want, we have with us always. So, I suppose, thought Jimmy Rose.

But all women are not vain, or if a little grain that way inclined, more than redeem it all with goodness. Such was the sweet girl that closed poor Jimmy's eyes. The only daughter of an opulent alderman, she knew Jimmy well, and saw to him in his declining days. During his last sickness, with her own hands she carried him jellies and blanc-mange; made tea for him in his attic, and turned the poor old gentleman in his bed. And well hadst thou deserved it, Jimmy, at that fair creature's hands; well merited to have thy old eyes closed by woman's fairy fingers, who through life, in riches and in poverty, was still woman's sworn champion and devotee.

I hardly know that I should mention here one little incident connected with this young lady's ministrations, and poor Jimmy's reception of them. But it is harm to neither; I will tell it.

Chancing to be in town, and hearing of Jimmy's illness, I went to see him. And there in his lone attic I found the lovely ministrant. Withdrawing upon seeing another visitor, she left me alone with him. She had brought some little delicacies, and also several books, of such a sort as are sent by serious-minded well-wishers to invalids in a serious crisis. Now whether it was repugnance at being considered next door to death, or whether it was but the natural peevishness brought on by the general misery of his state; however it was, as the gentle girl withdrew, Jimmy, with what small remains of strength were his, pitched the books into the furthest corner, murmuring, "Why will she bring me this sad old stuff? Does she take me for a pauper? Thinks she to salve a gentleman's heart with Poor Man's Plaster?"

Poor, poor Jimmy—God guard us all—poor Jimmy Rose!

Well, well, I am an old man, and I suppose these tears I drop are dribblets from my dotage. But Heaven be praised, Jimmy needs no man's pity now.

Jimmy Rose is dead!

Meantime, as I sit within the parlor of the peacocks—that chamber from which his husky voice had come ere threatening me with the pistol—I still must meditate upon his strange example, whereof the marvel is, how after that gay, dashing, nobleman's career, he could be content to crawl through life, and peep about among the marbles and mahoganies for contumelious tea and toast, where once like a very Warwick he had feasted the huzzaing world with Burgundy and venison.

And every time I look at the wilted resplendence of those proud peacocks on the wall, I bethink me of the withering change in Jimmy's once resplendent pride of state. But still again, every time I gaze upon those festoons of perpetual roses, mid which the faded peacocks hang, I bethink me of those undying roses which bloomed in ruined Jimmy's cheek.

Transplanted to another soil, all the unkind past forgot, God grant that Jimmy's roses may immortally survive!

1855

# LUCRETIA P. HALE

(1820–1900)

## *The Queen of the Red Chessmen*

THE BOX OF chessmen had been left open all night. That was a great oversight! For everybody knows that the contending chessmen are but too eager to fight their battles over again by midnight, if a chance is only allowed them.

It was at the Willows,—so called, not because the house is surrounded by willows, but because a little clump of them hangs over the pond close by. It is a pretty place, with its broad lawn in front of the door-way, its winding avenue hidden from the road by high trees. It is a quiet place, too; the sun rests gently on the green lawn, and the drooping leaves of the willows hang heavily over the water.

No one would imagine what violent contests were going on under the still roof, this very night. It was the night of the first of May. The moon came silently out from the shadows; the trees were scarcely stirring. The box of chessmen had been left on the balcony steps by the drawing-room window, and the window, too, that warm night, had been left open. So, one by one, all the chessmen came out to fight over again their evening's battles.

It was a famously carved set of chessmen. The bishops wore their mitres, the knights pranced on spirited steeds, the castles rested on the backs of elephants,—even the pawns mimicked the private soldiers of an army. The skilful carver had given to each piece, and each pawn, too, a certain individuality. That night there had been a close contest. Two well-matched players had guided the game, and it had ended with leaving a deep irritation on the conquered side.

It was Isabella, the Queen of the Red Chessmen, who had been obliged to yield. She was young and proud, and it was she, indeed, who held the rule; for her father, the old Red King, had grown too imbecile to direct affairs; he merely bore the name of sovereignty. And Isabella was loved by knights, pawns, and all; the bishops were willing to die in her cause, the castles would have crumbled to earth for her. Opposed to her, stood the detested White Queen. All the Whites, of course, were despised by her: but the haughty, self-sufficient queen angered her most.

The White Queen was reigning during the minority of her only son. The White Prince had reached the age of nineteen, but the strong mind of his mother had kept him always under restraint. A simple youth, he had always yielded to her control. He was pure-hearted and gentle, but never ventured to make a move of his own. He sought shelter under cover of his castles, while his more energetic mother went forth at the head of his army. She was dreaded by her subjects,—never loved by them. Her own pawn, it is true, had ventured much for her sake, had often with his own life redeemed her from captivity; but it was loyalty that bound even him,—no warmer feeling of devotion or love.

The Queen Isabella was the first to come out from her prison.

"I will stay here no longer," she cried; "the blood of the Reds grows pale in this inactivity."

She stood upon the marble steps; the May moon shone down upon her. She listened a moment to a slight murmuring within the drawing-room window. The Spanish lady, the Murillo-painted Spanish lady, had come down from her frame that bound her against the wall. Just for this one night in the year, she stepped out from the canvas to walk up and down the rooms majestically. She would not exchange a word with anybody; nobody understood her language. She could remember when Murillo looked at her, watched over her, created her with his pencil. She could have nothing to say to little paltry shepherdesses, and other articles of *virtù*, that came into grace and motion just at this moment.

The Queen of the Red Chessmen turned away, down into the avenue. The May moon shone upon her. Her feet trod upon unaccustomed ground; no black or white square hemmed her in; she felt a new liberty.

"My poor old father!" she exclaimed, "I will leave him behind; better let him slumber in an ignoble repose than wander over the board, a laughing-stock for his enemies. We have been conquered,—the foolish White Prince rules!"

A strange inspiration stole upon her; the breath of the May night hovered over her; the May moon shone upon her. She could move without waiting for the will of another; she was free. She passed down the avenue; she had left her old prison behind.

Early in the morning,—it was just after sunrise,—the kind Doctor Lester was driving home, after watching half the night out with a patient. He passed the avenue to the Willows, but drew up his horse just as he was leaving the entrance. He saw a young girl sitting under the hedge. She was without any bonnet, in a red dress, fitting closely and hanging heavily about her. She was so very beautiful, she looked so strangely lost and out of place here at this early hour, that the Doctor could not resist speaking to her.

"My child, how came you here?"

The young girl rose up, and looked round with uncertainty.

"Where am I?" she asked.

She was very tall and graceful, with an air of command, but with a strange, wild look in her eyes.

"The young woman must be slightly insane," thought the Doctor; "but she cannot have wandered far."

"Let me take you home," he said aloud. "Perhaps you come from the Willows?"

"Oh, don't take me back there!" cried Isabella, "they will imprison me again! I had rather be a slave than a conquered queen!"

"Decidedly insane!" thought the Doctor. "I must take her back to the Willows."

He persuaded the young girl to let him lift her into his chaise. She did not resist him; but when he turned up the avenue, she leaned back in despair. He was fortunate enough to find one of the servants up at the house, just sweeping the steps of the hall-door. Getting out of his chaise, he said confidentially to the servant,—

"I have brought back your young lady."

"Our young lady!" exclaimed the man, as the Doctor pointed out Isabella.

"Yes, she is a little insane, is she not?"

"She is not our young lady," answered the servant; "we have nobody in the house just now, but Mr. and Mrs. Fogerty, and Mrs. Fogerty's brother, the old geologist."

"Where did she come from?" inquired the Doctor.

"I never saw her before," said the servant, "and I certainly should remember. There's some foreign folks live down in the cottage, by the railroad; but they are not the like of her!"

The Doctor got into his chaise again, bewildered.

"My child," he said, "you must tell me where you came from."

"Oh, don't let me go back again!" said Isabella, clasping her hands imploringly. "Think how hard it must be never to take a move of one's own! to know how the game might be won, then see it lost through folly! Oh, that last game, lost through utter weakness! There was that one move! Why did he not push me down to the king's row? I might have checkmated the White Prince, shut in by his own castles and pawns,—it would have been a direct checkmate! Think of his folly! he stopped to take the queen's pawn with his bishop, and within one move of a checkmate!"

"Quite insane!" repeated the Doctor. "But I must have my breakfast. She seems quiet; I think I can keep her till after breakfast, and then I must try and find where the poor child's friends live. I don't know what Mrs. Lester will think of her."

They rode on. Isabella looked timidly round.

"You don't quite believe me," she said, at last. "It seems strange to you."

"It does," answered the Doctor, "seem very strange."

"Not stranger than to me," said Isabella,—"it is so very grand to me! All this motion! Look down at that great field there, not cut up into squares! If I only had my knights and squires there! I would be willing to give *her* as good a field, too; but I would show her where the true bravery lies. What a place for the castles, just to defend that pass!"

The Doctor whipped up his horse.

Mrs. Lester was a little surprised at the companion her husband had brought home to breakfast with him.

"Who is it?" she whispered.

"That I don't know,—I shall have to find out," he answered, a little nervously.

"Where is her bonnet?" asked Mrs. Lester; this was the first absence of conventionality she had noticed.

"You had better ask her," answered the Doctor.

But Mrs. Lester preferred leaving her guest in the parlor while she questioned her husband. She was somewhat disturbed when she found he had nothing more satisfactory to tell her.

"An insane girl! and what shall we do with her?" she asked.

"After breakfast I will make some inquiries about her," answered the Doctor.

"And leave her alone with us? that will never do! You must take her away directly,—at least to the Insane Asylum,—somewhere! What if she should grow wild while you were gone? She might kill us all! I will go in and tell her that she cannot stay here."

On returning to the parlor, she found Isabella looking dreamily out of the window. As Mrs. Lester approached, she turned.

"You will let me stay with you a little while, will you not?"

She spoke in a quiet tone, with an air somewhat commanding. It imposed upon nervous little Mrs. Lester. But she made a faint struggle.

"Perhaps you would rather go home," she said.

"I have no home now," said Isabella; "some time I may recover it; but my throne has been usurped."

Mrs. Lester looked round in alarm, to see if the Doctor were near.

"Perhaps you had better come in to breakfast," she suggested.

She was glad to place the Doctor between herself and their new guest.

Celia Lester, the only daughter, came down stairs. She had heard that her father had picked up a lost girl in the road. As she came down in her clean morning dress, she expected to have to hold her skirts away from some little squalid object of charity. She started when she saw the elegant-looking young girl who sat at the table. There was something in her air and manner that seemed to make the breakfast equipage, and the furniture of the room about her, look a little mean and poor. Yet the Doctor was very well off, and Mrs. Lester fancied she had everything quite in style. Celia stole into her place, feeling small in the presence of the stranger.

After breakfast, when the Doctor had somewhat refreshed himself by its good cheer from his last night's fatigue, Isabella requested to speak with him.

"Let me stay with you a little while," she asked, beseechingly; "I will do everything for you that you desire. You shall teach me anything;—I know I can learn all that you will show me, all that Mrs. Lester will tell me."

"Perhaps so,—perhaps that will be best," answered the Doctor, "until your friends inquire for you; then I must send you back to them."

"Very well, very well," said Isabella, relieved. "But I must tell you they will not inquire for me. I see you will not believe my story. If you only would listen to me, I could tell it all to you."

"That is the only condition I can make with you," answered the Doctor, "that you will not tell your story,—that you will never even think of it yourself. I am a physician. I know that it is not good for you to dwell upon such things. Do not talk of them to me, nor to my wife or daughter. Never speak of your story to any one who comes here. It will be better for you."

"Better for me," said Isabella, dreamily, "that no one should know! Perhaps so. I am, in truth, captive to the White Prince; and if he should come and demand me,—I should be half afraid to try the risks of another game."

"Stop, stop!" exclaimed the Doctor, "you are already forgetting the condition. I shall be obliged to take you away to some retreat, unless you promise me"——

"Oh, I will promise you anything," interrupted Isabella; "and you will see that I can keep my promise."

Meanwhile Mrs. Lester and Celia had been holding a consultation.

"I think she must be some one in disguise," suggested Celia.

Celia was one of the most unromantic of persons. Both she and her mother had passed their lives in an unvarying routine of duties. Neither of them had ever found time from their sewing even to read. Celia had her books of history laid out, that she meant to take up when she should get through her work; but it seemed hopeless that this time would ever come. It had never come to Mrs. Lester, and she was now fifty years old. Celia had never read any novels. She had tried to read them, but never was interested in them. So she had a vague idea of what romance was, conceiving of it only as something quite different from her every-day life. For this reason the unnatural event that was taking place this very day was gradually appearing to her something possible and natural. Because she knew there was such a thing as romance, and that it was something quite beyond her comprehension, she was the more willing to receive this event quietly from finding it incomprehensible.

"We can let her stay here to-day, at least," said Mrs. Lester. "We will keep John at work in the front door-yard, in case we should want him. And I will set Mrs. Anderson's boy to weeding in the border; we can call him, if we should want to send for help."

She was quite ashamed of herself, when she had uttered these words, and Isabella walked into the room, so composed, so refined in her manners.

"The Doctor says I may stay here a little while, if you will let me," said Isabella, as she took Mrs. Lester's hands.

"We will try to make you comfortable," replied Mrs. Lester.

"He says you will teach me many things,—I think he said, how to sew."

"How to sew! Was it possible she did not know how to sew?" Celia thought to herself. "How many servants she must have had, never to have learned how to sew, herself!"

And this occupation was directly provided, while the Doctor set forth on his day's duties, and at the same time to inquire about the strange apparition of the young girl. He was so convinced that there was a vein of insanity about her, that he was very sure that questioning her only excited her the more. Just as he had parted from her, some compunction seized her, and she followed him to the door.

"There is my father," said she.

"Your father! where shall I find him?" asked the Doctor.

"Oh, he could not help me," she replied; "it is a long time since he has been able to direct affairs. He has scarcely been conscious of my presence, and will hardly feel my absence, his mind is so weak."

"But where can I find him?" persisted the Doctor.

"He did not come out," said Isabella; "the White Queen would not allow it, indeed."

"Stop, stop!" exclaimed the Doctor, "we are on forbidden ground."

He drove away.

"So there is insanity in the family," he thought to himself. "I am quite interested in this case. A new form of monomania! I should be quite sorry to lose sight of it. I shall be loath to give her up to her friends."

But he was not yet put to that test. No one could give him any light with regard to the strange girl. He went first to the Willows, and found there so much confusion that he could hardly persuade any one to listen to his questions. Mrs. Fogerty's brother, the geologist, had been riding that morning, and had fallen from his horse and broken his leg. The Doctor arrived just in time to be of service in setting it. Then he must linger some time to see that the old gentleman was comfortable, so that he was obliged to stay nearly the whole morning. He was much amused at the state of disturbance in which he left the family. The whole house was in confusion, looking after some lost chessmen.

"There was nothing," said Mrs. Fogerty, apologetically, "that would soothe her brother so much as a game of chess. That, perhaps, might keep him quiet. He would be willing to play chess with Mr. Fogerty by the day together. It was so strange! they had a game the night before, and now some of the pieces could not be found. Her brother had lost the game, and to-day he was so eager to take his revenge!"

"How absurd!" thought the Doctor; "what trifling things people interest themselves in! Here is this old man more disturbed at losing his game of chess than he is at breaking his leg! It is different in my profession, where one deals with life and death. Here is this young girl's fate in my hands, and they talk to me of the loss of a few paltry chessmen!"

The "foreign people" at the cottage knew nothing of Isabella. No one had seen her the night before, or at any time. Dr. Lester even drove ten miles to Dr. Giles's Retreat for the Insane, to see if it were possible that a patient could have wandered away from there. Dr. Giles was deeply interested in the account Dr. Lester gave. He would very gladly take such a person under his care.

"No," said Dr. Lester, "I will wait awhile. I am interested in the young girl. It is not possible but that I shall in time find out from her, by chance, perhaps, who her friends are, and where she came from. She must have wandered away in some delirium of fever,—but it is very strange, for she appears perfectly calm now. Yet I hardly know in what state I shall find her."

He returned to find her very quiet and calm, learning from his wife and daughter how to sew. She seemed deeply interested in this new occupation, and had given all her time and thought to it. Celia and her mother privately confided to the Doctor their admiration of their strange guest. Her ways were so graceful and beautiful! all that she said seemed so new and singular! The Doctor, before he went away, had exhorted Mrs. Lester and Celia to ask her no questions about her former life, and everything had gone on very smoothly. And everything went on as smoothly for some weeks. Isabella seemed willing to be as silent as the Doctor, upon all exciting subjects. She appeared to be quite taken up with her sewing, much to Mrs. Lester's delight.

"She will turn out quite as good a seamstress as Celia," said she to the Doctor. "She sews steadily all the time, and nothing seems to please her so much as to finish a piece of work. She will be able to do much more than her own sewing, and may prove quite a help to us."

"I shall be very glad," said the Doctor, "if anything can be a help to prevent you and Celia from working yourselves to death. I shall be glad if you can ever have done with that eternal sewing. It is time that Celia should do something about cultivating her mind."

"Celia's mind is so well regulated," interrupted Mrs. Lester.

"We won't discuss that," continued the Doctor,—"we never come to an agreement there. I was going on to say that I am becoming so interested in Isabella, that I feel towards her as if she were my own. If she is of help to the family, that is very well,—it is the best thing for her to be able to make herself of use. But I don't care to make any profit to ourselves out of her help. Somehow I begin to think of her as belonging to us. Certainly she belongs to nobody else. Let us treat her as our own child. We have but one, yet God has given us means enough to care for many more. I confess I should find it hard to give Isabella up to any one else. I like to find her when I come home,—it is pleasant to look at her."

"And I, too, love her," said Mrs. Lester. "I like to see her as she sits quietly at her work."

So Isabella went on learning what it was to be one of the family, and becoming, as Mrs. Lester remarked, a very experienced seamstress. She seldom said anything as she sat at her work, but seemed quite occupied with her sewing; while Mrs. Lester and Celia kept up a stream of conversation, seldom addressing Isabella, as, indeed, they had few topics in common.

One day, Celia and Isabella were sitting together.

"Have you always sewed?" asked Isabella.

"Oh, yes," answered Celia,—"since I was quite a child."

"And do you remember when you were a child?" asked Isabella, laying down her work.

"Oh, yes, indeed," said Celia; "I used to make all my doll's dresses myself."

"Your doll's dresses!" repeated Isabella.

"Oh, yes," replied Celia,—"I was not ashamed to play with dolls in that way."

"I should like to see some dolls," said Isabella.

"I will show you my large doll," said Celia; "I have always kept it, because I fitted it out with such a nice set of clothes. And I keep it for children to play with."

She brought her doll, and Isabella handled it and looked at it with curiosity.

"So you dressed this, and played with it," said Isabella, inquiringly, "and moved it about as one would move a piece at chess?"

Celia started at this word "chess." It was one of the forbidden words. But Isabella went on:—

"Suppose this doll should suddenly have begun to speak, to move, and walk round, would not you have liked it?"

"Oh, no!" exclaimed Celia. "What! a wooden thing speak and move! It would have frightened me very much."

"Why should it not speak, if it has a mouth, and walk, if it has feet?" asked Isabella.

"What foolish questions you ask!" exclaimed Celia, "of course it has not life."

"Oh, life,—that is it!" said Isabella. "Well, what is life?"

"Life! why it is what makes us live," answered Celia. "Of course you know what life is."

"No, I don't know," said Isabella, "but I have been thinking about it lately, while I have been sewing,—what it is."

"But you should not think, you should talk more, Isabella," said Celia. "Mamma and I talk while we are at work, but you are always very silent."

"But you think sometimes?" asked Isabella.

"Not about such things," replied Celia. "I have to think about my work."

"But your father thinks, I suppose, when he comes home and sits in his study alone?"

"Oh, he reads when he goes into his study,—he reads books and studies them," said Celia.

"Do you know how to read?" asked Isabella.

"Do I know how to read!" cried Celia, angrily.

"Forgive me," said Isabella, quickly, "but I never saw you reading. I thought perhaps—women are so different here!"

She did not finish her sentence, for she saw Celia was really angry. Yet she had no idea of hurting her feelings. She had tried to accommodate herself to her new circumstances. She had observed a great deal, and had never been in the habit of asking questions. Celia was disturbed at having it supposed that she did not know how to read; therefore it must be a very important thing to know how to read, and she determined she must learn. She applied to the Doctor. He was astonished at her entire ignorance, but he was very glad to help her. Isabella gave herself up to her reading, as she had done before to her sewing. The Doctor was now the gainer. All the time he was away, Isabella sat in his study, poring over her books; when he returned, she had a famous lesson to recite to him. Then he began to tell her of books that he was interested in. He made Celia come in, for a history class. It was such a pleasure to him to find Isabella interested in what he could tell her of history!

"All this really happened," said Isabella to Celia once,—"these people really lived!"

"Yes, but they died," responded Celia, in an indifferent tone,—"and ever so long ago, too!"

"But did they die," asked Isabella, "if we can talk about them, and imagine how they looked? They live for us as much as they did then."

"That I can't understand," said Celia. "My uncle saw Napoleon when he was in Europe, long ago. But I never saw Napoleon. He is dead and gone to me, just as much as Alexander the Great."

"Well, who does live, if Alexander the Great, if Napoleon, and Columbus do not live?" asked Isabella, impatiently.

"Why, papa and mamma live," answered Celia, "and you"——

"And the butcher," interrupted Isabella, "because he brings you meat to eat; and Mr. Spool, because he keeps the thread store. Thank you for putting me in, too! Once"——

"Once!" answered Celia, in a dignified tone, "I suppose once you lived in a grander circle, and it appears to you we have nobody better than Mr. Spool and the butcher."

Isabella was silent, and thought of her "circle," her former circle. The circle here was large enough, the circumference not very great, but there were as many points in it as in a larger one. There were pleasant, motherly Mrs. Gibbs, and her agreeable daughters,—the Gresham boys, just in college,—the Misses Tarletan, fresh from a New York boarding-school,—Mr. Lovell, the young minister,—and the old Misses Pendleton, that made raspberry-jam,—together with Celia's particular friends, Anna and Selina Mountfort, who had a great deal of talking with Celia in private, but not a word to say to anybody in the parlor. All those, with many others in the background, had been speculating upon the riddle that Isabella presented,—"Who was she? and where did she come from?"

Nobody found any satisfactory answer. Neither Celia nor her mother would disclose anything. It is a great convenience in keeping a secret, not to know what it is. One can't easily tell what one does not know.

"The Doctor really has a treasure in his wife and daughter," said Mrs. Gibbs, "they keep his secrets so well! Neither of them will lisp a word about this handsome Isabella."

"I have no doubt she is the daughter of an Italian refugee," said one of the Misses Tarletan. "We saw a number of Italian refugees in New York."

This opinion became prevalent in the neighborhood. That Dr. Lester should be willing to take charge of an unknown girl did not astonish those who knew of his many charitable deeds. It was not more than he had done for his cousin's child, who had no especial claim upon him. He had adopted Lawrence Egerton, educated him, sent him to college, and was giving him every advantage in his study of the law. In the end Lawrence would probably marry Celia and the pretty property that the Doctor would leave behind for his daughter.

"She is one of my patients," the Doctor would say, to any one who asked him about her.

The tale that she was the daughter of an Italian refugee became more rife after Isabella had begun to study Italian. She liked to have the musical Italian words linger on her tongue. She quoted Italian poetry, read Italian history. In conversation, she generally talked of the present, rarely of the past or of the future. She listened with wonder to those who had a talent for reminiscence. How rich their past must be, that they should be willing to dwell in it! Her own she thought very meagre. If she wanted to live in the past, it must be in the past of great men, not in that of her own little self. So she read of great painters and great artists, and because she read of them she talked of them. Other people, in referring to bygone events, would say, "When I was in Trenton last summer,"—"In Cuba the spring that we were there"; but Isabella would say, "When Raphael died, or when Dante lived." Everybody liked to talk with her,—laughed with her at her enthusiasm. There was something inspiring, too, in this enthusiasm; it compelled attention, as her air and manner always attracted notice. By her side, the style and elegance of the Misses Tarletan faded out; here was a moon that quite extinguished the light of their little tapers. She became the centre of admiration; the young girls admired her, as they are prone to admire some one particular star. She never courted attention, but it was always given.

"Isabella attracts everybody," said Celia to her mother. "Even the old Mr. Spencers, who have never been touched by woman before, follow her, and act just as she wills."

Little Celia, who had been quite a belle hitherto, sunk into the shade by the side of the brilliant Isabella. Yet she followed willingly in the sunny wake that Isabella left behind. She expanded somewhat, herself, for she was quite ashamed to know nothing of all that Isabella talked about so earnestly. The sewing gave place to a little reading, to Mrs. Lester's horror. The Mountforts and the Gibbses met with Isabella and Celia to read and study, and went into town with them to lectures and to concerts.

A winter passed away and another summer came. Still Isabella was at Dr. Lester's; and with the lapse of time the harder did it become for the Doctor to question her of her past history,—the more, too, was she herself weaned from it.

The young people had been walking in the garden one evening.

"Let me sit by you here in the porch," said Lawrence Egerton to Celia,—"I want rest, for body and spirit. I am always in a battle-field when I am talking with Isabella. I must either fight with her or against her. She insists on my fighting all the time. I have to keep my weapons bright, ready for use, every moment. She will lead me, too, in conversation, sends me here, orders me there. I feel like a poor knight in chess, under the sway of a queen"——

"I don't know anything about chess," said Celia, curtly.

"It is a comfort to have you a little ignorant," said Lawrence. "Please stay in bliss awhile. It is repose, it is refreshment. Isabella drags one into the company of her heroes, and then one feels completely ashamed not to be on more familiar terms with them all. Her Mazzinis, her Tancreds, heroes false and true,—it makes no difference to her,—put one into a whirl between history and story. What a row she would make in Italy, if she went back there!"

"What could we do without her?" said Celia; "it was so quiet and commonplace before she came!"

"That is the trouble," replied Lawrence. "Isabella won't let anything remain commonplace. She pulls everything out of its place,—makes a hero or heroine out of a piece of clay. I don't want to be in heroics all the time. Even Homer's heroes ate their suppers comfortably. I think it was a mistake in your father, bringing her here. Let her stay in her sphere queening it, and leave us poor mortals to our bread and butter."

"You know you don't think so," expostulated Celia; "you worship her shoe-tie, the hem of her garment."

"But I don't want to," said Lawrence,—"it is a compulsory worship. I had rather be quiet."

"Lazy Lawrence!" cried Celia, "it is better for you. You would be the first to miss Isabella. You would find us quite flat without her brilliancy, and would be hunting after some other excitement."

"Perhaps so," said Lawrence. "But here she comes to goad us on again. Queen Isabella, when do the bull-fights begin?"

"I wish I were Queen Isabella!" she exclaimed. "Have you read the last accounts from Spain? I was reading them to the Doctor to-day. Nobody knows what to do there. Only think what an opportunity for the Queen to show herself a queen! Why will not she make of herself such a queen as the great Isabella of Castile was?"

"I can't say," answered Lawrence.

"Queens rule in chess," said Horace Gresham. "I always wondered that the king was made such a poor character there. He is not only ruled by his cabinet, bishops, and knights, but his queen is by far the more warlike character."

"Whoever plays the game rules,—you or Mr. Egerton," said Isabella, bitterly; "it is not the poor queen. She must yield to the power of the moving hand. I suppose it is so with us women. We see a great aim before us, but have not the power."

"Nonsense!" exclaimed Lawrence, "it is just the reverse. With some women,—for I won't be personal,—the aim, as you call it, is very small,—a poor amusement, another dress, a larger house"——

"You may stop," interrupted Isabella, "for you don't believe this. At least, keep some of your flings for the women that deserve them; Celia and I don't accept them."

"Then we'll talk of the last aim we were discussing,—the ride to-morrow."

The next winter was passed by Mrs. Lester, her daughter, and Isabella in Cuba. Lawrence Egerton accompanied them thither, and the Doctor hoped to go for them in the spring. They went on Mrs. Lester's account. She had worn herself out with her household labors,—very uselessly, the Doctor thought,—so he determined to send her away from them. Isabella and Celia were very happy all this winter and spring. With Isabella Spanish took the place of Italian studies. She liked talking in Spanish. They made some friends among the residents, as well as among the strangers, particularly the Americans. Of these last, they enjoyed most the society of Mrs. Blanchard and her son, Otho, who were at the same hotel with them.

The opera, too, was a new delight to Isabella, and even Celia was excited by it.

"It is a little too absurd, to see the dying scene of Romeo and Juliet sung out in an opera!" remarked Lawrence Egerton, one morning; "all the music of the spheres could not have made that scene, last night, otherwise than supremely ridiculous."

"I am glad you did not sit by us, then," replied Celia; "Isabella and I were crying."

"I dare say," said Lawrence, "I should be afraid to take you to sec a tragedy well acted. You would both be in hysterics before the killing was over."

"I should be really afraid," said Celia, "to see Romeo and Juliet finely performed. It would be too sad."

"It would be much better to end it up comfortably," said Lawrence. "Why should not Juliet marry her Romeo in peace?"

"It would be impossible!" exclaimed Isabella,—"impossible to bring together two such hostile families! Of course the result must be a tragedy."

"In romances," answered Lawrence, "that may be necessary; but not in real life."

"Why not in real life?" asked Isabella. "When two thunder-clouds meet, there must be an explosion."

"But we don't have such hostile families arrayed against each other now-a-days," said Lawrence. "The Bianchi and the Neri have died out; unless the feud lives between the whites and the blacks of the present day."

"Are you sure that it has died out everywhere?" asked Isabella.

"Certainly not," said Otho Blanchard; "my mother, Bianca Bianco, inherits her name from a long line of ancestry, and with it come its hatreds as well as its loves."

"You speak like an Italian or Spaniard," said Lawrence. "We are cold-blooded Yankees, and in our slow veins such passions do die out. I should have taken you for an American from your name."

"It is our name Americanized; we have made Americans of ourselves, and the Bianchi have become the Blanchards."

"The romance of the family, then," persisted Lawrence, "must needs become Americanized too. If you were to meet with a lovely young lady of the enemy's race, I think you would be willing to bury your sword in the sheath for her sake."

"I hope I should not forget the honor of my family," said Otho. "I certainly never could, as long as my mother lives; her feelings on the subject are stronger even than mine."

"I cannot imagine the possibility of such feelings dying out," said Isabella. "I cannot imagine such different elements amalgamating. It would be like fire and water uniting. Then there would be no longer any contest; the game of life would be over."

"Why will you make out life to be a battle always?" exclaimed Lawrence; "won't you allow us any peace? I do not find such contests all the time,—never, except when I am fighting with you."

"I had rather fight with you than against you," said Isabella, laughing. "But when one is not striving, one is sleeping."

"That reminds me that it is time for our siesta," said Lawrence; "so we need not fight any longer."

Afterwards Isabella and Celia were talking of their new friend Otho.

"He does not seem to me like a Spaniard," said Celia, "his complexion is so light; then, too, his name sounds German."

"But his passions are quick," replied Isabella. "How he colored up when he spoke of the honor of his family!"

"I wonder that you like him," said Celia; "when he is with his mother, he hardly ventures to say his soul is his own."

"I don't like his mother," said Isabella; "her manner is too imperious and unrefined, it appears to me. No wonder that Otho is ill at ease in her presence. It is evident that her way of talking is not agreeable to him. He is afraid that she will commit herself in some way."

"But he never stands up for himself," answered Celia; "he always yields to her. Now I should not think you would like that."

"He yields because she is his mother," said Isabella; "and it would not be becoming to contradict her."

"He yields to you, too," said Celia; "how happens that?"

"I hope he does not yield to me more than is becoming," answered Isabella, laughing; "perhaps that is why I like him. After all, I don't care to be always sparring, as I am with Lawrence Egerton. With Otho I find that I agree wonderfully in many things. Neither of us yields to the other, neither of us is obliged to convince the other."

"Now I should think you would find that stupid," said Celia. "What becomes of this desire of yours never to rest, always to be struggling after something?"

"We might strive together, we might struggle together," responded Isabella.

She said this musingly, not in answer to Celia, but to her own thoughts,—as she looked away, out from everything that surrounded her. The passion for ruling had always been uppermost in her mind; suddenly there dawned upon her the pleasure of being ruled. She became conscious of the pleasure of conquering all things for the sake of giving all to another. A new sense of peace stole upon her mind. Before, she had felt herself alone, even in the midst of the kindness of the home that had been given her. She had never dared to think or to speak of the past, and as little of the future. She had gladly flung herself into the details of every-day life. She had given her mind to the study of all that it required. She loved the Doctor, because he was always leading her on to fresh fields, always exciting her to a new knowledge. She loved him, too, for himself, for his tenderness and kindness to her. With Mrs. Lester and Celia she felt herself on a different footing. They admired her, but they never came near her. She led them, and they were always behind her.

With Otho she experienced a new feeling. He seemed, very much as she did herself, out of place in the world just around him. He was a foreigner,—was not yet acclimated to the society about him. He was willing to talk of other things than every-day events. He did not talk of "things," indeed, but he speculated, as though he lived a separate life from that of mere eating and drinking. He was not content with what seemed to every-day people possible, but was willing to believe that there were things not dreamed of in their philosophy.

"It is a satisfaction," said Lawrence once to Celia, "that Isabella has found somebody who will go high enough into the clouds to suit her. Besides, it gives me a little repose."

"And a secret jealousy at the same time; is it not so?" asked Celia. "He takes up too much of Isabella's time to please you."

"The reason he pleases her," said Lawrence, "is because he is more womanly than manly, and she thinks women ought to rule the world. Now if the world were made up of such as he, it would be very easily ruled. Isabella loves power too well to like to see it in others. Look at her when she is with Mrs. Blanchard! It is a splendid sight to see them together!"

"How can you say so? I am always afraid of some outbreak."

These families were, however, so much drawn together, that, when the Doctor came to summon his wife and daughter and Isabella home, Mrs. Blanchard was anxious to accompany them to New England. She wondered if it were not possible to find a country-seat somewhere near the Lesters, that she could occupy for a time. The Doctor knew that the Willows was to be vacant this spring. The Fogertys were all going to Europe, and would be very willing to let their place.

So it was arranged after their return. The Fogertys left for Europe, and Mrs. Blanchard took possession of the Willows. It was a pleasant walking distance from the Lesters, but it was several weeks before Isabella made her first visit there. She was averse to going into the house, but, in company with Celia, Lawrence, and Otho, walked about the grounds. Presently they stopped near a pretty fountain that was playing in the midst of the garden.

"That is a pretty place for an Undine," said Otho.

"The idea of an Undine makes me shiver," said Lawrence. "Think what a cold-blooded, unearthly being she would be!"

"Not after she had a soul!" exclaimed Isabella.

"An Undine with a soul!" cried Lawrence. "I conceive of them as malicious spirits, who live and die as the bubbles of water rise and fall."

"You talk as if there were such things as Undines," said Celia. "I remember once trying to read the story of Undine, but I never could finish it."

"It ends tragically," remarked Otho.

"Of course all such stories must," responded Lawrence; "of course it is impossible to bring the natural and the unnatural together."

"That depends upon what you call the natural," said Otho.

"We should differ, I suppose," said Lawrence, "if we tried to explain what we each call the natural. I fancy your 'real life' is different from mine."

"Pictures of real life," said Isabella, "are sometimes pictures of horses and dogs, sometimes of children playing, sometimes of fruits of different seasons heaped upon one dish, sometimes of watermelons cut open."

"That is hardly your picture of real life," said Lawrence, laughing,—"a watermelon cut open! I think you would rather choose the picture of the Water Fairies from the Düsseldorf Gallery."

"Why not?" said Isabella. "The life we see must be very far from being the only life that is."

"That is very true," answered Lawrence; "but let the fairies live their life by themselves, while we live our life in our own way. Why should they come to disturb our peace, since we cannot comprehend them, and they certainly cannot comprehend us?"

"You do not think it well, then," said Isabella, stopping in their walk, and looking down,—"you do not think it well that beings of different natures should mingle?"

"I do not see how they can," replied Lawrence. "I am limited by my senses; I can perceive only what they show me. Even my imagination can picture to me only what my senses can paint."

"Your senses!" cried Otho, contemptuously,—"it is very true, as you confess, you are limited by your senses. Is all this beauty around you created merely for you—and the other insects about us? I have no doubt it is filled with invisible life."

"Do let us go in!" said Celia. "This talk, just at twilight, under the shade of this shrubbery, makes me shudder. I am not afraid of the fairies. I never could read fairy stories when I was a child: they were tiresome to me. But talking in this way makes one timid. There might be strollers or thieves under all these hedges."

They went into the house, through the hall, and different apartments, till they reached the drawing-room. Isabella stood transfixed upon the threshold. It was all so familiar to her!—everything as she had known it before! Over the mantelpiece hung the picture of the scornful Spanish lady; a heavy book-case stood in one corner; comfortable chairs and couches were scattered round the room; beautiful landscapes against the wall seemed like windows cut into foreign scenery. There was an air of ease in the room, an old-fashioned sort of ease, such as the Fogertys must have loved.

"It is a pretty room, is it not?" said Lawrence. "You look at it as if it pleased you. How much more comfort there is about it than in the fashionable parlors of the day! It is solid, substantial comfort."

"You look at it as if you had seen it before," said Otho to Isabella. "Do you know the room impressed me in that way, too?"

"It is singular," said Lawrence, "the feeling, that 'all this has been before,' that comes over one at times. I have heard it expressed by a great many people."

"Have you, indeed, ever had this feeling?" asked Isabella.

"Certainly," replied Lawrence; "I say to myself sometimes, 'I have been through all this before!' and I can almost go on to tell what is to come next,—it seems so much a part of my past experience."

"It is strange it should be so with you,—and with you too," she said, turning to Otho.

"Perhaps we are all more alike than we have thought," said Otho.

Otho's mother appeared, and the conversation took another turn.

Isabella did not go to the Willows again, until all the Lester family were summoned there to a large party that Mrs. Blanchard gave. She called it a house-warming, although she had been in the house some time. It was a beautiful evening. A clear moonlight made it as brilliant outside on the lawn as the lights made the house within. There was a band of music stationed under the shrubbery, and those who chose could dance. Those who were more romantic wandered away down the shaded walks, and listened to the dripping of the fountain.

Lawrence and Isabella returned from a walk through the grounds, and stopped a moment on the terrace in front of the house. Just then a dark cloud appeared in the sky, threatening the moon. The wind, too, was rising, and made a motion among the leaves of the trees.

"Do you remember," asked Lawrence, "that child's story of the Fisherman and his Wife? how the fisherman went down to the sea-shore, and cried out,—

'O man of the sea.
Come listen to me!
For Alice, my wife,
The plague of my life,
Has sent me to beg a boon of thee!'

The sea muttered and roared;—do you remember? There was always something impressive to me in the descriptions, in the old story, of the changes in the sea, and of the tempest that rose up, more and more fearful, as the fisherman's wife grew more ambitious and more and more grasping in her desires, each time that the fisherman went down to the sea-shore. I believe my first impression of the sea came from that. The coming on of a storm is always associated with it. I always fancy that it is bringing with it something beside the tempest,—that there is something ruinous behind it."

"That is more fanciful than you usually are," said Isabella; "but, alas! I cannot remember your story, for I never read it."

"That is where your education and Celia's was fearfully neglected," said Lawrence; "you were not brought up on fairy stories and Mother Goose. You have not needed the first, as Celia has; but Mother Goose would have given a tone to your way of thinking, that is certainly wanting."

A little while afterwards, Isabella stood upon the balcony steps leading from the drawing-room. Otho was with her. The threatening clouds had driven almost every one into the house. There was distant thunder and lightning; but through the cloud-rifts, now and then, the moonlight streamed down. Isabella and Otho had been talking earnestly,—so earnestly, that they were quite unobservant of the coming storm, of the strange lurid light that hung around.

"It is strange that this should take place here!" said Isabella,—"that just here I should learn that you love me! Strange that my destiny should be completed in this spot!"

"And this spot has its strange associations with me," said Otho, "of which I must some time speak to you. But now I can think only of the present. Now, for the first time, do I feel what life is,—now that you have promised to be mine!"

Otho was interrupted by a sudden cry. He turned to find his mother standing behind him.

"You are here with Isabella! she has promised herself to you!" she exclaimed. "It is a fatality, a terrible fatality! Listen, Isabella! You are the Queen of the Red Chessmen; and he, Otho, is the King of the White Chessmen,—and I, their Queen. Can there be two queens? Can there be a marriage between two hostile families? Do you not see, if there were a marriage between the Reds and the Whites, there were no game? Look! I have found our old prison! The pieces would all be here,—but we, we are missing! Would you return to the imprisonment of this poor box,—to your old mimic life? No, my children, go back! Isabella, marry this Lawrence Egerton, who loves you. You will find what life is, then. Leave Otho, that he may find this same life also."

Isabella stood motionless.

"Otho, the White Prince! Alas! where is my hatred? But life without him! Even stagnation were better! I must needs be captive to the White Prince!"

She stretched out her hand to Otho. He seized it passionately. At this moment there was a grand crash of thunder. A gust of wind extinguished at once all the lights in the drawing-room. The terrified guests hurried into the hall, into the other rooms.

"The lightning must have struck the house!" they exclaimed.

A heavy rain followed; then all was still. Everybody began to recover his spirits. The servants relighted the candles. The drawing-room was found untenanted. It was time to go; yet there was a constraint upon all the party, who were eager to find their hostess and bid her good-bye.

But the hostess could not be found! Isabella and Otho, too, were missing! The Doctor and Lawrence went everywhere, calling for them, seeking them in the house, in the grounds. They were nowhere to be found,—neither that night, nor the next day, nor ever afterwards!

The Doctor found in the balcony a box of chessmen fallen down. It was nearly filled; but the red queen, and the white king and queen, were lying at a little distance. In the box was the red king, his crown fallen from his head, himself broken in pieces. The Doctor took up the red queen, and carried it home.

"Are you crazy?" asked his wife. "What are you going to do with that red queen?"

But the Doctor placed the figure on his study-table, and often gazed at it wistfully.

Whenever, afterwards, as was often the case, any one suggested a new theory to account for the mysterious disappearance of Isabella and the Blanchards, the Doctor looked at the carved image on his table and was silent.

1858

# EDWARD EVERETT HALE

(1822–1909)

---

## *The Man Without a Country*

I SUPPOSE that very few casual readers of the New York Herald of August 13th observed, in an obscure corner, among the "Deaths," the announcement,—

"NOLAN. Died, on board U. S. Corvette Levant, Lat. 2° 11' S., Long. 131° W., on the 11th of May, PHILIP NOLAN."

I happened to observe it, because I was stranded at the old Mission-House in Mackinaw, waiting for a Lake-Superior steamer which did not choose to come, and I was devouring to the very stubble all the current literature I could get hold of, even down to the deaths and marriages in the Herald. My memory for names and people is good, and the reader will see, as he goes on, that I had reason enough to remember Philip Nolan. There are hundreds of readers who would have paused at that announcement, if the officer of the Levant who reported it had chosen to make it thus:—"Died, May 11th, THE MAN WITHOUT A COUNTRY." For it was as "The Man without a Country" that poor Philip Nolan had generally been known by the officers who had him in charge during some fifty years, as, indeed, by all the men who sailed under them. I dare say there is many a man who has taken wine with him once a fortnight, in a three years' cruise, who never knew that his name was "Nolan," or whether the poor wretch had any name at all.

There can now be no possible harm in telling this poor creature's story. Reason enough there has been till now, ever since Madison's administration went out in 1817, for very strict secrecy, the secrecy of honor itself, among the gentlemen of the navy who have had Nolan in successive charge. And certainly it speaks well for the *esprit de corps* of the profession and the personal honor of its members, that to the press this man's story has been wholly unknown,—and, I think, to the country at large also. I have reason to think, from some investigations I made in the Naval Archives when I was attached to the Bureau of Construction, that every official report relating to him was burned when Ross burned the public buildings at Washington. One of the Tuckers, or possibly one of the Watsons, had Nolan in charge at the end of the war; and when, on returning from his cruise, he reported at Washington to one of the Crowninshields,—who was in the Navy Department when he came home,—he found that the Department ignored the whole business. Whether they really knew nothing about it, or whether it was a "*Non mi ricordo*," determined on as a piece of policy, I do not know. But this I do know, that since 1817, and possibly before, no naval officer has mentioned Nolan in his report of a cruise.

But, as I say, there is no need for secrecy any longer. And now the poor creature is dead, it seems to me worth while to tell a little of his story, by way of showing young Americans of to-day what it is to be

A MAN WITHOUT A COUNTRY.

Philip Nolan was as fine a young officer as there was in the "Legion of the West," as the Western division of our army was then called. When Aaron Burr made his first dashing expedition down to New Orleans in 1805, at Fort Massac, or somewhere above on the river, he met, as the Devil would have it, this gay, dashing, bright young fellow, at some dinner-party, I think. Burr marked him, talked to him, walked with him, took him a day or two's voyage in his flat-boat, and, in short, fascinated him. For the next year, barrack-life was very tame to poor Nolan. He occasionally availed of the permission the great man had given him to write to him. Long, high-worded, stilted letters the poor boy wrote and rewrote and copied. But never a line did he have in reply from the gay deceiver. The other boys in the garrison sneered at him, because he sacrificed in this unrequited affection for a politician the time which they devoted to Monongahela, sledge, and high-low-jack. Bourbon, euchre, and poker were still unknown. But one day Nolan had his revenge. This time Burr came down the river, not as an attorney seeking a place for his office, but as a disguised conqueror. He had defeated I know not how many district-attorneys; he had dined at I know not how many public dinners; he had been heralded in I know not how many Weekly Arguses, and it was rumored that he had an army behind him and an empire before him. It was a great day—his arrival—to poor Nolan. Burr had not been at the fort an hour before he sent for him. That evening he asked Nolan to take him out in his skiff, to show him a canebrake or a cotton-wood tree, as he said,—really to seduce him; and by the time the sail was over, Nolan was enlisted body and soul. From that time, though he did not yet know it, he lived as A MAN WITHOUT A COUNTRY.

What Burr meant to do I know no more than you, dear reader. It is none of our business just now. Only, when the grand catastrophe came, and Jefferson and the House of Virginia of that day undertook to break on the wheel all the possible Clarences of the then House of York, by the great treason-trial at Richmond, some of the lesser fry in that distant Mississippi Valley, which was farther from us than Puget's Sound is to-day, introduced the like novelty on their provincial stage, and, to while away the monotony of the summer at Fort Adams, got up, for *spectacles*, a string of court-martials on the officers there. One and another of the colonels and majors were tried, and, to fill out the list, little Nolan, against whom, Heaven knows, there was evidence enough,—that he was sick of the service, had been willing to be false to it, and would have obeyed any order to march any-whither with any one who would follow him, had the order only been signed, "By command of His Exc. A. Burr." The courts dragged on. The big flies escaped,—rightly for all I know. Nolan was proved guilty enough, as I say; yet you and I would never have heard of him, reader, but that, when the president of the court asked him at the close, whether he wished to say anything to show that he had always been faithful to the United States, he cried out, in a fit of frenzy,—

"D—n the United States! I wish I may never hear of the United States again!"

I suppose he did not know how the words shocked old Colonel Morgan, who was holding the court. Half the officers who sat in it had served through the Revolution, and their lives, not to say their necks, had been risked for the very idea which he so cavalierly cursed in his madness. He, on his part, had grown up in the West of those days, in the midst of "Spanish plot," "Orleans plot," and all the rest. He had been educated on a plantation where the finest company was a Spanish officer or a French merchant from Orleans. His education, such as it was, had been perfected in commercial expeditions to Vera Cruz, and I think he told me his father once hired an Englishman to be a private tutor for a winter on the plantation. He had spent half his youth with an older brother, hunting horses in Texas: and, in a word, to him "United States" was scarcely a reality. Yet he had been fed by "United States" for all the years since he had been in the army. He had sworn on his faith as a Christian to be true to "United States." It was "United States" which gave him the uniform he wore, and the sword by his side. Nay, my poor Nolan, it was only because "United States" had picked you out first as one of her own confidential men of honor, that "A. Burr" cared for you a straw more than for the flat-boat men who sailed his ark for him. I do not excuse Nolan; I only explain to the reader why he damned his country, and wished he might never hear her name again.

He never did hear her name but once again. From that moment, September 23, 1807, till the day he died, May 11, 1863, he never heard her name again. For that half century and more he was a man without a country.

Old Morgan, as I said, was terribly shocked. If Nolan had compared George Washington to Benedict Arnold, or had cried, "God save King George," Morgan would not have felt worse. He called the court into his private room, and returned in fifteen minutes, with a face like a sheet, to say,—

"Prisoner, hear the sentence of the Court! The Court decides, subject to the approval of the President, that you never hear the name of the United States again."

Nolan laughed. But nobody else laughed. Old Morgan was too solemn, and the whole room was hushed dead as night for a minute. Even Nolan lost his swagger in a moment. Then Morgan added,—

"Mr. Marshal, take the prisoner to Orleans in an armed boat, and deliver him to the naval commander there."

The Marshal gave his orders and the prisoner was taken out of court.

"Mr. Marshal," continued old Morgan, "see that no one mentions the United States to the prisoner. Mr. Marshal, make my respects to Lieutenant Mitchell at Orleans, and request him to order that no one shall mention the United States to the prisoner while he is on board ship. You will receive your written orders from the officer on duty here this evening. The court is adjourned without day."

I have always supposed that Colonel Morgan himself took the proceedings of the court to Washington City, and explained them to Mr. Jefferson. Certain it is that the President approved them,—certain, that is, if I may believe the men who say they have seen his signature. Before the Nautilus got round from New Orleans to the Northern Atlantic coast with the prisoner on board, the sentence had been approved, and he was a man without a country.

The plan then adopted was substantially the same which was necessarily followed ever after. Perhaps it was suggested by the necessity of sending him by water from Fort Adams and Orleans. The Secretary of the Navy—it must have been the first Crowninshield, though he is a man I do not remember—was requested to put Nolan on board a Government vessel bound on a long cruise, and to direct that he should be only so far confined there as to make it certain that he never saw or heard of the country. We had few long cruises then, and the navy was very much out of favor; and as almost all of this story is traditional, as I have explained, I do not know certainly what his first cruise was. But the commander to whom he was intrusted,—perhaps it was Tingey or Shaw, though I think it was one of the younger men,—we are all old enough now,—regulated the etiquette and the precautions of the affair, and according to his scheme they were carried out, I suppose, till Nolan died.

When I was second officer of the Intrepid, some thirty years after, I saw the original paper of instructions. I have been sorry ever since that I did not copy the whole of it. It ran, however, much in this way:—

"*Washington*," (with the date, which must have been late in 1807.)

"SIR,—You will receive from Lieutenant Neale the person of Philip Nolan, late a Lieutenant in the United States Army.

"This person on his trial by court-martial expressed with an oath the wish that he might 'never hear of the United States again.'

"The Court sentenced him to have his wish fulfilled.

"For the present, the execution of the order is intrusted by the President to this department.

"You will take the prisoner on board your ship, and keep him there with such precautions as shall prevent his escape.

"You will provide him with such quarters, rations, and clothing as would be proper for an officer of his late rank, if he were a passenger on your vessel on the business of his Government.

"The gentlemen on board will make any arrangements agreeable to themselves regarding his society. He is to be exposed to no indignity of any kind, nor is he ever unnecessarily to be reminded that he is a prisoner.

"But under no circumstances is he ever to hear of his country or to see any information regarding it; and you will specially caution all the officers under your command to take care, that in the various indulgences which may be granted, this rule, in which his punishment is involved, shall not be broken.

"It is the intention of the Government that he shall never again see the country which he has disowned. Before the end of your cruise you will receive orders which will give effect to this intention.

"Respectfully yours,
"W. SOUTHARD, for the
Secretary of the Navy."

If I had only preserved the whole of this paper, there would be no break in the beginning of my sketch of this story. For Captain Shaw, if it was he, handed it to his successor in the charge, and he to his, and I suppose the commander of the Levant has it to-day as his authority for keeping this man in this mild custody.

The rule adopted on board the ships on which I have met "the man without a country" was, I think, transmitted from the beginning. No mess liked to have him permanently, because his presence cut off all talk of home or of the prospect of return, of politics or letters, of peace or of war,—cut off more than half the talk men liked to have at sea. But it was always thought too hard that he should never meet the rest of us, except to touch hats, and we finally sank into one system. He was not permitted to talk with the men, unless an officer was by. With officers he had unrestrained intercourse, as far as they and he chose. But he grew shy, though he had favorites: I was one. Then the captain always asked him to dinner on Monday. Every mess in succession took up the invitation in its turn. According to the size of the ship, you had him at your mess more or less often at dinner. His breakfast he ate in his own state-room,—he always had a state-room,—which was where a sentinel or somebody on the watch could see the door. And whatever else he ate or drank, he ate or drank alone. Sometimes, when the marines or sailors had any special jollification, they were permitted to invite "Plain-Buttons," as they called him. Then Nolan was sent with some officer, and the men were forbidden to speak of home while he was there. I believe the theory was that the sight of his punishment did them good. They called him "Plain-Buttons," because, while he always chose to wear a regulation army-uniform, he was not permitted to wear the army-button, for the reason that it bore either the initials or the insignia of the country he had disowned.

I remember, soon after I joined the navy, I was on shore with some of the older officers from our ship and from the Brandywine, which we had met at Alexandria. We had leave to make a party and go up to Cairo and the Pyramids. As we jogged along, (you went on donkeys then,) some of the gentlemen (we boys called them "Dons," but the phrase was long since changed) fell to talking about Nolan, and some one told the system which was adopted from the first about his books and other reading. As he was almost never permitted to go on shore, even though the vessel lay in port for months, his time, at the best, hung heavy; and everybody was permitted to lend him books, if they were not published in America and made no allusion to it. These were common enough in the old days, when people in the other hemisphere talked of the United States as little as we do of Paraguay. He had almost all the foreign papers that came into the ship, sooner or later; only somebody must go over them first, and cut out any advertisement or stray paragraph that alluded to America. This was a little cruel sometimes, when the back of what was cut out might be as innocent as Hesiod. Right in the midst of one of Napoleon's battles, or one of Canning's speeches, poor Nolan would find a great hole, because on the back of the page of that paper there had been an advertisement of a packet for New York, or a scrap from the President's message. I say this was the first time I ever heard of this plan, which afterwards I had enough, and more than enough, to do with. I remember it, because poor Phillips, who was of the party, as soon as the allusion to reading was made, told a story of something which happened at the Cape of Good Hope on Nolan's first voyage; and it is the only thing I ever knew of that voyage. They had touched at the Cape, and had done the civil thing with the English Admiral and the fleet, and then, leaving for a long cruise up the Indian Ocean, Phillips had borrowed a lot of English books from an officer, which, in those days, as indeed in these, was quite a windfall. Among them, as the Devil would order, was the "Lay of the Last Minstrel," which they had all of them heard of, but which most of them had never seen. I think it could not have been published long. Well, nobody thought there could be any risk of anything national in that, though Phillips swore old Shaw had cut out the "Tempest" from Shakespeare before he let Nolan have it, because he said "the Bermudas ought to be ours, and, by Jove, should be one day." So Nolan was permitted to join the circle one afternoon when a lot of them sat on deck smoking and reading aloud. People do not do such things so often now; but when I was young we got rid of a great deal of time so. Well, so it happened that in his turn Nolan took the book and read to the others; and he read very well, as I know. Nobody in the circle knew a line of the poem, only it was all magic and Border chivalry, and was ten thousand years ago. Poor Nolan read steadily through the fifth canto, stopped a minute and drank something, and then began, without a thought of what was coming,—

> "Breathes there the man, with soul so dead,
> Who never to himself hath said,"—

It seems impossible to us that anybody ever heard this for the first time; but all these fellows did then, and poor Nolan himself went on, still unconsciously or mechanically,—

> "This is my own, my native land!"

Then they all saw something was to pay; but he expected to get through, I suppose, turned a little pale, but plunged on,—

> "Whose heart hath ne'er within him burned,
> As home his footsteps he hath turned
> From wandering on a foreign strand?—
> If such there breathe, go, mark him well."

By this time the men were all beside themselves, wishing there was any way to make him turn over two pages; but he had not quite presence of mind for that; he gagged a little, colored crimson, and staggered on,—

> "For him no minstrel raptures swell;
> High though his titles, proud his name,
> Boundless his wealth as wish can claim,
> Despite these titles, power, and pelf,
> The wretch, concentred all in self,"—

and here the poor fellow choked, could not go on, but started up, swung the book into the sea, vanished into his state-room, "and by Jove," said Phillips, "we did not see him for two months again. And I had to make up some beggarly story to that English surgeon why I did not return his Walter Scott to him."

That story shows about the time when Nolan's braggadocio must have broken down. At first, they said, he took a very high tone, considered his imprisonment a mere farce, affected to enjoy the voyage, and all that; but Phillips said that after he came out of his state-room he never was the same man again. He never read aloud again, unless it was the Bible or Shakespeare, or something else he was sure of. But it was not that merely. He never entered in with the other young men exactly as a companion again. He was always shy afterwards, when I knew him,—very seldom spoke, unless he was spoken to, except to a very few friends. He lighted up occasionally,—I remember late in his life hearing him fairly eloquent on something which had been suggested to him by one of Fléchier's sermons,—but generally he had the nervous, tired look of a heart-wounded man.

When Captain Shaw was coming home,—if, as I say, it was Shaw,—rather to the surprise of everybody they made one of the Windward Islands, and lay off and on for nearly a week. The boys said the officers were sick of salt-junk, and meant to have turtle-soup before they came home. But after several days the Warren came to the same rendezvous; they exchanged signals; she sent to Phillips and these homeward-bound men letters and papers, and told them she was outward-bound, perhaps to the Mediterranean, and took poor Nolan and his traps on the boat back to try his second cruise. He looked very blank when he was told to get ready to join her. He had known enough of the signs of the sky to know that till that moment he was going "home." But this was a distinct evidence of something he had not thought of, perhaps,—that there was no going home for him, even to a prison. And this was the first of some twenty such transfers, which brought him sooner or later into half our best vessels, but which kept him all his life at least some hundred miles from the country he had hoped he might never hear of again.

It may have been on that second cruise,—it was once when he was up the Mediterranean,—that Mrs. Graff, the celebrated Southern beauty of those days, danced with him. They had been lying a long time in the Bay of Naples, and the officers were very intimate in the English fleet, and there had been great festivities, and our men thought they must give a great ball on board the ship. How they ever did it on board the Warren I am sure I do not know. Perhaps it was not the Warren, or perhaps ladies did not take up so much room as they do now. They wanted to use Nolan's state-room for something, and they hated to do it without asking him to the ball; so the captain said they might ask him, if they would be responsible that he did not talk with the wrong people, "who would give him intelligence." So the dance went on, the finest party that had ever been known, I dare say; for I never heard of a man-of-war ball that was not. For ladies they had the family of the American consul, one or two travellers who had adventured so far, and a nice bevy of English girls and matrons, perhaps Lady Hamilton herself.

Well, different officers relieved each other in standing and talking with Nolan in a friendly way, so as to be sure that nobody else spoke to him. The dancing went on with spirit, and after a while even the fellows who took this honorary guard of Nolan ceased to fear any *contre-temps*. Only when some English lady—Lady Hamilton, as I said, perhaps—called for a set of "American dances," an odd thing happened. Everybody then danced contra-dances. The black band, nothing loath, conferred as to what "American dances" were, and started off with "Virginia Reel," which they followed with "Money-Musk," which, in its turn in those days, should have been followed by "The Old Thirteen." But just as Dick, the leader, tapped for his fiddles to begin, and bent forward, about to say, in true negro state, "'The Old Thirteen,' gentlemen and ladies!" as he had said "'Virginny Reel,' if you please!" and "'Money-Musk,' if you please!" the captain's boy tapped him on the shoulder, whispered to him, and he did not announce the name of the dance; he merely bowed, began on the air, and they all fell to,—the officers teaching the English girls the figure, but not telling them why it had no name.

But that is not the story I started to tell.—As the dancing went on, Nolan and our fellows all got at ease, as I said,—so much so, that it seemed quite natural for him to bow to that splendid Mrs. Graff, and say,—

"I hope you have not forgotten me, Miss Rutledge. Shall I have the honor of dancing?"

He did it so quickly, that Fellows, who was by him, could not hinder him. She laughed, and said,—

"I am not Miss Rutledge any longer, Mr. Nolan; but I will dance all the same," just nodded to Fellows, as if to say he must leave Mr. Nolan to her, and led him off to the place where the dance was forming.

Nolan thought he had got his chance. He had known her at Philadelphia, and at other places had met her, and this was a Godsend. You could not talk in contra-dances, as you do in cotillons, or even in the pauses of waltzing; but there were chances for tongues and sounds, as well as for eyes and blushes. He began with her travels, and Europe, and Vesuvius, and the French; and then, when they had worked down, and had that long talking-time at the bottom of the set, he said, boldly,—a little pale, she said, as she told me the story, years after,—

"And what do you hear from home, Mrs. Graff?"

And that splendid creature looked through him. Jove! how she must have looked through him!

"Home!! Mr. Nolan!!! I thought you were the man who never wanted to hear of home again!"—and she walked directly up the deck to her husband, and left poor Nolan alone, as he always was.—He did not dance again.

I cannot give any history of him in order; nobody can now; and, indeed, I am not trying to. These are the traditions, which I sort out, as I believe them, from the myths which have been told about this man for forty years. The lies that have been told about him are legion. The fellows used to say he was the "Iron Mask"; and poor George Pons went to his grave in the belief that this was the author of "Junius," who was being punished for his celebrated libel on Thomas Jefferson. Pons was not very strong in the historical line. A happier story than either of these I have told is of the War. That came along soon after. I have heard this affair told in three or four ways,—and, indeed, it may have happened more than once. But which ship it was on I cannot tell. However, in one, at least, of the great frigate-duels with the English, in which the navy was really baptized, it happened that a round-shot from the enemy entered one of our ports square, and took right down the officer of the gun himself, and almost every man of the gun's crew. Now you may say what you choose about courage, but that is not a nice thing to see. But, as the men who were not killed picked themselves up, and as they and the surgeon's people were carrying off the bodies, there appeared Nolan, in his shirt-sleeves, with the rammer in his hand, and, just as if he had been the officer, told them off with authority,—who should go to the cockpit with the wounded men, who should stay with him,—perfectly cheery, and with that way which makes men feel sure all is right and is going to be right. And he finished loading the gun with his own hands, aimed it, and bade the men fire. And there he stayed, captain of that gun, keeping those fellows in spirits, till the enemy struck,—sitting on the carriage while the gun was cooling, though he was exposed all the time,—showing them easier ways to handle heavy shot,—making the raw hands laugh at their own blunders,—and when the gun cooled again, getting it loaded and fired twice as often as any other gun on the ship. The captain walked forward by way of encouraging the men, and Nolan touched his hat and said,—

"I am showing them how we do this in the artillery, sir."

And this is the part of the story where all the legends agree; that the Commodore said,—

"I see you do, and I thank you, sir; and I shall never forget this day, sir, and you never shall, sir."

And after the whole thing was over, and he had the Englishman's sword, in the midst of the state and ceremony of the quarter-deck, he said,—

"Where is Mr. Nolan? Ask Mr. Nolan to come here."

And when Nolan came, the captain said,—

"Mr. Nolan, we are all very grateful to you to-day; you are one of us to-day; you will be named in the despatches."

And then the old man took off his own sword of ceremony, and gave it to Nolan, and made him put it on. The man told me this who saw it. Nolan cried like a baby, and well he might. He had not worn a sword since that infernal day at Fort Adams. But always afterwards, on occasions of ceremony, he wore that quaint old French sword of the Commodore's.

The captain did mention him in the despatches. It was always said he asked that he might be pardoned. He wrote a special letter to the Secretary of War. But nothing ever came of it. As I said, that was about the time when they began to ignore the whole transaction at Washington, and when Nolan's imprisonment began to carry itself on because there was nobody to stop it without any new orders from home.

I have heard it said that he was with Porter when he took possession of the Nukahiwa Islands. Not this Porter, you know, but old Porter, his father, Essex Porter,—that is, the old Essex Porter, not this Essex. As an artillery officer, who had seen service in the West, Nolan knew more about fortifications, embrasures, ravelins, stockades, and all that, than any of them did; and he worked with a right good-will in fixing that battery all right. I have always thought it was a pity Porter did not leave him in command there with Gamble. That would have settled all the question about his punishment. We should have kept the islands, and at this moment we should have one station in the Pacific Ocean. Our French friends, too, when they wanted this little watering-place, would have found it was preoccupied. But Madison and the Virginians, of course, flung all that away.

All that was near fifty years ago. If Nolan was thirty then, he must have been near eighty when he died. He looked sixty when he was forty. But he never seemed to me to change a hair afterwards. As I imagine his life, from what I have seen and heard of it, he must have been in every sea, and yet almost never on land. He must have known, in a formal way, more officers in our service than any man living knows. He told me once, with a grave smile, that no man in the world lived so methodical a life as he. "You know the boys say I am the Iron Mask, and you know how busy he was." He said it did not do for any one to try to read all the time, more than to do anything else all the time; but that he read just five hours a day. "Then," he said, "I keep up my note-books, writing in them at such and such hours from what I have been reading; and I include in these my scrap-books." These were very curious indeed. He had six or eight, of different subjects. There was one of History, one of Natural Science, one which he called "Odds and Ends." But they were not merely books of extracts from newspapers. They had bits of plants and ribbons, shells tied on, and carved scraps of bone and wood, which he had taught the men to cut for him, and they were beautifully illustrated. He drew admirably. He had some of the funniest drawings there, and some of the most pathetic, that I have ever seen in my life. I wonder who will have Nolan's scrap-books.

Well, he said his reading and his notes were his profession, and that they took five hours and two hours respectively of each day. "Then," said he, "every man should have a diversion as well as a profession. My Natural History is my diversion." That took two hours a day more. The men used to bring him birds and fish, but on a long cruise he had to satisfy himself with centipedes and cockroaches and such small game. He was the only naturalist I ever met who knew anything about the habits of the house-fly and the mosquito. All those people can tell you whether they are *Lepidoptera* or *Steptopotera*; but as for telling how you can get rid of them, or how they get away from you when you strike them,—why, Linnæus knew as little of that as John Foy the idiot did. These nine hours made Nolan's regular daily "occupation." The rest of the time he talked or walked. Till he grew very old, he went aloft a great deal. He always kept up his exercise; and I never heard that he was ill. If any other man was ill, he was the kindest nurse in the world; and he knew more than half the surgeons do. Then if anybody was sick or died, or if the captain wanted him to on any other occasion, he was always ready to read prayers. I have said that he read beautifully.

My own acquaintance with Philip Nolan began six or eight years after the War, on my first voyage after I was appointed a midshipman. It was in the first days after our Slave-Trade treaty, while the Reigning House, which was still the House of Virginia, had still a sort of sentimentalism about the suppression of the horrors of the Middle Passage, and something was sometimes done that way. We were in the South Atlantic on that business. From the time I joined, I believe I thought Nolan was a sort of lay chaplain,—a chaplain with a blue coat. I never asked about him. Everything in the ship was strange to me. I knew it was green to ask questions, and I suppose I thought there was a "Plain-Buttons" on every ship. We had him to dine in our mess once a week, and the caution was given that on that day nothing was to be said about home. But if they had told us not to say anything about the planet Mars or the Book of Deuteronomy, I should not have asked why; there were a great many things which seemed to me to have as little reason. I first came to understand anything about "the man without a country" one day when we overhauled a dirty little schooner which had slaves on board. An officer was sent to take charge of her, and, after a few minutes, he sent back his boat to ask that some one might be sent him who could speak Portuguese. We were all looking over the rail when the message came, and we all wished we could interpret, when the captain asked who spoke Portuguese. But none of the officers did; and just as the captain was sending forward to ask if any of the people could, Nolan stepped out and said he should be glad to interpret, if the captain wished, as he understood the language. The captain thanked him, fitted out another boat with him, and in this boat it was my luck to go.

When we got there, it was such a scene as you seldom see, and never want to. Nastiness beyond account, and chaos run loose in the midst of the nastiness. There were not a great many of the negroes; but by way of making what there were understand that they were free, Vaughan had had their hand-cuffs and ankle-cuffs knocked off, and, for convenience' sake, was putting them upon the rascals of the schooner's crew. The negroes were, most of them, out of the hold, and swarming all round the dirty deck, with a central throng surrounding Vaughan and addressing him in every dialect and *patois* of a dialect, from the Zulu click up to the Parisian of Beledeljereed.

As we came on deck, Vaughan looked down from a hogshead, on which he had mounted in desperation, and said,—

"For God's love, is there anybody who can make these wretches understand something? The men gave them rum, and that did not quiet them. I knocked that big fellow down twice, and that did not soothe him. And then I talked Choctaw to all of them together; and I 'll be hanged if they understood that as well as they understood the English."

Nolan said he could speak Portuguese, and one or two fine-looking Kroomen were dragged out, who, as it had been found already, had worked for the Portuguese on the coast at Fernando Po.

"Tell them they are free," said Vaughan; "and tell them that these rascals are to be hanged as soon as we can get rope enough."

Nolan "put that into Spanish,"—that is, he explained it in such Portuguese as the Kroomen could understand, and they in turn to such of the negroes as could understand them. Then there was such a yell of delight, clinching of fists, leaping and dancing, kissing of Nolan's feet, and a general rush made to the hogshead by way of spontaneous worship of Vaughan, as the *deus ex machina* of the occasion.

"Tell them," said Vaughan, well pleased, "that I will take them all to Cape Palmas."

This did not answer so well. Cape Palmas was practically as far from the homes of most of them as New Orleans or Rio Janeiro was; that is, they would be eternally separated from home there. And their interpreters, as we could understand, instantly said, "*Ah, non Palmas*," and began to propose infinite other expedients in most voluble language. Vaughan was rather disappointed at this result of his liberality, and asked Nolan eagerly what they said. The drops stood on poor Nolan's white forehead, as he hushed the men down, and said,—

"He says, 'Not Palmas.' He says, 'Take us home, take us to our own country, take us to our own house, take us to our own pickaninnies and our own women.' He says he has an old father and mother who will die if they do not see him. And this one says he left his people all sick, and paddled down to Fernando to beg the white doctor to come and help them, and that these devils caught him in the bay just in sight of home, and that he has never seen anybody from home since then. And this one says," choked out Nolan, "that he has not heard a word from his home in six months, while he has been locked up in an infernal barracoon."

Vaughan always said he grew gray himself while Nolan struggled through this interpretation. I, who did not understand anything of the passion involved in it, saw that the very elements were melting with fervent heat, and that something was to pay somewhere. Even the negroes themselves stopped howling, as they saw Nolan's agony, and Vaughan's almost equal agony of sympathy. As quick as he could get words, he said,—

"Tell them yes, yes, yes; tell them they shall go to the Mountains of the Moon, if they will. If I sail the schooner through the Great White Desert, they shall go home!"

And after some fashion Nolan said so. And then they all fell to kissing him again, and wanted to rub his nose with theirs.

But he could not stand it long; and getting Vaughan to say he might go back, he beckoned me down into our boat. As we lay back in the stern-sheets and the men gave way, he said to me,—"Youngster, let that show you what it is to be without a family, without a home, and without a country. And if you are ever tempted to say a word or to do a thing that shall put a bar between you and your family, your home, and your country, pray God in His mercy to take you that instant home to His own heaven. Stick by your family, boy; forget you have a self, while you do everything for them. Think of your home, boy; write and send, and talk about it. Let it be nearer and nearer to your thought, the farther you have to travel from it; and rush back to it, when you are free, as that poor black slave is doing now. And for your country, boy," and the words rattled in his throat, "and for that flag," and he pointed to the ship, "never dream a dream but of serving her as she bids you, though the service carry you through a thousand hells. No matter what happens to you, no matter who flatters you or who abuses you, never look at another flag, never let a night pass but you pray God to bless that flag. Remember, boy, that behind all these men you have to do with, behind officers, and government, and people even, there is the Country Herself, your Country, and that you belong to Her as you belong to your own mother.

Stand by Her, boy, as you would stand by your mother, if those devils there had got hold of her to-day!"

I was frightened to death by his calm, hard passion; but I blundered out, that I would, by all that was holy, and that I had never thought of doing anything else. He hardly seemed to hear me; but he did, almost in a whisper, say,—"Oh, if anybody had said so to me when I was of your age!"

I think it was this half-confidence of his, which I never abused, for I never told this story till now, which afterward made us great friends. He was very kind to me. Often he sat up, or even got up, at night, to walk the deck with me, when it was my watch. He explained to me a great deal of my mathematics, and I owe to him my taste for mathematics. He lent me books, and helped me about my reading. He never alluded so directly to his story again; but from one and another officer I have learned, in thirty years, what I am telling. When we parted from him in St. Thomas harbor, at the end of our cruise, I was more sorry than I can tell. I was very glad to meet him again in 1830; and later in life, when I thought I had some influence in Washington, I moved heaven and earth to have him discharged. But it was like getting a ghost out of prison. They pretended there was no such man, and never was such a man. They will say so at the Department now! Perhaps they do not know. It will not be the first thing in the service of which the Department appears to know nothing!

There is a story that Nolan met Burr once on one of our vessels, when a party of Americans came on board in the Mediterranean. But this I believe to be a lie; or, rather, it is a myth, *ben trovato*, involving a tremendous blowing-up with which he sunk Burr,—asking him how he liked to be "without a country." But it is clear, from Burr's life, that nothing of the sort could have happened; and I mention this only as an illustration of the stories which get a-going where there is the least mystery at bottom.

So poor Philip Nolan had his wish fulfilled. I know but one fate more dreadful: it is the fate reserved for those men who shall have one day to exile themselves from their country because they have attempted her ruin, and shall have at the same time to see the prosperity and honor to which she rises when she has rid herself of them and their iniquities. The wish of poor Nolan, as we all learned to call him, not because his punishment was too great, but because his repentance was so clear, was precisely the wish of every Bragg and Beauregard who broke a soldier's oath two years ago, and of every Maury and Barron who broke a sailor's. I do not know how often they have repented. I do know that they have done all that in them lay that they might have no country,—that all the honors, associations, memories, and hopes which belong to "country" might be broken up into little shreds and distributed to the winds. I know, too, that their punishment, as they vegetate through what is left of life to them in wretched Boulognes and Leicester Squares, where they are destined to upbraid each other till they die, will have all the agony of Nolan's, with the added pang that every one who sees them will see them to despise and to execrate them. They will have their wish, like him.

For him, poor fellow, he repented of his folly, and then, like a man, submitted to the fate he had asked for. He never intentionally added to the difficulty or delicacy of the charge of those who had him in hold. Accidents would happen; but they never happened from his fault. Lieutenant Truxton told me, that, when Texas was annexed, there was a careful discussion among the officers, whether they should get hold of Nolan's handsome set of maps, and cut Texas out of it,—from the map of the world and the map of Mexico. The United States had been cut out when the atlas was bought for him. But it was voted, rightly enough, that to do this would be virtually to reveal to him what had happened, or, as Harry Cole said, to make him think Old Burr had succeeded. So it was from no fault of Nolan's that a great botch happened at my own table, when, for a short time, I was in command of the George Washington corvette, on the South-American station. We were lying in the La Plata, and some of the officers, who had been on shore, and had just joined again, were entertaining us with accounts of their misadventures in riding the half-wild horses of Buenos Ayres. Nolan was at table, and was in an unusually bright and talkative mood. Some story of a tumble reminded him of an adventure of his own, when he was catching wild horses in Texas with his brother Stephen, at a time when he must have been quite a boy. He told the story with a good deal of spirit,—so much so, that the silence which often follows a good story hung over the table for an instant, to be broken by Nolan himself. For he asked, perfectly unconsciously,—

"Pray, what has become of Texas? After the Mexicans got their independence, I thought that province of Texas would come forward very fast. It is really one of the finest regions on earth; it is the Italy of this continent. But I have not seen or heard a word of Texas for near twenty years."

There were two Texan officers at the table. The reason he had never heard of Texas was that Texas and her affairs had been painfully cut out of his newspapers since Austin began his settlements; so that, while he read of Honduras and Tamaulipas, and till quite lately, of California,—this virgin province, in which his brother had travelled so far, and, I believe, had died, had ceased to be to him. Waters and Williams, the two Texas men, looked grimly at each other, and tried not to laugh. Edward Morris had his attention attracted by the third link in the chain of the captain's chandelier. Watrous was seized with a convulsion of sneezing. Nolan himself saw that something was to pay, he did not know what. And I, as master of the feast, had to say,—

"Texas is out of the map, Mr. Nolan. Have you seen Captain Back's curious account of Sir Thomas Roe's Welcome?"

After that cruise I never saw Nolan again. I wrote to him at least twice a year, for in that voyage we became even confidentially intimate; but he never wrote to me. The other men tell me that in those fifteen years he *aged* very fast, as well he might indeed, but that he was still the same gentle, uncomplaining, silent sufferer that he ever was, bearing as best he could his self-appointed punishment,—rather less social, perhaps, with new men whom he did not know, but more anxious, apparently, than ever to serve and befriend and teach the boys, some of whom fairly seemed to worship him. And now, it seems, the dear old fellow is dead. He has found a home at last, and a country.

Since writing this, and while considering whether or no I would print it, as a warning to the young Nolans and Vallandighams and Tatnals of to-day of what it is to throw away a country, I have received from Danforth, who is on board the Levant, a letter which gives an account of Nolan's last hours. It removes all my doubts about telling this story.

To understand the first words of the letter, the non-professional reader should remember that after 1817, the position of every officer who had Nolan in charge was one of the greatest delicacy. The government had failed to renew the order of 1807 regarding him. What was a man to do? Should he let him go? What, then, if he were called to account by the Department for violating the order of 1807? Should he keep him? What, then, if Nolan should be liberated some day, and should bring an action for false imprisonment or kidnapping against every man who had had him in charge? I urged and pressed this upon Southard, and I have reason to think that other officers did the same thing. But the Secretary always said, as they so often do at Washington, that there were no special orders to give, and that we must act on our own judgment. That means, "If you succeed, you will be sustained; if you fail, you will be disavowed." Well, as Danforth says, all that is over now, though I do not know but I expose myself to a criminal prosecution on the evidence of the very revelation I am making.

Here is the letter:—

LEVANT, 2° 2′ S. @ 131° W.

"DEAR FRED,—I try to find heart and life to tell you that it is all over with dear old Nolan. I have been with him on this voyage more than I ever was, and I can understand wholly now the way in which you used to speak of the dear old fellow. I could see that he was not strong, but I had no idea the end was so near. The doctor has been watching him very carefully, and yesterday morning came to me and told me that Nolan was not so well, and had not left his state-room,—a thing I never remember before. He had let the doctor come and see him as he lay there,—the first time the doctor had been in the stateroom,—and he said he should like to see me. O dear! do you remember the mysteries we boys used to invent about his room, in the old Intrepid days? Well, I went in, and there, to be sure, the poor fellow lay in his berth, smiling pleasantly as he gave me his hand, but looking very frail. I could not help a glance round, which showed me what a little shrine he had made of the box he was lying in. The stars and stripes were triced up above and around a picture of Washington, and he had painted a majestic eagle, with lightnings blazing from his beak and his foot just clasping the whole globe, which his wings overshadowed. The dear old boy saw my glance, and said, with a sad smile, 'Here, you see, I have a country!' And then he pointed to the foot of his bed, where I had not seen before a great map of the United States, as he had drawn it from memory, and which he had there to look upon as he lay. Quaint, queer old names were on it, in large letters: 'Indiana Territory,' 'Mississippi Territory,' and 'Louisiana Territory,' as I suppose our fathers learned such things: but the old fellow had patched in Texas, too; he had carried his western boundary all the way to the Pacific, but on that shore he had defined nothing.

"'O Danforth,' he said, 'I know I am dying. I cannot get home. Surely you will tell me something now?—Stop! stop! Do not speak till I say what I am sure you know, that there is not in this ship, that there is not in America,—God bless her!—a more loyal man than I. There cannot be a man who loves the old flag as I do, or prays for it as I do, or hopes for it as I do. There are thirty-four stars in it now, Danforth. I thank God for that, though I do not know what their names are. There has never been one taken away: I thank God for that. I know by that, that there has never been any successful Burr. O Danforth, Danforth,' he sighed out, 'how like a wretched night's dream a boy's idea of personal fame or of separate sovereignty seems, when one looks back on it after such a life as mine? But tell me,—tell me something,—tell me everything, Danforth, before I die!'

"Ingham, I swear to you that I felt like a monster that I had not told him everything before. Danger or no danger, delicacy or no delicacy, who was I, that I should have been acting the tyrant all this time over this dear, sainted old man, who had years ago expiated, in his whole manhood's life, the madness of a boy's treason? 'Mr. Nolan,' said I, 'I will tell you everything you ask about. Only, where shall I begin?'

"O the blessed smile that crept over his white face! and he pressed my hand and said, 'God bless you!' 'Tell me their names,' he said, and he pointed to the stars on the flag. 'The last I know is Ohio. My father lived in Kentucky. But I have guessed Michigan and Indiana and Mississippi,—that was where Fort Adams is,—they make twenty. But where are your other fourteen? You have not cut up any of the old ones, I hope?'

"Well, that was not a bad text, and I told him the names in as good order as I could, and he bade me take down his beautiful map and draw them in as I best could with my pencil. He was wild with delight about Texas, told me how his brother died there; he had marked a gold cross where he supposed his brother's grave was; and he had guessed at Texas. Then he was delighted as he saw California and Oregon;—that, he said, he had suspected partly, because he had never been permitted to land on that shore, though the ships were there so much. 'And the men,' said he, laughing, 'brought off a good deal besides furs.' Then he went back—heavens, how far!—to ask about the Chesapeake, and what was done to Barron for surrendering her to the Leopard, and whether Burr ever tried again,—and he ground his teeth with the only passion he showed. But in a moment that was over, and he said, 'God forgive me, for I am sure I forgive him.' Then he asked about the old war,—told me the true story of his serving the gun the day we took the Java,—asked about dear old David Porter, as he called him. Then he settled down more quietly, and very happily, to hear me tell in an hour the history of fifty years.

"How I wished it had been somebody who knew something! But I did as well as I could. I told him of the English war. I told him about Fulton and the steamboat beginning. I told him about old Scott, and Jackson; told him all I could think about the Mississippi, and New Orleans, and Texas, and his own old Kentucky. And do you think, he asked, who was in command of the 'Legion of the West.' I told him it was a very gallant officer named Grant, and that, by our last news, he was about to establish his head-quarters at Vicksburg. Then, 'Where was Vicksburg?' I worked that out on the map; it was about a hundred miles, more or less, above his old Fort Adams; and I thought Fort Adams must be a ruin now. 'It must be at old Vick's plantation,' said he; 'well, that is a change!'

"I tell you Ingham, it was a hard thing to condense the history of half a century into that talk with a sick man. And I do not now know what I told him,—of emigration, and the means of it,—of steamboats, and railroads, and telegraphs,—of inventions, and books, and literature,—of the colleges, and West Point, and the Naval School,—but with the queerest interruptions that ever you heard. You see it was Robinson Crusoe asking all the accumulated questions of fifty-six years!

"I remember he asked, all of a sudden, who was President now; and when I told him, he asked if Old Abe was General Benjamin Lincoln's son. He said he met old General Lincoln, when he was quite a boy himself, at some Indian treaty. I said no, that Old Abe was a Kentuckian like himself, but I could not tell him of what family; he had worked up from the ranks. 'Good for him!' cried Nolan; 'I am glad of that. As I have brooded and wondered, I have thought our danger was in keeping up those regular successions in the first families.' Then I got talking about my visit to Washington. I told him of meeting the Oregon Congressman, Harding; I told him about the Smithsonian, and the Exploring Expedition; I told him about the Capitol, and the statues for the pediment, and Crawford's Liberty, and Greenough's Washington: Ingham, I told him everything I could think of that would show the grandeur of his country and its prosperity; but I could not make up my mouth to tell him a word about this infernal Rebellion!

"And he drank it in, and enjoyed it as I cannot tell you. He grew more and more silent, yet I never thought he was tired or faint. I gave him a glass of water, but he just wet his lips, and told me not to go away. Then he asked me to bring the Presbyterian 'Book of Public Prayer,' which lay there, and said, with a smile, that it would open at the right place,—and so it did. There was his double red mark down the page; and I knelt down and read, and he repeated with me, 'For ourselves and our country, O gracious God, we thank Thee, that notwithstanding our manifold transgressions of Thy holy laws, Thou hast continued to us Thy marvellous kindness,'—and so to the end of that thanksgiving. Then he turned to the end of the same book, and I read the words more familiar to me,—'Most heartily we beseech Thee with Thy favor to behold and bless Thy servant, the President of the United States, and all others in authority,'—and the rest of the Episcopal Collect. 'Danforth,' said he, 'I have repeated those prayers night and morning, it is now fifty-five years.' And then he said he would go to sleep. He bent me down over him and kissed me; and he said,

'Look in my Bible, Danforth, when I am gone.' And I went away.

"But I had no thought it was the end. I thought he was tired and would sleep. I knew he was happy and I wanted him to be alone.

"But in an hour, when the doctor went in gently, he found Nolan had breathed his life away with a smile. He had something pressed close to his lips. It was his father's badge of the Order of the Cincinnati.

"We looked in his Bible, and there was a slip of paper, at the place where he had marked the text,—

"'They desire a country, even a heavenly: wherefore God is not ashamed to be called their God: for he hath prepared for them a city.'

"On this slip of paper he had written,—

"'Bury me in the sea; it has been my home, and I love it. But will not some one set up a stone for my memory at Fort Adams or at Orleans, that my disgrace may not be more than I ought to bear? Say on it,—

"'*In Memory of*

"'PHILIP NOLAN,

"'*Lieutenant in the Army of the United States.*

"'He loved his country as no other man has loved her; but no man deserved less at her hands.'"

1863

# ELIZABETH STODDARD

(1823–1902)

---

## *Lemorne* versus *Huell*

THE TWO MONTHS I spent at Newport with Aunt Eliza Huell, who had been ordered to the sea-side for the benefit of her health, were the months that created all that is dramatic in my destiny. My aunt was troublesome, for she was not only out of health, but in a lawsuit. She wrote to me, for we lived apart, asking me to accompany her—not because she was fond of me, or wished to give me pleasure, but because I was useful in various ways. Mother insisted upon my accepting her invitation, not because she loved her late husband's sister, but because she thought it wise to cotton to her in every particular, for Aunt Eliza was rich, and we—two lone women—were poor.

I gave my music-pupils a longer and earlier vacation than usual, took a week to arrange my wardrobe—for I made my own dresses—and then started for New York, with the five dollars which Aunt Eliza had sent for my fare thither. I arrived at her house in Bond Street at 7 A.M., and found her man James in conversation with the milkman. He informed me that Miss Huell was very bad, and that the housekeeper was still in bed. I supposed that Aunt Eliza was in bed also, but I had hardly entered the house when I heard her bell ring as she only could ring it—with an impatient jerk.

"She wants hot milk," said James, "and the man has just come."

I laid my bonnet down, and went to the kitchen. Saluting the cook, who was an old acquaintance, and who told me that the "divil" had been in the range that morning, I took a pan, into which I poured some milk, and held it over the gaslight till it was hot; then I carried it up to Aunt Eliza.

"Here is your milk, Aunt Eliza. You have sent for me to help you, and I begin with the earliest opportunity."

"I looked for you an hour ago. Ring the bell."

I rang it.

"Your mother is well, I suppose. She would have sent you, though, had she been sick in bed."

"She has done so. She thinks better of my coming than I do."

The housekeeper, Mrs. Roll, came in, and Aunt Eliza politely requested her to have breakfast for her niece as soon as possible.

"I do not go down of mornings yet," said Aunt Eliza, "but Mrs. Roll presides. See that the coffee is good, Roll."

"It is good generally, Miss Huell."

"You see that Margaret brought me my milk."

"Ahem!" said Mrs. Roll, marching out.

At the beginning of each visit to Aunt Eliza I was in the habit of dwelling on the contrast between her way of living and ours. We lived from "hand to mouth." Every thing about her wore a hereditary air; for she lived in my grandfather's house, and it was the same as in his day. If I was at home when these contrasts occurred to me I should have felt angry; as it was, I felt them as in a dream—the china, the silver, the old furniture, and the excellent fare soothed me.

In the middle of the day Aunt Eliza came down stairs, and after she had received a visit from her doctor, decided to go to Newport on Saturday. It was Wednesday; and I could, if I chose, make any addition to my wardrobe. I had none to make, I informed her. What were my dresses?—had I a black silk? she asked. I had no black silk, and thought one would be unnecessary for hot weather.

"Who ever heard of a girl of twenty-four having no black silk! You have slimsy muslins, I dare say?"

"Yes."

"And you like them?"

"For present wear."

That afternoon she sent Mrs. Roll out, who returned with a splendid heavy silk for me, which Aunt Eliza said should be made before Saturday, and it was. I went to a fashionable dressmaker of her recommending, and on Friday it came home, beautifully made and trimmed with real lace.

"Even the Pushers could find no fault with this," said Aunt Eliza, turning over the sleeves and smoothing the lace. Somehow she smuggled into the house a white straw-bonnet, with white roses; also a handsome mantilla. She held the bonnet before me with a nod, and deposited it again in the box, which made a part of the luggage for Newport.

On Sunday morning we arrived in Newport, and went to a quiet hotel in the town. James was with us, but Mrs. Roll was left in Bond Street, in charge of the household. Monday was spent in an endeavor to make an arrangement regarding the hire of a coach and coachman. Several livery-stable keepers were in attendance, but nothing was settled, till I suggested that Aunt Eliza should send for her own carriage. James was sent back the next day, and returned on Thursday with coach, horses, and William her coachman. That matter being finished, and the trunks being unpacked, she decided to take her first bath in the sea, expecting me to support her through the trying ordeal of the surf. As we were returning from the beach we met a carriage containing a number of persons with a family resemblance.

When Aunt Eliza saw them she angrily exclaimed, "Am I to see those Uxbridges every day?"

Of the Uxbridges this much I knew—that the two brothers Uxbridge were the lawyers of her opponents in the lawsuit which had existed three or four years. I had never felt any interest in it, though I knew that it was concerning a tract of ground in the city which had belonged to my grandfather, and which had, since his day, become very valuable. Litigation was a habit of the Huell family. So the sight of the Uxbridge family did not agitate me as it did Aunt Eliza.

"The sly, methodical dogs! but I shall beat Lemorne yet!"

"How will you amuse yourself then, aunt?"

"I'll adopt some boys to inherit what I shall save from his clutches."

The bath fatigued her so she remained in her room for the rest of the day; but she kept me busy with a hundred trifles. I wrote for her, computed interest, studied out bills of fare, till four o'clock came, and with it a fog. Nevertheless I must ride on the Avenue, and the carriage was ordered.

"Wear your silk, Margaret; it will just about last your visit through—the fog will use it up."

"I am glad of it," I answered.

"You will ride every day. Wear the bonnet I bought for you also."

"Certainly; but won't that go quicker in the fog than the dress?"

"Maybe; but wear it."

I rode every day afterward, from four to six, in the black silk, the mantilla, and the white straw. When Aunt Eliza went she was so on the alert for the Uxbridge family carriage that she could have had little enjoyment of the ride. Rocks never were a passion with her, she said, nor promontories, chasms, or sand. She came to Newport to be washed with salt-water; when she had washed up to the doctor's prescription she should leave, as ignorant of the peculiar pleasures of Newport as when she arrived. She had no fancy for its conglomerate societies, its literary cottages, its parvenue suits of rooms, its saloon habits, and its bathing herds.

I considered the rides a part of the contract of what was expected in my two months' performance. I did not dream that I was enjoying them, any more than I supposed myself to be enjoying a sea-bath while pulling Aunt Eliza to and fro in the surf. Nothing in the life around me stirred me, nothing in nature attracted me. I liked the fog; somehow it seemed to emanate from me instead of rolling up from the ocean, and to represent me. Whether I went alone or not, the coachman was ordered to drive a certain round; after that I could extend the ride in whatever direction I pleased, but I always said, "Any where, William." One afternoon, which happened to be a bright one, I was riding on the road which led to the glen, when I heard the screaming of a flock of geese which were waddling across the path in front of the horses. I started, for I was asleep probably, and, looking forward, saw the Uxbridge carriage, filled with ladies and children, coming toward me; and by it rode a gentleman on horseback. His horse was rearing among the hissing geese, but neither horse nor geese appeared to engage him; his eyes were fixed upon me. The horse swerved so near that its long mane almost brushed against me. By an irresistible impulse I laid my ungloved hand upon it, but did not look at the rider. Carriage and horseman passed on, and William resumed his pace. A vague idea took possession of me that I had seen the horseman before on my various drives. I had a vision of a man galloping on a black horse out of the fog, and into it again. I was very sure, however, that I had never seen him on so pleasant a day as this! William did not bring his horses to time; it was after six when I went into Aunt Eliza's parlor, and found her impatient for her tea and toast. She was crosser than the occasion warranted; but I understood it when she gave me the outlines of a letter she desired me to write to her lawyer in New York. Something had turned up, he had written her; the Uxbridges believed that they had ferreted out what would go against her. I told her that I had met the Uxbridge carriage.

"One of them is in New York; how else could they be giving me trouble just now?"

"There was a gentleman on horseback beside the carriage."

"Did he look mean and cunning?"

"He did not wear his legal beaver up, I think; but he rode a fine horse and sat it well."

"A lawyer on horseback should, like the beggar of the adage, ride to the devil."

"Your business now is the 'Lemorne?'"

"You know it is."

"I did not know but that you had found something besides to litigate."

"It must have been Edward Uxbridge that you saw. He is the brain of the firm."

"You expect Mr. Van Horn?"

"Oh, he must come; I can not be writing letters."

We had been in Newport two weeks when Mr. Van Horn, Aunt Eliza's lawyer, came. He said that he would see Mr. Edward Uxbridge. Between them they might delay a term, which he thought would be best. "Would Miss Huell ever be ready for a compromise?" he jestingly asked.

"Are you suspicious?" she inquired.

"No; but the Uxbridge chaps are clever."

He dined with us; and at four o'clock Aunt Eliza graciously asked him to take a seat in the carriage with me, making some excuse for not going herself.

"Hullo!" said Mr. Van Horn when we had reached the country road, "there's Uxbridge now." And he waved his hand to him.

It was indeed the black horse and the same rider that I had met. He reined up beside us, and shook hands with Mr. Van Horn.

"We are required to answer this new complaint?" said Mr. Van Horn.

Mr. Uxbridge nodded.

"And after that the judgment?"

Mr. Uxbridge laughed.

"I wish that certain gore of land had been sunk instead of being mapped in 1835."

"The surveyor did his business well enough, I am sure."

They talked together in a low voice for a few minutes, and then Mr. Van Horn leaned back in his seat again. "Allow me," he said, "to introduce you, Uxbridge, to Miss Margaret Huell, Miss Huell's niece. Huell *vs.* Brown, you know," he added, in an explanatory tone; for I was Huell *vs.* Brown's daughter.

"Oh!" said Mr. Uxbridge, bowing, and looking at me gravely. I looked at him also; he was a pale, stern-looking man, and forty years old certainly. I derived the impression at once that he had a domineering disposition, perhaps from the way in which he controlled his horse.

"Nice beast that," said Mr. Van Horn.

"Yes," he answered, laying his hand on its mane, so that the action brought immediately to my mind the recollection that I had done so too. I would not meet his eye again, however.

"How long shall you remain, Uxbridge?"

"I don't know. You are not interested in the lawsuit, Miss Huell?" he said, putting on his hat.

"Not in the least; nothing of mine is involved."

"We'll gain it for your portion yet, Miss Margaret," said Mr. Van Horn, nodding to Mr. Uxbridge, and bidding William drive on. He returned the next day, and we settled into the routine of hotel life. A few mornings after, she sent me to a matinée, which was given by some of the Opera people, who were in Newport strengthening the larynx with applications of brine. When the concert was half over, and the audience were making the usual hum and stir, I saw Mr. Uxbridge against a pillar, with his hands incased in pearl-colored gloves, and holding a shiny hat. He turned half away when he caught my eye, and then darted toward me.

"You have not been much more interested in the music than you are in the lawsuit," he said, seating himself beside me.

"The *tutoyer* of the Italian voice is agreeable, however."

"It makes one dreamy."

"A child."

"Yes, a child; not a man nor a woman."

"I teach music. I can not dream over 'one, two, three.'"

"*You*—a music teacher!"

"For six years."

I was aware that he looked at me from head to foot, and I picked at the lace on my invariable black silk; but what did it matter whether I owned that I was a genteel pauper, representing my aunt's position for two months, or not?

"Where?"

"In Waterbury."

"Waterbury differs from Newport."

"I suppose so."

"You suppose!"

A young gentleman sauntered by us, and Mr. Uxbridge called to him to look up the Misses Uxbridge, his nieces, on the other side of the hall.

"Paterfamilias Uxbridge has left his brood in my charge," he said. "I try to do my duty," and he held out a twisted pearl-colored glove, which he had pulled off while talking. What white nervous fingers he had! I thought they might pinch like steel.

"You suppose," he repeated.

"I do not look at Newport."

"Have you observed Waterbury?"

"I observe what is in my sphere."

"Oh!"

He was silent then. The second part of the concert began; but I could not compose myself to appreciation. Either the music or I grew chaotic. So many tumultuous sounds I heard—of hope, doubt, inquiry, melancholy, and desire; or did I feel the emotions which these words express? Or was there magnetism stealing into me from the quiet man beside me? He left me with a bow before the concert was over, and I saw him making his way out of the hall when it was finished.

I had been sent in the carriage, of course; but several carriages were in advance of it before the walk, and I waited there for William to drive up. When he did so, I saw by the oscillatory motion of his head, though his arms and whiphand were perfectly correct, that he was inebriated. It was his first occasion of meeting fellow-coachmen in full dress, and the occasion had proved too much for him. My hand, however, was on the coach door, when I heard Mr. Uxbridge say, at my elbow,

"It is not safe for you."

"Oh, Sir, it is in the programme that I ride home from the concert." And I prepared to step in.

"I shall sit on the box, then."

"But your nieces?"

"They are walking home, squired by a younger knight."

Aunt Eliza would say, I thought, "Needs must when a lawyer drives;" and I concluded to allow him to have his way, telling him that he was taking a great deal of trouble. He thought it would be less if he were allowed to sit inside; both ways were unsafe.

Nothing happened. William drove well from habit; but James was obliged to assist him to dismount. Mr. Uxbridge waited a moment at the door, and so there was quite a little sensation, which spread its ripples till Aunt Eliza was reached. She sent for William, whose only excuse was "dampness."

"Uxbridge knew my carriage, of course," she said, with a complacent voice.

"He knew me," I replied.

"You do not look like the Huells."

"I look precisely like the young woman to whom he was introduced by Mr. Van Horn."

"Oh ho!"

"He thought it unsafe for me to come alone under William's charge."

"Ah ha!"

No more was said on the subject of his coming home with me. Aunt Eliza had several fits of musing in the course of the evening while I read aloud to her, which had no connection with the subject of the book. As I put it down she said that it would be well for me to go to church the next day. I acquiesced, but remarked that my piety would not require the carriage, and that I preferred to walk. Besides, it would be well for William and James to attend divine service. She could not spare James, and thought William had better clean the harness, by way of penance.

The morning proved to be warm and sunny. I donned a muslin dress of home manufacture and my own bonnet, and started for church. I had walked but a few paces when the consciousness of being *free* and *alone* struck me. I halted, looked about me, and concluded that I would not go to church, but walk into the fields. I had no knowledge of the whereabouts of the fields; but I walked straight forward, and after a while came upon some barren fields, cropping with coarse rocks, along which ran a narrow road. I turned into it, and soon saw beyond the rough coast the blue ring of the ocean—vast, silent, and splendid in the sunshine. I found a seat on the ruins of an old stone-wall, among some tangled bushes and briers. There being no Aunt Eliza to pull through the surf, and no animated bathers near, I discovered the beauty of the sea, and that I loved it.

Presently I heard the steps of a horse, and, to my astonishment, Mr. Uxbridge rode past. I was glad he did not know me. I watched him as he rode slowly down the road, deep in thought. He let drop the bridle, and the horse stopped, as if accustomed to the circumstance, and pawed the ground gently, or yawed his neck for pastime. Mr. Uxbridge folded his arms and raised his head to look seaward. It seemed to me as if he were about to address the jury. I had dropped so entirely from my observance of the landscape that I jumped when he resumed the bridle and turned his horse to come back. I slipped from my seat to look among the bushes, determined that he should not recognize me; but my attempt was a failure—he did not ride by the second time.

"Miss Huell!" And he jumped from his saddle, slipping his arm through the bridle.

"I am a runaway. What do you think of the Fugitive Slave Bill?"

"I approve of returning property to its owners."

"The sea must have been God's temple first, instead of the groves."

"I believe the Saurians were an Orthodox tribe."

"Did you stop yonder to ponder the sea?"

"I was pondering 'Lemorne *vs.* Huell.'"

He looked at me earnestly, and then gave a tug at the bridle, for his steed was inclined to make a crude repast from the bushes.

"How was it that I did not detect you at once?" he continued.

"My apparel is Waterbury apparel."

"Ah!"

We walked up the road slowly till we came to the end of it; then I stopped for him to understand that I thought it time for him to leave me. He sprang into the saddle.

"Give us good-by!" he said, bringing his horse close to me.

"We are not on equal terms; I feel too humble afoot to salute you."

"Put your foot on the stirrup then."

A leaf stuck in the horse's forelock, and I pulled it off and waved it in token of farewell. A powerful light shot into his eyes when he saw my hand close on the leaf.

"May I come and see you?" he asked, abruptly. "I will."

"I shall say neither 'No' nor 'Yes.'"

He rode on at a quick pace, and I walked homeward, forgetting the sense of liberty I had started with, and proceeded straightway to Aunt Eliza.

"I have not been to church, aunt, but to walk beyond the town; it was not so nominated in the bond, but I went. The taste of freedom was so pleasant that I warn you there is danger of my 'striking.' When will you have done with Newport?"

"I am pleased with Newport now," she answered, with a curious intonation. "I like it."

"I do also."

Her keen eyes sparkled.

"Did you ever like any thing when you were with me before?"

"Never. I will tell you why I like it: because I have met, and shall probably meet, Mr. Uxbridge. I saw him to-day. He asked permission to visit me."

"Let him come."

"He will come."

But we did not see him either at the hotel or when we went abroad. Aunt Eliza rode with me each afternoon, and each morning we went to the beach. She engaged me every moment when at home, and I faithfully performed all my tasks. I clapped to the door on self-investigation—locked it against any analysis or reasoning upon any circumstance connected with Mr. Uxbridge. The only piece of treachery to my code that I was guilty of was the putting of the leaf which I brought home on Sunday between the leaves of that poem whose motto is,

"Mariana in the moated grange."

On Saturday morning, nearly a week after I saw him on my walk, Aunt Eliza proposed that we should go to Turo Street on a shopping excursion; she wanted a cap, and various articles besides. As we went into a large shop I saw Mr. Uxbridge at a counter buying gloves; her quick eye caught sight of him, and she edged away, saying she would look at some goods on the other side; I might wait where I was. As he turned to go out he saw me and stopped.

"I have been in New York since I saw you," he said. "Mr. Lemorne sent for me."

"There is my aunt," I said.

He shrugged his shoulders.

"I shall not go away soon again," he remarked. "I missed Newport greatly."

I made some foolish reply, and kept my eyes on Aunt Eliza, who dawdled unaccountably. He appeared amused, and after a little talk went away.

Aunt Eliza's purchase was a rose-colored moire antique, which she said was to be made for me; for Mrs. Bliss, one of our hotel acquaintances, had offered to chaperon me to the great ball which would come off in a few days, and she had accepted the offer for me.

"There will be no chance for you to take a walk instead," she finished with.

"I can not dance, you know."

"But you will be *there*."

I was sent to a dress-maker of Mrs. Bliss's recommending; but I ordered the dress to be made after my own design, long plain sleeves, and high plain corsage, and requested that it should not be sent home till the evening of the ball. Before it came off Mr. Uxbridge called, and was graciously received by Aunt Eliza, who could be gracious to all except her relatives. I could not but perceive, however, that they watched each other in spite of their lively conversation. To me he was deferential, but went over the ground of our acquaintance as if it had been the most natural thing in the world. But for my life-long habit of never calling in question the behavior of those I came in contact with, and of never expecting any thing different from that I received, I might have wondered over his visit. Every person's individuality was sacred to me, from the fact, perhaps, that my own individuality had never been respected by any person with whom I had any relation—not even by my own mother.

After Mr. Uxbridge went, I asked Aunt Eliza if she thought he looked mean and cunning? She laughed, and replied that she was bound to think that Mr. Lemorne's lawyer could not look otherwise.

When, on the night of the ball, I presented myself in the rose-colored moire antique for her inspection, she raised her eyebrows, but said nothing about it.

"I need not be careful of it, I suppose, aunt?"

"Spill as much wine and ice-cream on it as you like."

In the dressing-room Mrs. Bliss surveyed me.

"I think I like this mass of rose-color," she said. "Your hair comes out in contrast so brilliantly. Why, you have not a single ornament on!"

"It is so easy to dress without."

This was all the conversation we had together during the evening, except when she introduced some acquaintance to fulfill her matronizing duties. As I was no dancer I was left alone most of the time, and amused myself by gliding from window to window along the wall, that it might not be observed that I was a fixed flower. Still I suffered the annoyance of being stared at by wandering squads of young gentlemen, the "curled darlings" of the ball-room. I borrowed Mrs. Bliss's fan in one of her visits for a protection. With that, and the embrasure of a remote window where I finally stationed myself, I hoped to escape further notice. The music of the celebrated band which played between the dances recalled the chorus of spirits which charmed Faust:

"And the fluttering
Ribbons of drapery
Cover the plains,
Cover the bowers,
Where lovers,

Deep in thought,
Give themselves for life."

The voice of Mrs. Bliss broke its spell.

"I bring an old friend, Miss Huell, and he tells me an acquaintance of yours."

It was Mr. Uxbridge.

"I had no thought of meeting you, Miss Huell."

And he coolly took the seat beside me in the window, leaving to Mrs. Bliss the alternative of standing or of going away; she chose the latter.

"I saw you as soon as I came in," he said, "gliding from window to window, like a vessel hugging the shore in a storm."

"With colors at half-mast; I have no dancing partner."

"How many have observed you?"

"Several young gentlemen."

"Moths."

"Oh no, butterflies."

"They must keep away now."

"Are you Rhadamanthus?"

"And Charon, too. I would have you row in the same boat with me."

"Now you are fishing."

"Won't you compliment me. Did I ever look better?"

His evening costume *was* becoming, but he looked pale, and weary, and disturbed. But if we were engaged for a tournament, as his behavior indicated, I must do my best at telling. So I told him that he never looked better, and asked him how I looked. He would look at me presently, he said, and decide. Mrs. Bliss skimmed by us with nods and smiles; as she vanished our eyes followed her, and we talked vaguely on various matters, sounding ourselves and each other. When a furious redowa set in which cut our conversation into rhythm he pushed up the window and said, "Look out."

I turned my face to him to do so, and saw the moon at the full, riding through the strip of sky which our vision commanded. From the moon our eyes fell on each other. After a moment's silence, during which I returned his steadfast gaze, for I could not help it, he said:

"If we understand the impression we make upon each other, what must be said?"

I made no reply, but fanned myself, neither looking at the moon, nor upon the redowa, nor upon any thing.

He took the fan from me.

"Speak of yourself," he said.

"Speak you."

"I am what I seem, a man within your sphere. By all the accidents of position and circumstance suited to it. Have you not learned it?"

"I am not what I seem. I never wore so splendid a dress as this till to-night, and shall not again."

He gave the fan such a twirl that its slender sticks snapped, and it drooped like the broken wing of a bird.

"Mr. Uxbridge, that fan belongs to Mrs. Bliss."

He threw it out of the window.

"You have courage, fidelity, and patience—this character with a passionate soul. I am sure that you have such a soul?"

"I do not know."

"I have fallen in love with you. It happened on the very day when I passed you on the way to the Glen. I never got away from the remembrance of seeing your hand on the mane of my horse."

He waited for me to speak, but I could not; the balance of my mind was gone. Why should this have happened to me—a slave? As it had happened, why did I not feel exultant in the sense of power which the chance for freedom with him should give?

"What is it, Margaret? your face is as sad as death."

"How do you call me 'Margaret?'"

"As I would call my wife—Margaret."

He rose and stood before me to screen my face from observation. I supposed so, and endeavored to stifle my agitation.

"You are better," he said, presently. "Come go with me and get some refreshment." And he beckoned to Mrs. Bliss, who was down the hall with an unwieldy gentleman.

"Will you go to supper now?" she asked.

"We are only waiting for you," Mr. Uxbridge answered, offering me his arm.

When we emerged into the blaze and glitter of the supper-room I sought refuge in the shadow of Mrs. Bliss's companion, for it seemed to me that I had lost my own.

"Drink this Champagne," said Mr. Uxbridge. "Pay no attention to the Colonel on your left; he won't expect it."

"Neither must you."

"Drink."

The Champagne did not prevent me from reflecting on the fact that he had not yet asked whether I loved him.

The spirit chorus again floated through my mind:

"Where lovers,
Deep in thought,
Give themselves for life."

I was not allowed to *give* myself—I was *taken*.

"No heel-taps," he whispered, "to the bottom quaff."

"Take me home, will you?"

"Mrs. Bliss is not ready."

"Tell her that I must go."

He went behind her chair and whispered something, and she nodded to me to go without her.

When her carriage came up, I think he gave the coachman an order to drive home in a round-about way, for we were a long time reaching it. I kept my face to the window, and he made no effort to divert my attention. When we came to a street whose thick rows of trees shut out the moonlight my eager soul longed to leap out into the dark and demand of him his heart, soul, life, for *me*.

I struck him lightly on the shoulder; he seized my hand.

"Oh, I know you, Margaret; you are mine!"

"We are at the hotel."

He sent the carriage back, and said that he would leave me at my aunt's door. He wished that he could see her then. Was it magic that made her open the door before I reached it?

"Have you come on legal business?" she asked him.

"You have divined what I come for."

"Step in, step in; it's very late. I should have been in bed but for neuralgia. Did Mr. Uxbridge come home with you, Margaret?"

"Yes, in Mrs. Bliss's carriage; I wished to come before she was ready to leave."

"Well, Mr. Uxbridge is old enough for your protector, certainly."

"I *am* forty, ma'am."

"Do you want Margaret?"

"I do."

"You know exactly how much is involved in your client's suit?"

"Exactly."

"You know also that his claim is an unjust one."

"Do I?"

"I shall not be poor if I lose; if I gain, Margaret will be rich."

"'Margaret will be rich!'" he repeated, absently.

"What! have you changed your mind respecting the orphans, aunt?"

"She has, and is—nothing," she went on, not heeding my remark. "Her father married below his station; when he died his wife fell back to her place—for he spent his fortune—and there she and Margaret must remain, unless Lemorne is defeated."

"Aunt, for your succinct biography of my position many thanks."

"Sixty thousand dollars," she continued. "Van Horn tells me that, as yet, the firm of Uxbridge Brothers have only an income—no capital."

"It is true," he answered, musingly.

The clock on the mantle struck two.

"A thousand dollars for every year of my life," she said. "You and I, Uxbridge, know the value and beauty of money."

"Yes, there is beauty in money, and"—looking at me—"beauty without it."

"The striking of the clock," I soliloquized, "proves that this scene is not a phantasm."

"Margaret is fatigued," he said, rising. "May I come to-morrow?"

"It is my part only," replied Aunt Eliza, "to see that she is, or is not, Cinderella."

"If you have ever thought of me, aunt, as an individual, you must have seen that I am not averse to ashes."

He held my hand a moment, and then kissed me with a kiss of appropriation.

"He is in love with you," she said, after he had gone. "I think I know him. He has found beauty ignorant of itself; he will teach you to develop it."

The next morning Mr. Uxbridge had an interview with Aunt Eliza before he saw me.

When we were alone I asked him how her eccentricities affected him; he could not but consider her violent, prejudiced, warped, and whimsical. I told him that I had been taught to accept all that she did on this basis. Would this explain to him my silence in regard to her?

"Can you endure to live with her in Bond Street for the present, or would you rather return to Waterbury?"

"She desires my company while she is in Newport only. I have never been with her so long before."

"I understand her. Law is a game, in her estimation, in which cheating can as easily be carried on as at cards."

"Her soul is in this case."

"Her soul is not too large for it. Will you ride this afternoon?"

I promised, of course. From that time till he left Newport we saw each other every day, and though I found little opportunity to express my own peculiar feelings, he comprehended many of my wishes, and all my tastes. I grew fond of him hourly. Had I not reason? Never was friend so considerate, never was lover more devoted.

When he had been gone a few days, Aunt Eliza declared that she was ready to depart from Newport. The rose-colored days were ended! In two days we were on the Sound, coach, horses, servants, and ourselves.

It was the 1st of September when we arrived in Bond Street. A week from that date Samuel Uxbridge, the senior partner of Uxbridge Brothers, went to Europe with his family, and I went to Waterbury, accompanied by Mr. Uxbridge. He consulted mother in regard to our marriage, and appointed it in November. In October Aunt Eliza sent for me to come back to Bond Street and spend a week. She had some fine marking to do, she wrote. While there I noticed a restlessness in her which I had never before observed, and conferred with Mrs. Roll on the matter. "She do be awake nights a deal, and that's the reason," Mrs. Roll said. Her manner was the same in other respects. She said she would not give me any thing for my wedding outfit, but she paid my fare from Waterbury and back.

She could not spare me to go out, she told Mr. Uxbridge, and in consequence I saw little of him while there.

In November we were married. Aunt Eliza was not at the wedding, which was a quiet one. Mr. Uxbridge desired me to remain in Waterbury till spring. He would not decide about taking a house in New York till then; by that time his brother might return, and if possible we would go to Europe for a few months. I acquiesced in all his plans. Indeed I was not consulted; but I was happy—happy in him, and happy in every thing.

The winter passed in waiting for him to come to Waterbury every Saturday; and in the enjoyment of the two days he passed with me. In March Aunt Eliza wrote me that Lemorne was beaten! Van Horn had taken up the whole contents of his snuff-box in her house the evening before in amazement at the turn things had taken.

That night I dreamed of the scene in the hotel at Newport. I heard Aunt Eliza saying, "If I gain, Margaret will be rich." And I heard also the clock strike two. As it struck I said, "*My husband is a scoundrel*," and woke with a start.

1863

# FRANCIS PARKMAN

(1823–1893)

## *The Scalp-Hunter*

### *A Semi-Historical Sketch*

FAR BE IT from me to detract from the fair fame of our ancestors. Least of all, would I cast any reflection on those frontier heroes, the memory of whose exploits lives in the homely chronicles of DRAKE, or in the 'collections' of some Historical Society; or faintly survives in the mouldering pages of some obscure MS. Yet, if truth be told, their valiant deeds were not always achieved under the inspiration of pure patriotism. The backwoodsmen of a century since sometimes hunted Indians from the same motive that urges those of our time to hunt wolves; viz., the bounty on scalps. In the year of which I propose to treat, 1724, the bounty in New-Hampshire was, if my recollections do not fail me, ten pounds; not an eighth part of the sum which peaceful and scrupulous Pennsylvania long afterward offered in the day of her distress, when the savages of the West broke in upon her frontier. How far such measures are consonant with religion and morality, is a question which I gladly leave to be decided by pious philanthropists, who can form no conception of the circumstances that made them necessary; for I propose merely to relate plain facts, and leave reflections and inferences to my betters. Should I be called upon to produce authority for what I say, I am permitted to refer to an ancient manuscript diary, kept by the Rev. PHINEAS W. STONE, of Portsmouth, and preserved in the small but valuable library of the New-Hampshire Fraternity of the Л. Т. This, however, relates merely to the earlier part of our narrative. The remainder must be regarded as of a character somewhat less authentic, as it rests solely on the authority of a tradition preserved by a few old squaws of the St. Francis tribe; one of whom, rendered good-humored and loquacious by the benign influences of a bottle of rum, told the story at a hunting-camp near Lake Megantic.

A party of the tribe just mentioned came in July, 1724, to work their usual butcheries upon the back settlers of New-Hampshire. Eight white men undertook to chastise them, and secure the bounty. The savages were now retiring, which they did with remarkable celerity, and in an unusual direction. The whites plunged into the forests after them. For nearly a fortnight they hung on their rear, unable to find a good opportunity to attack. They traced them past Lake Winnipisiogee; and from the top of Red Mountain saw them cross the beautiful lake beyond, in two canoes, made hastily of bark for the purpose. Again striking their trail, they followed it some twenty miles farther, into the recesses of those wild mountains that stretch from the present town of Conway toward the great father of New-England hills. Meanwhile the savages lost all suspicion of pursuit, as was evident from their careless manner of encamping, and the great profusion of game which the frontiers-men found around their smouldering fires.

One hot afternoon, the party came to the brow of a precipitous hill, looking northward, which commanded a wide prospect of forests and lonely mountains. In all probability there was no human being within the range of a dozen leagues save themselves and their destined prey. In its terrible solitude it was a scene of more than Alpine sublimity; but what chiefly interested the hunters was a smoke that rose dense and distinct through the thick carpet of boughs at the bottom of a deep valley just below them. The afternoon sun was beating powerfully on the cliff where they sat, and filling the sultry air with the resinous odors of the spruce and pine that grew around. They watched till it had sunk behind the bristling firs on the ridge of the western mountain; and then, as the usual crimson hue of an American sunset, which had suffused the whole landscape, turned to a gray obscurity, and the half-starved wolves began to call and reply from opposite hills, they descended and groped their way toward their victims. With great difficulty and danger they managed to surround the fires of the savages. Their motives were none of the most magnanimous, it is true; but one cannot help admiring the hardihood of thus assailing a very superior force in a wilderness whose savage features were of themselves sufficient to fill with awe and terror any but the manliest heart.

It is useless to dwell on the incidents of the ignoble and desperate conflict that followed. The white men had to lie flat on the ground for hours, before the last savage had wrapped himself in his blanket, and lain down. They counted eleven Indians around the two fires. It was now near midnight; the damp air of the forest was very chill, and the fires had sunk to glowing piles of coals, that shed a dim ruddy light on the sleepers, the mossy trunks of the trees, and the thick undergrowth around the spot. The leader of the whites was about to give the signal, when an Indian turned in his sleep, murmured, and finally arose; awakened apparently by the cold. Dropping his blanket, he approached the fire, and stirred the embers with a stick; when a stream of crackling sparks flew upward, illuminating for a moment the distorted boughs and shadowy leaves. This sudden light was answered by a scream so piercing and unearthly, that the ferocious frontiers-men started at their posts; and with a loud flapping of wings among the branches overhead a huge dark bird sailed off into the depths of the forest. The Indian immediately took a handful of tobacco from a pouch by his side, and scattered it on the coals, as an offering to the Great Horned Owl, whose supposed connexion with the divinities of his national mythology procured it this remarkable honor. This was the poor fellow's last act of piety. At that instant, the white men poured upon the sleepers a deadly fire, and bursting in with a fierce shout, beat down those who rose with axes and rifle-butts. Of the eleven, all but two were killed at the camp, or at a short distance from it. One of these two bounded into the dark woods and escaped; the other was soon traced to a neighboring 'windfall,' where no man could follow him, among the decayed trunks and roots and tangled branches. The dogs of the white men, however, soon penetrated into its depths, killed the wounded wretch, and drew him out.

Thus was a deed achieved, of which the reverend gentleman before mentioned speaks in his diary with high praise, as an act of eminent service to God and man. The actors themselves felt well satisfied. Having peeled the trophy from each head, they tossed the carcasses into the bed of a cold and sluggish rivulet, that flowing from the clear springs in the heart of some granite mountain, glided lazily hard by, half hid by fallen trees, decaying logs and mosses, and the abundant vegetation that sprang from the rich forest soil. There they left them to be nibbled by the minute trout that darted in the pure icy waters; while seated around the rekindled fires, they ate the moose-meat which the Indians had left, and refreshed themselves with draughts from their rum-canteens. They ate and drank with the spirits of a party of successful wolf-hunters; and when they laid down, they slept the sound sleep of health and toil.

But the morning brought reflection and regrets. They grumbled over their bad luck. One savage had escaped. The most prominent figure in their group was an old man, who sat on a log, leaning lazily forward, with his elbows on his knees, while he extracted the rich marrow from a thigh-bone of moose with his jack-knife. A little torn straw hat was stuck jauntily on one side of his gray bristly head; his leathery countenance expressed a kind of reckless good-humor, which his present discontent did not wholly banish; though you might see that his features could readily assume the expression of anger and even ferocity. He was venting his wrath and uneasiness through his toothless jaws, in a succession of oaths and injurious expressions, uttered by no means in a surly manner, but in a reckless, boastful spirit, that had survived his youth. This old reprobate was eager for gain; had a keen relish for the chase; and was desirous, moreover, to exhibit his superiority to his fellow sportsmen. These motives combined to produce the resolution he presently expressed, to set out alone, and not rest till he had taken the scalp from the head of the remaining Indian. So, calling his dogs and shouldering his gun, he calmly marched away, without a word of leave-taking on either side; after that cold manner which his countrymen seem to have caught from their extirpated enemies, the aborigines, and which often hides as warm a heart as ever beat in the breast of man. His companions returned with great glory to the settlements, whither we will not follow; but turn to pursue the old man on his adventurous quest.

For four days, the staunch huntsman tracked the game northward, through forests and over mountains. Whatever were his faults, fear was not one of them. Neither the howlings of beasts, nor the deep solitude of his situation, nor any sense of his ferocious purpose, ever disturbed his rest. With his dogs for sentinels, he slept as quietly on a bed of spruce-boughs, to the music of some savage stream, as on the straw of his own frontier cabin.

His hardened muscles were never fatigued, though he struggled from sunrise to sunset through tangled brushwood and obscure ravines; over decaying logs, and the thousand pit-falls and impediments that annoy the forest traveller. His course lay always through the obscurity and dampness of the dense wood; except at times, when he would hear the noise of a stream below him, and emerge from the forest darkness into a beautiful sun-lit vista of trees and glancing waters. At such times, he could see that, as he proceeded, the mountains grew wilder and higher, and closed gradually around him.

Late one afternoon, when he had all day toiled stubbornly on in twilight, and was looking upward to catch glimpses of the bright sky through the leaves, he heard again the sound of water, and by the transparency in the screen of maple saplings before him, he knew the opening was near at hand. In a moment he put aside the slender boughs, and stepped out into the broad stony bed of the Saco, just where it emerges from the Notch of the White Mountains. It was a wild and beautiful scene. The tumbling waters, the long lines of birch trees, maples and beeches that reached their branches over it; the stiff pines that shot up into the air above them; the great pile of granite crags that rose from the woods, bristling with firs, three thousand feet sheer upward; all were tinged with the crimson of approaching evening; all lay in the quiet of the wilderness, which the ripple and murmur of the stream only made more impressive.

The old man did not trouble himself with the scenery. His feelings were those of bitter vexation; for he knew himself close upon his game, and here the savage had taken to the water and thrown his dogs off the scent. He dashed into the wide and shallow stream, and wading up the middle, sent a dog on either bank to search for the lost track. The very first angle he turned showed him his prey, wading naked and unarmed, for he had fled from the massacre without his gun. The old hunter did not repress a cry of fierce exultation, which the sleeping mountains prolonged: then, as the unhappy savage leaped splashing to the bank, he followed close, and set his dogs again on the track. They made the woods resound with their fearful baying: the old man held his gun poised for a shot; and the trio dashed on at a pace at which that tangled wood was never traversed before or since. He often tripped and fell; the thorns and branches tore away fragments of his clothing, and bared his gray head. Twilight soon came on. The old human bloodhound cared for none of these things. At length, suddenly and unexpectedly, he broke out from the woods, upon a broad surface of rocks, stones and gravel, interspersed with stunted bushes; while at a little distance on the right stood a forest of dead trees, bare and white, seeming in the dim light like a host of skeletons. All around towered high mountains, half clothed with shaggy forests; and their precipitous crags, old weather-stains, and scars of avalanches, gave them the aspect of savage desolation. The old hunter scarcely saw them. All that met his eye was the slender figure of the Indian, leaping like a frightened deer toward the base of the mountain on the left. He dashed after him at full speed, over piles of rock and stone, strewn by an ancient avalanche over the narrow valley, where none but a sleep-walker, or such a frantic sportsman, could have passed in safety. It was in the Notch, close to the place where the unfortunate Willeys afterward met their fate.

The game soon began to ascend the mountain, choosing the place where the avalanche had come down, and cut for itself a pathway, resembling, in all but its depth, the bed of a torrent. These mountains are every where channelled with such ravines, which often extend from top to bottom, and seem at a little distance like deep gashes cut in their sides. Most of them expand and grow shallow as they approach the base, where the torrent of earth and stone spread itself over the valley. Such was the case in the present instance. The Indian bounded up; the hunter and dogs followed. The sides of the ravine rapidly approached each other, and grew more abrupt and high; the ascent became steeper and more perilous. A little stream that trickled down the narrow and steep passage-way, and spread itself over the smooth rocks, made the foothold very precarious. The dogs were soon brought up. They stopped at the foot of a deep pitch of the rock, against which they pawed in vain efforts to ascend, and made the rocks echo with their cries. The eager old man climbed on. The sides of the ravine now towered over his head, leaving only a strip of the darkening sky visible between their opposite edges. His efforts soon brought him to a height whence the baying of the dogs sounded up the passage faint and distant. He caught frequent glimpses of the Indian, scrambling on before him; and once, getting a fair sight, he fired. The mountains bellowed back the report; but the Indian climbed on unhurt. Still the old man gained rapidly on him, clenching his jaws together with eagerness and longing.

At length, however, a long reach of the ravine stretched upward in the obscurity before him! He looked, and saw nothing of his prey. Furious with anger and disappointment at the renewed activity of the savage, he pressed on faster than before. A smooth rock, nearly perpendicular, soon arrested his progress. He did not dream of pausing, but began to work his way up the dangerous precipice, with his mind occupied by the sole thought of overtaking and slaying the Indian. With every faculty at its utmost tension, availing himself of every little point and crevice, he did what no man else could have done; he climbed half way up the steep wet face of the rock; but here he was obliged to pause; and for the first time, his blood cooled, and he was conscious of the peril of his situation. He moved his hand to the right and to the left, over the rock, clammy with the spreading water of the little streamlet, and found scarcely a crevice large enough to thrust a finger into, or a projection that a foot could rest against. He looked up; the edge of the precipice was twenty feet above his head. He looked down; there were the sharp projecting angles of the rocky sides of the ravine; and below, all lay in deep blackness, like a bottomless gulf. He tried to descend; but his foot moved vainly from side to side, searching for the place where it had last rested when he was climbing up. To ascend was perilous enough; to descend, impossible. His hair began to bristle. He listened, and heard from below the faint baying of the hounds. Hitherto he had clung to his gun by a sort of instinct, but now he let it drop. The oaken stock struck at the foot of the cliff with a dull shock, and splintered to pieces: there was a pause for an instant, and then came the clanging rattle of the barrel, as it bounded from side to side of the ravine, down the mountain. The old man thought he must soon follow it, and the thought gave him desperation. His alternative was to be dashed to pieces, or to gain the top of the rock; and to this fearful task he applied himself. His success was almost miraculous, as those who have seen the place will confess. He *did* reach the top; but all his limbs were aching with the strong and continued strain of every muscle; the ends of his fingers were worn to the bone; the flesh was rubbed from his knees; and his heart throbbed with a violence that, though unfelt while he was climbing, almost choked him when he laid himself down at the top. Poor wretch! It would have been better for him had he fallen. The level rock he had attained was not eight feet across. Beyond it, rose up another precipice, full sixty feet high, perpendicular, smooth, and wet; while on each side the loftier walls of the ravine destroyed every chance of escape. The old scalp-hunter was caught in his own trap. There was not a civilized man within more than ninety miles.

The Indian had escaped from the ravine at a point where its sides were less precipitous than elsewhere, and the long tough root of a spruce, hanging several yards from the top, helped him in the most dangerous part. He was now safe in the woods, on the surface of the mountain. The eager hunter had passed on, without dreaming that the game had given him the slip.

It is useless to dwell on his fate. In the morning he looked down the frightful gorge in front, and on the cliffs that imprisoned him, to see if no possibility of escape offered; for till then his hardy spirit had not quite despaired. The daylight dispelled every shadow of hope. At the edge of the ravine, a hundred feet over him, his startled eye encountered a human face, peering down upon him from behind a stunted pine that projected over the gulf. It was the Indian, who had seated himself there to exult in the fate of his enemy.

The old man spent two days in his prison. The afternoon of the second day was peculiarly beautiful: the atmosphere had a softness not common in New-England; and while the western mountains seemed enveloped in a blue, transparent haze, the warm sunlight poured full on the rugged slopes to the east. The desolate valley wore the mildest aspect its savage features could put on; like a sleeping warrior dreaming of his home. The evening brought a change. A thunder-gust came up, and in a few moments filled every gully and ravine with foaming waters, and drift-logs driving down to the valley. The old man was swept from his place in an instant, but the watchful Indian found him next morning wedged under a rock; and a week after, his gray hairs were fluttering in the wind from the top of a cabin in the Indian village of St. Francis, by the side of the St. Lawrence.

The Indians, it is well known, believed these mountains the abode of a malignant spirit; and this, they say, was the greeting he gave to the first white man who ever found his way into the Notch. The writer must not be understood to give his authority in support of so loose and frivolous a tradition, thereby putting in jeopardy his reputation as an antiquarian, and—what is of far more consequence than mere personal considerations—misleading, perchance, the unsuspecting reader, who has confided himself to his guidance. It is his duty to remind him that the White Mountains were visited long before, by one Neal, and his party, who found that country 'daunting terrible,' and made all haste to escape from the dismal neighborhood. It is not, however, recorded of this party, nor of any other, prior to 1724, that they visited the defile called the Notch; so that this Indian story may, after all, be entitled to as strict credence as any portion of the narrative whatever.

1845

# FRANCES E. W. HARPER

(1825–1911)

---

## *The Two Offers*

"WHAT IS the matter with you, Laura, this morning? I have been watching you this hour, and in that time you have commenced a half dozen letters and torn them all up. What matter of such grave moment is puzzling your dear little head, that you do not know how to decide?"

"Well, it is an important matter: I have two offers for marriage, and I do not know which to choose."

"I should accept neither, or to say the least, not at present."

"Why not?"

"Because I think a woman who is undecided between two offers, has not love enough for either to make a choice; and in that very hesitation, indecision, she has a reason to pause and seriously reflect, lest her marriage, instead of being an affinity of souls or a union of hearts, should only be a mere matter of bargain and sale, or an affair of convenience and selfish interest."

"But I consider them both very good offers, just such as many a girl would gladly receive. But to tell you the truth, I do not think that I regard either as a woman should the man she chooses for her husband. But then if I refuse, there is the risk of being an old maid, and that is not to be thought of."

"Well, suppose there is, is that the most dreadful fate that can befall a woman? Is there not more intense wretchedness in an ill-assorted marriage—more utter loneliness in a loveless home, than in the lot of the old maid who accepts her earthly mission as a gift from God, and strives to walk the path of life with earnest and unfaltering steps?"

"Oh! what a little preacher you are. I really believe that you were cut out for an old maid; that when nature formed you, she put in a double portion of intellect to make up for a deficiency of love; and yet you are kind and affectionate. But I do not think that you know anything of the grand, over-mastering passion, or the deep necessity of woman's heart for loving."

"Do you think so?" resumed the first speaker; and bending over her work she quietly applied herself to the knitting that had lain neglected by her side, during this brief conversation; but as she did so, a shadow flitted over her pale and intellectual brow, a mist gathered in her eyes, and a slight quivering of the lips, revealed a depth of feeling to which her companion was a stranger.

But before I proceed with my story, let me give you a slight history of the speakers. They were cousins, who had met life under different auspices. Laura Lagrange, was the only daughter of rich and indulgent parents, who had spared no pains to make her an accomplished lady. Her cousin, Janette Alston, was the child of parents, rich only in goodness and affection. Her father had been unfortunate in business, and dying before he could retrieve his fortunes, left his business in an embarrassed state. His widow was unacquainted with his business affairs, and when the estate was settled, hungry creditors had brought their claims and the lawyers had received their fees, she found herself homeless and almost penniless, and she who had been sheltered in the warm clasp of loving arms, found them too powerless to shield her from the pitiless pelting storms of adversity. Year after year she struggled with poverty and wrestled with want, till her toil-worn hands became too feeble to hold the shattered chords of existence, and her tear-dimmed eyes grew heavy with the slumber of death. Her daughter had watched over her with untiring devotion, had closed her eyes in death, and gone out into the busy, restless world, missing a precious tone from the voices of earth, a beloved step from the paths of life. Too self reliant to depend on the charity of relations, she endeavored to support herself by her own exertions, and she had succeeded. Her path for a while was marked with struggle and trial, but instead of uselessly repining, she met them bravely, and her life became not a thing of ease and indulgence, but of conquest, victory, and accomplishments. At the time when this conversation took place, the deep trials of her life had passed away. The achievements of her genius had won her a position in the literary world, where she shone as one of its bright particular stars. And with her fame came a competence of worldly means, which gave her leisure for improvement, and the riper development of her rare talents. And she, that pale intellectual woman, whose genius gave life and vivacity to the social circle, and whose presence threw a halo of beauty and grace around the charmed atmosphere in which she moved, had at one period of her life, known the mystic and solemn strength of an all-absorbing love. Years faded into the misty past, had seen the kindling of her eye, the quick flushing of her cheek, and the wild throbbing of her heart, at tones of a voice long since hushed to the stillness of death. Deeply, wildly, passionately, she had loved. Her whole life seemed like the pouring out of rich, warm and gushing affections. This love quickened her talents, inspired her genius, and threw over her life a tender and spiritual earnestness. And then came a fearful shock, a mournful waking from that "dream of beauty and delight." A shadow fell around her path; it came between her and the object of her heart's worship; first a few cold words, estrangement, and then a painful separation; the old story of woman's pride—digging the sepulchre of her happiness, and then a new-made grave, and her path over it to the spirit world; and thus faded out from that young heart her bright, brief and saddened dream of life. Faint and spirit-broken, she turned from the scenes associated with the memory of the loved and lost. She tried to break the chain of sad associations that bound her to the mournful past; and so, pressing back the bitter sobs from her almost breaking heart, like the dying dolphin, whose beauty is born of its death anguish, her genius gathered strength from suffering and wonderous power and brilliancy from the agony she hid within the desolate chambers of her soul. Men hailed her as one of earth's strangely gifted children, and wreathed the garlands of fame for her brow, when it was throbbing with a wild and fearful unrest. They breathed her name with applause, when through the lonely halls of her stricken spirit, was an earnest cry for peace, a deep yearning for sympathy and heart-support.

But life, with its stern realities, met her; its solemn responsibilities confronted her, and turning, with an earnest and shattered spirit, to life's duties and trials, she found a calmness and strength that she had only imagined in her dreams of poetry and song. We will now pass over a period of ten years, and the cousins have met again. In that calm and lovely woman, in whose eyes is a depth of tenderness, tempering the flashes of her genius, whose looks and tones are full of sympathy and love, we recognize the once smitten and stricken Janette Alston. The bloom of her girlhood had given way to a higher type of spiritual beauty, as if some unseen hand had been polishing and refining the temple in which her lovely spirit found its habitation; and this had been the fact. Her inner life had grown beautiful, and it was this that was constantly developing the outer. Never, in the early flush of womanhood, when an absorbing love had lit up her eyes and glowed in her life, had she appeared so interesting as when, with a countenance which seemed overshadowed with a spiritual light, she bent over the death-bed of a young woman, just lingering at the shadowy gates of the unseen land.

"Has he come?" faintly but eagerly exclaimed the dying woman. "Oh! how I have longed for his coming, and even in death he forgets me."

"Oh, do not say so, dear Laura, some accident may have detained him," said Janette to her cousin; for on that bed, from whence she will never rise, lies the once-beautiful and light-hearted Laura Lagrange, the brightness of whose eyes has long since been dimmed with tears, and whose voice had become like a harp whose every chord is tuned to sadness—whose faintest thrill and loudest vibrations are but the variations of agony. A heavy hand was laid upon her once warm and bounding heart, and a voice came whispering through her soul, that she must die. But, to her, the tidings was a message of deliverance—a voice, hushing her wild sorrows to the calmness of resignation and hope. Life had grown so weary upon her head—the future looked so hopeless—she had no wish to tread again the track where thorns had pierced her feet, and clouds overcast her sky; and she hailed the coming of death's angel as the footsteps of a welcome friend. And yet, earth had one object so very dear to her weary heart. It was her absent and recreant husband; for, since that conversation, she had accepted one of her offers, and become a wife. But, before she married, she learned that great lesson of human experience and woman's life, to love the man who bowed at her shrine, a willing worshipper. He had a pleasing address, raven hair, flashing eyes, a voice of thrilling sweetness, and lips of persuasive eloquence; and being well versed in the ways of the world, he won his way to her heart, and she became his bride, and he was proud of his prize. Vain and superficial in his character, he looked upon marriage not as a divine sacrament for the soul's development and human progression, but as the title-deed that gave him possession of the woman he thought he loved. But alas for her, the laxity of his principles had rendered him unworthy of the deep and undying devotion of a pure-hearted woman; but, for awhile, he hid from her his true character, and she blindly loved him, and for a short period was happy in the consciousness of being beloved; though sometimes a vague unrest would fill her soul, when, overflowing with a sense of the good, the beautiful, and the true, she would turn to him, but find no response to the deep yearnings of her soul—no appreciation of life's highest realities—its solemn grandeur and significant importance. Their souls never met, and soon she found a void in her bosom, that his earth-born love could not fill. He did not satisfy the wants of her mental and moral nature—between him and her there was no affinity of minds, no intercommunion of souls.

Talk as you will of woman's deep capacity for loving, of the strength of her affectional nature. I do not deny it; but will the mere possession of any human love, fully satisfy all the demands of her whole being? You may paint her in poetry or fiction, as a frail vine, clinging to her brother man for support, and dying when deprived of it; and all this may sound well enough to please the imaginations of school-girls, or love-lorn maidens. But woman—the true woman—if you would render her happy, it needs more than the mere development of her affectional nature. Her conscience should be enlightened, her faith in the true and right established, and scope given to her Heaven-endowed and God-given faculties. The true aim of female education should be, not a development of one or two, but all the faculties of the human soul, because no perfect womanhood is developed by imperfect culture. Intense love is often akin to intense suffering, and to trust the whole wealth of a woman's nature on the frail bark of human love, may often be like trusting a cargo of gold and precious gems, to a bark that has never battled with the storm, or buffetted the waves. Is it any wonder, then, that so many life-barks go down, paving the ocean of time with precious hearts and wasted hopes? that so many float around us, shattered and dismasted wrecks? that so many are stranded on the shoals of existence, mournful beacons and solemn warnings for the thoughtless, to whom marriage is a careless and hasty rushing together of the affections? Alas that an institution so fraught with good for humanity should be so perverted, and that state of life, which should be filled with happiness, become so replete with misery. And this was the fate of Laura Lagrange. For a brief period after her marriage her life seemed like a bright and beautiful dream, full of hope and radiant with joy. And then there came a change—he found other attractions that lay beyond the pale of home influences. The gambling saloon had power to win him from her side, he had lived in an element of unhealthy and unhallowed excitements, and the society of a loving wife, the pleasures of a well-regulated home, were enjoyments too tame for one who had vitiated his tastes by the pleasures of sin. There were charmed houses of vice, built upon dead men's loves, where, amid a flow of song, laughter, wine, and careless mirth, he would spend hour after hour, forgetting the cheek that was paling through his neglect, heedless of the tear-dimmed eyes, peering anxiously into the darkness, waiting, or watching his return.

The influence of old associations was upon him. In early life, home had been to him a place of ceilings and walls, not a true home, built upon goodness, love and truth. It was a place where velvet carpets hushed his tread, where images of loveliness and beauty invoked into being by painter's art and sculptor's skill, pleased the eye and gratified the taste, where magnificence surrounded his way and costly clothing adorned his person; but it was not the place for the true culture and right development of his soul. His father had been too much engrossed in making money, and his mother in spending it, in striving to maintain a fashionable position in society, and shining in the eyes of the world, to give the proper direction to the character of their wayward and impulsive son. His mother put beautiful robes upon his body, but left ugly scars upon his soul; she pampered his appetite, but starved his spirit. Every mother should be a true artist, who knows how to weave into her child's life images of grace and beauty, the true poet capable of writing on the soul of childhood the harmony of love and truth, and teaching it how to produce the grandest of all poems—the poetry of a true and noble life. But in his home, a love for the good, the true and right, had been sacrificed at the shrine of frivolity and fashion. That parental authority which should have been preserved as a string of precious pearls, unbroken and unscattered, was simply the administration of chance. At one time obedience was enforced by authority, at another time by flattery and promises, and just as often it was not enforced at all. His early associations were formed as chance directed, and from his want of home-training, his character received a bias, his life a shade, which ran through every avenue of his existence, and darkened all his future hours. Oh, if we would trace the history of all the crimes that have o'ershadowed this sin-shrouded and sorrow-darkened world of ours, how many might be seen arising from the wrong home influences, or the weakening of the home ties. Home should always be the best school for the affections, the birthplace of high resolves, and the altar upon which lofty aspirations are kindled, from whence the soul may go forth strengthened, to act its part aright in the great drama of life, with conscience enlightened, affections cultivated, and reason and judgment dominant. But alas for the young wife. Her husband had not been blessed with such a home. When he entered the arena of life, the voices from home did not linger around his path as angels of guidance about his steps; they were not like so many messages to invite him to deeds of high and holy worth. The memory of no sainted mother arose between him and deeds of darkness; the earnest prayers of no father arrested him in his downward course: and before a year of his married life had waned, his young wife had learned to wait and mourn his frequent and uncalled-for absence. More than once had she seen him come home from his midnight haunts, the bright intelligence of his eye displaced by the drunkard's stare, and his manly gait changed to the inebriate's stagger; and she was beginning to know the bitter agony that is compressed in the mournful words, a drunkard's wife. And then there came a bright but brief episode in her experience; the angel of life gave to her existence a deeper meaning and loftier significance: she sheltered in the warm clasp of her loving arms, a dear babe, a precious child, whose love filled every chamber of her heart, and felt the fount of maternal love gushing so new within her soul. That child was hers. How overshadowing was the love with which she bent over its helplessness, how much it helped to fill the void and chasms in her soul. How many lonely hours were beguiled by its winsome ways, its answering smiles and fond caresses. How exquisite and solemn was the feeling that thrilled her heart when she clasped the tiny hands together and taught her dear child to call God "Our Father."

What a blessing was that child. The father paused in his headlong career, awed by the strange beauty and precocious intellect of his child; and the mother's life had a better expression through her ministrations of love. And then there came hours of bitter anguish, shading the sunlight of her home and hushing the music of her heart. The angel of death bent over the couch of her child and beaconed it away. Closer and closer the mother strained her child to her wildly heaving breast, and struggled with the heavy hand that lay upon its heart. Love and agony contended with death, and the language of the mother's heart was,

"Oh, Death, away! that innocent is mine;
I cannot spare him from my arms
To lay him, Death, in thine.
I am a mother, Death; I gave that darling birth
I could not bear his lifeless limbs
Should moulder in the earth."

But death was stronger than love and mightier than agony and won the child for the land of crystal founts and deathless flowers, and the poor, stricken mother sat down beneath the shadow of her mighty grief, feeling as if a great light had gone out from her soul, and that the sunshine had suddenly faded around her path. She turned in her deep anguish to the father of her child, the loved and cherished dead. For awhile his words were kind and tender, his heart seemed subdued, and his tenderness fell upon her worn and weary heart like rain on perishing flowers, or cooling waters to lips all parched with thirst and scorched with fever; but the change was evanescent, the influence of unhallowed associations and evil habits had vitiated and poisoned the springs of his existence. They had bound him in their meshes, and he lacked the moral strength to break his fetters, and stand erect in all the strength and dignity of a true manhood, making life's highest excellence his ideal, and striving to gain it.

And yet moments of deep contrition would sweep over him, when he would resolve to abandon the wine-cup forever, when he was ready to forswear the handling of another card, and he would try to break away from the associations that he felt were working his ruin; but when the hour of temptation came his strength was weakness, his earnest purposes were cobwebs, his well-meant resolutions ropes of sand, and thus passed year after year of the married life of Laura Lagrange. She tried to hide her agony from the public gaze, to smile when her heart was almost breaking. But year after year her voice grew fainter and sadder, her once light and bounding step grew slower and faltering. Year after year she wrestled with agony, and strove with despair, till the quick eyes of her brother read, in the paling of her cheek and the dimming eye, the secret anguish of her worn and weary spirit. On that wan, sad face, he saw the death-tokens, and he knew the dark wing of the mystic angel swept coldly around her path. "Laura," said her brother to her one day, "you are not well, and I think you need our mother's tender care and nursing. You are daily losing strength, and if you will go I will accompany you." At first, she hesitated, she shrank almost instinctively from presenting that pale sad face to the loved ones at home. That face was such a tell-tale; it told of heart-sickness, of hope deferred, and the mournful story of unrequited love. But then a deep yearning for home sympathy woke within her a passionate longing for love's kind words, for tenderness and heart-support, and she resolved to seek the home of her childhood, and lay her weary head upon her mother's bosom, to be folded again in her loving arms, to lay that poor, bruised and aching heart where it might beat and throb closely to the loved ones at home. A kind welcome awaited her. All that love and tenderness could devise was done to bring the bloom to her cheek and the light to her eye; but it was all in vain; her's was a disease that no medicine could cure, no earthly balm would heal. It was a slow wasting of the vital forces, the sickness of the soul. The unkindness and neglect of her husband, lay like a leaden weight upon her heart, and slowly oozed away its life-drops. And where was he that had won her love, and then cast it aside as a useless thing, who rifled her heart of its wealth and spread bitter ashes upon its broken altars? He was lingering away from her when the death-damps were gathering on her brow, when his name was trembling on her lips! lingering away! when she was watching his coming, though the death films were gathering before her eyes, and earthly things were fading from her vision. "I think I hear him now," said the dying woman, "surely that is his step;" but the sound died away in the distance. Again she started from an uneasy slumber, "that is his voice! I am so glad he has come." Tears gathered in the eyes of the sad watchers by that dying bed, for they knew that she was deceived. He had not returned. For her sake they wished his coming. Slowly the hours waned away, and then came the sad, soul-sickening thought that she was forgotten, forgotten in the last hour of human need, forgotten when the spirit, about to be dissolved, paused for the last time on the threshold of existence, a weary watcher at the gates of death. "He has forgotten me," again she faintly murmured, and the last tears she would ever shed on earth sprung to her mournful eyes, and clasping her hands together in silent anguish, a few broken sentences issued from her pale and quivering lips. They were prayers for strength and earnest pleading for him who had desolated her young life, by turning its sunshine to shadows, its smiles to tears. "He has forgotten me," she murmured again, "but I can bear it, the bitterness of death is passed, and soon I hope to exchange the shadows of death for the brightness of eternity, the rugged paths of life for the golden streets of glory, and the care and turmoils of earth for the peace and rest of heaven." Her voice grew fainter and fainter, they saw the shadows that never deceive flit over her pale and faded face, and knew that the death angel waited to soothe their weary one to rest, to calm the throbbing of her bosom and cool the fever of her brain. And amid the silent hush of their grief the freed spirit, refined through suffering, and brought into divine harmony through the spirit of the living Christ, passed over the dark waters of death as on a bridge of light, over whose radiant arches hovering angels bent. They parted the dark locks from her marble brow, closed the waxen lids over the once bright and laughing eye, and left her to the dreamless slumber of the grave. Her cousin turned from that death-bed a sadder and wiser woman. She resolved more earnestly than ever to make the world better by her example, gladder by her presence, and to kindle the fires of her genius on the altars of universal love and truth. She had a higher and better object in all her writings than the mere acquisition of gold, or acquirement of fame. She felt that she had a high and holy mission on the battle-field of existence, that life was not given her to be frittered away in nonsense, or wasted away in trifling pursuits. She would willingly espouse an unpopular cause but not an unrighteous one. In her the down-trodden slave found an earnest advocate; the flying fugitive remembered her kindness as he stepped cautiously through our Republic, to gain his freedom in a monarchial land, having broken the chains on which the rust of centuries had gathered. Little children learned to name her with affection, the poor called her blessed, as she broke her bread to the pale lips of hunger. Her life was like a beautiful story, only it was clothed with the dignity of reality and invested with the sublimity of truth. True, she was an old maid, no husband brightened her life with his love, or shaded it with his neglect. No children nestling lovingly in her arms called her mother. No one appended Mrs. to her name; she was indeed an old maid, not vainly striving to keep up an appearance of girlishness, when departed was written on her youth. Not vainly pining at her loneliness and isolation: the world was full of warm, loving hearts, and her own beat in unison with them. Neither was she always sentimentally sighing for something to love, objects of affection were all around her, and the world was not so wealthy in love that it had no use for her's; in blessing others she made a life and benediction, and as old age descended peacefully and gently upon her, she had learned one of life's most precious lessons, that true happiness consists not so much in the fruition of our wishes as in the regulation of desires and the full development and right culture of our whole natures.

1859

# ROSE TERRY COOKE

(1827–1892)

---

## *My Visitation*

"Is not this she of whom,
When first she came, all flushed you said to me,
*  *  *  *  *  *  *

Now could you share your thought; now should men see
Two women faster welded in one love
Than pairs of wedlock?" *The Princess.*

If this story is incoherent—arranged rather for the writer's thought than for the reader's eye—it is because the brain which dictated it reeled with the sharp assaults of memory, that living anguish that abides while earth passes away into silence; and because the hand that wrote it trembled with electric thrills from a past that can not die, forever fresh in the soul it tested and tortured—powerful after the flight of years as in its first agony, to fill the dim eye with tears, and throb the languid pulses with fresh fever and passion.

Take, then, the record as it stands, and ask not from a cry of mortal pain the liquid cadence and accurate noting of an operatic bravura.

The first time *It* came was in broad day. I was ill, unable to rise; the day was cold; autumnal sunshine, pure and still, streamed through the house and came in at both the south windows of my room, the curtains drawn wide to receive it, for the ague of sickness is worse to me than its pain, and not yet had my preparations for winter enabled me to have a fire. Every thing was clear and chill; Aunt Mary, down stairs in the parlor, sat and knitted, as it was her custom to do of an afternoon; Uncle Seth was not at home; the servant had gone to mass, for it was some feast-day of her Church—no sound or echo disturbed the solitude.

There is something peculiar in a silent day of autumn; melancholy pierces its fine sting through the rays of sunshine; sadness cries in the cricket's monotonous voice; separation and death symbolize in the slow leaves that quit the bough reluctantly, and lie down in dust to be over-trodden—to rot. I can endure any silence better than this hush of decay; it fills me with preternatural horror; it is as if a tomb opened and breathed out its dank, morbid breath across the murmur of life, to paralyze and to chill.

But that day I had taken refuge from the awe and foreboding, the ticking of the clock, the dust-motes floating on light, the startling crack that now and then a springing board or an ill-hung window made. I had taken a book. I was deep in Shirley; it excited, it affected me; it is always to me like a brief and voluntary brain-fever to read that book. Jane Eyre is insanity for the time. Villette is like the scarlet fever; it possesses, it chokes, flushes, racks you; it leaves you weak and in vague pain, apprehensive of some bad result; but it was Shirley I read, so forgetting every thing. I am not lonely usually, yet I know when I am alone; there is an indescribable freedom in the sense of solitude, no alien sphere crosses and disturbs mine, no intrusive influence distorts the orbit; I am myself—or I was, then. Presently, as I lay there, the clock struck three. I was to take some potion at that hour. I must rise and get it. I set one foot on the floor, and was putting a shoe upon the other cautiously, when it occurred to me, why was I so careful? and I remembered that it had seemed to me something was on the bed when I moved—my kitten perhaps. I looked, there was nothing there; but I was not alone in the room—there was something else I could not see. I did not hear, but I knew it.

A horror of flesh and sense crept over me; but I was ashamed; I treated it with contempt. Shivering, I walked to the shelf, reached the cup, swallowed my nauseous dose—now tasteless—and went back to bed. It is not worth denying that I trembled. I am a coward. I am always afraid, even when I face the fear; so, shaking, I lay down. My throat was parched, my lips beaded with a sweat of terror, but the consciousness of solitude returned in time to save me from faintness. *It* had gone. And that was the first time.

Here, perhaps, it is best to interpolate my own story, as much of it as is needful to the understanding of this visitation.

I was an orphan, living in the family of my guardian and uncle by marriage, Mr. Van Alstyne. I was not an orphan till fifteen years of happy life at home had fitted me to feel the whole force of such a bereavement. My parents had died within a year of each other, and at the time my story begins I had been ten years under my uncle's roof. He was kind, gentle, generous, and good; all that he could be, not being my father.

It is not necessary to say that I grieved long and deeply over my loss; my nature is intense as well as excitable, and I had no mother. What that brief sentence expresses many will feel; many, more blessed, can not imagine. It is to all meaning enough to define my longing for what I had not, my solitude in all that I had, my eager effort to escape from both longing and solitude.

After I had been a year under my guardian's care, Eleanor Wyse, a far-off cousin of Mr. Van Alstyne, came to board at the house and go to school with me. She was fifteen, I sixteen, but she was far the oldest. In the same family as we were, in the same classes, there were but two ways for us to take, either rivalry or friendship; between two girls of so much individuality there was no neutral ground, and within a month I had decided the matter by falling passionately in love with Eleanor Wyse.

I speak advisedly in the use of that term; no other phrase expresses the blind, irrational, all-enduring devotion I gave to her; no less vivid word belongs to that madness. If I had not been in love with her I should have seen her as I can now—as what she really was; for I believe in physiognomy. I believe that God writes the inner man upon the outer as a restraint upon society; what the moulding of feature lacks, expression, subtle traitor, supplies; and it is only years of repression, of training, of diplomacy, that put the flesh totally in the power of the spirit, and enable man or woman to seem what they are not, what they would be thought.

Eleanor's face was very beautiful; its Greek outline, straight and clear, cut to a perfect contour; the white brow; the long, melancholy eye, with curved, inky lashes; the statuesque head, its undulant, glittering hair bound in a knot of classic severity; the proud, serene mouth, full of carved beauty, opening its scarlet lips to reveal tiny pearl-grains of teeth of that rare delicacy and brilliance that carry a fatal warning; the soft, oval cheek, colorless but not pale, opaque and smooth, betraying Southern blood; the delicate throat, shown whiter under the sweeping shadow and coil of her black-brown tresses; the erect, stately, perfect figure, slight as became her years, but full of strength and promise; all these captivated my intense adoration of beauty. I did not see the label of the sculptor; I did not perceive in that cold, strict chiseling the assertion that its material was marble. I believed the interpretation of its hieroglyphic legend would have run thus: "This is the head of young Pallas; power, intellect, purity are her ægis; the daughter of Jove has not yet tasted passion; virgin, stainless, strong for sacrifice and victory, let the ardent and restless hearts of women seek her to be calmed and taught. *Evoe Athena!*" Nor did I like to see the goddess moved; expression did not become her; the soul that pierced those deep eyes was eager, unquiet, despotic; nothing divine, indeed, yet, in my eyes, it was the unresting, hasting meteor that flashed and faded through mists of earth toward its rest—where I knew not, but its flickering seemed to me atmospheric, not intrinsic.

I looked up to Eleanor with respect as well as fervor. She was full of noble theories. To hear her speak you would have been inwardly shamed by the great and pure thoughts she expressed, the high standard by which she measured all. Truth, disinterestedness, honor, purity, humility, found in her a priestess garmented in candor. If I thought an evil thought, I was thereafter ashamed to see her; if I was indolent or selfish, her presence reproached me; her will, irresistible and mighty, awoke me; if she was kind in speech or act—if she spoke to me caressingly—if she put her warm lips upon my cheek—I was thrilled with joy; her presence affected me, as sunshine does, with a sense of warm life and delight; when we rode, walked, or talked together, I wished the hour eternal; and when she fell into some passion, and burned me with bitter words, stinging me into retort by their injustice, their hard cruelty, it was I who repented—I who humiliated myself—I who, with abundant tears, asked her pardon, worked, plead, prayed to obtain it; and if some spasmodic conscientiousness roused her to excuse herself—to say she had been wrong—my hand closed her lips: I could not hear that: the fault was mine, mine only. I was glad to be clay as long as she was queen and deity.

I do not think this passion of mine moved Eleanor much. She liked to talk with me; our minds mated, our tastes were alike. I had no need to explain my phrases to her, or to do more than indicate my thoughts; she was receptive and appreciative of thought, not of emotion. Me she never knew. I had no reserve in my nature—none of what is commonly called pride; what I felt I said, to the startling of good usual persons; and because I said it, Eleanor did not think I felt it. To her organization utterance and simplicity were denied; she could not speak her emotions if she would; she would not if she could; and she had no faith in words from others. My demonstrations annoyed her; she could not return them; they could not be ignored; there was a certain spice of life and passion in them that asserted itself poignantly and disturbed her. My services she liked better; yet there was in her the masculine contempt for spaniels; she despised a creature that would endure a blow, mental or physical, without revenging itself; and from her I endured almost any repulse, and forgot it.

She was with us in the house three years, and in that time she learned to love me after a fashion of her own, and I, still blind, adored her more. She found in me a receptivity that suited her, and a useful power of patient endurance. Her will made me a potent instrument. What she wanted she must have, and her want was my law. No time, no pains, no patience were wanting in me to fulfill her ends. I served her truly, and I look back upon it with no regret; futile or fertile, such devotion widens and ripens the soul that it inhabits. No aftershock of anguish can contract the space or undo the maturity; and even in my deepest humiliation before her sublime theories and superhuman ideals I unconsciously grew better myself. A capacity for worship implies much, and results in much.

Yet I think I loved her without much selfishness. I desired nothing better than to see her appreciated and admired. It was inexplicable to me when she was not; and I charged the coolness with which she was spoken of, and the want of enthusiasm for her person and character in general society, to her own starry height above common people, and their infinite distance from her nature.

So these years passed by. We went to school; we finished our school-days; we came out into the world; for, in the mean time, her mother had died, and her father removed to Bangor. She liked the place as a residence, and it had become home to her of late. I hoped it was pleasanter for her to be near me. When Eleanor was about twenty a nephew of Uncle Van Alstyne's came to make us a visit; he was no new acquaintance; he had come often in his boyhood, but since we grew up he had been in college, at the seminary, last in Germany for two years' study, and we did not know him well in his maturer character until this time. Herman Van Alstyne was quiet and plain, but of great capacity; I saw him much, and liked him. Love did not look at us. I was absorbed in Eleanor; so was he; but to her he was of no interest. I think she respected him, but her manner was careless and cold, even neglectful. Herman perceived the repulsion. At first he had taken pains to interest her—to mould her traits—to develop some inner nature in which he had faith; but the stone was intractable; neither ductile nor docile was Pallas; her soul yielded no more to him than the strong sea yields place or submission to the winged wind that smites it in passing.

He was with us three months waiting for a call he said, but stricter chains held him till he broke them with one blow and went to a Western parish.

He had not offered himself to Eleanor and been refused. Wisely he refrained from bringing the matter to a foreknown crisis: he spared himself the pain and Eleanor the regret of a refusal that he regarded truly as certain. I was sorry for the whole affair, for I believed she would scarcely know a better man, but it passed away; I promised to write him when his mother found the correspondence wearying, and we interchanged a few letters at irregular intervals till we met again, letters into which Eleanor's name found no entrance.

Three years after he left I went, early in July, to spend some weeks at the sea-side, for I was not strong; in the last few years my health had failed slowly, but progressively, till I was alarmingly weak, and ordered to breathe salt air and use sea-bathing as the best hope of restoration. I do not know why I should reserve the cause of this long languor and sinking: it was nothing wrong in me that I owed it to the breaking of a brief engagement. A young girl, totally inexperienced, I had loved a man and been taught by himself to despise him—a tragedy both trite and sharp; one that is daily reacted, noted, and forgotten by observers, to find a cold record in marble or the catalogues of insane asylums, another perhaps in the eternal calendar of the heavens above. I was too strong in nature to grace either of these mortal lists, and I loved Eleanor too well. I had always loved her more than that man; and when the episode was over, I discovered in myself that I never could have loved any man as I did her, and I went out into the world in this conviction, finding that life had not lost all its charms—that so long as she lived for me I should neither die nor craze. But the shock and excitement of the affair shattered my nervous system and undermined my health, and the listless, aimless life of a young lady offered no reactive agency to help me: so I went from home to new scenes and fresh atmosphere.

The air of Gloucester Beach strengthened me day by day. The exquisite scenery was a pleasure endless and pure. I asked nothing better than to sit upon some tide-washed rock and watch the creeping waves slide back in half-articulate murmur from the repelling shore, or, eager with the strength of flood, fling themselves, in mock anger, against cliff and crag, only to break in wreaths of silver spray and foam-bells—to glitter and fall in a leap of futile mirth, then rustling in the shingle and sea-weed with vague whispers, that

"Song half asleep or speech half awake,"

which has lulled so many restless hearts to a momentary quiet, singing them the long lullaby that preludes a longer slumber.

It was excitement enough to walk alone upon the beach when a hot cloudy night drooped over land and sea; when the soft trance and enchantment of summer lulled cloud and wave into stillness absolute and cherishing, when the sole guide I had in that warm gloom was the white edge of surf, and the only sound that smote the quiet, the still-recurring, apprehensive dash, as wave after wave raced, leaped, panted, and hissed after its forerunner.

The Beach House was almost empty at that early season, and I enjoyed all this alone, not without constant yearnings for Eleanor; wanting her, even this scenery lost a charm, and I gave it but faint admiration since I could not see it with her eyes. It must be a very pure love of nature that can exist alone, and without flaw, in the absence of association. The austere soul of the great mother offers no sympathy to the petulant passion or irrational grief of her children. It is only to the heart that has proved itself strong and lofty that her potent and life-giving traits reveal themselves. In this love, as in all others, save only the love of God, the return that is yielded is measured by the power of the adorer, not his want. Truly,

"Nature never did betray
The heart that loved her;"

but she has many and many a time betrayed the partial love—scoffed at the divided worship.

After I had been a fortnight at the Beach, I was joined by Herman Van Alstyne. He had come on from the West to recruit his own health, suffering from a long intermittent fever, by sea-air; and hearing I was at Gloucester, had come there, and asked my leave to remain, gladly accorded to him. We had always been good friends, and my unspoken sympathy with his liking for, and loss of, Eleanor had established a permanent bond between us. In the constant association into which we were now thrown I learned daily to like him better. He was very weak indeed, quite unable to walk or drive far, and the connection of our families was a sufficient excuse to others for our intimacy. I delighted to offer him any kindness or service in my power, and he repaid me well by the charm of his society.

We spent our mornings always together in some niche of the lofty cliff that towered from the tide below in bare grandeur, reflecting the sun from its abrupt brown crags till every fibre of grass rooted in their crevices grew blanched, and the solitary streamer of bramble or wild creeper became crisp long ere autumn. But this heat was my element; the slow blood quickened in my veins under its vital glow; I felt life stealing back to its deserted and chilly conduits; I basked like a cactus or a lizard into brighter tints and a gayer existence.

There we often sat till noon, talking or silent as we would; for though there was a peculiar charm in the appreciative, thoughtful conversation of Herman Van Alstyne, a better and a rarer trait he possessed in full measure—the power of "a thousand silences."

Or, perhaps, under the old cedars that shed aromatic scents upon the sun-thrilled air, and strewed bits of dry, sturdy leaves upon the short grass that carpeted the summit of the cliff, we preferred shadow to sunshine; and while I rested against some ragged bole, and inhaled all odor and health, he read to me some quaint German story, some incredibly exquisite bit of Tennyson, some sensitively musical passage of Kingsley, or, better and more apt, a song or a poem of Shelley's—vivid, spiritual, supernatural; the ideal of poetry; the leaping flame-tongue of lonely genius hanging in mid-air, self-poised, self-containing, glorious, and unattainable.

I have never known so delicate an apprehension as Mr. Van Alstyne possessed; his nobler traits I was afterward to know—to feel; but now it suited me thoroughly to be so well understood—to feel that I might utter the wildest imagination, or the most unexpected peculiarity of opinion, and never once be asked to explain what I meant—to reduce into social formulas that which was not social but my own. If there is one rest above another to a weary mind it is this freedom from shackles, this consciousness of true response. Never did I perceive a charm in the landscape that he had not noticed before or simultaneously with me; the same felicity of diction or of thought in what we read struck us as with one stroke; we liked the same people, read the same books, agreed in opinion so far as to disagree on and discuss many points without a shadow of impatience or an uncandid expression. We talked together as few men talk—perhaps no women—

"Talked at large of worldly fate,
And drew truly every trait"

—but we never spoke of Eleanor.

And so the summer wore on. I perceived a gradual change creep over Herman's manner in its process; he watched me continually. I felt his eyes fixed on me whenever I sat sewing or reading; I never looked up without meeting them. He grew absent and fitful. I did not know what had happened. I accused myself of having pained him. I feared he was ill. I never once thought of the true trouble; and one day it came—he asked me to marry him.

Never was any woman more surprised. I had not thought of the thing. I could not speak at first. I drew from him the hand he attempted to grasp. I did not collect my stricken and ashamed thoughts till, looking up, I saw him perfectly pale, his eyes dark with emotion, waiting, in rigid self-control, for my answer.

I could not, in justice to him or to myself, be less than utterly candid. I told him how much I liked him; how grieved I was that I could have mistaken his feeling for me so entirely; and then I said what I then believed—that I could not marry him—for I had but the lesser part of a heart to give any man. I loved a woman too well to love or to marry. A deep flush of relief crossed his brow.

"Is that the only objection you offer to me?" asked he, calmly.

"It is enough," said I. "If you think that past misery of mine interferes against you, you are in the wrong. I know now that I never loved that man as a woman should love the man she marries, and had I done so, the utter want of respect or trust I feel for him now would have silenced the love forever."

"I did not think of that," said he. "I needed but one assurance—that, except for Miss Wyse, you might have loved me; is it so?"

I could not tell him—I did not know. The one present and all-absorbing passion of my soul was Eleanor; beside her, no rival could enter. I shuddered at the possibility of loving a man so utterly, and then placing myself at his mercy for life. I felt that my safety lay in my freedom from any such tie to Eleanor. She made me miserable often enough as it was; what might she not do were I in her power always? Yet this face of the subject I did not suggest to Mr. Van Alstyne; it was painful enough to be kept to myself. I told him plainly that I could not love another as I did her; that I would not if I could.

He looked at me, not all unmoved, though silently; a gentle shading of something like pity stole across his regard, fixed and keen at first. He neither implored nor deprecated, but lifted my hand reverently to his lips, and said, in a tone of supreme calmness, "I can wait."

I should have combated the hope implied in those words. I was afterward angry with myself for enduring them; but at the moment uncertainty, shaped out of instinct and apprehension, closed my lips; I could not speak, and he left me. I went to my room more moved than I liked to acknowledge; and when he went away the next morning, though I felt the natural relief from embarrassment—knowing that I should not meet him as before—I still missed him, as a part of my daily life.

A month longer at the Beach protracted my stay into autumn; and then, with refreshed health and new strength, I returned home—home! whose chief charm lay in the prospect of seeing Eleanor.

It is true that this hope was not unalloyed. I am possessed of a nature singularly instinctive, and for some weeks past a certain shadow had crept into her letters that pained me. No word or phrase denoted change; but I perceived the uncertain aura, and was irrationally harassed by a trouble too vague for expression.

When I reached Bangor it lay waiting for me sufficiently tangible and legible in the shape of a note from Eleanor.

* * * * * *

And here must I leave a blank. The forgiveness which stirs me to this record refuses to define for alien eyes what that trouble was. All that I can say to justify the extreme and piteous result which followed is, that Eleanor Wyse had utterly, cruelly, and deliberately deceived me; and when it was no longer possible to do so, had been obliged by circumstances to show me what she had done.

Of that day it is best to say but little: the world cracked and reeled under me; I returned from a brief stupor into one bitter, blind tempest of contempt; and in its strength I answered her note concisely and coldly. An hour's time brought me a rejoinder not worth answering, simply perfidious—a regret, "deep and true," that she had been compelled to grieve me, to "reserve" from me any thing.

True! I had believed in truth, in goodness, in disinterested love, in principle; where now were such faiths swept? Verily, over the cliff into the sea! I was morally destroyed; I made shipwreck of myself and my life; my whole soul was a salt raging wave, tideless and foaming, without rest, without intent, without faith or hope in God—for he who loses faith in man loses faith in man's Maker—and this had Eleanor Wyse done for me.

Doubtless, to many, this emotion of mine will seem exaggerated. Let them remember that it was the loss of all that bound to life a lonely, morbid, intense, and excitable woman. Need I say more? If, after many years, with the kind help of nobler men and women, and the great patience of God, I have worn my way, inch by inch, back to some foothold of belief, I feel even yet—in some recoils of memory, some recurring habit of my soul—the reflex influence of those wretched days, months, years, when I suspected every one—"hateful, and hating," of a truth.

Death is hard to bear when its angel breathes upon the face we love, and extinguishes therein the fiery spark of life; but what is death compared to such dissolution as treachery brings? If Eleanor Wyse had died when I loved her and trusted her, I should have gone mourning softly all my days, but not in pain; to find her untrue admitted no remedy, no palliation. Truth was the ruling passion of my mind; that, and nothing else, contented me. Its absence or its loss were the loss and absence of all in those whom I loved; and it was only within a brief time, as years go, that I had grown into the discovery that men are liars in spite of education or policy; what was it, then, to know this of my ideal—of Eleanor?

But let those helpless, miserable weeks go by. If I detail so much as I have, it is to show the reason of my righteous indignation—of my tenacious memory. After a time I supposed that I forgave Eleanor. I thought myself good, most Pharisaically good, to have forgiven such an injury. I made some little comedy of friendship for visible use; I visited her, though not as often as I had done before. I saw her try to supply, with the love of others, the lavish devotion and service I had given her; I saw her fail and suffer in the consciousness of want and dissatisfaction, and, self-righteously, I forgave again! Senseless that I was!—as if forgiveness rankled and grew bitter in one's heart—as if pardon, full and pure, rejoiced in the retributions of this life—fed itself with salt recollections of the past, and evil foreshadowings of the future; as if it could exist without love, without forgetfulness; as if good deeds were its pledge, or good words its seal!

No! I never forgave her. I never forgot one pang she inflicted on me, one untruth she uttered; I never trusted her word or her smile again. I gathered up every circumstance of the past, and hunted it to its source; I discovered that she had not simply deceived but deluded me, and laughed at me in the process.

How my blood boiled over these revelations! how my flesh failed with my heart! Slow, persistent fever gnawed me; my nights were without sleep or rest; my days laggard and delirious. Why I did not go crazy is yet unexplained to myself. I think I did, only that there was a method in my madness that won for it the milder name of nervousness. I was ill—I tottered on the very tempting brink of death, without awe or regret; I made no effort to live, nor any to die, except to pray that I might—the only prayer that ever passed my seared lips. I was sent away from home again; and while I was gone Eleanor married a certain Mr. Mason, of Bangor, and they removed to Illinois—in time, still further West. I was no better for this absence; and, impatient of strangers and intrusive acquaintance, I came home, and, strange as it may seem, I missed Eleanor! Habit is the anchor of half the love in this world, and my habit of loving her survived the love—or held it, perhaps—for I missed her sorrowfully.

I found Herman Van Alstyne at my uncle's when I came, and I was glad—glad of any thing to break the desperate monotony of sorrow. He knew nothing more than every one knew of this affair, except that he knew me, and from that gathered intuitively a part of the truth; and, by long patience, unwearied and delicate care—watching, waiting, forbearing, and enduring—he brought me nearer a certain degree of calm than I had believed possible, when a sudden summons called him away from Bangor; and it was during his absence that *It* began to come; as I said in the beginning, more than two years after I had lost Eleanor.

I lay still in my bed on that day of which I had spoken; the long stress of misery that I had undergone in the past years resulted in so much physical exhaustion as to have brought on the exquisite tortures of neuralgia, and it was a sudden access of this chronic rack that to-day held me prisoner. The draught I had taken was an anodyne, and under its influence I fell asleep. I must have slept an hour, when I woke abruptly with a renewed sense of something in the dusk beside me, at my pillow. I screamed as I woke into this terror, and instantly Aunt Mary came in. A cold sigh crossed my cheek; I shivered with a horror strange and unearthly. Aunt Mary asked if I had been asleep? I said yes. If I had been dreaming painfully? I did not answer that. I asked for some water, and getting it she forgot her question; but I could not bear to be alone. I begged her to sit beside me and to sleep with me, for I could not endure solitude; perpetual apprehension made me cringe in every nerve and fibre. I started at the slightest stir of leaf or insect upon the pane, and the repining autumn wind seemed to come over mile on mile of graves, bringing thence no mealy scent of white daisies—no infant-breathing violet odors—no frutescent perfume of sweet-briar, nor funereal smells of cypress, and plaintive whispers of fir and pine; but wave after wave of cries from half-free souls; sobbing with dull pain, and moans of deprecating anguish; a cry that neither heaven nor earth answered, but which crept—a live desolation—into the ear attent, and the brain morbidly excited.

Yet gradually this left me. I kept by some kindly human presence all day, and feared night no more till—

Let me say that all this time I was imperceptibly growing better than I had been. Hope, the very ministrant of Heaven, was by tiny crevice and unguarded postern stealing into my heart, though I knew it not, and softening all my hard thoughts of Eleanor, for I am moved to the outer world rather by my own moods than theirs; sorrow and pain make me selfish and unkind; peace, joy, even unconscious hope, expand my love for all mankind. I am better, more tender, more benevolent to others, when I receive some light and life within.

One night I was all alone; the low, unearthly glimmer of a waning moon lit the naked earth, a few leaves rustled on the fitful wind that lulled, and rose, and lulled again, with almost articulate meaning. I lay listening; a long pause came, of most significant quiet—a faint sigh crossed my brow. *It* was there beside me!—unseen, unheard, but felt in the secretest recesses of life and consciousness; a spirit, whereat my marrow curdled, my heart was constricted, my blood refused to run, my breath failed—fluttered—was it death? I sprung from my pillow; the presence drew farther away. I could see nothing, but I felt that something yearning, restless, pained, and sad regarded me. I began to gather courage. I began to pity a soul that had cast off life yet could not die to life; and now it drew nearer, as if some magnetism, born of my kindlier sympathies, melted the barrier between us, close—closer—till something rustled like a light touch the cover of my bed, stirred at my ear! Good Heaven! could I bear that? I could not shriek or cry, I fell forward upon my face. It went, and the wind began its wail; now reproachful sobs filled it: the moon sank, rain gathered overhead, and dripped with sullen persistence all night upon the roof, for all night I heard it.

It is tedious to recount each instance of this visitation. For weeks it staid beside me. I felt it on my bed at night; I felt it by my chair in the day; it swept past me in the garden paths, a cold waft of air; it watched me through the window-blinds; it hung over me sleeping; yet never was I wonted to the presence; every day thrilled me with fresh surprise, and daily it grew, for daily it became more perceivable.

At first I felt only a sense of alien life in a room otherwise solitary; then a breath of air, air from some other sphere than this, penetrative, dark, chilling; then a sound, not of voice, or pulse, but of motion in some inanimate thing, the motion of contact; then came a touch, the gentlest, faintest approach of lips or fingers, I knew not which, to my brow; and last, a growing, gathering, flickering into sight. I saw nothing at first, directly; from the oblique glance that fear impelled I drew an impression of quivering air beside me; then of a shadow, frail and variant; then a shapeless shape of mist, a cloud, dark and portentous and significant; and next those sidelong glances revealed to me an expression; no face, no feature, but, believe it who can, an expression, earnest, melancholy, beseeching; a look that pierced me, that pleaded with my soul's depth, that entreated shelter, succor, consolation, which even in my terror I longed to give.

I might perhaps have suffered physically more than I did from this visiting, but the winged hope of which I spoke before upheld me still, daily, with stronger hands.

Herman had returned to Bangor after a brief absence, and was there still. I could not see him so constantly as I did and refuse my admiration to those traits that ever rule and satisfy me. Mr. Van Alstyne passed with some people for a philosopher, with some for a reformer: there were those who called him singular and self-opinionated; there were others who revered him for his devout nature and stainless life. He was more than any of these, he was a true man: and even in his plain exterior the eye that knew him found a charm peculiar and salient; the deep-sunken, clear, earnest eyes, kindled with a spark of profound depth and meaning; the thin, sharply cut, aquiline outline; the flexible, pure, refined mouth; the bronzed coloring; the overhanging brow—all these wore beauty indefinable, fired by the sweet and vivid smile of the irradiate soul within. In his presence, calm, restful, and strengthening, no subterfuge or evasion could live. He was just, direct, and tenderly strong; it was to him, to him it is, that I owed and owe a new and higher life than I had known before; he saw my sinking and lonely soul, but he saw its self-recuperative power, and with the most delicate and careful tenderness beguiled that motive force into action. He did far more than that; he recalled to me the higher motives that anguish had well-nigh scourged out from my horizon; he taught me as a father teaches his little child a newer trust in the Father of us all. I returned to those divine consolations that he laid before me with a pierced and penitent heart; and in knowing that I was prayed and cared for on earth, I learned anew that God is more tender and more patient than his creatures, and the logic of strong emotion made the truth living and potent. In all this was I drawn toward Herman by the strongest tie that can bind one heart to another—a tie that overarches and outlasts all the fleeting passions of time, for it is the adamantine link of eternity; and had I lost him then, I should have felt for all my life that there was a relation between us, undying and sure, to be renewed and acknowledged at length where such relations respire their native air, where there is neither marrying nor giving in marriage.

But it pleased God that I should live to receive my heart's desire; what began in gratitude ended in love. I might have shrunk from admitting so potent a guest again into my soul, had any other soul sent the messenger thither; but I trusted him when I disbelieved every other creature, and with this trust had crept back to me my faith in God, in good, in life and its ends. Truly, so far as man can do it, he saved my soul alive!

Now it was the early part of December. It was still haunting me. I could see more—eyes, deep and pleading, the outline of a head, pure lineaments, seemed hovering beside me, but if I turned for a direct look they were gone. I did not fear it; my happy faith and Herman shielded me.

The year drew on. The day before Christmas came, still, crisp, but yet warm for its season; no snow shrouded the earth; the far-off sun beamed out benign and pale; the few dry leaves lay quiet as they fell; the firs upon the lawn with curved boughs waited for their ermine, stately and dark. Herman asked me to walk with him. I cloaked and hooded myself, and we went away, away into the deep woods. What we said in that sweet silence of a leafless, sunny forest is known to us two: it is not for you, reader, friendly though you be; it is enough to tell you that I had promised to be his wife, that I was homesick no more.

It was well for me that this happened that day—should I not rather say God ordered it?—for as ever in this life sorrow tramples upon the foregoing footsteps of joy, so I found upon my return a household in tears. Mr. Mason, Eleanor's husband, had written, at last, two months after it happened, and another month had the letter been in coming—ah! how ever shall I say it? Eleanor was dead! her latest breath had gasped out a cry for me!

If Death is the Spoiler, so is he the Restorer; who shall dare to soil the shroud with any thing but tears? I could do no more but weep; but I mourned for Eleanor again as I had never thought to do; evil, treachery, anguish, and distrust vanished—I remembered only love.

For hours I could not see or speak with Herman, the flood of misery overpowered me; and he too sorrowed, deeply, but serenely. It was late in the evening before I recovered any sort of composure. He sent to my chamber a brief penciled request, and I went down; worn out with weeping, I obeyed like a child. I ate the food he brought me; I drank the restorative draught; quiet, but languid, I laid my head upon his breast, and, held by the firm grasp of his arm, I rested, and he consoled me; a deep and vital draught of peace slaked my soul's feverish thirst. Such peace had I never known, for it was the daughter of experience and trust.

You who, full of youth and its intact passion, give a careless hour to these pages, wonder not that I could find it just to give so noble a man a heart once given and wasted! Know that it is not the flower of any tropic palm that is fit to feed and sustain man, but the ripened clusters of its fruitage—the result of time, and sun, and storm. The first blush, the earliest kiss, the tender and timid glance are sweet indeed; but the true household fire, deep and abiding, is oftenest kindled in the heart matured by passion and by pain, tested in the stress of life, deepened and strengthened by manifold experience; and such a heart receives no unworthy guest, lights its altar-fire for no idol of wood or clay. I felt that I rendered Herman Van Alstyne far nobler and higher homage, that I did him purer justice in loving him now than it had ever been in my power to do before.

First love is a honeyed and dewy romance, fit for novels and school-girls; but of the myriad women who have lived to curse their marriage-day nine-tenths have been those who married in their ignorant girlhood, and married boys.

I have digressed to honor Herman, to vindicate myself. That Christmas-eve I lay sheltered and at rest on his arm, till the toll of midnight rang clear upon my ear. I could forever sing the angels' song now, that for years had been a blank repetition to my wretched and ungodly soul.

"Peace on earth!" was no more a chimera; I knew it at heart. "Good will to men!" that was spontaneous; I loved all in and for one. "Glory to God in the highest!" What did that ask to utter it but a full thankfulness that bore me upward like the flood-tide of a summer sea?

Blessed as I was, my common sense reminded me that it was far into the night, that I ought to sleep; so I said good-night to Herman, and crept with weak steps to my room. I fell asleep to dream of him, of Eleanor, of peace, and I woke into the deep silence that always preceded—*It*.

I woke knowing what stood beside me. Keen starlight pierced the pane, and shed a dim, obscure perception of place and outline over my room. A long, restful, sobbing sigh parted my lips; I perceived *It* was at hand; fear fled; terror died out; I turned my eyes—oh God! it was Eleanor!

Wan—frail—a flowing outline of shadow, but the face in every faultless line and vivid expression; now an expression of intense longing, of wistful prayer, of pleading that would never be denied.

I lifted my heavy arms toward the vision; it swayed and bent above me: the white lips parted; no murmur nor sound clave them, yet they spoke—"Forgive! forgive!"

"Eleanor! Yes love, darling! yes, forever, as I hope to be forgiven!" I cried out aloud. A gleam of rapture and rest relaxed the brow, the sad eyes; love ineffable glowed along each lineament, and transfused to splendor the frigid moulding of snow.

I closed my eyes to crush inward the painful tears, and a touch of lips sealed them with sacred and unearthly repose. I looked again; *It* had gone forever. The Christmas bells pealed loud and clear for dawn, and my thoughts rung their own joy bells beside the steeple chimes. Herman and Eleanor both loved me—I had forgiven; I was forgiven.

Yet must day and space echo that word once more. Hear me, Eleanor! hear me, from that mystic country where thou hast fled before!

I repeat that forgiveness again. So may Heaven pardon me in the hour of need; so may God look upon me with strong affection in the parting of soul and body, even as I pardon and love thee, Eleanor, with a truth and faith eternal! Thee, forever loved, but, ah! not now forever lost?

1858

# ROSE TERRY COOKE

(1827–1892)

## *Too Late*

"'Tis true 'tis pity! pity 'tis 'tis true!"

In one of those scanty New England towns that fill a stranger with the acutest sense of desolation, more desolate than the desert itself, because there are human inhabitants to suffer from its solitude and listlessness, there stood, and still stands, a large red farm-house, with sloping roof, and great chimney in the middle, where David Blair lived. Perhaps Wingfield was not so forlorn to him as to another, for he had Scotch blood in his veins, and his shrewd thrift found full exercise in redeeming the earth from thorns and briers, and eating his bread under the full force of the primeval curse. He was a "dour" man, with a long, grim visage that would have become any Covenanter's conventicle in his native land; and his prayers were as long and grim as his face. Of life's graces and amenities he had no idea; they would have been scouted as profane vanities had they blossomed inside his threshold. Existence to him was a heavy and dreadful responsibility; a drear and doubtful working out of his own salvation; a perpetual fleeing from the wrath to come, that seemed to dog his heels and rear threatening heads at every turn. A cowardly man, with these ever-present terrors, would have taken refuge in some sweet and lulling sin or creed, some belief of a universal salvation, some epicurean "let us eat and drink, for to-morrow we die," or some idea in nothing beyond the grave.

But David Blair was full of courage. Like some knotty, twisted oak, that offers scant solace to the eye, he endured, oak-like, all storms, and bent not an atom to any fierce blast of nature or Providence; for he made a distinction between them. His wife was a neat, quiet, subdued woman, who held her house and her husband in as much reverence as a Feejee holds his idols. Like most women, she had an instinctive love for grace and beauty, but from long repression it was only a blind and groping instinct. Her house was kept in a state of spotless purity, but was bald as any vineless rock within. Flies never intruded there; spiders still less. The windows of the "best room" were veiled and double-veiled with green paper shades and snow-white cotton curtains, and the ghastly light that strayed in through these obstructions revealed a speckless, but hideous, homespun carpet, four straight-backed chairs, with horse-hair seats, an equally black and shining sofa, and a round mahogany table with a great Bible in the midst. No vases, no shells, no ornament of useless fashion stood on the white wooden mantelpiece over the open fireplace; no stencil border broke the monotonous whitewash of the walls. You could see your face in a state of distortion and jaundice anywhere in the andirons, so brilliant were their brassy columns; and the very bricks of the chimney were scraped and washed from the soot of the rare fire. You could hardly imagine that even the leaping, laughing wood-fire could impart any cheer to the funereal order of that chill and musty apartment. Bedroom, kitchen, shed, wood-house,—all shared this scrupulous array. The processes that in other households are wont to give cheery tokens of life, and bounty, and natural appetites and passions, seemed here to be carried on under protest. No flour was spilled when Thankful Blair made bread; no milk ever slopped from an overfull pail; no shoe ever brought in mud or sand across the mats that lay inside and outside of every door. The very garret preserved an aspect of serenity, since all its bundles of herbs hung evenly side by side, and the stores of nuts had each their separate boundaries, lest some jarring door or intrusive mouse should scatter them.

In the midst of all this order there was yet a child, if little Hannah Blair ever was a child in more than name. From her babyhood she was the model of all Wingfield babies: a child that never fretted; that slept nights through all the pangs and perils of teething; that had every childish disease with perfect decency and patience; was a child to be held up to every mother's admiration. Poor little soul! the mother love that crushed those other babies with kisses; that romped and laughed with them, when she was left straight and solemn in her cradle; that petted, and slapped, and spoiled, and scolded all those common children, Thankful Blair kept under lock and key in her inmost heart.

"Beware of idols!" was the stern warning that had fallen on her first outburst of joy at the birth of one living child at last, and from that time the whole tenor of her husband's speech and prayer had been that they both might be saved from the awful sin of idolatry, and be enabled to bring up their child in the fear of the Lord, a hater of sin and a follower of the Law: the gospel that a baby brought to light was not yet theirs! So Hannah grew to girlhood, a feminine reproduction of her father. Keen, practical insight is not the most softening trait for a woman to possess. It is iron and steel in the soul that does not burn with love mighty and outflowing enough to fuse all other elements in its own glow, and as Hannah grew older and read her mother's repressed nature through and through, the tender heart, the timid conscience, the longing after better and brighter things than life offered to her, only moved her child to an unavowed contempt for a soul so weak and so childish. In a certain way Hannah Blair loved her mother, but it was more as if she had been her child than her parent. Toward her father her feelings were far different. She respected him; he was her model. She alone knew, from a like experience, what reserved depth of feeling lay unawakened under his rigid exterior; she knew, for there were times when her own granite nature shuddered through and through with volcanic forces; when her only refuge against generous indignation or mighty anger was in solitary prayer and grievous wrestlings of the flesh against the spirit as well as the spirit against the flesh. So Hannah grew up to womanhood. Tall and slight as any woodland sapling, but without the native grace of a free growth, her erect and alert figure pleased only by its alacrity and spotless clothing. She was "dredful spry," as old Moll Thunder, the half-breed Indian woman used to say,—"dredful spry; most like squaw—so still, so straight; blue eyes, most like ice. Ho! Moll better walk a chalk 'fore Miss Hanner!"

And Moll spoke from bitter experience, for old Deacon Campbell himself never gave her severer lectures on her ungodly life and conversation than dropped with cutting distinctness from those prim, thin, red lips. Yet Hannah Blair was not without charms for the youth of Wingfield. Spare as she was, her face had the fresh bloom of youth upon its high, straight features; her eyes were blue and bright; her hair, smoothed about her small head, glittered like fresh flax, and made a heavy coil, that her slender white throat seemed over-small to sustain. She was cool, serene, rather unapproachable to lovers or love-makers; but she was David Blair's only child, and his farm lay fair and wide on the high plains of Wingfield. She was well-to-do and pious,—charms which hold to this day potent sway over the youth of her native soil,—and after she was eighteen no Sunday night passed in solitude in the Blair keeping-room; for young men of all sorts and sizes ranged themselves against the wall, sometimes four at once, tilted their chairs, twirled their thumbs, crossed one foot and then the other over their alternate knees, dropping sparse remarks about the corn, or the weather, or the sermon, sometimes even the village politics; but one and all stared at Hannah, as she sat upright by the fireplace or the window, arrayed in a blue-stuff gown or a flowered chintz, as the season might be, and sitting as serene, as cool, as uninteresting as any cherub on a tombstone, till the old Dutch clock struck nine, the meeting-house bell tolled, and the young men, one and all, made their awkward farewells and went home, uttering, no doubt, a sigh of relief when the painful pleasure was over.

By and by the Wingfield store, long kept by Uncle Gid Mayhew, began to have a look of new life, for the old man's only son, Charley Mayhew, had come home from Boston, where he had been ten years in a dry-goods shop, to take the business off his father's hands. Just in time, too, for the store was scarce set to rights in symmetrical fashion when Uncle Gid was struck with paralysis and put to bed for the rest of his life,—a brief one at that. Wingfield gossips shook their heads and muttered that the new order of things was enough to kill him. After so many years of dust and confusion, to see the pepper-corns, candy, and beeswax sorted out into fresh, clean jars; the shoes and ribbons, cut nails and bar-soap, neatly disentangled and arranged; the ploughs, harrows, cheeses, hoes and bales of cotton and calico divorced and placed at different ends of the store; the grimy windows washed, and the dirty floor cleaned and swept,—was perhaps a shock to the old man, but not enough to kill him. His eighty years of vegetation sufficed for that; but he left behind him this son, so full of life, and spirit, and fun, so earnest at work, so abounding in energy, but withal so given over to frolic in its time, that it seemed as if even Wingfield stagnation never could give him a proper dulness or paralyze his handsome face and manly figure. Of course Charley Mayhew fell in love with Hannah Blair.

A mischievous desire at first to wake up those cold blue eyes and flush that clear, set face with blushes soon deepened into a very devoted affection. The ranks of Sunday-night lovers began to look at him with evil eyes, for not even the formality of the best parlor restrained his fun, or the impassive visage of David Blair awed him into silence. Even Hannah began to glow and vivify in his presence; a warmer color flushed her cheeks, her thin lips relaxed in real smiles; her eyes shone with deeper and keener gleams than the firelight lent them, and, worst of all, the sheepish suitors themselves could not help an occasional giggle, a broad grin, or even a decided horse-laugh, at his sallies; and when at last David Blair himself relaxed into an audible laugh, and declared to Charley he was "a master hand at telling stories," the vexed ranks gave it up, allowed that the conquering hero had come, and left Charley Mayhew a free field thereafter, which of course he improved. But even after Hannah Blair had promised in good, set terms to be his wife, and David had given his slow consent, it was doubtful to Charley if this treasure was his merely out of his own determined persistence or with any genuine feeling of her own, any real response of heart; for the maiden was so inaccessible, so chill, so proper, that his warm, impulsive nature dashed against hers and recoiled as the wild sea from a rocky coast. Yet after many days the rock does show signs of yielding; there are traces on its surface, though it needs years to soften and disintegrate its nature. They were a handsome couple, these two, and admiring eyes followed them in their walks. Never had Hannah's face mantled with so rich a color, or her eyes shone with so deep and soft a blue; the stern, red lips relaxed into a serene content, and here and there a tint of gayety about her dress—a fresh ribbon, a flower at her throat, a new frill—told of her shy blossom-time. She was one of those prim, old-fashioned pinks, whose cold color, formal shape, stiff growth, and dagger-shaped gray-green leaves, stamp them the quaint old-maid sisterhood of flowers, yet which hold in their hearts a breath of passionate spice, an odor of the glowing Orient or the sweet and ardent South, that seems fitter for the open-breasted roses, looking frankly and fervently up to the sun.

No, not even her lover knew the madness of Hannah Blair's hungry heart, now for the first time fed,—a madness that filled her with sweet delirium, that she regarded as nothing less than a direct Satanic impulse, against which she fought and prayed, all in vain; for God was greater than her heart, and he had filled it with that love which every wife and mother needs, strong enough to endure all things, to be forever faithful and forever fresh. But no vine-planted and grass-strewn volcano ever showed more placidly than Hannah Blair. Her daily duties were done with such exactness and patience, her lover's demands so coolly set aside till those duties were attended to, her face kept so calm even when the blood thrilled to her finger-tips at the sound of his voice, that, long as her mother had known her, she looked on with wonder, and admired afar off the self-control she never could have exhibited. For Hannah's wooing was carried on in no such style as her mother's had been. Thankful Parsons had accepted David Blair from a simple sense of duty, and he had asked her because she was meek and pious, had a good farm, and understood cows; no troublesome sentiment, no turbulent passion, disturbed their rather dull courtship. A very different wooer was this handsome, merry young fellow, with his dark curls and keen, pleasant eyes, who came into the house like a fresh, dancing breeze, and stirred its dusty stagnation into absolute sparkle. Mrs. Blair loved him dearly already; her repressed heart opened to him all its motherly instincts. She cooked for him whatever she observed he liked, with simple zeal and pleasure. She unconsciously smiled to hear his voice. Deeply she wondered at Hannah, who, day by day, stitched on her quilts, her sheets, her pillow-cases, and her napery, with as diligent sternness as ever she applied to more irksome tasks, and never once blushed or smiled over the buying or shaping of her personal bridal gear, only showing, if possible, a keener eye for business, a more infallible judgment of goods and prices, wear and tear, use and fitness, than ever before.

So the long winter wore away. Hannah's goods lay piled in the "spare chamber,"—heaps of immaculate linen, homespun flannel, patchwork of gayest hues, and towels woven and hemmed by her own hands; and in the clothes-press, whose deep drawers were filled with her own garments in neat array, hung the very wedding dress of dove-colored paduasoy, the great Leghorn bonnet, with white satin ribbons, and the black silk cardinal. Hannah had foregone all the amusements of the past months, at no time consonant to her taste, in order to construct these treasures for her new life. In vain had Charley coaxed her to share in the sleighing frolics, the huskings, the quilting-bees of the neighborhood. It did not once enter into his mind that Hannah had rather be alone with the fulness of her great joy than to have its sacred rapture intermeddled with by the kindly or unkindly jokes and jeers of other people. He never knew that her delight was full even to oppression, when she sat by herself and sewed like an automaton, setting with every stitch a hope or a thought of her love and life.

It was spring now. The long, cold winter had passed at last; the woods began to bud, the pastures grew green even in Wingfield, and brave little blossoms sprung up in the very moisture of the just melted snow-drifts. May had brought the robins and the swallows back; here and there an oriole darted like a flake of fire from one drooping elm to another; the stiff larches put out little crimson cones; the gracious elm boughs grew dusk and dense with swelling buds, and the maple hung out its dancing yellow tassels high in air. The swamps were transfigured with vivid verdure and lit with rank yellow blossoms, where

> "The wild marsh marigold shone like fire,"—

the quaint, sad-colored trillium made its protest in fence corners and by the low buttresses of granite on the hills far and near, and the rough-leaved arbutus nestled its baby faces of sweetest bloom deep in the gray grass and stiff moss beds. The day drew near for the wedding. It was to be the last Wednesday in May.

"Darned unlucky!" muttered Moll Thunder, drying her ragged shoes before Mrs. Blair's kitchen fire, having just brought a fagot of herbs and roots for the brewing of root-beer,—even then a favorite beverage in New England, as it is to-day. "Darned unlucky! Married in May, repent alway. Guess Hanner pretty good like ter set up 'ginst ole debbil heself. No good, no good; debbil pretty good strong. Moll knows! He! he! he!"

Mrs. Blair shivered. She was superstitious, like all women, and old Moll was a born witch, everybody knew. But then her daughter's pure, fair, and resolute face rose up before her, and the superstitious fear flickered and went out. She thought Hannah altogether beyond the power of "ole debbil." At last the last Wednesday came,—a day as serene and lovely as if new created; flying masses of white cloud chased each other through the azure sky, and cast quick shadows on the long, green range of hills that shut in Wingfield on the west. Shine and shadow added an exquisite grace of expression to the shades of tender green veiling those cruel granite rocks; a like flitting grace at last transfigured Hannah Blair's cold-featured face. The apple-trees blossomed everywhere with festive garlands of faint pink bloom, and filled the air with their bitter-sweet, subtle odor, clean and delicate, yet the parent of that luscious, vinous, oppressive perfume that autumn should bring from the heaps of gold and crimson fruit, as yet unformed below those waxen petals.

To-day at last Hannah had resolved to give her beating heart one day of freedom,—one long day of unrestrained joy,—if she could bear the freedom of that ardent rapture, so long, so conscientiously repressed. For once in her life she sung about her work; psalm-tunes, indeed, but one can put a deal of vitality into Mear and Bethesda; and Cambridge, with its glad, exultant repeat, has all the capacity of a love-song. Mrs. Blair heard it from the kitchen where she was watching the last pan of cake come to crisp perfection in the brick oven. The old words had a curious adaptation to the sweet, intense triumph of the air, and Hannah carried the three parts of the tune as they came in with a flexibility of voice new to her as to her sole hearer:—

"'Twas in the watches of the night
I thought upon thy power;
I kept thy lovely face in sight
Amid the darkest hour!"

What a subdued ecstasy rose and fell in her voice as she swept and garnished the old house.

"Amid the darkest hour!"

Oh, there could never be a dark hour for her again, she thought,—never a doubt, or fear, or trouble.

"My beloved is mine and I am his,"

rose to her lips from the oldest of all love-songs. Half profane she seemed to herself; but to-day her deeper nature got the better of her deep prejudices; she was at heart, for once, a simple, love-smitten girl.

The quiet wedding was to be after tea. Nobody was asked, for the few relatives David Blair possessed were almost strangers to him, and lived far away. His wife had been an only child, and Hannah had made no girl friends in the village. The minister was to come at eight o'clock, and the orthodox cake and wine handed round after the ceremony. The young couple were to go to their own house, and settle down at once to the duties and cares of life. Charley had been ordered not to appear till tea-time, and after the dinner was eaten and everything put to rights Mrs. Blair went to her room to plait a cap-ruffle, and Hannah sat down in the spare room by herself, to rest, she said; really to dream, to hope, to bury her face in her trembling hand, and let a mighty wave of rapture overflow her whole entranced soul. The cap-ruffle troubled Mrs. Blair much. Twice it had to be taken from the prim plaits and relaid, then to be sprinkled and ironed out. This involved making a fresh fire to heat the flat-iron, and it got to be well on in the afternoon, and Mrs. Blair was tired. There was nobody to reflect on her waste of time, so she lay down a moment on the bed. David had gone to plough a lot on the furthest part of the farm. He neglected work for no emergency. As a godless neighbor said once, "Dave Blair would sow rye on the edge of hell if he thought he could get the cattle there to plough it up!" A daughter's wedding-day was no excuse for idleness in him. So Mrs. Blair was safe in her nap.

Meantime, as Hannah sat a little withdrawn from the open window, where for once the afternoon sun streamed in unguardedly, and the passionate warble of the song-sparrows, and the indescribable odor of spring followed too, she was suddenly half aware of an outside shadow, and a letter skimmed through the window, and fell at her feet. Scarce roused from her dream, she looked at it fixedly a moment before she stooped to pick it up. Its coming was so sudden, so startling, it did not once occur to her to look out and see who brought it. She hesitated before she broke the broad, red seal, and swept her hand across her eyes as if to brush away the dreams that had filled and clouded them. But the first few words brought back to those eyes their native steely glint, and, as she read on, life, light, love, withdrew their tender glories from her face. It settled into stone, into flint. Her mouth set in lines of dreadful implacable portent, her cheek paled to the whiteness of a marble monument, and the red lips faded to pale, cold purple. What she read in that letter neither man nor woman save the writer and the reader ever knew, for when it was read Hannah Blair walked like an unrepentant conspirator to the stake, fearless, careless, hopeless, out into the small, silent kitchen, and laying that missive of evil on the smouldering coals, stood by stark and stiff till every ash was burned or floated up the chimney. Then she turned, and said in the voice of one who calls from his grave:—

"Mother!"

Mrs. Blair sprung from her doze at the sound. Her mother instinct was keen as the hen's who hears the hawk scream in the sky, and knows her brood in danger. She was on the threshold of the kitchen door almost as soon as Hannah spoke; and her heart sank to its furthest depth when she saw the face before her. Death would have left no such traces—given her no such shock. This was death in life, and it spoke, slowly, deliberately, with an awful distinctness.

"Mother, when Charles Mayhew comes here to-night, you must tell him I will not marry him."

"What?" half screamed the terrified woman, doubtful of her own hearing. Again the cold, relentless tones, in accents as clear and certain as the voice of fate itself:—

"When Charles Mayhew comes here to-night you must see him, and tell him I will not marry him."

"Hanner, I can't! I can't! What for? What do you mean? What is it?"

The words syllabled themselves again out of the thin, rigid lips:—

"I will not marry him."

"Oh, I can't tell him! he will die! I *cannot*, Hanner. You must tell him yourself—you must! you must!"

Still the same answer, only the words lessening each time:—

"I will not!"

"But, Hanner, child, stop and think—do. All your things made; you're published; the minister's spoke to. Why do you act so? You can't, Hanner. Oh, I never can tell him! What shall I say? What will he do? Oh, dear! You must tell him yourself; I can't—I won't! I aint goin' to; you must!"

A shade of mortal weariness stole across the gray, still face, most like the relaxation of the features after death; but that was all the shrill tirade produced, except the dull, cold repetition:—

"I will not!"

And then Hannah Blair turned and crept up the narrow stairway to her bedroom; her mother, stunned with terror and amazement, still with a mother's alert ear, heard the key grate in the lock, the window shut quietly down, and heard no more. The house was silent even to breathlessness. In her desperation Mrs. Blair began to wish that David would come; and then the unconscious spur of life-long habit stung her into action. It was five o'clock, and she must get tea; for tea must be prepared though the crack of doom were impending. So she built the fire, filled the kettle, hung it on the crane, laid the table, all with the accuracy of habit, her ear strained to its utmost to hear some voice, some sigh, some movement from that bolted chamber above. All in vain. There might have been a corpse there for any sound of life, and Mrs. Blair felt the awe of death creep over her as she listened. For once it was glad relief to hear David coming with the oxen; to see them driven to their shed; to watch his gaunt, erect figure come up the path to the back door; but how hard it was to tell him. He asked no question, he made no comment, but the cold, gray eye quickened into fire like the sudden glitter of lightning, and without a word he strode up the stair to Hannah's room.

"Hannah!"

There was no answer. David Blair was ill-used to disobedience. His voice was sterner than ever as he repeated the call:—

"Hannah, open your door!"

Slowly the key turned, slowly the door opened, and the two faced each other. The strong man recoiled. Was this his child,—this gray, rigid masque, this old woman? But he had a duty to do.

"Hannah, why is this?"

"I cannot tell you, father."

"But you must see Charles Mayhew."

"I will not!"

Still calm, but inexpressibly bitter and determined, like one repeating a dreadful lesson after some tyrant's torture. David Blair could not speak. He stood still on that threshold, without speech or motion, and softly as it had opened, the door closed in his face, the key turned, he was shut out,—not merely from the chamber, but forever from the deepest recess of Hannah's heart and life, if indeed he had ever, even in imagination, entered there. He stood a moment in silent amazement, and then went down into the kitchen utterly speechless. He swallowed his supper mechanically, reached down his hat, but on the door-step turned and said:—

"Thankful, you must tell Charles Mayhew: Hannah will not; I cannot. It is women's work—yea, it was a woman that first time in Paradise!"

And with this scriptural sneer he left his frightened wife to do the thing he dared not. Not the first man who has done so, nor the last. An hour later the joyful bridegroom came in, his dark eyes full of happy light, his handsome figure set off by a new suit of clothes, the like of which Wingfield never had seen, much less originated; his face fairly radiant; but it clouded quickly as a storm-reflecting lake when he saw the cold, wet face of Mrs. Blair, the reddened eyes, the quivering lips, and felt the close, yet trembling pressure of the kind old arms, for the first time clasped round his neck as he stooped toward her. How Thankful Blair contrived to tell him what she had to tell she never knew. It was forced from her lips in incoherent snatches; it was received at first with total incredulity, and she needed to repeat it again and again; to recall Hannah's words, to describe, as she best might, her ghastly aspect, her hollow, hoarse voice, her reply to her father. At last Charles Mayhew began to believe—to rave, to give way to such passionate, angry grief that Thankful Blair trembled, and longed for Parson Day to come, or for David to return. But neither thing happened, for David had warned the parson, and then hidden his own distress and dismay as far as he could get from the house in his own woodland, sitting on a log for hours, lest in coming back to the house he should face the man he could not but pity and fear both; for what reason or shadow of excuse could he offer to him for his daughter's cruel and mysterious conduct? So Mrs. Blair had to bear the scene alone. At last the maddened man insisted on going upstairs to Hannah's door; but that her mother withstood. He should not harass Hannah; she would keep her from one more anguish, if she stood in the door-way and resisted physically.

"But I will see her! I will speak to her! I will know myself what this means! I am not a fool or a dog, to be thrown aside for nothing!"

And with this he rushed out of the kitchen door, round the end of the house, to the grass-plat below Hannah's window. Well he knew that little window, with its white curtain, where he had so often watched the light go out from the hill-side, where he always lingered in his homeward walks. The curtain was down now, and no ray of light quivered from behind it.

"Hannah! Hannah! *my* Hannah!" he called, with anguish in every tone. "Hannah, look at me! only just look at me! tell me one word!" And then came the fondest pleadings, the most passionate remonstrances—all in vain. He might as well have agonized by her coffin side—by her grass-grown grave. Now a different mood inspired him, and he poured out threats and commands till the cool moonlight air seemed quivering with passion and rage. Still there was no voice nor answer, nor any that replied. The calmness of immortal repose lay upon this quiet dwelling, though the torment and tumult without stormed like a tempest. Was there, then, neither tumult nor torment within? At last, when hours—ages it seemed to the desperate man—had passed by, nature could endure no more. The apathy of exhaustion stole over him; he felt a despair, that was partly bodily weariness, take entire possession of him; he ceased to adjure, to remonstrate, to cry out.

"Good-by, Hannah; good-by!" he called at length. The weak, sad accents beat like storm-weary birds vainly against that blank, deaf window. Nothing spoke to him, not even the worn-out and helpless woman who sat on the kitchen door-step with her apron over her head, veiling her hopeless distress, nor lifting that homely screen to see a ruined man creep away from his own grave,—the grave of all his better nature, to be seen there no more; for from that hour no creature in Wingfield ever saw or heard of him again.

There was a mighty stir among the gossips of the village for once. Not often did so piquant and mysterious a bit of scandal regale them at sewing societies, at tea-fights, even at prayer-meetings, for it became a matter of certain religious interest, since all the parties therein were church-members. But in vain did all the gossips lay their heads together. Nothing was known beyond the bare facts that at the last minute Hannah Blair had "gi'n the mitten" to Charley Mayhew, and he had then and there disappeared. His store was sold to a new-comer from Grenville Centre, who was not communicative,—perhaps because he had nothing to tell,—and Charley dropped out of daily talk before long, as one who is dead and buried far away; as we all do, after how brief a time, how vanishing a grief. As for the Blairs, they endured in stoical silence, and made no sign. Sunday saw both the old people in their places early; nobody looked for Hannah, but before the bell ceased its melancholy toll, just before Parson Day ambled up the broad aisle, her slender figure, straight and still as ever, came up to her seat in the square pew. True her face was colorless; the shadow of death lingered there yet; and though her eyes shone with keener glitter than ever, and her lips burned like a scarlet streak, an acute observer would have seen upon her face traces of a dreadful conflict: lines around the mouth that years of suffering might have grown; a relaxation of the muscles about the eye and temple; a look as of one who sees only something afar off, who is absent from the body as far as consciousness goes. There she sat,—through short prayer and long prayer, hymn, psalm, and sermon, and the battery of looks, both direct and furtive, that assailed her,—all unmoved. And at home it was the same,—utterly listless, cold, silent, she took up her life again; day by day did her weary round of household duties with the same punctilious neatness and despatch; spun and knit, and turned cheeses; for her mother had been broken down visibly for a time by this strange and sad catastrophe, and was more incapable than ever in her life before of earnest work, so Hannah had her place to supply in part as well as her own. We hear of martyrs of the stake, the fagot, the arena, the hunger-maddened beasts, the rising tide, the rack, and our souls shudder, our flesh creeps; we wonder and adore. I think the gladdest look of her life would have illuminated Hannah Blair's face had it been possible now to exchange her endurance for any of these deaths; but it is women who must endure; for them are those secret agonies no enthusiasm gilds, no hope assuages, no sympathy consoles. God alone stoops to this anguish, and he not always; for there is a stubborn pride that will not lift its eyes to heaven lest it should be a tacit acknowledgment that they were fixed once upon poor earth. For these remains only the outlook daily lessening to all of us,—the outlook whose vista ends in a grave.

But the unrelenting days stole on; their dead march, with monotonous tramp, left traces on even Hannah's wretched, haughty soul. They trampled down the past in thick dust; it became ashes under their feet. Her life from torture subsided into pain; then into bitterness, stoicism, contempt,—at last into a certain treadmill of indifference; only not indifference from the strong, cruel grasp she still found it needful to keep upon thought and memory: once let that iron hand relax its pressure, and chaos threatened her again; she dared not. Lovers came no more to Hannah; a certain instinct of their sure fate kept them away; the store of linen and cotton she had gathered, her mother's careful hands had packed away directly in the great garret. The lavender silk, the cardinal, the big bonnet, had been worn to church, year after year, in the same spirit in which a Hindoo woman puts on her gorgeous garments and her golden ornaments for suttee. Mrs. Blair looked on in solemn wonder, but said not a word. Nor were these bridal robes worn threadbare ten years after, when another change came to Hannah's life; when Josiah Maxwell, a well-to-do bachelor from Newfield, the next village, was "recommended" to her, and came over to try his chance. Josiah was a personable, hale, florid man of forty; generous, warm-hearted, a little blustering perhaps, but thoroughly good, and a rich man for those days. He had a tannery, a foundry, and a flourishing farm. Newfield was a place of great water-privileges, sure to grow; it was pretty, bright, and successful; the sleepy, mullein-growing farms of Wingfield had in them no such cheer or life. Hannah was thirty years old; the matter was set before her purely as a matter of business. Josiah wanted a pious, capable wife. He had been too busy to fall in love all his life; now he was too sensible (he thought); so he looked about him calmly, after royal fashion, and, hearing good report of Hannah Blair, proceeded to make her acquaintance and visit her. She, too, was a rational woman; feeling she had long set aside as a weak indulgence of the flesh; all these long and lonely years had taught her a lesson—more than one. She had learned, that a nature as strong, as dominant, as full of power and pride as hers must have some outlet or burn itself out, and here was a prospect offered that appealed to her native instincts, save and except that one so long trodden under foot. She accepted Mr. Maxwell; listened to his desire for a short engagement favorably; took down the stores prepared for a past occasion from the chests in the garret, washed and bleached them with her own hands; and purchased once more her bridal attire, somewhat graver, much more costly than before,—a plum-colored satin dress, a white merino shawl, a hat of chip with rich white ribbons. Moll Thunder, who served as chorus to this homely tragedy, was at hand with her quaint, shrewd comment, as she brought Mrs. Blair her yearly tribute of hickory nuts the week before the wedding.

"He! he! She look pretty much fine; same as cedar tree out dere, all red vine all ober; nobody tink him ole cedar been lightnin'-struck las' year. He! he! Haint got no heart in him—pretty much holler."

One bright October day Hannah was married. Parson Day's successor performed the ceremony in the afternoon, and the "happy couple" went home to Newfield in a gig directly. Never was a calmer bride, a more matter-of-fact wedding. Sentiment was at a discount in the Blair family; if David felt anything at parting with his only child, he repressed its expression; and since that day her mother never could forget, Hannah had wrought in poor Mrs. Blair's mind a sort of terror toward her that actually made her absence a relief, and the company of the little "bound girl" she had taken to bring up a pleasant substitute for Hannah's stern, quiet activity. Everybody was suited; it was almost a pleasure to Mrs. Maxwell to rule over her sunny farmhouse and become a model to all backsliding house-keepers about her. Her butter always "came;" her bread never soured; her hens laid and set, her chickens hatched, in the most exemplary manner; nobody had such a garden, such a loom and wheel, such spotless linen, such shiny mahogany; there was never a hole in her husband's garments or a button off his shirt; the one thing that troubled her was that her husband—good, honest, tender man—had during their first year of married life fallen thoroughly in love with her; it was not in his genial nature to live in the house a year with even a cat and not love it. Hannah was a handsome woman, and his wife; what could one expect? But she did not expect it; she was bored and put out by his demonstrations; almost felt a cold contempt for the love he lavished on her, icy and irresponsive as she was, though all the time ostensibly submissive. Josiah felt after a time that he had made a mistake; but he had the sense to adapt himself to it, and to be content, like many another idolater, with worship instead of response. Not even the little daughter born in the second year of their marriage thawed the heart so long frost-sealed in Hannah's breast; she had once worshipped a false god, and endured the penalty; henceforward she would be warned. Baby was baptized Dorothy, after her father's dead mother, and by every one but Hannah that quaint style was softened into Dolly. Never was a child better brought up, everybody said,—a rosy, sturdy, saucy little creature, doing credit to fresh air and plain food; a very romp in the barn and fields with her father, whom she loved with all her warm, wayward heart; but, alas! a child whose strong impulses, ardent feeling, violent temper, and stormy will were never to know the softening, tempering sweetness of real mother love. She knew none of those tender hours of caressing and confidence that even a very little child enjoys in the warmth of any mother-heart, if not its own mother's; no loving arms clasped her to a mother's bosom to soothe her baby-griefs, to rest her childish weariness. There were even times when Hannah Maxwell seemed to resent her existence; to repel her affection, though her duty kept her inexorably just to the child. Dolly was never punished for what she had not done, but always for nearly everything she did do, and services were exacted from her that made her childhood a painful memory to all her later life. Were there butter or eggs wanted from Wingfield on any emergency, at five years old Dolly would be mounted on the steady old horse that Josiah had owned fifteen years, and, with saddle-bags swinging on either side, sent over to her grandfather's at Wingfield to bring home the supplies,—a long and lonely road of five full-measured miles for the tiny creature to traverse; and one could scarce believe the story did it not come direct to these pages from her own lips. In vain was Josiah's remonstrance; for by this time Hannah was fully the head of the house, and the first principle of her rule was silent obedience. All her husband could do was to indulge and spoil Dolly in private, persistently and bravely. Alas for her, there was one day in the week when even father could not interfere to help his darling. Sunday was a sound of terror in her ears: first the grim and silent breakfast, where nobody dared smile, and where even a fixed routine of food, not in itself enticing, became at last tasteless by mere habit; codfish-cakes and tea, of these, "as of all carnal pleasure, cometh satiety at the last," according to the monk in "Hypatia;" then, fixed in a high, stiff-backed chair, the pretty little vagrant must be still, and read her Bible till it was time to ride to church; till she was taken down and arrayed in spotlessness and starch, and set bodkinwise into the gig beside her silent mother and subdued father.

Once at meeting, began the weariest routine of all. Through all the long services, her little fat legs swinging from the high seat, Dolly was expected to sit perfectly quiet; not a motion was allowed, not a whisper permitted; she dared not turn her head to watch a profane butterfly or a jolly bumblebee wandering about that great roof or tall window. Of course she did do it instinctively, recovering herself with a start of terror and a glance at her mother's cold blue eyes, always fixed on Parson Buck, but always aware of all going on beside her, as Dolly knew too well. At noon, after a hurried lunch of gingerbread and cheese, the child was taken to the nearest house, there to sit through the noon prayer-meeting, her weary legs swinging this time off the edge of the high bed, and her wearier ears dinned with long prayers. Then, as soon as the bell tolled, off to the meeting-house to undergo another long sermon, till, worn out mentally and physically, the last hour of the *séance* became a struggle with sleep, painful in the extreme, as well in present resistance as in certainty of results; for, soon as poor Dolly reached home, after another silent drive, she was invariably taken into the spare bedroom, and soundly whipped for being restless in meeting. And, adding insult to injury, after dinner, enjoyed with the eager appetite of a healthy child used to three meals on a week-day, she was required to repeat that theological torture,—the Assembly's Catechism,—from end to end. But in spite of all this, partly because Sunday came only once a week, partly because of her father's genial nature and devoted affection for his girl, which grew deeper and stronger constantly, Dolly did not miss of her life as many a morbid character might have in her place. She grew up a rosy, sunny, practical young woman, with a dominant temper toward everybody but her mother. Plump, healthy, and pretty, her cheeriness and usefulness would have made her popular had she been a poor man's daughter,—and by this time Josiah Maxwell was the richest man in the town; so Dolly had plenty of lovers, and in due time married a fine young fellow, and settled down at home with her parents, who were almost as much pleased with Mr. Henderson as was their daughter. But all this time Mrs. Maxwell preserved the calm austerity of her manner, even to her child. She did her duty by Dolly. She prepared for her marriage with liberal hand and unerring judgment; but no caress, no sympathetic word, no slightest expression of affection, soothed the girl's agitated heart or offered her support in this tender, yet exciting, crisis of her life.

Hannah Maxwell made her life a matter of business,—it had been nothing else to her for years; it was an old habit at sixty; and she was well over that age when one day Dolly, rocking her first baby to sleep, was startled to see her mother, who sat in her upright chair reading the county paper, fall quietly to the floor and lie there. Baby was left to fret while her mother ran to the old lady and lifted her spare, thin shape to the sofa; but she did not need to do more, for Mrs. Maxwell's eyes opened and her hand clasped tight on Dolly's.

"Do not call any one," she whispered faintly, and, leaning on her daughter's shoulder, her whole body shook with agonized sobs. At last that heart of granite had broken in her breast; lightning-struck so long ago, now it crumbled. With her head still on Dolly's kind arm, she told her then and there the whole story of her one love, her solitary passion, and its fatal ending. She still kept to herself the contents of that anonymous letter, only declaring that she knew, and the writer must have been aware she would know, from the handwriting as well as the circumstances detailed, who wrote it, and that the information it conveyed of certain lapses from virtue on the part of Charles Mayhew must be genuine.

"O Dolly!" groaned the smitten woman, "when he stood under my window and called me I was wrung to my heart's core. The pains of hell gat hold upon me. I was upon the floor, with my arms wound about the bed-rail and my teeth shut like a vice, lest I should listen to the voice of nature, and, going to the window to answer him, behold his face. Had I seen him I must have gone down and done what I thought a sin; so I steeled myself to resist, although I thought flesh would fail in the end; but it did not. I conquered then and after. Oh, how long it has been! I meant to do right, Dolly; but to-day, when I saw in the paper that he died last week in a barn over Goshen way, a lonely, drunken pauper—Dolly, my heart came out of its grave and smote me. Had I been a meeker woman, having mercy instead of judgment, I might have helped him to right ways. I might have saved him—I loved him so."

The last words struck upon her hearer with the force of a blow, so burning, so eager, so intense was the emphasis: "I loved him *so*!"

Ah, who could ever know the depths out of which that regretful utterance sprang!

"Dear mother, dear mother," sobbed Dolly, altogether overcome by this sudden revelation of gulfs she had never dreamed of,—a heart which, long repressed, convulsively burst at last, and revealed its bleeding arteries.

"Dear, good mother, don't feel so—don't! You meant right. Try to forgive yourself. If you made a mistake then, try to forget it now. Try to believe it was all for the best—do, dear."

But all she got for answer was—"Dolly, it is too late!"

1875

# ROSE TERRY COOKE

(1827–1892)

## *How Celia Changed Her Mind*

"If there 's anything on the face of the earth I *do* hate, it 's an old maid!"

Mrs. Stearns looked up from her sewing in astonishment.

"Why, Miss Celia!"

"Oh, yes! I know it. I 'm one myself, but all the same, I hate 'em worse than p'ison. They ain't nothing nor nobody; they 're cumberers of the ground." And Celia Barnes laid down her scissors with a bang, as if she might be Atropos herself, ready to cut the thread of life for all the despised class of which she was a notable member.

The minister's wife was genuinely surprised at this outburst; she herself had been well along in life before she married, and though she had been fairly happy in the uncertain relationship to which she had attained, she was, on the whole, inclined to agree with St. Paul, that the woman who did not marry "doeth better." "I don't agree with you, Miss Celia," she said gently. "Many, indeed, most of my best friends are maiden ladies, and I respect and love them just as much as if they were married women."

"Well, I don't. A woman that 's married is somebody; she 's got a place in the world; she ain't everybody's tag; folks don't say, 'Oh, it 's nobody but that old maid Celye Barnes;' it 's 'Mis' Price,' and 'Mis' Simms,' or 'Thomas Smith's wife,' as though you was somebody. I don't know how 't is elsewheres, but here in Bassett you might as well be a dog as an old maid. I allow it might be better if they all had means or eddication: money 's 'a dreadful good thing to have in the house,' as I see in a book once, and learning is sort of comp'ny to you if you 're lonesome; but then lonesome you be, and you 've got to be, if you're an old maid, and it can't be helped noway."

Mrs. Stearns smiled a little sadly, thinking that even married life had its own loneliness when your husband was shut up in his study, or gone off on a long drive to see some sick parishioner or conduct a neighborhood prayer-meeting, or even when he was the other side of the fireplace absorbed in a religious paper or a New York daily, or meditating on his next sermon, while the silent wife sat unnoticed at her mending or knitting. "But married women have more troubles and responsibilities than the unmarried, Miss Celia," she said. "You have no children to bring up and be anxious about, no daily dread of not doing your duty by the family whom you preside over, and no fear of the supplies giving out that are really needed. Nobody but your own self to look out for."

"That 's jest it," snapped Celia, laying down the boy's coat she was sewing with a vicious jerk of her thread. "There 't is! Nobody to home to care if you live or die; nobody to peek out of the winder to see if you 're comin', or to make a mess of gruel or a cup of tea for you, or to throw ye a feelin' word if you 're sick nigh unto death. And old maids is just as li'ble to up and die as them that 's married. And as to responsibility, I ain't afraid to tackle that. Never! I don't hold with them that cringe and crawl and are skeert at a shadder, and won't do a living thing that they had ought to do because they 're 'afraid to take the responsibility.' Why, there 's Mrs. Deacon Trimble, she durst n't so much as set up a prayer-meetin' for missions or the temp'rance cause, because 't was 'sech a reesponsibility to take the lead in them matters.' I suppose it 's somethin' of a responsible chore to preach the gospel to the heathen, or grab a drinkin' feller by the scruff of his neck and haul him out of the horrible pit anyway, but if it 's dooty it 's got to be done, whether or no; and I ain't afraid of pitchin' into anything the Lord sets me to do!"

"Except being an old maid," said Mrs. Stearns.

Celia darted a sharp glance at her over her silver-rimmed spectacles, and pulled her needle through and through the seams of Willy's jacket with fresh vigor, while a thoughtful shadow came across her fine old face. Celia was a candid woman, for all her prejudices, a combination peculiarly characteristic of New England, for she was a typical Yankee. Presently she said abruptly, "I had n't thought on 't in that light." But then the minister opened the door, and the conversation stopped.

Parson Stearns was tired and hungry and cross, and his wife knew all that as soon as she saw his face. She had learned long ago that ministers, however good they may be, are still men; so to-day she had kept her husband's dinner warm in the under-oven, and had the kettle boiling to make him a cup of tea on the spot to assuage his irritation in the shortest and surest way; but though the odor of a savory stew and the cheerful warmth of the cooking-stove greeted him as he preceded her through the door into the kitchen, he snapped out, sharply enough for Celia to hear him through the half-closed door, "What do you have that old maid here for so often?"

"There!" said Celia to herself,—"there 't is! *He* don't look upon 't as a dispensation, if she doos. Men-folks run the world, and they know it. There ain't one of the hull caboodle but what despises an onmarried woman! Well, 't ain't altogether my fault. I would n't marry them that I could; I could n't—not and be honest; and them that I would hev had did n't ask me. I don't know as I 'm to blame, after all, when you look into 't."

And she went on sewing Willy's jacket, contrived with pains and skill out of an old coat of his father's, while Mrs. Stearns poured out her husband's tea in the kitchen, replenished his plate with stew, and cut for him more than one segment of the crisp, fresh apple-pie, and urged upon him the squares of new cheese that legitimately accompany this deleterious viand of the race and country, the sempiternal, insistent, flagrant, and alas! also fragrant pie.

Celia Barnes was the tailoress of the little scattered country town of Bassett. Early left an orphan, without near relatives or money, she had received the scantiest measure of education that our town authorities deal to the pauper children of such organizations. She was ten years old when her mother, a widow for almost all those ten years, left her to the tender mercies of the selectmen of Bassett. The selectmen of our country towns are almost irresponsible governors of their petty spheres, and gratify the instinct of oligarchy peculiar to, and conservative of, the human race. Men must be governed and tyrannized over,—it is an inborn necessity of their nature; and while a republic is a beautiful theory, eminently fitted for a race who are "non Angli, sed Angeli," it has in practice the effect of producing more than Russian tyranny, but on smaller scales and in far and scattered localities. Nowhere are there more despots than among village selectmen in New England. Those who have wrestled with their absolute monarchism in behalf of some charity that might abstract a few of the almighty dollars made out of poverty and distress from their official pockets know how positive and dogmatic is their use of power—*experto crede*. The Bassett "first selectman" promptly bound out little Celia Barnes to a hard, imperious woman, who made a white slave of the child, and only dealt out to her the smallest measure of schooling demanded by law, because the good old minister, Father Perkins, interfered in the child's behalf.

As she was strong and hardy and resolute, Celia lived through her bondage, and at the "free" age of eighteen apprenticed herself to old Miss Polly Mariner, the Bassett tailoress, and being deft with her fingers and quick of brain, soon outran her teacher, and when Polly died, succeeded to her business.

She was a bright girl, not particularly noticeable among others, for she had none of that delicate flower-like New England beauty which is so peculiar, so charming, and so evanescent; her features were tolerably regular, her forehead broad and calm, her gray eyes keen and perceptive, and she had abundant hair of an uncertain brown; but forty other girls in Bassett might have been described in the same way; Celia's face was one to improve with age; its strong sense, capacity for humor, fine outlines of a rugged sort, were always more the style of fifty than fifteen, and what she said of herself was true.

She had been asked to marry an old farmer with five uproarious boys, a man notorious in East Bassett for his stinginess and bad temper, and she had promptly declined the offer. Once more fate had given her a chance. A young fellow of no character, poor, "shiftless," and given to cider as a beverage, had considered it a good idea to marry some one who would make a home for him and earn his living. Looking about him for a proper person to fill this pleasant situation, he pounced on Celia—and she returned the attention!

"Marry *you*? I wonder you 've got the sass to ask any decent girl to marry ye, Alfred Hatch! What be you good for, anyway? I don't know what under the canopy the Lord spares you for,—only He doos let the tares grow amongst the wheat, Scripter says, and I 'm free to suppose He knows why, but I don't. No, *sir*! Ef you was the last man in the livin' universe I would n't tech ye with the tongs. If you 'd got a speck of grit into you,

you 'd be ashamed to ask a woman to take ye in and support ye, for that 's what it comes to. You go 'long! I can make my hands save my head so long as I hev the use of 'em, and I haven't no call to set up a private poor-house!"

So Alfred Hatch sneaked off, much like a cur that has sought to share the kennel of a mastiff, and been shortly and sharply convinced of his presumption.

Here ended Celia's "chances," as she phrased it. Young men were few in Bassett; the West had drawn them away with its subtle attraction of unknown possibilities, just as it does to-day, and Celia grew old in the service of those established matrons who always want clothes cut over for their children, carpet rags sewed, quilts quilted, and comfortables tacked. She was industrious and frugal, and in time laid up some money in the Dartford Savings' Bank; but she did not, like many spinsters, invest her hard-earned dollars in a small house. Often she was urged to do so, but her reasons were good for refusing.

"I should be so independent? Well, I 'm as independent now as the law allows. I 've got two good rooms to myself, south winders, stairs of my own and outside door, and some privileges. If I had a house there 'd be taxes, and insurance, and cleanin' off snow come winter-time, and hoein' paths; and likely enough I should be so fur left to myself that I should set up a garden, and make my succotash cost a dollar a pint a-hirin' of a man to dig it up and hoe it down. Like enough, too, I should be gettin' flower seeds and things; I 'm kinder fond of blows in the time of 'em. My old fish-geran'um is a sight of comfort to me as 't is, and there would be a bill of expense again. Then you can't noway build a house with only two rooms in 't, it would be all outside; and you might as well try to heat the universe with a cookin'-stove as such a house. Besides, how lonesome I should be! It 's forlorn enough to be an old maid anyway, but to have it sort of ground into you, as you may say, by livin' all alone in a hull house, that ain't necessary nor agreeable. Now, if I 'm sick or sorry, I can just step downstairs and have aunt Nabby to help or hearten me. Deacon Everts he did set to work one time to persuade me to buy a house; he said 't was a good thing to be able to give somebody shelter 't was poorer 'n I was. Says I, 'Deacon, I 've worked for my livin' ever sence I remember, and I know there 's no use in anybody bein' poorer than I be. I have n't no call to take any sech in and do for 'em. I give what I can to missions,—home ones,—and I 'm willin', cheerfully willin', to do a day's work now and again for somebody that is strivin' with too heavy burdens; but as for keepin' free lodgin' and board, I sha'n't do it.' 'Well, well, well,' says he, kinder as if I was a fractious young one, and a-sawin' his fat hand up and down in the air till I wanted to slap him, 'just as you 'd ruther, Celye,—just as you 'd ruther. I don't mean to drive ye a mite, only, as Scripter says, "Provoke one another to love and good works."'

"That did rile me! Says I: 'Well, you 've provoked me full enough, though I don't know as you 've done it in the Scripter sense; and mabbe I should n't have got so fur provoked if I hadn't have known that little red house your grandsir' lived and died in was throwed back on your hands just now, and advertised for sellin'. I see the "Mounting County Herald," Deacon Everts.' He shut up, I tell ye. But I sha'n't never buy no house so long as aunt Nabby lets me have her two south chambers, and use the back stairway and the north door continual."

So Miss Celia had kept on in her way till now she was fifty, and to-day making over old clothes at the minister's. The minister's wife had, as we have seen, little romance or wild happiness in her life; it is not often the portion of country ministers' wives; and, moreover, she had two step-daughters who were girls of sixteen and twelve when she married their father. Katy was married herself now, this ten years, and doing her hard duty by an annual baby and a struggling parish in Dakota; but Rosabel, whose fine name had been the only legacy her dying mother left the day-old child she had scarce had time to kiss and christen before she went to take her own "new name" above, was now a girl of twenty-two, pretty, headstrong, and rebellious. Nature had endowed her with keen dark eyes, crisp dark curls, a long chin, and a very obstinate mouth, which only her red lips and white even teeth redeemed from ugliness; her bright color and her sense of fun made her attractive to young men wherever she encountered one of that rare species. Just now she was engaged in a serious flirtation with the station-master at Bassett Centre,—an impecunious youth of no special interest to other people and quite unable to maintain a wife. But out of the "strong necessity of loving," as it is called, and the want of young society or settled occupation, Rosa Stearns chose to fall in love with Amos Barker, and her father considered it a "fall" indeed. So, with the natural clumsiness of a man and a father, Parson Stearns set himself to prevent the matter, and began by forbidding Rosabel to see or speak or write to the youth in question, and thereby inspired in her mind a burning desire to do all three. Up to this time she had rather languidly amused herself by mild and gentle flirtations with him, such as looking at him side-wise in church on Sunday, meeting him accidentally on his way to and from the station, for she spent at least half her time at her aunt's in Bassett Centre, and had even taught the small school there during the last six months. She had also sent him her tintype, and his own was secreted in her bureau drawer. He had invited her to go with him to two sleigh-rides and one sugaring-off, and always came home with her from prayer-meeting and singing-school; but like a wise youth he had never yet proposed to marry her in due form, not so much because he was wise as because he was thoughtless and lazy; and while he enjoyed the society of a bright girl, and liked to dangle after the prettiest one in Bassett, and the minister's daughter too, he did not love work well enough to shoulder the responsibility of providing for another those material but necessary supplies that imply labor of an incessant sort.

Rosabel, in her first inconsiderate anger at her father's command, sat down and wrote a note to Amos, eminently calculated to call out his sympathy with her own wrath, and promptly mailed it as soon as it was written. It ran as follows:—

DEAR FRIEND,—Pa has forbidden me to speak to you any more, or to correspond with you. I suppose I must submit so far; but he did not say I must return your picture [the parson had not an idea that she possessed that precious thing], so I shall keep it to remind me of the pleasant hours we have passed together.

"Fare thee well, and if forever,
Still forever fare thee well!"

Your true friend, ROSABEL STEARNS.

P. S.—I think pa is *horrid*!

So did Amos as he read this heart-rending missive, in which the postscript, according to the established sneer at woman's postscripts, carried the whole force of the epistle.

Now Amos had made a friend of Miss Celia by once telegraphing for her trunk, which she had lost on her way home from the only journey of her life, a trip to Boston, whither she had gone, on the strength of the one share of B. & A. R. R. stock she held, to spend the allotted three days granted to stockholders on their annual excursions, presumably to attend the annual meeting. Amos had put himself to the immense trouble of sending two messages for Miss Celia, and asked her nothing for the civility, so that ever after, in the fashion of solitary women, she held herself deeply in his debt. He knew that she was at work for Mrs. Stearns when he received Rosa's epistle, for he had just been over to Bassett on the train—there was but a mile to traverse—to get her to repair his Sunday coat, and not found her at home, but had no time to look her up at the parson's, as he must walk back to his station. Now he resolved to take his answer to Rosa to Miss Celia in the evening, and so be sure that his abused sweetheart received it, for he had read too many dime novels to doubt that her tyrannic father would intercept their letters, and drive them both to madness and despair. That well-meaning but rather dull divine never would have thought of such a thing; he was a puffy, absent-minded, fat little man, with a weak, squeaky voice, and a sudden temper that blazed up like a bunch of dry weeds at a passing spark, and went out at once in flattest ashes. It had been Mrs. Stearns's step-motherly interference that drove him into his harshness to Rosa. She meant well and he meant well, but we all know what good intentions with no further sequel of act are good for, and nobody did more of that "paving" than these two excellent but futile people.

Miss Celia was ready to do anything for Amos Barker, and she considered it little less than a mortal sin to stand in the way of any marriage that was really desired by two parties. That Amos was poor did not daunt her at all; she had the curious faith that possesses some women, that any man can be prosperous if he has the will so to be; and she had a high opinion of this youth, based on his civility to her. It may be said of men, as of elephants, that it is lucky they do not know their own power; for how many more women would become their worshipers and slaves than are so to-day if they knew the abject gratitude the average woman feels for the least attention, the smallest kindness, the faintest expression of affection or good will. We are all, like the Syrophenician woman, glad and ready to eat of the crumbs which fall from the children's table, so great is our faith—in men.

Miss Celia took the note in her big basket over to the minister's the very next day after that on which we introduced her to our readers. She was perhaps more rejoiced to contravene that reverend gentleman's orders than if she had not heard his querulous and contemptuous remark about her through the crack of the door on the previous afternoon; and it was with a sense of joy that, after all, an old maid could do something, that she slipped the envelope into Rosa's hands, and told her to put it quickly into her pocket, the very first moment she found herself alone with that young woman.

Many a hasty word had Parson Stearns spoken in the suddenness of his petulant temper, but never one that bore direr fruit than that when he called Celia Barnes "that old maid."

For of course Amos and Rosabel found in her an ardent friend. They had the instinct of distressed lovers to cajole her with all their confidences, caresses, and eager gratitude, and for once she felt herself dear and of importance. Amos consulted her on his plans for the future, which of course pointed westward, where he had a brother editing and owning a newspaper. This brother had before offered him a place in his office, but Amos had liked better the easy work of a station-master in a tiny village. Now his ambition was aroused, for the time at least. He wanted to make a home for Rosabel, but, alack! he had not one cent to pay their united expenses to Peoria, and a lion stood in the way. Here again Celia stepped in: she had some money laid up; she would lend it to them.

I do not say that at this stage she had no misgivings, but even these were set at rest by a conversation she had with Mrs. Stearns some six weeks after the day on which Celia had so fully expressed her scorn of spinsters. She was there again to tack a comfortable for Rosabel's bed, and bethought herself that it was a good time to feel her way a little concerning Mrs. Stearns's opinion of things.

"They do say," she remarked, stopping to snip off her thread and twist the end of it through her needle's eye, "that your Rosy don't go with Amos Barker no more. Is that so?"

"Yes," said Mrs. Stearns, with a half sigh. "Husband was rather prompt about it; he don't think Amos Barker ever 'll amount to much, and he thinks his people are not just what they should be. You know his father never was very much of a man, and his grandfather is a real old reprobate. Husband says he never knew anything but crows come out of a crow's nest, and so he told Rosa to break acquaintance with him."

"Who does he like to hev come to see her?" asked Celia, with a grim set of her lips, stabbing her needle fiercely through the unoffending calico.

Mrs. Stearns laughed rather feebly. "I don't think he has anybody on his mind, Miss Celia. I don't think there are any young men in Bassett. I dare say Rosa will never marry. I wish she would, for she is n't happy here, and I can't do much to help it, with all my cares."

"And you can't feel for her as though she was your own, if you try ever so," confidently asserted Celia.

"No, I suppose not. I try to do my duty by her, and I am sorry for her; but I know all the time an own mother would understand her better and make it easier for her. Mr. Stearns is peculiar, and men don't know just how to manage girls."

It was a cautious admission, but Miss Celia had sharp eyes, and knew very well that Rosabel neither loved nor respected her father, and that they were now on terms of real if unavowed hostility.

"Well," said she, "I don' know but you will have to have one of them onpleasant creturs, an old maid, in your fam'ly. I declare for 't, I 'd hold a Thanksgiving Day all to myself ef I 'd escaped that marcy."

"You may not always think so, Celia."

"I don't know what 'll change me. 'T will be something I don't look forrard to now," answered Celia obstinately.

Mrs. Stearns sighed. "I hope Rosa will do nothing worse than to live unmarried," she said; but she could not help wishing silently that some worthy man would carry the perverse and annoying girl out of the parsonage for good.

After this Celia felt a certain freedom to help Rosabel; she encouraged the lovers to meet at her house, helped plan their elopement, sewed for the girl, and at last went with them as far as Brimfield when they stole away one evening, saw them safely married at the Methodist parsonage there, and bidding them good-speed, returned to Bassett Centre on the midnight train, and walked over to her own dwelling in the full moonshine of the October night, quite fearless and entirely exultant.

But she was not to come off unscathed. There was a scene of wild commotion at the parsonage next day, when Rosa's letter, modeled on that of the last novel heroine she had become acquainted with, was found on her bureau, as per novel aforesaid.

With her natural thoughtlessness she assured her parents that she "fled not uncompanioned," that her "kind and all but maternal friend, Miss Celia Barnes, would accompany her to the altar, and give her support and her countenance to the solemn ceremony that should make Rosabel Stearns the blessed wife of Amos Barker!"

It was all the minister could do not to swear as he read this astounding letter. His flabby face grew purple; his fat, sallow hands shook with rage; he dared not speak, he only sputtered, for he knew that profane and unbecoming words would surely leap from his tongue if he set it free; but he must—he really must—do or say something! So he clapped on his old hat, and with coat tails flying in the breeze, and rage in every step, set out to find Celia Barnes; and find her he did.

It would be unpleasant, and it is needless, to depict this encounter; language both unjust and unsavory smote the air and reverberated along the highway, for he met the spinster on her road to an engagement at Deacon Stiles's. Suffice it to say that both freed their minds with great enlargement of opinion, and the parson wound up with,—

"And I never want to see you again inside of my house, you confounded old maid!"

"There! that 's it!" retorted Celia. "Ef I was n't an old maid, you would n't no more have darst to 'a' talked to me this way than nothin'. Ef I 'd had a man to stand up to ye you 'd have been dumber 'n Balaam's ass a great sight,—afore it seen the angel, I mean. I swow to man, I b'lieve I 'd marry a hitchin'-post if 't was big enough to trounce ye. You great lummox, if I could knock ye over you would n't peep nor mutter agin, if I be a woman!"

And with a burst of furious tears that asserted her womanhood Miss Celia went her way. Her hands were clinched under her blanket-shawl, her eyes red with angry rain, and as she walked on she soliloquized aloud:—

"I declare for 't, I b'lieve I 'd marry the Old Boy himself if he 'd ask me. I 'm sicker 'n ever of bein' an old maid!"

"Be ye?" queried a voice at her elbow. "P'r'aps, then, you might hear to me if I was to speak my mind, Celye."

Celia jumped. As she said afterward, "I vum I thought 't was the Enemy, for certain; and to think 't was only Deacon Everts!"

"Mercy me!" she said now; "is 't you, deacon?"

"Yes, it 's me; and I think 't is a real providence I come up behind ye just in the nick of time. I 've sold my farm only last week, and I 've come to live on the street in that old red house of grandsir's, that you mistrusted once I wanted you to buy. I'm real lonesome sence I lost my partner" (he meant his wife), "and I 've been a-hangin' on by the edges the past two year; hired help is worse than nothing onto a farm, and hard to get at that; so I sold out, and I 'm a-movin' yet, but the old house looks forlorn enough, and I was intendin' to look about for a second; so if you 'll have me, Celye, here I be."

Celia looked at him sharply; he was an apple-faced little man, with shrewd, twinkling eyes, a hard, dull red still lingering on his round cheeks in spite of the deep wrinkles about his pursed-up lips and around his eyelids; his mouth gave him a consequential and self-important air, to which the short stubbly hair, brushed up "like a blaze" above his forehead, added; and his old blue coat with brass buttons, his homespun trousers, the old-fashioned aspect of his unbleached cotton shirt, all attested his frugality. Indeed, everybody knew that Deacon Everts was "near," and also that he had plenty of money, that is to say, far more than he could spend. He had no children, no near relations; his first wife had died two years since, after long invalidism, and all her relations had moved far west. All this Celia knew and now recalled; her wrath against Parson Stearns was yet fresh and vivid; she remembered that Simeon Everts was senior deacon of the church, and had it in his power to make the minister extremely uncomfortable if he chose. I have never said Celia was a very good woman; her religion was of the dormant type not uncommon nowadays; she kept up its observances properly, and said her prayers every day, bestowed a part of her savings on each church collection, and was rated as a church-member "in good and regular standing;" but the vital transforming power of that Christianity which means to "love the Lord thy God with all thy heart, and mind, and soul, and strength, and thy neighbor as thyself," had no more entered into her soul than it had into Deacon Everts's; and while she would have honestly admitted that revenge was a very wrong sentiment, and entirely improper for any other person to cherish, she felt that she did well to be angry with Parson Stearns, and had a perfect right to "pay him off" in any way she could.

Now here was her opportunity. If she said "Yes" to Deacon Everts, he would no doubt take her part. Her objections to housekeeping were set aside by the fact that the house-owner himself would have to do those heavy labors about the house which she must otherwise have hired a man to do; and the cooking and the indoor work for two people could not be so hard as to sew from house to house for her daily bread. In short, her mind was slowly turning favorably toward this sudden project, but she did not want this wooer to be too sure; so she said: "W-e-ll, 't is a life sentence, as you may say, deacon, and I want to think on 't a spell. Let 's see,—to-day 's Tuesday; I 'll let ye know Thursday night, after prayer-meetin'."

"Well," answered the deacon.

Blessed Yankee monosyllable that means so much and so little; that has such shades of phrase and intention in its myriad inflections; that is "yes," or "no," or "perhaps," just as you accent it; that is at once preface and peroration, evasion and definition! What would all New England speech be without "well"? Even as salt without any savor, or pepper with no pungency.

Now it meant to Miss Celia assent to her proposition; and in accordance the deacon escorted her home from meeting Thursday night, and received for reward a consenting answer. This was no love affair, but a matter of mere business. Deacon Everts needed a housekeeper, and did not want to pay out wages for one; and Miss Celia's position she expressed herself as she put out her tallow candle on that memorable night, and breathed out on the darkness the audible aspiration, "Thank goodness, I sha'n't hev to die an old maid!"

There was no touch of sanctifying love or consoling affection, or even friendly comradeship, in this arrangement; it was as truly a *marriage de convenance* as was ever contracted in Paris itself, and when the wedding day came, a short month afterward, the sourest aspect of November skies threatening a drenching pour, the dead and sodden leaves that strewed the earth, the wailing northeast wind, even the draggled and bony old horse behind which they jogged over to Bassett Centre, seemed fit accompaniments to the degraded ceremony performed by a justice of the peace, who concluded this merely legal compact, for Miss Celia stoutly refused to be married by Parson Stearns; she would not be accessory to putting one dollar in his pocket, even as her own wedding fee. So she went home to the little red house on Bassett Street, and begun her married life by scrubbing the dust and dirt of years from the kitchen table, making biscuit for tea, washing up the dishes, and at last falling asleep during the deacon's long nasal prayer, wherein he wandered to the ends of the earth, and prayed fervently for the heathen, piteously unconscious that he was little better than a heathen himself.

It did not take many weeks to discover to Celia what is meant by "the curse of a granted prayer." She could not at first accept the situation at all; she was accustomed to enough food, if it was plain and simple, when she herself provided it; but now it was hard to get such viands as would satisfy a healthy appetite.

"You 've used a sight of pork, Celye," the deacon would remonstrate. "My first never cooked half what you do. We shall come to want certain, if you 're so free-handed."

"Well, Mr. Everts, there was n't a mite left to set by. We eat it all, and I did n't have no more 'n I wanted, if you did."

"We must mortify the flesh, Celye. It 's hullsome to get up from your victuals hungry. Ye know what Scripter says, 'Jeshurun waxed fat an' kicked.'"

"Well, I ain't Jeshurun, but I expect I shall be more likely to kick if I don't have enough to eat, when it 's only pork 'n' potatoes."

"My first used to say them was the best, for steady victuals, of anything, and she never used but two codfish and two quarts of m'lasses the year round; and as for butter, she was real sparin'; she 'd fry our bread along with the salt pork, and 't was just as good."

"Look here!" snapped Celia. "I don't want to hear no more about your 'first.' I 'm ready to say I wish 't she 'd ha' been your last too."

"Well, well, well! this is onseemly contention, Celye," sputtered the alarmed deacon. "Le' 's dwell together in unity so fur as we can, Mis' Everts. I have n't no intention to starve ye, none whatever. I only want to be keerful, so as we sha'n't have to fetch up in the poor-us."

"No need to have a poor-house to home," muttered Celia.

But this is only a mild specimen of poor Celia's life as a married woman. She did not find the honor and glory of "Mrs." before her name a compensation for the thousand evils that she "knew not of" when she fled to them as a desirable change from her single blessedness. Deacon Everts entirely refused to enter into any of her devices against Parson Stearns; he did not care a penny about Celia's wrongs, and he knew very well that no other man than dreamy, unpractical Mr. Stearns, who eked out his minute pittance by writing school-books of a primary sort, would put up with four hundred dollars a year from his parish; yet that was all Bassett people would pay. If they must have the gospel, they must have it at the lowest living rates, and everybody would not assent to that.

So Celia found her revenge no more feasible after her marriage than before, and, gradually absorbed in her own wrongs and sufferings, her desire to reward Mr. Stearns in kind for his treatment of her vanished; she thought less of his futile wrath and more of her present distresses every day.

For Celia, like everybody who profanes the sacrament of marriage, was beginning to suffer the consequences of her misstep. As her husband's mean, querulous, loveless character unveiled itself in the terrible intimacy of constant and inevitable companionship, she began to look woefully back to the freedom and peace of her maiden days. She learned that a husband is by no means his wife's defender always, not even against reviling tongues. It did not suit Deacon Everts to quarrel with any one, whatever they said to him, or of him and his; he "did n't want no enemies," and Celia bitterly felt that she must fight her own battles; she had not even an ally in her husband. She became not only defiant, but also depressed; the consciousness of a vital and life-long mistake is not productive of cheer or content; and now, admitted into the freemasonry of married women, she discovered how few among them were more than household drudges, the servants of their families, worked to the verge of exhaustion, and neither thanked nor rewarded for their pains. She saw here a woman whose children were careless of, and ungrateful to her, and her husband coldly indifferent; there was one on whom the man she had married wreaked all his fiendish temper in daily small injuries, little vexatious acts, petty tyrannies, a "street-angel, house-devil" of a man, of all sorts the most hateful. There were many whose lives had no other outlook than hard work until the end should come, who rose up to labor and lay down in sleepless exhaustion, and some whose days were a constant terror to them from the intemperate brutes to whom they had intrusted their happiness, and indeed their whole existence.

It was no worse with Celia than with most of her sex in Bassett; here and there, there were of course exceptions, but so rare as to be shining examples and objects of envy. Then, too, after two years, there came forlorn accounts of poor Rosabel's situation at the west. Amos Barker had done his best at first to make his wife comfortable, but change of place or new motives do not at once, if ever, transform an indolent man into an active and efficient one. He found work in his brother's office, but it was the hard work of collecting bills all about the country; the roads were bad, the weather as fluctuating as weather always is, the climate did not agree with him, and he got woefully tired of driving about from dawn till after dark, to dun unwilling debtors. Rosa had chills and fever and babies with persistent alacrity; she had indeed enough to eat, with no appetite, and a house, with no strength to keep it. She grew untidy, listless, hysterical; and her father, getting worried by her despondent and infrequent letters, actually so far roused himself as to sell his horse, and with this sacrificial money betook himself to Mound Village, where he found Rosabel with two babies in her arms, dust an inch deep on all her possessions, nothing but pork, potatoes, and corn bread in the pantry, and a slatternly negress washing some clothes in a kitchen that made the parson shudder.

The little man's heart was bigger than his soul. He put his arms about Rosa and the dingy babies, and forgave her all; but he had to say, even while he held them closely and fondly to his breast, "Oh, Rosy, I told you what would happen if you married that fellow."

Of course Rosa resented the speech, for, after all, she had loved Amos; perhaps could love him still if the poverty and malaria and babies could have all been eliminated from her daily life.

Fortunately the parson's horse had sold well, for it was strong and young, and the rack of venerable bones with which he replaced it was bought very cheap at a farmer's auction, so he had money enough to carry Rosa and the two children home to Bassett, where two months after she added another feeble, howling cipher to the miserable sum of humanity.

Miss—no, Mrs.—Celia's conscience stung her to the quick when she encountered this ghastly wreck of pretty Rosabel Stearns, now called Mrs. Barker. She remembered with deep regret how she had given aid and comfort to the girl who had defied and disobeyed parental counsel and authority, and so brought on herself all this misery. She fancied that Parson Stearns glared at her with eyes of bitter accusation and reproach, and not improbably he did, for beside his pity and affection for his daughter, it was no slight burden to take into his house a feeble woman with two children helpless as babies, and to look forward to the expense and anxiety of another soon to come. And Mrs. Stearns had never loved Rosa well enough to be complacent at this addition to her family cares. She gave the parson no sympathy. It would have been her way to let Rosabel lie on the bed she had made, and die there if need be. But the poor worn-out creature died at home, after all, and the third baby lay on its mother's breast in her coffin: they had gone together.

Celia felt almost like a murderess when she heard that Rosabel Barker was dead. She did not reflect that in all human probability the girl would have married Amos if she, Celia, had refused to help or encourage her. It began to be an importunate question in our friend's mind whether she herself had not made a mistake too; whether the phrase "single blessedness" was not an expression of a vital truth rather than a scoff. Celia was changing her mind no doubt, surely if slowly.

Meantime Deacon Everts did not find all the satisfaction with his "second" that he had anticipated. Celia had a will of her own, quite undisciplined, and it was too often asserted to suit her lord and master. Secretly he planned devices to circumvent her purposes, and sometimes succeeded. In prayer-meeting and in Sunday-school the idea haunted him; his malice lay down and rose up with him. Even when he propounded to his Bible class the important question, "How fur be the heathen *ree*-sponsible for what they dun know?" and asked them "to ponder on 't through the comin' week," he chuckled inwardly at the thought that Celia could not evade *her* responsibility; she knew enough, and would be judged accordingly: the deacon was not a merciful man.

At last he hit upon that great legal engine whereby men do inflict the last deadly kick upon their wives: he would remodel his will. Yes, he would leave those gathered thousands to foreign missions; he would leave behind him the indisputable testimony and taunt that he considered the wife of his bosom less than the savages and heathen afar off. He forgot conveniently that the man "who provideth not for his own household hath denied the faith, and is worse than an infidel." And in his delight of revenge he also forgot that the law of the land provides for a man's wife and children in spite of his wicked will. Nor did he remember that his life-insurance policy for five thousand dollars was made out in his wife's name, simply as his wife, her own name not being specified. He had paid the premium always from his "first's" small annual income, and agreed that it should be written for her benefit, but he supposed that at her death it had reverted to him. He forgot that he still had a wife when he mentioned that policy in his assets recorded in the will, and to save money he drew that evil document up himself, and had it signed down at "the store" by three witnesses.

Celia had borne her self-imposed yoke for four years, when it was suddenly broken. A late crop of grass was to be mowed in mid-July on the meadow which appertained to the old house, and the deacon, now some seventy years old, to save hiring help, determined to do it by himself. The grass was heavy and over-ripe, the day extremely hot and breathless, and the grim Mower of Man trod side by side with Simeon Everts, and laid him too, all along by the rough heads of timothy and the purpled feather-tops of the blue-grass. He did not come home at noon or at night, and when Celia went down to the lot to call him he heard no summons of hers; he had answered a call far more imperative and final.

After the funeral Celia found his will pushed back in the deep drawer of an old secretary, where he kept his one quill pen, a bottle of dried ink, a lump of chalk, some rat-poison, and various other odds and ends.

She was indignant enough at its tenor; but it was easily broken, and she not only had her "thirds," but the life policy reverted to her also, as it was made out to Simeon Everts's wife, and surely she had occupied that position for four wretched years. Then, also, she had a right to her support for one year out of the estate, and the use of the house for that time.

Oh, how sweet was her freedom! With her characteristic honesty she refused to put on mourning, and even went to the funeral in her usual gray Sunday gown and bonnet. "I won't lie, anyhow!" she answered to Mrs. Stiles's remonstrance. "I ain't a mite sorry nor mournful. I could ha' wished he 'd had time to repent of his sins, but sence the Lord saw fit to cut him short, I don't feel to rebel ag'inst it. I wish 't I 'd never married him, that 's all!"

"But, Celye, you got a good livin'."

"I earned it."

"And he 's left ye with means too."

"He done his best not to. I don't owe him nothing for that; and I earned that too,—the hull on 't. It 's poor pay for what I've lived through; and I 'm a'most a mind to call it the wages of sin, for I done wrong, ondeniably wrong, in marryin' of him; but the Lord knows I 've repented, and said my lesson, if I did get it by the hardest."

Yet all Bassett opened eyes and mouth both when on the next Thanksgiving Day Celia invited every old maid in town—seven all told—to take dinner with her. Never before had she celebrated this old New England day of solemn revel. A woman living in two small rooms could not "keep the feast," and rarely had she been asked to any family conclave. We Yankees are conservative at Thanksgiving if nowhere else, and like to gather our own people only about the family hearth; so Celia had but once or twice shared the turkeys of her more fortunate neighbors.

Now she called in Nabby Hyde and Sarah Gillett, Ann Smith, Celestia Potter, Delia Hills, Sophronia Ann Jenkins and her sister Adelia Ann, ancient twins, who lived together on next to nothing, and were happy.

Celia bloomed at the head of the board, not with beauty, but with gratification. "Well," she said, as soon as they were seated, "I sent for ye all to come because I wanted to have a good time, for one thing, and because it seems as though I 'd ought to take back all the sassy and disagreeable things I used to be forever flingin' at old maids. 'I spoke in my haste,' as Scripter says, and also in my ignorance, I 'm free to confess. I feel as though I could keep Thanksgivin' to-day with my hull soul. I 'm so thankful to be an old maid ag'in!"

"I thought you was a widder," snapped Sally Gillett.

Celia flung a glance of wrath at her, but scorned to reply.

"And I 'm thankful too that I 'm spared to help ondo somethin' done in that ignorance. I 've got means, and, as I 've said before, I earned 'em. I don't feel noway obleeged to him for 'em; he did n't mean it. But now I can I 'm goin' to adopt Rosy Barker's two children, and fetch 'em up to be dyed-in-the-wool old maids; and every year, so long as I live, I 'm goin' to keep an old maids' Thanksgivin' for a kind of a burnt-offering, sech as the Bible tells about, for I 've changed my mind clear down to the bottom, and I go the hull figure with the 'postle Paul when he speaks about the onmarried, 'It is better if she so abide.' Now let 's go to work at the victuals."

1892

# FITZ-JAMES O'BRIEN

(1828–1862)

## *The Lost Room*

IT WAS OPPRESSIVELY WARM. The sun had long disappeared, but seemed to have left its vital spirit of heat behind it. The air rested; the leaves of the acacia-trees that have shrouded my windows, hung plumb-like on their delicate stalks. The smoke of my cigar scarce rose above my head, but hung about me in a pale blue cloud, which I had to dissipate with languid waves of my hand. My shirt was open at the throat, and my chest heaved laboriously in the effort to catch some breaths of fresher air. The very noises of the city seemed to be wrapped in slumber, and the shrilling of the mosquitoes were the only sounds that broke the stillness.

As I lay with my feet elevated on the back of a chair, wrapped in that peculiar frame of mind in which thought assumes a species of lifeless motion, the strange fancy seized me of making a languid inventory of the principal articles of furniture in my room. It was a task well suited to the mood in which I found myself. Their forms were duskily defined in the dim twilight that floated shadowily through the chamber; it was no labor to note and particularize each, and from the place where I sat I could command a view of all my possessions without even turning my head.

There was, *imprimus*, that ghostly lithograph by Calame. It was a mere black spot on the white wall, but my inner vision scrutinized every detail of the picture. A wild, desolate, midnight heath, with a spectral oak-tree in the centre of the foreground. The wind blows fiercely, and the jagged branches, clothed scantily with ill-grown leaves, are swept to the left continually by its giant force. A formless wrack of clouds streams across the awful sky, and the rain sweeps almost parallel with the horizon. Beyond, the heath stretches off into endless blackness, in the extreme of which either fancy or art has conjured up some undefinable shapes that seem riding into space. At the base of the huge oak stands a shrouded figure. His mantle is wound by the blast in tight folds around his form, and the long cock's feather in his hat is blown upright, till it seems as if it stood on end with fear. His features are not visible, for he has grasped his cloak with both hands, and drawn it from either side across his face. The picture is seemingly objectless. It tells no tale, but there is a weird power about it that haunts one, and it was for that I bought it.

Next to the picture comes the round blot that hangs below it, which I know to be a smoking-cap. It has my coat of arms embroidered on the front, and for that reason I never wear it; though, when properly arranged on my head with its long blue silken tassel hanging down by my cheek, I believe it becomes me well. I remember the time when it was in the course of manufacture. I remember the tiny little hands that pushed the colored silks so nimbly through the cloth that was stretched on the embroidery-frame—the vast trouble I was put to to get a colored copy of my armorial bearings for the heraldic work which was to decorate the front of the band—the pursings up of the little mouth, and the contractions of the young forehead, as their possessor plunged into a profound sea of cogitation touching the way in which the cloud should be represented from which the armed hand, that is my crest, issues—the heavenly moment when the tiny hands placed it on my head, in a position that I could not bear for more than a few seconds, and I, king-like, immediately assumed my royal prerogative after the coronation, and instantly levied a tax on my only subject, which was, however, not paid unwillingly. Ah! the cap is there, but the embroiderer has fled; for Atropos was severing the web of life above her head while she was weaving that silken shelter for mine!

How uncouthly the huge piano that occupies the corner at the left of the door looms out in the uncertain twilight! I neither play nor sing, yet I own a piano. It is a comfort to me to look at it, and to feel that the music *is* there, although I am not able to break the spell that binds it. It is pleasant to know that Bellini and Mozart, Cimarosa, Porpora, Glück, and all such—or at least their souls—sleep in that unwieldy case. There lie embalmed, as it were, all operas, sonatas, oratorios, notturnos, marches, songs, and dances, that ever climbed into existence through the four bars that wall in melody. Once I was entirely repaid for the investment of my funds in that instrument which I never use. Blokeeta, the composer, came to see me. Of course his instincts urged him as irresistibly to my piano as if some magnetic power lay within it compelling him to approach. He tuned it, he played on it. All night long, until the gray and spectral dawn rose out of the depths of the midnight, he sat and played, and I lay smoking by the window listening. Wild, unearthly, and sometimes insufferably painful, were the improvisations of Blokeeta. The chords of the instrument seemed breaking with anguish. Lost souls shrieked in his dismal preludes; the half-heard utterances of spirits in pain, that groped at inconceivable distances from any thing lovely or harmonious, seemed to rise dimly up out of the waves of sound that gathered under his hands. Melancholy human love wandered out on distant heaths, or beneath dank and gloomy cypresses, murmuring its unanswered sorrow, or hateful gnomes sported and sang in the stagnant swamps, triumphing in unearthly tones over the knight whom they had lured to his death. Such was Blokeeta's night's entertainment; and when he at length closed the piano, and hurried away through the cold morning, he left a memory about the instrument from which I could never escape.

Those snow-shoes, that hang in the space between the mirror and the door, recall Canadian wanderings. A long race through the dense forests over the frozen snow, through whose brittle crust the slender hoofs of the cariboo that we were pursuing sank at every step, until the poor creature despairingly turned at bay in a small juniper coppice, and we heartlessly shot him down. And I remember how Gabriel, the *habitant*, and François, the half-breed, cut his throat, and how the hot blood rushed out in a torrent over the snowy soil; and I recall the snow *cabane* that Gabriel built, where we all three slept so warmly, and the great fire that glowed at our feet painting all kinds of demoniac shapes on the black screen of forest that lay without, and the deer-steaks that we roasted for our breakfast, and the savage drunkenness of Gabriel in the morning, he having been privately drinking out of my brandy-flask all the night long.

That long haftless dagger that dangles over the mantle-piece makes my heart swell. I found it when a boy, in a hoary old castle in which one of my maternal ancestors once lived. That same ancestor—who, by-the-way, yet lives in history—was a strange old sea-king, who dwelt on the extremest point of the southwestern coast of Ireland. He owned the whole of that fertile island called Inniskeiran, which directly faces Cape Clear, where between them the Atlantic rolls furiously, forming what the fishermen of the place call "the Sound." An awful place in winter is that same Sound. On certain days no boat can live there for a moment, and Cape Clear is frequently cut off for days from any communication with the main land.

This old sea-king—Sir Florence O'Driscoll by name—passed a stormy life. From the summit of his castle he watched the ocean, and when any richly laden vessels, bound from the south to the industrious Galway merchants, hove in sight, Sir Florence hoisted the sails of his galley, and it went hard with him if he did not tow into harbor ship and crew. In this way he lived; not a very honest mode of livelihood certainly, according to our modern ideas, but quite reconcilable with the morals of the time. As may be supposed, Sir Florence got into trouble. Complaints were laid against him at the English Court by the plundered merchants, and the Irish viking set out for London to plead his own cause before good Queen Bess, as she was called. He had one powerful recommendation; he was a marvelously handsome man. Not Celtic by descent, but half Spanish, half Danish in blood, he had the great northern stature with the regular features, flashing eyes, and dark hair of the Iberian race. This may account for the fact that his stay at the English Court was much longer than was necessary, as also for the tradition, which a local historian mentions, that the English Queen evinced a preference for the Irish chieftain of other nature than that usually shown from monarch to subject.

Previous to his departure Sir Florence had intrusted the care of his property to an Englishman named Hull. During the long absence of the knight this person managed to ingratiate himself with the local authorities, and gain their favor so far that they were willing to support him in almost any scheme. After a protracted stay Sir Florence, pardoned of all his misdeeds, returned to his home. Home no longer. Hull was in possession, and refused to yield an acre of the lands he had so nefariously acquired. It was no use appealing to the law, for its officers were in the opposite interest. It was no use appealing to the Queen, for she had another lover, and had forgotten the poor Irish knight by this time; and so the viking passed the best portion of his life in unsuccessful attempts to reclaim his vast estates, and was eventually, in his old age, obliged to content himself with his castle by the sea, and the island of Inniskeiran, the only spot of which the usurper was unable to deprive him. So this old story of my kinsman's fate looms up out of the darkness that enshrouds that haftless dagger hanging on the wall.

It was somewhat after the foregoing fashion that I dreamily made the inventory of my personal property. As I turned my eyes on each object, one after the other, or the places where they lay—for the room was now so dark that it was almost impossible to see with any distinctness—a crowd of memories connected with each rose up before me, and, perforce, I had to indulge them. So I proceeded but slowly, and at last my cigar shortened to a hot and bitter morsel that I could barely hold between my lips, while it seemed to me that the night grew each moment more insufferably oppressive. While I was revolving some impossible means of cooling my wretched body, the cigar stump began to burn my lips. I flung it angrily through the open window, and stooped out to watch it falling. It first lighted on the leaves of the acacia, sending out a spray of red sparkles, then rolling off, it fell plump on the dark walk in the garden, faintly illuminating for a moment the dusky trees and breathless flowers. Whether it was the contrast between the red flash of the cigar stump and the silent darkness of the garden, or whether it was that I detected by the sudden light a faint waving of the leaves, I know not, but something suggested to me that the garden was cool. I will take a turn there, thought I, just as I am; it can not be warmer than this room, and however still the atmosphere, there is always a feeling of liberty and spaciousness in the open air that partially supplies one's wants. With this idea running through my head I arose, lit another cigar, and passed out into the long, intricate corridors that led to the main stair-case. As I crossed the threshold of my room, with what a different feeling I should have passed it had I known that I was never to set foot in it again!

I lived in a very large house, in which I occupied two rooms on the second floor. The house was old-fashioned, and all the floors communicated by a huge circular stair-case that wound up through the centre of the building, while at every landing long rambling corridors stretched off into mysterious nooks and corners. This palace of mine was very high, and its resources, in the way of crannies and windings, seemed to be interminable. Nothing seemed to stop any where. Cul de sacs were unknown on the premises. The corridors and passages, like mathematical lines, seemed capable of indefinite extension, and the object of the architect must have been to erect an edifice in which people might go ahead forever. The whole place was gloomy, not so much because it was large, but because an unearthly nakedness seemed to pervade the structure. The staircases, corridors, halls, and vestibules all partook of a desert-like desolation. There was nothing on the walls to break the sombre monotony of those long vistas of shade. No carvings on the wainscoting, no moulded masks peering down from the simply severe cornices, no marble vases on the landings. There was an eminent dreariness and want of life—so rare in an American establishment—all over the abode. It was Hood's haunted house put in order, and newly painted. The servants, too, were shadowy and chary of their visits. Bells rang three times before the gloomy chambermaid could be induced to present herself, and the negro waiter, a ghoul-like looking creature from Congo, obeyed the summons only when one's patience was exhausted, or one's want satisfied in some other way. When he did come, one felt sorry that he had not staid away altogether, so sullen and savage did he appear. He moved along the echoless floors with a slow, noiseless shamble, until his dusky figure, advancing from the gloom, seemed like some reluctant afreet, compelled, by the superior power of his master, to disclose himself. When the doors of all the chambers were closed, and no light illuminated the long corridor, save the red, unwholesome glare of a small oil lamp on a table at the end, where late lodgers lit their candles, one could not by any possibility conjure up a sadder or more desolate prospect.

Yet the house suited me. Of meditative and sedentary habits, I rather enjoyed the extreme quiet. There were but few lodgers, from which I infer that the landlord did not drive a very thriving trade; and these, probably oppressed by the sombre spirit of the place, were quiet and ghost-like in their movements. The proprietor I scarcely ever saw. My bills were deposited by unseen hands every month on my table while I was out walking or riding, and my pecuniary response was intrusted to the attendant afreet. On the whole, when the bustling, wide-awake spirit of New York is taken into consideration, the sombre, half-vivified character of the house in which I lived was an anomaly that no one appreciated better than I who lived there.

I felt my way down the wide, dark stair-case in my pursuit of zephyrs. The garden, as I entered it, did feel somewhat cooler than my own room, and I puffed my cigar along the dim, cypress-shrouded walks with a sensation of comparative relief. It was very dark. The tall-growing flowers that bordered the path were so wrapped in gloom as to present the aspect of solid pyramidal masses, all the details of leaves and blossoms being buried in an embracing darkness, while the trees had lost all form, and seemed like masses of overhanging cloud. It was a place and time to excite the imagination; for in the impenetrable cavities of endless gloom there was room for the most riotous fancies to play at will. I walked and walked, and the echoes of my footsteps on the ungraveled and mossy path suggested a double feeling. I felt alone and yet in company at the same time. The solitariness of the place made itself distinct enough in the stillness, broken alone by the hollow reverberations of my step, while those very reverberations seemed to imbue me with an undefined feeling that I was not alone. I was not, therefore, much startled when I was suddenly accosted from beneath the solid darkness of an immense cypress by a voice saying,

"Will you give me a light, Sir?"

"Certainly," I replied, trying in vain to distinguish the speaker amidst the impenetrable dark.

Somebody advanced, and I held out my cigar. All I could gather definitively about the individual that thus accosted me was, that he must have been of extremely small stature; for I, who am by no means an overgrown man, had to stoop considerably in handing him my cigar. The vigorous puff that he gave his own lighted up my Havana for a moment, and I fancied that I caught a glimpse of a pale, weird countenance, immersed in a background of long, wild hair. The flash was, however, so momentary that I could not even say certainly whether this was an actual impression or the mere effort of imagination to embody that which the senses had failed to distinguish.

"Sir, you are out late," said this unknown to me, as he, with a half-uttered thanks, handed me back my cigar, for which I had to grope in the gloom.

"Not later than usual," I replied, dryly.

"Hum! you are fond of late wanderings, then?"

"That is just as the fancy seizes me."

"Do you live here?"

"Yes."

"Queer house, isn't it?"

"I have only found it quiet."

"Hum! But you *will* find it queer, take my word for it." This was earnestly uttered; and I felt, at the same time, a bony finger laid on my arm that cut it sharply, like a blunted knife.

"I can not take your word for any such assertion," I replied, rudely, shaking off the bony finger with an irrepressible motion of disgust.

"No offense, no offense," muttered my unseen companion rapidly, in a strange, subdued voice, that would have been shrill had it been louder; "your being angry does not alter the matter. You will find it a queer house. Every body finds it a queer house. Do you know who live there?"

"I never busy myself, Sir, about other people's affairs," I answered, sharply, for the individual's manner, combined with my utter uncertainty as to his appearance, oppressed me with an irksome longing to be rid of him.

"Oh! you don't? Well, I do. I know what they are—well, well, well;" and as he pronounced the three last words his voice rose with each, until, with the last, it reached a shrill shriek that echoed horribly among the lonely walks. "Do you know what they eat?" he continued.

"No, Sir—nor care."

"Oh! but you will care. You must care. You shall care. I'll tell you what they are. They are enchanters. They are ghouls. They are cannibals. Did you never remark their eyes, and how they gloated on you when you passed? Did you never remark the food that they served up at your table? Did you never, in the dead of night, hear muffled and unearthly footsteps gliding along the corridors, and stealthy hands turning the handle of your door? Does not some magnetic influence fold itself continually around you when they pass, and send a thrill through spirit and body, and a cold shiver that no sunshine will chase away? Oh, you have! You have felt all these things! I know it!"

The earnest rapidity, the subdued tones, the eagerness of accent with which all this was uttered, impressed me most uncomfortably. I really seemed as if I could recall all those weird occurrences and influences of which he spoke; and I shuddered in spite of myself in the midst of that impenetrable darkness that surrounded me.

"Hum!" said I, assuming, without knowing it, a confidential tone, "may I ask how you know of these things?"

"How I know them? Because I am their enemy. Because they tremble at my whisper. Because I hang upon their track with the perseverance of a blood-hound and the stealthiness of a tiger—because—because—I was *of* them once!"

"Wretch!" I cried, excitedly, for involuntarily his eager tones had wrought me up to a high pitch of spasmodic nervousness, "then you mean to say that you—"

As I uttered this word, obeying an uncontrollable impulse, I stretched forth my hand in the direction of the speaker and made a blind clutch. The tips of my fingers seemed to touch a surface as smooth as glass, that glided suddenly from under them. A sharp, angry hiss sounded through the gloom, followed by a whirring noise, as if some projectile passed rapidly by, and the next moment I felt instinctively that I was alone.

A most disagreeable sensation instantly assailed me. A prophetic instinct that some terrible misfortune menaced me; an eager and overpowering anxiety to get back to my own room without loss of time. I turned and ran blindly along the dark cypress alley, every dusky clump of flowers that rose blackly in the borders making my heart each moment cease to beat. The echoes of my own footsteps seemed to redouble and assume the sounds of unknown pursuers following fast upon my track. The boughs of lilac-bushes and syringas that here and there stretched partly across the walk, seemed to have been furnished suddenly with hooked hands that sought to grasp me as I flew by, and each moment I expected to behold some awful and impassable barrier fall right across my track, and wall me up forever.

At length I reached the wide entrance. With a single leap I sprang up the four or five steps that formed the stoop, and dashing along the hall, up the wide, echoing stairs, and again along the dim funereal corridors until I paused, breathless and panting, at the door of my room. Once so far, I stopped for an instant and leaned heavily against one of the panels, panting lustily after my late run. I had, however, scarcely rested my whole weight against the door, when it suddenly gave way, and I staggered in head-foremost. To my utter astonishment the room that I had left in profound darkness was now a blaze of light. So intense was the illumination that, for a few seconds while the pupils of my eyes were contracting under the sudden change, I saw absolutely nothing save the dazzling glare. This fact in itself coming on me with such utter suddenness, was sufficient to prolong my confusion, and it was not until after several moments had elapsed that I perceived the room was not alone illuminated but occupied. And such occupants! Amazement at the scene took such possession of me that I was incapable of either moving or uttering a word. All that I could do was to lean against the wall, and stare blankly at the whole business.

It might have been a scene out of Faublas, or Grammont's Memoirs, or happened in some palace of Minister Fouque.

Round a large table in the centre of the room, where I had left a student-like litter of books and papers, were seated half a dozen persons. Three were men, and three were women. The table was heaped with a prodigality of luxuries. Luscious Eastern fruits were piled up in silver filagree vases, through whose meshes their glowing rinds shone in the contrasts of a thousand hues. Small silver dishes that Benvenuto might have designed, filled with succulent and aromatic meats, were distributed upon a cloth of snowy damask. Bottles of every shape, slender ones from the Rhine, stout fellows from Holland, sturdy ones from Spain, and quaint basket-woven flasks from Italy, absolutely littered the board. Drinking glasses of every size and hue filled up the interstices, and the thirsty German flagon stood side by side with the aerial bubbles of Venetian glass that rested so lightly on their thread-like stems. An odor of luxury and sensuality floated through the apartment. The lamps that burned in every vacant spot where room for one could be found, seemed to diffuse a subtle incense on the air, and in a large vase that stood on the floor I saw a mass of magnolias, tuberoses, and jasmines grouped together, stifling each other with their honeyed and heavy fragrance.

The inhabitants of my room seemed beings well suited to so sensual an atmosphere. The women were strangely beautiful, and all were attired in dresses of the most fantastic devices and brilliant hues. Their figures were round, supple, and elastic; their eyes dark and languishing; their lips full, ripe, and of the richest bloom. The three men wore half-masks, so that all I could distinguish were heavy jaws, pointed beards, and brawny throats that rose like massive pillars out of their doublets. All six lay reclining on Roman couches about the table, drinking down the purple wines in large draughts, and tossing back their heads and laughing wildly.

I stood, I suppose, for some three minutes, with my back against the wall staring vacantly at the bacchanal vision, before any of the revelers appeared to notice my presence. At length, without any expression to indicate whether I had been observed from the beginning or not, two of the women arose from their couches, and, approaching, took each a hand and led me to the table. I obeyed their motions mechanically. I sat on a couch between them as they indicated. I unresistingly permitted them to wind their arms about my neck.

"You must drink," said one, pouring out a large glass of red wine, "here is Clos Vougeot of a rare vintage; and here," pushing a flask of amber-hued wine before me, "is Lachrima Christi."

"You must eat," said the other, drawing the silver dishes toward her. "Here are cutlets stewed with olives, and here are slices of a *filet* stuffed with bruised sweet chestnuts;" and as she spoke, she, without waiting for a reply, proceeded to help me.

The sight of the food recalled to me the warnings I had received in the garden. This sudden effort of memory restored to me my other faculties at the same instant. I sprang to my feet, thrusting the women from me with each hand.

"Demons!" I almost shouted, "I will have none of your accursed food. I know you. You are cannibals, you are ghouls, you are enchanters. Begone, I tell you! Leave my room in peace!"

A shout of laughter from all six was the only effect that my passionate speech produced. The men rolled on their couches, and their half-masks quivered with the convulsions of their mirth. The women shrieked, and tossed the slender wine-glasses wildly aloft, and turned to me and flung themselves on my bosom, fairly sobbing with laughter.

"Yes," I continued, as soon as the noisy mirth had subsided, "yes, I say, leave my room instantly! I will have none of your unnatural orgies here!"

"His room!" shrieked the woman on my right.

"His room!" echoed she on my left.

"His room! He calls it his room!" shouted the whole party, as they rolled once more into jocular convulsions.

"How know you that it is your room?" said one of the men who sat opposite to me, at length, after the laughter had once more somewhat subsided.

"How do I know?" I replied, indignantly. "How do I know my own room? How could I mistake it, pray? There's my furniture—my piano—"

"He calls that a piano!" shouted my neighbors, again in convulsions as I pointed to the corner where my huge piano, sacred to the memory of Blokeeta, used to stand. "Oh, yes! It is his room. There—there is his piano!"

The peculiar emphasis they laid on the word "piano" caused me to scrutinize the article I was indicating more thoroughly. Up to this time, though utterly amazed at the entrance of these people into my chamber, and connecting them somewhat with the wild stories I had heard in the garden, I still had a sort of indefinite idea that the whole thing was a masquerading freak got up in my absence, and that the bacchanalian orgy I was witnessing was nothing more than a portion of some elaborate hoax of which I was to be the victim. But when my eyes turned to the corner where I had left a huge and cumbrous piano, and beheld a vast and sombre organ lifting its fluted front to the very ceiling, and convinced myself, by a hurried process of memory, that it occupied the very spot in which I had left my own instrument, the little self-possession that I had left forsook me. I gazed around me bewildered.

In like manner every thing was changed. In the place of that old haftless dagger, connected with so many historic associations personal to myself, I beheld a Turkish yataghan dangling by its belt of crimson silk, while the jewels in the hilt blazed as the lamplight played upon them. In the spot where hung my cherished smoking-cap, memorial of a buried love, a knightly casque was suspended, on the crest of which a golden dragon stood in the act of springing. That strange lithograph by Calame was no longer a lithograph, but it seemed to me that the portion of the wall which it had covered, of the exact shape and size, had been cut out, and, in place of the picture, a *real* scene on the same scale, and with real actors, was distinctly visible. The old oak was there, and the stormy sky was there; but I saw the branches of the oak sway with the tempest, and the clouds drive before the wind. The wanderer in his cloak was gone; but in his place I beheld a circle of wild figures, men and women, dancing with linked hands around the bole of the great tree, chanting some wild fragment of a song, to which the winds roared an unearthly chorus. The snow-shoes, too, on whose sinewy woof I had sped for many days amidst Canadian wastes, had vanished, and in their place lay a pair of strange up-curled papooshes, that had, perhaps, been many a time shuffled off at the doors of mosques, beneath the steady blaze of an Orient sun.

All was changed. Wherever my eyes turned they missed familiar objects, yet encountered strange representatives. Still in all the substitutes there seemed to me a reminiscence of what they replaced. They seemed only for a time transmuted into other shapes, and there lingered around them the atmosphere of what they once had been. Thus I could have sworn the room to have been mine, yet there was nothing in it that I could rightly claim. Every thing reminded me of some former possession that it was not. I looked for the acacia at the window, and lo! long, silken palm-leaves swayed in through the open lattice; yet they had the same motion and the same air of my favorite tree, and seemed to murmur to me, "Though we seem to be palm-leaves, yet are we acacia-leaves; yea, those very ones on which you used to watch the butterflies alight and the rain patter while you smoked and dreamed!" So in all things. The room was, yet was not mine; and a sickening consciousness of my utter inability to reconcile its identity with its appearance overwhelmed me, and choked my reason.

"Well, have you determined whether or not this is your room?" asked the girl on my left, proffering me a huge tumbler creaming over with Champagne, and laughing wickedly as she spoke.

"It is mine," I answered, doggedly, striking the glass rudely with my hand, and dashing the aromatic wine over the white cloth. "I know that it is mine; and ye are jugglers and enchanters that want to drive me mad."

"Hush! hush!" she said, gently, not in the least angered at my rough treatment. "You are excited. Alf shall play something to soothe you."

At her signal one of the men arose and sat down at the organ. After a short, wild, spasmodic prelude, he began what seemed to me to be a symphony of recollections. Dark and sombre, and all through full of quivering and intense agony, it appeared to recall a dark and dismal night, on a cold reef, around which an unseen but terribly audible ocean broke with eternal fury. It seemed as if a lonely pair were on the reef, one living, the other dead; one clasping his arms around the tender neck and naked bosom of the other, striving to warm her into life, when his own vitality was being each moment sucked from him by the icy breath of the storm. Here and there a terrible wailing minor key would tremble through the chords like the shriek of sea-birds, or the warning of advancing death. While the man played I could scarce restrain myself. It seemed to be Blokeeta whom I listened to, and on whom I gazed. That wondrous night of pleasure and pain that I had once passed listening to him seemed to have been taken up again at the spot where it had broken off and the same hand was continuing it. I stared at the man called Alf. There he sat with his cloak and doublet, and long rapier and mask of black velvet. But there was something in the air of the peaked beard, a familiar mystery in the wild mass of raven hair that fell as if wind-blown over his shoulders, which riveted my memory.

"Blokeeta! Blokeeta!"—I shouted, starting up furiously from the couch on which I was lying, and bursting the fair arms that were linked around my neck as if they had been hateful chains—"Blokeeta! my friend, speak to me I entreat you! Tell these horrid enchanters to leave me. Say that I hate them. Say that I command them to leave my room!"

The man at the organ stirred not in answer to my appeal. He ceased playing, and the dying sound of the last note he had touched faded off into a melancholy moan. The other men and the women burst once more into peals of mocking laughter.

"Why will you persist in calling this your room?" said the woman next me, with a smile meant to be kind, but to me inexpressibly loathsome. "Have we not shown you by the furniture, by the general appearance of the place, that you are mistaken, and that this can not be your apartment? Rest content, then, with us. You are welcome here, and need no longer trouble yourself about your room."

"Rest content!" I answered, madly; "live with ghosts! eat of awful meats, and see awful sights! Never, never! You have cast some enchantment over the place that has disguised it; but for all that I know it to be my room. You shall leave it!"

"Softly, softly!" said another of the sirens. "Let us settle this amicably. This poor gentleman seems obstinate and inclined to make an uproar. Now we do not want an uproar. We love the night and its quiet; and there is no night that we love so well as that on which the moon is coffined in clouds. Is it not so, my brothers?"

An awful and sinister smile gleamed on the countenances of her unearthly audience, and seemed to glide visibly from underneath their masks.

"Now," she continued, "I have a proposition to make. It would be ridiculous for us to surrender this room simply because this gentleman states that it is his; and yet I feel anxious to gratify, as far as may be fair, his wild assertion of ownership. A room, after all, is not much to us; we can get one easily enough, but still we would be loth to give this apartment up to so imperious a demand. We are willing, however, to *risk* its loss. That is to say"—turning to me—"I propose that we play for the room. If you win, we will immediately surrender it to you just as it stands; if, on the contrary, you lose, you shall bind yourself to depart and never molest us again."

Agonized at the ever-darkening mysteries that seemed to thicken around me, and despairing of being able to dissipate them by the mere exercise of my own will, I caught almost gladly at the chance thus presented to me. The idea of my loss or my gain scarce entered into my calculations. All I felt was an indefinite knowledge that I might, in the way proposed, regain, in an instant, that quiet chamber and that peace of mind which I had so strangely been deprived of.

"I agree!" I cried, eagerly; "I agree. Any thing to rid myself of such unearthly company!"

The woman touched a small golden bell that stood near her on the table, and it had scarce ceased to tinkle when a negro dwarf entered with a silver tray on which were dice-boxes and dice. A shudder passed over me as I thought in this stunted African I could trace a resemblance to the ghoul-like black servant to whose attendance I had been accustomed.

"Now," said my neighbor, seizing one of the dice-boxes and giving me the other, "the highest wins. Shall I throw first?"

I nodded assent. She rattled the dice, and I felt an inexpressible load lifted from my heart as she threw fifteen.

"It is your turn," she said, with a mocking smile; "but before you throw, I repeat the offer I made you before. Live with us. Be one of us. We will initiate you into our mysteries and enjoyments—enjoyments of which you can form no idea unless you experience them. Come; it is not too late yet to change your mind. Be with us!"

My reply was a fierce oath as I rattled the dice with spasmodic nervousness and flung them on the board. They rolled over and over again, and during that brief instant I felt a suspense, the intensity of which I have never known before or since. At last they lay before me. A shout of the same horrible, maddening laughter rang in my ears. I peered in vain at the dice, but my sight was so confused that I could not distinguish the amount of the cast. This lasted for a few moments. Then my sight grew clear, and I sank back almost lifeless with despair as I saw that I had thrown but *twelve*!

"Lost! lost!" screamed my neighbor, with a wild laugh. "Lost! lost!" shouted the deep voices of the masked men. "Leave us, coward!" they all cried; "you are not fit to be one of us. Remember your promise; leave us!"

Then it seemed as if some unseen power caught me by the shoulders and thrust me toward the door. In vain I resisted. In vain I screamed and shouted for help. In vain I implored them for pity. All the reply I had were those mocking peals of merriment, while, under the invisible influence, I staggered like a drunken man toward the door. As I reached the threshold the organ pealed out a wild triumphal strain. The power that impelled me concentrated itself into one vigorous impulse that sent me blindly staggering out into the echoing corridor, and, as the door closed swiftly behind me, I caught one glimpse of the apartment I had left forever. A change passed like a shadow over it. The lamps died out, the siren women and masked men vanished, the flowers, the fruits, the bright silver and bizarre furniture faded swiftly, and I saw again, for the tenth of a second, my own old chamber restored. There was the acacia waving darkly; there was the table littered with books; there was the ghostly lithograph, the dearly-beloved smoking cap, the Canadian snow-shoes, the ancestral dagger. And there, at the piano, organ no longer, sat Blokeeta playing.

The next instant the door closed violently, and I was left standing in the corridor stunned and despairing.

As soon as I had partially recovered my comprehension I rushed madly to the door with the dim idea of beating it in. My fingers beat against a cold and solid wall. There was no door! I felt all along the corridor for many yards on both sides. There was not even a crevice to give me hope. I rushed down stairs shouting madly. No one answered. In the vestibule I met the negro; I seized him by the collar, and demanded my room. The demon showed his white and awful teeth, which were filed into a saw-like shape, and extricating himself from my grasp with a sudden jerk, fled down the passage with a gibbering laugh. Nothing but echo answered to my despairing shrieks. The lonely garden resounded with my cries as I strode madly through the dark walks, and the tall funereal cypresses seemed to bury me beneath their heavy shadows. I met no one. Could find no one. I had to bear my sorrow and despair alone.

Since that awful hour I have never found my room. Every where I look for it, yet never see it. Shall I ever find it?

1858

# FITZ-JAMES O'BRIEN

(1828–1862)

---

## *What Was It?*

### *A Mystery*

It is, I confess, with considerable diffidence that I approach the strange narrative which I am about to relate. The events which I purpose detailing are of so extraordinary and unheard-of a character that I am quite prepared to meet with an unusual amount of incredulity and scorn. I accept all such beforehand. I have, I trust, the literary courage to face unbelief. I have, after mature consideration, resolved to narrate, in as simple and straightforward a manner as I can compass, some facts that passed under my observation in the month of July last, and which, in the annals of the mysteries of physical science, are wholly unparalleled.

I live at No. — Twenty-sixth Street, in this city. The house is in some respects a curious one. It has enjoyed for the last two years the reputation of being haunted. It is a large and stately residence, surrounded by what was once a garden, but which is now only a green inclosure used for bleaching clothes. The dry basin of what has been a fountain, and a few fruit-trees, ragged and unpruned, indicate that this spot, in past days, was a pleasant, shady retreat, filled with fruits and flowers and the sweet murmur of waters.

The house is very spacious. A hall of noble size leads to a vast spiral staircase winding through its centre; while the various apartments are of imposing dimensions. It was built some fifteen or twenty years since by Mr. A——, the well-known New York merchant, who five years ago threw the commercial world into convulsions by a stupendous bank fraud. Mr. A——, as every one knows, escaped to Europe, and died not long after of a broken heart. Almost immediately after the news of his decease reached this country, and was verified, the report spread in Twenty-sixth Street that No. — was haunted. Legal measures had dispossessed the widow of its former owner, and it was inhabited merely by a care-taker and his wife, placed there by the house-agent into whose hands it had passed for purposes of renting or sale. These people declared that they were troubled with unnatural noises. Doors were opened without any visible agency. The remnants of furniture scattered through the various rooms were, during the night, piled one upon the other by unknown hands. Invisible feet passed up and down the stairs in broad daylight, accompanied by the rustle of unseen silk dresses and the gliding of viewless hands along the massive balusters. The care-taker and his wife declared they would live there no longer. The house-agent laughed, dismissed them, and put others in their place. The noises and supernatural manifestations continued. The neighborhood caught up the story, and the house remained untenanted for three years. Several parties negotiated for it; but somehow, always before the bargain was closed, they heard the unpleasant rumors, and declined to treat any further.

It was in this state of things that my landlady—who at that time kept a boarding-house in Bleecker Street, and who wished to move farther up town—conceived the bold idea of renting No. — Twenty-sixth Street. Happening to have in her house rather a plucky and philosophical set of boarders, she laid her scheme before us, stating candidly every thing she had heard respecting the ghostly qualities of the establishment to which she wished to remove us. With the exception of one or two timid persons—a sea-captain and a returned Californian, who immediately gave notice that they would leave—every one of Mrs. Moffat's guests declared that they would accompany her in her chivalric incursion into the abode of spirits.

Our removal was effected in the month of May, and we were all charmed with our new residence. The portion of Twenty-sixth Street where our house is situated—between Seventh and Eighth Avenues—is one of the pleasantest localities in New York. The gardens back of the houses, running down nearly to the Hudson, form, in the summer time, a perfect avenue of verdure. The air is pure and invigorating, sweeping, as it does, straight across the river from the Weehawken heights, and even the ragged garden which surrounded the house on two sides, although displaying on washing-days rather too much clothes-line, still gave us a piece of green sward to look at, and a cool retreat in the summer evenings, where we smoked our cigars in the dusk, and watched the fire-flies flashing their dark-lanterns in the long grass.

Of course we had no sooner established ourselves at No. — than we began to expect the ghosts. We absolutely awaited their advent with eagerness. Our dinner conversation was supernatural. One of the boarders, who had purchased Mrs. Crowe's "Night Side of Nature" for his own private delectation, was regarded as a public enemy by the entire household for not having bought twenty copies. The man led a life of supreme wretchedness while he was perusing the volume. A system of espionage was established, of which he was the victim. If he incautiously laid the book down for an instant and left the room, it was immediately seized and read aloud in secret places to a select few. I found myself a person of immense importance, it having leaked out that I was tolerably well versed in the history of supernaturalism, and had once written a story, entitled "The Pot of Tulips," for *Harper's Monthly*, the foundation of which was a ghost. If a table or a wainscot panel happened to warp when we were assembled in the large drawing-room, there was an instant silence, and every one was prepared for an immediate clanking of chains and a spectral form.

After a month of psychological excitement, it was with the utmost dissatisfaction that we were forced to acknowledge that nothing in the remotest degree approaching the supernatural had manifested itself. Once the black butler asseverated that his candle had been blown out by some invisible agency while in the act of undressing himself for the night; but as I had more than once discovered this colored gentleman in a condition when one candle must have appeared to him like two, I thought it possible that, by going a step farther in his potations, he might have reversed this phenomenon, and seen no candle at all where he ought to have beheld one.

Things were in this state when an incident took place so awful and inexplicable in its character that my reason fairly reels at the bare memory of the occurrence. It was the 10th of July. After dinner was over I repaired, with my friend Dr. Hammond, to the garden to smoke my evening pipe. Independent of certain mental sympathies which existed between the Doctor and myself, we were linked together by a secret vice. We both smoked opium. We knew each other's secret, and respected it.

We enjoyed together that wonderful expansion of thought; that marvelous intensifying of the perceptive faculties; that boundless feeling of existence when we seem to have points of contact with the whole universe; in short, that unimaginable spiritual bliss, which I would not surrender for a throne, and which I hope you, reader, will never—never taste.

Those hours of opium happiness which the Doctor and I spent together in secret were regulated with a scientific accuracy. We did not blindly smoke the drug of Paradise, and leave our dreams to chance. While smoking we carefully steered our conversation through the brightest and calmest channels of thought. We talked of the East, and endeavored to recall the magical panorama of its glowing scenery. We criticised the most sensuous poets, those who painted life ruddy with health, brimming with passion, happy in the possession of youth, and strength, and beauty. If we talked of Shakspeare's "Midsummer Night's Dream," we lingered over Ariel and avoided Caliban. Like the Gebers, we turned our faces to the East, and saw only the sunny side of the world.

This skillful coloring of our train of thought produced in our subsequent visions a corresponding tone. The splendors of Arabian fairy-land dyed our dreams. We paced that narrow strip of grass with the tread and port of kings. The song of the *Rana arborea* while he clung to the bark of the ragged plum-tree sounded like the strains of divine orchestras. Houses, walls, and streets melted like rain-clouds, and vistas of unimaginable glory stretched away before us. It was a rapturous companionship. We each of us enjoyed the vast delight more perfectly because, even in our most ecstatic moments, we were ever conscious of each other's presence. Our pleasures, while individual, were still twin, vibrating and moving in musical accord.

On the evening in question, the 10th of July, the Doctor and myself found ourselves in an unusually metaphysical mood. We lit our large meerschaums, filled with fine Turkish tobacco, in the core of which burned a little black nut of opium, that, like the nut in the fairy tale, held within its narrow limits wonders beyond the reach of kings; we paced to and fro, conversing. A strange perversity dominated the currents of our thought. They would *not* flow through the sun-lit channels into which we strove to divert them. For some unaccountable reason they constantly diverged into dark and lonesome beds, where a continual gloom brooded. It was in vain that, after our old fashion, we flung ourselves on the shores of the East, and talked of its gay bazaars, of the splendors of the time of Haroun, of harems and golden palaces. Black afreets continually arose from the depths of our talk, and expanded, like the one the fisherman released from the copper vessel, until they blotted every thing bright from our vision. Insensibly we yielded to the occult force that swayed us, and indulged in gloomy speculation. We had talked some time upon the proneness of the human mind to mysticism and the almost universal love of the Terrible, when Hammond suddenly said to me:

"What do you consider to be the greatest element of Terror?"

The question, I own, puzzled me. That many things were terrible, I knew. Stumbling over a corpse in the dark; beholding, as I once did, a woman floating down a deep and rapid river, with wildly-lifted arms and awful, upturned face, uttering, as she sank, shrieks that rent one's heart, while we, the spectators, stood frozen at a window which overhung the river at a height of sixty feet, unable to make the slightest effort to save her, but dumbly watching her last supreme agony and her disappearance. A shattered wreck, with no life visible, encountered floating listlessly on the ocean, is a terrible object, for it suggests huge terror, the proportions of which are vailed. But it now struck me for the first time that there must be one great and ruling embodiment of fear, a King of Terrors to which all others must succumb. What might it be? To what train of circumstances would it owe its existence?

"I confess, Hammond," I replied to my friend, "I never considered the subject before. That there must be one Something more terrible than any other thing, I feel. I can not attempt, however, even the most vague definition."

"I am somewhat like you, Harry," he answered. "I feel my capacity to experience a terror greater than any thing yet conceived by the human mind. Something combining in fearful and unnatural amalgamation hitherto supposed incompatible elements. The calling of the voices in Brockden Brown's novel of 'Wieland' is awful; so is the picture of the Dweller of the

Threshold in Bulwer's 'Zanoni;' but," he added, shaking his head gloomily, "there is something more horrible still than these."

"Look here, Hammond," I rejoined; "let us drop this kind of talk for Heaven's sake. We shall suffer for it, depend on it."

"I don't know what's the matter with me to-night," he replied, "but my brain is running upon all sorts of weird and awful thoughts. I feel as if I could write a story like Hoffmann to-night, if I were only master of a literary style."

"Well, if we are going to be Hoffmanesque in our talk I'm off to bed. Opium and nightmares should never be brought together. How sultry it is! Good-night, Hammond."

"Goodnight, Harry. Pleasant dreams to you."

"To you, gloomy wretch, afreets, ghouls, and enchanters."

We parted, and each sought his respective chamber. I undressed quickly and got into bed, taking with me, according to my usual custom, a book, over which I generally read myself to sleep. I opened the volume as soon as I had laid my head upon the pillow, and instantly flung it to the other side of the room. It was Goudon's "History of Monsters"—a curious French work, which I had lately imported from Paris, but which, in the state of mind I was then in, was any thing but an agreeable companion. I resolved to go to sleep at once; so turning down my gas until nothing but a little blue point of light glimmered on the top of the tube, I composed myself to rest once more.

The room was in total darkness. The atom of gas that still remained lighted did not illuminate a distance of three inches round the burner. I desperately drew my arm across my eyes, as if to shut out even the darkness, and tried to think of nothing. It was in vain. The confounded themes touched on by Hammond in the garden kept obtruding themselves on my brain. I battled against them. I erected ramparts of would-be blankness of intellect to keep them out. They still crowded upon me. While I was lying still as a corpse, hoping that by a perfect physical inaction I would hasten mental repose, an awful incident occurred. A Something dropped, as it seemed, from the ceiling, plumb upon my chest, and the next instant I felt two bony hands encircling my throat, endeavoring to choke me.

I am no coward, and am possessed of considerable physical strength. The suddenness of the attack instead of stunning me strung every nerve to its highest tension. My body acted from instinct, before my brain had time to realize the terrors of my position. In an instant I wound two muscular arms around the creature, and squeezed it, with all the strength of despair, against my chest. In a few seconds the bony hands that had fastened on my throat loosened their hold, and I was free to breathe once more. Then commenced a struggle of awful intensity. Immersed in the most profound darkness, totally ignorant of the nature of the Thing by which I was so suddenly attacked, finding my grasp slipping every moment by reason, it seemed to me, of the entire nakedness of my assailant, bitten with sharp teeth in the shoulder, neck, and chest, having every moment to protect my throat against a pair of sinewy, agile hands, which my utmost efforts could not confine—these were a combination of circumstances to combat which required all the strength and skill and courage that I possessed.

At last, after a silent, deadly, exhausting struggle, I got my assailant under by a series of incredible efforts of strength. Once pinned, with my knee on what I made out to be its chest, I knew that I was victor. I rested for a moment to breathe. I heard the creature beneath me panting in the darkness, and felt the violent throbbing of a heart. It was apparently as exhausted as I was, that was one comfort. At this moment I remembered that I usually placed under my pillow, before going to bed, a large, yellow silk pocket-handkerchief, for use during the night. I felt for it instantly; it was there. In a few seconds more I had, after a fashion, pinioned the creature's arms.

I now felt tolerably secure. There was nothing more to be done but to turn on the gas, and, having first seen what my midnight assailant was like, arouse the household. I will confess to being actuated by a certain pride in not giving the alarm before; I wished to make the capture alone and unaided.

Never loosing my hold for an instant, I slipped from the bed to the floor, dragging my captive with me. I had but a few steps to make to reach the gas-burner; these I made with the greatest caution, holding the creature in a grip like a vice. At last I got within arm's-length of the tiny speck of blue light, which told me where the gas-burner lay. Quick as lightning I released my grasp with one hand and let on the full flood of light. Then I turned to look at my captive.

I can not even attempt to give any definition of my sensations the instant after I turned on the gas. I suppose I must have shrieked with terror, for in less than a minute afterward my room was crowded with the inmates of the house. I shudder now as I think of that awful moment. *I saw nothing!* Yes; I had one arm firmly clasped round a breathing, panting, corporeal shape, my other hand gripped with all its strength a throat as warm, and apparently fleshly, as my own; and yet, with this living substance in my grasp, with its body pressed against my own, and all in the bright glare of a large jet of gas, I absolutely beheld nothing! Not even an outline—a vapor!

I do not, even at this hour, realize the situation in which I found myself. I can not recall the astounding incident thoroughly. Imagination in vain tries to compass the awful paradox.

It breathed. I felt its warm breath upon my cheek. It struggled fiercely. It had hands. They clutched me. Its skin was smooth, just like my own. There it lay, pressed close up against me, solid as stone—and yet utterly invisible!

I wonder that I did not faint or go mad on the instant. Some wonderful instinct must have sustained me; for, absolutely, in place of loosening my hold on the terrible Enigma, I seemed to gain an additional strength in my moment of horror, and tightened my grasp with such wonderful force that I felt the creature shivering with agony.

Just then Hammond entered my room at the head of the household. As soon as he beheld my face—which, I suppose, must have been an awful sight to look at—he hastened forward, crying,

"Great Heaven, Harry! what has happened?"

"Hammond! Hammond!" I cried, "come here. Oh! this is awful! I have been attacked in bed by something or other, which I have hold of; but I can't see it—I can't see it!"

Hammond, doubtless struck by the unfeigned horror expressed in my countenance, made one or two steps forward with an anxious yet puzzled expression. A very audible titter burst from the remainder of my visitors. This suppressed laughter made me furious. To laugh at a human being in my position! It was the worst species of cruelty. *Now*, I can understand why the appearance of a man struggling violently, as it would seem, with an airy nothing, and calling for assistance against a vision, should have appeared ludicrous. *Then*, so great was my rage against the mocking crowd that had I the power I would have stricken them dead where they stood.

"Hammond! Hammond!" I cried again, despairingly, "for God's sake come to me. I can hold the—the Thing but a short while longer. It is overpowering me. Help me. Help me!"

"Harry," whispered Hammond, approaching me, "you have been smoking too much opium."

"I swear to you Hammond that this is no vision," I answered, in the same low tone. "Don't you see how it shakes my whole frame with its struggles? If you don't believe me convince yourself. Feel it—touch it."

Hammond advanced and laid his hand in the spot I indicated. A wild cry of horror burst from him. He had felt it!

In a moment he had discovered somewhere in my room a long piece of cord, and was the next instant winding it, and knotting it about the body of the unseen being that I clasped in my arms.

"Harry," he said, in a hoarse, agitated voice, for, though he preserved his presence of mind, he was deeply moved, "Harry, it's all safe now. You may let go, old fellow, if you're tired. The Thing can't move."

I was utterly exhausted, and I gladly loosed my hold.

Hammond stood holding the ends of the cord that bound the Invisible, twisted round his hand, while before him, self-supporting, as it were, he beheld a rope laced and interlaced, and stretching tightly around a vacant space. I never saw a man look so thoroughly stricken with awe. Nevertheless his face expressed all the courage and determination which I knew him to possess. His lips, although white, were set firmly, and one could perceive at a glance that, although stricken with fear, he was not daunted.

The confusion that ensued among the guests of the house, who were witnesses of this extraordinary scene between Hammond and myself—who beheld the pantomime of binding this struggling Something—who beheld me almost sinking from physical exhaustion when my task of jailer was over—the confusion and terror that took possession of the by-standers, when they saw all this, was beyond description. Many of the weaker ones fled from the apartment. The few who remained behind clustered near the door, and could not be induced to approach Hammond and his Charge. Still incredulity broke out through their terror. They had not the courage to satisfy themselves, and yet they doubted. It was in vain that I begged of some of the men to come near and convince themselves by touch of the existence of a living being in that room which was invisible. They were incredulous, but did not dare to undeceive themselves. How could a solid, living, breathing body be invisible? they asked. My reply was this. I gave a sign to Hammond, and both of us—conquering our fearful repugnance to touching the invisible creature—lifted it from the ground, manacled as it was, and took it to my bed. Its weight was about that of a boy of fourteen.

"Now my friends," I said, as Hammond and myself held the creature suspended over the bed, "I can give you self-evident proof that here is a solid, ponderable body which, nevertheless, you can not see. Be good enough to watch the surface of the bed attentively."

I was astonished at my own courage in treating this strange event so calmly; but I had recovered from my first terror, and felt a sort of scientific pride in the affair which dominated every other feeling.

The eyes of the by-standers were immediately fixed on my bed. At a given signal Hammond and I let the creature fall. There was the dull sound of a heavy body alighting on a soft mass. The timbers of the bed creaked. A deep impression marked itself distinctly on the pillow, and on the bed itself. The crowd who witnessed this gave a sort of low, universal cry, and rushed from the room. Hammond and I were left alone with our Mystery.

We remained silent for some time, listening to the low, irregular breathing of the creature on the bed, and watching the rustle of the bedclothes as it impotently struggled to free itself from confinement. Then Hammond spoke.

"Harry, this is awful."

"Ay, awful."

"But not unaccountable."

"Not unaccountable! What do you mean? Such a thing has never occurred since the birth of the world. I know not what to think, Hammond. God grant that I am not mad, and that this is not an insane fantasy!"

"Let us reason a little, Harry. Here is a solid body which we touch, but which we can not see. The fact is so unusual that it strikes us with terror. Is there no parallel, though, for such a phenomenon? Take a piece of pure glass. It is tangible and transparent. A certain chemical coarseness is all that prevents its being so entirely transparent as to be totally invisible. It is not *theoretically impossible*, mind you, to fabricate a glass which shall not reflect a single ray of light—a glass so pure and homogeneous in its atoms that the rays from the sun shall pass through it as they do through the air, refracted but not reflected. We do not see the air, and yet we feel it."

"That's all very well, Hammond, but these are inanimate substances. Glass does not breathe, air does not breathe. *This* thing has a heart that palpitates. A will that moves it. Lungs that play and inspire and respire."

"You forget the strange phenomena of which we have so often heard of late," answered the Doctor, gravely. "At the meetings called 'spirit circles,' invisible hands have been thrust into the hands of those persons round the table—warm, fleshly hands that seemed to pulsate with mortal life."

"What? Do you think, then, that this thing is—"

"I don't know what it is," was the solemn reply; "but please the gods I will, with your assistance, thoroughly investigate it."

We watched together, smoking many pipes, all night long by the bedside of the unearthly being that tossed and panted until it was apparently wearied out. Then we learned by the low, regular breathing that it slept.

The next morning the house was all astir. The boarders congregated on the landing outside my room, and Hammond and myself were lions. We had to answer a thousand questions as to the state of our extraordinary prisoner, for as yet not one person in the house except ourselves could be induced to set foot in the apartment.

The creature was awake. This was evidenced by the convulsive manner in which the bed-clothes were moved in its efforts to escape. There was something truly terrible in beholding, as it were, those second-hand indications of the terrible writhings and agonized struggles for liberty, which themselves were invisible.

Hammond and myself had racked our brains during the long night to discover some means by which we might realize the shape and general appearance of the Enigma. As well as we could make out by passing our hands over the creature's form, its outlines and lineaments were human. There was a mouth; a round, smooth head without hair; a nose, which, however, was little elevated above the cheeks; and its hands and feet felt like those of a boy. At first we thought of placing the being on a smooth surface and tracing its outline with chalk, as shoemakers trace the outline of the foot. This plan was given up as being of no value. Such an outline would give not the slightest idea of its conformation.

A happy thought struck me. We would take a cast of it in plaster of Paris. This would give us the solid figure, and satisfy all our wishes. But how to do it? The movements of the creature would disturb the setting of the plastic covering, and distort the mould. Another thought. Why not give it chloroform? It had respiratory organs—that was evident by its breathing. Once reduced to a state of insensibility, we could do with it what we would. Doctor X—— was sent for; and after the worthy physician had recovered from the first shock of amazement, he proceeded to administer the chloroform. In three minutes afterward we were enabled to remove the fetters from the creature's body, and a well-known modeler of this city was busily engaged in covering the invisible form with the moist clay. In five minutes more we had a mould, and before evening a rough *fac-simile* of the Mystery. It was shaped like a man. Distorted, uncouth, and horrible, but still a man. It was small, not over four feet and some inches in height, and its limbs betrayed a muscular development that was unparalleled. Its face surpassed in hideousness any thing I had ever seen. Gustave Doré, or Callot, or Tony Johannot never conceived any thing so horrible. There is a face in one of the latter's illustrations to "*Un voyage ou il vous plaira*," which somewhat approaches the countenance of this creature, but does not equal it. It was the physiognomy of what I should have fancied a ghoul to be. It looked as if it was capable of feeding on human flesh.

Having satisfied our curiosity, and bound every one in the house over to secrecy, it became a question what was to be done with our Enigma? It was impossible that we should keep such a horror in our house; it was equally impossible that such an awful being should be let loose upon the world. I confess that I would have gladly voted for the creature's destruction. But who would shoulder the responsibility? Who would undertake the execution of this horrible semblance of a human being? Day after day this question was deliberated gravely. The boarders all left the house. Mrs. Moffat was in despair, and threatened Hammond and myself with all sorts of legal penalties if we did not remove the Horror. Our answer was, "We will go if you like, but we decline taking this creature with us. Remove it yourself if you please. It appeared in your house. On you the responsibility rests." To this there was, of course, no answer. Mrs. Moffat could not obtain for love or money a person who would even approach the Mystery.

The most singular part of the transaction was, that we were entirely ignorant of what the creature habitually fed on. Every thing in the way of nutriment that we could think of was placed before it, but was never touched. It was awful to stand by, day after day, and see the clothes lost and hear the hard breathing, and know that it was starving.

Ten, twelve days, a fortnight passed, and it still lived. The pulsations of the heart, however, were daily growing fainter, and had now nearly ceased altogether. It was evident that the creature was dying for want of sustenance. While this terrible life-struggle was going on I felt miserable. I could not sleep of nights. Horrible as the creature was, it was pitiful to think of the pangs it was suffering.

At last it died. Hammond and I found it cold and stiff one morning in the bed. The heart had ceased to beat, the lungs to inspire. We hastened to bury it in the garden. It was a strange funeral, the dropping of that viewless corpse into the damp hole. The cast of its form I gave to Doctor X——, who keeps it in his museum in Tenth Street.

As I am on the eve of a long journey from which I may not return, I have drawn up this narrative of an event the most singular that has ever come to my knowledge.

HARRY ESCOTT.

[Note.—It is rumored that the proprietors of a well-known museum in this city have made arrangements with Dr. X—— to exhibit to the public the singular cast which Mr. Escott deposited with him. So extraordinary a history can not fail to attract universal attention.]

1859

# REBECCA HARDING DAVIS

(1831–1910)

---

## *Life in the Iron-Mills*

"Is this the end?
O Life, as futile, then, as frail!
What hope of answer or redress?"

A CLOUDY DAY: do you know what that is in a town of iron-works? The sky sank down before dawn, muddy, flat, immovable. The air is thick, clammy with the breath of crowded human beings. It stifles me. I open the window, and, looking out, can scarcely see through the rain the grocer's shop opposite, where a crowd of drunken Irishmen are puffing Lynchburg tobacco in their pipes. I can detect the scent through all the foul smells ranging loose in the air.

The idiosyncrasy of this town is smoke. It rolls sullenly in slow folds from the great chimneys of the iron-founderies, and settles down in black, slimy pools on the muddy streets. Smoke on the wharves, smoke on the dingy boats, on the yellow river,—clinging in a coating of greasy soot to the house-front, the two faded poplars, the faces of the passers-by. The long train of mules, dragging masses of pig-iron through the narrow street, have a foul vapor hanging to their reeking sides. Here, inside, is a little broken figure of an angel pointing upward from the mantel-shelf; but even its wings are covered with smoke, clotted and black. Smoke everywhere! A dirty canary chirps desolately in a cage beside me. Its dream of green fields and sunshine is a very old dream,—almost worn out, I think.

From the back-window I can see a narrow brick-yard sloping down to the river-side, strewed with rain-butts and tubs. The river, dull and tawny-colored, (*la belle rivière!*) drags itself sluggishly along, tired of the heavy weight of boats and coal-barges. What wonder? When I was a child, I used to fancy a look of weary, dumb appeal upon the face of the negro-like river slavishly bearing its burden day after day. Something of the same idle notion comes to me to-day, when from the street-window I look on the slow stream of human life creeping past, night and morning, to the great mills. Masses of men, with dull, besotted faces bent to the ground, sharpened here and there by pain or cunning; skin and muscle and flesh begrimed with smoke and ashes; stooping all night over boiling caldrons of metal, laired by day in dens of drunkenness and infamy; breathing from infancy to death an air saturated with fog and grease and soot, vileness for soul and body. What do you make of a case like that, amateur psychologist? You call it an altogether serious thing to be alive: to these men it is a drunken jest, a joke,—horrible to angels perhaps, to them commonplace enough. My fancy about the river was an idle one: it is no type of such a life. What if it be stagnant and slimy here? It knows that beyond there waits for it odorous sunlight,—quaint old gardens, dusky with soft, green foliage of apple-trees, and flushing crimson with roses,—air, and fields, and mountains. The future of the Welsh puddler passing just now is not so pleasant. To be stowed away, after his grimy work is done, in a hole in the muddy graveyard, and after that,—*not* air, nor green fields, nor curious roses.

Can you see how foggy the day is? As I stand here, idly tapping the window-pane, and looking out through the rain at the dirty back-yard and the coal-boats below, fragments of an old story float up before me,—a story of this house into which I happened to come to-day. You may think it a tiresome story enough, as foggy as the day, sharpened by no sudden flashes of pain or pleasure. I know: only the outline of a dull life, that long since, with thousands of dull lives like its own, was vainly lived and lost: thousands of them,—massed, vile, slimy lives, like those of the torpid lizards in yonder stagnant water-butt.—Lost? There is a curious point for you to settle, my friend, who study psychology in a lazy, *dilettante* way. Stop a moment. I am going to be honest. This is what I want you to do. I want you to hide your disgust, take no heed to your clean clothes, and come right down with me,—here, into the thickest of the fog and mud and foul effluvia. I want you to hear this story. There is a secret down here, in this nightmare fog, that has lain dumb for centuries: I want to make it a real thing to you. You, Egoist, or Pantheist, or Arminian, busy in making straight paths for your feet on the hills, do not see it clearly,—this terrible question which men here have gone mad and died trying to answer. I dare not put this secret into words. I told you it was dumb. These men, going by with drunken faces, and brains full of unawakened power, do not ask it of Society or of God. Their lives ask it; their deaths ask it. There is no reply. I will tell you plainly that I have a great hope; and I bring it to you to be tested. It is this: that this terrible dumb question is its own reply; that it is not the sentence of death we think it, but, from the very extremity of its darkness, the most solemn prophecy which the world has known of the Hope to come. I dare make my meaning no clearer, but will only tell my story. It will, perhaps, seem to you as foul and dark as this thick vapor about us, and as pregnant with death; but if your eyes are free as mine are to look deeper, no perfume-tinted dawn will be so fair with promise of the day that shall surely come.

My story is very simple,—only what I remember of the life of one of these men,—a furnace-tender in one of Kirby & John's rolling-mills,—Hugh Wolfe. You know the mills? They took the great order for the lower Virginia railroads there last winter; run usually with about a thousand men. I cannot tell why I choose the half-forgotten story of this Wolfe more than that of myriads of these furnace-hands. Perhaps because there is a secret, underlying sympathy between that story and this day with its impure fog and thwarted sunshine,—or perhaps simply for the reason that this house is the one where the Wolfes lived. There were the father and son,—both hands, as I said, in one of Kirby & John's mills for making railroad-iron,—and Deborah, their cousin, a picker in some of the cotton-mills. The house was rented then to half a dozen families. The Wolfes had two of the cellar-rooms. The old man, like many of the puddlers and feeders of the mills, was Welsh,—had spent half of his life in the Cornish tin-mines. You may pick the Welsh emigrants, Cornish miners, out of the throng passing the windows, any day. They are a trifle more filthy; their muscles are not so brawny; they stoop more. When they are drunk, they neither yell, nor shout, nor stagger, but skulk along like beaten hounds. A pure, unmixed blood, I fancy, shows itself in the slight angular bodies and sharply-cut facial lines. It is nearly thirty years since the Wolfes lived here. Their lives were like those of their class: incessant labor, sleeping in kennel-like rooms, eating rank pork and molasses, drinking—God and the distillers only know what;

with an occasional night in jail, to atone for some drunken excess. Is that all of their lives?—of the portion given to them and these their duplicates swarming the streets to-day?—nothing beneath?—all? So many a political reformer will tell you,—and many a private reformer, too, who has gone among them with a heart tender with Christ's charity, and come out outraged, hardened.

One rainy night, about eleven o'clock, a crowd of half-clothed women stopped outside of the cellar-door. They were going home from the cotton-mill.

"Good-night, Deb," said one, a mulatto, steadying herself against the gas-post. She needed the post to steady her. So did more than one of them.

"Dah 's a ball to Miss Potts' to-night. Ye 'd best come."

"Inteet, Deb, if hur 'll come, hur 'll hef fun," said a shrill Welsh voice in the crowd.

Two or three dirty hands were thrust out to catch the gown of the woman, who was groping for the latch of the door.

"No."

"No? Where 's Kit Small, then?"

"Begorra! on the spools. Alleys behint, though we helped her, we dud. An wid ye! Let Deb alone! It 's ondacent frettin' a quite body. Be the powers, an' we 'll have a night of it! there 'll be lashin's o' drink,—the Vargent be blessed and praised for 't!"

They went on, the mulatto inclining for a moment to show fight, and drag the woman Wolfe off with them; but, being pacified, she staggered away.

Deborah groped her way into the cellar, and, after considerable stumbling, kindled a match, and lighted a tallow dip, that sent a yellow glimmer over the room. It was low, damp,—the earthen floor covered with a green, slimy moss,—a fetid air smothering the breath. Old Wolfe lay asleep on a heap of straw, wrapped in a torn horse-blanket. He was a pale, meek little man, with a white face and red rabbit-eyes. The woman Deborah was like him; only her face was even more ghastly, her lips bluer, her eyes more watery. She wore a faded cotton gown and a slouching bonnet. When she walked, one could see that she was deformed, almost a hunchback. She trod softly, so as not to waken him, and went through into the room beyond. There she found by the half-extinguished fire an iron saucepan filled with cold boiled potatoes, which she put upon a broken chair with a pint-cup of ale. Placing the old candlestick beside this dainty repast, she untied her bonnet, which hung limp and wet over her face, and prepared to eat her supper. It was the first food that had touched her lips since morning. There was enough of it, however: there is not always. She was hungry,—one could see that easily enough,—and not drunk, as most of her companions would have been found at this hour. She did not drink, this woman,—her face told that too,—nothing stronger than ale. Perhaps the weak, flaccid wretch had some stimulant in her pale life to keep her up,—some love or hope, it might be, or urgent need. When that stimulant was gone, she would take to whiskey. Man cannot live by work alone. While she was skinning the potatoes, and munching them, a noise behind her made her stop.

"Janey!" she called, lifting the candle and peering into the darkness. "Janey, are you there?"

A heap of ragged coats was heaved up, and the face of a young girl emerged, staring sleepily at the woman.

"Deborah," she said, at last, "I 'm here the night."

"Yes, child. Hur 's welcome," she said, quietly eating on.

The girl's face was haggard and sickly; her eyes were heavy with sleep and hunger: real Milesian eyes they were, dark, delicate blue, glooming out from black shadows with a pitiful fright.

"I was alone," she said, timidly.

"Where 's the father?" asked Deborah, holding out a potato, which the girl greedily seized.

"He 's beyant,—wid Haley,—in the stone house." (Did you ever hear the word *jail* from an Irish mouth?) "I came here. Hugh told me never to stay me-lone."

"Hugh?"

"Yes."

A vexed frown crossed her face. The girl saw it, and added quickly,—

"I have not seen Hugh the day, Deb. The old man says his watch lasts till the mornin'."

The woman sprang up, and hastily began to arrange some bread and flitch in a tin pail, and to pour her own measure of ale into a bottle. Tying on her bonnet, she blew out the candle.

"Lay ye down, Janey dear," she said, gently, covering her with the old rags. "Hur can eat the potatoes, if hur 's hungry."

"Where are ye goin', Deb? The rain 's sharp."

"To the mill, with Hugh's supper."

"Let him bide till th' morn. Sit ye down."

"No, no,"—sharply pushing her off. "The boy 'll starve."

She hurried from the cellar, while the child wearily coiled herself up for sleep. The rain was falling heavily, as the woman, pail in hand, emerged from the mouth of the alley, and turned down the narrow street, that stretched out, long and black, miles before her. Here and there a flicker of gas lighted an uncertain space of muddy footwalk and gutter; the long rows of houses, except an occasional lager-bier shop, were closed; now and then she met a band of mill-hands skulking to or from their work.

Not many even of the inhabitants of a manufacturing town know the vast machinery of system by which the bodies of workmen are governed, that goes on unceasingly from year to year. The hands of each mill are divided into watches that relieve each other as regularly as the sentinels of an army. By night and day the work goes on, the unsleeping engines groan and shriek, the fiery pools of metal boil and surge. Only for a day in the week, in half-courtesy to public censure, the fires are partially veiled; but as soon as the clock strikes midnight, the great furnaces break forth with renewed fury, the clamor begins with fresh, breathless vigor, the engines sob and shriek like "gods in pain."

As Deborah hurried down through the heavy rain, the noise of these thousand engines sounded through the sleep and shadow of the city like far-off thunder. The mill to which she was going lay on the river, a mile below the city-limits. It was far, and she was weak, aching from standing twelve hours at the spools. Yet it was her almost nightly walk to take this man his supper, though at every square she sat down to rest, and she knew she should receive small word of thanks.

Perhaps, if she had possessed an artist's eye, the picturesque oddity of the scene might have made her step stagger less, and the path seem shorter; but to her the mills were only "summat deilish to look at by night."

The road leading to the mills had been quarried from the solid rock, which rose abrupt and bare on one side of the cinder-covered road, while the river, sluggish and black, crept past on the other. The mills for rolling iron are simply immense tent-like roofs, covering acres of ground, open on every side. Beneath these roofs Deborah looked in on a city of fires, that burned hot and fiercely in the night. Fire in every horrible form: pits of flame waving in the wind; liquid metal-flames writhing in tortuous streams through the sand; wide caldrons filled with boiling fire, over which bent ghastly wretches stirring the strange brewing; and through all, crowds of half-clad men, looking like revengeful ghosts in the red light, hurried, throwing masses of glittering fire. It was like a street in Hell. Even Deborah muttered, as she crept through, "'T looks like t' Devil's place!" It did,—in more ways than one.

She found the man she was looking for, at last, heaping coal on a furnace. He had not time to eat his supper; so she went behind the furnace, and waited. Only a few men were with him, and they noticed her only by a "Hyur comes t' hunchback, Wolfe."

Deborah was stupid with sleep; her back pained her sharply; and her teeth chattered with cold, with the rain that soaked her clothes and dripped from her at every step. She stood, however, patiently holding the pail, and waiting.

"Hout, woman! ye look like a drowned cat. Come near to the fire,"—said one of the men, approaching to scrape away the ashes.

She shook her head. Wolfe had forgotten her. He turned, hearing the man, and came closer.

"I did no' think; g' me my supper, woman."

She watched him eat with a painful eagerness. With a woman's quick instinct, she saw that he was not hungry,—was eating to please her. Her pale, watery eyes began to gather a strange light.

"Is 't good, Hugh? T' ale was a bit sour, I feared."

"No, good enough." He hesitated a moment. "Ye 're tired, poor lass! Bide here till I go. Lay down there on that heap of ash, and go to sleep."

He threw her an old coat for a pillow, and turned to his work. The heap was the refuse of the burnt iron, and was not a hard bed; the half-smothered warmth, too, penetrated her limbs, dulling their pain and cold shiver.

Miserable enough she looked, lying there on the ashes like a limp, dirty rag,—yet not an unfitting figure to crown the scene of hopeless discomfort and veiled crime: more fitting, if one looked deeper into the heart of things,—at her thwarted woman's form, her colorless life, her waking stupor that smothered pain and hunger,—even more fit to be a type of her class. Deeper yet if one could look; was there nothing worth reading in this wet, faded thing, half covered with ashes? no story of a soul filled with groping, passionate love, heroic unselfishness, fierce jealousy? of years of weary trying to please the one human being whom she loved, to gain one look of real heart-kindness from him? If anything like this were hidden beneath the pale, bleared eyes, and dull, washed-out-looking face, no one had ever taken the trouble to read its faint signs: not the half-clothed furnace-tender, Wolfe, certainly. Yet he was kind to her: it was his nature to be kind, even to the very rats that swarmed in the cellar: kind to her in just the same way. She knew that. And it might be that very knowledge had given to her face its apathy and vacancy more than her low, torpid life. One sees that dead, vacant look steal sometimes over the rarest, finest of women's faces,—in the very midst, it may be, of their warmest summer's day; and then one can guess at the secret of intolerable solitude that lies hid beneath the delicate laces and brilliant smile. There was no warmth, no brilliancy, no summer for this woman; so the stupor and vacancy had time to gnaw into her face perpetually. She was young, too, though no one guessed it; so the gnawing was the fiercer.

She lay quiet in the dark corner, listening, through the monotonous din and uncertain glare of the works, to the dull plash of the rain in the far distance,—shrinking back whenever the man Wolfe happened to look towards her. She knew, in spite of all his kindness, that there was that in her face and form which made him loathe the sight of her. She felt by instinct, although she could not comprehend it, the finer nature of the man, which made him among his fellow-workmen something unique, set apart. She knew, that, down under all the vileness and coarseness of his life, there was a groping passion for whatever was beautiful and pure,—that his soul sickened with disgust at her deformity, even when his words were kindest. Through this dull consciousness, which never left her, came, like a sting, the recollection of the dark blue eyes and lithe figure of the little Irish girl she had left in the cellar. The recollection struck through even her stupid intellect with a vivid glow of beauty and of grace. Little Janey, timid, helpless, clinging to Hugh as her only friend: that was the sharp thought, the bitter thought, that drove into the glazed eyes a fierce light of pain. You laugh at it? Are pain and jealousy less savage realities down here in this place I am taking you to than in your own house or your own heart,—your heart, which they clutch at sometimes? The note is the same, I fancy, be the octave high or low.

If you could go into this mill where Deborah lay, and drag out from the hearts of these men the terrible tragedy of their lives, taking it as a symptom of the disease of their class, no ghost Horror would terrify you more. A reality of soul-starvation, of living death, that meets you every day under the besotted faces on the street—I can paint nothing of this, only give you the outside outlines of a night, a crisis in the life of one man: whatever muddy depth of soul-history lies beneath you can read according to the eyes God has given you.

Wolfe, while Deborah watched him as a spaniel its master, bent over the furnace with his iron pole, unconscious of her scrutiny, only stopping to receive orders. Physically, Nature had promised the man but little. He had already lost the strength and instinct vigor of a man, his muscles were thin, his nerves weak, his face (a meek, woman's face) haggard, yellow with consumption. In the mill he was known as one of the girl-men: "Molly Wolfe" was his *sobriquet*. He was never seen in the cock-pit, did not own a terrier, drank but seldom; when he did, desperately. He fought sometimes, but was always thrashed, pommelled to a jelly. The man was game enough, when his blood was up: but he was no favorite in the mill; he had the taint of school-learning on him,—not to a dangerous extent, only a quarter or so in the free-school in fact, but enough to ruin him as a good hand in a fight.

For other reasons, too, he was not popular. Not one of themselves, they felt that, though outwardly as filthy and ash-covered; silent, with foreign thoughts and longings breaking out through his quietness in innumerable curious ways: this one, for instance. In the neighboring furnace-buildings lay great heaps of the refuse from the ore after the pig-metal is run. *Korl* we call it here: a light, porous substance, of a delicate, waxen, flesh-colored tinge. Out of the blocks of this korl, Wolfe, in his off-hours from the furnace, had a habit of chipping and moulding figures,—hideous, fantastic enough, but sometimes strangely beautiful: even the mill-men saw that, while they jeered at him. It was a curious fancy in the man, almost a passion. The few hours for rest he spent hewing and hacking with his blunt knife, never speaking, until his watch came again,—working at one figure for months, and, when it was finished, breaking it to pieces perhaps, in a fit of disappointment. A morbid, gloomy man, untaught, unled, left to feed his soul in grossness and crime, and hard, grinding labor.

I want you to come down and look at this Wolfe, standing there among the lowest of his kind, and see him just as he is, that you may judge him justly when you hear the story of this night. I want you to look back, as he does every day, at his birth in vice, his starved infancy; to remember the heavy years he has groped through as boy and man,—the slow, heavy years of constant, hot work. So long ago he began, that he thinks sometimes he has worked there for ages. There is no hope that it will ever end. Think that God put into this man's soul a fierce thirst for beauty,—to know it, to create it; to *be*—something, he knows not what,—other than he is. There are moments when a passing cloud, the sun glinting on the purple thistles, a kindly smile, a child's face, will rouse him to a passion of pain,—when his nature starts up with a mad cry of rage against God, man, whoever it is that has forced this vile, slimy life upon him. With all this groping, this mad desire, a great blind intellect stumbling through wrong, a loving poet's heart, the man was by habit only a coarse, vulgar laborer, familiar with sights and words you would blush to name. Be just: when I tell you about this night, see him as he is. Be just,—not like man's law, which seizes on one isolated fact, but like God's judging angel, whose clear, sad eye saw all the countless cankering days of this man's life, all the countless nights, when, sick with starving, his soul fainted in him, before it judged him for this night, the saddest of all.

I called this night the crisis of his life. If it was, it stole on him unawares. These great turning-days of life cast no shadow before, slip by unconsciously. Only a trifle, a little turn of the rudder, and the ship goes to heaven or hell.

Wolfe, while Deborah watched him, dug into the furnace of melting iron with his pole, dully thinking only how many rails the lump would yield. It was late,—nearly Sunday morning; another hour, and the heavy work would be done,—only the furnaces to replenish and cover for the next day. The workmen were growing more noisy, shouting, as they had to do, to be heard over the deep clamor of the mills. Suddenly they grew less boisterous,—at the far end, entirely silent. Something unusual had happened. After a moment, the silence came nearer; the men stopped their jeers and drunken choruses. Deborah, stupidly lifting up her head, saw the cause of the quiet. A group of five or six men were slowly approaching, stopping to examine each furnace as they came. Visitors often came to see the mills after night: except by growing less noisy, the men took no notice of them. The furnace where Wolfe worked was near the bounds of the works; they halted there hot and tired: a walk over one of these great founderies is no trifling task. The woman, drawing out of sight, turned over to sleep. Wolfe, seeing them stop, suddenly roused from his indifferent stupor, and watched them keenly. He knew some of them: the overseer, Clarke,—a son of Kirby, one of the mill-owners,—and a Doctor May, one of the town-physicians. The other two were strangers. Wolfe came closer. He seized eagerly every chance that brought him into contact with this mysterious class that shone down on him perpetually with the glamour of another order of being. What made the difference between them? That was the mystery of his life. He had a vague notion that perhaps to-night he could find it out. One of the strangers sat down on a pile of bricks, and beckoned young Kirby to his side.

"This *is* hot, with a vengeance. A match, please?"—lighting his cigar. "But the walk is worth the trouble. If it were not that you must have heard it so often, Kirby, I would tell you that your works look like Dante's Inferno."

Kirby laughed.

"Yes. Yonder is Farinata himself in the burning tomb,"—pointing to some figure in the shimmering shadows.

"Judging from some of the faces of your men," said the other, "they bid fair to try the reality of Dante's vision, some day."

Young Kirby looked curiously around, as if seeing the faces of his hands for the first time.

"They 're bad enough, that 's true. A desperate set, I fancy. Eh, Clarke?"

The overseer did not hear him. He was talking of net profits just then,—giving, in fact, a schedule of the annual business of the firm to a sharp peering little Yankee, who jotted down notes on a paper laid on the crown of his hat: a reporter for one of the city papers, getting up a series of reviews of the leading manufactories. The other gentlemen had accompanied them merely for amusement. They were silent until the notes were finished, drying their feet at the furnaces, and sheltering their faces from the intolerable heat. At last the overseer concluded with—

"I believe that is a pretty fair estimate, Captain."

"Here, some of you men!" said Kirby, "bring up those boards. We may as well sit down, gentlemen, until the rain is over. It cannot last much longer at this rate."

"Pig-metal,"—mumbled the reporter,—"um!—coal facilities,—um!—hands employed, twelve hundred,—bitumen,—um!—all right, I believe, Mr. Clarke;—sinking-fund,—what did you say was your sinking-fund?"

"Twelve hundred hands?" said the stranger, the young man who had first spoken. "Do you control their votes, Kirby?"

"Control? No." The young man smiled complacently. "But my father brought seven hundred votes to the polls for his candidate last November. No force-work, you understand,—only a speech or two, a hint to form themselves into a society, and a bit of red and blue bunting to make them a flag. The Invincible Roughs,—I believe that is their name. I forget the motto: 'Our country's hope,' I think."

There was a laugh. The young man talking to Kirby sat with an amused light in his cool gray eye, surveying critically the half-clothed figures of the puddlers, and the slow swing of their brawny muscles. He was a stranger in the city,—spending a couple of months in the borders of a Slave State, to study the institutions of the South,—a brother-in-law of Kirby's,—Mitchell. He was an amateur gymnast,—hence his anatomical eye; a patron, in a *blasé* way, of the prize-ring; a man who sucked the essence out of a science or philosophy in an indifferent, gentlemanly way; who took Kant, Novalis, Humboldt, for what they were worth in his own scales; accepting all, despising nothing, in heaven, earth, or hell, but one-idead men; with a temper yielding and brilliant as summer water, until his Self was touched, when it was ice, though brilliant still. Such men are not rare in the States.

As he knocked the ashes from his cigar, Wolfe caught with a quick pleasure the contour of the white hand, the blood-glow of a red ring he wore. His voice, too, and that of Kirby's, touched him like music,—low, even, with chording cadences. About this man Mitchell hung the impalpable atmosphere belonging to the thoroughbred gentleman. Wolfe, scraping away the ashes beside him, was conscious of it, did obeisance to it with his artist sense, unconscious that he did so.

The rain did not cease. Clarke and the reporter left the mills; the others, comfortably seated near the furnace, lingered, smoking and talking in a desultory way. Greek would not have been more unintelligible to the furnace-tenders, whose presence they soon forgot entirely. Kirby drew out a newspaper from his pocket and read aloud some article, which they discussed eagerly. At every sentence, Wolfe listened more and more like a dumb, hopeless animal, with a duller, more stolid look creeping over his face, glancing now and then at Mitchell, marking acutely every smallest sign of refinement, then back to himself, seeing as in a mirror his filthy body, his more stained soul.

Never! He had no words for such a thought, but he knew now, in all the sharpness of the bitter certainty, that between them there was a great gulf never to be passed. Never!

The bell of the mills rang for midnight. Sunday morning had dawned. Whatever hidden message lay in the tolling bells floated past these men unknown. Yet it was there. Veiled in the solemn music ushering the risen Saviour was a key-note to solve the darkest secrets of a world gone wrong,—even this social riddle which the brain of the grimy puddler grappled with madly to-night.

The men began to withdraw the metal from the caldrons. The mills were deserted on Sundays, except by the hands who fed the fires, and those who had no lodgings and slept usually on the ash-heaps. The three strangers sat still during the next hour, watching the men cover the furnaces, laughing now and then at some jest of Kirby's.

"Do you know," said Mitchell, "I like this view of the works better than when the glare was fiercest? These heavy shadows and the amphitheatre of smothered fires are ghostly, unreal.

One could fancy these red smouldering lights to be the half-shut eyes of wild beasts, and the spectral figures their victims in the den."

Kirby laughed. "You are fanciful. Come, let us get out of the den. The spectral figures, as you call them, are a little too real for me to fancy a close proximity in the darkness,—unarmed, too."

The others rose, buttoning their overcoats, and lighting cigars.

"Raining still," said Doctor May, "and hard. Where did we leave the coach, Mitchell?"

"At the other side of the works.—Kirby, what 's that?"

Mitchell started back, half-frightened, as, suddenly turning a corner, the white figure of a woman faced him in the darkness,—a woman, white, of giant proportions, crouching on the ground, her arms flung out in some wild gesture of warning.

"Stop! Make that fire burn there!" cried Kirby, stopping short.

The flame burst out, flashing the gaunt figure into bold relief.

Mitchell drew a long breath.

"I thought it was alive," he said, going up curiously.

The others followed.

"Not marble, eh?" asked Kirby, touching it.

One of the lower overseers stopped.

"Korl, Sir."

"Who did it?"

"Can't say. Some of the hands; chipped it out in off-hours."

"Chipped to some purpose, I should say. What a flesh-tint the stuff has! Do you see, Mitchell?"

"I see."

He had stepped aside where the light fell boldest on the figure, looking at it in silence. There was not one line of beauty or grace in it: a nude woman's form, muscular, grown coarse with labor, the powerful limbs instinct with some one poignant longing. One idea: there it was in the tense, rigid muscles, the clutching hands, the wild, eager face, like that of a starving wolf's. Kirby and Dr. May walked around it, critical, curious. Mitchell stood aloof, silent. The figure touched him strangely.

"Not badly done," said Doctor May. "Where did the fellow learn that sweep of the muscles in the arm and hand? Look at them! They are groping,—do you see?—clutching: the peculiar action of a man dying of thirst."

"They have ample facilities for studying anatomy," sneered Kirby, glancing at the half-naked figures.

"Look," continued the Doctor, "at this bony wrist, and the strained sinews of the instep! A working-woman,—the very type of her class."

"God forbid!" muttered Mitchell.

"Why?" demanded May. "What does the fellow intend by the figure? I cannot catch the meaning."

"Ask him," said the other, dryly. "There he stands,"—pointing to Wolfe, who stood with a group of men, leaning on his ash-rake.

The Doctor beckoned him with the affable smile which kind-hearted men put on, when talking to these people.

"Mr. Mitchell has picked you out as the man who did this,—I'm sure I don't know why. But what did you mean by it?"

"She be hungry."

Wolfe's eyes answered Mitchell, not the Doctor.

"Oh-h! But what a mistake you have made, my fine fellow! You have given no sign of starvation to the body. It is strong,—terribly strong. It has the mad, half-despairing gesture of drowning."

Wolfe stammered, glanced appealingly at Mitchell, who saw the soul of the thing, he knew. But the cool, probing eyes were turned on himself now,—mocking, cruel, relentless.

"Not hungry for meat," the furnace-tender said at last.

"What then? Whiskey?" jeered Kirby, with a coarse laugh.

Wolfe was silent a moment, thinking.

"I dunno," he said, with a bewildered look. "It mebbe. Summat to make her live, I think,—like you. Whiskey ull do it, in a way."

The young man laughed again. Mitchell flashed a look of disgust somewhere,—not at Wolfe.

"May," he broke out impatiently, "are you blind? Look at that woman's face! It asks questions of God, and says, 'I have a right to know.' Good God, how hungry it is!"

They looked a moment; then May turned to the mill-owner:—

"Have you many such hands as this? What are you going to do with them? Keep them at puddling iron?"

Kirby shrugged his shoulders. Mitchell's look had irritated him.

"*Ce n'est pas mon affaire.* I have no fancy for nursing infant geniuses. I suppose there are some stray gleams of mind and soul among these wretches. The Lord will take care of his own; or else they can work out their own salvation. I have heard you call our American system a ladder which any man can scale. Do you doubt it? Or perhaps you want to banish all social ladders, and put us all on a flat table-land,—eh, May?"

The Doctor looked vexed, puzzled. Some terrible problem lay hid in this woman's face, and troubled these men. Kirby waited for an answer, and, receiving none, went on, warming with his subject.

"I tell you, there 's something wrong that no talk of '*Liberté*' or '*Egalité*' will do away. If I had the making of men, these men who do the lowest part of the world's work should be machines,—nothing more,—hands. It would be kindness. God help them! What are taste, reason, to creatures who must live such lives as that?" He pointed to Deborah, sleeping on the ash-heap. "So many nerves to sting them to pain. What if God had put your brain, with all its agony of touch, into your fingers, and bid you work and strike with that?"

"You think you could govern the world better?" laughed the Doctor.

"I do not think at all."

"That is true philosophy. Drift with the stream, because you cannot dive deep enough to find bottom, eh?"

"Exactly," rejoined Kirby. "I do not think. I wash my hands of all social problems,—slavery, caste, white or black. My duty to my operatives has a narrow limit,—the pay-hour on Saturday night. Outside of that, if they cut korl, or cut each other's throats, (the more popular amusement of the two,) I am not responsible."

The Doctor sighed,—a good honest sigh, from the depths of his stomach.

"God help us! Who is responsible?"

"Not I, I tell you," said Kirby, testily. "What has the man who pays them money to do with their souls' concerns, more than the grocer or butcher who takes it?"

"And yet," said Mitchell's cynical voice, "look at her! How hungry she is!"

Kirby tapped his boot with his cane. No one spoke. Only the dumb face of the rough image looking into their faces with the awful question, "What shall we do to be saved?" Only Wolfe's face, with its heavy weight of brain, its weak, uncertain mouth, its desperate eyes, out of which looked the soul of his class,—only Wolfe's face turned towards Kirby's. Mitchell laughed,—a cool, musical laugh.

"Money has spoken!" he said, seating himself lightly on a stone with the air of an amused spectator at a play. "Are you answered?"—turning to Wolfe his clear, magnetic face.

Bright and deep and cold as Arctic air, the soul of the man lay tranquil beneath. He looked at the furnace-tender as he had looked at a rare mosaic in the morning; only the man was the more amusing study of the two.

"Are you answered? Why, May, look at him! '*De profundis clamavi*.' Or, to quote in English, 'Hungry and thirsty, his soul faints in him.' And so Money sends back its answer into the depths through you, Kirby! Very clear the answer, too!—I think I remember reading the same words somewhere:—washing your hands in Eau de Cologne, and saying, 'I am innocent of the blood of this man. See ye to it!'"

Kirby flushed angrily.

"You quote Scripture freely."

"Do I not quote correctly? I think I remember another line, which may amend my meaning: 'Inasmuch as ye did it unto one of the least of these, ye did it unto me.' Deist? Bless you, man, I was raised on the milk of the Word. Now, Doctor, the pocket of the world having uttered its voice, what has the heart to say? You are a philanthropist, in a small way,—*n'est ce pas*? Here, boy, this gentleman can show you how to cut korl better,—or your destiny. Go on, May!"

"I think a mocking devil possesses you to-night," rejoined the Doctor, seriously.

He went to Wolfe and put his hand kindly on his arm. Something of a vague idea possessed the Doctor's brain that much good was to be done here by a friendly word or two: a latent genius to be warmed into life by a waited-for sunbeam. Here it was: he had brought it. So he went on complacently:—

"Do you know, boy, you have it in you to be a great sculptor, a great man?—do you understand?" (talking down to the capacity of his hearer: it is a way people have with children, and men like Wolfe,)—"to live a better, stronger life than I, or Mr. Kirby here? A man may make himself anything he chooses. God has given you stronger powers than many men,—me, for instance."

May stopped, heated, glowing with his own magnanimity. And it was magnanimous. The puddler had drunk in every word, looking through the Doctor's flurry, and generous heat, and self-approval, into his will, with those slow, absorbing eyes of his.

"Make yourself what you will. It is your right."

"I know," quietly. "Will you help me?"

Mitchell laughed again. The Doctor turned now, in a passion,—

"You know, Mitchell, I have not the means. You know, if I had, it is in my heart to take this boy and educate him for—"

"The glory of God, and the glory of John May."

May did not speak for a moment; then, controlled, he said,—

"Why should one be raised, when myriads are left?—I have not the money, boy," to Wolfe, shortly.

"Money?" He said it over slowly, as one repeats the guessed answer to a riddle, doubtfully. "That is it? Money?"

"Yes, money,—that is it," said Mitchell, rising, and drawing his furred coat about him. "You've found the cure for all the world's diseases.—Come, May, find your good-humor, and come home. This damp wind chills my very bones. Come and preach your Saint-Simonian doctrines to-morrow to Kirby's hands. Let them have a clear idea of the rights of the soul, and I 'll venture next week they 'll strike for higher wages. That will be the end of it."

"Will you send the coach-driver to this side of the mills?" asked Kirby, turning to Wolfe.

He spoke kindly: it was his habit to do so. Deborah, seeing the puddler go, crept after him. The three men waited outside. Doctor May walked up and down, chafed. Suddenly he stopped.

"Go back, Mitchell! You say the pocket and the heart of the world speak without meaning to these people. What has its head to say? Taste, culture, refinement? Go!"

Mitchell was leaning against a brick wall. He turned his head indolently, and looked into the mills. There hung about the place a thick, unclean odor. The slightest motion of his hand marked that he perceived it, and his insufferable disgust. That was all. May said nothing, only quickened his angry tramp.

"Besides," added Mitchell, giving a corollary to his answer, "it would be of no use. I am not one of them."

"You do not mean"—said May, facing him.

"Yes, I mean just that. Reform is born of need, not pity. No vital movement of the people's has worked down, for good or evil; fermented, instead, carried up the heaving, cloggy mass. Think back through history, and you will know it. What will this lowest deep—thieves, Magdalens, negroes—do with the light filtered through ponderous Church creeds, Baconian theories, Goethe schemes? Some day, out of their bitter need will be thrown up their own light-bringer,—their Jean Paul, their Cromwell, their Messiah."

"Bah!" was the Doctor's inward criticism. However, in practice, he adopted the theory; for, when, night and morning, afterwards, he prayed that power might be given these degraded souls to rise, he glowed at heart, recognizing an accomplished duty.

Wolfe and the woman had stood in the shadow of the works as the coach drove off. The Doctor had held out his hand in a frank, generous way, telling him to "take care of himself, and to remember it was his right to rise." Mitchell had simply touched his hat, as to an equal, with a quiet look of thorough recognition. Kirby had thrown Deborah some money, which she found, and clutched eagerly enough. They were gone now, all of them. The man sat down on the cinder-road, looking up into the murky sky.

"'T be late, Hugh. Wunnot hur come?"

He shook his head doggedly, and the woman crouched out of his sight against the wall. Do you remember rare moments when a sudden light flashed over yourself, your world, God? when you stood on a mountain-peak, seeing your life as it might have been, as it is? one quick instant, when custom lost its force and every-day usage? when your friend, wife, brother, stood in a new light? your soul was bared, and the grave,—a foretaste of the nakedness of the Judgment-Day? So it came before him, his life, that night. The slow tides of pain he had borne gathered themselves up and surged against his soul. His squalid daily life, the brutal coarseness eating into his brain, as the ashes into his skin: before, these things had been a dull aching into his consciousness; to-night, they were reality. He gripped the filthy red shirt that clung, stiff with soot, about him, and tore it savagely from his arm. The flesh beneath was muddy with grease and ashes,—and the heart beneath that! And the soul? God knows.

Then flashed before his vivid poetic sense the man who had left him,—the pure face, the delicate, sinewy limbs, in harmony with all he knew of beauty or truth. In his cloudy fancy he had pictured a Something like this. He had found it in this Mitchell, even when he idly scoffed at his pain: a Man all-knowing, all-seeing, crowned by Nature, reigning,—the keen glance of his eye falling like a sceptre on other men. And yet his instinct taught him that he too— He! He looked at himself with sudden loathing, sick, wrung his hands with a cry, and then was silent. With all the phantoms of his heated, ignorant fancy, Wolfe had not been vague in his ambitions. They were practical, slowly built up before him out of his knowledge of what he could do. Through years he had day by day made this hope a real thing to himself,—a clear, projected figure of himself, as he might become.

Able to speak, to know what was best, to raise these men and women working at his side up with him: sometimes he forgot this defined hope in the frantic anguish to escape,—only to escape,—out of the wet, the pain, the ashes, somewhere, anywhere,—only for one moment of free air on a hillside, to lie down and let his sick soul throb itself out in the sunshine. But to-night he panted for life. The savage strength of his nature was roused; his cry was fierce to God for justice.

"Look at me!" he said to Deborah, with a low, bitter laugh, striking his puny chest savagely. "What am I worth, Deb? Is it my fault that I am no better? My fault? My fault?"

He stopped, stung with a sudden remorse, seeing her hunchback shape writhing with sobs. For Deborah was crying thankless tears, according to the fashion of women.

"God forgi' me, woman! Things go harder wi' you nor me. It 's a worse share."

He got up and helped her to rise; and they went doggedly down the muddy street, side by side.

"It 's all wrong," he muttered, slowly,—"all wrong! I dunnot understan'. But it 'll end some day."

"Come home, Hugh!" she said, coaxingly; for he had stopped, looking around bewildered.

"Home,—and back to the mill!" He went on saying this over to himself, as if he would mutter down every pain in this dull despair.

She followed him through the fog, her blue lips chattering with cold. They reached the cellar at last. Old Wolfe had been drinking since she went out, and had crept nearer the door. The girl Janey slept heavily in the corner. He went up to her, touching softly the worn white arm with his fingers. Some bitterer thought stung him, as he stood there. He wiped the drops from his forehead, and went into the room beyond, livid, trembling. A hope, trifling, perhaps, but very dear, had died just then out of the poor puddler's life, as he looked at the sleeping, innocent girl,—some plan for the future, in which she had borne a part. He gave it up that moment, then and forever. Only a trifle, perhaps, to us: his face grew a shade paler,—that was all. But, somehow, the man's soul, as God and the angels looked down on it, never was the same afterwards.

Deborah followed him into the inner room. She carried a candle, which she placed on the floor, closing the door after her. She had seen the look on his face, as he turned away; her own grew deadly. Yet, as she came up to him, her eyes glowed. He was seated on an old chest, quiet, holding his face in his hands.

"Hugh!" she said, softly.

He did not speak.

"Hugh, did hur hear what the man said,—him with the clear voice? Did hur hear? Money, money,—that it wud do all?"

He pushed her away,—gently, but he was worn out; her rasping tone fretted him.

"Hugh!"

The candle flared a pale yellow light over the cobwebbed brick walls, and the woman standing there. He looked at her. She was young, in deadly earnest; her faded eyes, and wet, ragged figure caught from their frantic eagerness a power akin to beauty.

"Hugh, it is true! Money ull do it! Oh, Hugh, boy, listen till me! He said it true! It is money!"

"I know. Go back! I do not want you here."

"Hugh, it is t' last time. I 'll never worrit hur again."

There were tears in her voice now, but she choked them back.

"Hear till me only to-night! If one of t' witch people wud come, them we heard of t' home, and gif hur all hur wants, what then? Say, Hugh!"

"What do you mean?"

"I mean money."

Her whisper shrilled through his brain.

"If one of t' witch dwarfs wud come from t' lane moors to-night, and gif hur money, to go out,—*out*, I say,—out, lad, where t' sun shines, and t' heath grows, and t' ladies walk in silken gownds, and God stays all t' time,—where t' man lives that talked to us to-night,—Hugh knows,—Hugh could walk there like a king!"

He thought the woman mad, tried to check her, but she went on, fierce in her eager haste.

"If *I* were t' witch dwarf, if I had t' money, wud hur thank me? Wud hur take me out o' this place wid hur and Janey? I wud not come into the gran' house hur wud build, to vex hur wid t' hunch,—only at night, when t' shadows were dark, stand far off to see hur."

"Poor Deb! poor Deb!" he said, soothingly.

"It is here," she said, suddenly jerking into his hand a small roll. "I took it! I did it! I shall be hanged! I shall be burnt in hell, if anybody knows I took it! Me, me! not hur! Out of his pocket, as he leaned against t' bricks. Hur knows?"

She thrust it into his hand, and then, her errand done, began to gather chips together to make a fire, choking down hysteric sobs.

"Has it come to this?"

That was all he said. The Welsh Wolfe blood was honest. The roll was a small green pocket-book containing one or two gold pieces, and a check for an incredible amount, as it seemed to the poor puddler. He laid it down, hiding his face again in his hands.

"Hugh, don't be angry wud me! It 's only poor Deb,—hur knows?"

He took the long skinny fingers kindly in his.

"Angry? God help me, no! Let me sleep. I am tired."

He threw himself heavily down on the wooden bench, stunned with pain and weariness. She brought some old rags to cover him.

It was late on Sunday evening before he awoke. I tell God's truth, when I say he had then no thought of keeping this money. Deborah had hid it in his pocket. He found it there. She watched him eagerly, as he took it out.

"I must gif it to him," he said, reading her face.

"Hur knows," she said with a bitter sigh of disappointment. "But it is hur right to keep it."

His right! The word struck him. Doctor May had used the same. He washed himself, and went out to find this man Mitchell. His right! Why did this chance word cling to him so obstinately? Do you hear the fierce devils whisper in his ear, as he went slowly down the darkening street?

The evening came on, slow and calm. He seated himself at the end of an alley leading into one of the larger streets. His brain was clear to-night, keen, intent, mastering. It would not start back, cowardly, from any hellish temptation, but meet it face to face. Therefore the great temptation of his life came to him veiled by no sophistry, but bold, defiant, owning its own vile name, trusting to one bold blow for victory.

He did not deceive himself. Theft! That was it. At first the word sickened him; then he grappled with it. Sitting there on a broken cart-wheel, the fading day, the noisy groups, the church-bells' tolling passed before him like a panorama, while the sharp struggle went on within. This money! He took it out, and looked at it. If he gave it back, what then? He was going to be cool about it.

People going by to church saw only a sickly mill-boy watching them quietly at the alley's mouth. They did not know that he was mad, or they would not have gone by so quietly: mad with hunger; stretching out his hands to the world, that had given so much to them, for leave to live the life God meant him to live. His soul within him was smothering to death; he wanted so much, thought so much, and *knew*—nothing. There was nothing of which he was certain, except the mill and things there. Of God and heaven he had heard so little, that they were to him what fairy-land is to a child: something real, but not here; very far off. His brain, greedy, dwarfed, full of thwarted energy and unused powers, questioned these men and women going by, coldly, bitterly, that night. Was it not his right to live as they,—a pure life, a good, true-hearted life, full of beauty and kind words? He only wanted to know how to use the strength within him. His heart warmed, as he thought of it. He suffered himself to think of it longer. If he took the money?

Then he saw himself as he might be, strong, helpful, kindly. The night crept on, as this one image slowly evolved itself from the crowd of other thoughts and stood triumphant. He looked at it. As he might be! What wonder, if it blinded him to delirium,—the madness that underlies all revolution, all progress, and all fall?

You laugh at the shallow temptation? You see the error underlying its argument so clearly,—that to him a true life was one of full development rather than self-restraint? that he was deaf to the higher tone in a cry of voluntary suffering for truth's sake than in the fullest flow of spontaneous harmony? I do not plead his cause. I only want to show you the mote in my brother's eye: then you can see clearly to take it out.

The money,—there it lay on his knee, a little blotted slip of paper, nothing in itself; used to raise him out of the pit; something straight from God's hand. A thief! Well, what was it to be a thief? He met the question at last face to face, wiping the clammy drops of sweat from his forehead. God made this money—the fresh air, too—for his children's use. He never made the difference between poor and rich. The Something who looked down on him that moment through the cool gray sky had a kindly face, he knew,—loved his children alike. Oh, he knew that!

There were times when the soft floods of color in the crimson and purple flames, or the clear depth of amber in the water below the bridge, had somehow given him a glimpse of another world than this,—of an infinite depth of beauty and of quiet somewhere,—somewhere,—a depth of quiet and rest and love. Looking up now, it became strangely real. The sun had sunk quite below the hills, but his last rays struck upward, touching the zenith. The fog had risen, and the town and river were steeped in its thick, gray damp; but overhead, the sun-touched smoke-clouds opened like a cleft ocean,—shifting, rolling seas of crimson mist, waves of billowy silver veined with blood-scarlet, inner depths unfathomable of glancing light. Wolfe's artist-eye grew drunk with color. The gates of that other world! Fading, flashing before him now! What, in that world of Beauty,

Content, and Right, were the petty laws, the mine and thine, of mill-owners and mill-hands?

A consciousness of power stirred within him. He stood up. A man,—he thought, stretching out his hands,—free to work, to live, to love! Free! His right! He folded the scrap of paper in his hand. As his nervous fingers took it in, limp and blotted, so his soul took in the mean temptation, lapped it in fancied rights, in dreams of improved existences, drifting and endless as the cloud-seas of color. Clutching it, as if the tightness of his hold would strengthen his sense of possession, he went aimlessly down the street. It was his watch at the mill. He need not go, need never go again, thank God!—shaking off the thought with unspeakable loathing.

Shall I go over the history of the hours of that night? how the man wandered from one to another of his old haunts, with a half-consciousness of bidding them farewell,—lanes and alleys and back-yards where the mill-hands lodged,—noting, with a new eagerness, the filth and drunkenness, the pig-pens, the ash-heaps covered with potato-skins, the bloated, pimpled women at the doors,—with a new disgust, a new sense of sudden triumph, and, under all, a new, vague dread, unknown before, smothered down, kept under, but still there? It left him but once during the night, when, for the second time in his life, he entered a church. It was a sombre Gothic pile, where the stained light lost itself in far-retreating arches; built to meet the requirements and sympathies of a far other class than Wolfe's. Yet it touched, moved him uncontrollably. The distances, the shadows, the still, marble figures, the mass of silent, kneeling worshippers, the mysterious music, thrilled, lifted his soul with a wonderful pain. Wolfe forgot himself, forgot the new life he was going to live, the mean terror gnawing underneath. The voice of the speaker strengthened the charm; it was clear, feeling, full, strong. An old man, who had lived much, suffered much; whose brain was keenly alive, dominant; whose heart was summer-warm with charity. He taught it to-night. He held up Humanity in its grand total; showed the great world-cancer to his people. Who could show it better? He was a Christian reformer; he had studied the age thoroughly; his outlook at man had been free, world-wide, over all time. His faith stood sublime upon the Rock of Ages; his fiery zeal guided vast schemes by which the Gospel was to be preached to all nations. How did he preach it to-night? In burning, light-laden words he painted Jesus, the incarnate Life, Love, the universal Man: words that became reality in the lives of these people,—that lived again in beautiful words and actions, trifling, but heroic. Sin, as he defined it, was a real foe to them; their trials, temptations, were his. His words passed far over the furnace-tender's grasp, toned to suit another class of culture; they sounded in his ears a very pleasant song in an unknown tongue. He meant to cure this world-cancer with a steady eye that had never glared with hunger, and a hand that neither poverty nor strychnine-whiskey had taught to shake. In this morbid, distorted heart of the Welsh puddler he had failed.

Eighteen centuries ago, the Master of this man tried reform in the streets of a city as crowded and vile as this, and did not fail. His disciple, showing Him to-night to cultured hearers, showing the clearness of the God-power acting through Him, shrank back from one coarse fact; that in birth and habit the man Christ was thrown up from the lowest of the people: his flesh, their flesh; their blood, his blood; tempted like them, to brutalize day by day; to lie, to steal: the actual slime and want of their hourly life, and the wine-press he trod alone.

Yet, is there no meaning in this perpetually covered truth? If the son of the carpenter had stood in the church that night, as he stood with the fishermen and harlots by the sea of Galilee, before His Father and their Father, despised and rejected of men, without a place to lay His head, wounded for their iniquities, bruised for their transgressions, would not that hungry mill-boy at least, in the back seat, have "known the man"? That Jesus did not stand there.

Wolfe rose at last, and turned from the church down the street. He looked up; the night had come on foggy, damp; the golden mists had vanished, and the sky lay dull and ash-colored. He wandered again aimlessly down the street, idly wondering what had become of the cloud-sea of crimson and scarlet. The trial-day of this man's life was over, and he had lost the victory. What followed was mere drifting circumstance,—a quicker walking over the path,—that was all. Do you want to hear the end of it? You wish me to make a tragic story out of it? Why, in the police-reports of the morning paper you can find a dozen such tragedies; hints of shipwrecks unlike any that ever befell on the high seas; hints that here a power was lost to heaven,—that there a soul went down where no tide can ebb or flow. Commonplace enough the hints are,—jocose sometimes, done up in rhyme.

Doctor May, a month after the night I have told you of, was reading to his wife at breakfast from this fourth column of the morning-paper: an unusual thing,—these police-reports not being, in general, choice reading for ladies; but it was only one item he read.

"Oh, my dear! You remember that man I told you of, that we saw at Kirby's mill?—that was arrested for robbing Mitchell? Here he is; just listen:—'Circuit Court. Judge Day. Hugh Wolfe, operative in Kirby & John's Loudon Mills. Charge, grand larceny. Sentence, nineteen years hard labor in penitentiary.'—Scoundrel! Serves him right! After all our kindness that night! Picking Mitchell's pocket at the very time!"

His wife said something about the ingratitude of that kind of people, and then they began to talk of something else.

Nineteen years! How easy that was to read! What a simple word for Judge Day to utter! Nineteen years! Half a lifetime!

Hugh Wolfe sat on the window-ledge of his cell, looking out. His ankles were ironed. Not usual in such cases; but he had made two desperate efforts to escape. "Well," as Haley, the jailer, said, "small blame to him! Nineteen years' imprisonment was not a pleasant thing to look forward to." Haley was very good-natured about it, though Wolfe had fought him savagely.

"When he was first caught," the jailer said afterwards, in telling the story, "before the trial, the fellow was cut down at once,—laid there on that pallet like a dead man, with his hands over his eyes. Never saw a man so cut down in my life. Time of the trial, too, came the queerest dodge of any customer I ever had. Would choose no lawyer. Judge gave him one, of course. Gibson it was. He tried to prove the fellow crazy; but it would n't go. Thing was plain as daylight: check found on him. 'T was a hard sentence,—all the law allows; but it was for 'xample's sake. These mill-hands are gettin' onbearable. When the sentence was read, he just looked up, and said the money was his by rights, and that all the world had gone wrong. That night, after the trial, a gentleman came to see him here, name of

Mitchell,—him as he stole from. Talked to him for an hour. Thought he came for curiosity, like. After he was gone, thought Wolfe was remarkable quiet, and went into his cell. Found him very low; bed all bloody. Doctor said he had been bleeding at the lungs. He was as weak as a cat; yet, if ye 'll b'lieve me, he tried to get a-past me and get out. I just carried him like a baby, and threw him on the pallet. Three days after, he tried it again: that time reached the wall. Lord help you! he fought like a tiger,—giv' some terrible blows. Fightin' for life, you see; for he can't live long, shut up in the stone crib down yonder. Got a death-cough now. 'T took two of us to bring him down that day; so I just put the irons on his feet. There he sits, in there. Goin' to-morrow, with a batch more of 'em. That woman, hunchback, tried with him,—you remember?—she 's only got three years. 'Complice. But *she 's* a woman, you know. He 's been quiet ever since I put on irons: giv' up, I suppose. Looks white, sick-lookin'. It acts different on 'em, bein' sentenced. Most of 'em gets reckless, devilish-like. Some prays awful, and sings them vile songs of the mills, all in a breath. That woman, now, she 's desper't'. Been beggin' to see Hugh, as she calls him, for three days. I 'm a-goin' to let her in. She don't go with him. Here she is in this next cell. I 'm a-goin' now to let her in."

He let her in. Wolfe did not see her. She crept into a corner of the cell, and stood watching him. He was scratching the iron bars of the window with a piece of tin which he had picked up, with an idle, uncertain, vacant stare, just as a child or idiot would do.

"Tryin' to get out, old boy?" laughed Haley. "Them irons will need a crowbar beside your tin, before you can open 'em."

Wolfe laughed, too, in a senseless way.

"I think I 'll get out," he said.

"I believe his brain 's touched," said Haley, when he came out.

The puddler scraped away with the tin for half an hour. Still Deborah did not speak. At last she ventured nearer, and touched his arm.

"Blood?" she said, looking at some spots on his coat with a shudder.

He looked up at her. "Why, Deb!" he said, smiling,—such a bright, boyish smile, that it went to poor Deborah's heart directly, and she sobbed and cried out loud.

"Oh, Hugh, lad! Hugh! dunnot look at me, when it wur my fault! To think I brought hur to it! And I loved hur so! Oh, lad, I dud!"

The confession, even in this wretch, came with the woman's blush through the sharp cry.

He did not seem to hear her,—scraping away diligently at the bars with the bit of tin.

Was he going mad? She peered closely into his face. Something she saw there made her draw suddenly back,—something which Haley had not seen, that lay beneath the pinched, vacant look it had caught since the trial, or the curious gray shadow that rested on it. That gray shadow,—yes, she knew what that meant. She had often seen it creeping over women's faces for months, who died at last of slow hunger or consumption. That meant death, distant, lingering: but this— Whatever it was the woman saw, or thought she saw, used as she was to crime and misery, seemed to make her sick with a new horror. Forgetting her fear of him, she caught his shoulders, and looked keenly, steadily, into his eyes.

"Hugh!" she cried, in a desperate whisper,—"oh, boy, not that! for God's sake, not *that*!"

The vacant laugh went off his face, and he answered her in a muttered word or two that drove her away. Yet the words were kindly enough. Sitting there on his pallet, she cried silently a hopeless sort of tears, but did not speak again. The man looked up furtively at her now and then. Whatever his own trouble was, her distress vexed him with a momentary sting.

It was market-day. The narrow window of the jail looked down directly on the carts and wagons drawn up in a long line, where they had unloaded. He could see, too, and hear distinctly the clink of money as it changed hands, the busy crowd of whites and blacks shoving, pushing one another, and the chaffering and swearing at the stalls. Somehow, the sound, more than anything else had done, wakened him up,—made the whole real to him. He was done with the world and the business of it. He let the tin fall, and looked out, pressing his face close to the rusty bars. How they crowded and pushed! And he,—he should never walk that pavement again! There came Neff Sanders, one of the feeders at the mill, with a basket on his arm. Sure enough, Neff was married the other week. He whistled, hoping he would look up; but he did not. He wondered if Neff remembered he was there,—if any of the boys thought of him up there, and thought that he never was to go down that old cinder-road again. Never again! He had not quite understood it before; but now he did. Not for days or years, but never!—that was it.

How clear the light fell on that stall in front of the market! and how like a picture it was, the dark-green heaps of corn, and the crimson beets, and golden melons! There was another with game: how the light flickered on that pheasant's breast, with the purplish blood dripping over the brown feathers! He could see the red shining of the drops, it was so near. In one minute he could be down there. It was just a step. So easy, as it seemed, so natural to go! Yet it could never be—not in all the thousands of years to come—that he should put his foot on that street again! He thought of himself with a sorrowful pity, as of some one else. There was a dog down in the market, walking after his master with such a stately, grave look!—only a dog, yet he could go backwards and forwards just as he pleased: he had good luck! Why, the very vilest cur, yelping there in the gutter, had not lived his life, had been free to act out whatever thought God had put into his brain; while he— No, he would not think of that! He tried to put the thought away, and to listen to a dispute between a countryman and a woman about some meat; but it would come back. He, what had he done to bear this?

Then came the sudden picture of what might have been, and now. He knew what it was to be in the penitentiary,—how it went with men there. He knew how in these long years he should slowly die, but not until soul and body had become corrupt and rotten,—how, when he came out, if he lived to come, even the lowest of the mill-hands would jeer him,—how his hands would be weak, and his brain senseless and stupid. He believed he was almost that now. He put his hand to his head, with a puzzled, weary look. It ached, his head, with thinking. He tried to quiet himself. It was only right, perhaps; he had done wrong. But was there right or wrong for such as he? What was right? And who had ever taught him? He thrust the whole matter away. A dark, cold quiet crept through his brain. It was all wrong; but let it be! It was nothing to him more than the others. Let it be!

The door grated, as Haley opened it.

"Come, my woman! Must lock up for t' night. Come, stir yerself!"

She went up and took Hugh's hand.

"Good-night, Deb," he said, carelessly.

She had not hoped he would say more; but the tired pain on her mouth just then was bitterer than death. She took his passive hand and kissed it.

"Hur 'll never see Deb again!" she ventured, her lips growing colder and more bloodless.

What did she say that for? Did he not know it? Yet he would not be impatient with poor old Deb. She had trouble of her own, as well as he.

"No, never again," he said, trying to be cheerful.

She stood just a moment, looking at him. Do you laugh at her, standing there, with her hunchback, her rags, her bleared, withered face, and the great despised love tugging at her heart?

"Come you!" called Haley, impatiently.

She did not move.

"Hugh!" she whispered.

It was to be her last word. What was it?

"Hugh, boy, not THAT!"

He did not answer. She wrung her hands, trying to be silent, looking in his face in an agony of entreaty. He smiled again, kindly.

"It is best, Deb. I cannot bear to be hurted any more."

"Hur knows," she said, humbly.

"Tell my father good-by; and—and kiss little Janey."

She nodded, saying nothing, looked in his face again, and went out of the door. As she went, she staggered.

"Drinkin' to-day?" broke out Haley, pushing her before him. "Where the Devil did you get it? Here, in with ye!" and he shoved her into her cell, next to Wolfe's, and shut the door.

Along the wall of her cell there was a crack low down by the floor, through which she could see the light from Wolfe's. She had discovered it days before. She hurried in now, and, kneeling down by it, listened, hoping to hear some sound. Nothing but the rasping of the tin on the bars. He was at his old amusement again. Something in the noise jarred on her ear, for she shivered as she heard it. Hugh rasped away at the bars. A dull old bit of tin, not fit to cut korl with.

He looked out of the window again. People were leaving the market now. A tall mulatto girl, following her mistress, her basket on her head, crossed the street just below, and looked up. She was laughing; but, when she caught sight of the haggard face peering out through the bars, suddenly grew grave, and hurried by. A free, firm step, a clear-cut olive face, with a scarlet turban tied on one side, dark, shining eyes, and on the head the basket poised, filled with fruit and flowers, under which the scarlet turban and bright eyes looked out half-shadowed. The picture caught his eye. It was good to see a face like that. He would try to-morrow, and cut one like it. *To-morrow!* He threw down the tin, trembling, and covered his face with his hands. When he looked up again, the daylight was gone.

Deborah, crouching near by on the other side of the wall, heard no noise. He sat on the side of the low pallet, thinking. Whatever was the mystery which the woman had seen on his face, it came out now slowly, in the dark there, and became fixed,—a something never seen on his face before. The evening was darkening fast. The market had been over for an hour; the rumbling of the carts over the pavement grew more infrequent: he listened to each, as it passed, because he thought it was to be for the last time. For the same reason, it was, I suppose, that he strained his eyes to catch a glimpse of each passer-by, wondering who they were, what kind of homes they were going to, if they had children,—listening eagerly to every chance word in the street, as if—(God be merciful to the man! what strange fancy was this?)—as if he never should hear human voices again.

It was quite dark at last. The street was a lonely one. The last passenger, he thought, was gone. No,—there was a quick step: Joe Hill, lighting the lamps. Joe was a good old chap; never passed a fellow without some joke or other. He remembered once seeing the place where he lived with his wife. "Granny Hill" the boys called her. Bedridden she was; but so kind as Joe was to her! kept the room so clean!—and the old woman, when he was there, was laughing at "some of t' lad's foolishness." The step was far down the street; but he could see him place the ladder, run up, and light the gas. A longing seized him to be spoken to once more.

"Joe!" he called out of the grating. "Good-by, Joe!"

The old man stopped a moment, listening uncertainly; then hurried on. The prisoner thrust his hand out of the window, and called again, louder; but Joe was too far down the street. It was a little thing; but it hurt him,—this disappointment.

"Good-by, Joe!" he called, sorrowfully enough.

"Be quiet!" said one of the jailers, passing the door, striking on it with his club.

Oh, that was the last, was it?

There was an inexpressible bitterness on his face, as he lay down on the bed, taking the bit of tin, which he had rasped to a tolerable degree of sharpness, in his hand,—to play with, it may be. He bared his arms, looking intently at their corded veins and sinews. Deborah, listening in the next cell, heard a slight clicking sound, often repeated. She shut her lips tightly, that she might not scream; the cold drops of sweat broke over her, in her dumb agony.

"Hur knows best," she muttered at last, fiercely clutching the boards where she lay.

If she could have seen Wolfe, there was nothing about him to frighten her. He lay quite still, his arms outstretched, looking at the pearly stream of moonlight coming into the window. I think in that one hour that came then he lived back over all the years that had gone before. I think that all the low, vile life, all his wrongs, all his starved hopes, came then, and stung him with a farewell poison that made him sick unto death. He made neither moan nor cry, only turned his worn face now and then to the pure light, that seemed so far off, as one that said, "How long, O Lord? how long?"

The hour was over at last. The moon, passing over her nightly path, slowly came nearer, and threw the light across his bed on his feet. He watched it steadily, as it crept up, inch by inch, slowly. It seemed to him to carry with it a great silence. He had been so hot and tired there always in the mills! The years had been so fierce and cruel! There was coming now quiet and coolness and sleep. His tense limbs relaxed, and settled in a calm languor. The blood ran fainter and slow from his heart. He did not think now with a savage anger of what might be and was not; he was conscious only of deep stillness creeping over him. At first he saw a sea of faces: the mill-men,—women he had known, drunken and bloated,—Janey's timid and pitiful,—poor old Debs: then they floated together like a mist, and faded away, leaving only the clear, pearly moonlight.

Whether, as the pure light crept up the stretched-out figure, it brought with it calm and peace, who shall say? His dumb soul was alone with God in judgment. A Voice may have spoken for it from far-off Calvary, "Father, forgive them, for they know not what they do!" Who dare say? Fainter and fainter the heart rose and fell, slower and slower the moon floated from behind a cloud, until, when at last its full tide of white splendor swept over the cell, it seemed to wrap and fold into a deeper stillness the dead figure that never should move again. Silence deeper than the Night! Nothing that moved, save the black, nauseous stream of blood dripping slowly from the pallet to the floor!

There was outcry and crowd enough in the cell the next day. The coroner and his jury, the local editors, Kirby himself, and boys with their hands thrust knowingly into their pockets and heads on one side, jammed into the corners. Coming and going all day. Only one woman. She came late, and outstayed them all. A Quaker, or Friend, as they call themselves. I think this woman was known by that name in heaven. A homely body, coarsely dressed in gray and white. Deborah (for Haley had let her in) took notice of her. She watched them all—sitting on the end of the pallet, holding his head in her arms—with the ferocity of a watch-dog, if any of them touched the body. There was no meekness, no sorrow, in her face; the stuff out of which murderers are made, instead. All the time Haley and the woman were laying straight the limbs and cleaning the cell, Deborah sat still, keenly watching the Quaker's face. Of all the crowd there that day, this woman alone had not spoken to her,—only once or twice had put some cordial to her lips. After they all were gone, the woman, in the same still, gentle way, brought a vase of wood-leaves and berries, and placed it by the pallet, then opened the narrow window. The fresh air blew in, and swept the woody fragrance over the dead face. Deborah looked up with a quick wonder.

"Did hur know my boy wud like it? Did hur know Hugh?"

"I know Hugh now."

The white fingers passed in a slow, pitiful way over the dead, worn face. There was a heavy shadow in the quiet eyes.

"Did hur know where they 'll bury Hugh?" said Deborah in a shrill tone, catching her arm.

This had been the question hanging on her lips all day.

"In t' town-yard? Under t' mud and ash? T' lad 'll smother, woman! He wur born on t' lane moor, where t' air is frick and strong. Take hur out, for God's sake, take hur out where t' air blows!"

The Quaker hesitated, but only for a moment. She put her strong arm around Deborah and led her to the window.

"Thee sees the hills, friend, over the river? Thee sees how the light lies warm there, and the winds of God blow all the day? I live there,—where the blue smoke is, by the trees. Look at me." She turned Deborah's face to her own, clear and earnest. "Thee will believe me? I will take Hugh and bury him there to-morrow."

Deborah did not doubt her. As the evening wore on, she leaned against the iron bars, looking at the hills that rose far off, through the thick sodden clouds, like a bright, unattainable calm. As she looked, a shadow of their solemn repose fell on her face: its fierce discontent faded into a pitiful, humble quiet. Slow, solemn tears gathered in her eyes: the poor weak eyes turned so hopelessly to the place where Hugh was to rest, the grave heights looking higher and brighter and more solemn than ever before. The Quaker watched her keenly. She came to her at last, and touched her arm.

"When thee comes back," she said, in a low, sorrowful tone, like one who speaks from a strong heart deeply moved with remorse or pity, "thee shall begin thy life again,—there on the hills. I came too late; but not for thee,—by God's help, it may be."

Not too late. Three years after, the Quaker began her work. I end my story here. At evening-time it was light. There is no need to tire you with the long years of sunshine, and fresh air, and slow, patient Christ-love, needed to make healthy and hopeful this impure body and soul. There is a homely pine house, on one of these hills, whose windows overlook broad, wooded slopes and clover-crimsoned meadows,—niched into the very place where the light is warmest, the air freest. It is the Friends' meeting-house. Once a week they sit there, in their grave, earnest way, waiting for the Spirit of Love to speak, opening their simple hearts to receive His words. There is a woman, old, deformed, who takes a humble place among them: waiting like them: in her gray dress, her worn face, pure and meek, turned now and then to the sky. A woman much loved by these silent, restful people; more silent than they, more humble, more loving. Waiting: with her eyes turned to hills higher and purer than these on which she lives,—dim and far off now, but to be reached some day. There may be in her heart some latent hope to meet there the love denied her here,—that she shall find him whom she lost, and that then she will not be all-unworthy. Who blames her? Something is lost in the passage of every soul from one eternity to the other,—something pure and beautiful, which might have been and was not: a hope, a talent, a love, over which the soul mourns, like Esau deprived of his birthright. What blame to the meek Quaker, if she took her lost hope to make the hills of heaven more fair?

Nothing remains to tell that the poor Welsh puddler once lived, but this figure of the mill-woman cut in korl. I have it here in a corner of my library. I keep it hid behind a curtain,—it is such a rough, ungainly thing. Yet there are about it touches, grand sweeps of outline, that show a master's hand. Sometimes,—to-night, for instance,—the curtain is accidentally drawn back, and I see a bare arm stretched out imploringly in the darkness, and an eager, wolfish face watching mine: a wan, woful face, through which the spirit of the dead korl-cutter looks out, with its thwarted life, its mighty hunger, its unfinished work. Its pale, vague lips seem to tremble with a terrible question. "Is this the End?"—they say,—"nothing beyond?—no more?" Why, you tell me you have seen that look in the eyes of dumb brutes,—horses dying under the lash. I know.

The deep of the night is passing while I write. The gas-light wakens from the shadows here and there the objects which lie scattered through the room: only faintly, though; for they belong to the open sunlight. As I glance at them, they each recall some task or pleasure of the coming day. A half-moulded child's head; Aphrodite; a bough of forest-leaves; music; work; homely fragments, in which lie the secrets of all eternal truth and beauty. Prophetic all! Only this dumb, woful face seems to belong to and end with the night. I turn to look at it. Has the power of its desperate need commanded the darkness away? While the room is yet steeped in heavy shadow, a cool, gray light suddenly touches its head like a blessing hand, and its groping arm points through the broken cloud to the far East, where, in the flickering, nebulous crimson, God has set the promise of the Dawn.

1861

# LOUISA MAY ALCOTT

(1832–1888)

## *Perilous Play*

"If some one does not propose a new and interesting amusement, I shall die of ennui!" said pretty Belle Daventry, in a tone of despair. "I have read all my books, used up all my Berlin wools, and it's too warm to go to town for more. No one can go sailing yet, as the tide is out; we are all nearly tired to death of cards, croquet, and gossip, so what shall we do to while away this endless afternoon? Doctor Meredith, I command you to invent and propose a new game in five minutes."

"To hear is to obey," replied the young man, who lay in the grass at her feet, as he submissively slapped his forehead, and fell a-thinking with all his might.

Holding up her finger to preserve silence, Belle pulled out her watch, and waited with an expectant smile. The rest of the young party, who were indolently scattered about under the elms, drew nearer, and brightened visibly, for Doctor Meredith's inventive powers were well known, and something refreshingly novel might be expected from him. One gentleman did not stir, but, then, he lay within ear-shot, and merely turned his fine eyes from the sea to the group before him. His glance rested a moment on Belle's piquant figure, for she looked very pretty with her bright hair blowing in the wind, one plump white arm extended to keep order, and one little foot, in a distracting slipper, just visible below the voluminous folds of her dress. Then the glance passed to another figure, sitting somewhat apart in a cloud of white muslin, for an airy burnoose floated from head and shoulders, showing only a singularly charming face. Pale, and yet brilliant, for the Southern eyes were magnificent, the clear olive cheeks contrasted well with darkest hair; lips like a pomegranate flower, and delicate, straight brows, as mobile as the lips. A cluster of crimson flowers, half falling from the loose black braids, and a golden bracelet of Arabian coins on the slender wrist, were the only ornaments she wore, and became her better than the fashionable frippery of her companions. A book lay on her lap, but her eyes, full of a passionate melancholy, were fixed on the sea, which glittered round an island green and flowery as a summer paradise. Rose St. Just was as beautiful as her Spanish mother, but had inherited the pride and reserve of her English father; and this pride was the thorn which repelled lovers from the human flower. Mark Done sighed as he looked, and, as if the sigh, low as it was, roused her from her reverie, Rose flashed a quick glance at him, took up her book, and went on reading the legend of "The Lotus Eaters."

"Time is up now, doctor," cried Belle, pocketing her watch with a flourish.

"Ready to report," answered Meredith, sitting up, and producing a little box of tortoise-shell and gold.

"How mysterious! What is it? Let me see, first!" And Belle removed the cover, looking like an inquisitive child. "Only bonbons; how stupid! That won't do, sir. We don't want to be fed with sugar-plums. We demand to be amused."

"Eat six of these despised bonbons, and you *will* be amused in a new, delicious and wonderful manner," said the young doctor, laying half a dozen on a green leaf, and offering them to her.

"Why, what are they?" she asked, looking at them askance.

"Hasheesh; did you never hear of it?"

"Oh, yes; it's that Indian stuff which brings one fantastic visions, isn't it? I've always wanted to see and taste it, and now I will," cried Belle, nibbling at one of the bean-shaped comfits with its green heart.

"I advise you not to try it. People do all sorts of queer things when they take it. I wouldn't for the world," said a prudent young lady, warningly, as all examined the box and its contents.

"Six can do no harm, I give you my word. I take twenty before I can enjoy myself, and some people even more. I've tried many experiments, both on the sick and the well, and nothing ever happened amiss, though the demonstrations were immensely interesting," said Meredith, eating his sugar-plums with a tranquil air, which was very convincing to others.

"How shall I feel?" asked Belle, beginning on her second comfit.

"A heavenly dreaminess comes over one, in which they move as if on air. Everything is calm and lovely to them: no pain, no care, no fear of anything, and while it lasts one feels like an angel half-asleep."

"But if one takes too much, how then?" said a deep voice, behind the doctor.

"Hum! Well, that's not so pleasant, unless one likes phantoms, frenzies, and a touch of nightmare, which seems to last a thousand years. Ever try it, Done?" replied Meredith, turning toward the speaker, who was now leaning on his arm and looking interested.

"Never. I'm not a good subject for experiments. Too nervous a temperament to play pranks with."

"I should say ten would be about your number. Less than that seldom affects men. Ladies go off sooner, and don't need so many. Miss St. Just, may I offer you a taste of Elysium? I owe my success to you," said the doctor, approaching her deferentially.

"To me! And how?" she asked, lifting her large eyes with a slight smile.

"I was in the depths of despair when my eye caught the title of your book, and I was saved. For I remembered that I had hasheesh in my pocket."

"Are you a lotus-eater?" she said, permitting him to lay the six charmed bonbons on the page.

"My faith, no! I use it for my patients. It is very efficacious in nervous disorders, and is getting to be quite a pet remedy with us."

"I do not want to forget the past, but to read the future. Will hasheesh help me to do that?" asked Rose, with an eager look, which made the young man flush, wondering if he bore any part in her hopes of that vailed future.

"Alas, no. I wish it could, for I, too, long to know my fate," he answered, very low, as he looked into the lovely face before him.

The soft glance changed to one of cool indifference, and Rose gently brushed the hasheesh off her book, saying, with a little gesture of dismissal:

"Then I have no desire to taste Elysium."

The white morsels dropped into the grass at her feet; but Doctor Meredith let them lie, and turning sharply, went back to sun himself in Belle's smiles.

"I've eaten all mine, and so has Evelyn. Mr. Norton will see goblins, I know, for he has taken quantities. I'm glad of it, for he does not believe in it, and I want to have him convinced by making a spectacle of himself for our amusement," said Belle, in great spirits at the new plan.

"When does the trance come on?" asked Evelyn, a shy girl, already rather alarmed at what she had done.

"About three hours after you take your dose, though the time varies with different people. Your pulse will rise, heart beat quickly, eyes darken and dilate, and an uplifted sensation will pervade you generally. Then these symptoms change, and the bliss begins. I've seen people sit or lie in one position for hours, rapt in a delicious dream, and wake from it as tranquil as if they had not a nerve in their bodies."

"How charming! I'll take some every time I'm worried. Let me see. It's now four, so our trances will come about seven, and we will devote the evening to manifestations," said Belle.

"Come, Done, try it. We are all going in for the fun. Here's your dose," and Meredith tossed him a dozen bonbons, twisted up in a bit of paper.

"No, thank you; I know myself too well to risk it. If you are all going to turn hasheesh-eaters, you'll need some one to take care of you, so I'll keep sober," tossing the little parcel back.

It fell short, and the doctor, too lazy to pick it up, let it lie, merely saying, with a laugh:

"Well, I advise any bashful man to take hasheesh when he wants to offer his heart to any fair lady, for it will give him the courage of a hero, the eloquence of a poet, and the ardor of an Italian. Remember that, gentlemen, and come to me when the crisis approaches."

"Does it conquer the pride, rouse the pity, and soften the hard hearts of the fair sex?" asked Done.

"I dare say now is your time to settle the fact, for here are two ladies who have imbibed, and in three hours will be in such a seraphic state of mind that 'No' will be an impossibility to them."

"Oh, mercy on us; what *have* we done? If that's the case, I shall shut myself up till my foolish fit is over. Rose, you haven't taken any; I beg you to mount guard over me, and see that I don't disgrace myself by any nonsense. Promise me you will," cried Belle, in half real, half feigned alarm at the consequences of her prank.

"I promise," said Rose, and floated down the green path as noiselessly as a white cloud, with a curious smile on her lips.

"Don't tell any of the rest what we have done, but after tea let us go into the grove and compare notes," said Norton, as Done strolled away to the beach, and the voices of approaching friends broke the summer quiet.

At tea, the initiated glanced covertly at one another, and saw, or fancied they saw, the effects of the hasheesh, in a certain suppressed excitement of manner, and unusually brilliant eyes. Belle laughed often, a silvery ringing laugh, pleasant to hear; but when complimented on her good spirits, she looked distressed, and said she could not help her merriment; Meredith was quite calm, but rather dreamy; Evelyn was pale, and her next neighbor heard her heart beat; Norton talked incessantly, but as he talked uncommonly well, no one suspected anything. Done and Miss St. Just watched the others with interest, and were very quiet, especially Rose, who scarcely spoke, but smiled her sweetest, and looked very lovely.

The moon rose early, and the experimenters slipped away to the grove, leaving the outsiders on the lawn as usual. Some bold spirit asked Rose to sing, and she at once complied, pouring out Spanish airs in a voice that melted the hearts of her audience, so full of fiery sweetness or tragic pathos was it. Done seemed quite carried away, and lay with his face in the grass, to hide the tears that would come; till, afraid of openly disgracing himself, he started up and hurried down to the little wharf, where he sat alone, listening to the music with a countenance which plainly revealed to the stars the passion which possessed him. The sound of loud laughter from the grove, followed by entire silence, caused him to wonder what demonstrations were taking place, and half resolve to go and see. But that enchanting voice held him captive, even when a boat put off mysteriously from a point near by, and sailed away like a phantom through the twilight.

Half an hour afterward, a white figure came down the path, and Rose's voice broke in on his midsummer night's dream. The moon shone clearly now, and showed him the anxiety in her face as she said hurriedly:

"Where is Belle?"

"Gone sailing, I believe."

"How could you let her go? She was not fit to take care of herself?"

"I forgot that."

"So did I; but I promised to watch over her, and I must. Which way did they go?" demanded Rose, wrapping the white mantle about her, and running her eye over the little boats moored below.

"You will follow her?"

"Yes."

"I'll be your guide, then. They went toward the lighthouse; it is too far to row; I am at your service. Oh, say yes," cried Done, leaping into his own skiff, and offering his hand persuasively.

She hesitated an instant and looked at him. He was always pale, and the moonlight seemed to increase this pallor, but his hat-brim hid his eyes, and his voice was very quiet. A loud peal of laughter floated over the water, and, as if the sound decided her, she gave him her hand and entered the boat. Done smiled triumphantly as he shook out the sail, which caught the freshening wind, and sent the boat dancing along a path of light.

How lovely it was! All the indescribable allurements of a perfect summer night surrounded them; balmy airs, enchanting moonlight, distant music, and, close at hand, the delicious atmosphere of love, which made itself felt in the eloquent silences that fell between them. Rose seemed to yield to the subtle charm, and leaned back on the cushioned seat, with her beautiful head uncovered, her face full of dreamy softness, and her hands lying loosely clasped before her. She seldom spoke, showed no further anxiety for Belle, and soon seemed to forget the object of her search, so absorbed was she in some delicious thought which wrapped her in its peace.

Done sat opposite, flushed now, restless, and excited, for his eyes glittered; the hand on the rudder shook, and his voice sounded intense and passionate, even in the utterance of the simplest words. He talked continually and with unusual brilliancy, for, though a man of many accomplishments, he was too indolent or too fastidious to exert himself, except among his peers. Rose seemed to look without seeing, to listen without hearing, and, though she smiled blissfully, the smiles were evidently not for him.

On they sailed, scarcely heeding the bank of black cloud piled up in the horizon, the rising wind, or the silence which proved their solitude. Rose moved once or twice, and lifted her hand as if to speak, but sank back mutely, and the hand fell again, as if it had not energy enough to enforce her wish. A cloud sweeping over the moon, a distant growl of thunder, and the slight gust that struck the sail, seemed to rouse her. Done was singing now like one inspired, his hat at his feet, hair in disorder, and a strangely rapturous expression in his eyes, which were fixed on her. She started, shivered, and seemed to recover herself with an effort.

"Where are they?" she asked, looking vainly for the island heights and the other boat.

"They have gone to the beach, I fancy, but we will follow." As Done leaned forward to speak, she saw his face, and shrank back with a sudden flush, for in it she read clearly what she had felt, yet doubted until now. He saw the tell-tale blush and gesture, and said impetuously: "You know it now; you cannot deceive me longer, or daunt me with your pride! Rose, I love you, and dare tell you so to-night!"

"Not now—not here—I will not listen. Turn back, and be silent, I entreat you, Mr. Done," she said, hurriedly.

He laughed a defiant laugh, and took her hand in his, which was burning and throbbing with the rapid heat of his pulse.

"No, I *will* have my answer here, and now, and never turn back till you give it; you have been a thorny Rose, and given me many wounds. I'll be paid for my heartache with sweet words, tender looks, and frank confessions of love, for, proud as you are, you do love me, and dare not deny it."

Something in his tone terrified her; she snatched her hand away, and drew beyond his reach, trying to speak calmly, and to meet coldly the ardent glances of the eyes which were strangely darkened and dilated with uncontrollable emotion.

"You forget yourself. I shall give no answer to an avowal made in such terms. Take me home instantly," she said, in a tone of command.

"Confess you love me, Rose."

"Never!"

"Ah! I'll have a kinder answer, or——" Done half rose and put out his hand to grasp and draw her to him, but the cry she uttered seemed to arrest him with a sort of shock. He dropped into his seat, passed his hand over his eyes, and shivered nervously, as he muttered in an altered tone: "I meant nothing; it's the moonlight; sit down, I'll control myself—upon my soul I will!"

"If you do not, I shall go overboard. Are you mad, sir?" cried Rose, trembling with indignation.

"Then, I shall follow you, for I *am* mad, Rose, with love—hasheesh!"

His voice sank to a whisper, but the last word thrilled along her nerves, as no sound of fear had ever done before. An instant she regarded him with a look which took in every sign of unnatural excitement, then she clasped her hands with an imploring gesture, saying, in a tone of despair:

"Why did I come? How will it end? Oh, Mark, take me home before it is too late!"

"Hush! Be calm; don't thwart me, or I may get wild again. My thoughts are not clear, but I understand you. There, take my knife, and if I forget myself, kill me. Don't go overboard; you are too beautiful to die, my Rose!"

He threw her the slender hunting-knife he wore, looked at her a moment with a far-off look, and trimmed the sail like one moving in a dream. Rose took the weapon, wrapped her cloak closely about her, and, crouching as far away as possible, kept her eye on him, with a face in which watchful terror contended with some secret trouble and bewilderment more powerful than her fear.

The boat moved round, and began to beat up against wind and tide; spray flew from her bow, the sail bent and strained in the gusts that struck it with perilous fitfulness. The moon was nearly hidden by scudding clouds, and one-half the sky was black with the gathering storm. Rose looked from threatening heavens to treacherous sea, and tried to be ready for any danger, but her calm had been sadly broken, and she could not recover it. Done sat motionless, uttering no word of encouragement, though the frequent flaws almost tore the rope from his hand, and the water often dashed over him.

"Are we in any danger?" asked Rose at last, unable to bear the silence, for he looked like a ghostly helmsman, seen by the fitful light, pale now, wild-eyed, and speechless.

"Yes, great danger."

"I thought you were a skillful boatman."

"I am when I am myself; now I am rapidly losing the control of my will, and the strange quiet is coming over me. If I had been alone I should have given up sooner, but for your sake I've kept on."

"Can't you work the boat?" asked Rose, terror-struck by the changed tone of his voice, the slow, uncertain movements of his hands.

"No. I see everything through a thick cloud; your voice sounds far away, and my one desire is to lay my head down and sleep."

"Let me steer—I can, I must!" she cried, springing toward him, and laying her hand on the rudder.

He smiled and kissed the little hand, saying, dreamily, "You could not hold it a minute; sit by me, love; let us turn the boat again, and drift away together—anywhere, anywhere out of the world."

"Oh, Heaven, what will become of us!" and Rose wrung her hands in real despair. "Mr. Done—Mark—dear Mark, rouse yourself and listen to me. Turn, as you say, for it is certain death to go on so. Turn, and let us drift down to the lighthouse; they will hear and help us. Quick, take down the sail, get out the oars, and let us try to reach there before the storm breaks."

As Rose spoke, he obeyed her like a dumb animal; love for her was stronger even than the instinct of self-preservation, and for her sake he fought against the treacherous lethargy which was swiftly overpowering him. The sail was lowered, the boat brought round, and with little help from the ill-pulled oars, it drifted rapidly out to sea with the ebbing tide.

As she caught her breath after this dangerous manœuver was accomplished, Rose asked, in a quiet tone, she vainly tried to render natural:

"How much hasheesh did you take?"

"All that Meredith threw me. Too much; but I was possessed to do it, so I hid the roll and tried it," he answered, peering at her with a weird laugh.

"Let us talk; our safety lies in keeping awake, and I dare not let you sleep," continued Rose, dashing water on her own hot forehead with a sort of desperation.

"Say you love me; that would wake me from my lost sleep, I think. I have hoped and feared, waited and suffered so long. Be pitiful, and answer, Rose."

"I do; but I should not own it now."

So low was the soft reply, he scarcely heard it, but he felt it, and made a strong effort to break from the hateful spell that bound him. Leaning forward, he tried to read her face in a ray of moonlight breaking through the clouds: he saw a new and tender warmth in it, for all the pride was gone, and no fear marred the eloquence of those soft, Southern eyes.

"Kiss me, Rose, then I shall believe it. I feel lost in a dream, and you, so changed, so kind, may be only a fair phantom. Kiss me, love, and make it real."

As if swayed by a power more potent than her will, Rose bent to meet his lips. But the ardent pressure seemed to startle her from a momentary oblivion of everything but love. She covered up her face and sank down, as if overwhelmed with shame, sobbing through passionate tears:

"Oh, what am I doing? I am mad, for I, too, have taken hasheesh."

What he answered she never heard, for a rattling peal of thunder drowned his voice, and then the storm broke loose. Rain fell in torrents, the wind blew fiercely, sky and sea were black as ink, and the boat tossed from wave to wave almost at their mercy. Giving herself up for lost, Rose crept to her lover's side and clung there, conscious only that they would bide together through the perils their own folly brought them. Done's excitement was quite gone now; he sat like a statue, shielding the frail creature whom he loved, with a smile on his face, which looked awfully emotionless when the lightning gave her glimpses of its white immobility. Drenched, exhausted, and half senseless with danger, fear and exposure, Rose saw at last a welcome glimmer through the gloom, and roused herself to cry for help.

"Mark, wake and help me! Shout, for God's sake—shout and call them, for we are lost if we drift by!" she cried, lifting his head from his breast, and forcing him to see the brilliant beacons streaming far across the troubled water.

He understood her, and springing up, uttered shout after shout, like one demented. Fortunately, the storm had lulled a little; the lighthouse-keeper heard and answered. Rose seized the helm, Done the oars, and with one frantic effort, guided the boat into quieter waters, where it was met by the keeper, who towed it to the rocky nook which served as harbor.

The moment a strong, steady face met her eyes, and a gruff, cheery voice hailed her, Rose gave way, and was carried up to the house, looking more like a beautiful drowned Ophelia than a living woman.

"Here, Sally, see to the poor thing; she's had a rough time on't. I'll take care of her sweetheart—and a nice job I'll have, I reckon, for if he ain't mad or drunk, he's had a stroke of lightenin, and looks as if he wouldn't get his bearin' in a hurry," said the old man, as he housed his unexpected guests, and stood staring at Done, who looked about him like one dazed. "You jest turn in yonder and sleep it off, mate. We'll see to the lady, and right up your boat in the morning," the old man added.

"Be kind to Rose. I frightened her. I'll not forget you. Yes, let me sleep and get over this cursed folly as soon as possible," muttered this strange visitor.

Done threw himself down on the rough couch and tried to sleep, but every nerve was overstrained, every pulse beating like a trip-hammer, and everything about him was intensified and exaggerated with awful power. The thunder-shower seemed a wild hurricane, the quaint room a wilderness peopled with tormenting phantoms, and all the events of his life passed before him in an endless procession, which nearly maddened him. The old man looked weird and gigantic, his own voice sounded shrill and discordant, and the ceaseless murmur of Rose's incoherent wanderings haunted him like parts of a grotesque but dreadful dream.

All night he lay motionless, with staring eyes, feverish lips, and a mind on the rack, for the delicate machinery which had been tampered with revenged the wrong by torturing the foolish experimenter. All night Rose wept and sang, talked and cried for help in a piteous state of nervous excitement, for with her the trance came first, and the after-agitation was increased by the events of the evening. She slept at last, lulled by the old woman's motherly care, and Done was spared one tormenting fear, for he dreaded the consequences of this folly on her, more than upon himself.

As day dawned he rose, haggard and faint, and staggered out. At the door he met the keeper, who stopped him to report that the boat was in order, and a fair day coming. Seeing doubt and perplexity in the old man's eye, Done told him the truth, and added that he was going to the beach for a plunge, hoping by that simple tonic to restore his unstrung nerves.

He came back feeling like himself again, except for a dull headache, and a heavy sense of remorse weighing on his spirits, for he distinctly recollected all the events of the night. The old woman made him eat and drink, and in an hour he felt ready for the homeward trip.

Rose slept late, and when she woke soon recovered herself, for her dose had been a small one. When she had breakfasted and made a hasty toilet, she professed herself anxious to return at once. She dreaded yet longed to see Done, and when the time came armed herself with pride, feeling all a woman's shame at what had passed, and resolving to feign forgetfulness of the incidents of the previous night. Pale and cold as a statue she met him, but the moment he began to say humbly, "Forgive me, Rose," she silenced him with an imperious gesture and the command, "Don't speak of it; I only remember that it was very horrible, and wish to forget it all as soon as possible."

"All, Rose?" he added, significantly.

"Yes, *all.* No one would care to recall the follies of a hashish dream," she answered, turning hastily to hide the scarlet flush that would rise, and the eyes that would fall before his own.

"*I* never can forget, but I will be silent if you bid me."

"I do. Let us go. What will they think at the island? Mr. Done, give me your promise to tell no one, now or ever, that I tried that dangerous experiment. I will guard your secret also." She spoke eagerly and looked up imploringly.

"I promise," and he gave her his hand, holding her own with a wistful glance, till she drew it away and begged him to take her home.

Leaving hearty thanks and a generous token of their gratitude, they sailed away with a fair wind, finding in the freshness of the morning a speedy cure for tired bodies and excited minds. They said little, but it was impossible for Rose to preserve her coldness. The memory of the past night broke down her pride, and Done's tender glances touched her heart. She half hid her face behind her hand, and tried to compose herself for the scene to come, for as she approached the island, she saw Belle and her party waiting for them on the shore.

"Oh, Mr. Done, screen me from their eyes and questions as much as you can! I'm so worn out and nervous, I shall betray myself. You will help me?" And she turned to him with a confiding look, strangely at variance with her usual calm self-possession.

"I'll shield you with my life, if you will tell me why you took the hasheesh," he said, bent on knowing his fate.

"I hoped it would make me soft and lovable, like other women. I'm tired of being a lonely statue," she faltered, as if the truth was wrung from her by a power stronger than her will.

"And I took it to gain courage to tell my love. Rose, we have been near death together; let us share life together, and neither of us be any more lonely or afraid?"

He stretched his hand to her with his heart in his face, and she gave him hers with a look of tender submission, as he said ardently, "Heaven bless hasheesh, if its dreams end like this!"

1869

# LOUISA MAY ALCOTT

(1832–1888)

## *How I Went Out to Service*

WHEN I WAS eighteen I wanted something to do. I had tried teaching for two years, and hated it; I had tried sewing, and could not earn my bread in that way, at the cost of health; I tried story-writing and got five dollars for stories which now bring a hundred; I had thought seriously of going upon the stage, but certain highly respectable relatives were so shocked at the mere idea that I relinquished my dramatic aspirations.

"What *shall* I do?" was still the question that perplexed me. I was ready to work, eager to be independent, and too proud to endure patronage. But the right task seemed hard to find, and my bottled energies were fermenting in a way that threatened an explosion before long.

My honored mother was a city missionary that winter, and not only served the clamorous poor, but often found it in her power to help decayed gentlefolk by quietly placing them where they could earn their bread without the entire sacrifice of taste and talent which makes poverty so hard for such to bear. Knowing her tact and skill, people often came to her for companions, housekeepers, and that class of the needy who do not make their wants known through an intelligence office.

One day, as I sat dreaming splendid dreams, while I made a series of little petticoats out of the odds and ends sent in for the poor, a tall, ministerial gentleman appeared, in search of a companion for his sister. He possessed an impressive nose, a fine flow of language, and a pair of large hands, encased in black kid gloves. With much waving of these somber members, Mr. R. set forth the delights awaiting the happy soul who should secure this home. He described it as a sort of heaven on earth. "There are books, pictures, flowers, a piano, and the best of society," he said. "This person will be one of the family in all respects, and only required to help about the lighter work, which my sister has done herself hitherto, but is now a martyr to neuralgia and needs a gentle hand to assist her."

My mother, who never lost her faith in human nature, spite of many impostures, believed every word, and quite beamed with benevolent interest as she listened and tried to recall some needy young woman to whom this charming home would be a blessing. I also innocently thought:

"That sounds inviting. I like housework and can do it well. I should have time to enjoy the books and things I love, and D—— is not far away from home. Suppose I try it."

So, when my mother turned to me, asking if I could suggest any one, I became as red as a poppy and said abruptly:

"Only myself."

"Do you really mean it?" cried my astonished parent.

"I really do if Mr. R. thinks I should suit," was my steady reply, as I partially obscured my crimson countenance behind a little flannel skirt, still redder.

The Reverend Josephus gazed upon me with the benign regard which a bachelor of five and thirty may accord a bashful damsel of eighteen. A smile dawned upon his countenance, "sicklied o'er with the pale cast of thought," or dyspepsia; and he softly folded the black gloves, as if about to bestow a blessing, as he replied, with emphasis:

"I am sure you would, and we should think ourselves most fortunate if we could secure your society, and—ahem—services for my poor sister."

"Then I'll try it," responded the impetuous maid.

"We will talk it over a little first, and let you know to-morrow, sir," put in my prudent parent, adding, as Mr. R—— arose: "What wages do you pay?"

"My dear madam, in a case like this let us not use such words as those. Anything you may think proper we shall gladly give. The labor is very light, for there are but three of us and our habits are of the simplest sort. I am a frail reed and may break at any moment; so is my sister, and my aged father cannot long remain; therefore, money is little to us, and any one who comes to lend her youth and strength to our feeble household will not be forgotten in the end, I assure you." And, with another pensive smile, a farewell wave of the impressive gloves, the Reverend Josephus bowed like a well-sweep and departed.

"My dear, are you in earnest?" asked my mother.

"Of course, I am. Why not try this experiment? It can but fail, like all the others."

"I have no objection; only I fancied you were rather too proud for this sort of thing."

"I am too proud to be idle and dependent, ma'am. I'll scrub floors and take in washing first. I do housework at home for love; why not do it abroad for money? I like it better than teaching. It is healthier than sewing and surer than writing. So why not try it?"

"It is going out to service, you know, though you are called a companion. How does that suit?"

"I don't care. Every sort of work that is paid for is service; and I don't mind being a companion, if I can do it well. I may find it is my mission to take care of neuralgic old ladies and lackadaisical clergymen. It does not sound exciting, but it's better than nothing," I answered, with a sigh; for it *was* rather a sudden downfall to give up being a Siddons and become a Betcinder.

How my sisters laughed when they heard the new plan! But they soon resigned themselves, sure of fun, for Lu's adventures were the standing joke of the family. Of course, the highly respectable relatives held up their hands in holy horror at the idea of one of the clan degrading herself by going out to service. Teaching a private school was the proper thing for an indigent gentlewoman. Sewing even, if done in the seclusion of home and not mentioned in public, could be tolerated. Story-writing was a genteel accomplishment and reflected credit upon the name. But leaving the paternal roof to wash other people's teacups, nurse other people's ails, and obey other people's orders for hire—this, this was degradation; and headstrong Louisa would disgrace her name forever if she did it.

Opposition only fired the revolutionary blood in my veins, and I crowned my iniquity by the rebellious declaration:

"If doing this work hurts my respectability, I wouldn't give much for it. My aristocratic ancestors don't feed or clothe me and my democratic ideas of honesty and honor won't let me be idle or dependent. You need not know me if you are ashamed of me, and I won't ask you for a penny; so, if I never do succeed in anything, I shall have the immense satisfaction of knowing I am under no obligation to any one."

In spite of the laughter and the lamentation, I got ready my small wardrobe, consisting of two calico dresses and one delaine, made by myself, also several large and uncompromising blue aprons and three tidy little sweeping-caps; for I had some English notions about housework and felt that my muslin hair-protectors would be useful in some of the "light labors" I was to undertake. It is needless to say they were very becoming. Then, firmly embracing my family, I set forth one cold January day, with my little trunk, a stout heart, and a five-dollar bill for my fortune.

"She will be back in a week," was my sister's prophecy, as she wiped her weeping eye.

"No, she won't, for she has promised to stay the month out and she will keep her word," answered my mother, who always defended the black sheep of her flock.

I heard both speeches, and registered a tremendous vow to keep that promise, if I died in the attempt—little dreaming, poor innocent, what lay before me.

Josephus meantime had written me several remarkable letters, describing the different members of the family I was about to enter. His account was peculiar; but I believed every word of it and my romantic fancy was much excited by the details he gave. The principal ones are as follows, condensed from the voluminous epistles which he evidently enjoyed writing:

"You will find a stately mansion, fast falling to decay, for my father will have nothing repaired, preferring that the old house and its master should crumble away together. I have, however, been permitted to rescue a few rooms from ruin; and here I pass my recluse life, surrounded by the things I love. This will naturally be more attractive to you than the gloomy apartments my father inhabits, and I hope you will here allow me to minister to your young and cheerful nature when your daily cares are over. I need such companionship and shall always welcome you to my abode.

"Eliza, my sister, is a child at forty, for she has lived alone with my father and an old servant all her life. She is a good creature, but not lively, and needs stirring up, as you will soon see. Also I hope by your means to rescue her from the evil influence of Puah, who, in my estimation, is a *wretch*. She has gained entire control over Eliza, and warps her mind with great skill, prejudicing her against *me*, and thereby desolating my home. Puah hates *me* and always has. Why I know not, except that I will not yield to her control. She ruled here for years while I was away, and my return upset all her nefarious plans. It will always be my firm opinion that she has tried to *poison me*, and may again. But even this dark suspicion will not deter me from my duty. I cannot send her away, for both my deluded father and my sister have entire faith in her, and I cannot shake it. She is faithful and kind to them, so I submit and remain to guard them, even at the risk of my life.

"I tell you these things because I wish you to know all and be warned, for this old hag has a specious tongue, and I should grieve to see you deceived by her lies. Say nothing, but watch her silently, and help me to thwart her evil plots; but do not trust her, or beware."

Now this was altogether romantic and sensational, and I felt as if about to enter one of those delightfully dangerous houses we read of in novels, where perils, mysteries, and sins freely disport themselves, till the newcomer sets all to rights, after unheard of trials and escapes.

I arrived at twilight, just the proper time for the heroine to appear; and, as no one answered my modest solo on the rusty knocker, I walked in and looked about me. Yes, here was the long, shadowy hall, where the ghosts doubtless walked at midnight. Peering in at an open door on the right, I saw a parlor full of ancient furniture, faded, dusty, and dilapidated. Old portraits stared at me from the walls and a damp chill froze the marrow of my bones in the most approved style.

"The romance opens well," I thought, and, peeping in at an opposite door, beheld a luxurious apartment, full of the warm glow of firelight, the balmy breath of hyacinths and roses, the white glimmer of piano keys, and tempting rows of books along the walls.

The contrast between the two rooms was striking, and, after an admiring survey, I continued my explorations, thinking that I should not mind being "ministered to" in that inviting place when my work was done.

A third door showed me a plain, dull sitting-room, with an old man napping in his easy-chair. I heard voices in the kitchen beyond, and, entering there, beheld Puah the fiend. Unfortunately for the dramatic effect of the tableaux, all I saw was a mild-faced old woman, buttering toast, while she conversed with her familiar, a comfortable gray cat.

The old lady greeted me kindly, but I fancied her faded blue eye had a weird expression and her amiable words were all a snare, though I own I was rather disappointed at the commonplace appearance of this humble Borgia.

She showed me to a tiny room, where I felt more like a young giantess than ever, and was obliged to stow away my possessions as snugly as in a ship's cabin. When I presently descended, armed with a blue apron and "a heart for any fate," I found the old man awake and received from him a welcome full of ancient courtesy and kindliness. Miss Eliza crept in like a timid mouse, looking so afraid of her buxom companion that I forgot my own shyness in trying to relieve hers. She was so enveloped in shawls that all I could discover was that my mistress was a very nervous little woman, with a small button of pale hair on the outside of her head and the vaguest notions of work inside. A few spasmodic remarks and many awkward pauses brought us to teatime, when Josephus appeared, as tall, thin, and cadaverous as ever. After his arrival there was no more silence, for he preached all suppertime something in this agreeable style.

"My young friend, our habits, as you see, are of the simplest. We eat in the kitchen, and all together, in the primitive fashion; for it suits my father and saves labor. I could wish more order and elegance; but *my* wishes are not consulted and I submit. I live above these petty crosses, and, though my health suffers from bad cookery, I do not murmur. Only, I must say, in passing, that if you *will* make your battercakes green with saleratus, Puah, I shall feel it my duty to throw them out of the window. *I* am used to poison; but I cannot see the coats of this blooming girl's stomach destroyed, as mine have been. And, speaking of duties, I may as well mention to you, Louisa (I call you so in a truly fraternal spirit), that I like to find my study in order when I come down in the morning; for I often need a few moments of solitude before I face the daily annoyances of my life. I shall permit *you* to perform this light task, for *you* have some idea of order (I see it in the formation of your brow), and feel sure that *you* will respect the sanctuary of thought. Eliza is so blind she does not see dust, and Puah enjoys devastating the one poor refuge I can call my own this side the grave. We are all waiting for you, sir. My father keeps up the old formalities, you observe; and I endure them, though *my* views are more advanced."

The old gentleman hastily finished his tea and returned thanks, when his son stalked gloomily away, evidently oppressed with the burden of his wrongs, also, as I irreverently fancied, with the seven "green" flapjacks he had devoured during the sermon.

I helped wash up the cups, and during that domestic rite Puah chatted in what I should have considered a cheery, social way had I not been darkly warned against her wiles.

"You needn't mind half Josephus says, my dear. He likes to hear himself talk and always goes on so before folks. I sometimes thinks his books and new idees have sort of muddled his wits, for he is as full of notions as a paper is of pins; and he gets dreadfully put out if we don't give in to 'em. But, gracious me! they are so redicklus sometimes and so selfish I can't allow him to make a fool of himself or plague Lizy. She don't dare to say her soul is her own; so I have to stand up for her. His pa don't know half his odd doings; for I try to keep the old gentleman comfortable and have to manage 'em all, which is not an easy job, I do assure you."

I had a secret conviction that she was right, but did not commit myself in any way, and we joined the social circle in the sitting-room. The prospect was not a lively one, for the old gentleman nodded behind his newspaper; Eliza, with her head pinned up in a little blanket, slumbered on the sofa, Puah fell to knitting silently; and the plump cat dozed under the stove. Josephus was visible, artistically posed in the luxurious recesses of his cell, with the light beaming on his thoughtful brow, as he pored over a large volume or mused with upturned eye.

Having nothing else to do, I sat and stared at him, till, emerging from a deep reverie, with an effective start, he became conscious of my existence and beckoned me to approach the "sanctuary of thought" with a melodramatic waft of his large hand.

I went, took possession of an easy-chair, and prepared myself for elegant conversation. I was disappointed, however; for Josephus showed me a list of his favorite dishes, sole fruit of all that absorbing thought, and, with an earnestness that flushed his saffron countenance, gave me hints as to the proper preparation of these delicacies.

I mildly mentioned that I was not a cook; but was effectually silenced by being reminded that I came to be generally useful, to take his sister's place, and see that the flame of life which burned so feebly in this earthly tabernacle was fed with proper fuel. Mince pies, Welsh rarebits, sausages, and strong coffee did not strike me as strictly spiritual fare; but I listened meekly and privately resolved to shift this awful responsibility to Puah's shoulders.

Detecting me in gape, after an hour of this high converse, he presented me with an overblown rose, which fell to pieces before I got out of the room, pressed my hand, and dismissed me with a fervent "God bless you, child. Don't forget the dropped eggs for breakfast."

I was up betimes next morning and had the study in perfect order before the recluse appeared, enjoying a good prowl among the books as I worked and becoming so absorbed that I forgot the eggs, till a gusty sigh startled me, and I beheld Josephus, in dressing gown and slippers, languidly surveying the scene.

"Nay, do not fly," he said, as I grasped my duster in guilty haste. "It pleases me to see you here and lends a sweet, domestic charm to my solitary room. I like that graceful cap, that housewifely apron, and I beg you will wear them often; for it refreshes my eye to see something tasteful, young, and womanly about me. Eliza makes a bundle of herself and Puah is simply detestable."

He sank languidly into a chair and closed his eyes, as if the mere thought of his enemy was too much for him. I took advantage of this momentary prostration to slip away, convulsed with laughter at the looks and words of this bald-headed sentimentalist.

After breakfast I fell to work with a will, eager to show my powers and glad to put things to rights, for many hard jobs had evidently been waiting for a stronger arm than Puah's and a more methodical head than Eliza's.

Everything was dusty, moldy, shiftless, and neglected, except the domain of Josephus. Up-stairs the paper was dropping from the walls, the ancient furniture was all more or less dilapidated, and every hole and corner was full of relics tucked away by Puah, who was a regular old magpie. Rats and mice reveled in the empty rooms and spiders wove their tapestry undisturbed, for the old man would have nothing altered or repaired and his part of the house was fast going to ruin.

I longed to have a grand "clearing up"; but was forbidden to do more than to keep things in livable order. On the whole, it was fortunate, for I soon found that my hands would be kept busy with the realms of Josephus, whose ethereal being shrank from dust, shivered at a cold breath, and needed much cosseting with dainty food, hot fires, soft beds, and endless service, else, as he expressed it, the frail reed would break.

I regret to say that a time soon came when I felt supremely indifferent as to the breakage, and very skeptical as to the fragility of a reed that ate, slept, dawdled, and scolded so energetically. The rose that fell to pieces so suddenly was a good symbol of the rapid disappearance of all the romantic delusions I had indulged in for a time. A week's acquaintance with the inmates of this old house quite settled my opinion, and further developments only confirmed it.

Miss Eliza was a nonentity and made no more impression on me than a fly. The old gentleman passed his days in a placid sort of doze and took no notice of what went on about him. Puah had been a faithful drudge for years, and, instead of being a "wretch," was, as I soon satisfied myself, a motherly old soul, with no malice in her. The secret of Josephus's dislike was that the reverend tyrant ruled the house, and all obeyed him but Puah, who had nursed him as a baby, boxed his ears as a boy, and was not afraid of him even when he became a man and a minister. I soon repented of my first suspicions, and grew fond of her, for without my old gossip I should have fared ill when my day of tribulation came.

At first I innocently accepted the fraternal invitations to visit the study, feeling that when my day's work was done I earned a right to rest and read. But I soon found that this was not the idea. I was not to read; but to be read to. I was not to enjoy the flowers, pictures, fire, and books; but to keep them in order for my lord to enjoy. I was also to be a passive bucket, into which he was to pour all manner of philosophic, metaphysical, and sentimental rubbish. I was to serve his needs, soothe his sufferings, and sympathize with all his sorrows—be a galley slave, in fact.

As soon as I clearly understood this, I tried to put an end to it by shunning the study and never lingering there an instant after my work was done. But it availed little, for Josephus demanded much sympathy and was bound to have it. So he came and read poems while I washed dishes, discussed his pet problems all meal-times, and put reproachful notes under my door, in which were comically mingled complaints of neglect and orders for dinner.

I bore it as long as I could, and then freed my mind in a declaration of independence, delivered in the kitchen, where he found me scrubbing the hearth. It was not an impressive attitude for an orator, nor was the occupation one a girl would choose when receiving calls; but I have always felt grateful for the intense discomfort of that moment, since it gave me courage to rebel outright. Stranded on a small island of mat, in a sea of soapsuds, I brandished a scrubbing brush, as I indignantly informed him that I came to be a companion to his sister, not to him, and I should keep that post or none. This I followed up by reproaching him with the delusive reports he had given me of the place and its duties, and assuring him that I should not stay long unless matters mended.

"But I offer you lighter tasks, and you refuse them," he begun, still hovering in the doorway, whither he had hastily retired when I opened my batteries.

"But I don't like the tasks, and consider them much worse than hard work," was my ungrateful answer, as I sat upon my island, with the softsoap conveniently near.

"Do you mean to say you prefer to scrub that hearth to sitting in my charming room while I read Hegel to you?" he demanded, glaring down upon me.

"Infinitely," I responded promptly, and emphasized my words by beginning to scrub with a zeal that made the bricks white with foam.

"Is it possible!" and, with a groan at my depravity, Josephus retired, full of ungodly wrath.

I remember that I immediately burst into jocund song, so that no doubt might remain in his mind, and continued to warble cheerfully till my task was done. I also remember that I cried heartily when I got to my room, I was so vexed, disappointed, and tired. But my bower was so small I should soon have swamped the furniture if I had indulged copiously in tears; therefore I speedily dried them up, wrote a comic letter home, and waited with interest to see what would happen next.

Far be it from me to accuse one of the nobler sex of spite or the small revenge of underhand annoyances and slights to one who could not escape and would not retaliate; but after that day a curious change came over the spirit of that very unpleasant dream. Gradually all the work of the house had been slipping into my hands; for Eliza was too poorly to help or direct, and Puah too old to do much besides the cooking. About this time I found that even the roughest work was added to my share, for Josephus was unusually feeble and no one was hired to do his chores. Having made up my mind to go when the month was out, I said nothing, but dug paths, brought water from the well, split kindlings, made fires, and sifted ashes, like a true Cinderella.

There never had been any pretense of companionship with Eliza, who spent her days mulling over the fire, and seldom exerted herself except to find odd jobs for me to do—rusty knives to clean, sheets to turn, old stockings to mend, and, when all else failed, some paradise of moths and mice to be cleared up; for the house was full of such "glory holes."

If I remonstrated, Eliza at once dissolved into tears and said she must do as she was told; Puah begged me to hold on till spring, when things would be much better; and pity pleaded for the two poor souls. But I don't think I could have stood it if my promise had not bound me, for when the fiend said "Budge" honor said "Budge not," and I stayed.

But, being a mortal worm, I turned now and then when the ireful Josephus trod upon me too hard, especially in the matter of boot-blacking. I really don't know why that is considered such humiliating work for a woman; but so it is, and there I drew the line. I would have cleaned the old man's shoes without a murmur; but he preferred to keep their native rustiness intact. Eliza never went out, and Puah affected carpet-slippers of the Chinese-junk pattern. Josephus, however, plumed himself upon his feet, which, like his nose, were large, and never took his walks abroad without having his boots in a high state of polish. He had brushed them himself at first; but soon after the explosion I discovered a pair of muddy boots in the shed, set suggestively near the blacking-box. I did not take the hint, feeling instinctively that this amiable being was trying how much I would bear for the sake of peace.

The boots remained untouched; and another pair soon came to keep them company, whereat I smiled wickedly as I chopped just kindlings enough for my own use. Day after day the collection grew, and neither party gave in. Boots were succeeded by shoes, then rubbers gave a pleasing variety to the long line, and then I knew the end was near.

"Why are not my boots attended to?" demanded Josephus, one evening, when obliged to go out.

"I'm sure I don't know," was Eliza's helpless answer.

"I told Louizy I guessed you'd want some of 'em before long," observed Puah, with an exasperating twinkle in her old eye.

"And what did she say?" asked my lord with an ireful whack of his velvet slippers as he cast them down.

"Oh! she said she was so busy doing your other work you'd have to do that yourself; and I thought she was about right."

"Louizy" heard it all through the slide, and could have embraced the old woman for her words, but kept still till Josephus had resumed his slippers with a growl and retired to the shed, leaving Eliza in tears, Puah chuckling, and the rebellious handmaid exulting in the china-closet.

Alas! for romance and the Christian virtues, several pairs of boots were cleaned that night, and my sinful soul enjoyed the spectacle of the reverend bootblack at his task. I even found my "fancy work," as I called the evening job of paring a bucketful of hard russets with a dull knife, much cheered by the shoebrush accompaniment played in the shed.

Thunder-clouds rested upon the martyr's brow at breakfast, and I was as much ignored as the cat. And what a relief that was! The piano was locked up, so were the bookcases, the newspapers mysteriously disappeared, and a solemn silence reigned at table, for no one dared to talk when that gifted tongue was mute. Eliza fled from the gathering storm and had a comfortable fit of neuralgia in her own room, where Puah nursed her, leaving me to skirmish with the enemy.

It was not a fair fight, and that experience lessened my respect for mankind immensely. I did my best, however—grubbed about all day and amused my dreary evenings as well as I could; too proud even to borrow a book, lest it should seem like a surrender. What a long month it was, and how eagerly I counted the hours of that last week, for my time was up Saturday, and I hoped to be off at once. But when I announced my intention such dismay fell upon Eliza that my heart was touched, and Puah so urgently begged me to stay till they could get some one that I consented to remain a few days longer, and wrote posthaste to my mother, telling her to send a substitute quickly or I should do something desperate.

That blessed woman, little dreaming of all the woes I had endured, advised me to be patient, to do the generous thing, and be sure I should not regret it in the end. I groaned, submitted, and did regret it all the days of my life.

Three mortal weeks I waited; for, though two other victims came, I was implored to set them going, and tried to do it. But both fled after a day or two, condemning the place as a very hard one and calling me a fool to stand it another hour. I entirely agreed with them on both points, and, when I had cleared up after the second incapable lady, I tarried not for the coming of a third, but clutched my property and announced my departure by the next train.

Of course, Eliza wept, Puah moaned, the old man politely regretted, and the younger one washed his hands of the whole affair by shutting himself up in his room and forbidding me to say farewell because he "could not bear it." I laughed, and fancied it done for effect then; but I soon understood it better and did not laugh.

At the last moment, Eliza nervously tucked a sixpenny pocket-book into my hand and shrouded herself in the little blanket with a sob. But Puah kissed me kindly and whispered, with an odd look: "Don't blame us for anything. Some folks is liberal and some ain't." I thanked the poor old soul for her kindness to me and trudged gayly away to the station, whither my property had preceded me on a wheelbarrow, hired at my own expense.

I never shall forget that day. A bleak March afternoon, a sloppy, lonely road, and one hoarse crow stalking about a field, so like Josephus that I could not resist throwing a snowball at him. Behind me stood the dull old house, no longer either mysterious or romantic in my disenchanted eyes; before me rumbled the barrow, bearing my dilapidated wardrobe; and in my pocket reposed what I fondly hoped was, if not a liberal, at least an honest return for seven weeks of the hardest work I ever did.

Unable to resist the desire to see what my earnings were, I opened the purse and beheld *four dollars.*

I have had a good many bitter minutes in my life; but one of the bitterest came to me as I stood there in the windy road, with the sixpenny pocket-book open before me, and looked from my poor chapped, grimy, chill-blained hands to the paltry sum that was considered reward enough for all the hard and humble labor they had done.

A girl's heart is a sensitive thing. And mine had been very full lately; for it had suffered many of the trials that wound deeply yet cannot be told; so I think it was but natural that my first impulse was to go straight back to that sacred study and fling this insulting money at the feet of him who sent it. But I was so boiling over with indignation that I could not trust myself in his presence, lest I should be unable to resist the temptation to shake him, in spite of his cloth.

No, I would go home, show my honorable wounds, tell my pathetic tale, and leave my parents to avenge my wrongs. I did so; but over that harrowing scene I drop a veil, for my feeble pen refuses to depict the emotions of my outraged family. I will merely mention that the four dollars went back and the reverend Josephus never heard the last of it in that neighborhood.

My experiment seemed a dire failure and I mourned it as such for years; but more than once in my life I have been grateful for that serio-comico experience, since it has taught me many lessons. One of the most useful of these has been the power of successfully making a companion, not a servant, of those whose aid I need, and helping to gild their honest wages with the sympathy and justice which can sweeten the humblest and lighten the hardest task.

1874

# FRANK R. STOCKTON

(1834–1902)

---

## *The Lady, or the Tiger?*

IN THE very olden time, there lived a semi-barbaric king, whose ideas, though somewhat polished and sharpened by the progressiveness of distant Latin neighbors, were still large, florid, and umtrammelled, as became the half of him which was barbaric. He was a man of exuberant fancy, and, withal, of an authority so irresistible that, at his will, he turned his varied fancies into facts. He was greatly given to self-communing; and, when he and himself agreed upon any thing, the thing was done. When every member of his domestic and political systems moved smoothly in its appointed course, his nature was bland and genial; but whenever there was a little hitch, and some of his orbs got out of their orbits, he was blander and more genial still, for nothing pleased him so much as to make the crooked straight, and crush down uneven places.

Among the borrowed notions by which his barbarism had become semified was that of the public arena, in which, by exhibitions of manly and beastly valor, the minds of his subjects were refined and cultured.

But even here the exuberant and barbaric fancy asserted itself. The arena of the king was built, not to give the people an opportunity of hearing the rhapsodies of dying gladiators, nor to enable them to view the inevitable conclusion of a conflict between religious opinions and hungry jaws, but for purposes far better adapted to widen and develop the mental energies of the people. This vast amphitheatre, with its encircling galleries, its mysterious vaults, and its unseen passages, was an agent of poetic justice, in which crime was punished, or virtue rewarded, by the decrees of an impartial and incorruptible chance.

When a subject was accused of a crime of sufficient importance to interest the king, public notice was given that on an appointed day the fate of the accused person would be decided in the king's arena,—a structure which well deserved its name;

for, although its form and plan were borrowed from afar, its purpose emanated solely from the brain of this man, who, every barleycorn a king, knew no tradition to which he owed more allegiance than pleased his fancy, and who ingrafted on every adopted form of human thought and action the rich growth of his barbaric idealism.

When all the people had assembled in the galleries, and the king, surrounded by his court, sat high up on his throne of royal state on one side of the arena, he gave a signal, a door beneath him opened, and the accused subject stepped out into the amphitheatre. Directly opposite him, on the other side of the enclosed space, were two doors, exactly alike and side by side. It was the duty and the privilege of the person on trial, to walk directly to these doors and open one of them. He could open either door he pleased: he was subject to no guidance or influence but that of the aforementioned impartial and incorruptible chance. If he opened the one, there came out of it a hungry tiger, the fiercest and most cruel that could be procured, which immediately sprang upon him, and tore him to pieces, as a punishment for his guilt. The moment that the case of the criminal was thus decided, doleful iron bells were clanged, great wails went up from the hired mourners posted on the outer rim of the arena, and the vast audience, with bowed heads and downcast hearts, wended slowly their homeward way, mourning greatly that one so young and fair, or so old and respected, should have merited so dire a fate.

But, if the accused person opened the other door, there came forth from it a lady, the most suitable to his years and station that his majesty could select among his fair subjects; and to this lady he was immediately married, as a reward of his innocence. It mattered not that he might already possess a wife and family, or that his affections might be engaged upon an object of his own selection: the king allowed no such subordinate arrangements to interfere with his great scheme of retribution and reward. The exercises, as in the other instance, took place immediately, and in the arena. Another door opened beneath the king, and a priest, followed by a band of choristers, and dancing maidens blowing joyous airs on golden horns and treading an epithalamic measure, advanced to where the pair stood, side by side; and the wedding was promptly and cheerily solemnized. Then the gay brass bells rang forth their merry peals, the people shouted glad hurrahs, and the innocent man, preceded by children strewing flowers on his path, led his bride to his home.

This was the king's semi-barbaric method of administering justice. Its perfect fairness is obvious. The criminal could not know out of which door would come the lady: he opened either he pleased, without having the slightest idea whether, in the next instant, he was to be devoured or married. On some occasions the tiger came out of one door, and on some out of the other. The decisions of this tribunal were not only fair, they were positively determinate: the accused person was instantly punished if he found himself guilty; and, if innocent, he was rewarded on the spot, whether he liked it or not. There was no escape from the judgments of the king's arena.

The institution was a very popular one. When the people gathered together on one of the great trial days, they never knew whether they were to witness a bloody slaughter or a hilarious wedding. This element of uncertainty lent an interest to the occasion which it could not otherwise have attained. Thus, the masses were entertained and pleased, and the thinking part of the community could bring no charge of unfairness against this plan; for did not the accused person have the whole matter in his own hands?

This semi-barbaric king had a daughter as blooming as his most florid fancies, and with a soul as fervent and imperious as his own. As is usual in such cases, she was the apple of his eye, and was loved by him above all humanity. Among his courtiers was a young man of that fineness of blood and lowness of station common to the conventional heroes of romance who love royal maidens. This royal maiden was well satisfied with her lover, for he was handsome and brave to a degree unsurpassed in all this kingdom; and she loved him with an ardor that had enough of barbarism in it to make it exceedingly warm and strong. This love affair moved on happily for many months, until one day the king happened to discover its existence. He did not hesitate nor waver in regard to his duty in the premises. The youth was immediately cast into prison, and a day was appointed for his trial in the king's arena. This, of course, was an especially important occasion; and his majesty, as well as all the people, was greatly interested in the workings and development of this trial. Never before had such a case occurred; never before had a subject dared to love the daughter of a king. In after-years such things became commonplace enough; but then they were, in no slight degree, novel and startling.

The tiger-cages of the kingdom were searched for the most savage and relentless beasts, from which the fiercest monster might be selected for the arena; and the ranks of maiden youth and beauty throughout the land were carefully surveyed by competent judges, in order that the young man might have a fitting bride in case fate did not determine for him a different destiny. Of course, everybody knew that the deed with which the accused was charged had been done. He had loved the princess, and neither he, she, nor any one else thought of denying the fact; but the king would not think of allowing any fact of this kind to interfere with the workings of the tribunal, in which he took such great delight and satisfaction. No matter how the affair turned out, the youth would be disposed of; and the king would take an æsthetic pleasure in watching the course of events, which would determine whether or not the young man had done wrong in allowing himself to love the princess.

The appointed day arrived. From far and near the people gathered, and thronged the great galleries of the arena; and crowds, unable to gain admittance, massed themselves against its outside walls. The king and his court were in their places, opposite the twin doors,—those fateful portals, so terrible in their similarity.

All was ready. The signal was given. A door beneath the royal party opened, and the lover of the princess walked into the arena. Tall, beautiful, fair, his appearance was greeted with a low hum of admiration and anxiety. Half the audience had not known so grand a youth had lived among them. No wonder the princess loved him! What a terrible thing for him to be there!

As the youth advanced into the arena, he turned, as the custom was, to bow to the king: but he did not think at all of that royal personage; his eyes were fixed upon the princess, who sat to the right of her father. Had it not been for the moiety of barbarism in her nature, it is probable that lady would not have been there; but her intense and fervid soul would not allow her to be absent on an occasion in which she was so terribly interested. From the moment that the decree had gone forth, that her lover should decide his fate in the king's arena, she had thought of nothing, night or day, but this great event and the various subjects connected with it. Possessed of more power, influence, and force of character than any one who had ever before been interested in such a case, she had done what no other person had done,—she had possessed herself of the secret of the doors. She knew in which of the two rooms, that lay behind those doors, stood the cage of the tiger, with its open front, and in which waited the lady. Through these thick doors, heavily curtained with skins on the inside, it was impossible that any noise or suggestion should come from within to the person who should approach to raise the latch of one of them; but gold, and the power of a woman's will, had brought the secret to the princess.

And not only did she know in which room stood the lady ready to emerge, all blushing and radiant, should her door be opened, but she knew who the lady was. It was one of the fairest and loveliest of the damsels of the court who had been selected as the reward of the accused youth, should he be proved innocent of the crime of aspiring to one so far above him; and the princess hated her. Often had she seen, or imagined that she had seen, this fair creature throwing glances of admiration upon the person of her lover, and sometimes she thought these glances were perceived and even returned. Now and then she had seen them talking together; it was but for a moment or two, but much can be said in a brief space; it may have been on most unimportant topics, but how could she know that? The girl was lovely, but she had dared to raise her eyes to the loved one of the princess; and, with all the intensity of the savage blood transmitted to her through long lines of wholly barbaric ancestors, she hated the woman who blushed and trembled behind that silent door.

When her lover turned and looked at her, and his eye met hers as she sat there paler and whiter than any one in the vast ocean of anxious faces about her, he saw, by that power of quick perception which is given to those whose souls are one, that she knew behind which door crouched the tiger, and behind which stood the lady. He had expected her to know it. He understood her nature, and his soul was assured that she would never rest until she had made plain to herself this thing, hidden to all other lookers-on, even to the king. The only hope for the youth in which there was any element of certainty was based upon the success of the princess in discovering this mystery; and the moment he looked upon her, he saw she had succeeded, as in his soul he knew she would succeed.

Then it was that his quick and anxious glance asked the question: "Which?" It was as plain to her as if he shouted it from where he stood. There was not an instant to be lost. The question was asked in a flash; it must be answered in another.

Her right arm lay on the cushioned parapet before her. She raised her hand, and made a slight, quick movement toward the right. No one but her lover saw her. Every eye but his was fixed on the man in the arena.

He turned, and with a firm and rapid step he walked across the empty space. Every heart stopped beating, every breath was held, every eye was fixed immovably upon that man. Without the slightest hesitation, he went to the door on the right, and opened it.

Now, the point of the story is this: Did the tiger come out of that door, or did the lady?

The more we reflect upon this question, the harder it is to answer. It involves a study of the human heart which leads us through devious mazes of passion, out of which it is difficult to find our way. Think of it, fair reader, not as if the decision of the question depended upon yourself, but upon that hot-blooded, semi-barbaric princess, her soul at a white heat beneath the combined fires of despair and jealousy. She had lost him, but who should have him?

How often, in her waking hours and in her dreams, had she started in wild horror, and covered her face with her hands as she thought of her lover opening the door on the other side of which waited the cruel fangs of the tiger!

But how much oftener had she seen him at the other door! How in her grievous reveries had she gnashed her teeth, and torn her hair, when she saw his start of rapturous delight as he opened the door of the lady! How her soul had burned in agony when she had seen him rush to meet that woman, with her flushing cheek and sparkling eye of triumph; when she had seen him lead her forth, his whole frame kindled with the joy of recovered life; when she had heard the glad shouts from the multitude, and the wild ringing of the happy bells; when she had seen the priest, with his joyous followers, advance to the couple, and make them man and wife before her very eyes; and when she had seen them walk away together upon their path of flowers, followed by the tremendous shouts of the hilarious multitude, in which her one despairing shriek was lost and drowned!

Would it not be better for him to die at once, and go to wait for her in the blessed regions of semi-barbaric futurity?

And yet, that awful tiger, those shrieks, that blood!

Her decision had been indicated in an instant, but it had been made after days and nights of anguished deliberation. She had known she would be asked, she had decided what she would answer, and, without the slightest hesitation, she had moved her hand to the right.

The question of her decision is one not to be lightly considered, and it is not for me to presume to set myself up as the one person able to answer it. And so I leave it with all of you: Which came out of the opened door,—the lady, or the tiger?

1882

# FRANK R. STOCKTON

(1834–1902)

---

## *The Discourager of Hesitancy*

### *A Continuation of "The Lady, or the Tiger?"*

IT WAS NEARLY a year after the occurrence of that event in the arena of the semi-barbaric King known as the incident of the lady or the tiger* that there came to the palace of this monarch a deputation of five strangers from a far country. These men, of venerable and dignified aspect and demeanor, were received by a high officer of the court, and to him they made known their errand.

"Most noble officer," said the speaker of the deputation, "it so happened that one of our countrymen was present here, in your capital city, on that momentous occasion when a young man who had dared to aspire to the hand of your King's daughter had been placed in the arena, in the midst of the assembled multitude, and ordered to open one of two doors, not knowing whether a ferocious tiger would spring out upon him, or a beauteous lady would advance, ready to become his bride. Our fellow-citizen who was then present was a man of super-sensitive feelings, and at the moment when the youth was about to open the door he was so fearful lest he should behold a horrible spectacle, that his nerves failed him, and he fled precipitately from the arena, and mounting his camel rode homeward as fast as he could go.

"We were all very much interested in the story which our countryman told us, and we were extremely sorry that he did not wait to see the end of the affair. We hoped, however, that in a few weeks some traveler from your city would come among us and bring us further news; but up to the day when we left our country, no such traveler had arrived. At last it was determined that the only thing to be done was to send a deputation to this country, and to ask the question: 'Which came out of the open door, the lady, or the tiger?'"

* See THE CENTURY MAGAZINE for November, 1882.

When the high officer had heard the mission of this most respectable deputation, he led the five strangers into an inner room, where they were seated upon soft cushions, and where he ordered coffee, pipes, sherbet, and other semi-barbaric refreshments to be served to them. Then, taking his seat before them, he thus addressed the visitors:

"Most noble strangers, before answering the question you have come so far to ask, I will relate to you an incident which occurred not very long after that to which you have referred. It is well known in all regions hereabouts that our great King is very fond of the presence of beautiful women about his court. All the ladies-in-waiting upon the Queen and Royal Family are most lovely maidens, brought here from every part of the kingdom. The fame of this concourse of beauty, unequaled in any other royal court, has spread far and wide; and had it not been for the equally wide-spread fame of the systems of impetuous justice adopted by our King, many foreigners would doubtless have visited our court.

"But not very long ago there arrived here from a distant land a prince of distinguished appearance and undoubted rank. To such an one, of course, a royal audience was granted, and our King met him very graciously, and begged him to make known the object of his visit. Thereupon the Prince informed his Royal Highness that, having heard of the superior beauty of the ladies of his court, he had come to ask permission to make one of them his wife.

"When our King heard this bold announcement, his face reddened, he turned uneasily on his throne, and we were all in dread lest some quick words of furious condemnation should leap from out his quivering lips. But by a mighty effort he controlled himself; and after a moment's silence he turned to the Prince, and said: 'Your request is granted. To-morrow at noon you shall wed one of the fairest damsels of our court.' Then turning to his officers, he said: 'Give orders that everything be prepared for a wedding in this palace at high noon to-morrow. Convey this royal Prince to suitable apartments. Send to him tailors, boot-makers, hatters, jewelers, armorers; men of every craft, whose services he may need. Whatever he asks, provide. And let all be ready for the ceremony to-morrow.'

"'But, your Majesty,' exclaimed the Prince, 'before we make these preparations, I would like——'

"'Say no more!' roared the King. 'My royal orders have been given, and nothing more is needed to be said. You asked a boon; I granted it; and I will hear no more on the subject. Farewell, my Prince, until to-morrow noon.'

"At this the King arose, and left the audience chamber, while the Prince was hurried away to the apartments selected for him. And here came to him tailors, hatters, jewelers, and every one who was needed to fit him out in grand attire for the wedding. But the mind of the Prince was much troubled and perplexed.

"'I do not understand,' he said to his attendants, 'this precipitancy of action. When am I to see the ladies, that I may choose among them? I wish opportunity, not only to gaze upon their forms and faces, but to become acquainted with their relative intellectual development.'

"'We can tell you nothing,' was the answer. 'What our King thinks right, that will he do. And more than this we know not.'

"'His Majesty's notions seem to be very peculiar,' said the Prince, 'and, so far as I can see, they do not at all agree with mine.'

"At that moment an attendant whom the Prince had not noticed before came and stood beside him. This was a broad-shouldered man of cheery aspect, who carried, its hilt in his right hand, and its broad back resting on his broad arm, an enormous scimeter, the upturned edge of which was keen and bright as any razor. Holding this formidable weapon as tenderly as though it had been a sleeping infant, this man drew closer to the Prince and bowed.

"'Who are you?' exclaimed his Highness, starting back at the sight of the frightful weapon.

"'I,' said the other, with a courteous smile, 'am the Discourager of Hesitancy. When our King makes known his wishes to any one, a subject or visitor, whose disposition in some little points may be supposed not to wholly coincide with that of his Majesty, I am appointed to attend him closely, that, should he think of pausing in the path of obedience to the royal will, he may look at me, and proceed.'

"The Prince looked at him, and proceeded to be measured for a coat.

"The tailors and shoemakers and hatters worked all night; and the next morning, when everything was ready, and the hour of noon was drawing nigh, the Prince again anxiously inquired of his attendants when he might expect to be introduced to the ladies.

"'The King will attend to that,' they said. 'We know nothing of the matter.'

"'Your Highness,' said the Discourager of Hesitancy, approaching with a courtly bow, 'will observe the excellent quality of this edge.' And drawing a hair from his head, he dropped it upon the upturned edge of his scimeter, upon which it was cut in two at the moment of touching.

"The Prince glanced and turned upon his heel.

"Now came officers to conduct him to the grand hall of the palace, in which the ceremony was to be performed. Here the Prince found the King seated on the throne, with his nobles, his courtiers, and his officers standing about him in magnificent array. The Prince was led to a position in front of the King, to whom he made obeisance, and then said:

"'Your Majesty, before I proceed further——'

"At this moment an attendant, who had approached with a long scarf of delicate silk, wound it about the lower part of the Prince's face so quickly and adroitly that he was obliged to cease speaking. Then, with wonderful dexterity, the rest of the scarf was wound around the Prince's head, so that he was completely blindfolded. Thereupon the attendant quickly made openings in the scarf over the mouth and ears, so that the Prince might breathe and hear; and fastening the ends of the scarf securely, he retired.

"The first impulse of the Prince was to snatch the silken folds from his head and face; but as he raised his hands to do so, he heard beside him the voice of the Discourager of Hesitancy, who gently whispered: 'I am here, your Highness.' And, with a shudder, the arms of the Prince fell down by his side.

"Now before him he heard the voice of a priest, who had begun the marriage service in use in that semi-barbaric country. At his side he could hear a delicate rustle, which seemed to proceed from fabrics of soft silk. Gently putting forth his hand, he felt folds of such silk close beside him. Then came the voice of the priest requesting him to take the hand of the lady by his side; and reaching forth his right hand, the Prince received within it another hand so small, so soft, so delicately fashioned, and so delightful to the touch, that a thrill went through his being.

Then, as was the custom of the country, the priest first asked the lady would she have this man to be her husband. To which the answer gently came in the sweetest voice he ever heard: 'I will.'

"Then ran raptures rampant through the Prince's blood. The touch, the tone, enchanted him. All the ladies of that court were beautiful; the Discourager was behind him; and through his parted scarf he boldly answered: 'Yes, I will.'

"Whereupon the priest pronounced them man and wife.

"Now the Prince heard a little bustle about him; the long scarf was rapidly unrolled from his head; and he turned, with a start, to gaze upon his bride. To his utter amazement, there was no one there. He stood alone. Unable on the instant to ask a question or say a word, he gazed blankly about him.

"Then the King arose from his throne, and came down, and took him by the hand.

"'Where is my wife?' gasped the Prince.

"'She is here,' said the King, leading him to a curtained doorway at the side of the hall.

"The curtains were drawn aside, and the Prince, entering, found himself in a long apartment, near the opposite wall of which stood a line of forty ladies, all dressed in rich attire, and each one apparently more beautiful than the rest.

"Waving his hand towards the line, the King said to the Prince: 'There is your bride! Approach, and lead her forth! But, remember this: that if you attempt to take away one of the unmarried damsels of our court, your execution shall be instantaneous. Now, delay no longer. Step up and take your bride.'

"The Prince, as in a dream, walked slowly along the line of ladies, and then walked slowly back again. Nothing could he see about any one of them to indicate that she was more of a bride than the others. Their dresses were all similar; they all blushed; they all looked up, and then looked down. They all had charming little hands. Not one spoke a word. Not one lifted a finger to make a sign. It was evident that the orders given them had been very strict.

"'Why this delay?' roared the King. 'If I had been married this day to one so fair as the lady who wedded you, I should not wait one second to claim her.'

"The bewildered Prince walked again up and down the line. And this time there was a slight change in the countenances of two of the ladies. One of them among the fairest gently smiled as he passed her. Another, just as beautiful, slightly frowned.

"'Now,' said the Prince to himself, 'I am sure that it is one of those two ladies whom I have married. But which? One smiled. And would not any woman smile when she saw, in such a case, her husband coming towards her? But, then, were she not his bride, would she not smile with satisfaction to think he had not selected her, and that she had not led him to an untimely doom? But then, on the other hand, would not any woman frown when she saw her husband come towards her and fail to claim her? Would she not knit her lovely brows? And would she not inwardly say, "It is I! Don't you know it? Don't you feel it? Come!" But if this woman had not been married, would she not frown when she saw the man looking at her? Would she not say to herself, "Don't stop at me! It is the next but one. It is two ladies above. Go on!" And then again, the one who married me did not see my face. Would she not smile if she thought me comely? While if I wedded the one who frowned, could she restrain her disapprobation if she did not like me? Smiles invite the approach of true love. A frown is a reproach to a tardy advance. A smile——'

"'Now, hear me!' loud cried the King. 'In ten seconds, if you do not take the lady we have given you, she, who has just been made your bride, shall be your widow.'

"And, as the last word was uttered, the Discourager of Hesitancy stepped close behind the Prince, and whispered: 'I am here!'

"Now the Prince could not hesitate an instant; and he stepped forward and took one of the two ladies by the hand.

"Loud rang the bells; loud cheered the people; and the King came forward to congratulate the Prince. He had taken his lawful bride.

"Now, then," said the high officer to the deputation of five strangers from a far country, "when you can decide among yourselves which lady the Prince chose, the one who smiled or the one who frowned, then will I tell you which came out of the opened door, the lady or the tiger!"

At the latest accounts the five strangers had not yet decided.

1885

# HARRIET PRESCOTT SPOFFORD

(1835–1921)

## *Her Story*

WELLNIGH THE WORST of it all is the mystery.

If it were true, that accounts for my being here. If it were not true, then the best thing they could do with me was to bring me here. Then, too, if it were true, they would save themselves by hurrying me away; and if it were not true— You see, just as all roads lead to Rome, all roads led me to this Retreat. If it were true, it was enough to craze me; and if it were not true, I was already crazed. And there it is! I can't make out, sometimes, whether I am really beside myself or not; for it seems that whether I was crazed or sane, if it were true, they would naturally put me out of sight and hearing—bury me alive, as they have done, in this Retreat. They? Well, no—he. She stayed at home, I hear. If she had come with us, doubtless I should have found reason enough to say to the physician at once that she was the mad woman, not I—she, who, for the sake of her own brief pleasure, could make a whole after-life of misery for three of us. She— Oh no, don't rise, don't go. I am quite myself, I am perfectly calm. Mad! There was never a drop of crazy blood in the Ridgleys or the Bruces, or any of the generations behind them, and why should it suddenly break out like a smothered fire in me? That is one of the things that puzzle me—why should it come to light all at once in me if it were not true?

Now, I am not going to be incoherent. It was too kind in you to be at such trouble to come and see me in this prison, this grave. I will not cry out once: I will just tell you the story of it all exactly as it was, and you shall judge. If I can, that is—oh, if I can! For sometimes, when I think of it, it seems as if Heaven itself would fail to take my part if I did not lift my own voice. And I cry, and I tear my hair and my flesh, till I know my anguish weighs down their joy, and the little scale that holds that joy flies up under the scorching of the sun, and God sees the festering thing for what it is! Ah, it is not injured reason that cries out in that way: it is a breaking heart!

How cool your hand is, how pleasant your face is, how good it is to see you! Don't be afraid of me: I am as much myself, I tell you, as you are. What an absurdity! Certainly any one who heard me make such a speech would think I was insane and without benefit of clergy. To ask you not to be afraid of me because I am myself. Isn't it what they call a vicious circle? And then to cap the climax by adding that I am as much myself as you are myself! But no matter—you know better. Did you say it was ten years? Yes, I knew it was as much as that—oh, it seems a hundred years! But we hardly show it: your hair is still the same as when we were at school; and mine— Look at this lock— I cannot understand why it is only sprinkled here and there: it ought to be white as the driven snow. My babies are almost grown women, Elizabeth. How could he do without me all this time? Hush now! I am not going to be disturbed at all; only that color of your hair puts me so in mind of his: perhaps there was just one trifle more of gold in his. Do you remember that lock that used to fall over his forehead and which he always tossed back so impatiently. I used to think that the golden Apollo of Rhodes had just such massive, splendid locks of hair as that; but I never told him; I never had the face to praise him; she had. She could exclaim how like ivory the forehead was—that great wide forehead—how that keen aquiline was to be found in the portrait of the Spencer of two hundred years ago. She could tell of the proud lip, of the fire burning in the hazel eye. She knew how, by a silent flattery, as she shrank away and looked up at him, to admire his haughty stature, and make him feel the strength and glory of his manhood and the delicacy of her womanhood.

She was a little thing—a little thing, but wondrous fair. Fair, did I say? No: she was dark as an Egyptian, but such perfect features, such rich and splendid color, such great soft eyes—so soft, so black—so superb a smile; and then such hair! When she let it down, the backward curling ends lay on the ground and she stood on them, or the children lifted them and carried them behind her as pages carry a queen's train. If I had my two hands twisted in that hair! Oh, how I hate that hair! It would make as good a bowstring as ever any Carthaginian woman's made.

Ah, that is atrocious! I am sure you think so. But living all these lonesome years as I have done seems to double back one's sinfulness upon one's self. Because one is sane it does not follow that one is a saint. And when I think of my innocent babies playing with the hair that once I saw him lift and pass across his lips! But I will not think of it!

Well, well! I was a pleasant thing to look at myself once on a time, you know, Elizabeth. He used to tell me so: those were his very words. I was tall and slender, and if my skin was pale it was clear with a pearly clearness, and the lashes of my gray eyes were black as shadows; but now those eyes are only the color of tears.

I never told a syllable about it—I never could. It was so deep down in my heart, that love I had for him: it slept there so dark and still and full, for he was all I had in the world. I was alone, an orphan—if not friendless, yet quite dependent. I see you remember it all. I did not even sit in the pew with my cousin's family,—there were so many to fill it,—but down in one beneath the gallery, you know. And altogether life was a thing to me that hardly seemed worth the living. I went to church one Sunday, I recollect, idly and dreamingly as usual. I did not look off my book till a voice filled my ear—a strange new voice, a deep sweet voice, that invited you and yet commanded you—a voice whose sound divided the core of my heart, and sent thrills that were half joy, half pain, coursing through me. And then I looked up and saw him at the desk. He was reading the first lesson: "Fear not, for I have redeemed thee, I have called thee by thy name: thou art mine." And I saw the bright hair, the bright upturned face, the white surplice, and I said to myself, It is a vision, it is an angel; and I cast down my eyes. But the voice went on, and when I looked again he was still there. Then I bethought me that it must be the one who was coming to take the place of our superannuated rector—the last of a fine line, they had been saying the day before, who, instead of finding his pleasure otherwise, had taken all his wealth and prestige into the Church.

Why will a trifle melt you so—a strain of music, a color in the sky, a perfume? Have you never leaned from the window at evening, and had the scent of a flower float by and fill you with as keen a sorrow as if it had been disaster touching you? Long ago, I mean—we never lean from any windows here. I don't know how, but it was in that same invisible way that this voice melted me; and when I heard it saying, "Behold, I will do a new thing; now it shall spring forth; shall ye not know it? I will even make a way in the wilderness, and rivers in the desert," I was fairly crying. Oh, nervous tears, I dare say. The doctor here would tell you so, at any rate. And that is what I complain of here: they give a physiological reason for every emotion—they could give you a chemical formula for your very soul, I have no doubt. Well, perhaps they were nervous tears, for certainly there was nothing to cry for, and the mood went as suddenly as it came—changed to a sort of exaltation, I suppose—and when they sang the psalm, and he had swept in, in his black gown, and had mounted the pulpit stairs, and was resting that fair head on the big Bible in his silent prayer, I too was singing—singing like one possessed:

"Then, to thy courts when I repair,
My soul shall rise on joyful wing,
The wonders of thy love declare,
And join the strain which angels sing."

And as he rose I saw him searching for the voice unconsciously, and our eyes met. Oh, it was a fresh young voice, let it be mine or whose. I can hear it now as if it were someone else singing. Ah, ah, it has been silent so many years! Does it make you smile to hear me pity myself? It is not myself I am pitying: it is that fresh young girl that loved so. But it used to rejoice me to think that I loved him before I laid eyes on him.

He came to my cousin's in the week—not to see Sylvia or to see Laura: he talked of church-music with my cousin, and then crossed the room and sat down by me. I remember how I grew cold and trembled—how glad, how shy I was; and then he had me sing; and at first Sylvia sang with us, but by and by we sang alone—I sang alone. He brought me yellow old church music, written in quaint characters: he said those characters, those old square breves, were a text guarding secrets of enchantment as much as the text of Merlin's book did; and so we used to find it. Once he brought a copy of an old Roman hymn, written only in the Roman letters: he said it was a hymn which the ancients sang to Maia, the mother-earth, and which the Church fathers adopted, singing it stealthily in the hidden places of the Catacombs; and together we translated it into tones. A rude but majestic thing it was.

And once— The sunshine was falling all about us in the bright lonely room, and the shadows of the rose leaves at the window were dancing over us. I had been singing a Gloria while he walked up and down the room, and he came up behind me: he stooped and kissed me on the mouth. And after that there was no more singing, for, lovely as the singing was, the love was lovelier yet. Why do I complain of such a hell as this is now? I had my heaven once—oh, I had my heaven once! And as for the other, perhaps I deserve it all, for I saw God only through him: it was he that waked me to worship. I had no faith but Spencer's faith; if he had been a heathen, I should have been the same, and creeds and systems might have perished for me had he only been spared from the wreck. And he had loved me from the first moment that his eyes met mine. "When I looked at you," he said, "singing that simple hymn that first day, I felt as I do when I look at the evening star leaning out of the clear sunset lustre: there is something in your face as pure, as remote, as shining. It will always be there," he said, "though you should live a hundred years." He little knew, he little knew!

But he loved me then—oh yes, I never doubted that. There were no happier lovers trod the earth. We took our pleasure as lovers do: we walked in the fields; we sat on the river's side; together we visited the poor and sick; he read me the passages he liked best in his writing from week to week; he brought me the verse from which he meant to preach, and up in the organ-loft I improvised to him the thoughts that it inspired in me. I did that timidly indeed: I could not think my thoughts were worth his hearing till I forgot myself, and only thought of him and the glory I would have revealed to him, and then the great clustering chords and the full music of the diapason swept out beneath my hands—swept along the aisles and swelled up the raftered roof as if they would find the stars, and sunset and twilight stole around us there as we sat still in the succeeding silence. I was happy: I was humble too. I wondered why I had been chosen for such a blest and sacred lot. It was so blessed to be allowed to minister one delight to him. I had a little print of the angel of the Lord appearing to Mary with the lily of annunciation in his hand, and I thought— I dare not tell you what I thought. I made an idol of my piece of clay.

When the leaves had turned we were married, and he took me home. Ah, what a happy home it was! Luxury and beauty filled it. When I first went into it and left the chill October night without, fires blazed upon the hearths; flowers bloomed in every room; a marble Eros held a light up, searching for his Psyche. "*Our* love has found its soul," said he. He led me to the music-room—a temple in itself, for its rounded ceiling towered to the height of the house. There were golden organ-pipes and banks of keys fit for St. Cecilia's use; there were all the delightful outlines of violin and piccolo and harp and horn for any who would use them; there was a pianoforte near the door for me—one such as I had never touched before; and there were cases on all sides filled with the rarest musical works. The floor was bare and inlaid; the windows were latticed in stained glass, so that no common light of day ever filtered through, but light bluer than the sky, gold as the dawn, purple as the night; and then there were vast embowering chairs, in any of which he could hide himself away while I made my incantation, as he sometimes called it, of the great spirits of song. As I tried the piano that night he tuned the old Amati which he himself now and then played upon, and together we improvised our own epithalamium. It was the violin that took the strong assuring part with strains of piercing sweetness, and the music of the piano flowed along in a soft cantabile of undersong. It seemed to me as if his part was like the flight of some white and strong-winged bird above a sunny brook.

But he had hardly created this place for the love of me alone. He adored music as a regenerator; he meant to use it so among his people: here were to be pursued those labors which should work miracles when produced in the open church. For he was building a church with the half of his fortune—a church full of restoration of the old and creation of the new: the walls within were to be a frosty tracery of vines running to break into the gigantic passion-flower that formed the rose-window; the lectern a golden globe upon a tripod, clasped by a silver dove holding on outstretched wings the book.

I have feared, since I have been here, that Spencer's piety was less piety than partisanship: I have doubted if faith were so much alive in him as the love of a great perfect system, and the pride in it I know he always felt. But I never thought about it then: I believed in him as I would have believed in an apostle. So stone by stone the church went up, and stone by stone our lives followed it—lives of such peace, such bliss! Then fresh hopes came into it—sweet trembling hopes; and by and by our first child was born. And if I had been happy before, what was I then? There are some compensations in this world: such happiness could not come twice, such happiness as there was in that moment when I lay, painless and at peace, with the little cheek nestled beside my own, while he bent above us both, proud and glad and tender. It was a dear little baby—so fair, so bright! and when she could walk she could sing. Her sister sang earlier yet; and what music their two shrill sweet voices made as they sat in their little chairs together at twilight before the fire, their curls glistening and their red shoes glistening, while they sang the evening hymn, Spencer on one side of the hearth and I upon the other! Sometimes we let the dear things sit up for a later hour in the music-room—for many a canticle we tried and practised there that hushed hearts and awed them when the choir gave them on succeeding Sundays—and always afterward I heard them singing in their sleep, just as a bird stirs in his nest and sings his stave in the night. Oh, we were happy then; and it was then she came.

She was the step-child of his uncle, and had a small fortune of her own, and Spencer had been left her guardian; and so she was to live with us—at any rate, for a while. I dreaded her coming. I did not want the intrusion; I did not like the things I heard about her; I knew she would be a discord in our harmony. But Spencer, who had only seen her once in her childhood, had been told by some one who travelled in Europe with her that she was delightful and had a rare intelligence. She was one of those women often delightful to men indeed, but whom other women—by virtue of their own kindred instincts, it may be, perhaps by virtue of temptations overcome—see through and know for what they are. But she had her own way of charming: she was the being of infinite variety—to-day glad, to-morrow sad, freakish, and always exciting you by curiosity as to her next caprice, and so moody that after a season of the lowering weather of one of her dull humors you were ready to sacrifice something for the sake of the sunshine that she knew how to make so vivid and so sweet. Then, too, she brought forward her forces by detachment. At first she was the soul of domestic life, sitting at night beneath the light and embossing on web-like muslin designs of flower and leaf which she had learned in her convent, listening to Spencer as he read, and taking from the little wallet of her work-basket apropos scraps which she had preserved from the sermon of some Italian father of the Church or of some French divine. As for me, the only thing I knew was my poor music; and I used to burn with indignation when she interposed that unknown tongue between my husband and myself. Presently her horses came, and then, graceful in her dark riding-habit, she would spend a morning fearlessly subduing one of the fiery fellows, and dash away at last with plume and veil streaming behind her. In the early evening she would dance with the children—witch-dances they were—with her round arms linked above her head, and her feet weaving the measure in and out as deftly as any flashing-footed Bayadere might do—only when Spencer was there to see: at other times I saw she pushed the little hindering things aside without a glance.

By and by she began to display a strange dramatic sort of power: she would rehearse to Spencer scenes that she had met with from day to day in the place, giving now the old church-warden's voice and now the sexton's, their gestures and very faces; she could tell the ailments of half the old women in the parish who came to me with them, and in their own tone and manner to the life; she told us once of a street-scene, with the crier crying a lost child, the mother following with lamentations, the passing strangers questioning, the boys hooting, and the child's reappearance, followed by a tumult, with kisses and blows and cries, so that I thought I saw it all; and presently she had found the secret and vulnerable spot of every friend we had, and could personate them all as vividly as if she did it by necromancy.

One night she began to sketch our portraits in charcoal: the likenesses were not perfect; she exaggerated the careless elegance of Spencer's attitude; perhaps the primness of my own. But yet he saw there the ungraceful trait for the first time, I think. And so much led to more: she brought out her portfolios, and there were her pencil-sketches from the Rhine and from the Guadalquivir, rich water-colors of Venetian scenes, interiors of old churches, and sheet after sheet covered with details of church architecture. Spencer had been admiring all the others—in spite of something that I thought I saw in them, a something that was not true, a trait of her own identity, for I had come to criticise her sharply—but when his eye rested on those sheets I saw it sparkle, and he caught them up and pored over them one by one.

"I see you have mastered the whole thing," he said: "you must instruct me here." And so she did. And there were hours, while I was busied with servants and accounts or with the children, when she was closeted with Spencer in the study, criticising, comparing, making drawings, hunting up authorities; other hours when they walked away together to the site of the new church that was building, and here an arch was destroyed, and there an aisle was extended, and here a row of cloisters sketched into the plan, and there a row of windows, till the whole design was reversed and made over. And they had the thing between them, for, admire and sympathize as I might, I did not know. At first Spencer would repeat the day's achievement to me, but the contempt for my ignorance which she did not deign to hide soon put an end to it when she was present.

It was this interest that now unveiled a new phase of her character: she was devout. She had a little altar in her room; she knew all about albs and chasubles; she would have persuaded Spencer to burn candles in the chancel; she talked of a hundred mysteries and symbols; she wanted to embroider a stole to lay across his shoulders. She was full of small church sentimentalities, and as one after another she uttered them, it seemed to me that her belief was no sound fruit of any system—if it were belief, and not a mere bunch of fancies—but only, as you might say, a rotten windfall of the Romish Church: it had none of the round splendor of that Church's creed, none of the pure simplicity of ours: it would be no stay in trouble, no shield in temptation. I said as much to Spencer.

"You are prejudiced," said he: "her belief is the result of long observation abroad, I think. She has found the need of outward observances: they are, she has told me, a shrine to the body of her faith, like that commanded in the building of the tabernacle, where the ark of the covenant was enclosed in the holy of holies."

"And you didn't think it profane in her to speak so? But I don't believe it, Spencer," I said. "She has no faith: she has some sentimentalisms."

"You are prejudiced," he repeated. "She seems to me a wonderful and gifted being."

"Too gifted," I said. "Her very gifts are unnatural in their abundance. There must be scrofula there to keep such a fire in the blood and sting the brain to such action: she will die in a madhouse, depend upon it." Think of my saying such a thing as that!

"I have never heard you speak so before," he replied coldly. "I hope you do not envy her her powers."

"I envy her nothing," I cried. "For she is as false as she is beautiful!" But I did—oh I did!

"Beautiful?" said Spencer. "Is she beautiful? I never thought of that."

"You are very blind, then," I said with a glad smile.

Spencer smiled too. "It is not the kind of beauty I admire," said he.

"Then I must teach you, sir," said she. And we both started to see her in the doorway, and I, for one, did not know, till shortly before I found myself here, how much or how little she had learned of what we said.

"Then I must teach you, sir," said she again. And she came deliberately into the firelight and paused upon the rug, drew out the silver arrows and shook down all her hair about her, till the great snake-like coils unrolled upon the floor.

"Hyacinthine," said Spencer.

"Indeed it is," said she. "The very color of the jacinth, with that red tint in its darkness that they call black in the shade and gold in the sun. Now look at me."

"Shut your eyes, Spencer," I cried, and laughed.

But he did not shut his eyes. The firelight flashed over her: the color in her cheeks and on her lips sprang ripe and red in it as she held the hair away from them with her rosy finger-tips; her throat curved small and cream-white from the bosom that the lace of her dinner-dress scarcely hid; and the dark eyes glowed with a great light as they lay full on his.

"You mustn't call it vanity," said she. "It is only that it is impossible, looking at the picture in the glass, not to see it as I see any other picture. But for all that, I know it is not every fool's beauty: it is no daub for the vulgar gaze, but a masterpiece that it needs the educated eye to find. I could tell you how this nostril is like that in a famous marble, how the curve of this cheek is that of a certain Venus, the line of this forehead like the line in the dreamy Antinous' forehead. Are you taught? Is it—?"

Then she twisted her hair again and fastened the arrows, and laughed and turned away to look over the evening paper. But as for Spencer, as he lay back in his lordly way, surveying the vision from crown to toe, I saw him flush—I saw him flush and start and quiver, and then he closed his eyes and pressed his fingers on them, and lay back again and said not a word.

She began to read aloud something concerning services at the recent dedication of a church. I was called out as she read. When I came back, a half hour afterward, they were talking. I stopped at my worktable in the next room for a skein of floss that she had asked me for, and I heard her saying, "You cannot expect me to treat you with reverence. You are a married priest, and you know what opinion I necessarily must have of married priests." Then I came in and she was silent.

But I knew, I always knew, that if Spencer had not felt himself weak, had not found himself stirred, if he had not recognized that, when he flushed and quivered before her charm, it was the flesh and not the spirit that tempted him, he would not have listened to her subtle invitation to austerity. As it was, he did. He did—partly in shame, partly in punishment; but to my mind the listening was confession. She had set the wedge that was to sever our union—the little seed in a mere idle cleft that grows and grows and splits the rock asunder.

Well, I had my duties, you know. I never felt my husband's wealth a reason why I should neglect them any more than another wife should neglect her duties. I was wanted in the parish, sent for here and waited for there: the dying liked to see me comfort their living, the living liked to see me touch their dead; some wanted help, and others wanted consolation; and where I felt myself too young and unlearned to give advice, I could at least give sympathy. Perhaps I was the more called upon for such detail of duty because Spencer was busy with the greater things, the church-building and the sermons—sermons that once on a time lifted you and held you on their strong wings. But of late Spencer had been preaching old sermons. He had been moody and morose too: sometimes he seemed oppressed with melancholy. He had spoken to me strangely, had looked at me as if he pitied me, had kept away from me. But she had not regarded his moods: she had followed him in his solitary strolls, had sought him in his study; and she had ever a mystery or symbol to be interpreted, the picture of a private chapel that she had heard of when abroad, or the ground-plan of an ancient one, or some new temptation to his ambition, as I divine. And soon he was himself again.

I was wrong to leave him so to her, but what was there else for me to do? And as for those duties of mine, as I followed them I grew restive; I abridged them, I hastened home. I was impatient even with the detentions the children caused. I could not leave them to their nurses, for all that; but they kept me away from him, and he was alone with her.

One day at last he told me that his mind was troubled by the suspicion that his marriage was a mistake; that on his part at least it had been wrong; that he had been thinking a priest should have the Church only for his bride, and should wait at the altar mortified in every affection; that it was not for hands that were full of caresses and lips that were covered with kisses to touch the sacrament, to offer praise. But for answer I brought my children and put them in his arms. I was white and cold and shaking, but I asked him if they were not justification enough. And I told him that he did his duty better abroad for the heartening of a wife at home, and that he knew better how to interpret God's love to men through his own love for his children. And I laid my head on his breast beside them, and he clasped us all and we cried together, he and I.

But that was not enough, I found. And when our good bishop came, who had always been like a father to Spencer, I led the conversation to that point one evening, and he discovered Spencer's trouble, and took him away and reasoned with him. The bishop was a power with Spencer, and I think that was the end of it.

The end of that, but only the beginning of the rest. For she had accustomed him to the idea of separation from me—the idea of doing without me. He had put me away from himself once in his mind: we had been one soul, and now we were two.

One day, as I stood in my sleeping-room with the door ajar, she came in. She had never been there before, and I cannot tell you how insolently she looked about her. There was a bunch of flowers on a stand that Spencer himself placed there for me every morning. He had always done so, and there had been no reason for breaking off the habit; and I had always worn one of them at my throat. She advanced a hand to pull out a blossom. "Do not touch them," I cried: "my husband puts them there."

"Suppose he does," said she lightly. "For how long?" Then she overlooked me with a long sweeping glance of search and contempt, shrugged her shoulders, and with a French sentence that I did not understand turned back and coolly broke off the blossom she had marked and hung it in her hair. I could not take her by the shoulders and put her from the room. I could not touch the flowers that she had desecrated. I left the room myself, and left her in it, and went down to dinner for the first time without the flower at my throat. I saw Spencer's eye note the omission: perhaps he took it as a release from me, for he never put the flowers in my room again after that day.

Nor did he ask me any more into his study, as he had been used, or read his sermons to me. There was no need of his talking over the church-building with me—he had her to talk it over with. And as for our music, that had been a rare thing since she arrived, for her conversation had been such as to leave but little time for it, and somehow when she came into the music-room and began to dictate to me the time in which I should take an Inflammatus and the spirit in which I should sing a ballad, I could not bear it. Then, too, to tell you the truth, my voice was hoarse and choked with tears full half the time.

It was some weeks after the flowers ceased that our youngest child fell ill. She was very ill—I don't think Spencer knew how ill. I dared not trust her with any one, and Spencer said no one could take such care of her as her mother could; so, although we had nurses in plenty, I hardly left the room by night or day. I heard their voices down below, I saw them go out for their walks. It was a hard fight, but I saved her.

But I was worn to a shadow when all was done—worn with anxiety for her, with alternate fevers of hope and fear, with the weight of my responsibility as to her life; and with anxiety for Spencer too, with a despairing sense that the end of peace had come, and with the total sleeplessness of many nights. Now, when the child was mending and gaining every day, I could not sleep if I would.

The doctor gave me anodynes, but to no purpose: they only nerved me wide awake. My eyes ached, and my brain ached, and my body ached, but it was of no use: I could not sleep. I counted the spots on the wall, the motes upon my eyes, the notes of all the sheets of music I could recall. I remembered the Eastern punishment of keeping the condemned awake till they die, and wondered what my crime was; I thought if I could but sleep I might forget my trouble, or take it up freshly and master it. But no, it was always there—a heavy cloud, a horror of foreboding. As I heard that woman's step go by the door I longed to rid the house of it, and I dinted my palms with my nails till she had passed.

I did not know what to do. It seemed to me that I was wicked in letting the thing go on, in suffering Spencer to be any longer exposed to her power; but then I feared to take a step lest I should thereby rivet the chains she was casting on him. And then I longed so for one hour of the old dear happiness—the days when I and the children had been all and enough. I did not know what to do; I had no one to counsel with; I was wild within myself, and all distraught. Once I thought if I could not rid the house of her I could rid it of myself; and as I went through a dark passage and chanced to look up where a bright-headed nail glittered, I questioned if it would bear my weight. For days the idea haunted me. I fancied that when I was gone perhaps he would love me again, and at any rate I might be asleep and at rest. But the thought of the children prevented me, and one other thought—I was not certain that even my sorrows would excuse me before God.

I went down to dinner again at last. How she glowed and abounded in her beauty as she sat there! And I—I must have been very thin and ghastly: perhaps I looked a little wild in all my bewilderment and hurt. His heart smote him, it may be, for he came round to where I sat by the fire afterward and smoothed my hair and kissed my forehead. He could not tell all I was suffering then—all I was struggling with; for I thought I had better put him out of the world than let him, who was once so pure and good, stay in it to sin. I could have done it, you know. For though I still lay with the little girl, I could have stolen back into our own room with the chloroform, and he would never have known. I turned the handle of the door one night, but the bolt was slipped. I never thought of killing her, you see: let her live and sin, if she would. She was the thing of slime and sin, a splendid tropical growth of the passionate heat and the slime: it was only her nature. But then we think it no harm to kill reptiles, however splendid.

But it was by that time that the voices had begun to talk with me—all night long, all day. It was they, I found, that had kept me so sleepless. Go where I might, they were ever before me. If I went to the woods, I heard them in the whisper of every pine tree. If I went down to the seashore, I heard them in the plash of every wave. I heard them in the wind, in the singing of my ears, in the children's breath as I hung above them,—for I had decided that if I went out of the world I would take the children with me. If I sat down to play, the things would twist the chords into discords; if I sat down to read, they would come between me and the page.

Then I could see the creatures: they had wings like bats. I did not dare speak of them, although I fancied she suspected me, for once she said, as I was kissing my little girl, "When you are gone to a madhouse, don't think they'll have many such kisses." Did she say it? or did I think she said it? I did not answer her, I did not look up: I suppose I should have flown at her throat if I had.

I took the children out with me on my rambles: we went for miles; sometimes I carried one, sometimes the other. I took such long, long walks to escape those noisome things: they would never leave me till I was quite tired out. Now and then I was gone the whole day; and all the time that I was gone he was with her, I knew, and she was tricking out her beauty and practising her arts.

I went to a little festival with them, for Spencer insisted. And she made shadow-pictures on the wall, wonderful things with her perfect profile and her perfect arms and her subtle curves—she out of sight, the shadow only seen. Now it was Isis, I remember, and now it was the head and shoulders and trailing hair of a floating sea-nymph. And then there were charades in which she played; and I can't tell you the glorious thing she looked when she came on as Helen of Troy with all her "beauty shadowed in white veils," you know—that brown and red beauty with its smiles and radiance under the wavering of the flower-wrought veil. I sat by Spencer, and I felt him shiver. He was fighting and struggling too within himself, very likely; only he knew that he was going to yield after all—only he longed to yield while he feared. But as for me, I saw one of those bat-like things perched on her ear as she stood before us, and when she opened her mouth to speak I saw them flying in and out. And I said to Spencer, "She is tormenting me. I cannot stay and see her swallowing the souls of men in this way." And I would have gone, but he held me down fast in my seat. But if I was crazy then—as they say I was, I suppose—it was only with a metaphor, for she was sucking Spencer's soul out of his body.

But I was not crazy. I should admit I might have been if I alone had seen those evil spirits. But Spencer saw them too. He never told me so, but—there are subtle ways—I knew he did; for when I opened the church door late, as I often did at that time after my long walks, they would rush in past me with a whizz, and as I sat in the pew I would see him steadily avoid looking at me; and if he looked by any chance, he would turn so pale that I have thought he would drop where he stood; and he would redden afterward as though one had struck him. He knew then what I endured with them; but I was not the one to speak of it. Don't tell me that his color changed and he shuddered so because I sat there mumbling and nodding to myself. It was because he saw those things mopping and mowing beside me and whispering in my ear. Oh what loathsomeness the obscene creatures whispered! Foul quips and evil words I had never heard before, ribald songs and oaths; and I would clap my hands over my mouth to keep from crying out at them. Creatures of the imagination, you may say. It is possible. But they were so vivid that they seem real to me even now. I burn and tingle as I recall them. And how could I have imagined such sounds, such shapes, of things I had never heard or seen or dreamed?

And Spencer was very unhappy, I am sure. I was the mother of his children, and if he loved me no more, he had an old kindness for me still, and my distress distressed him. But for all that the glamour was on him, and he could not give up that woman and her beauty and her charm. Once or twice he may have thought about sending her away, but perhaps he could not bring himself to do it—perhaps he reflected it was too late, and now it was no matter. But every day she stayed he was the more like wax in her hands. Oh, he was weaker than water that is poured out. He was abandoning himself, and forgetting earth and heaven and hell itself, before a passion—a passion that soon would cloy, and then would sting.

It was the spring season: I had been out several hours. The sunset fell while I was in the wood, and the stars came out; and at one time I thought I would lie down there on last year's leaves and never get up again. But I remembered the children, and went home to them. They were in bed and asleep when I took off my shoes and opened the door of their room—breathing so sweetly and evenly, the little yellow heads close together on one pillow, their hands tossed about the coverlid, their parted lips, their rosy cheeks. I knelt to feel the warm breath on my own cold cheek, and then the voices began whispering again: "If only they never waked! they never waked!"

And all I could do was to spring to my feet and run from the room. I ran shoeless down the great staircase and through the long hall. I thought I would go to Spencer and tell him all—all my sorrows, all the suggestions of the voices, and maybe in the endeavor to save me he would save himself. And I ran down the long dimly-lighted drawing-room, led by the sound I heard, to the music-room, whose doors were open just beyond. It was lighted only by the pale glimmer from the other room and by the moonlight through the painted panes. And I paused to listen to what I had never listened to there—the sound of the harp and a voice with it. Of course they had not heard me coming, and I hesitated and looked, and then I glided within the door and stood just by the open piano there.

She sat at the harp singing—the huge gilded harp. I did not know she sang—she had kept that for her last reserve—but she struck the harp so that it sang itself, like some great prisoned soul, and her voice followed it—oh so rich a voice! My own was white and thin, I felt, beside it. But mine had soared, and hers still clung to earth—a contralto sweet with honeyed sweetness—

the sweetness of unstrained honey that has the earth-taste and the heavy blossom-dust yet in it—sweet, though it grew hoarse and trembling with passion. He sat in one of the great arm-chairs just before her: he was white with feeling, with rapture, with forgetfulness; his eyes shone like stars. He moved restlessly, a strange smile kindled all his face: he bent toward her, and the music broke off in the middle as they threw their arms around each other, and hung there lip to lip and heart to heart. And suddenly I crashed down both my hands on the keyboard before me, and stood and glared upon them.

And I never knew anything more till I woke up here.

And that is the whole of it. That is the puzzle of it—was it a horrid nightmare, an insane vision, or was it true? Was it true that I saw Spencer, my white, clean lover, my husband, a man of God, the father of our spotless babies,—was it true that I saw him so, or was it only some wild, vile conjuration of disease? Oh, I would be willing to have been crazed a lifetime, a whole lifetime, only to wake one moment before I died and find that that had never been!

Well, well, well! When time passed and I became more quiet, I told the doctor here about the voices—I never told him of Spencer or of her—and he bade me dismiss care. He said I was ill—excitement and sleeplessness had surcharged my nerves with that strange magnetic fluid that has worked so much mischief in the world. There was no organic disease, you see; only when my nerves were rested and right, my brain would be right. And the doctor gave me medicines and books and work, and when I saw the bat-like things again I was to go instantly to him. And after a little while I was not sure that I did see them. And in a little while longer they had ceased to come altogether. And I have had no more of them. I was on my parole then in the parlor, at the table, in the grounds. I felt that I was cured of whatever had ailed me: I could escape at any moment that I wished.

And it came Christmas time. A terrible longing for home overcame me—for my children. I thought of them at this time when I had been used to take such pains for their pleasure. I thought of the little empty stockings, the sad faces; I fancied I could hear them crying for me. I forgot all about my word of honor. It seemed to me that I should die, that I might as well die, if I could not see my little darlings, and hold them on my knees, and sing to them while the chimes were ringing in the Christmas Eve. And winter was here and there was so much to do for them. And I walked down the garden, and looked out at the gate, and opened it and went through. And I slept that night in a barn—so free, so free and glad! And the next day an old farmer and his sons, who thought they did me a service, brought me back, and of course I shrieked and raved. And so would you.

But since then I have been in this ward and a prisoner. I have my work, my amusement. I send such little things as I can make to my girls. I read. Sometimes of late I sing in the Sunday service. The place is a sightly place; the grounds, when we are taken out, are fine; the halls are spacious and pleasant.

Pleasant—but ah, when you have trodden them ten years!

And so, you see, if I were a clod, if I had no memory, no desires, if I had never been happy before, I might be happy now. I am confident the doctor thinks me well. But he has no orders to let me go. Sometimes it is so wearisome. And it might be worse if lately I had not been allowed a new service. And that is to try to make a woman smile who came here a year ago. She is a little woman, swarthy as a Malay, but her hair, that grows as rapidly as a fungus grows in the night, is whiter than leprosy: her eyebrows are so long and white that they veil and blanch her dark dim eyes; and she has no front teeth. A stone from a falling spire struck her from her horse, they say. The blow battered her and beat out reason and beauty. Her mind is dead: she remembers nothing, knows nothing; but she follows me about like a dog: she seems to want to do something for me, to propitiate me. All she ever says is to beg me to do her no harm. She will not go to sleep without my hand in hers. Sometimes, after long effort, I think there is a gleam of intelligence, but the doctor says there was once too much intelligence, and her case is hopeless.

Hopeless, poor thing!—that is an awful word: I could not wish it said for my worst enemy.

In spite of these ten years I cannot feel that it has yet been said for me.

If I am strange just now, it is only the excitement of seeing you, only the habit of the strange sights and sounds here. I should be calm and well enough at home. I sit and picture to myself that some time Spencer will come for me—will take me to my girls, my fireside, my music. I shall hear his voice, I shall rest in his arms, I shall be blest again. For, oh, Elizabeth, I do forgive him all!

Or if he will not dare to trust himself at first, I picture to myself how he will send another—some old friend who knew me before my trouble—who will see me and judge, and carry back report that I am all I used to be—some friend who will open the gates of heaven to me, or close the gates of hell upon me—who will hold my life and my fate.

If—oh if it should be you, Elizabeth!

1860

# MARK TWAIN

(1835–1910)

## *The Facts Concerning the Recent Carnival of Crime in Connecticut*

I WAS FEELING BLITHE, almost jocund. I put a match to my cigar, and just then the morning's mail was handed in. The first superscription I glanced at was in a handwriting that sent a thrill of pleasure through and through me. It was aunt Mary's; and she was the person I loved and honored most in all the world, outside of my own household. She had been my boyhood's idol; maturity, which is fatal to so many enchantments, had not been able to dislodge her from her pedestal; no, it had only justified her right to be there, and placed her dethronement permanently among the impossibilities. To show how strong her influence over me was, I will observe that long after everybody else's "*do*-stop-smoking" had ceased to affect me in the slightest degree, aunt Mary could still stir my torpid conscience into faint signs of life when she touched upon the matter. But all things have their limit, in this world. A happy day came at last, when even aunt Mary's words could no longer move me. I was not merely glad to see that day arrive; I was more than glad—I was grateful; for when its sun had set, the one alloy that was able to mar my enjoyment of my aunt's society was gone. The remainder of her stay with us that winter was in every way a delight. Of course she pleaded with me just as earnestly as ever, after that blessed day, to quit my pernicious habit, but to no purpose whatever; the moment she opened the subject I at once became calmly, peacefully, contentedly indifferent—absolutely, adamantinely indifferent. Consequently the closing weeks of that memorable visit melted away as pleasantly as a dream, they were so freighted, for me, with tranquil satisfaction. I could not have enjoyed my pet vice more if my gentle tormentor had been a smoker herself, and an advocate of the practice. Well, the sight of her handwriting reminded me that I was getting very hungry to see her again. I easily guessed what I should find in her letter. I opened it. Good! just as I expected; she was coming! Coming this very day, too, and by the morning train; I might expect her any moment.

I said to myself, "I am thoroughly happy and content, now. If my most pitiless enemy could appear before me at this moment, I would freely right any wrong I may have done him."

Straightway the door opened, and a shriveled, shabby dwarf entered. He was not more than two feet high. He seemed to be about forty years old. Every feature and every inch of him was a trifle out of shape; and so, while one could not put his finger upon any particular part and say, "This is a conspicuous deformity," the spectator perceived that this little person was a deformity as a whole—a vague, general, evenly-blended, nicely-adjusted deformity. There was a fox-like cunning in the face and the sharp little eyes, and also alertness and malice. And yet, this vile bit of human rubbish seemed to bear a sort of remote and ill-defined resemblance to me! It was dully perceptible in the mean form, the countenance, and even the clothes, gestures, manner, and attitudes of the creature. He was a far-fetched, dim suggestion of a burlesque upon me, a caricature of me in little. One thing about him struck me forcibly, and most unpleasantly: he was covered all over with a fuzzy, greenish mold, such as one sometimes sees upon mildewed bread. The sight of it was nauseating.

He stepped along with a chipper air, and flung himself into a doll's chair in a very free and easy way, without waiting to be asked. He tossed his hat into the waste basket. He picked up my old chalk pipe from the floor, gave the stem a wipe or two on his knee, filled the bowl from the tobacco-box at his side, and said to me in a tone of pert command,—

"Gimme a match!"

I blushed to the roots of my hair; partly with indignation, but mainly because it somehow seemed to me that this whole performance was very like an exaggeration of conduct which I myself had sometimes been guilty of in my intercourse with familiar friends;—but never, never with strangers, I observed to myself. I wanted to kick the pygmy into the fire, but some incomprehensible sense of being legally and legitimately under his authority forced me to obey his order. He applied the match to the pipe, took a contemplative whiff or two, and remarked, in an irritatingly familiar way,—

"Seems to me it 's devilish odd weather for this time of year."

I flushed again, and in anger and humiliation as before; for the language was hardly an exaggeration of some that I have uttered in my day, and moreover was delivered in a tone of voice and with an exasperating drawl that had the seeming of a deliberate travesty of my style. Now there is nothing I am quite so sensitive about as a mocking imitation of my drawling infirmity of speech. I spoke up sharply and said,—

"Look here, you miserable ash-cat! you will have to give a little more attention to your manners, or I will throw you out of the window!"

The manikin smiled a smile of malicious content and security, puffed a whiff of smoke contemptuously toward me, and said, with a still more elaborate drawl,—

"Come—go gently, now; don't put on *too* many airs with your betters."

This cool snub rasped me all over, but it seemed to subjugate me, too, for a moment. The pygmy contemplated me a while with his weasel eyes, and then said, in a peculiarly sneering way,—

"You turned a tramp away from your door this morning."

I said crustily,—

"Perhaps I did, perhaps I did n't. How do *you* know?"

"Well, I know. It is n't any matter *how* I know."

"Very well. Suppose I *did* turn a tramp away from the door—what of it?"

"Oh, nothing; nothing in particular. Only you lied to him."

"I *did n't*! That is, I"—

"Yes, but you did; you lied to him."

I felt a guilty pang,—in truth I had felt it forty times before that tramp had traveled a block from my door,—but still I resolved to make a show of feeling slandered; so I said,—

"This is a baseless impertinence. I said to the tramp"—

"There—wait. You were about to lie again. *I* know what you said to him. You said the cook was gone down town and there was nothing left from breakfast. Two lies. You knew the cook was behind the door, and plenty of provisions behind *her*."

This astonishing accuracy silenced me; and it filled me with wondering speculations, too, as to how this cub could have got his information. Of course he could have culled the conversation from the tramp, but by what sort of magic had he contrived to find out about the concealed cook? Now the dwarf spoke again:—

"It was rather pitiful, rather small, in you to refuse to read that poor young woman's manuscript the other day, and give her an opinion as to its literary value; and she had come so far, too, and *so* hopefully. Now *was n't* it?"

I felt like a cur! And I had felt so every time the thing had recurred to my mind, I may as well confess. I flushed hotly and said,—

"Look here, have you nothing better to do than prowl around prying into other people's business? Did that girl tell you that?"

"Never mind whether she did or not. The main thing is, you did that contemptible thing. And you felt ashamed of it afterwards. Aha! you feel ashamed of it *now*!"

This with a sort of devilish glee. With fiery earnestness I responded,—

"I told that girl, in the kindest, gentlest way, that I could not consent to deliver judgment upon *any* one's manuscript, because an individual's verdict was worthless. It might underrate a work of high merit and lose it to the world, or it might overrate a trashy production and so open the way for its infliction upon the world. I said that the great public was the only tribunal competent to sit in judgment upon a literary effort, and therefore it must be best to lay it before that tribunal in the outset, since in the end it must stand or fall by that mighty court's decision any way."

"Yes, you said all that. So you did, you juggling, small-souled shuffler! And yet when the happy hopefulness faded out of that poor girl's face, when you saw her furtively slip beneath her shawl the scroll she had so patiently and honestly scribbled at,—so ashamed of her darling now, so proud of it before,—when you saw the gladness go out of her eyes and the tears come there, when she crept away so humbly who had come so"—

"Oh, peace! peace! peace! Blister your merciless tongue, haven't all these thoughts tortured me enough, without *your* coming here to fetch them back again?"

Remorse! remorse! It seemed to me that it would eat the very heart out of me! And yet that small fiend only sat there leering at me with joy and contempt, and placidly chuckling. Presently he began to speak again. Every sentence was an accusation, and every accusation a truth. Every clause was freighted with sarcasm and derision, every slow-dropping word burned like vitriol. The dwarf reminded me of times when I had flown at my children in anger and punished them for faults which a little inquiry would have taught me that others, and not they, had committed. He reminded me of how I had disloyally allowed old friends to be traduced in my hearing, and been too craven to utter a word in their defense. He reminded me of many dishonest things which I had done; of many which I had procured to be done by children and other irresponsible persons; of some which I had planned, thought upon, and longed to do, and been kept from the performance by fear of consequences only. With exquisite cruelty he recalled to my mind, item by item, wrongs and unkindnesses I had inflicted and humiliations I had put upon friends since dead, "who died thinking of those injuries, maybe, and grieving over them," he added, by way of poison to the stab.

"For instance," said he, "take the case of your younger brother, when you two were boys together, many a long year ago. He always lovingly trusted in you with a fidelity that your manifold treacheries were not able to shake. He followed you about like a dog, content to suffer wrong and abuse if he might only be with you; patient under these injuries so long as it was your hand that inflicted them. The latest picture you have of him in health and strength must be such a comfort to you! You pledged your honor that if he would let you blindfold him no harm should come to him; and then, giggling and choking over the rare fun of the joke, you led him to a brook thinly glazed with ice, and pushed him in; and how you did laugh! Man, you will never forget the gentle, reproachful look he gave you as he struggled shivering out, if you live a thousand years! Oho! you see it now, you see it *now*!"

"Beast, I have seen it a million times, and shall see it a million more! and may you rot away piecemeal, and suffer till doomsday what I suffer now, for bringing it back to me again!"

The dwarf chuckled contentedly, and went on with his accusing history of my career. I dropped into a moody, vengeful state, and suffered in silence under the merciless lash. At last this remark of his gave me a sudden rouse:—

"Two months ago, on a Tuesday, you woke up, away in the night, and fell to thinking, with shame, about a peculiarly mean and pitiful act of yours toward a poor ignorant Indian in the wilds of the Rocky Mountains in the winter of eighteen hundred and"—

"Stop a moment, devil! Stop! Do you mean to tell me that even my very *thoughts* are not hidden from you?"

"It seems to look like that. Did n't you think the thoughts I have just mentioned?"

"If I did n't, I wish I may never breathe again! Look here, friend—look me in the eye. Who *are* you?"

"Well, who do you think?"

"I think you are Satan himself. I think you are the devil."

"No."

"No? Then who *can* you be?"

"Would you really like to know?"

"*Indeed* I would."

"Well, I am your *Conscience*!"

In an instant I was in a blaze of joy and exultation. I sprang at the creature, roaring,—

"Curse you, I have wished a hundred million times that you were tangible, and that I could get my hands on your throat once! Oh, but I will wreak a deadly vengeance on"—

Folly! Lightning does not move more quickly than my Conscience did! He darted aloft so suddenly that in the moment my fingers clutched the empty air he was already perched on the top of the high book-case, with his thumb at his nose in token of derision. I flung the poker at him, and missed. I fired the boot-jack. In a blind rage I flew from place to place, and snatched and hurled any missile that came handy; the storm of books, inkstands, and chunks of coal gloomed the air and beat about the manikin's perch relentlessly, but all to no purpose; the nimble figure dodged every shot; and not only that, but burst into a cackle of sarcastic and triumphant laughter as I sat down exhausted. While I puffed and gasped with fatigue and excitement, my Conscience talked to this effect:—

"My good slave, you are curiously witless—no, I mean characteristically so. In truth, you are always consistent, always yourself, always an ass. Otherwise it must have occurred to you that if you attempted this murder with a sad heart and a heavy conscience, I would droop under the burdening influence instantly. Fool, I should have weighed a ton, and could not have budged from the floor; but instead, you are so cheerfully anxious to kill me that your conscience is as light as a feather; hence I am away up here out of your reach. I can almost respect a mere ordinary sort of fool; but *you*—pah!"

I would have given anything, then, to be heavy-hearted, so that I could get this person down from there and take his life, but I could no more be heavy-hearted over such a desire than I could have sorrowed over its accomplishment. So I could only look longingly up at my master, and rave at the ill-luck that denied me a heavy conscience the one only time that I had ever wanted such a thing in my life. By and by I got to musing over the hour's strange adventure, and of course my human curiosity began to work. I set myself to framing in my mind some questions for this fiend to answer. Just then one of my boys entered, leaving the door open behind him, and exclaimed,—

"My! what *has* been going on, here! The book-case is all one riddle of"—

I sprang up in consternation, and shouted,—

"Out of this! Hurry! Jump! Fly! Shut the door! Quick, or my Conscience will get away!"

The door slammed to, and I locked it. I glanced up and was grateful, to the bottom of my heart, to see that my owner was still my prisoner. I said,—

"Hang you, I might have lost you! Children are the heedlessest creatures. But look here, friend, the boy did not seem to notice you at all; how is that?"

"For a very good reason. I am invisible to all but you."

I made mental note of that piece of information with a good deal of satisfaction. I could kill this miscreant now, if I got a chance, and no one would know it. But this very reflection made me so light-hearted that my Conscience could hardly keep his seat, but was like to float aloft toward the ceiling like a toy balloon. I said, presently,—

"Come, my Conscience, let us be friendly. Let us fly a flag of truce for a while. I am suffering to ask you some questions."

"Very well. Begin."

"Well, then, in the first place, why were you never visible to me before?"

"Because you never asked to see me before; that is, you never asked in the right spirit and the proper form before. You were just in the right spirit this time, and when you called for your most pitiless enemy I was that person by a very large majority, though you did not suspect it."

"Well, did that remark of mine turn you into flesh and blood?"

"No. It only made me visible to you. I am unsubstantial, just as other spirits are."

This remark prodded me with a sharp misgiving. If he was unsubstantial, how was I going to kill him? But I dissembled, and said persuasively,—

"Conscience, it is n't sociable of you to keep at such a distance. Come down and take another smoke."

This was answered with a look that was full of derision, and with this observation added:—

"Come where you can get at me and kill me? The invitation is declined with thanks."

"All right," said I to myself; "so it seems a spirit *can* be killed, after all; there will be one spirit lacking in this world, presently, or I lose my guess." Then I said aloud,—

"Friend"—

"There; wait a bit. I am not your friend, I am your enemy; I am not your equal, I am your master. Call me 'my lord,' if you please. You are too familiar."

"I don't like such titles. I am willing to call you *sir*. That is as far as"—

"We will have no argument about this. Just obey; that is all. Go on with your chatter."

"Very well, my lord,—since nothing but my lord will suit you,—I was going to ask you how long you will be visible to me?"

"Always!"

I broke out with strong indignation: "This is simply an outrage. That is what I think of it. You have dogged, and dogged, and *dogged* me, all the days of my life, invisible. That was misery enough; now to have such a looking thing as you tagging after me like another shadow all the rest of my days is an intolerable prospect. You have my opinion, my lord; make the most of it."

"My lad, there was never so pleased a conscience in this world as I was when you made me visible. It gives me an inconceivable advantage. *Now*, I can look you straight in the eye, and call you names, and leer at you, jeer at you, sneer at you; and *you* know what eloquence there is in visible gesture and expression, more especially when the effect is heightened by audible speech. I shall always address you henceforth in your o-w-n s-n-i-v-e-l-i-n-g d-r-a-w-l—baby!"

I let fly with the coal-hod. No result. My lord said,—

"Come, come! Remember the flag of truce!"

"Ah, I forgot that. I will try to be civil; and *you* try it, too, for a novelty. The idea of a *civil* conscience! It is a good joke; an excellent joke. All the consciences *I* have ever heard of were nagging, badgering, fault-finding, execrable savages! Yes; and always in a sweat about some poor little insignificant trifle or other—destruction catch the lot of them, *I* say! I would trade mine for the small-pox and seven kinds of consumption, and be glad of the chance. Now tell me, why *is* it that a conscience can't haul a man over the coals once, for an offense, and then let him alone? Why is it that it wants to keep on pegging at him, day and night and night and day, week in and week out, forever and ever, about the same old thing? There is no sense in that, and no reason in it. I think a conscience that will act like that is meaner than the very dirt itself."

"Well, *we* like it; that suffices."

"Do you do it with the honest intent to improve a man?"

That question produced a sarcastic smile, and this reply:—

"No, sir. Excuse me. We do it simply because it is 'business.' It is our trade. The *purpose* of it *is* to improve the man, but *we* are merely disinterested agents. We are appointed by authority, and have n't anything to say in the matter. We obey orders and leave the consequences where they belong. But I am willing to admit this much: we *do* crowd the orders a trifle when we get a chance, which is most of the time. We enjoy it. We are instructed to remind a man a few times of an error; and I don't mind acknowledging that we try to give pretty good measure. And when we get hold of a man of a peculiarly sensitive nature, oh, but we do haze him! I have known consciences to come all the way from China and Russia to see a person of that kind put through his paces, on a special occasion. Why, I knew a man of that sort who had accidentally crippled a mulatto baby; the news went abroad, and I wish you may never commit another sin if the consciences did n't flock from all over the earth to enjoy the fun and help his master exercise him. That man walked the floor in torture for forty-eight hours, without eating or sleeping, and then blew his brains out. The child was perfectly well again in three weeks."

"Well, you are a precious crew, not to put it too strong. I think I begin to see, now, why you have always been a trifle inconsistent with me. In your anxiety to get all the juice you can out of a sin, you make a man repent of it in three or four different ways. For instance, you found fault with me for lying to that tramp, and I suffered over that. But it was only yesterday that I told a tramp the square truth, to wit, that, it being regarded as bad citizenship to encourage vagrancy, I would give him nothing. What did you do *then*? Why, you made me say to myself, 'Ah, it would have been so much kinder and more blameless to ease him off with a little white lie, and send him away feeling that if he could not have bread, the gentle treatment was at least something to be grateful for!' Well, I suffered all day about *that*. Three days before, I had fed a tramp, and fed him freely, supposing it a virtuous act. Straight off you said, 'O false citizen, to have fed a tramp!' and I suffered as usual. I gave a tramp work; you objected to it,—*after* the contract was made, of course; you never speak up beforehand. Next, I *refused* a tramp work; you objected to *that*. Next, I proposed to kill a tramp; you kept me awake all night, oozing remorse at every pore. Sure I was going to be right *this* time, I sent the next tramp away with my benediction; and I wish you may live as long as I do, if you did n't make me smart all night again because I did n't kill him. Is there *any* way of satisfying that malignant invention which is called a conscience?"

"Ha, ha! this is luxury! Go on!"

"But come, now, answer me that question. *Is* there any way?"

"Well, none that I propose to tell *you*, my son. Ass! I don't care *what* act you may turn your hand to, I can straightway whisper a word in your ear and make you think you have committed a dreadful meanness. It is my *business*—and my joy—to make you repent of *every*thing you do. If I have fooled away any opportunities it was not intentional; I beg to assure you it was not intentional."

"Don't worry; you have n't missed a trick that *I* know of. I never did a thing in all my life, virtuous or otherwise, that I didn't repent of within twenty-four hours. In church last Sunday I listened to a charity sermon. My first impulse was to give three hundred and fifty dollars; I repented of that and reduced it a hundred; repented of that and reduced it another hundred; repented of that and reduced it another hundred; repented of that and reduced the remaining fifty to twenty-five; repented of that and came down to fifteen; repented of that and dropped to two dollars and a half; when the plate came around at last, I repented once more and contributed ten cents. Well, when I got home, I did wish to goodness I had that ten cents back again! You never *did* let me get through a charity sermon without having something to sweat about."

"Oh, and I never shall, I never shall. You can always depend on me."

"I think so. Many and many's the restless night I've wanted to take you by the neck. If I could only get hold of you now!"

"Yes, no doubt. But I am not an ass; I am only the saddle of an ass. But go on, go on. You entertain me more than I like to confess."

"I am glad of that. (You will not mind my lying a little, to keep in practice.) Look here; not to be too personal, I think you are about the shabbiest and most contemptible little shriveled-up reptile that can be imagined. I am grateful enough that you are invisible to other people, for I should die with shame to be seen with such a mildewed monkey of a conscience as *you* are. Now if you were five or six feet high, and"—

"Oh, come! who is to blame?"

"*I* don't know."

"Why, you are; nobody else."

"Confound you, I was n't consulted about your personal appearance."

"I don't care, you had a good deal to do with it, nevertheless. When you were eight or nine years old, I was seven feet high and as pretty as a picture."

"I wish you had died young! So you have grown the wrong way, have you?"

"Some of us grow one way and some the other. You had a large conscience once; if you 've a small conscience now, I reckon there are reasons for it. However, both of us are to blame, you and I. You see, you used to be conscientious about a great many things; morbidly so, I may say. It was a great many years ago. You probably do not remember it, now. Well, I took a great interest in my work, and I so enjoyed the anguish which certain pet sins of yours afflicted you with, that I kept pelting at you until I rather overdid the matter. You began to rebel. Of course I began to lose ground, then, and shrivel a little,—diminish in stature, get moldy, and grow deformed. The more I weakened, the more stubbornly you fastened on to those particular sins; till at last the places on my person that represent those vices became as callous as shark skin. Take smoking, for instance. I played that card a little too long, and I lost. When people plead with you at this late day to quit that vice, that old callous place seems to enlarge and cover me all over like a shirt of mail. It exerts a mysterious, smothering effect; and presently I, your faithful hater, your devoted Conscience, go sound asleep! Sound? It is no name for it. I could n't hear it thunder at such a time. You have some few other vices—perhaps eighty, or maybe ninety—that affect me in much the same way."

"This is flattering; you must be asleep a good part of your time."

"Yes, of late years. I should be asleep *all* the time, but for the help I get."

"Who helps you?"

"Other consciences. Whenever a person whose conscience I am acquainted with tries to plead with you about the vices you are callous to, I get my friend to give his client a pang concerning some villainy of his own, and that shuts off his meddling and starts him off to hunt personal consolation. My field of usefulness is about trimmed down to tramps, budding authoresses, and that line of goods, now; but don't you worry—I 'll harry you on *them* while they last! Just you put your trust in me."

"I think I can. But if you had only been good enough to mention these facts some thirty years ago, I should have turned my particular attention to sin, and I think that by this time I should not only have had you pretty permanently asleep on the entire list of human vices, but reduced to the size of a homœopathic pill, at that. That is about the style of conscience *I* am pining for. If I only had you shrunk down to a homœopathic pill, and could get my hands on you, would I put you in a glass case for a keepsake? No, sir. I would give you to a yellow dog! That is where *you* ought to be—you and all your tribe. You are not fit to be in society, in my opinion. Now another question. Do you know a good many consciences in this section?"

"Plenty of them."

"I would give anything to see some of them! Could you bring them here? And would they be visible to me?"

"Certainly not."

"I suppose I ought to have known that, without asking. But no matter, you can describe them. Tell me about my neighbor Thompson's conscience, please."

"Very well. I know him intimately; have known him many years. I knew him when he was eleven feet high and of a faultless figure. But he is very rusty and tough and misshapen, now, and hardly ever interests himself about anything. As to his present size—well, he sleeps in a cigar box."

"Likely enough. There are few smaller, meaner men in this region than Hugh Thompson. Do you know Robinson's conscience?"

"Yes. He is a shade under four and a half feet high; used to be a blonde; is a brunette, now, but still shapely and comely."

"Well, Robinson is a good fellow. Do you know Tom Smith's conscience?"

"I have known him from childhood. He was thirteen inches high, and rather sluggish, when he was two years old—as nearly all of us are, at that age. He is thirty-seven feet high, now, and the stateliest figure in America. His legs are still racked with growing-pains, but he has a good time, nevertheless. Never sleeps. He is the most active and energetic member of the New England Conscience Club; is president of it. Night and day you can find him pegging away at Smith, panting with his labor, sleeves rolled up, countenance all alive with enjoyment. He has got his victim splendidly dragooned, now. He can make poor Smith imagine that the most innocent little thing he does is an odious sin; and then he sets to work and almost tortures the soul out of him about it."

"Smith is the noblest man in all this section, and the purest; and yet is always breaking his heart because he cannot be good!

Only a conscience *could* find pleasure in heaping agony upon a spirit like that. Do you know my aunt Mary's conscience?"

"I have seen her at a distance, but am not acquainted with her. She lives in the open air altogether, because no door is large enough to admit her."

"I can believe that. Let me see. Do you know the conscience of that publisher who once stole some sketches of mine for a 'series' of his, and then left me to pay the law expenses I had to incur in order to choke him off?"

"Yes. He has a wide fame. He was exhibited, a month ago, with some other antiquities, for the benefit of a recent Member of the Cabinet's conscience, that was starving in exile. Tickets and fares were high, but I traveled for nothing by pretending to be the conscience of an editor, and got in for half price by representing myself to be the conscience of a clergyman. However, the publisher's conscience, which was to have been the main feature of the entertainment, was a failure—as an exhibition. He was there, but what of that? The management had provided a microscope with a magnifying power of only thirty thousand diameters, and so nobody got to see him, after all. There was great and general dissatisfaction, of course, but"—

Just here there was an eager footstep on the stair; I opened the door, and my aunt Mary burst into the room. It was a joyful meeting, and a cheery bombardment of questions and answers concerning family matters ensued. By and by my aunt said,—

"But I am going to abuse you a little now. You promised me, the day I saw you last, that you would look after the needs of the poor family around the corner as faithfully as I had done it myself. Well, I found out by accident that you failed of your promise. *Was* that right?"

In simple truth, I never had thought of that family a second time! And now such a splintering pang of guilt shot through me! I glanced up at my Conscience. Plainly, my heavy heart was affecting him. His body was drooping forward; he seemed about to fall from the book-case. My aunt continued:—

"And think how you have neglected my poor *protégée* at the almshouse, you dear, hard-hearted promise-breaker!" I blushed scarlet, and my tongue was tied. As the sense of my guilty negligence waxed sharper and stronger, my Conscience began to sway heavily back and forth; and when my aunt, after a little pause, said in a grieved tone, "Since you never once went to see her, maybe it will not distress you now to know that that poor child died, months ago, utterly friendless and forsaken!" my Conscience could no longer bear up under the weight of my sufferings, but tumbled headlong from his high perch and struck the floor with a dull, leaden thump. He lay there writhing with pain and quaking with apprehension, but straining every muscle in frantic efforts to get up. In a fever of expectancy I sprang to the door, locked it, placed my back against it, and bent a watchful gaze upon my struggling master. Already my fingers were itching to begin their murderous work.

"Oh, what *can* be the matter!" exclaimed my aunt, shrinking from me, and following with her frightened eyes the direction of mine. My breath was coming in short, quick gasps now, and my excitement was almost uncontrollable. My aunt cried out,—

"Oh, do not look so! You appall me! Oh, what can the matter be? What is it you see? Why do you stare so? Why do you work your fingers like that?"

"Peace, woman!" I said, in a hoarse whisper. "Look elsewhere; pay no attention to me; it is nothing—nothing. I am often this way. It will pass in a moment. It comes from smoking too much."

My injured lord was up, wild-eyed with terror, and trying to hobble toward the door. I could hardly breathe, I was so wrought up. My aunt wrung her hands, and said,—

"Oh, I knew how it would be; I knew it would come to this at last! Oh, I implore you to crush out that fatal habit while it may yet be time! You must not, you shall not be deaf to my supplications longer!" My struggling Conscience showed sudden signs of weariness! "Oh, promise me you will throw off this hateful slavery of tobacco!" My Conscience began to reel drowsily, and grope with his hands—enchanting spectacle! "I beg you, I beseech you, I implore you! Your reason is deserting you! There is madness in your eye! It flames with frenzy! Oh, hear me, hear me, and be saved! See, I plead with you on my very knees!" As she sank before me my Conscience reeled again, and then drooped languidly to the floor, blinking toward me a last supplication for mercy, with heavy eyes. "Oh, promise, or you are lost! Promise, and be redeemed! Promise! Promise and live!" With a long-drawn sigh my conquered Conscience closed his eyes and fell fast asleep!

With an exultant shout I sprang past my aunt, and in an instant I had my life-long foe by the throat. After so many years of waiting and longing, he was mine at last. I tore him to shreds and fragments. I rent the fragments to bits. I cast the bleeding rubbish into the fire, and drew into my nostrils the grateful incense of my burnt-offering. At last, and forever, my Conscience was dead!

I was a free man! I turned upon my poor aunt, who was almost petrified with terror, and shouted,—

"Out of this with your paupers, your charities, your reforms, your pestilent morals! You behold before you a man whose life-conflict is done, whose soul is at peace; a man whose heart is dead to sorrow, dead to suffering, dead to remorse; a man WITHOUT A CONSCIENCE! In my joy I spare you, though I could throttle you and never feel a pang! Fly!"

She fled. Since that day my life is all bliss. Bliss, unalloyed bliss. Nothing in all the world could persuade me to have a conscience again. I settled all my old outstanding scores, and began the world anew. I killed thirty-eight persons during the first two weeks—all of them on account of ancient grudges. I burned a dwelling that interrupted my view. I swindled a widow and some orphans out of their last cow, which is a very good one, though not thoroughbred, I believe. I have also committed scores of crimes, of various kinds, and have enjoyed my work exceedingly, whereas it would formerly have broken my heart and turned my hair gray, I have no doubt.

In conclusion I wish to state, by way of advertisement, that medical colleges desiring assorted tramps for scientific purposes, either by the gross, by cord measurement, or per ton, will do well to examine the lot in my cellar before purchasing elsewhere, as these were all selected and prepared by myself, and can be had at a low rate, because I wish to clear out my stock and get ready for the spring trade.

1876

# MARK TWAIN

(1835–1910)

---

## *The Invalid's Story*[*]

I SEEM SIXTY and married, but these effects are due to my condition and sufferings, for I am a bachelor, and only forty-one. It will be hard for you to believe that I, who am now but a shadow, was a hale, hearty man two short years ago,—a man of iron, a very athlete!—yet such is the simple truth. But stranger still than this fact is the way in which I lost my health. I lost it through helping to take care of a box of guns on a two-hundred-mile railway journey one winter's night. It is the actual truth, and I will tell you about it.

I belong in Cleveland, Ohio. One winter's night, two years ago, I reached home just after dark, in a driving snow-storm, and the first thing I heard when I entered the house was that my dearest boyhood friend and schoolmate, John B. Hackett, had died the day before, and that his last utterance had been a desire that I would take his remains home to his poor old father and mother in Wisconsin. I was greatly shocked and grieved, but there was no time to waste in emotions; I must start at once. I took the card, marked "Deacon Levi Hackett, Bethlehem, Wisconsin," and hurried off through the whistling storm to the railway station. Arrived there I found the long white-pine box which had been described to me; I fastened the card to it with some tacks, saw it put safely aboard the express car, and then ran into the eating-room to provide myself with a sandwich and some cigars. When I returned, presently, there was my coffin-box *back again*, apparently, and a young fellow examining around it, with a card in his hand, and some tacks and a hammer! I was astonished and puzzled. He began to nail on his card, and I rushed out to the express car, in a good deal of a state of mind, to ask for an explanation. But no—there was my

* Left out of these "Rambling Notes," when originally published in the "Atlantic Monthly," because it was feared that the story was not true, and at that time there was no way of proving that it was not.—M. T.

box, all right, in the express car; it had n't been disturbed. [The fact is that without my suspecting it a prodigious mistake had been made. I was carrying off a box of *guns* which that young fellow had come to the station to ship to a rifle company in Peoria, Illinois, and *he* had got my corpse!] Just then the conductor sung out "All aboard," and I jumped into the express car and got a comfortable seat on a bale of buckets. The expressman was there, hard at work,—a plain man of fifty, with a simple, honest, good-natured face, and a breezy, practical heartiness in his general style. As the train moved off a stranger skipped into the car and set a package of peculiarly mature and capable Limburger cheese on one end of my coffin-box—I mean my box of guns. That is to say, I know *now* that it was Limburger cheese, but at that time I never had heard of the article in my life, and of course was wholly ignorant of its character. Well, we sped through the wild night, the bitter storm raged on, a cheerless misery stole over me, my heart went down, down, down! The old expressman made a brisk remark or two about the tempest and the arctic weather, slammed his sliding doors to, and bolted them, closed his window down tight, and then went bustling around, here and there and yonder, setting things to rights, and all the time contentedly humming "Sweet By and By," in a low tone, and flatting a good deal. Presently I began to detect a most evil and searching odor stealing about on the frozen air. This depressed my spirits still more, because of course I attributed it to my poor departed friend. There was something infinitely saddening about his calling himself to my remembrance in this dumb pathetic way, so it was hard to keep the tears back. Moreover, it distressed me on account of the old expressman, who, I was afraid, might notice it. However, he went humming tranquilly on, and gave no sign; and for this I was grateful. Grateful, yes, but still uneasy; and soon I began to feel more and more uneasy every minute, for every minute that went by that odor thickened up the more, and got to be more and more gamey and hard to stand. Presently, having got things arranged to his satisfaction, the expressman got some wood and made up a tremendous fire in his stove. This distressed me more than I can tell, for I could not but feel that it was a mistake. I was sure that the effect would be deleterious upon my poor departed friend. Thompson—the expressman's name was

Thompson, as I found out in the course of the night—now went poking around his car, stopping up whatever stray cracks he could find, remarking that it did n't make any difference what kind of a night it was outside, he calculated to make *us* comfortable, anyway. I said nothing, but I believed he was not choosing the right way. Meantime he was humming to himself just as before; and meantime, too, the stove was getting hotter and hotter, and the place closer and closer. I felt myself growing pale and qualmish, but grieved in silence and said nothing. Soon I noticed that the "Sweet By and By" was gradually fading out; next it ceased altogether, and there was an ominous stillness. After a few moments Thompson said,—

"Pfew! I reckon it ain't no cinnamon 't I 've loaded up thishyer stove with!"

He gasped once or twice, then moved toward the cof—gunbox, stood over that Limburger cheese part of a moment, then came back and sat down near me, looking a good deal impressed. After a contemplative pause, he said, indicating the box with a gesture,—

"Friend of yourn?"

"Yes," I said with a sigh.

"He 's pretty ripe, *ain't* he!"

Nothing further was said for perhaps a couple of minutes, each being busy with his own thoughts; then Thompson said, in a low, awed voice,—

"Sometimes it 's uncertain whether they 're really gone or not,—*seem* gone, you know—body warm, joints limber—and so, although you *think* they 're gone, you don't really know. I've had cases in my car. It 's perfectly awful, becuz *you* don't know what minute they 'll rise right up and look at you!" Then, after a pause, and slightly lifting his elbow toward the box,—"But *he* ain't in no trance! No, sir, I go bail for *him*!"

We sat some time, in meditative silence, listening to the wind and the roar of the train; then Thompson said, with a good deal of feeling,—

"Well-a-well, we 've all got to go, they ain't no getting around it. Man that is born of woman is of few days and far between, as Scriptur' says. Yes, you look at it any way you want to, it 's awful solemn and cur'us: they ain't *nobody* can get around it; *all 's* got to go—just *everybody*, as you may say. One day you 're hearty and strong"—here he scrambled to his feet and broke a pane and stretched his nose out at it a moment or two, then sat down again while I struggled up and thrust my nose out at the same place, and this we kept on doing every now and then—"and next day he 's cut down like the grass, and the places which knowed him then knows him no more forever, as Scriptur' says. Yes-'ndeedy, it 's awful solemn and cur'us; but we 've all got to go, one time or another; they ain't no getting around it."

There was another long pause; then,—

"What did he die of?"

I said I did n't know.

"How long has he ben dead?"

It seemed judicious to enlarge the facts to fit the probabilities; so I said,—

"Two or three days."

But it did no good; for Thompson received it with an injured look which plainly said, "Two or three *years*, you mean." Then he went right along, placidly ignoring my statement, and gave his views at considerable length upon the unwisdom of putting off burials too long. Then he lounged off toward the box, stood a moment, then came back on a sharp trot and visited the broken pane, observing,—

"'T would 'a' ben a dum sight better, all around, if they 'd started him along last summer."

Thompson sat down and buried his face in his red silk handkerchief, and began to slowly sway and rock his body like one who is doing his best to endure the almost unendurable. By this time the fragrance—if you may call it fragrance—was just about suffocating, as near as you can come at it. Thompson's face was turning gray; I knew mine had n't any color left in it. By and by Thompson rested his forehead in his left hand, with his elbow on his knee, and sort of waved his red handkerchief towards the box with his other hand, and said,—

"I 've carried a many a one of 'em,—some of 'em considerable overdue, too,—but, lordy, he just lays over 'em all!—and does it *easy*. Cap., they was heliotrope to *him*!"

This recognition of my poor friend gratified me, in spite of the sad circumstances, because it had so much the sound of a compliment.

Pretty soon it was plain that something had got to be done. I suggested cigars. Thompson thought it was a good idea. He said,—

"Likely it 'll modify him some."

We puffed gingerly along for a while, and tried hard to imagine that things were improved. But it was n't any use. Before very long, and without any consultation, both cigars were quietly dropped from our nerveless fingers at the same moment. Thompson said, with a sigh,—

"No, Cap., it don't modify him worth a cent. Fact is, it makes him worse, becuz it appears to stir up his ambition. What do you reckon we better do, now?"

I was not able to suggest anything; indeed, I had to be swallowing and swallowing, all the time, and did not like to trust myself to speak. Thompson fell to maundering, in a desultory and low-spirited way, about the miserable experiences of this night; and he got to referring to my poor friend by various titles,—sometimes military ones, sometimes civil ones; and I noticed that as fast as my poor friend's effectiveness grew, Thompson promoted him accordingly,—gave him a bigger title. Finally he said,—

"I 've got an idea. Suppos'n' we buckle down to it and give the Colonel a bit of a shove towards t' other end of the car?—about ten foot, say. He would n't have so much influence, then, don't you reckon?"

I said it was a good scheme. So we took in a good fresh breath at the broken pane, calculating to hold it till we got through; then we went there and bent down over that deadly cheese and took a grip on the box. Thompson nodded "All ready," and then we threw ourselves forward with all our might; but Thompson slipped, and slumped down with his nose on the cheese, and his breath got loose. He gagged and gasped, and floundered up and made a break for the door, pawing the air and saying, hoarsely, "Don't hender me!—gimme the road! I 'm a-dying; gimme the road!" Out on the cold platform I sat down and held his head a while, and he revived. Presently he said,—

"Do you reckon we started the Gen'rul any?"

I said no; we had n't budged him.

"Well, then, *that* idea 's up the flume. We got to think up something else. He 's suited wher' he is, I reckon; and if that 's the way he feels about it, and has made up his mind that he don't wish to be disturbed, you bet you he 's a-going to have his own way in the business. Yes, better leave him right wher' he is, long as he wants it so; becuz he holds all the trumps, don't you know, and so it stands to reason that the man that lays out to alter his plans for him is going to get left."

But we could n't stay out there in that mad storm; we should have frozen to death. So we went in again and shut the door, and began to suffer once more and take turns at the break in the window. By and by, as we were starting away from a station where we had stopped a moment Thompson pranced in cheerily, and exclaimed,—

"We 're all right, now! I reckon we 've got the Commodore this time. I judge I 've got the stuff here that 'll take the tuck out of him."

It was carbolic acid. He had a carboy of it. He sprinkled it all around everywhere; in fact he drenched everything with it, rifle-box, cheese, and all. Then we sat down, feeling pretty hopeful. But it was n't for long. You see the two perfumes began to mix, and then—well, pretty soon we made a break for the door; and out there Thompson swabbed his face with his bandanna and said in a kind of disheartened way,—

"It ain't no use. We can't buck agin *him*. He just utilizes everything we put up to modify him with, and gives it his own flavor and plays it back on us. Why, Cap., don't you know, it 's as much as a hundred times worse in there now than it was when he first got a-going. I never *did* see one of 'em warm up to his work so, and take such a dumnation interest in it. No, sir, I never did, as long as I 've ben on the road; and I 've carried a many a one of 'em, as I was telling you."

We went in again, after we were frozen pretty stiff; but my, we could n't *stay* in, now. So we just waltzed back and forth, freezing, and thawing, and stifling, by turns. In about an hour we stopped at another station; and as we left it Thompson came in with a bag, and said,—

"Cap., I 'm a-going to chance him once more,—just this once; and if we don't fetch him this time, the thing for us to do, is to just throw up the sponge and withdraw from the canvass. That 's the way *I* put it up."

He had brought a lot of chicken feathers, and dried apples, and leaf tobacco, and rags, and old shoes, and sulphur, and assafœtida, and one thing or another; and he piled them on a breadth of sheet iron in the middle of the floor, and set fire to them. When they got well started, I could n't see, myself, how even the corpse could stand it. All that went before was just simply poetry to that smell,—but mind you, the original smell stood up out of it just as sublime as ever,—fact is, these other smells just seemed to give it a better hold; and my, how rich it was! I did n't make these reflections there—there was n't time—made them on the platform. And breaking for the platform, Thompson got suffocated and fell; and before I got him dragged out, which I did by the collar, I was mighty near gone myself. When we revived, Thompson said dejectedly,—

"We got to stay out here, Cap. We got to do it. They ain't no other way. The Governor wants to travel alone, and he 's fixed so he can outvote us."

And presently he added,—

"And don't you know, we 're *pisoned*. It 's *our* last trip, you can make up your mind to it. Typhoid fever is what 's going to come of this. I feel it a-coming right now. Yes, sir, we 're elected, just as sure as you 're born."

We were taken from the platform an hour later, frozen and insensible, at the next station, and I went straight off into a virulent fever, and never knew anything again for three weeks. I found out, then, that I had spent that awful night with a harmless box of rifles and a lot of innocent cheese; but the news was too late to save *me*; imagination had done its work, and my health was permanently shattered; neither Bermuda nor any other land can ever bring it back to me. This is my last trip; I am on my way home to die.

[1877]

# MARK TWAIN

(1835–1910)

---

## *Jim Baker's Blue-Jay Yarn*

ANIMALS TALK to each other, of course. There can be no question about that; but I suppose there are very few people who can understand them. I never knew but one man who could. I knew he could, however, because he told me so himself. He was a middle-aged, simple-hearted miner who had lived in a lonely corner of California, among the woods and mountains, a good many years, and had studied the ways of his only neighbors, the beasts and the birds, until he believed he could accurately translate any remark which they made. This was Jim Baker. According to Jim Baker, some animals have only a limited education, and use only very simple words, and scarcely ever a comparison or a flowery figure; whereas, certain other animals have a large vocabulary, a fine command of language and a ready and fluent delivery; consequently these latter talk a great deal; they like it; they are conscious of their talent, and they enjoy "showing off." Baker said, that after long and careful observation, he had come to the conclusion that the blue-jays were the best talkers he had found among birds and beasts. Said he:—

"There's more *to* a blue-jay than any other creature. He has got more moods, and more different kinds of feelings than other creature; and mind you, whatever a blue-jay feels, he can put into language. And no mere commonplace language, either, but rattling, out-and-out book-talk—and bristling with metaphor, too—just bristling! And as for command of language—why *you* never see a blue-jay get stuck for a word. No man ever did. They just boil out of him! And another thing: I've noticed a good deal, and there's no bird, or cow, or anything that uses as good grammar as a blue-jay. You may say a cat uses good grammar. Well, a cat does—but you let a cat get excited, once; you let a cat get to pulling fur with another cat on a shed, nights, and you'll hear grammar that will give you the lockjaw. Ignorant people think it's the *noise* which fighting cats make that is so aggravating, but it ain't so; it's the sickening grammar they use. Now I've never heard a jay use bad grammar but very seldom; and when they do, they are as ashamed as a human; they shut right down and leave.

"You may call a jay a bird. Well, so he is, in a measure—because he's got feathers on him, and don't belong to no church, perhaps; but otherwise he is just as much a human as you be. And I'll tell you for why. A jay's gifts, and instincts, and feelings, and interests, cover the whole ground. A jay hasn't got any more principle than a Congressman. A jay will lie, a jay will steal, a jay will deceive, a jay will betray; and four times out of five, a jay will go back on his solemnest promise. The sacredness of an obligation is a thing which you can't cram into no blue-jay's head. Now on top of all this, there's another thing: a jay can out-swear any gentleman in the mines. You think a cat can swear. Well, a cat can; but you give a blue-jay a subject that calls for his reserve-powers, and where is your cat? Don't talk to *me*—I know too much about this thing. And there's yet another thing: in the one little particular of scolding—just good, clean, out-and-out scolding—a blue-jay can lay over anything, human or divine. Yes, sir, a jay is everything that a man is. A jay can cry, a jay can laugh, a jay can feel shame, a jay can reason and plan and discuss, a jay likes gossip and scandal, a jay has got a sense of humor, a jay knows when he is an ass just as well as you do—maybe better. If a jay ain't human, he better take in his sign, that's all. Now I'm going to tell you a perfectly true fact about some blue-jays."

## BAKER'S BLUE-JAY YARN

"When I first begun to understand jay language correctly, there was a little incident happened here. Seven years ago, the last man in this region but me, moved away. There stands his house,—been empty ever since; a log house, with a plank roof—just one big room, and no more; no ceiling—nothing between the rafters and the floor. Well, one Sunday morning I was sitting out here in front of my cabin, with my cat, taking the sun, and looking at the blue hills, and listening to the leaves rustling so lonely in the trees, and thinking of the home away yonder in the States, that I hadn't heard from in thirteen years, when a blue jay lit on that house, with an acorn in his mouth, and says, 'Hello, I reckon I've struck something.' When he spoke, the acorn dropped out of his mouth and rolled down the roof, of course, but he didn't care; his mind was all on the thing he had struck. It was a knot-hole in the roof. He cocked his head to one side, shut one eye and put the other one to the hole, like a 'possum looking down a jug; then he glanced up with his bright eyes, gave a wink or two with his wings—which signifies gratification, you understand,—and says, 'It looks like a hole, it's located like a hole,—blamed if I don't believe it *is* a hole!'

"Then he cocked his head down and took another look; he glances up perfectly joyful, this time; wink his wings and his tail both, and says, 'O, no, this ain't no fat thing, I reckon! If I ain't in luck!—why it's a perfectly elegant hole!' So he flew down and got that acorn, and fetched it up and dropped it in, and was just tilting his head back, with the heavenliest smile on his face, when all of a sudden he was paralyzed into a listening attitude and that smile faded gradually out of his countenance like breath off'n a razor, and the queerest look of surprise took its place. Then he says, 'Why I didn't hear it fall!' He cocked his eye at the hole again, and took a long look; raised up and shook his head; stepped around to the other side of the hole and took another look from that side; shook his head again. He studied a while, then he just went into the *de*tails—walked round and round the hole and spied into it from every point of the compass. No use. Now he took a thinking attitude on the comb of the roof and scratched the back of his head with his right foot a minute, and finally says, 'Well, it's too many for *me*, that's certain; must be a mighty long hole; however, I ain't got no time to fool around here, I got to 'tend to business; I reckon it's all right—chance it, anyway.'

"So he flew off and fetched another acorn and dropped it in, and tried to flirt his eye to the hole quick enough to see what become of it, but he was too late. He held his eye there as much as a minute; then he raised up and sighed, and says, 'Consound it, I don't seem to understand this thing, no way; however, I'll tackle her again.' He fetched another acorn, and done his level best to see what become of it, but he couldn't. He says, 'Well, *I* never struck no such a hole as this, before; I'm of the opinion it's a totally new kind of a hole.' Then he begun to get mad. He held in for a spell, walking up and down the comb of the roof and shaking his head and muttering to himself; but his feelings got the upper hand of him, presently, and he broke loose and cussed himself black in the face. I never see a bird take on so about a little thing. When he got through he walks to the hole and looks in again for half a minute; then he says, 'Well, you're a long hole, and a deep hole, and a mighty singular hole altogether—but I've started in to fill you, and I'm d—d if I *don't* fill you, if it takes a hundred years!'

"And with that, away he went. You never see a bird work so since you was born. He laid into his work like a nigger, and the way he hove acorns into that hole for about two hours and a half was one of the most exciting and astonishing spectacles I ever struck. He never stopped to take a look any more—he just hove 'em in and went for more. Well at last he could hardly flop his wings, he was so tuckered out. He comes a-drooping down, once more, sweating like an ice-pitcher, drops his acorn in and says, '*Now* I guess I've got the bulge on you by this time!' So he bent down for a look. If you'll believe me, when his head come up again he was just pale with rage. He says, 'I've shoveled acorns enough in there to keep the family thirty years, and if I can see a sign of one of 'em I wish I may land in a museum with a belly full of sawdust in two minutes!'

"He just had strength enough to crawl up on to the comb and lean his back agin the chimbly, and then he collected his impressions and begun to free his mind. I see in a second that what I had mistook for profanity in the mines was only just the rudiments, as you may say.

"Another jay was going by, and heard him doing his devotions, and stops to inquire what was up. The sufferer told him the whole circumstance, and says, 'Now yonder's the hole, and if you don't believe me, go and look for yourself.' So this fellow went and looked, and comes back and says, 'How many did you say you put in there?' 'Not any less than two tons,' says the sufferer. The other jay went and looked again. He couldn't seem to make it out, so he raised a yell, and three more jays come. They all examined the hole, they all made the sufferer tell it over again, then they all discussed it, and got off as many leather-headed opinions about it as an average crowd of humans could have done.

"They called in more jays; then more and more, till pretty soon this whole region 'peared to have a blue flush about it.

There must have been five thousand of them; and such another jawing and disputing and ripping and cussing, you never heard. Every jay in the whole lot put his eye to the hole and delivered a more chuckle-headed opinion about the mystery than the jay that went there before him. They examined the house all over, too. The door was standing half open, and at last one old jay happened to go and light on it and look in. Of course that knocked the mystery galley-west in a second. There lay the acorns, scattered all over the floor. He flopped his wings and raised a whoop. 'Come here!' he says, 'Come here, everybody; hang'd if this fool hasn't been trying to fill up a house with acorns!' They all came a-swooping down like a blue cloud, and as each fellow lit on the door and took a glance, the whole absurdity of the contract that that first jay had tackled hit him home and he fell over backwards suffocating with laughter, and the next jay took his place and done the same.

"Well, sir, they roosted around here on the house-top and the trees for an hour, and guffawed over that thing like human beings. It ain't any use to tell me a blue-jay hasn't got a sense of humor, because I know better. And memory, too. They brought jays here from all over the United States to look down that hole, every summer for three years. Other birds too. And they could all see the point, except an owl that come from Nova Scotia to visit the Yo Semite, and he took this thing in on his way back. He said he couldn't see anything funny in it. But then he was a good deal disappointed about Yo Semite, too."

1880

BIOGRAPHICAL NOTES

NOTE ON THE TEXTS

NOTES

INDEX OF AUTHORS AND STORY TITLES

# *Biographical Notes*

**Louisa May Alcott** (November 29, 1832–March 6, 1888) b. Germantown, Pennsylvania, but spent her early life in and around Boston. Second of four daughters of Abigail May Brown Alcott and educational reformer Amos Bronson Alcott. Became teacher and began publishing poetry and stories in 1850s. Supported abolitionism, temperance, women's suffrage, and women's rights. First published story appeared in 1852 in the *Olive Branch*, a weekly Boston newspaper. Traveled to Washington, DC, in December 1862 to serve as a nurse in an army hospital but soon fell ill with typhoid fever and returned to Massachusetts; described her nursing experiences in *Hospital Sketches* (1863). In addition to writing war-related stories, stories for young adults, and domestic fiction, published sensation stories anonymously or pseudonymously in serial publications, including *The Flag of Our Union*, *Frank Leslie's Chimney Corner*, and *Frank Leslie's Illustrated Newspaper*. Became editor of the children's magazine *Merry's Museum* in 1868; later that year *Little Women* appeared and made Alcott internationally famous. Other novels included *An Old-Fashioned Girl* (1870), *Little Men* (1871), *Work* (1873), and *Jo's Boys* (1886). Alcott never married. Died in Boston.

**William Austin** (March 2, 1778–June 27, 1841) b. Lunenberg, Massachusetts. Third child of Margaret Rand Austin and Nathaniel Austin, a pewterer. After graduation from Harvard College in 1789 appointed schoolmaster and chaplain in the navy. Served aboard the *United States Ship Constitution*. After his chaplaincy ended, studied law at Lincoln's Inn in London. While overseas produced a series of observations about English people and politics, published first serially and then in book form as *Letters from London* (1804). Began to practice law in Charlestown, Massachusetts, after returning to America and continued to do so until his death. Wounded in a duel with James Henderson Elliot on March 31, 1806, after Austin published accusations of treason against Elliot's father. Published *An Essay on the Human Character of Jesus Christ,* a work of Unitarian theology. Married twice; had fourteen children, twelve by his second wife, Lucy Jones Austin. Elected to Massachusetts State Senate in 1821, 1822, and 1823. Published a half dozen works of short fiction, though none achieved the fame or influence of "Peter Rugg, the Missing Man," first published in three parts (1824–27) in *New-England*

*Galaxy*. The story of Peter Rugg—retold many times—became part of New England folklore. Died in Charlestown.

**Charles Brockden Brown** (January 17, 1771–February 22, 1810) b. Philadelphia. Son of Miriam Churchman Brown and James Brown, prosperous merchant. Classically educated and precocious student, began writing poetry at an early age. Studied law. Helped found Society for the Attainment of Useful Knowledge. Abandoned legal studies and embarked on literary career; read William Godwin, Condorcet, and other social thinkers. In 1798, published *Alcuin*, philosophical dialogue arguing for educational and professional equality for women, and *Wieland; or the Transformation*, novel involving mesmerism, religious obsession, and murder. Subsequent novels include *Ormond; or, the Secret Witness* (1799), *Edgar Huntly; or, Memoirs of a Sleep-Walker* (1799), *Arthur Mervyn; or, Memoirs of the Year 1793* (1799–1800), *Clara Howard* (1801), and *Jane Talbot* (1801). Wrote a dozen shorter works of fiction, including "Thessalonica: A Roman Story" (1799), "Lesson on Concealment" (1800), and "Somnambulism: A Fragment" (1805). Published short-lived quarterly *The American Review and Literary Journal* (1801–2); started another journal, *The Literary Magazine, and American Register* (1803–7); and launched the semiannual *The American Register, or General Repository of History, Politics, & Science* (1807–10). Wrote series of political tracts critical of Jefferson's administration. Married Elizabeth Linn in 1804; had four children. Died of tuberculosis in Philadelphia.

**Lydia Maria Child** (February 11, 1802–October 20, 1880) b. Medford, Massachusetts. Daughter of Susannah Rand Francis and Convers Francis, baker; sister of prominent Unitarian minister Convers Francis. After mother's death in 1814, sent to live with older sister in Norridgewock, Maine. Moved to Boston in 1821 to rejoin brother Convers; met Emerson, then a student at Harvard; developed interest in Swedenborgianism, joining Boston Society of the New Jerusalem in 1822. *Hobomok* (1824), novel about Native Americans in seventeenth-century New England, established reputation as writer. A second novel, *The Rebels, or Boston Before the Revolution* (1825), was less well received. Edited first American children's magazine, *The Juvenile Miscellany* (1826–34); during same period ran private school in Watertown, Massachusetts; made acquaintance of Margaret Fuller. Married David Lee Child, lawyer and newspaper editor, in 1828; no children. Wrote financially successful household manual, *The Frugal Housewife* (1829). Became increasingly involved in abolitionist movement, and published series of controversial antislavery works: *An Appeal in Favor of That Class of Americans called Africans* (1833), *The Oasis* (1834), and *An Anti-Slavery Catechism* (1836). Published two-volume *History of the Condition of Women in Various Ages and Nations* (1835) and *Philothea* (1836), philosophical novel set in ancient Athens. Moved to New York to edit *The National Anti-Slavery Standard* (1841–44), boarding with family of abolitionist Isaac T. Hopper; newspaper articles collected in successful *Letters from New York* (1843); resigned from *Standard* following disagreements with other abolitionists. While in New York, enjoyed renewed friendship with Margaret Fuller. In 1850 reunited with husband (whom she had seen only sporadically since coming to New York) and returned with him to Massachusetts. After many years of work, published three-volume history *The Progress of Religious Ideas Through Successive Ages* in 1855. In October 1859, following John Brown's raid on Harpers Ferry, offered to help nurse Brown in prison, resulting in controversy summarized in *Correspondence Between Lydia Maria Child, Governor Wise, and Mrs. Mason* (1860). Wrote introduction for and edited fugitive enslaved person Harriet Jacobs's *Incidents in the Life of a Slave Girl* (1860); also published *The Duty of Disobedience to the Fugitive Slave Act* (1860) and *The Right Way, the Safe Way* (1860), pamphlet urging freeing of enslaved people. Closely involved in politics of Reconstruction under Johnson and Grant administrations. *A Romance of the Republic* (1867) gave fictional account of mulatto life in New Orleans. Final book, religious anthology *Aspirations of the World*, published 1878. Died in Wayland, Massachusetts.

**Rose Terry Cooke** (February 17, 1827–July 18, 1892) b. West Hartford, Connecticut. Elder of two daughters of Anne Hurlbut Terry and Henry Wadsworth Terry. At age six, moved with family into the Wadsworth mansion, owned by paternal grandmother, in Hartford. Educated at Hartford Female Seminary, graduated 1843; officially joined Congregational Church. Taught briefly in Hartford and then four years at a Presbyterian church school in Burlington, New Jersey, where she also worked as governess for minister's family. In 1848, received inheritance from a great-uncle, which enabled her to devote herself to writing poetry and fiction, and to establish a home in Hartford. In 1852, began publishing poems in the *New-York Daily Tribune*, where Charles A. Dana was editor. Beginning in 1855—though earlier stories may have appeared pseudonymously—Cooke published her stories of New England life in various periodicals, including *Harper's New Monthly Magazine*, *Putnam's Magazine*, *The Galaxy*, and *The Atlantic Monthly*, whose inaugural issue in November 1857 carried her story "Sally Parson's Duty." In the late 1850s, after her sister Alice fell ill, Cooke reared Alice's two children. *Poems*, first verse collection, published 1861. In April 1873 married Rollin H. Cooke, a widower sixteen years her junior. Moved to Winsted, Connecticut, where she continued to write and where husband worked in a bank. Writing helped to support the family, which suffered financial setbacks as result of husband's and father-in-law's business failures. Close friend of Harriet Prescott Spofford and James T. and Annie Fields; work admired by William Dean Howells. Wrote two adult novels, *Happy Dodd* (1878) and *Steadfast* (1889), and one novel for children, *No* (1886). Many of her stories were collected in *Somebody's Neighbors* (1881), *Root-Bound and Other Sketches* (1885), *The Sphinx's Children and Other People's* (1886), and *Huckleberries Gathered from New England Hills* (1891). Family moved again in 1887 to Pittsfield, Massachusetts. Cooke died after suffering several bouts of influenza.

**Rebecca Harding Davis** (June 24, 1831–September 29, 1910) b. Rebecca Harding in Washington, Pennsylvania. Daughter of Rachel Leet Wilson Harding and Richard W. Harding. Early years spent in Big Spring (now Huntsville), Alabama. In 1837 family moved to steel-manufacturing town of Wheeling, Virginia (West Virginia after June 20, 1863, when the western part of the state was admitted to the Union). Educated at Washington Female Seminary, 1845–48. "Life in the Iron-Mills"—first published story and first of many stories and novels that embraced realism and reform—appeared in *The Atlantic Monthly* in 1861, making its author famous. *Peterson's Magazine*, *Harper's New Monthly Magazine*, and *Scribner's Magazine*, in addition to *The Atlantic Monthly*, were outlets for her essays and fiction of all lengths. Also published stories for children in *The Youth's Companion* and *St. Nicholas*. At age thirty-two, in 1863, married lawyer L. Clarke Davis of Philadelphia; they had three children. Couple lived primarily on income from her writing. In 1868 began long association with the *New-York Tribune* as a contributing editor. Published twelve novels, including *Waiting for the Verdict* (1868), *John Andross* (1874), and *A Law Unto Herself* (1878). *Silhouettes of American Life*, a collection of stories, appeared in 1891. *Bits of Gossip*, an autobiography, appeared in 1904. Died of a stroke in Mt. Kisco, New York, at the home of her son, journalist Richard Harding Davis.

**Frederick Douglass** (February 1818–February 20, 1895) b. Frederick Bailey in Talbot County, Maryland. Son of an enslaved mother and an unknown white man. Worked on farms and in Baltimore shipyards. Escaped to Philadelphia in 1838. Married Anna Murray, a free woman from Maryland, and settled in New Bedford, Massachusetts, where he took the name Douglass. Became a lecturer for the American Anti-Slavery Society, led by William Lloyd Garrison, in 1841. Published *Narrative of the Life of Frederick Douglass, An American Slave* (1845). Began publishing *North Star*, first in a series of antislavery newspapers, in Rochester, New York, in 1847. Broke with Garrison and became an ally of Gerrit Smith, who advocated an antislavery interpretation of the Constitution and participation in electoral politics. Inspired by actual events, *The Heroic Slave*, Douglass's only work of fiction, appeared in 1852. Published *My Bondage and My Freedom* (1855). Advocated emancipation and the enlistment of Black soldiers at the outbreak of the Civil War. Met with Abraham Lincoln in Washington in August 1863 and again in August 1864; wrote public letter supporting his reelection in September 1864. Continued his advocacy of racial equality and women's rights after the Civil War. Served as U.S. marshal for the District of Columbia, 1877–81, and as its recorder of deeds, 1881–86. Published *Life and Times of Frederick Douglass* (1881). After the death of his wife Anna, married Helen Pitts in 1884. Served as minister resident and consul general to Haiti, 1889–91. Died in Washington, DC.

**Edward Everett Hale** (April 3, 1822–June 10, 1909) b. Boston, Massachusetts. Son of writer Sarah Preston Everett Hale and Nathan Hale, editor and publisher of the *Boston Daily Advertiser*; younger brother of Lucretia P. Hale, with whom he collaborated on various writing projects, including novel *Margaret Percival in America* (1850). Educated at the Boston Latin School, Harvard College, and Harvard Divinity School. Ordained in the Unitarian ministry in 1846, served as pastor of the Church of Unity in Worcester, Massachusetts. Married Emily Baldwin Perkins in 1852; they had nine children. Left Church of Unity in 1856 to become pastor at South Congregational Church, Boston, where he served until his retirement. Published many works of fiction, travel, autobiography, and history. Used his fame, writings, and the two magazines he started, *Old and New* (1870–75) and *Lend a Hand* (1886–97), to promote social reforms and many charitable causes. His short fiction appeared in leading magazines and was collected in various volumes, including *If, Yes, and Perhaps* (1868), *His Level Best and Other Stories* (1872), and *The Brick Moon and Other Stories* (1899). Patriotic tale "The Man Without a Country" appeared first in *The Atlantic Monthly*, in December 1863, when the outcome of the Civil War remained uncertain. *In His Name* (1873) and *East and West* (1892) were two of his most popular novels. Died in Roxbury, Massachusetts.

**Lucretia P. Hale** (September 2, 1820–June 12, 1900) b. Boston, Massachusetts. Daughter of writer Sarah Preston Everett Hale and Nathan Hale, editor and publisher of the *Boston Daily Advertiser*; older sister of writer, clergyman, and reformer Edward Everett Hale. Educated at the Emerson School for Girls in Boston. From an early age, assisted father with various editorial tasks for his paper. Collaborated with Edward on novel *Margaret Percival in America* (1850). Began writing articles and stories in 1850s for leading magazines, including *The Atlantic Monthly*. Worked with Edward on his magazine *Old and New* (1870–75). Her popular stories of the Peterkin family appeared in *Our Young Folks* and *St. Nicholas*, popular children's magazines, and were later collected in *The Peterkin Papers* (1880) and *The Last of the Peterkins* (1886). Other writings included devotionals and a series of game and sewing books. Died in McLean Hospital in Belmont, Massachusetts.

**Frances E. W. Harper** (September 24, 1825–February 22, 1911) b. Baltimore, Maryland. Parents were free Blacks; given name Frances Ellen Watkins; she was orphaned at early age. Attended school run by uncle, the Rev. William Watkins (Methodist minister and frequent contributor to *The Liberator*). Found work in a bookshop in Baltimore. Published collection of poetry, *Forest Leaves* (1845). In 1850 took position teaching sewing at Union Seminary, near Columbus, Ohio, a school for free Blacks founded by the African Methodist Episcopal Church. Two years later left for Little York, Pennsylvania, where she obtained another teaching position. Met Black abolitionist William Grant Still, who became close friend. In 1854 moved to Philadelphia and became active in antislavery movement, working under Still's direction for Underground Railroad. *Poems on Miscellaneous Subjects* (1854), published with a preface by William Lloyd Garrison, enjoyed wide circulation and went through several editions. Lectured widely, initially for Maine Antislavery Society, and then throughout New England, in Canada, and in western states. "The Two Offers," the first short story published by an African American woman, appeared in the September and October 1859 issues of *The Anglo-African Magazine*. Poems, stories, lectures, and speeches appeared regularly in abolitionist press. Married widower Fenton Harper in 1860 and settled in Columbus, Ohio; they had a daughter. After husband's death in 1864, resumed career as lecturer and organizer; toured South frequently in late 1860s and early 1870s. Published two volumes of narrative poetry, *Moses: A Story of the Nile* (1869) and *Sketches of Southern Life* (1872) as well as the verse collection *Poems* (1871). In 1871 settled permanently in Philadelphia. Founder and assistant superintendent of YMCA Sabbath School from 1872. Active in many social and political organizations in later years; associates included Frederick Douglass, Ida B. Wells-Barnett, Harriet Tubman, Susan B. Anthony, and Elizabeth Cady Stanton. Novel *Iola Leroy, or Shadows Uplifted* published in 1892; later poetry collected in *Atlanta Offering* (1895). Addressed World Congress of Representative Women in 1893 at World's Columbian Exposition in Chicago. In 1896 helped found National Association of Colored Women, of which she became vice president the following year. Buried in Philadelphia's Eden Cemetery.

**Nathaniel Hawthorne** (July 4, 1804–May 19, 1864) b. Salem, Massachusetts. Second of three children of Elizabeth Manning Hathorne and Nathaniel Hathorne. Father, a ship's captain, died of fever in Surinam when Hawthorne was four. Mother and children moved into her parents' home and were henceforth dependent on Manning relatives. Educated at home for a number of years following a schoolyard injury. Educated at Bowdoin College, 1821–25, where he began first novel, *Fanshawe*. Devoted himself to writing short fiction, eventually collected in *Twice-Told Tales* (1837). Took job at Boston Custom House. Joined utopian community Brook Farm and left after eight months. Married Sophia Peabody in 1842; they had three children. Settled in Concord, Massachusetts, where he became acquainted with Emerson, Thoreau, and their circle. Story collection *Mosses from an Old Manse* (1846), followed by *The Scarlet Letter* (1850), *The House of the Seven Gables* (1851), and *The Blithedale Romance* (1852), inspired by experiences at Brook Farm. During residence in Lenox, Massachusetts, formed friendship with Herman Melville, who had reviewed his work enthusiastically. Wrote campaign biography for presidential campaign of Bowdoin friend Franklin Pierce; appointed American consul at Liverpool after Pierce's election. Kept extensive notebooks of travels in England, France, and Italy. Last completed novel, *The Marble Faun*, published in 1860. Returned to America in 1860. Died while on a tour of the White Mountains in New Hampshire—a trip taken with friend and former president Franklin Pierce.

**Washington Irving** (April 3, 1783–November 28, 1859) b. New York City. Youngest of eight surviving children of Sarah Sanders Irving and William Irving, a successful merchant. Studied law in desultory fashion while beginning to contribute sketches to the *Morning Chronicle* under pseudonym "Jonathan Oldstyle, Gent." Traveled to Europe where he befriended painter Washington Allston and met Madame de Stäel. With James Kirke Paulding and brother William Irving, wrote *Salmagundi* (1807–8), a collection of comic pieces.

*A History of New York* (1809), attributed to fictional author Diedrich Knickerbocker, became an instant success. Edited *Analectic Magazine*, 1813–15. Traveled to England, where his brother Peter ran Liverpool office of family mercantile business. Extended stay for years due in part to firm's difficulties. Wrote *The Sketch Book of Geoffrey Crayon, Gent.* (1819), including "Rip Van Winkle" and "The Legend of Sleepy Hollow"; book's success made him an international celebrity. Published *Bracebridge Hall* (1822) and *Tales of a Traveller* (1824). Traveled to Spain, where in 1826 he became an attaché to the American legation in Madrid. Published *Life and Voyages of Columbus* (1828), *A Chronicle of the Conquest of Granada* (1829), *Voyages and Discoveries of the Companions of Columbus* (1830), and *The Alhambra* (1832). Returned to United States in 1832 and made a trip west into Indian Territory, described in *A Tour on the Prairie* (1834). Settled in Tarrytown, New York, eventually building residence called Sunnyside. Served as minister to Spain, 1842–45. Later books included *Astoria* (1836), *Adventures of Captain Bonneville* (1837), and multivolume biographies of Muhammad and George Washington. Died of heart attack at Sunnyside. Buried at Sleepy Hollow Cemetery.

**Herman Melville** (August 1, 1819–September 28, 1891) b. New York City. Son of Maria Gansevoort Melvill, daughter of American Revolutionary hero General Peter Gansevoort, and Allan Melvill, importer and merchant. Father's business failed in financial panic of 1830; family forced to move to Albany where father died in 1832. Educated sporadically in New York City and upstate New York. Worked as clerk, bookkeeper, and schoolteacher before joining crew of trading ship *St. Lawrence* in 1839, traveling to Liverpool and back. Sailed to South Seas on whaling ship *Acushnet* in 1841; deserted with a shipmate at Nuku Hiva in the Marquesas. After a month in Taipi valley, sailed on Australian whaling ship *Lucy Ann*, but sent ashore in Tahiti as mutineer; escaped, and explored Tahiti. Sailed to Hawaii where he worked at various jobs in Honolulu before enlisting in U.S. Navy. Sailed to Boston on frigate *United States*; discharged October 1844. *Typee*, fictionalized account of Marquesas experiences, published to great success in 1846; *Omoo*, a sequel, appeared the following year. Married Elizabeth Shaw, daughter of Massachusetts Chief Justice Lemuel Shaw; they had four children. Published *Mardi* (1849), *Redburn* (1849), and *White-Jacket* (1850). Met Nathaniel Hawthorne, whose work he admired. Bought farm, which he named "Arrowhead," near Pittsfield, Massachusetts. *Moby-Dick* was published in 1851. Its indifferent reception was followed by the failure of *Pierre, or The Ambiguities* (1852), *Israel Potter* (1855), and *The Piazza*

*Tales* (1856), which included "Bartleby, the Scrivener." Made a year-long trip to Europe and the Holy Land with father-in-law's financial help. Last published novel, *The Confidence-Man*, appeared in 1857. Moved with family to New York City in 1863; collection of Civil War poems, *Battle-Pieces and Aspects of the War*, published in 1866. Worked as deputy inspector of customs at port of New York, 1866–85. Son, Malcolm, died of self-inflicted gunshot wound in 1867. Long poem *Clarel: A Poem and a Pilgrimage* published in 1867. Died in New York City. Left *Billy Budd, Sailor* in manuscript (first published 1924), along with a number of poems.

**Fitz-James O'Brien** (1828?–April 6, 1862) b. Michael O'Brien in County Cork, Ireland. Only child of Eliza O'Driscoll O'Brien and James O'Brien, county coroner. Educated at University of Dublin. Changed his name to "Fitz-James" after arriving penniless (having squandered an inheritance) in United States in 1852. He frequented Bohemian circles at Pfaff's Cellar in New York. Began contributing articles, stories, and poems to *Harper's New Monthly Magazine*, *The New-York Saturday Press*, *Putnam's Magazine*, *Vanity Fair*, and *The Atlantic Monthly*. To *The Atlantic Monthly* he contributed two of his best-known stories, "The Diamond Lens" (1858), about a man who falls in love with a woman he sees in a drop of water under a microscope, and "The Wonder Smith" (1859), in which fractious toys rebel against their owners. Joined 7th Regiment of New York National Guard at the outbreak of the Civil War, and after the regiment returned without seeing action, was appointed to staff of General Frederick W. Lander. Wounded in a skirmish in early 1862, and died soon after in Cumberland, Maryland. Critic William Winter, a friend of O'Brien, collected his *Poems and Stories* in 1881.

**Francis Parkman** (September 16, 1823–November 8, 1893) b. on Beacon Hill, in Boston. First son of Caroline Hall Parkman and the Rev. Francis Parkman, a Unitarian pastor. For health reasons lived on farm of maternal grandparents outside of Medford, Massachusetts, 1831–36. After graduation from Harvard College, studied law at Dane Law School (later Harvard Law School). Published anonymously in *The Knickerbocker* five tales using as background earlier wilderness excursions to White Mountains, Adirondacks, and Maine. Upon return from a western trip, suffered a breakdown, the first of many that plagued him for remainder of his life. Published *The California and Oregon Trail* serially (1847–49) and then in book form (1849); "California" added by publisher Putnam to exploit gold-rush fever—subsequently issued as *The Oregon Trail.* Married Catherine Scollay Bigelow in 1850. Following year the couple settled in Brookline,

Massachusetts. They had three children. After death of James Fenimore Cooper in 1851, published an appreciation of his works in *North American Review*. Published *The History of the Conspiracy of Pontiac and the Indian War After the Conquest of Canada* (1851), the first in a series of books about conflict between France and England for control of North America. *Vassall Morton*, only novel, appeared in 1856. After death of wife in 1858, moved with mother and sisters into house on Walnut Street, Boston, and then to a new house on Chestnut Street. *Pioneers of France in New World* published 1865, established his reputation as an historian. Later books include *The Jesuits in North America in the Seventeenth Century* (1867), *The Discovery of the Great West* (1869), and *The Old Régime in Canada* (1874). *Montcalm and Wolfe* (1884) and *A Half-Century of Conflict* (1892)—his final two books—completed his history of the conflict between France and England. Died at summer home on Jamaica Pond, after suffering an attack of appendicitis.

**James Kirke Paulding** (August 22, 1778–April 6, 1860) b. Great Nine Partners, Putnam County, New York. Son of Catherine Ogden Paulding and William Paulding. Raised in Tarrytown; moved around 1796 to New York City. Worked in a public office and became friendly with Washington Irving and Irving's brother William (who had married Paulding's sister Julia in 1793), collaborating with them on *Salmagundi* (1807–8). *The Diverting History of John Bull and Brother Jonathan* (1812), a humorous history in vein of *Irving's History of New York*, was followed by *The Lay of the Scottish Fiddle* (1813), a parody of Sir Walter Scott's *Lay of the Last Minstrel*. Served as major in New York militia during War of 1812. After the war, published other works critical of English politics and culture, including *The United States and England* (1815) and *A Sketch of Old England by a New-England Man* (1822), as well as account of a journey through Virginia, *Letters from the South* (1817); long narrative poem in heroic couplets, *The Backwoodsman* (1818); and unsuccessful sequel to Irving collaboration written by Paulding alone, *Salmagundi, Second Series* (1819–20). Served as secretary of Board of Navy Commissioners under Madison, 1815–23. In 1818 married Gertrude Kemble. First novel, *Koningsmarke: The Long Finne* (1823), initiated a series of fictional accounts of American life, including *The Dutchman's Fireside* (1831) and *Westward Ho!* (1832). Wrote more than seventy stories, some collected in *Tales of the Good Woman* (1829) and *Chronicles of the City of Gotham* (1830); several plays; a biography, *A Life of Washington* (1835); and *Slavery in the United States* (1836), a defense of the southern view. From 1823 to 1838 served as naval agent for New York City; appointed secretary of the navy by Martin Van Buren in

1837. Published two more historical novels, *The Old Continental* (1846) and *The Puritan and His Daughters* (1849). After the end of Van Buren's term as president, toured the West with him. Retired to Hyde Park, New York, in 1846. Died at Placentia, his farm in Hyde Park.

**Edgar Allan Poe** (January 19, 1809–October 7, 1849) b. Boston, Massachusetts. Second of three children of Elizabeth Arnold and David Poe, traveling actors. Father abandoned family in 1809. Mother moved frequently before her death in Richmond, Virginia, in December 1811. Poe was separated from his siblings and taken into the home of Richmond tobacco merchant John Allan and his wife, Frances; they served as foster parents but did not legally adopt him. Accompanied the Allans to Great Britain, attended schools in London, 1815–20, before returning with family to Richmond. Entered University of Virginia; lost money while gambling. Allan refused to honor debts. Moved to Boston; published anonymously first book of verse, *Tamerlane and Other Poems* (1827). Enlisted in U.S. Army. He was dismissed from West Point after eight months for neglect of duty. Lived in Baltimore with aunt Maria Clemm and her eight-year-old daughter Virginia. Published *Al Aaraaf, Tamerlane and Minor Poems* (1829). Began to publish short fiction in magazines, and in 1833 "Ms. Found in a Bottle" won a competition. Obtained editorial position with the *Southern Literary Messenger*, contributing stories (including "Berenice" and "Morella"), reviews, and poems. Married Virginia (then thirteen) in 1835. Resigned from *Messenger* after quarreling with editor and moved with Virginia and Mrs. Clemm to New York, then to Philadelphia. Became co-editor of *Burton's Gentleman's Magazine*. In 1838–39 wrote "Ligeia," "The Fall of the House of Usher," and "William Wilson," among other stories. Novel *The Narrative of Arthur Gordon Pym* was published in 1838; story collection *Tales of the Grotesque and Arabesque* appeared in 1839. Became literary editor of *Graham's Magazine* (1841–42), where he published "The Murders in the Rue Morgue" and "The Masque of the Red Death." Moved back to New York in 1844, working for *New-York Evening Mirror* and as editor of *The Broadway Journal*. Achieved fame with publication of "The Raven" in 1845. Later stories include "The Tell-Tale Heart," "The Black Cat," "The Premature Burial," "The Purloined Letter," "The Facts in the Case of M. Valdemar," and "The Cask of Amontillado." Published collections *Prose Romances* (1843) and *Tales* (1845). After years of illness, Virginia died of tuberculosis in 1847. Published metaphysical treatise *Eureka* (1848); returned to Richmond. In October 1849 stopped in

Baltimore on the way to New York on literary business. He was found in a delirious condition and died shortly thereafter.

**Catharine Maria Sedgwick** (December 28, 1789–July 31, 1867) b. in Stockbridge, Massachusetts. Sixth of seven children of Pamela Dwight Sedgwick, daughter of prominent Massachusetts family, and Theodore Sedgwick, a lawyer and politician. As a child, cared for by former enslaved woman whose freedom Sedgwick's father helped to win in court. Attended boarding schools. After death of parents, lived in homes of her brothers and their families. Briefly engaged but never married; devoted her time instead to her writing and brothers' families. First novel, *A New-England Tale* (1822), an immediate success, was inspired by her conversion from Calvinism to Unitarianism. Second novel, *Redwood: A Tale* (1824). *Hope Leslie; or, Early Times in Massachusetts* (1827), a frontier romance, expanded readership and reputation. Further novels include *Clarence; or, A Tale of Our Own Times* (1830) and *The Linwoods; or, "Sixty Years Since" in America* (1835), a story of the American Revolution. Comparing Sedgwick to American pioneers Irving, Cooper, Paulding, Bryant, and Halleck, Poe called her "one of our most celebrated and most meritorious writers . . . at a period when *American* reputation in letters was regarded as a phenomenon." In addition to her novels for adults, produced steady stream of children's fiction and short stories—the latter collected in volumes including *Tales and Sketches* (1835) and *Tales and Sketches*, second series (1844). A final, sixth novel, *Married or Single?*, appeared in 1857. Died in West Roxbury, Massachusetts, in home of beloved niece Katharine.

**James McCune Smith** (April 18, 1813–November 17, 1865) b. into slavery in New York City. Son of a white father and an enslaved woman named Lavinia. While still legally a bondman, attended New York African Free-School No. 2, on Mulberry Street. Freed at age fourteen by the Emancipation Act of New York on July 4, 1827. Worked as a blacksmith's apprentice, while studying Latin and Greek in the evenings. Went overseas in 1833 to attend University of Glasgow, where he faced fewer racial barriers; earned a BA in 1835, an MA in 1836, and his MD in 1837. After graduation returned to New York, where he opened a general medical and surgical practice. Became member of William Lloyd Garrison's Anti-Slavery Society; gave a keynote address on Haitian Revolution at the 1838 annual meeting. In early 1840s, married Malvina Barnet, a free woman of color who shared commitment to abolition movement; they had eleven children. In 1846 appointed physician of Colored Orphan Asylum in New York. Friendship with abolitionist Gerrit Smith led to his involvement in National Liberty Party, and later in Radical Abolition Party. Through Smith met Frederick Douglass, who invited him to serve as the New York correspondent of *Frederick Douglass' Paper.* Edited other black abolitionist newspapers, including *The Colored American* and *The Anglo-African Magazine.* In 1850s, these papers were outlets for Smith's essays of cultural criticism. His "Heads of Colored People," a series of ten sketches, appeared in *Frederick Douglass' Paper,* from 1852 to 1854. Douglass complained that his friend's unromanticized "Heads" were not "flattering to national pride" and he might get "a rap or two over his head with a broom-stick, or a few drops of moderately hot '*suds*' upon his neatly attired person." Died of congestive heart failure in New York.

**Harriet Prescott Spofford** (April 3, 1835–August 14, 1921) b. Elizabeth Josephine Prescott in Calais, Maine (name later changed to please grandmother, Harriet Delesdernier Prescott). Eldest child of Sarah Bridges Prescott and Joseph N. Prescott. Moved with grandmother to Newburyport, Massachusetts. After graduation from Putnam Free School in Newburyport, rejoined family, now living in Derry, New Hampshire, where she attended Pinkerton Academy. Family returned to Newburyport. Worked to support her invalid parents through writing. Story "In the Cellar" was highly praised by other writers when published in *The Atlantic Monthly* in 1859. The following year "The Amber Gods" and "Circumstance" were published. Of the first of these stories, Emily Dickinson remarked that "it is the only thing I ever read in my life that I didn't think I could have imagined myself," and of the second: "It followed me, in the Dark." Published novels *Sir Rohan's Ghost* (1860) and *Azarian* (1864). Married Richard Spofford, a Boston lawyer, in 1865 and moved with him to Deer Island in Amesbury, Massachusetts. Continued to publish fiction prolifically, but later work was not as well received. Published memoir, *A Little Book of Friends,* in 1916. Died on Deer Island.

**Frank R. Stockton** (April 5, 1834–April 20, 1902) b. Frank Richard Stockton in Philadelphia, Pennsylvania. Third son of Emily Hepsibeth Drean Stockton, a school administrator, and William Smith Stockton, a Methodist minister. Educated in the city's public schools. Early story won top honors from *Boys' and Girls' Journal.* In 1852 became wood engraver, supporting himself doing illustration work. Continued to pursue writing interests, publishing several stories in literary magazines, including prestigious *Southern Literary Messenger.* In 1860, left engraving business and married Marian Edwards Tuttle, a teacher at the Philadelphia school for girls founded by his mother. Moved with his bride to New Jersey, where he produced some of his first literary work. "Ting-a-Ling," a fantastical tale about a fairy, published in *The Riverside Magazine for Young People* (1867), later appeared in book form in 1870 with other fanciful tales. Became assistant editor and main contributor to children's section of the weekly illustrated magazine *Hearth and Home*. In 1873 began editing and contributing to *St. Nicholas*, a magazine for young readers. In 1878 left position at magazine due to failing eyesight, a condition that would also oblige him to dictate work for the rest of his life. First major success, episodic novel *Rudder Grange* (1879), was aimed at more mature readers. Published in 1882 in *The Century Illustrated Monthly Magazine*, story "The Lady, or the Tiger?" brought wide acclaim. Its metafictional "continuation," "The Discourager of Hesitancy," followed three years later in *The Century*. Also wrote science fiction, *The Great War Syndicate* (1889) being the most notable. Around 1899, moved with his wife to Charles Town, West Virginia. Died in Washington, DC of cerebral hemorrhage.

**Elizabeth Stoddard** (May 6, 1823–August 1, 1902) b. Elizabeth Drew Barstow in Mattapoisett, Massachusetts. Daughter of Elizabeth S. Drew Barstow and Wilson Barstow, a shipbuilder. Studied at Wheaton Seminary, Norton, Massachusetts. Married poet Richard Henry Stoddard in 1852. The following year they settled in New York City, where their literary circle included Thomas Bailey Aldrich and William Dean Howells. Two of the couple's three children died in infancy. Published a column of cultural and political commentary in *Daily Alta California*, 1854–58. About this time began to publish stories and poems. Writings appeared in many magazines, including *The Aldine*, *Harper's New Monthly Magazine*, *Harper's Bazar*, and *The Atlantic Monthly*. Published novels *The Morgesons* (1862), *Two Men* (1865), and *Temple House* (1867); also produced book for children, *Lolly Dinks's Doings* (1874), as well as a poetry collection, *Poems* (1895). Looking backward at her work at the end of the century, William Dean Howells lamented that "she has failed of the recognition her work merits, and which will be hers when Time begins to look about him for work worth remembering." Died of pneumonia in her home in New York City.

**Harriet Beecher Stowe** (June 14, 1811–July 1, 1896) b. in Litchfield, Connecticut. Seventh child and fourth daughter of Roxana Foote Beecher and Lyman Beecher, one of New England's leading Evangelical clergymen. Enrolled in Miss Sarah Pierce's School in Litchfield. In 1825 experienced religious rebirth or conversion while hearing one of her father's sermons. Attended Hartford Female Seminary, founded by older sister Catharine, which offered advanced courses of study in classics, languages, and mathematics. Moved in 1832 with the rest of the Beecher family to frontier and border city of Cincinnati, where father was appointed president of Lane Theological Seminary. In years before her marriage supported herself by teaching. In 1836 married Calvin Stowe, professor of biblical literature at Lane; they had seven children. Began to publish stories in national periodicals, especially *Godey's Lady's Book*. *The Mayflower; or, Sketches of Scenes and Characters among the Descendants of the Pilgrims* (1843) gathered fifteen stories. Moved to Maine in 1850 after Calvin accepted teaching position at Bowdoin; two years later family moved again, to Andover, Massachusetts, where husband took new appointment at Andover Theological Seminary. In 1851 *Uncle Tom's Cabin; or, Life among the Lowly*, first novel, appeared in installments in *The National Era*. Published in book form the following year, it went on to become the world's second most popular book, second only to Bible. Ten years later, Stowe traveled to Washington, DC, where she met with President Lincoln. In years after the conclusion of the Civil War, began to winter in Mandarin, Florida, and built new home in Hartford, Connecticut. Other novels include *Dred: A Tale of the Great Dismal Swamp* (1856), *The Minister's Wooing* (1859), *The Pearl of Orr's Island* (1862), and *Oldtown Folks* (1869). Story collection *Oldtown Fireside Stories* appeared in 1872. Died of stroke in Hartford.

**Thomas Bangs Thorpe** (March 1, 1815–September 20, 1878) b. Westfield, Massachusetts. First son of Rebecca Farnham Thorp and the Rev. Thomas Thorp, a circuit Methodist preacher. Studied painting with artist John Quidor before attending Wesleyan University, 1834–35. Partly for health reasons, moved in 1836 to Baton Rouge, Louisiana, where he lived for next twenty years. Married Anna Maria Hinckley in 1838; they had three children. Enjoyed some success as painter of portraits and still lifes. At this time, also began writing stories for *Spirit of the Times*, *The Knickerbocker*, and other magazines. With appearance of "The Big Bear of Arkansas" (1841) in *Spirit of the Times*, his reputation as a writer of humorous stories set in the old Southwest grew. Served in Mexican-American War. Many of his stories were collected in *The Mysteries of the Backwoods* (1846) and *The Hive of the "Bee-Hunter": A Repository of Sketches, Including Peculiar American Character, Scenery, and Rural Sports* (1854). Published *The Master's House: A Tale of Southern Life*, an antislavery reform novel, in 1854. After the death of first wife, married Jane Fosdick, in 1857. Moved to New York in 1858. Worked in New York Customs

House. During Civil War, returned to occupied New Orleans as customs officer. Died in New York of complications from Bright's disease.

**Mark Twain** (November 30, 1835–April 21, 1910) b. Samuel Langhorne Clemens in Florida, Missouri. Third of four children of Jane Lampton Clemens and John Marshall Clemens. At age four moved with family to Mississippi River port village of Hannibal, Missouri, where father worked unsuccessfully as storekeeper and farmer. Educated locally; after father's death in 1847 worked as apprentice printer. From 1851 published sketches and squibs in papers published by his brother Orion and elsewhere. Worked as journeyman printer, 1853–57, in St. Louis, New York, Philadelphia, and elsewhere. In 1857 became cub pilot on Mississippi riverboat; granted pilot's license in 1859; continued to work on river until traffic disrupted by outbreak of Civil War. Accompanied brother Orion (newly appointed secretary to Nevada Territory) to Carson City, serving as Orion's secretary, speculating in mining stocks, and prospecting; contributed writing to newspapers in Keokuk, Iowa, and Carson City and Virginia City, Nevada. First used pseudonym "Mark Twain" in 1863. In San Francisco contributed to *The Golden Era* and *The Californian*, and began to publish work in eastern publications such as *The Mercury*, *The New-York Saturday Press*, and *Harper's New Monthly Magazine*; reported on five-month trip to Sandwich Islands (Hawaii) for Sacramento *Union*. Achieved reputation as public lecturer and humorist. In 1867 sailed on first American cruise ship, *Quaker City*, for tour of Europe and Holy Land; published first collection, *The Celebrated Jumping Frog of Calaveras County and Other Sketches*. Account of *Quaker City* tour published with great success as *The Innocents Abroad* (1869). In 1870 married Livy Langdon, with whom he had four children. Settled in Hartford, Connecticut, the following year. *Roughing It*, based on his western experiences, published in 1872. From 1873 traveled frequently with family in Europe, sometimes for years at a time. *The Gilded Age* (1873), written in collaboration with Charles Dudley Warner, followed by novels and travel books, including *The Adventures of Tom Sawyer* (1876), *A Tramp Abroad* (1880), *The Prince and the Pauper* (1882), *Life on the Mississippi* (1883), *Adventures of Huckleberry Finn* (1885), *A Connecticut Yankee in King Arthur's Court* (1889), *Tom Sawyer Abroad* (1892), *The Tragedy of Pudd'nhead Wilson* (1894), *Tom Sawyer, Detective* (1895), *Personal Recollections of Joan of Arc* (1896), and *Following the Equator* (1897). Close literary associates included William Dean Howells, George Washington Cable, and Richard Watson Gilder. Business investments, including establishment of publishing house

(Charles L. Webster & Company) and development of typesetting machine, led to heavy financial losses. Published *What Is Man?* privately and anonymously in 1906. Final years spent at Stormfield, his house in Redding, Connecticut.

**Nathaniel Parker Willis** (January 20, 1806–January 20, 1867) b. Portland, Maine. Son of Hannah Parker and Nathaniel Willis. Father and paternal grandfather both newspaper publishers. Raised in Boston; attended Boston Latin School and Phillips Andover. Published first poems at age seventeen in father's newspaper. Entered Yale in 1823 and published first book, *Sketches*, volume of biblical paraphrases in verse, in 1827, the year of his graduation. For Samuel G. Goodrich edited *The Legendary* of 1828 and *The Token* of 1829 before establishing *The American Monthly Magazine* (1829–31) in Boston, writing most of it himself. Continued to build poetic reputation with *Fugitive Poetry* (1829) and *Poems Delivered before the Society of United Brothers* (1831). Moved to New York in 1831; contributing editor on George Pope Morris's *New-York Mirror*, 1831–36. In 1831, went to Europe as foreign correspondent for *Mirror*, detailing travels in Europe and Asia Minor in newspaper pieces eventually collected in *Pencillings by the Way* (1835). Toured western Europe and Middle East; settled in England. In 1835 married Mary Stace, daughter of General William Stace; they had a daughter. Returned to America in 1836. Two plays were produced in New York, *Bianca Visconti* (1837) and *Tortesa, or the Usurer Matched* (1839); the latter enjoyed some popularity. Journalistic pieces and travel sketches collected in *Inklings of Adventure* (1836), *A l'Abri; or, the Tent Pitch'd* (1839), *American Scenery* (1840), *Loiterings of Travel* (1840), and *The Scenery and Antiquities of Ireland* (1842). Collections of poetry included *Melanie* (1835), *Poems of Passion* (1843), *The Lady Jane, and Other Humorous Poetry* (1843), *Poems, Sacred, Passionate, and Humorous* (1844), and *Poems of Early and After Years* (1848). With Dr. T. O. Porter, founded weekly *The Corsair* (1839–40); after its failure, again entered into partnership with Morris as co-owner and co-editor of *The New Mirror* (1843–44), succeeded by *Evening Mirror* and its supplement *Weekly Mirror*. Employed Edgar Allan Poe as subeditor on *Evening Mirror*; the two became friends. A year after first wife Mary's death in childbirth in 1845, married Cornelia Grinnell, twenty years his junior; with Cornelia had two daughters and two sons. From 1846, again in partnership with Morris on *National Press* (soon renamed *The Home Journal*). Achieved fame as chronicler of New York fashionable life and writer of short fiction, in the pages of the *Journal* and in such collections as *Lectures on Fashion* (1844), *Dashes at Life with a Free Pencil* (1845), *Rural Letters* (1849),

*People I Have Met* (1850), *Life Here and There* (1850), *Hurry-Graphs* (1851), and *Fun Jottings* (1853). Characterized in James Russell Lowell's *A Fable for Critics* as "the topmost bright bubble on the wave of the town." In 1849, published article defending Poe's reputation from the attacks of Rufus Griswold. In 1853, moved to country home Idlewild near Tarrytown, New York. With Morris, edited *The Prose and Poetry of Europe and America* (1857). Following death of Morris in 1864, took on full editorship of *Home Journal.* Pallbearers at Willis's funeral included Richard Henry Dana, Henry Wadsworth Longfellow, Oliver Wendell Holmes, and James Russell Lowell.

# *Note on the Texts*

This volume, the first of a two-volume set, gathers forty-six American stories written or published in the nineteenth century. The stories are presented in the order of their authors' birth dates, and, when an author is represented by multiple stories, by the order of their original publication or, in a few instances, of their composition. This volume gathers work from Charles Brockden Brown (b. 1771) to Mark Twain (b. 1835). A companion volume gathers work from Bret Harte (b. 1836) to Alice Dunbar-Nelson (b. 1875).

The choice of text for each story selected for inclusion in this volume has been made on the basis of a study of its textual history and a comparison of editions printed within the author's lifetime, along with relevant manuscripts, broadside and periodical appearances, and posthumous editions. In general, texts have been taken from the earliest book edition prepared with the author's participation; revised editions are sometimes followed, in light of the degree of authorial supervision and the stage of the writer's career at which the revisions were made, but the preference has been for the authorially approved book version closest to the date of composition. Texts from periodicals and anthologies sources have been used when a story was not printed in one of the author's books during his or her lifetime, or when such a book version is not authoritative. Modern scholarly editions are also used when their texts are likely to reflect the authors' intentions more comprehensively than any earlier edition.

The following is a list of the sources of the texts included in this volume, presented in the order of their appearance in this volume.

Charles Brockden Brown: Somnambulism: A Fragment. *Literary Magazine and American Register*, May 1805.

William Austin: Peter Rugg, the Missing Man. "Anti-Calvinist Allegory: A Critical Edition of William Austin's 'Peter Rugg, the Missing Man' (1824–1827)," a doctoral dissertation by Joseph A. Zimbalatti (1992), Fordham University, 1–48; copyright © 1978; used by permission of Joseph A. Zimbalatti. First published in three parts in *New-England Galaxy*, September 10, 1824, September 1, 1826, and January 19, 1827.

James Kirke Paulding: The End of the World: A Vision. *Graham's Magazine*, March 1843.

Washington Irving: The Little Man in Black. *The Complete Works of Washington Irving* (*CWWI*) (Boston: Twayne Publishers), Vol. 6 (1977), ed. Bruce I.

Granger and Martha Hartzog, 277–83. First published in *Salmagundi*, November 24, 1807. Rip Van Winkle. *CWWI*, Vol. 8 (1978), ed. Haskell Springer, 28–42. First published in *The Sketch Book of Geoffrey Crayon, Gent.* (New York: C. S. Van Winkle, 1819–20). The Legend of Sleepy Hollow. *CWWI*, Vol. 8, 272–97. First published in *The Sketch Book of Geoffrey Crayon, Gent.* (New York: C. S. Van Winkle, 1819–20). The Devil and Tom Walker. *CWWI*, Vol. 10 (1987), ed. Judith Giblin Haig, 217–26. First published in *Tales of a Traveller* (Philadelphia: H. C. Carey and I. Lee, 1824).

Catharine Maria Sedgwick: Cacoethes Scribendi. *Tales and Sketches* (Philadelphia: Carey, Lea, and Blanchard, 1835), 165–81. First published in *The Atlantic Souvenir* (Philadelphia: Carey, Lea and Lea, 1830).

Lydia Maria Child: Hilda Silfverling: A Fantasy. *Fact and Fiction: A Collection of Stories* (New York: C. S. Francis and Co., 1846; Boston: J. H. Francis, 1846), 205–40. First published in *The Columbian Lady's and Gentleman's Magazine*, October 1845.

Nathaniel Hawthorne: Young Goodman Brown. *The Centenary Edition of the Works of Nathaniel Hawthorne* (*CEWNH*) (Columbus: Ohio State University Press), Vol. 10 (1974), ed. William Charvat, Roy Harvey Pearce, Claude M. Simpson, Fredson Bowers, 74–90. First published in *The New-England Magazine*, April 1835. Collected in *Mosses from an Old Manse* (New York and London: Wiley and Putnam, 1846). Wakefield. *CEWNH*, Vol. 9 (1974), ed. William Charvat, Roy Harvey Pearce, Claude M. Simpson, Fredson Bowers, 130–40. First published in *The New-England Magazine*, May 1835. Collected in *Twice-told Tales* (Boston: American Stationers Company, 1837). The Minister's Black Veil: A Parable. *CEWNH*, Vol. 9, 37–53. First published in *The Token and Atlantic Souvenir* (Boston: Charles Bowen, 1836). Collected in *Twice-told Tales* (Boston: American Stationers Company, 1837). Rappaccini's Daughter. *CEWNH*, Vol. 10, 91–128. First published in *United States Magazine and Democratic Review*, December 1844. Collected in *Mosses from an Old Manse* (New York and London: Wiley and Putnam, 1846). *CEWNH* texts copyright © 1974. Used by permission of Ohio State University Press.

Nathaniel Parker Willis: The Lunatic's Skate. *Inklings of Adventure* (New York: Saunders and Otley, 1836), 208–22. First published in *The New Monthly Magazine and Literary Journal*, November 1834.

Edgar Allan Poe: Ligeia. *The Collected Works of Edgar Allan Poe* (*CWEAP*) (Cambridge, MA: Belknap Press), ed. T. O. Mabbott, Vol. 2 (1978), 310–30. First published in *The American Museum of Science, Literature, and the Arts*, September 1838. Collected in *Tales of the Grotesque and Arabesque*, Vol. I (Philadelphia: Lea and Blanchard, 1840) and *Tales* (New York: Wiley and Putnam, 1845). The Fall of the House of Usher. *Tales* (New York: Wiley and Putnam, 1845), 64–82. First published in *Burton's Gentleman's Magazine and American Monthly Review*, September 1839. Collected in *Tales of the Grotesque and*

*Arabesque*, Vol. I (Philadelphia: Lea and Blanchard, 1840) and *Tales* (New York: Wiley and Putnam, 1845). The Man of the Crowd. *Tales* (New York: Wiley and Putnam, 1845), 219–28. First published simultaneously in *The Casket* and *Burton's Gentleman's Magazine and American Monthly Review*, December 1840. The Masque of the Red Death. *Broadway Journal*, July 19, 1845. First published in *Graham's Magazine*, May 1842, as "The Masque of the Red Death: A Fantasy." The Purloined Letter. *CWEAP*, Vol. 3 (1978), 974–93. First published in *The Gift: A Christmas, New Year, and Birthday Present* (Philadelphia: Carey and Hart, 1844). Collected in *Tales* (New York: Wiley and Putnam, 1845). *CWEAP* texts copyright © 1978 by the President and Fellows of Harvard College. Used by permission of Harvard University Press.

Harriet Beecher Stowe: The Minister's Housekeeper. *Oldtown Fireside Stories* (Boston: James R. Osgood and Company, 1872), 53–78.

James McCune Smith: Heads of the Colored People, No. 3: The Washerwoman. *Frederick Douglass' Paper*, June 17, 1852. Heads of the Colored People, No. 4: The Sexton. *Frederick Douglass' Paper*, July 16, 1852.

Thomas Bangs Thorpe: The Big Bear of Arkansas. *The Hive of "The Bee-Hunter," A Repository of Sketches, Including Peculiar American Character, Scenery, and Rural Sports* (New York: D. Appleton and Company, 1854), 72–93. First published in *Spirit of the Times*, March 27, 1841.

Frederick Douglass: The Heroic Slave. *The Heroic Slave: A Cultural and Critical Edition*, ed. Robert S. Levine, John Stauffer, and John R. McKivigan (New Haven: Yale University Press, 2015), 3–51; copyright © 2015; used by permission of Yale University Press. First published in *Autographs for Freedom*, ed. Julia Griffiths (Boston: John P. Jewett and Company, 1853).

Herman Melville: Bartleby, the Scrivener: A Story of Wall-Street. *The Northwestern-Newberry Edition of The Writings of Herman Melville* (*NNEWHM*) (Evanston and Chicago: Northwestern University Press and The Newberry Library), Vol. 9 (1987), ed. Harrison Hayford, Alma A. MacDougall, G. Thomas Tanselle, 13–45. First published in two parts in *Putnam's Magazine*, November–December 1853. Collected in *The Piazza Tales* (New York: Dix and Edwards, 1856). The Two Temples. *NNEWHM*, Vol. 9, 303–15. Unpublished in Melville's lifetime. Jimmy Rose. *NNEWHM*, Vol. 9, 336–45. First published in *Harper's New Monthly Magazine*, November 1855. *NNEWHM* texts copyright © 1978 by Northwestern University Press and The Newberry Library. Used by permission of Northwestern University Press and The Newberry Library.

Lucretia P. Hale: The Queen of the Red Chessmen. *The Atlantic Monthly*, February 1858.

Edward Everett Hale: The Man Without a Country. *The Man Without a Country* (Boston: Ticknor and Fields, 1865), 3–23. First published in *The Atlantic Monthly*, December 1863.

Elizabeth Stoddard: Lemorne *versus* Huell. *Harper's New Monthly Magazine*, March 1863.

Francis Parkman: The Scalp-Hunter: A Semi-Historical Sketch. *The Knickerbocker, or New-York Monthly Magazine*, April 1845.

Frances E. W. Harper: The Two Offers. *The Anglo-African Magazine*, September–October 1859.

Rose Terry Cooke: My Visitation. *Harper's New Monthly Magazine*, July 1858. Too Late. *The Sphinx's Children and Other People's* (Boston: Ticknor and Company, 1886), 229–56. First published in *The Galaxy*, January 1875. How Celia Changed Her Mind. *Huckleberries Gathered from New England Hills* (Boston and New York: Houghton, Mifflin and Company, 1892), 284–315.

Fitz-James O'Brien: The Lost Room. *Harper's New Monthly Magazine*, September 1858. What Was It? *Harper's New Monthly Magazine*, March 1859.

Rebecca Harding Davis: Life in the Iron-Mills. *Atlantic Tales: A Collection of Stories from The Atlantic Monthly* (Boston: Ticknor and Fields, 1865), 50–92. First published anonymously, in a redacted form, in *The Atlantic Monthly*, April 1861.

Louisa May Alcott: Perilous Play. *Frank Leslie's Chimney Corner*, February 13, 1869. How I Went Out to Service. *The Independent*, June 4, 1874.

Frank R. Stockton: The Lady, or the Tiger? *The Lady, or the Tiger? and Other Stories* (New York: Charles Scribner's Sons, 1884), 1–10. First published in *The Century Illustrated Monthly Magazine*, November 1882. The Discourager of Hesitancy: A Continuation of "The Lady, or the Tiger?" *The Century Illustrated Monthly Magazine*, July 1885.

Harriet Prescott Spofford: Her Story. *Old Madame and Other Tragedies* (Boston: Richard G. Badger and Company, 1900), 205–49. First published in two parts in *The Atlantic Monthly*, January–February 1860.

Mark Twain: The Facts Concerning the Recent Carnival of Crime in Connecticut. *The Atlantic Monthly*, June 1876. The Invalid's Story. *The Stolen White Elephant* (Boston: James R. Osgood and Company, Boston, 1882), 94–104. Jim Baker's Blue-Jay Yarn. *A Tramp Abroad* (Hartford, CT: American Publishing Company, 1880), 36–42.

This volume presents the texts of the original printings chosen for inclusion here, but it does not attempt to reproduce nontextual features of their typographic design. The texts are presented without change, except for the correction of typographical errors. Spelling, punctuation, and capitalization are often expressive features and are not altered, even when inconsistent or irregular. The following is a list of typographical errors corrected, cited by page and line number: 10.6, it but; 44.36–37, warrantee; 90.19, piece his; 131.26, marriage.; 132.33–34, countrywoman; 133.16, beseiged; 135.5, varience; 145.3, wont; 149.32, smiling." One; 152.3, him.; 152.7, to-morrow.; 154.28, winesses; 159.33, that it it made; 252.7, had became; 317.16, Sure; 322.29, "Wal,; 325.7, shirits; 326.11, her tried; 328.6, lots, would; 328.9, men. John; 328.10, and thousand; 328.25, scalp. from; 329.6, Phillips; 329.12–13. He happened; 329.20, along People; 329.21, months, to; 329.34, druggists; 330.14, midnight, they; 330.29, mans; 330.30, masters; 331.3, and it *that*; 336.23, its an; 337.34, I once; 474.13, side. "Nay; 477.25–26, gentleman; 510.38, "I struck; 524.39–40, developement; 529.5–6, enforced all; 531.14, dimning; 540.32, lest a; 557.29, disentegrate; 609.11, sate; 615.7, Hoffman; 641.29, sky; 642.3, griped; 661.21, a a dozen; 745.1, his month.

# *Notes*

In the notes below, the reference numbers denote page and line of this volume (the line count includes chapter headings but not section breaks). Biblical quotations are keyed to the King James Version. Quotations from Shakespeare are keyed to *The Riverside Shakespeare*, ed. G. Blakemore Evans (Boston: Houghton Mifflin, 1974).

21.3 *Peter Rugg, the Missing Man*] Originally published in three parts in the weekly *New-England Galaxy* (1824–27) and attributed to "Jonathan Dunwell." Not until the story was reprinted in *The Boston Book* (1841), a gift book of verse and prose, did its three parts appear together under the author's name. There is no evidence, however, that Austin was involved in the latter publication. The text used here, based on the *New-England Galaxy* publications, follows the modern critical edition prepared by Joseph A. Zimbalatti. See also the Note on the Texts.

24.13 heaven sometimes . . . mark on a man] After Cain kills Abel, God places a mark on him in Genesis 4:15: "And the Lord said unto him, Therefore whosoever slayeth Cain, vengeance shall be taken on him sevenfold. And the Lord set a mark upon Cain, lest any finding him should kill him."

32.38–39 Flying Childers] First great thoroughbred racehorse, foaled in 1715 by Colonel Leonard of Doncaster, England.

34.19 Congo beauty.] A beautiful Black woman.

37.7 great eclipse.] A total solar eclipse that stretched across North America on June 16, 1806.

37.12 the late war] The War of 1812 (June 18, 1812–February 17, 1815), fought between the United States and Great Britain and its First Nation allies.

37.30–31 eighteen-pounder . . . Brattle-street church."] During the Revolutionary War, the tower of the Brattle Street Church (1698–1872) was struck by a cannonball while British troops occupied the building. In his *History of the Church in Brattle Street, Boston* (1851), Samuel Kirkland Lothrop, a pastor of the church, records: "When the church was repaired, in 1825, [the cannonball] was inserted, by order of the Standing Committee, in the spot where it struck."

38.3 McAdamised.] Scottish road builder John L. McAdam (1756–1836) invented the process of "McAdamisation," which involved putting down an initial layer of large gravel and then placing on top of it a carpet of finer grained stone that was hand-rammed into place. McAdamisation came into use in 1810.

40.5–6 Boston folks are full of notions."] Early American proverb that can be traced back to the seventeenth century: "The Boston folks are deucid lads, And always full of notions" (*Maryland Journal, and Baltimore Advertiser*, February 26, 1788).

40.17 President Monroe wore on his late tour.] In early June 1817, three months after his inauguration as the fifth president of the United States, James Monroe embarked on a tour of the northern states. Newspapers reported widely on his dress, including a hat and cockade of the Revolutionary era.

40.24 Nantucket coach] Better known as a Nantucket sleigh: a whaleboat being dragged by a harpooned whale.

45.27 temple of Solomon.] 1 Kings 6 describes the grandeur of Solomon's temple.

45.33–34 Neptune . . . Ceres . . . Pomona . . . Flora] Neptune, Roman god of the sea. Ceres, Roman goddess of grain, agriculture, and the earth. Pomona, Roman goddess of fruit. Flora, Roman goddess of flowers.

46.11–12 seven wise men of Greece.] The Seven Sages of Ancient Greece (620–c. 550 BCE); philosophers, statesmen, and lawgivers celebrated for their maxims and practical advice.

47.14 a seventy-four.] Two-deck warship of the late seventeenth century, in French or British navy, designed to carry seventy-four guns.

48.12–13 a Winslow . . . a Sargent . . . a Sewall . . . a Dudley.] Scions of distinguished New England families tracing lineage back to the Plymouth Colony or the Massachusetts Bay Colony.

49.23–24 get rid of it . . . like the Bankrupt Law.] The Bankruptcy Act of 1841, a response to the Panic of 1837, was the first federal law in the United States to permit voluntary bankruptcy; due to creditor concerns it was repealed in 1843.

51.12–13 Shylock demanding his pound of flesh] See *The Merchant of Venice*, I.iii.143–51.

54.18 Job's comforters] Eliphaz, Bildad, and Zophar increase Job's suffering by offering explanations for his suffering. See Job 16:2: "I have heard many such things: miserable comforters are ye all."

54.28 canvass backs] Canvasback ducks, a prized game dish in nineteenth-century America.

60.3 *The Little Man in Black*] First published in the November 24, 1807, issue of *Salmagundi*, the magazine created and written by Washington Irving, James Kirke Paulding, and Irving's younger brother William Irving Jr. Irving and his collaborators used a variety of pseudonyms, including Launcelot Langstaff,

Esq., to whom "The Little Man in Black" was credited. Scholarly consensus attributes sole authorship of the story to Irving.

61.21 wandering Jew—] Jew of medieval legend who mocked Jesus on his way to the cross and was condemned to roam the earth until the Second Coming.

68.4–8 By woden . . . My sepulchre—] From the play *The Ordinary* (published posthumously in 1651) by English playwright William Cartwright (1611–1642), III.i.57–61.

69.2–3 Peter Stuyvesant . . . Fort Christina.] Under Dutch colonial governor Peter Stuyvesant (c. 1610–1672), the Dutch attacked and captured the Swedish stronghold of Fort Christina in 1655, ending the official Swedish colonial presence in North America.

77.35 red night cap] Conical red cap known as a "Liberty cap," which was worn by French and American revolutionaries; said to be derived from the Phrygian bonnets worn by emancipated slaves among the Romans.

78.15 Bunker's hill—] Battle of Bunker Hill, fought on June 17, 1775, during the siege of Boston; an early colonial victory in the American Revolution.

79.27 Stoney Point—] Battle of Stony Point, fought on July 16, 1779, in which "Mad" Anthony Wayne's Continentals captured the steep Hudson River promontory, Stony Point, fortified by the British.

81.10–11 Vanderhonk . . . descendent of the historian of that name] Adrian Van Der Donk (1618–1655), author of *Description of New Netherland* (*as it is Today*) [1655; *Beschryvinge Van Nieuw-Nederlant (Ghelijck het tegenwoordigh in Staet is)*].

83.1 Frederick *der Rothbart* . . . Kyphosis Mountain] Frederick Barbarossa, Holy Roman Emperor (1152–90), sleeps, according to legend, in a cave in the Kyffhäuser mountains of Thuringia. When his beard has grown three times around the stone table at which he is sleeping, he will awake and lead Germany to preeminence in the world.

85.6–9 A pleasing . . . summer sky.] From Canto I of *Castle of Indolence* (1748) by Scottish poet James Thomson (1700–1748).

89.28–29 lion bold . . . lamb did hold] Cf. Isaiah 11:6–9.

103.37 Saint Vitus] Roman martyr (d. c. 303) during the reign of Diocletian; venerated beginning in the fifth century.

105.16–17 unfortunate Major André] During the American Revolution, Major John André, British intelligence officer, was hanged on October 2, 1780, in Tappan, New York.

106.25 extracts from . . . Cotton Mather] Among the many writings of American Puritan leader Cotton Mather (1663–1728) are several essays and books on witchcraft, witch trials, and cases of demonic possession.

111.8–9 "If I can . . . am safe."] Popular superstition held that supernatural beings cannot cross running water.

115.12 Kidd the pirate.] William Kidd (c. 1645–1701), Scottish pirate who, according to legend, left a buried treasure somewhere in Atlantic Canada or New England.

115.23–24 year 1727 . . . when earthquakes were prevalent in New England.] On the evening of October 29, 1727, New England experienced a severe earthquake that was felt as far south as Philadelphia and resulted in extensive property damage; the event was widely interpreted as a sign of God's wrath.

123.15 Governor Belcher] Jonathan Belcher (1682–1757), governor of Massachusetts, 1730–41.

123.16–17 The country . . . Land Bank] In 1740, despite the objections of Governor Belcher, the Land Bank began to issue 50,000 pounds of notes that were unauthorized by the Crown.

127.3 *Cacoethes Scribendi*] Latin: Irresistible itch for writing.

127.4 Glory and gain . . . tribe provoke.] Alexander Pope, *The Dunciad* (rev. ed. 1742–43), 2.33.

127.6 "literary emporium."] Boston, a cultural center.

127.21–23 "What . . . a spirit."] *The Tempest*, I.ii.410–12.

129.22–23 create a soul . . . ribs of death] See Milton's *Comus* (1634): "I was all ear, / And took in strains that might create a soul / Under the ribs of Death" (lines 560–62).

129.30–31 Crichton] James Crichton (1560–1582), called "the Admirable Crichton," a Scottish scholar, linguist, and adventurer, renowned for many accomplishments.

130.21–22 certain erratic female lecturer on . . . marriage] Frances "Fanny" Wright (1795–1852), a Scottish-born American lecturer and social reformer who opposed traditional marriage and advocated for sexual freedom.

131.17–18 the season . . . annuals.] Late autumn, when literary annuals, also known as gift books, were published in advance of the holidays. ("Cacoethes Scribendi" appeared in the 1830 issue of *The Atlantic Souvenir.*)

131.35 North American Review] Boston literary magazine, founded in 1815.

132.30 Atalanta . . . onward way.] In Greek mythology, Atalanta's suitor Hippomenes was able to outrun her and win her hand, having distracted her with three golden apples.

133.13 coup d'essai] French: first attempt.

133.14 Saturday night book] Book of meditations intended to be read on Saturday evening, before Sunday morning church services.

133.18 the French war] French and Indian War (1754–63), fought between France and Britain, and their colonial and Native American allies, for control of North American territories.

133.18–19 'Annals of the Parish.'] Novel (1821) by Scottish writer John Galt (1779–1839), taking the form of a pastor's diary chronicling the astonishing changes in his parish over the past fifty years (1760–1810).

133.33 Cambridge] Harvard College.

134.15 "Full many . . . ray serene,"] From "Elegy Written in a Country Churchyard" by English poet Thomas Gray (1716–1771).

134.30–31 La Roche] Pious Swiss clergyman and gentle, loving father in Scottish writer Henry Mackenzie's "The Story of La Roche" (1779).

134.32 Meg Merrilies] Demented gypsy woman in Sir Walter Scott's novel *Guy Mannering* (1815).

134.33 Ichabod Crane] Awkward, ridiculous schoolmaster in Washington Irving's "The Legend of Sleepy Hollow."

135.10 Otway] Thomas Otway (1652–1685), English dramatist best known for the Restoration tragedy *Venice Preserv'd, or, A Plot Discover'd* (1682).

135.10 Tasso] Torquato Tasso (1544–1595), Italian poet whose works include his 1581 masterpiece about the First Crusade, *La Gerusalemme liberata* (Italian: Jerusalem Delivered).

135.11 lean sheaf . . . full one.] See Genesis 41.5–7.

135.13 Mr. D'Israeli] Isaac D'Israeli (1766–1848), English novelist and biographer (father of British Prime Minister Benjamin Disraeli).

136.17 Waverley novel] One in a series of popular historical novels by Sir Walter Scott.

136.27 Babel . . . forsaken it] See Genesis 11:1–9.

136.28 Lancaster school] School employing monitorial methods of English-born American educator Joseph Lancaster (1778–1838), in which more advanced students tutored other children under the direction of an adult supervisor.

136.34–35 "There are tongues in the trees,"] *As You Like It*, II.i.15–17.

137.21–22 'no matter how blue . . . hide them.'"] Widely circulated witticism, attributed to various writers, including Scottish judge and writer Francis Jeffery (1773–1850). In the preface to *Harry and Lucy Concluded* (1825), Maria

Edgeworth writes: "All that can be said or thought upon the subject by the other sex, is comprised in the Edinburgh wit's declaration 'I do not care how blue a lady's stockings may be, if her petticoats are but long enough.'"

137.36–38 the 'Legendary;' . . . the 'Token;' . . . the 'Remember Me;'] Periodical gift books.

138.19 by-talk] Side conversation.

139.7 *coup de theatre.*] French: dramatic turn of events.

139.40 'c'est le premier pas qui coute.'"] French: the first step is the most difficult.

146.4 Fourier] Charles Fourier (1772–1837), French economic reformer and utopian social theorist.

148.24 the Nereides] In Greek mythology, sea nymphs; daughters of the sea god Nereus and of Doris, daughter of Oceanus.

159.17–19 "The lark . . . the ground."] From "The Gardener's Daughter" (1842) by English poet Alfred, Lord Tennyson (1809–1892).

160.39 *Lessing] The German philosopher, playwright, and scholar Gotthold Ephraim Lessing (1729–1781).

162.40 Niobe] In Greek mythology, a mortal woman who commits suicide, or turns to stone while weeping, after the murder of her children.

163.6 Odin and Frigga,"] In Norse mythology, divine couple.

167.35–36 King William's] King William III (1650–1702), also known as William of Orange, stadtholder of the United Provinces of the Netherlands, 1672–1702, and, after the Glorious Revolution of 1688, King of England, Ireland, and Scotland, 1689–1702. He ruled Great Britain and Ireland jointly with his wife, Queen Mary II, until her death in 1694.

168.9 wot'st of."] Archaic: know of.

169.30–31 Goody Cloyse . . . at night-fall!'] In the 1692 witchcraft trials, whose records Hawthorne knew well, "spectral evidence" was admitted—such evidence holding that Satan could assume the appearance of innocent persons. Goody Cloyse, Goody Cory, and Martha Carrier, all named in Hawthorne's story, were tried and sentenced in 1692 on the basis of such evidence.

194.15–17 If ever . . . wedding-knell.] Hawthorne refers to his own sketch, "The Wedding-Knell." It appeared in the same volume of *The Token* (1836) as "The Minister's Black Veil"; both stories were collected in *Twice-told Tales* (1837).

199.7–8 Governor Belcher's administration] See note 123.15.

202.5–203.26 We do not . . . worthy of all praise.] When "Rappaccini's Daughter" was collected in the 1846 edition of *Mosses from an Old Manse*, Hawthorne deleted these paragraphs, which refer to the *United States Magazine and Democratic Review* (as *La Revue Anti-Aristocratique*) and to its editor John L. O'Sullivan (as the Comte de Bearhaven). The tale had first appeared in O'Sullivan's journal in 1844, but in 1846 Hawthorne was looking for a political appointment and may have judged it best to appear apolitical. He secured his custom house appointment, only to be dismissed from it in 1849 for his supposedly political activities. In 1854, with his friend Franklin Pierce in the presidency and with his Liverpool consular appointment, he reinserted these paragraphs in the edition of *Mosses* issued that year. *Aubépine* is French for "hawthorn," and the publications of Aubépine listed are French renderings of the titles of some of Hawthorne's writings.

205.20–21 Vertumnus] Obscure Etruscan or Latin god, his function unknown.

224.37 most virulent . . . Borgias innocuous.] During the Italian Renaissance, the Borgias, a powerful Italian family of Spanish origins, were notorious for using poisons such as cantarella to do away with rivals and gain political advantage.

229.40–230.1 If they should be cruel . . . kind to them?] Cf. Hamlet, III.iv.178.

233.17 the great Channing] William Ellery Channing (1780–1842), prominent Unitarian preacher and theologian.

233.35 "That two . . . they seem;"] See Lord Byron's *Childe Harold's Pilgrimage* (1812–18), III.114.

234.14 *montagnes Russes*] French: literally "Russian mountains"; an amusement ride, a predecessor to the modern-day roller coaster.

234.30–31 "spirit-bird" . . . of Thalaba] In the Eleventh Book of Robert Southey's epic poem *Thaler the Destroyer* (1801), a green bird alights on the titular character's arm: "And when, beneath the noon, / The icey glitter of the snow / Dazzled his aching sight, / Then on his arm alighted the Green Bird / And spread before his eyes / Her plumage of refreshing hue."

240.20–21 a volume of "Ivanhoe," . . . just then appeared] Published anonymously (as were all Sir Walter Scott's Waverley novels prior to 1827), *Ivanhoe* appeared in three volumes in 1819.

244.4–9 And the will . . . *Joseph Glanvill*] Glanvill (1636–1680), an Anglican clergyman, believed in the preexistence of souls; however, the quotation appears to be Poe's invention.

245.2 *Ashtophet*] Likely, Poe means Ashtoreth, or Astarte, a Canaanite goddess associated with fertility and love.

245.16 Delos] In Greek mythology, the sacred Aegean island was the birthplace of Apollo (god of music, light, and healing) and his twin sister Artemis (goddess of the hunt, wild animals, and the moon).

245.32–33 Homeric epithet, "hyacinthine!"] In Alexander Pope's English translation of Homer's *Odyssey*.

246.31–32 more profound . . . well of Democritus—] The Greek philosopher Democritus (460–c. 370 BCE) posited that matter was made up of a variety of particles too small to be seen.

246.35 twin stars of Leda] Castor and Pollux, brightest stars in Gemini (in Greek mythology, Castor and Pollux are the sons of Leda, a Spartan queen seduced or raped by Zeus).

247.18–20 a star of the sixth magnitude . . . in Lyra] Epsilon Lyrae, also known as the Double Double, in the constellation Lyra.

250.14 The music of the spheres.] Pythagoras (569–475 BCE) theorized that the universe is governed by musical ratios, and that together the movements of celestial bodies produce a harmonious sound.

253.26–27 ghastly forms which belong to . . . the Norman] Grotesque figures such as *Loup-garou* (French: a werewolf) in Norman transformation legends.

260.4–5 Son cœur . . . il résonne.] Adapted from "Le Refus," lines 41–42, by French poet and songwriter Pierre-Jean de Béranger (1780–1857): "His heart is a hanging lute; / As soon as it is touched, it responds."

264.4 *ennuyé*] French: bored, suffering from ennui.

267.30 concrete reveries of Fuseli] Swiss painter Henry Fuseli (1741–1825) is renowned for his nightmarish, highly detailed paintings of supernatural subjects.

271.5–6 *Vigiliae . . . Maguntinae.*] In approximate translation: Vigils for the Dead in the Liturgy of the Church in Mainz. Like the other nine titles mentioned, the *Vigiliae* is authentic although the "mad ritual" attributed to it in the next paragraph is not.

279.4 Ce grand Malheur . . . être seul.] From *Les Caractères*, section 99, by French essayist and moralist Jean de La Bruyère (1645–1696): "That great evil, to be unable to be alone."

279.22 the αχλυς ος πριν επηεν—] More correctly: ἀχλὺς ἣ πρὶν ἐπῆεν. Greek: "Darkness which before was upon [them]." In Homer's *Iliad*, V.127, Pallas Athena speaks these words, removing the haze from the eyes of Diomedes, to allow him to clearly distinguish between gods and men in battle.

282.16–17 the statue in Lucian . . . with filth—] Poe refers to a passage in the twenty-fourth section of *Somnium* ("The Dream, or The Cock") by the Greek rhetorician and satirist Lucian (125–c. 180).

283.22–24 Retzsch, had he viewed it . . . the fiend.] Friedrich August Moritz Retzsch (1799–1857), a German painter and engraver, was noted especially for his etchings of Goethe's *Faust.*

284.5 *roquelaire*] French: knee-length cloak.

284.7–8 follow the stranger . . . should go.] Cf. Luke 9:57: "And it came to pass, that, as they went in the way, a certain man said unto him, Lord, I will follow thee whithersoever thou goest."

287.24 'Hortulus Animæ,'] In Isaac D'Israeli's *Curiosities of Literature,* where Poe probably read about it, Grüninger's book (1500) is described as a volume of puerile religious meditations that are accompanied by frivolous or ribald illustrations.

290.38 "Hernani."] *Hernani, or l'Honneur castillan,* a verse play by French writer Victor Hugo, which was controversial when it premiered at the Comédie Française in 1830 (seen by some as an attack on neoclassical principles).

292.19 vesture was dabbled in *blood*—] Cf. Revelation 19:13: "And he was clothed with a vesture dipped in blood: and his name is called The Word of God."

293.31–32 Red Death. . . . come like a thief in the night.] Cf. 1 Thessalonians 5:1–2: "But of the times and the seasons, brethren, ye have no need that I write unto you. For yourselves know perfectly that the day of the Lord so cometh as a thief in the night."

294.4–5 Nil sapientiae . . . Seneca.] Latin: There is nothing wisdom hates more than cleverness. Though the maxim is sometimes attributed to Seneca, there is no evidence he wrote it.

294.17–18 Rue Morgue . . . Marie Rogêt.] Poe refers to his two earlier stories that feature *Le Chevalier* C. Auguste Dupin: "The Murders in the Rue Morgue" (1841) and "The Mystery of Marie Rogêt" (1842).

297.29 *au fait*] French: well informed.

302.2–3 Procrustean bed] In Greek mythology, the ironsmith Procrustes, son of the god Poseidon, stretched or amputated the limbs of his victims to fit the dimensions of the bed he offered them.

304.3 La Bruyère] The text reads "La Bougive" in Poe's *Tales* (1845). Correction made by Thomas Ollive Mabbott for his authoritative text, which is printed here. Jean de La Bruyère (1645–1696) was a French philosopher and moralist.

305.16–17 *Non distributio medii*] Latin: literally, the undistributed middle; the logical fallacy of the undistributed middle (if all A's are B's, all B's may not necessarily be A's).

305.31–33 "'*Il y a à parier . . . grand nombre.*' ] From *Maximes et Pensées*, II.42, by Sébastien-Rock Nicolas, called Chamfort (1740–1794): "You can count on the fact that all popular notions and accepted conventions are stupid since the majority has found them acceptable."

306.25 Bryant, in his very learned 'Mythology,'] English mythographer Jacob Bryant's *A New System of Antient Mythology* (Third Edition, 1807).

307.40 *vis inertiæ*] Latin: force of inertia.

311.17 *facilis descensus Averni*] Virgil, *Aeneid*, 6.126 (Latin: "the descent to Avernus is easy").

311.20 *monstrum horrendum*] Virgil, *Aeneid*, 3.658 (Latin: "a terrifying monster").

311.35–36 Un dessein . . . de Thyeste.] From *Atrée et Thyeste* (1707), V.iv.13–15, by French poet and dramatist Prosper-Jolyot de Crébillon (1674–1762): So deadly a scheme is worthy of Thyestes, if not of Atreus.

312.4 Sam Lawson] Loafer and teller of yarns in Stowe's collection *Sam Lawson's Oldtown Fireside Stories* (1871).

315.5 Cambridge College] Harvard; more particularly, the Divinity School.

317.37 Arminians and Socinians] Heterodox Christians: Arminians were adherents to the anti-Calvinist idea that an individual could merit salvation through actions; Socinians rejected the doctrines of the divinity of Christ, the Trinity, original sin, the complete omniscience of God, and the propitiatory atonement of Christ.

321.14–15 Aaron's rod . . . and blossomed] See Numbers 17:8.

323.20–21 'spite of envy of the Jews, as the hymn says.] In Psalm 118.v, by English Congregational minister and hymn writer Isaac Watts (1674–1748): "See what a living stone / The builders did refuse! / Yet God hath built His church thereon, / In spite of envious Jews."

325.3 *Heads of the Colored People.*] James McCune Smith's series of ten sketches, which appeared in *Frederick Douglass' Paper*, 1852–54.

325.22 Pappy Thompson, or Brother Paul, or Sammy Cornish] George Donisthorpe Thompson (1804–1878), British abolitionist who toured the United States in 1834–35 and again in 1850–51 after the passage of the Fugitive Slave Law. Paul Cuffe (1759–1817), African American Quaker sea captain, maritime entrepreneur, and philanthropist who was involved in efforts to establish Sierra Leone as a refuge for free people of color. Samuel Eli Cornish (1795–1858), African American Presbyterian minister, abolitionist, and co-editor of *Freedom's Journal*, the nation's first Black newspaper.

325.24–25 Watts' Hymns, the Life of Christ] *Hymns and Spiritual Songs* (1707) by English hymn writer Isaac Watts. *Prayers and Meditations on the Life of Christ* by Thomas à Kempis (c. 1380–1471), German-born Dutch priest and theologian.

325.25–26 nice 'greasy novel' . . . circulating library] In the eighteenth and nineteenth centuries, circulating libraries made books, especially novels (a popular new genre), more accessible and affordable; patrons paid membership fees or onetime rental fees. The novel in question is not literally greasy (well-thumbed) but rather crowd-pleasing.

326.7–8 *Prie Dieu*] French: literally "pray to god"; a prayer bench.

327.1 Ethiop's] A Black person, Douglass's Black readers.

327.5–6 "face the devil" . . . Burn's prophylactic.] In Robert Burns's poem "Tam o' Shanter" (1791), Tam, after an evening of revels at the local public house, is fortified with whisky for the long ride home: "Inspiring bold John Barleycorn! / What dangers thou canst make us scorn! /Wi' tippenny, we fear nae evil; / Wi' usquabae, we'll face the devil!"

327.18 through it. . . .] After the conclusion of the sketch, Communipaw's letter goes on to criticize the "titled nobility" and Ethiop.

328.10 *nondum*] Latin: not yet.

328.29 *alae, nariculum*] Latin: wings, a small ship.

328.30 papilionaceous] Obsolete: butterfly-like.

328.33–329.4 "The sexton, he . . . of all."] From "The Sexton's Daughter" (1838), I.V and IX, by Scottish poet John Sterling (1806–1844).

330.10 New York African Society for mutual relief] Society organized by New York City's Black leaders in 1808 to provide health and life insurance for its members.

331.4 been mistaken.] Communipaw's letter continues beyond the sketch to condemn newspaper editor and publisher Horace Greeley.

332.22 Wolvereens, Suckers, Hoosiers, Buckeyes, and Corncrackers] Persons from Michigan, Illinois, Indiana, Ohio, and Kentucky, respectively.

346.3 "*The Heroic Slave*"] Douglass's only work of fiction, inspired by the life of Madison Washington, the leader of the revolt on board the domestic slave-trading ship *Creole* in 1841 that resulted in the liberation of more than a hundred enslaved people. It was first published in *Autographs for Freedom* (1853), an anthology of antislavery writing whose thirty-six contributors included Harriet Beecher Stowe, John Greenleaf Whittier, Lewis Tappan, and William H. Seward. The collection was edited by Julia Griffiths, Douglass's friend and business manager, who conceived of the volume as a means to raise funds for *Frederick Douglass' Paper* and the Rochester Ladies' Anti-Slavery Society.

346.5–8 Oh! child of grief . . . lingers there?] The opening stanza of a much-anthologized popular poem, "God Is Love."

346.18–19 a certain distinguished citizen . . . of New York] Perhaps a reference to Martin Van Buren of Kinderhook, New York, who, unlike his southern predecessors in the presidency, served just one term.

346.20 the Old Dominion] Virginia.

346.30–31 he who led all the . . . colonies] George Washington.

348.31–32 The North Star . . . follow it.] Refugees from slavery used Polaris, or the north star, as a directional guide toward freedom. Douglass fittingly named his first newspaper *The North Star* (1847–51).

349.10 "black, but comely."] Song of Solomon 1:5.

351.8–14 "The gaudy, blabbing . . . in the air."] *2 Henry VI*, IV.i.1–7.

353.19–20 Canada . . . rights of men] Those who escaped from slavery in the United States often fled to the British provinces of Canada, where they found refuge and built free communities.

357.17 the dismal swamps] Large wetlands region of southeast Virginia and northeast North Carolina, where for decades fugitives from slavery established maroon communities.

358.16 city of refuge] A phrase with biblical resonances; see, for examples, Numbers 35:11–34, Deuteronomy 19:3–13.

360.25 the raven's cry] Cf. Psalm 147:9.

360.27–28 With thee, O father . . . possible] Cf. Matthew 19:26.

360.30–31 "I have seen the affliction . . . deliver them,"] Cf. Acts 7:34.

360.39–40 the man who prays in secret] See Matthew 6:5–6.

361.2–3 Zacheus . . . the tree.] See Luke 19:1–10. The biblical tax collector Zacchaeus climbed a tree to view Jesus, who beckoned him to descend and receive him at his house.

362.31 the *Great Bear*] Ursa Major, the constellation of stars containing the Big Dipper.

363.11–14 the laws of Ohio . . . escape through that State.] Because of its location between Kentucky and Canada, Ohio was a crucial route for fugitives from slavery. To combat the active Underground Railroad in their state, Ohio lawmakers passed measures that rewarded slave catchers and penalized those found harboring refugees.

363.22 the Lake] Lake Erie.

364.7 buffaloes] Warm coverings made from buffalo hides.

364.17–18 the emancipating queen] Queen Victoria (1819–1901), the head of the British Empire, including the Canadian provinces.

364.33–34 "to deliver the spoiled . . . spoiler,"] Cf. Jeremiah 21:12.

364.34–35 given bread to the hungry . . . naked] Cf. Ezekiel 18:7; Matthew 25:36.

365.3 CANADA WEST] Ontario.

365.15–16 —His head was . . . far away!] Lord Byron, *Childe Harold's Pilgrimage* (1812–18), 4.141.

367.1 Dryburgh Abbey.] A Scottish monastery of the twelfth century and the burial place of Sir Walter Scott. Douglass visited the abbey in 1846.

370.9 *rencontres*] A hostile meeting, sometimes an impromptu duel.

370.15–16 "a sweet morsel," under . . . tongues.] Cf. Job 20:12.

370.38–39 cast such a pearl . . . swine] Cf. Matthew 7:6.

371.5–6 "without compromise and without concealment,"] This motto appeared on the masthead of the *National Anti-Slavery Standard*, a New York abolitionist newspaper.

371.9 Erasmus] Amid the often-violent theological disputes of the early Reformation, Dutch humanist Desiderius Erasmus (1466–1536) sought to avoid extremes, preaching tolerance and compromise.

371.15–16 boring him . . . questions] That is, drilling him.

372.1–2 that the earth . . . such wickedness] Cf. Numbers 26:10.

373.6 foreheads "*villainously low*,"] Cf. *The Tempest*, IV.i.249.

377.10–11 gladly shaking off . . . Old Virginia] Cf. Mark 6:11.

377.13–17 Oh, where's the slave so lowly . . . them slowly?] Thomas Moore, "Where Is the Slave" (1848).

377.19–20 ——Know ye not . . . strike the blow.] Lord Byron, *Childe Harold's Pilgrimage* (1812–18), 2.76.

377.32 Guinea] A word used to refer to the coast of West Africa.

378.5 *ocean birds*] Sailors.

378.25 the *caboose*.] A cast-iron stove on a merchantman's deck used to prepare meals.

378.33 Old Point] Referring to Old Point Comfort in Virginia's Hampton Roads, site of Fortress Monroe, which had large guns and fortifications.

379.21–22 were you a slave in Algiers] In the late eighteenth century, the great European trading powers France and Great Britain paid tribute to the Barbary States (Morocco, Algiers, Tunis, and Tripoli) in return for being left alone by pirates in the Mediterranean. This made smaller and less wealthy trading states, like the fledgling United States, vulnerable to having their ships seized and crews enslaved.

381.11 caulkers] Skilled craftsmen who made wooden ships airtight with packing material. Douglass had trained as a caulker in Baltimore.

383.34 Nassau] The capital of the Bahamas, a British colony.

384.38 binnacle] A case that contained the ship's compass and other navigational instruments.

386.29 Imprimis] Latin: In the first place.

387.3 late John Jacob Astor] Astor (1786–1848), German-born entrepreneur, founder of The American Fur Company, died five years prior to the publication of "Bartleby." He was the first American multimillionaire and the richest man in the country at the time of his death.

387.14–21 State of New York . . . premature act] The New York Court of Chancery, a civil court established in the colonial era, was abolished in 1847. The Master in Chancery presided over cases in matters of equity (chancery), including those involving wills and trusts, divorces and legal separations, and property. Holders of this position could take in substantial fees along with acquiring other privileges. Melville's brothers Gansevoort and Allan Melville were employed by the New York Court of Chancery.

390.24 the Tombs] Formally, the Halls of Justice; the main New York City detention center, built in 1838 in the Egyptian Revival style. "The Tombs" earned its nickname because it was rumored to be based on a specific Egyptian tomb.

395.18 into a pillar of salt] See Genesis 19:26.

402.13 Petra] City located in modern-day Jordan. Capital city of the Nabatean Kingdom from the second century BCE, it declined during Roman rule and lay deserted and in ruins for many centuries until European explorers "rediscovered" it in 1812.

402.18–19 Marius . . . Carthage!] Gaius Marius (157–86 BCE), Roman general and consul engaged in civil wars against Sulla. In 88 BCE, defeated and driven from Rome to refuge in Africa, he landed at Carthage (which had been destroyed in 146 BCE by Roman armies) and found bitter consolation in the sight of the once-great city in ruins.

403.2–3 pigeon-holes] Small open compartment in a desk or cabinet for keeping letters or documents.

411.22–23 Adams . . . the hapless Colt.] John C. Colt was convicted of the Broadway office murder of Samuel Adams in 1841. On the day scheduled for his hanging, he was married and committed suicide in his cell in the Tombs.

411.38–39 "A new commandment . . . another."] John 13:34.

412.27–28 "Edwards . . . Necessity."] Both works named, by Jonathan Edwards (1703–1758) and Joseph Priestley (1733–1804), published in 1754 and 1778 respectively, argue, on different grounds, that man's will is not free.

418.16 rockaway] Horse-drawn carriage: a light four-wheel model open on both sides, with a fixed top projecting forward to protect the driver in bad weather, and a heavier version enclosed at the sides and rear with a door on each side.

420.9 Mr. Cutlets] This volume uses the Northwestern-Newberry text of "Bartleby," which follows the *Putnam's Magazine* version of this scene. The book version was revised (possibly by an editor) to omit the name "Mr. Cutlets" from the lawyer's introduction and to alter the grub-man's invitation from "May Mrs. Cutlets and I have the pleasure of your company to dinner, sir, in Mrs. Cutlets' private room?" to "What will you have for dinner today?"

420.27 Monroe Edwards?"] American slave trader and swindler (1808–1847), known as "The Gentleman Forger," who was apprehended and confined in the Tombs in 1842. After his conviction, he was sent to Sing-Sing prison, where he died.

420.35 in quest of Bartleby] A single, spoiled fair-copy page of the manuscript, in the hand of Melville's sister Augusta, has an earlier and briefer version of the lawyer's second visit. In it he finds Bartleby dead in his cell, not in the yard, with a tombstone that does not appear in the published version.

421.24 "With kings and counsellors,"] Job 3:14.

423.3 *The Two Temples*] After Melville submitted "The Two Temples" to *Putnam's Monthly*, the magazine's editor, Charles F. Briggs, wrote to Melville on May 12, 1854, saying he was "very loth to reject it." The following day in a note to Melville from George Palmer Putnam, the publisher suggested that through revision, offense to "some of our church readers" might be "avoided." "The Two Temples" was not published in the author's lifetime. It first appeared in Volume XIII of the Standard, or Constable, Edition of Melville's *Works* (London, 1924). The text presented here is the one established by the Northwestern-Newberry editors, based on the fair-copy manuscript, corrected and revised by Melville.

423.4 Sheridan Knowles] James Sheridan Knowles (1784–1862), Irish dramatist and actor.

424.26 "the Tombs."] See note 390.24.

424.39 Jacob's ladder] Genesis 28:10–22.

425.11 "Venite, exultemus Domine".] Psalms 95:1. Latin: "O come, let us sing unto the Lord." Set to music, it is an opening invitation to prayer in the daily liturgy of both the Anglican Church and the Catholic Church.

426.12 Pharisee] Member of an ancient Jewish sect known for its strict adherence to the written law. Often refers to a self-righteous person, one who claims a superior sanctity.

427.1 Talma's] François Joseph Talma (1763–1826), celebrated French actor and manager at the Comédie-Française, introduced a new realism in costume and scenery, as well as a simpler, less theatrical style in performance.

427.13 "Ye are the salt of the earth."] Matthew 5:13.

428.14 Pisgah] The summit of Mount Nebo, from which Moses looked into the Promised Land of Canaan, which God had forbidden him to enter. (Deuteronomy 34:1–4.)

428.15 Puseyitish] Tending toward Puseyism, the doctrines propounded by Edward Pusey (1800–1882), Anglican cleric. One of the leaders of the Oxford movement, he advocated for increased ritualism—along lines similar to Catholicism—in the Anglican Church.

428.17 Hagar . . . Ishmael.—] See Genesis 16. Hagar, the Egyptian handmaiden of Abraham's barren wife, Sarah, had a child by Abraham, named Ishmael. Mother and son fled into the desert.

430.18 Charmian] Cleopatra's attendant in Shakespeare's *Antony and Cleopatra*.

430.24 Esculapius] Aesculapius, Roman god of healing and medicine.

431.20 Tartarean] In Greek mythology, pertaining to Tartarus, the deepest, most infernal region of Hades, where sinners are sent for punishment.

431.38 Macready . . . Richelieu.] In 1838, William Charles Macready (1793–1873), eminent English stage actor and theater manager, brought Edward Bulwer-Lytton's drama *Richelieu* to the stage, playing the title role. It became a continuing part of his repertoire.

432.23 Phlegethon] In Greek mythology, a river of fire, one of the five rivers in the underworld.

437.12 soft-warfle] "Warfle," variant ear-spelling of "waffle."

438.30 Prince Esterhazies] Nikolaus I, Prince Esterházy (1714–1790), Hungarian prince noted for his sartorial extravagance, which included a famous diamond-studded jacket.

438.31 Orders of the Golden Fleece.] Catholic order of chivalry founded in 1430 by Philip the Good, Duke of Burgundy. The members of the Order became known throughout Europe for their fine dress. The Order's gold medallion featured precious jewels, such as sapphires, diamonds, and opals.

439.34–35 Cosmo the Magnificent] Melville confuses Cosmo de' Medici (1389–1464) and Lorenzo de' Medici (1449–92), known as "Lorenzo the Magnificent."

447.7 Warwick] Richard Neville, 16th Earl of Warwick (1428–1471), known as "The Kingmaker." He wielded great influence and power during the treacherous years of the War of the Roses.

449.22–23 Murillo-painted Spanish lady] Bartolomé Esteban Murillo (1617–1682) was a Spanish painter of the Baroque period, known equally for his religious works and paintings of contemporary subjects, such as *Two Women at a Window* (c. 1655–1660).

461.22 Her Mazzinis, her Tancreds] Giuseppe Mazzini (1805–1872), Genoese revolutionary, founder of the secret society Young Italy. An uncompromising republican, he worked for the unification of the various Italian states. The Kingdom of Italy was established in 1861. Tancred (c. 1075–1112), Italo-Norman leader of the First Crusade and, later, Prince of Galilee. Torquato Tasso, in his book-length poem *Jerusalem Delivered*, depicts him as an epic hero.

463.24 "The Bianchi and the Neri] Tuscan factions of the Guelph party, which supported the Papacy in its power struggles with the Holy Roman Emperor (whose supporters were called Ghibellines) in the twelfth and thirteenth centuries. Once the Guelphs prevailed, infighting began, splitting the party into the Neri ("Blacks"), who continued to back Pope Boniface VIII, and the Bianchi ("Whites"), who came to oppose him.

466.21 Undine] Female figure in European folklore, a water nymph who becomes human when she falls in love with a man but is fated to die if he is unfaithful to her. Undines lack an immortal soul; marrying a human shortens their earthly life, but they thereby gain an immortal soul. In some traditions, mermaids are related to undines.

468.34–40 the Fisherman and his Wife? . . . beg a boon of thee!'] The story appears in *Grimm's Fairy Tales*, originally published as *Children's and Household Tales* in 1812. The verse refrain has been translated into English variously by many hands.

472.4 Ross burned . . . Washington.] During the War of 1812, Major General Robert Ross (1766–1814) led the British forces that captured Washington, D.C., on August 24, 1814. He ordered the burning of all public buildings, including the White House, the Capitol, and the Library of Congress.

472.10–11 "*Non mi ricordo,*"] Italian: I don't remember.

472.34 Monongahela, sledge, and high-low jack.] Monongahela, a rye whiskey produced in southwestern Pennsylvania and northwestern Maryland, known for its high rye content. Sledge and high-low jack, variants of the English "all-fours" card games, the object of which is to score points by winning tricks with valuable cards in them, somewhat like bridge.

473.8–9 Nolan was enlisted body and soul.] Philip Nolan supported the former Vice President Aaron Burr's supposed efforts to form parts of the newly acquired Louisiana Territory into a separate country, for which Burr was charged with treason in 1807 by the U.S. government under President Thomas Jefferson. Ultimately, Burr was acquitted, but the repercussions of his alleged dealings demolished his reputation.

473.14–15 Clarences of . . . House of York] George Plantagenet (1449–1478), Duke of Clarence, was a member of the then-ruling family of England, the House of York. His brother, King Edward IV, had him arrested on the charge of treason. He was convicted and executed.

473.40–474.1 "Spanish plot," "Orleans Plot,"] Rumors frequently circulated around the Gulf Coast of Spanish designs on the Louisiana Territory. Spain, already controlling Mexico and much of the Caribbean, had made claims of ownership to the French region as well.

478.1 Canning's] George Canning (1770–1827), Tory parliamentarian and, briefly, Prime Minister of England, known for his powerful and effective oratory.

478.15–16 "Lay of the Last Minstrel,"] Narrative poem (1805) in six cantos by Sir Walter Scott (1771–1832). The lines quoted hereafter are canto 6, lines 1–12.

479.33 Fléchier's] Esprit Fléchier (1632–1710), French preacher and Bishop of Nîmes.

480.34 Lady Hamilton] Dame Emma Hamilton (1765–1815), born Amy Lyon, an English maid, model, dancer, and actress as well as the mistress of a series of wealthy men, before marrying Sir William Hamilton, British Ambassador to Naples in 1791. Her long relationship with Lord Horatio Nelson, during her marriage, produced a daughter, Horatia.

482.9–11 "Iron Mask" . . . the author of "Junius,"] The Man in the Iron Mask, arrested in 1669 during the reign of Louis XIV, was a never-identified French prisoner. Strict measures were taken to keep his imprisonment secret, but the idea that his face was covered with a mask for the thirty-four years of his imprisonment (d. 1703) belongs to legend. Alexandre Dumas (père) published a popular novel based on the subject in 1847. "Junius" is the pseudonym of the unidentified author of a series of provocative letters published in a London newspaper, from 1769 to 1772, to inform readers of the Englishman's historical and constitutional rights and liberties, and to point up where and how the government had infringed on these rights. He also promoted causes and interests of the Whig party, including a more sympathetic attitude toward the grievances of American colonies.

483.26 Nukahiwa Islands] Nukahiva, largest island in the Marquesas Island group of French Polynesia in the central South Pacific.

484.35 John Foy the idiot] In "The Idiot Boy," a 1798 poem by William Wordsworth, the mentally challenged protagonist is named Johnny Foy.

485.5 our Slave-Trade treaty] An 1800 act of Congress made it illegal for Americans to engage in the slave trade between nations and gave U.S. authorities the right to seize ships that were caught transporting enslaved people. The "Act Prohibiting the Importation of Slaves" took effect in 1808. The domestic trade in enslaved people, however, persisted between ports within the United States.

486.2 Beledeljereed] Coinage from the Arabic term *Beled el jerid*, meaning "The Land of Dates." It referred to the southern part of Algeria.

486.12 Kroomen] Sailors from the Kru people, a West African ethnic group, living along the coast of Liberia and the Ivory Coast.

486.25 Cape Palmas."] Headland on the extreme southeast end of the coast of Liberia.

487.5 barracoon."] Type of barracks used by slave traders for the internment of captives along the coast of West Africa awaiting forced transport across the Atlantic.

488.27–28 *ben trovato*] Italian: well-found; figuratively, a felicitous or clever invention.

489.1–2 Bragg and Beauregard . . . two years ago] North Carolinian Braxton Bragg (1817–1876) and Louisianan Pierre Gustave Toutant-Beauregard (1818–1893) were West Point graduates and U.S. Army officers. In choosing to fight for the Confederacy, they were in violation of their oath of allegiance to the United States of America.

489.2 Maury and Barron] Matthew Fontaine Maury (1806–1873), U.S. naval officer. With the outbreak of the Civil War, Maury, a Virginian, resigned his commission as a U.S. Navy commander and joined the Confederacy. He spent the war acquiring ships for the Confederacy. Commodore James Barron (1768–1851), high-ranking U.S. naval officer. In 1807 he surrendered his frigate, USS *Chesapeake*, to the British ship HMS *Leopard* during a skirmish, which resulted in his court-martial for failure to properly prepare his ship for action.

490.32–33 Vallandighams and Tatnals] Clement L. Vallandigham (1820–1871) was a Democratic U.S. congressman from Ohio, 1858–63, and a leader of the "Peace Democrats" opposing Lincoln and the war. Lincoln banished

Vallandigham to rebel territory in 1863. Josiah Tatnall III (1795—1871) distinguished himself as a naval officer and ship's captain for decades prior to the Civil War. His loyalty to his home state of Georgia led him to resign his commission and join the Confederate Navy in 1861. He commanded the ironclad CSS *Virginia* during the Battle of Hampton Roads.

494.16 Exploring Expedition] United States Exploring Expedition (1838–1842), an exploring and surveying expedition of the Pacific Ocean and surrounding lands conducted by the United States.

494.17–18 Crawford's Liberty and Greenough's Washington] Thomas Crawford (1814–1857) sculpted the classical female figure called the Statue of Freedom, which sits atop the dome of the U.S. Capitol. Horatio Greenough (1805–1852) sculpted the large marble statue of George Washington, "Enthroned Washington," that was commissioned by the U.S. Congress in 1832 (and completed in 1840). Originally, it stood in the U.S. Capitol rotunda and now resides at the National Museum of American History.

495.9 Order of the Cincinnati.] The nation's oldest patriotic organization, founded in 1783 by officers of the Continental Army to commemorate the American Revolution. Membership is open only to those descended from officers in the Continental Army.

497.37 Pushers] Lace made by a Pusher machine, created by Samuel Clark and James Mart in 1812. The machines could make a perfect copy of handmade lace net.

500.13 beaver] Face guard of a helmet, typically worn down when entering battle.

501.40 *tutoyer*] French: to address someone familiarly. More specifically, to use the informal "tu" rather than formal "vous."

504.30–31 What do . . . Fugitive Slave Bill?"] The Fugitive Slave Act of 1850, a more stringent version of the Fugitive Slave Act of 1793, imposed heavy penalties on persons who helped runaway enslaved people but was resisted by abolitionists and countered in many northern states by the passage of "personal liberty laws." It denied alleged fugitives any jury trial. Their cases were instead heard by federal commissioners who received $5 if they decided for the defendant and $10 if they decided for the claimant.

504.35 Saurians] Suborder of reptiles that includes lizards.

506.3–4 poem whose motto is . . . moated grange."] "Mariana," an 1830 poem by Alfred, Lord Tennyson. The poem takes its epigraph from Shakespeare's *Measure for Measure,* III.i, in which Mariana, abandoned by her fiancé, Angelo, is reported to have taken refuge in a "moated grange."

507.29 "curled darlings"] In Shakespeare's *Othello,* Brabantio's description of the suitors who were vying for the hand of his daughter, Desdemona. See *Othello,* I.ii.68.

507.35–508.2 "And the fluttering . . . for life."] Goethe's play *Faust,* I, lines 1,464–69.

508.19 Rhadamanthus] In Greek mythology, the son of Zeus and Europa and King of Crete, known for his wisdom. He later became one of the three judges of the dead, who devise the laws governing the underworld.

508.20 Charon] In Greek mythology, the boatman who ferries the souls of the dead to the underworld across the river Acheron.

508.31 redowa] Either of two popular ballroom dances from nineteenth-century Bohemia: a triple-time dance resembling a waltz, or a 2/4-time dance resembling a polka.

514.1 Francis Parkman] "The Scalp-Hunter" was published anonymously in the April 1845 issue of *The Knickerbocker.*

519.18–19 unfortunate Willeys . . . their fate.] Samuel Willey (b. 1788), his wife, and five children moved to Crawford Notch, a relatively desolate rural area in the White Mountains of New Hampshire in 1825. Severe rainstorms in August 1826 triggered a landslide of rock and soil, which buried parts of the Willey property. The house was untouched, but the bodies of Willey, his wife, and two of the five children were found outside. The bodies of the other three were never located.

525.13 "dream of beauty and delight."] From the first stanza of "There Never Was an Earthly Dream": "There never was an earthly dream / Of beauty and delight / That mingled not too soon with clouds, / As sun's rays with the night; / That faded not from that fond heart / Where once it loved to stay, / And left that heart more desolate / For having felt its sway." The poem appeared without attribution in dozens of American newspapers throughout the 1840s and 1850s, sometimes with *The Knickerbocker* given as the source.

534.4–8 "Is not . . . pairs of wedlock?"] Alfred, Lord Tennyson, *The Princess,* Part 6, lines 232–33 and 235–37. A narrative poem published in 1847, in which the heroine, Ida, abjures the world of men and founds a university for women only—one that no man may enter.

535.10–13 Shirley . . . Jane Eyre . . . Villette] Novels by Charlotte Brontë, published in 1849, 1847, and 1853, respectively.

537.10 *Evoe Athena!*"] "Evoe" is a cry of joy in Bacchic rites. Athena is the Greek goddess of wisdom, sometimes called Pallas Athena in honor of her triumph over a giant of that name. "Evoe Athena!" is therefore a cry celebrating female power.

540.19 "Song half asleep or speech half awake,"] Cf. line 22 in third stanza of Robert Browning's "Garden Fancies I: The Flower's Name" (1844): "Speech half-asleep or song half-awake?"

541.4–5 "Nature never . . . loved her;] William Wordsworth, "Lines Composed a Few Miles Above Tintern Abbey" (1798), lines 122–23.

542.3 Kingsley] Charles Kingsley (1819–1875), English novelist and social reformer, best remembered for his novel *The Water Babies* (1863).

542.24–25 "Talked at large . . . every trait"] Ralph Waldo Emerson, "Hermione" (1847), lines 38–39.

545.25 Pharisaically] See note 426.12.

553.4 "'Tis true . . . 'tis true!"] *Hamlet*, II.ii.97–98.

553.15–16 Covenanter's conventicle] Following the restoration of episcopacy in Scotland by Charles II in 1662, Presbyterian Covenanters began holding their services—conventicles—in the open air.

553.33 Feejee] Alternative spelling of Fiji, island in the South Pacific and any of its inhabitants.

559.25 "The wild marsh marigold shone like fire,"] Cf. line 31 in Alfred, Lord Tennyson's "The May Queen" (1832, 1842): "And the wild marsh-marigold shines like fire in swamps and hollows gray."

560.24 Mear and Bethesda; and Cambridge] Names of tunes used as settings for the hymns frequently sung in colonial New England.

560.31–34 "'Twas in the watches . . . darkest hour!"] "Midnight Thoughts Recollected," a hymn written by Congregational minister Isaac Watts (1674–1748) and set to an English folk tune. The hymn takes its opening from Psalm 63:6.

561.3 "My beloved is mine and I am his,"] Song of Solomon 2:16.

567.27 suttee] Ritual once practiced in India in which a widow throws herself onto her husband's funeral pyre.

568.34 "bound girl"] Young female legally obligated to work as an indentured servant, for a set period of time in exchange for food, shelter, and sometimes education.

570.14 "Hypathia;"] 1853 novel by Charles Kingsley (1819–1875), set in fifth-century Alexandria. It explores through the eyes of Philammon, a monk and disciple of the pagan female philosopher Hypathia, the clash between Christian and pagan values.

571.2–3 Assembly's Catechism] The Westminster Catechism (1643–47), written by English and Scottish theologians and laymen and intended to bring the Church of England and the Church of Scotland into greater conformity. It became a central teaching tool in the Calvinist traditions in both England and America. The "Larger" Catechism, for clergy and adults, consists of

196 questions and answers; the "Shorter," for beginners and children, contains only 100 and was widely used in America.

573.11 Atropos] In Greek mythology, the eldest of Three Fates, often referred to as "The Inflexible One." Clotho attends the moment of birth, Lachesis spins out the actions and events of individual lives with threads of various lengths, and Atropos finally cuts the thread of life with a pair of scissors.

573.18–19 the woman . . . "doeth better."] See 1 Corinthians 7:38.

575.36–37 "non Angli, sed Angeli,"] Latin: "not Angles, but Angels." Attributed to Pope Gregory the Great upon seeing fair-skinned English children being sold as slaves in Rome. According to Bede, in his *Ecclesiastical History*, the sight led Gregory to send St. Augustine (of Canterbury) on his mission to Christianize Britain in 597.

576.4–5 *experto crede.*] Virgil, *Aeneid*, 2.238 ("trust the expert").

576.37 the tares grow amongst the wheat] Matthew 13:24–30.

578.9–10 "Provoke . . . good works."'] Hebrews 10:24.

579.34–35 "Fare thee well . . . fare thee well!"] Opening lines of Lord Byron's poem "Fare Thee Well," enclosed in a letter to his wife upon the finalization of their legal separation in 1816.

580.7 B. & A. R. R.] Boston and Albany Railroad.

581.5 Syrophenician woman] Mark 7:25–30. Woman from Phoenicia (currently coastal Syria, Lebanon, and northern Israel).

583.39–584.1 Balaam's ass . . . angel] See Numbers 22:21–38.

584.35 "near,"] Parsimonious, stingy.

586.35–36 'Jeshrun waxed fat an' kicked.'"] Deuteronomy 32:15.

590.23–24 "who provideth not . . . an infidel."] 1 Timothy 5:8.

592.29 'It is better if she so abide.'] 1 Corinthians 7:8.

593.25 *imprimus*] See note 386.29.

593.25 Calame] Alexandre Calame (1810–1864), Swiss landscape painter.

594.29 Atropos] See note 573.11.

594.37 Bellini . . . Cimarosa, Porpora, Glück] Vincenzo Bellini (1801–1835), an Italian opera composer of the early Romantic era. Domenico Cimarosa (1749–1801), Italian composer of the Classical period who wrote more than eighty operas. Nicola Porpora (1686–1768), Italian composer and singing teacher of the Baroque period. Christoph Willibald von Gluck (1714–1787), composer of French and Italian operas in the early Classical period.

595.29 *habitant*] French: literally, an inhabitant; an early French settler in Canada, particularly Quebec, or in Louisiana.

596.11 Sir Florence O'Driscoll] Sir Fineen O'Driscoll (d. 1629), Irish clan chief knighted by Queen Elizabeth I.

598.19–20 Hood's haunted house . . . newly painted.] "The Haunted House" (1844), a long poem by English poet Thomas Hood (1799–1845), depicts a gloomy, decayed, mold- and insect-ridden domicile.

599.5 afreet] In Islamic mythology, powerful demon or djinn, often associated with the spirits of the dead.

602.21–22 Faublas, or Grammont's Memoirs . . . Minister Fouque.] *Les amours du chevalier de Faublas* is a trilogy of novels (1787–90) by French writer Jean-Baptiste Louvet de Couvray (1760–1797) that follow the amorous adventures of the Chevalier de Faublas. *Mémoires de la vie du comte de Grammont* (1713), a historical memoir by French writer Anthony Hamilton (c. 1645–1719), chronicles the adventures of a libertine count. Nicolas Fouquet (1615–1680), wealthy French nobleman and superintendent of finances under Louis XIV, built on his estate at Vaux-le-Vicomte a magnificent chateau, which in its scope and design is considered a forerunner of Versailles Palace.

603.25–26 Clos Vougeot . . . Lachrima Christi."] Clos de Vougeot, a burgundy wine. Lachrima Christi, a Neapolitan wine produced on the slopes of Mount Vesuvius. *Lachrima Christi* means "tears of Christ" in Latin.

612.6–7 Mrs. Crowe's "Night Side of Nature"] Book (1848) by English author Catherine Ann Crowe (1790–1872); an investigation of supernatural phenomena, particularly ghosts and their significance, as well as dreams and presentiments.

612.16–17 "The Pot of Tulips," for *Harper's Monthly*] Fitz-James O'Brien's story of the same title appeared in the November 1855 issue of *Harper's New Monthly Magazine*.

613.23–24 *Rana arborea*] Latin: species of European tree frog.

614.4 Haroun] Harun al-Rashid, fifth Abbasid caliph (c. 763–809, r. 786–809), renowned as a patron of arts and letters. He makes frequent appearances as a character in *The Arabian Nights*.

614.6–7 the fisherman released from the copper vessel] See "The Fisherman and the Genie," trickster tale in *The Arabian Nights*.

615.7 Hoffman] E.T.A. Hoffmann (1776–1822), renowned German Romantic author of fantasy stories and Gothic horror.

621.29–30 Gustave Doré, or Callot, or Tony Johannot] Gustave Doré (1832–1883), French printmaker and painter whose highly imaginative, sometimes frightening illustrations graced editions of works by Dante, Poe, and Rabelais among many others. Jacques Callot (c. 1592–1635), French engraver and printmaker who produced a series of shocking images called "Grotesque Dwarves." Antoine Johannot (1803–1852), French engraver and illustrator, commonly known as "Tony," who created the images for Thomas Wright's *A History of Caricatures and Grotesques.*

621.31–32 "*Un voyage ou il vous plaira,*"] French illustrated book (1843) by Alfred de Musset and Pierre-Jules Hetzel (P.-J. Stahl), with sixty-three full-page wood engravings after drawings by Tony Johannot. The French title means "A trip you will enjoy."

623.4–6 "Is this the end . . . redress?"] From Alfred, Lord Tennyson's *In Memoriam: A.H.H.* (1850), an elegy for the poet's friend Arthur Henry Hallam (who died at age twenty-two). The first line is taken from canto XII, line 16; the second and third lines are from canto LVI, lines 25 and 27.

624.16 puddler] Worker in iron manufacturing, specializing in heating and stirring pig iron in a furnace to convert it into wrought iron.

626.21 "Begorra!] Alteration of "By God!"

627.22 Milesian] According to legend, the last race of Gaelic people to settle Ireland, arriving from Iberia. Descended from Mil Espáine, Gaelic warrior from Scythia in the second millennium BCE.

627.37 flitch] Piece of meat cut from the side of a pig to make bacon.

628.24–25 "gods in pain."] See Homer's *Iliad,* Book V. The goddess Dione catalogues for her wounded daughter, Aphrodite, those gods who have suffered pain at the hands of mortals.

633.33 Farinata] Farinata degli Uberti (1212–1264), Italian aristocrat, leader of Florence's Ghibelline faction (see note 463.24). Dante, who opposed that faction, places him in the sixth circle of Hell in his *Inferno* both for being a Ghibelline and for being an Epicurean—two blows against papal authority. His punishment is eternal imprisonment in a fiery coffin.

634.37 Kant, Novalis, Humboldt] Immanuel Kant (1724–1804), German philosopher whose systematic work in epistemology, ethics, and aesthetics set the terms for much of nineteenth- and twentieth-century philosophy. Novalis, pen name of Georg Philipp Friedrich Freiherr von Hardenberg (1772–1801), German Romantic poet, novelist, philosopher, and mystic. Friedrich Wilhelm Christian Karl Ferdinand von Humboldt (1767–1835), German philosopher, linguist, educational reformer, and diplomat.

639.17–18 '*De profundis clamavi.*'] Latin: "Out of the depths I have cried." Followed by *ad te, Domine* ("to you, O Lord"), the opening of Psalm 130.

639.18–19 'Hungry and thirsty . . . faints in him.'] Psalm 107:5.

639.22–23 "I am innocent . . . See ye to it!'] Matthew 27:24.

639.27–28 'Inasmuch as ye did it . . . unto me.'] Matthew 25:40.

640.28 Saint-Simonian doctrines] Henri de Saint-Simon (1760–1825) was a French aristocrat, political and economic theorist, and a founder of Christian socialism. He believed science and technology could solve most of humanity's problems, improving the conditions of the poorest classes. He advocated a meritocratic social hierarchy and the complete emancipation of women and their equality with men.

641.14 Jean Paul] Johann Paul Friedrich Richter (1763–1825), German Romantic poet who wrestled with the problem of nihilism.

646.15–16 the mote in my brother's eye] See Matthew 7:3–5.

648.14–30 Eighteen centuries ago . . . stand there.] When Davis's "Life in the Iron-Mills" first appeared (anonymously) in the April 1861 issue of *The Atlantic Monthly*, these two paragraphs were removed by James T. Fields or another editor. Davis restored the cuts when the story was reprinted under her name in *Atlantic Tales: A Collection of Stories from The Atlantic Monthly* (Ticknor and Fields, 1865). Almost all modern editions of Davis's story print the 1861 magazine text. This volume prints the unredacted 1865 text from *Atlantic Tales.* The holograph manuscript, held at the Huntington Library in San Marino, California, provides another, different version of the redacted text:

> Years ago, a mechanic tried reform in the alleys of a city as swarming and vile as this mill town, who did not fail. Could Wolfe have seen him as He was, that night, what then? A social Pariah, a man of the lowest caste, thrown up from among them, dying with their pain, starving with their hunger, tempted as they are to drink, to steal, to curse God and die. Theirs by blood, by birth. The son, they said, of Joseph the carpenter, his mother and sisters there among them. Terribly alone, one who loved and was not loved, and suffered from that pain; who dared to be pure and honest in that devil's den; who dared to die for us though he was a physical coward and feared death. If He had stood in the church that night, would not the wretch in the torn shirt there in the pew have "known the man"? His brother first. And then, unveiled his God.

656.7–8 "Father, forgive them . . . they do!"] Luke 23:34: Christ begs forgiveness for his tormentors.

658.14 Esau deprived of his birthright.] See Genesis 25:29–34.

661.10 "The Lotus Eaters."] In Greek mythology, inhabitants of an island who eat the leaves of the lotus tree, which induces a blissful lethargy and forgetfulness. In *Odyssey*, Book IX, Odysseus encounters such a tribe during his return from Troy. Odysseus, whose advance scouts partake of the lotus, must forcibly drag his men back to their ship. See also Alfred, Lord Tennyson's eponymous poem.

673.3 *How I Went Out to Service*] Based on Alcott's uncomfortable, sexually charged experiences as a companion at a house in Dedham for James Richardson, a demanding and abusive elderly lawyer who had been a classmate of Thoreau's at Harvard and an admirer of Bronson Alcott. Alcott had envisioned a genteel job whose duties included reading to Richardson; instead, she was told to black his boots. Adding insult to injury, Richardson paid her only four dollars when she left his employment. Two years later, hoping to launch her writing career, Alcott showed the story to publisher James T. Fields, who advised her to "stick to your teaching, Miss Alcott. You can't write."

674.19 "sicklied o'er . . . cast of thought,"] *Hamlet*, III.i.84.

675.17 Siddons . . . Betcinder.] Sarah Siddons (1775–1831), Welsh actress, the most celebrated tragedienne of her time on the English stage. Betcinder, a Cinderella figure, a household drudge.

676.2–3 delaine] From French: de laine ("of wool"); also a breed of Merino sheep producing high-quality wool for women's dresses.

678.7 Borgia.] See note 224.37.

678.11 "a heart for any fate,"] Henry Wadsworth Longfellow, "A Psalm of Life" (1838), line 34.

688.2–3 every barleycorn a king] Roughly, fully a king, as in "every inch a king" (*King Lear*, IV.vi.107) except that a barleycorn, an old English unit of measurement, is equal to a third of an inch.

702.25–26 "Fear not . . . thou art mine."] Isaiah 43:1.

703.15–18 "Then, to thy courts . . . angels sing."] From "My Opening Eyes with Rapture See," a hymn written by English bookseller and hymn writer James Hutton (1715–1795).

705.11 St. Cecilia's] Cecilia, the patron saint of music, thought to have been martyred in the second or third century CE, sang to God "in her heart" while the musicians at her wedding played their instruments.

705.22 Amati] Distinguished family of violin makers from the sixteenth to eighteenth centuries, based in Cremona, Italy.

707.18 Bayadere] Female Hindu dancer, especially one at a southern Indian temple, who dances before images of the gods.

708.1 Guadalquivir] River in southern Spain.

710.8 Antinous'] Greek youth celebrated for his masculine beauty; lover of the Roman Emperor Hadrian, who deified Antinous after his death.

712.29 Inflammatus] Latin: Ignited, set alight. Specific section or movement in a musical composition, often found in religious or sacred music, evoking a sense of fervent passion or divine fire.

736.3 33–35 *Left out . . . M.T.] "The Invalid's Story" was originally intended as part of Twain's series "Some Rambling Notes of an Idle Excursion," which appeared in *The Atlantic Monthly* in 1877. Editor William Dean Howells found the story too offensive to be published in the magazine. It first appeared in Twain's collection *The Stolen White Elephant* (1882).

737.22 "Sweet By and By,"] Hymn (1868), with lyrics by American songwriter Sanford Filmore Bennett (1836–1898) and music by his friend and collaborator Joseph P. Webster (1819–1875).

738.37–38 Man that is born . . . and far between.] See Job 14:1.

739.5–6 cut down like the grass . . . no more forever] See Psalm 103:15–16.

# *Index of Authors and Story Titles*

*This book is set in 10 point ITC Galliard, a face designed for digital composition by Matthew Carter and based on the sixteenth-century face Granjon. The paper is acid-free lightweight opaque that will not turn yellow or brittle with age. The binding is sewn, which allows the book to open easily and lie flat. The binding board is covered in Brillianta, a woven rayon cloth made by Van Heek–Scholco Textielfabrieken, Holland. Composition by Westchester Publishing Services. Printing by Sheridan, Grand Rapids, MI. Binding by Dekker Bookbinding, Wyoming, MI. Designed by Bruce Campbell.*

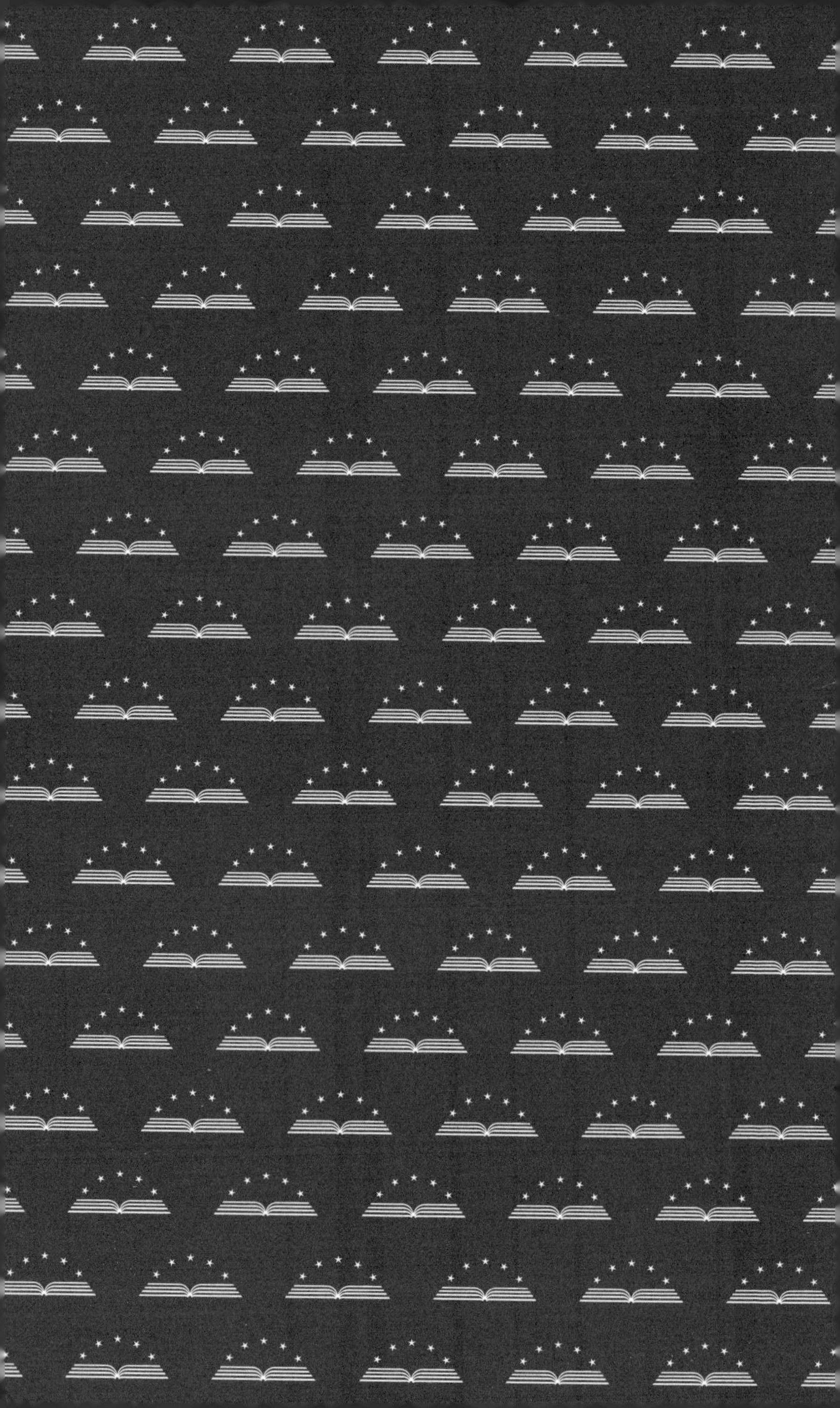